LIONHEART

LIONHEART

SHARON PENMAN

MACMILLAN

First published 2011 by G.P. Putnam's Sons,
a division of Penguin Group (USA) Inc.

First published in Great Britain 2012 by Macmillan
an imprint of Pan Macmillan, a division of Macmillan Publishers Limited
Pan Macmillan, 20 New Wharf Road, London N1 9RR
Basingstoke and Oxford
Associated companies throughout the world
www.panmacmillan.com

ISBN 978-0-230-76478-1

1 3 5 7 9 8 6 4 2

A CIP catalogue record for this book is available from
the British Library.

Book design by Nicole Laroche

Printed and bound by CPI Group (UK) Ltd, Croydon, CR0 4YY

Visit **www.panmacmillan.com** to read more about all our books
and to buy them. You will also find features, author interviews and
news of any author events, and you can sign up for e-newsletters
so that you're always first to hear about our new releases.

To Jill Davies

CAST OF CHARACTERS
As of 1189

ROYAL HOUSE OF ENGLAND

HENRY FITZ EMPRESS (1133–1189), King of England, Duke of Normandy, Count of Anjou

ELEANOR (b. 1124), Duchess of Aquitaine in her own right, Henry's queen and former consort of the French king, Louis VII

Their children:

WILLIAM (1153–1156)

HENRY (Hal in the novel) (1155–1182)

RICHARD (b. September 1157), Duke of Aquitaine, Count of Poitou, crowned King of England in September 1189

GEOFFREY (1158–1186), Duke of Brittany upon his marriage to Constance

JOHN (b. December 1166), Count of Mortain, also known as John Lackland

MATILDA (Tilda) (1156–1189), Duchess of Saxony and Bavaria, mother of Richenza

ELEANOR (Leonora) (b. 1161), Queen of Castile

JOANNA (b. October 1165), Queen of Sicily

ENGLISH ROYAL COURT

GEOFFREY (Geoff), Henry's illegitimate son, Archbishop of York

WILLIAM MARSHAL, one of Richard's justiciars, wed to Isabel de Clare, Countess of Pembroke

GUILLAUME LONGCHAMP, Bishop of Ely, Richard's chancellor

ROYAL HOUSE OF FRANCE

PHILIPPE II (b. 1165), King of France

ISABELLE, his queen, daughter of the Count of Hainaut

LOUIS CAPET, Philippe's father, former husband of Eleanor, deceased

ALYS CAPET, Philippe's half-sister, betrothed to Richard in childhood

AGNES CAPET, Philippe's sister, wed in childhood to the heir to the Greek Empire, today known as Byzantium

MARIE, Countess of Champagne, half-sister to Philippe and to Richard, daughter of Eleanor and Louis, mother of Henri

BRITTANY

CONSTANCE, Duchess of Brittany, widow of Geoffrey, now wed to the Earl of Chester

Her children by Geoffrey:

ARTHUR and ELEANOR (Aenor)

NAVARRE

SANCHO VI, King of Navarre

SANCHO, his eldest son and heir

BERENGARIA, his daughter (b. c. 1170)

SICILY

WILLIAM II DE HAUTEVILLE, King of Sicily

JOANNA, his queen, Richard's sister

WILLIAM I, William's father, deceased

MARGARITA OF NAVARRE, William's mother, deceased

CONSTANCE DE HAUTEVILLE, William's aunt and heir, wed to Heinrich von Hohenstaufen, King of Germany and heir of Frederick Barbarossa, Holy Roman Emperor

TANCRED, Count of Lecce, illegitimate cousin of William

SYBILLA, Tancred's wife

ROGER, Tancred's son

CYPRUS

ISAAC COMNENUS, self-proclaimed emperor

SOPHIA DE HAUTEVILLE, his empress, illegitimate daughter of the late king, William I of Sicily

ANNA COMNENA, Isaac's daughter

SARACENS

AL-MALIK AL-NASIR SALAH AL-DĪN, ABU' AL-MUZAFFAR YUSUF IBN AYYUB, Sultan of Egypt, known to crusaders and history as Saladin

AL-MALIK AL-'ĀDIL, SAIF AL-DĪN ABŪ-BAKR AHMAD IBN AYYUB, Saladin's brother

BAHĀ' AL-DĪN IBN SHADDĀD, a member of Saladin's inner circle and author of *The Rare and Excellent History of Saladin*

OUTREMER

BALDWIN IV, the "Leper King," deceased

SYBILLA, his sister, Queen of Jerusalem

GUY DE LUSIGNAN, King of Jerusalem, her husband

ISABELLA, Sybilla's half-sister

HUMPHREY DE TORON, her husband

BALIAN D'IBELIN, Lord of Nablus, wed to Maria Comnena, former Queen of Jerusalem and mother of Isabella

CONRAD OF MONTFERRAT, Italian-born Lord of Tyre, cousin of the French king, Philippe

AMAURY and JOFFROI DE LUSIGNAN, Guy's older brothers and vassals of King Richard

GARNIER DE NABLUS, Grand Master of the Knights Hospitaller

ROBERT DE SABLÉ, Grand Master of the Knights Templar

JOSCIUS, Archbishop of Tyre

CRUSADERS WITH RICHARD

HENRI, Count of Champagne, nephew to both Richard and Philippe

ANDRÉ DE CHAUVIGNY, Richard's cousin

ROBERT BEAUMONT, Earl of Leicester

HUBERT WALTER, Bishop of Salisbury

PRÉAUX BROTHERS, Guilhem, Jean, and Pierre, Norman knights

JACQUES D'AVESNES, Flemish lord

CRUSADERS WITH PHILIPPE

HUGH, Duke of Burgundy, cousin to Philippe

PHILIP, Bishop of Beauvais, cousin to Philippe

ROBERT, Count of Dreux, brother to Beauvais

MATHIEU DE MONTMORENCY, young French lord

GUILLAUME DES BARRES, renowned French knight

JAUFRE, son of the Count of Perche, wed to Richard's niece Richenza, a.k.a. Matilda

LEOPOLD VON BABENBERG, Duke of Austria

KINGDOM
of
SICILY

Naples

Mileto

Bagnara

Messina

Reggio

Palermo

Catania

Straits of Messina (Faro)

AL-MALIK AL-'ĀDIL, SAIF AL-DĪN ABŪ-BAKR AHMAD IBN AYYUB, Saladin's brother

BAHĀ' AL-DĪN IBN SHADDĀD, a member of Saladin's inner circle and author of *The Rare and Excellent History of Saladin*

OUTREMER

BALDWIN IV, the "Leper King," deceased

SYBILLA, his sister, Queen of Jerusalem

GUY DE LUSIGNAN, King of Jerusalem, her husband

ISABELLA, Sybilla's half-sister

HUMPHREY DE TORON, her husband

BALIAN D'IBELIN, Lord of Nablus, wed to Maria Comnena, former Queen of Jerusalem and mother of Isabella

CONRAD OF MONTFERRAT, Italian-born Lord of Tyre, cousin of the French king, Philippe

AMAURY and JOFFROI DE LUSIGNAN, Guy's older brothers and vassals of King Richard

GARNIER DE NABLUS, Grand Master of the Knights Hospitaller

ROBERT DE SABLÉ, Grand Master of the Knights Templar

JOSCIUS, Archbishop of Tyre

CRUSADERS WITH RICHARD

HENRI, Count of Champagne, nephew to both Richard and Philippe

ANDRÉ DE CHAUVIGNY, Richard's cousin

ROBERT BEAUMONT, Earl of Leicester

HUBERT WALTER, Bishop of Salisbury

PRÉAUX BROTHERS, Guilhem, Jean, and Pierre, Norman knights

JACQUES D'AVESNES, Flemish lord

CRUSADERS WITH PHILIPPE

HUGH, Duke of Burgundy, cousin to Philippe

PHILIP, Bishop of Beauvais, cousin to Philippe

ROBERT, Count of Dreux, brother to Beauvais

MATHIEU DE MONTMORENCY, young French lord

GUILLAUME DES BARRES, renowned French knight

JAUFRE, son of the Count of Perche, wed to Richard's niece Richenza, a.k.a. Matilda

LEOPOLD VON BABENBERG, Duke of Austria

KINGDOM
of
SICILY

Naples

Mileto

Bagnara

Messina

Reggio

Palermo

Catania

Straits of Messina (Faro)

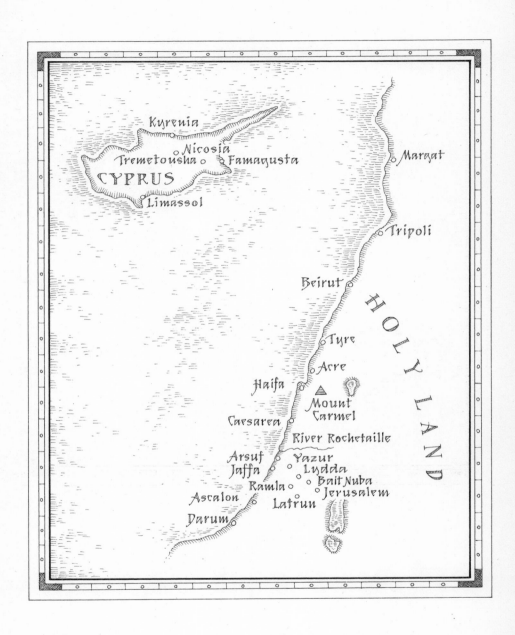

CYPRUS

Kyrenia

Nicosia
Tremetousha   Famagusta

Limassol

Margat

Tripoli

Beirut

HOLY LAND

Tyre

Acre

Haifa

Mount
Carmel

Caesarea

River Rochetaille

Arsuf   Yazur
Jaffa   Lydda
Ramla   Bait Nuba
Ascalon   Jerusalem
Latrun
Darum

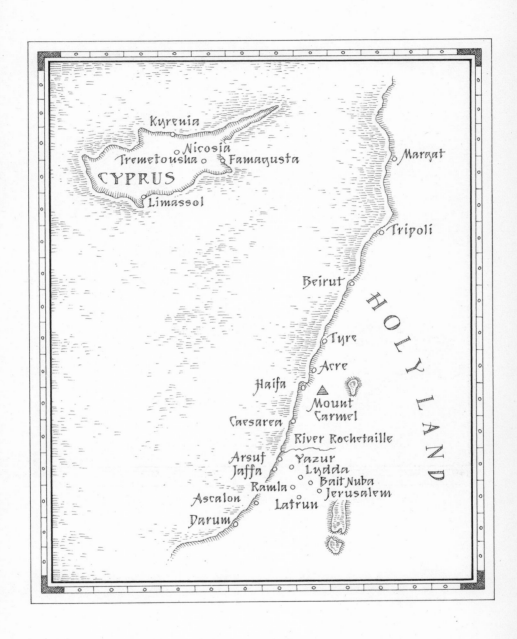

Kyrenia

Nicosia

Tremetousha   Famagusta

CYPRUS

Limassol

Margat

Tripoli

Beirut

HOLY LAND

Tyre

Acre

Haifa

Mount
Carmel

Caesarea

River Rochetaille

Arsuf   Yazur
Jaffa   Lydda

Ramla   Bait Nuba
Jerusalem

Ascalon   Latrun

Darum

PROLOGUE

heirs was a story that would rival the legend of King Arthur and Guinevere, his faithless queen. He was Henry, firstborn son of the Count of Anjou and the Empress Maude, and from an early age, he'd seemed to be one of Fortune's favorites. Whilst still Duke of Normandy, he'd dared to steal a queen, and by the time he was twenty-one, he'd claimed the crown that had eluded the Empress Maude. She was Eleanor, Duchess of Aquitaine, a great heiress and a great beauty who trailed scandal in her wake, her tragedy that she was a woman born in an age in which power was the preserve of men. The French king Louis had rejected Eleanor for her failure to give him a male heir. She gave Henry five, four of whom survived to manhood. They ruled over an empire that stretched from Scotland to the Mediterranean Sea, and for a time, their union seemed blessed.

Henry loved his sons, but not enough to share power with them. Nor would he give Eleanor a say in the governance of her beloved Aquitaine. The result would be the Great Rebellion of 1173, in which Henry's three eldest sons rose up against him, urged on by their mother, his own queen, an act of betrayal unheard of in their world. Henry won the war, but at great cost. His sons he could forgive; Eleanor he could not, for she'd inflicted a wound that would never fully heal.

Henry sought to make peace with his sons, but they were bitter that he continued to hold their mother prisoner and resentful that he kept them under a tight rein. Because he felt he could no longer trust them, he tried to bribe or coerce them into staying loyal. A great king, he would prove to be a failure as a father, for he was unable to learn from his mistakes.

His eldest and best-loved son, Hal—beguiling and handsome and utterly irresponsible—died in another rebellion against his sire, repenting when he was on his deathbed, when it was too late.

Upon Hal's death, the heir apparent was his brother Richard, who'd been raised in Eleanor's Aquitaine, meant from birth to rule over her duchy. Geoffrey, the third brother, had been wed to a great heiress of his own, Constance, the Duchess of Brittany. And then there was John, called John Lackland by his father in jest, for by the time he was born, there was little left for a younger fourth son. Henry was bound and determined to provide for John, too, and he unwittingly unleashed the furies that would bring about his ruin.

Henry demanded that Richard yield up Aquitaine to John, reasoning that Richard no longer needed the duchy now that he was to inherit an empire. But Richard loved Aquitaine, as he loved his imprisoned mother, and he would never forgive Henry for trying to take the duchy from him.

Henry made the same mistake with Geoffrey, withholding a large portion of his wife's Breton inheritance to ensure Geoffrey's good behavior. He only succeeded in driving Geoffrey into rebellion, too, and he'd allied himself with Philippe, the young French king, when he was killed in a tournament outside Paris.

The king who'd once jested about his surfeit of sons now had only two. When he stubbornly refused to recognize Richard as his heir, his son began to suspect that he meant to disinherit him in favor of John. Following in the footsteps of his brothers Hal and Geoffrey, Richard turned to the French king for aid, and it eventually came to war. By then, Henry was ailing and did not want to fight his own son. Richard no longer trusted him, though, and Henry was forced to make a humiliating surrender. But the worst was still to come. As Henry lay feverish and wretched at Chinon Castle, he learned that John, the son for whom he'd sacrificed so much, had betrayed him, making a private peace with Richard and King Philippe. Henry died two days later, crying, "Shame upon a conquered king." Few mourned. As was the way of their world, eyes were already turning from the sunset to the rising sun, to the man acclaimed as one of the best battle commanders in all of Christendom, Richard, first of that name to rule England since the Conquest.

Chapter 1

JULY 1189

Aboard the Galley San Niccolò

licia had been fearful long before she faced death in the Straits of Messina. She'd been afraid since the spring, when she'd lost her father and the only home she'd ever known. Even the arrival of her brother Arnaud did not ease her anxiety, for he was ill equipped to assume responsibility for a little sister. Arnaud was a warrior monk, one of that famed brotherhood-in-arms known as the Knights Templar, returning to Outremer to join the struggle to free the Holy City of Jerusalem from the infidels known as Saracens or Turks. Unable either to provide for Alicia's future or to abandon her, he'd felt compelled to take her with him. Alicia was grateful, but bewildered, too, for she did not know what awaited her in the Holy Land, and she suspected that her brother did not know, either. As he was her only lifeline, she had no choice but to trust in Arnaud and God as they left France behind.

The overland journey had been hard upon a young girl unaccustomed to travel. Arnaud had been kind in a distracted sort of way, though, and his fellow Templars had done their best to shield her from the rigors of the road, so some of her anxiety had begun to subside by the time they reached Genoa. But her fear came rushing back as soon as she set foot upon the wet, quaking deck of the *San Niccolò*.

Arnaud was pleased that he'd been able to book passage on a galley, explaining to Alicia that it would not be becalmed like naves and busses that relied solely upon sails, showing her the two banks of oars on each side of the ship. Alicia saw only how low it rode in the water, and she no longer worried about her uncertain prospects in Outremer, sure that she'd never survive the sea voyage.

She'd become seasick even before the Genoese lighthouse had receded into the distance. During the day, she huddled miserably in her small allotted space on the deck, obeying Arnaud's orders not to mingle with the other passengers, trying to settle her queasy stomach by nibbling on the twice-baked ship's biscuits. While some of the passengers had brought their own food, Arnaud had not, for he took seriously his Templar vows of poverty, obedience, and abstinence. The nights were by far the worst, and Alicia dreaded to see the sun sink into the sea behind them. She slept poorly, kept awake by the creaking and groaning of the ship's timbers, the relentless pounding of waves against the hull, the snoring of their neighbors, and the skittering sounds made by rats and mice unseen in the darkness. Each passenger was provided with a terra-cotta chamber pot and, with every breath she took, she inhaled the rank smells of urine and vomit and sweat. Lying awake as the hours dragged by until dawn, scratching flea bites and blinking back tears as she remembered the peaceful and familiar life that had once been hers, she yearned for the comfort of her brother's embrace, but Templars were forbidden to show physical affection to women, even their own mothers and sisters.

While most of the passengers were males, merchants and pilgrims and swaggering youths who'd taken the cross and boasted endlessly about the great deeds they'd perform in the Holy Land, there were several women returning to Tyre with their husbands after visiting family back in France, and even a few female pilgrims determined to fulfill their vows in the midst of war. One kindly matron would have taken Alicia under her wing, touched by the girl's youth, but Alicia was too shy to respond, not wanting to displease Arnaud.

She did listen to the other woman's cheerful conversation, though, marveling that she seemed so blithe about coming back to a land under siege. The port of Tyre and a few scattered castles were all that was left to the Christians in the Holy Land. Acre, Jaffa, and the sacred city of Jerusalem had all fallen to the infidels. On their journey, Alicia had heard her brother rant about the wickedness of the Saracens, bitterly cursing the man who led them, the Sultan of Egypt and Syria, Salah al-Dīn, known to the Christians as Saladin. Every time Alicia heard the name of Arnaud's godless nemesis, she shivered. Arnaud's courage was beyond question. He didn't even seem afraid of the perilous, hungry sea. If he died fighting the infidels, his entry into Paradise would be assured. But what would happen to her?

Arnaud had told her that their voyage to Tyre would take about thirty-five days, explaining that the prevailing winds blew from the west and they'd make faster time with the wind at their back. Voyages from the Holy Land took much longer, he said, since ships were sailing into the wind. When he added casually that it mattered naught to them since they'd not be returning to France, Alicia felt a pang of dismay, for she did not know if she wanted to live out her life in the alien, war-torn kingdom known as Outremer—the Land beyond the Sea. She'd overheard Arnaud talking about her to one of his Templar companions, saying that he knew the abbess of Our Lady of Tyre and she might be willing to take his sister in as a boarder and later as a novice. Alicia realized she could not stay with Arnaud in Tyre, for women were banned from their temples and commanderies, even orphaned little sisters. But she was not sure she wanted to be a nun. Shouldn't that be a free choice, not a last resort? Wouldn't it please the Lord Christ more if His brides came to Him willingly, not because they had nowhere else to go?

The weather had remained clear for the first week, but as they approached the isle of Sicily, they could see smoke rising up into the sky. Alicia's brother told her this was Sicily's famous Mountain of Fire, which many claimed to be one of the portals of Hell, for it belched smoke and noxious fumes and even liquid flames that spilled over the slope and burned a path of destruction down to the sea. Arnaud and his companions had already alarmed her by relating the ancient legend of Scylla, a six-headed sea monster who lurked in a cave facing the Straits of Messina. Directly opposite her was Charybdis, a whirlpool waiting to suck ships into its maw. If ships trying to avoid Charybdis ventured too close to Scylla's cave, she seized these unlucky vessels and feasted upon the captured sailors. Realizing belatedly that this was no story for his young sister's ears, Arnaud had hastened to reassure her that the tale was merely folklore. She wanted to believe him, but a land that harbored fiery mountains might easily shelter sea monsters, too, and each time she eyed the distant Sicilian coastline, she surreptitiously made the sign of the cross.

The other passengers were increasingly uneasy as they drew closer to the Faro, the straits separating Sicily from the mainland. Even the sailors seemed on edge, for at its narrowest point, it was only two miles wide and the currents were notoriously turbulent, seething like a "boiling cauldron" one merchant said grimly. *Like Charybdis,* Alicia thought, wondering which was worse, to be drowned or devoured, and wondering, too, what other trials lay ahead.

She was not long in finding out. A darkening sky warned of a coming storm, and the ship's master ordered that the sails be lowered as the wind rose and black, ominous clouds clustered overhead. The rain held off, but the sea soon pitched and rolled wildly, their ship sinking into troughs so deep that they were walled in by water. As the galley floundered, they were drenched by the waves breaking over the gunwales, bruised and battered against the heaving deck, tossed about like so many rag dolls. Sure that death was imminent, passengers and sailors alike offered up desperate prayers, but by now the wind was so loud they could not even hear their own words. Alicia was so petrified that her throat had closed up, and she could neither pray nor weep, waiting mutely for Scylla or Charybdis to claim the *San Niccolò* and end their suffering.

When the ship suddenly shuddered and stopped dead in the water, she was sure that they had been seized by Scylla's bloody talons. But the sailors were yelling and scrambling across the deck, and after a time, she could comprehend what Arnaud was shouting into her ear. "We've run aground!"

Grappling for boat hooks and oars, the crew sought to push off from the shoal. But as the galley fought for its life, one of its two masts snapped in half and plunged into the sea. The ship's master lurched toward Arnaud and the other Templars. Knowing he could not compete with the howling wind, he relied upon gestures, pointing toward the longboat tethered in the stern and then toward the knights' scabbards. Arnaud was quick to understand. They were going to launch the longboat and try to reach the shore, less than half a mile away, and the master wanted them to maintain order, to keep the panicked passengers from mobbing the boat. Grasping Alicia by her shoulders, he pulled her to her feet, holding her tightly as they headed for the stern.

Alicia could never clearly recall her final moments upon the *San Niccolò*. She had only snatches of memory—the men kept at bay by the drawn swords of the Templars, the most important of the passengers scrambling into the longboat, the eerie calm of the ship's master and the ashen-faced sailors. Once the affluent merchants, the women, an archdeacon, and several priests had climbed aboard, the master gestured for the Templars to join them. They were men who'd tested their courage against Saracen steel, and they did not hesitate now, sheathing their swords and clambering into the longboat. Alicia was too frozen with fear to move. Arnaud picked her up as if she were a feather, telling her to close her eyes as the longboat was lowered into the heaving sea.

Her memory went blank at that point, and the next thing she remembered, the current had thrust their little craft onto the Sicilian shoreline. The oarsmen leaped out into the water and began to drag the boat up onto the beach, and soon the passengers were jumping to safety, falling to their knees and thanking the Almighty for their deliverance. People seemed to have appeared from nowhere, helping the shipwreck survivors away from the crashing waves. An elderly man speaking a tongue that was utterly incomprehensible to Alicia jerked off his own mantle and wrapped her in it. She tried to thank him, but her teeth were chattering too much for speech. Someone else was offering a wineskin and she obeyed unthinkingly, gasping as the liquid burned its way down her throat. But where was Arnaud?

When she saw her brother standing by the beached longboat, she stumbled toward him, crying out in horror as she realized what was happening. Several of the sailors had balked, but the others were going back for the doomed passengers and their shipmates, and the Templars were going with them.

Arnaud turned as she screamed his name. He was saying that they were needed to help man the oars, saying there were Christian pilgrims still on the ship and it was his duty to rescue them, that it would shame him to stay on shore whilst the sailors braved the sea again. Alicia didn't understand, didn't even hear his words. Sobbing, she clung to him with all her feeble strength, begging him not to go, and he finally had to tear himself away, kissing her upon the forehead before he shoved her back onto the sand. "God will protect me," he insisted, with a grimace that he meant as a smile, and then scrambled into the longboat as they launched it out onto the churning waves.

By the time Alicia got to her feet, her brother was gone. Others had joined her at the water's edge, watching as the longboat fought the storm. It had almost reached the trapped ship when it was slammed by a monster wave. Alicia began to scream even before the longboat disappeared into its roiling depths. Hands were gripping her now, pulling her away, but she paid them no heed. Her eyes frantically searching the raging sea, she continued to scream for her brother.

THE MALE SURVIVORS of the *San Niccolò* wreck were given shelter at the monastery of San Salvatore dei Greci overlooking the harbor, and the injured women had been taken to the convent of Santa Maria della Valle, just west of Messina. Having strangers in their midst was always disruptive for the nuns, but it was the arrival of William de Hauteville and his entourage that created the real excitement, especially among the novices, for not even nuns were immune to his potent appeal of beauty, high birth, and gallant good manners.

"We were expecting a visit from you, my lord," the mother abbess said with a fond smile, for she'd known William for most of his thirty-six years. "You've always been very generous to those poor souls shipwrecked in your domains, and I was sure you'd be no less openhanded with the survivors of the *San Niccolò*."

"I do but follow the teachings of Our Lord Christ," William said, with becoming modesty and a dazzling smile. "'Be ye therefore merciful, as Your Father also is merciful.'" They were walking in the gardens, lush with summer blooms, for

Sicily had been blessed with a mild climate. William paused to pluck a fragrant flower and presented it to the elderly abbess with a flourish. "Have your hosteller speak with my steward, my lady abbess, and he will reimburse your abbey for the expenses you've incurred in caring for these castaways. I've given orders that men should search the beaches for the dead, but I doubt that their bodies will be recovered. It is a sad fate to be denied a Christian burial, especially for the Knights of God. They deserved better than that."

Abbess Blanche was in full agreement; she shared William's admiration for the Templars. Their deaths seemed all the more tragic because their sacrifice had been needless. The galley had not gone down as quickly as all feared, and once the storm passed, the local people rowed out in small boats and ferried the stranded survivors to shore, charging exorbitant fees for that service. Only then did the *San Niccolò* break up and sink quietly beneath the waves.

"Our costs have been minimal, my lord, for only three of the women passengers were injured. One broke her arm when she was flung against the tiller, and the second sprained her ankle when she jumped out of the longboat. But the third . . ." The abbess shook her head and sighed. "We know very little about her, for the other passengers say she kept to herself. They could tell me only her name—Alicia de Sezanne—and that she is the sister of one of the drowned Templars. She is just a child and I fear that she is all alone in the world now, may Our Blessed Mother pity her plight."

"She has no family?" William frowned. "Poor little lass. If her brother was a Templar, she must be gently born. Surely she has kin somewhere? What did she tell you?"

"Nothing, my lord. She has not spoken a word for a fortnight. Indeed, I am not even sure if she hears what we say to her, and if the passengers had not told me otherwise, I'd think she was a deaf-mute. It has been a struggle to get her to eat even a few swallows of soup. She just lies there. . . . I do not know what will become of the child, truly I do not. What if her grief has driven her mad?"

She paused then, hoping that William would come up with a solution, and he did not disappoint her. "Suppose I ask my wife to come and see the lass?" he said thoughtfully. "She may be able to break through the girl's shell. She is very good at that, you know."

"What a wonderful idea, my lord! Do you think the Lady Joanna would be willing?"

His smile was both indulgent and affectionate. "My wife has never been able to resist a bird with a broken wing."

JOANNA PAUSED in the doorway of the infirmary, beset by sudden doubts. What was she to say to the child? What comfort could she offer? "How old did you say she was, Sister Heloise?"

"We cannot be sure, Madame, but we think she looks to be about ten years or so, mayhap eleven."

Too young to understand why God had taken her brother, Joanna thought, and then smiled, without any humor. She was nigh on twenty-four, and she did not understand, either. "Take me to her," she said, and followed the young nun across the chamber toward a corner bed. She was touched by her first sight of that small, forlorn figure, lying so still that it was a relief to see the faint rise and fall of her chest. The girl seemed pathetically fragile and frail, her face turned toward the wall, and when Joanna spoke her name, she did not respond. Signaling for Sister Heloise to bring a chair over, Joanna sat beside the bed and pondered what to say.

"I am so very sorry for your brother's death, Alicia. You can be proud of his courage, and . . . and it must be some comfort to know that he is in the Almighty's Embrace. My confessor assured me that one of God's Knights would be spared Purgatory, that Heaven's Gates would be opened wide to him. . . ." There was no indication that Alicia had even heard her, and Joanna's words trailed off. How could she expect the lass to find consolation in theology? All Alicia knew was that her brother was dead and she was abandoned and alone.

"I would not presume to say I know what you are feeling, Alicia. I can tell you this, though, that I know what it is like to lose a brother. I have grieved for three of mine, and for a sister, too. . . ." Despite herself, her voice wavered at the last, for the death of her sister was still a raw wound. "I wish I could tell you that the pain will eventually heal. But that would be a lie. This is a sorrow you will take to your grave. In time, though, you'll learn to live with it, and that is all we can hope for."

She waited then, to no avail. Trying a new tack, she said quietly, "The world must be a very frightening place to you now. I cannot begin to imagine how alone you must feel. But you are not as alone as you think, Alicia. I promise you that."

Again her words were swallowed up in silence. She was usually good with children. Of course she'd never dealt with one so damaged before. "We share something else in common, lass. I was your age when I first came to Sicily, just eleven years old. I remember the journey all too well, for I had never been so wretched." She was following her instincts now, speaking in the soothing tones she'd have used to calm a nervous filly. "I was so sick, Alicia, feeding the fish day and night.

Were you seasick, too? It got so bad for me that we had to put into port at Naples and continue our journey on land. For years I had dreadful dreams about that trip and my husband had great difficulty in coaxing me to set foot on a ship again. I remember arguing with him that the Almighty had not intended man to fly, or else he'd have given us wings, and since we did not have gills like fish, clearly we were not meant to venture out onto the sea, either. He just laughed, but then he's never been seasick a day in his life. . . ."

She continued on in that vein for a while, speaking lightly of inconsequential matters in the hope of forging a connection, however tenuous, with this mute, motionless little girl. At last she had to concede defeat, and after exchanging regretful looks with Sister Heloise, she started to rise from the chair. It was then that Alicia spoke. Her words were mumbled, inaudible, but they were words, the first anyone had heard her utter since her brother drowned.

Trying to hide her excitement, Joanna said as calmly as she could, "I am sorry, Alicia. I could not hear you. Can you repeat yourself?"

"I am twelve," Alicia said, softly but distinctly, "not eleven."

Joanna almost laughed, remembering how affronted she'd been to be taken for younger than she was, a mortal insult for most children. "*Mea culpa*," she said. "But in my defense, it is not easy to tell how old you are when you will not look at me." She waited, then, holding her breath, until the bed creaked and Alicia slowly turned away from the wall. Joanna could see why the nuns had mistaken her age. She had round cheeks, a rosebud mouth, and freckles sprinkled over an upturned nose, a child's face, innocent and open to hurt. Joanna doubted that she'd begun her flux yet, for her lean and angular little body showed no signs of approaching womanhood.

"I am Joanna," she said, for she'd found that with children, the simplest approach was often the best. "I am here to help you."

Alicia had to squint, for she'd not looked into direct light for days and sun was flooding into the chamber, enveloping Joanna in a golden glow. She was the most beautiful woman Alicia had ever seen, and the most glamorous, with flawless, fair skin, copper-color hair covered by an embroidered silk veil, emerald-green eyes, and graceful white fingers adorned with jewels. Alicia was dumbfounded, not sure if this glorious vision was a figment of her fevered imagination. "Are you real?" she blurted out, and the vision laughed, revealing a deep dimple that flashed like a shooting star, and assured her she was very much a flesh-and-blood woman.

The flesh-and-blood women in Alicia's world did not look like this one. "May I . . . may I ask you a question? Did you truly lose three brothers?"

"I spoke the truth, Alicia. My eldest brother died ere I was even born, but my other brothers had reached manhood when death claimed them. Hal was stricken with the bloody flux, and Geoffrey was killed in a French tournament. And this summer my elder sister Tilda died of a fever. Indeed, I only learned of her death a few weeks ago." Joanna bit her lip, for the shock of Tilda's death had yet to abate; her sister had been just thirty-three.

Alicia regarded her solemnly. "You said the hurt never goes away. Will I grieve for Arnaud to the end of my days?" She was reassured when Joanna gave her the same straightforward answer, telling her the truth rather than what she wanted to hear. "Did you love your brothers?"

"Very much, Alicia. They were all older than me, except for my brother Johnny, and they spoiled me outrageously, as I imagine Arnaud did with you."

"No . . ." Alicia hesitated, but with gentle encouragement, she continued and eventually Joanna learned the history of this woebegone orphan. She came from Champagne, where her father had served as steward for one of the count's vassals. He'd died that past spring, leaving Alicia and two older brothers, Odo, his eldest and heir, and Arnaud, who'd been long gone from their lives, serving God in distant lands. Odo had not wanted to be burdened with her, she confided to Joanna, and he and his wife had arranged to marry her off to a neighbor, a widower who was willing to overlook her lack of a marriage portion. She had not wanted to wed him, for his breath reeked and he was very old, "even older than my papa! And I did not think I was ready to be a wife. Odo and Yvette paid me no heed, though, and were making ready to post the banns when Arnaud arrived from Paris."

Arnaud had been outraged by the match, and he quarreled bitterly with Odo, demanding that he provide a marriage portion so they could find her a suitable husband when she was of a proper age to wed. But Odo had turned a deaf ear. Arnaud knew Odo would wed her to the neighbor as soon as he was gone, and so he took her with him. "I think he had a nunnery in mind. He promised, though, to look after me, to make sure that I was always safe. . . ."

Tears had begun to well in Alicia's eyes, the first she'd shed since that awful day on the beach. Joanna gathered the child into her arms and held Alicia as she wept. But she had a practical streak, too, and glancing over Alicia's heaving shoulder, she caught the nun's eye and mouthed a silent command to fetch food from the abbey kitchen. Sister Heloise gladly obeyed, first hastening to find the abbess and give her the good news that the Lady Joanna had succeeded where everyone else had failed. She'd coaxed this unhappy child from the shadows back into the light.

AFTER A FORTNIGHT in bed, Alicia was surprised by how weak she felt when she first ventured outside. Tiring quickly, she sank down on a bench in the cloisters, taking pleasure in the warmth of the Sicilian sun upon her face. Brightly colored birds flitted from bush to bush and she tracked their passage with interest. It helped, she had discovered, to focus only upon the moment, and she resolutely refused to let herself dwell upon her fears, to think of the future she so dreaded. For now, the kindness of the nuns and her beautiful benefactor was enough.

Growing drowsy, she stretched out on the bench and soon fell asleep. When she awoke, she got hastily to her feet and greeted the abbess in the deferential manner that she'd copied from the nuns. Smiling, Blanche bade her sit back down again, saying she needed to regain her strength for the journey, and Alicia went suddenly cold. "A journey?" she whispered. "I am leaving here?"

"In two days' time. I do not suppose you can ride a mule? No matter, I am sure Lady Joanna can provide a horse litter for you. Her lord husband has already returned to Palermo, but she remained behind, waiting till you were well enough to travel."

Alicia didn't understand. "Why is she taking me to Palermo?"

"Well, that is where she and Lord William live, child. They have a palace here in Messina, too, but their favorite home is in Palermo."

"Am I . . . am I to live with her?" That seemed too much to hope for, though. "Why would she want me?"

That was a question some of Blanche's nuns had been asking, too. But not the abbess. She had no doubt that this bedraggled, pitiful kitten had stirred Joanna's thwarted maternal instincts. "Why not? There is always room for young women in the royal household, and taking you in would be a way to honor your brother, too. He died a martyr's death, for he was on his way to the Holy Land and he sacrificed himself to save his fellow Christians."

By now Alicia was thoroughly confused. "Does the Lady Joanna live in the royal household, then?"

The abbess looked at her in surprise. "You do not know who she is?"

Alicia flushed, taking those incredulous words as an implied rebuke. "I thought of her as my guardian angel," she said, staring down at the ground.

"Well, she is indeed that," the older woman acknowledged. "But your angel wears a crown, not a halo. Lady Joanna is the daughter of the English king, Henry Fitz Empress, and the queen of William de Hauteville, the King of Sicily."

CHAPTER 2

AUGUST 1189

Palermo, Sicily

licia had no memories of her mother, who'd died when she was three. It took no time at all for Joanna to fill that empty place in the girl's heart, for no one had ever shown her such kindness. She was so completely under Joanna's spell that she was even able to overcome her panic when Joanna revealed that they'd have to travel to Palermo by ship, explaining that it was only about one hundred and forty miles, but the roads were so bad that the journey could take up to four weeks by land. They'd stay within sight of the shoreline, she promised, and although it took more courage than Alicia thought she had, she followed the young Sicilian queen onto the royal galley, for drowning was no longer her greatest fear.

She felt at times as if she'd lost touch with reality, for there was a dream-like quality to the weeks after the sinking of the *San Niccolò*. She'd never met a man as charming as Joanna's husband, had never seen a city as beautiful as Palermo, had never imagined that people could live in such comfort and luxury, and at first Sicily seemed truly like the biblical land of milk and honey.

On the voyage to Palermo, Joanna had enjoyed telling Alicia about the history of her island home. Sicily was a jewel set in a turquoise sea, she'd said poetically, but its beauty and riches had been both a blessing and a curse, for it had been captured in turn by the Carthaginians, the ancient Greeks, the Romans, Germanic tribes, the Greek empire of Constantinople, and then the Saracens. In God's Year 1061, a Norman-French adventurer named Roger de Hauteville had been the one to launch an invasion from the mainland. It was so successful that in 1130, his son and namesake had himself crowned as Sicily's first king, whose domains would soon encompass all of southern Italy, too.

"He was my lord husband's grandfather," Joanna said, smiling at Alicia's won-derment. But it was not Sicily's turbulent past that amazed the girl; it was that the Kingdom of Sicily was younger than her own father, who'd died the day after his sixty-fourth birthday. How could such a magical realm have been in existence for less than six decades?

She was captivated by Palermo, set in a fertile plain of olive groves and date palms, its size beyond her wildest imaginings; her brother had told her that Paris had fifty thousand citizens, but Joanna said Palermo's population was more than twice that number. Alicia was impressed by the limestone houses that gleamed in the sun like white doves, by the number of public baths, the orchards of exotic fruit that she'd never tasted: oranges, lemons, limes, and pomegranates. But it was the royal palaces that utterly dazzled her, ringing the city like a necklace of opu-lent, shining pearls.

Joanna and William's primary residence was set in a precinct known as the Galca, which held palaces, churches, chapels, gardens, fountains, a menagerie of exotic animals, and the ruins of an ancient Roman amphitheater. The royal apart-ments were situated in a section of the main palace called the Joharia, flanked by two sturdy towers. A red marble staircase led to the first floor, with an entrance to the king's chapel, where Alicia came often to pray for her brother's soul and to marvel at its magnificence. The nave was covered with brilliant mosaic stones dramatizing scenes from the Old and New Testaments, the floor inlaid with cir-cles of green serpentine and red porphyry encased in white marble, and the ceil-ing honeycombed; one of the walls even contained a water clock, a device quite unknown in France.

The palace itself was splendidly decorated with vivid mosaic depictions of hunters, leopards, lions, centaurs, and peacocks. Alicia's father had once taken her to the Troyes residence of the Count of Champagne, and she'd come away con-vinced that no one in Christendom lived as well as Lord Henri. She now knew better. Joanna's coffers were filled with the finest silks, her chambers lit by lamps of brass and crystal and scented by silver incense burners, her jewelry kept in ivory boxes as well crafted as the treasures they held. She bathed in a copper bath-tub, read books whose covers were studded with gemstones, played with her dogs in gardens fragrant with late-blooming flowers, shaded by citrus trees, and adorned with elegant marble fountains. She even had a table of solid gold, set with silver plate and delicacies like sugar-coated almonds, dates, hazelnuts, mel-ons, figs, pomegranates, oranges, shrimp, and marzipan tortes. Alicia could not envision a more luxurious world than the one Joanna had married into; nor could she imagine a woman more deserving of it than the Sicilian queen, her "angel with a crown."

But if she embraced Joanna and her handsome husband wholeheartedly, some of her initial enthusiasm for their lush, green kingdom soon dimmed. While there was much to admire, there were aspects of Sicilian life that she found startling and others that profoundly shocked her. Palermo seemed like the biblical Babel, for not only were there three official languages—Latin, Greek, and Arabic—people also spoke Norman-French and the Italian dialect of Lombardy. Even the realm's religious life was complex and confusing, for the Latin Catholic Church vied with the Greek Orthodox Church for supremacy, and Palermo was home, too, to mosques and synagogues.

There had been Jews in Champagne, of course, but they were only allowed to earn their living as moneylenders. The Jewish community in Palermo was numerous, prosperous, and engaged in occupations forbidden to them in France; they were craftsmen, doctors, merchants, and dominated the textile industry. Alicia found it disconcerting to see them mingling so freely with the other citizens of the city, for her brother had told her that the French king, Philippe, had banished the Jews from Paris and he'd spoken of their exile with obvious approval.

She was uncomfortable in the city markets, for while they offered a vast variety of enticing goods, they offered slaves for sale, too. They were Saracens, not Christians, and Alicia took comfort in that. But she still found the sight of those manacled men and women to be unsettling, for slavery was not known in France.

There was so much in Sicily that was foreign to her. It was easy to appreciate the island's beauty and affluence, the mild climate, the prosperity of its people. Although its diversity was like nothing she'd ever experienced, she did not feel threatened by it. But she did not think that she could ever accept the presence of Saracen infidels living so freely in a Christian country, even allowed to be judged by Islamic law.

Every time she saw a turbaned Arab sauntering the city streets, she shrank back in alarm. When she heard the cries of the *muezzin* summoning Muslims to their prayers, she hastily crossed herself, as if to ward off the evil eye. She was baffled that there should be Arabic phrases on the gold *tari*, the coinage of the realm. She did not understand why young Sicilian women adopted Saracen fashions, often wearing face veils in public and decorating their fingers with henna. She was stunned when she learned that Muslims served in King William's army and navy, and some were actively involved in his government. They were known as the Palace Saracens, men of odd appearance, uncommonly tall, with high-pitched voices and smooth skin, lacking any facial hair. She'd heard them called eunuchs; when one of Joanna's ladies had explained the meaning of that foreign word, she'd been horrified, and for the first time she wondered if she'd ever feel truly at home in this alien land.

Her brother had said Saracens were the enemies of God, telling her how they'd desecrated Christian churches after capturing Jerusalem, exposing the precious fragment of the True Cross to jeering crowds in the streets of Damascus. The abbess had assured her that Arnaud died a martyr to his faith. So how could King William find so much to admire in Saracen culture? Why was he fluent in the tongue of the infidels and a patron of Arab poets? How could he entrust his very life to unbelievers? For he not only had a personal bodyguard of black Muslim slaves, his palace cooks, his physicians, and his astrologers were all Saracens, too.

Bewildered and deeply troubled, Alicia yearned to confide her fears to Joanna. She dared not do so, though, because of the Lady Mariam, with slanting eyes, hair like polished jet, and the blood of Saracens running through her veins. She spoke French as well as Arabic, and accompanied Joanna to church. But she was one of them, a godless infidel. And yet it was painfully obvious to Alicia that Joanna loved her. Of Joanna's ladies, only two were truly her intimates—Dame Beatrix, a tart-tongued Angevin in her middle years who'd been with Joanna since childhood, and the Lady Mariam. The Saracen.

As the weeks passed, Alicia found herself becoming obsessed with the Lady Mariam, a flesh-and-blood symbol of all that she could not understand about Sicilian society. She studied the young woman covertly, watching suspiciously as Mariam dutifully attended Mass and prayed to the God of the Christians. She thought her scrutiny was unobtrusive, until the day Mariam glanced over at her during the priest's invocation and winked. Alicia was so flustered that she fled the church, feigning illness to explain her abrupt departure. But after that, she had to know Mariam's secrets, had to know how she'd embedded herself in the very heart of a Christian queen's household.

While Joanna continued to treat her with affection, her other ladies had paid Alicia little heed, either jealous of Joanna's favor or considering her too young to be of any interest. Alicia had been observing them for weeks, though, so she knew which ones to approach: Emma d'Aleramici and Bethlem de Greci. They'd shown Alicia only the most grudging courtesy. But they loved to gossip and she hoped that would matter more to them than her relative insignificance.

She was right. Emma and Bethlem were more than willing to tell her of Mariam's scandalous history. Mariam was King William's half-sister, they confided gleefully, born to a slave girl in his late father's *harim*. William's widowed mother had shown little interest in her son's young, homesick bride, and so he'd turned Joanna's care over to his aunt Constance, who was only twenty-four years old herself. It was Constance who'd chosen Mariam as a companion for Joanna, Bethlem revealed. Apparently she'd thought the fact that they were the same age was more important than her dubious background and tainted blood, Emma added, and that was how Mariam had insinuated herself into the queen's favor.

Emma and Bethlem's spitefulness awakened in Alicia an unexpected emotion, a flicker of sympathy for Mariam. She was impressed, too, to find out that Mariam had royal blood. But what was a *harim*? They were happy to enlighten her, explaining that all of the Sicilian kings had adopted the shameful custom of the Arab emirs, keeping Saracen slave girls for their pleasure. Mariam's mother was one of these debased women, and Mariam the fruit of the first King William's lust. And when Alicia cried out that surely Queen Joanna's lord husband did not keep a *harim*, too, they laughed at her naïveté. Of course he did, they told her, and why not? What man would not want a bedmate who was subject to his every whim? A bedmate who could never say no, whose very existence depended upon pleasing him, upon fulfilling all of his secret desires, no matter how depraved.

Alicia did not know what they meant. What a man and woman did in bed was a mystery to her, something that happened once they were married. She knew that not all men were faithful to their wives, had heard her eldest brother Odo's servants gossiping about his roving eye. But her brother's wife was skeletal thin and sharp-tongued and Alicia could not remember ever hearing her laugh. Whereas Joanna was beautiful and lively and loving. How could William want any woman but the one he'd wed?

As it happened, Joanna was pondering that very question on a mild November night, lying awake and restless beside her sleeping husband. She had no basis for comparison, but she wondered sometimes if their love-making was lacking something. It was pleasant enough, but never fully satisfying; she was always left wanting more, even if she was not sure what that was. She did not let herself dwell upon these thoughts, though, choosing to laugh at herself instead. What did she expect? That flesh-and-blood men and women burned with the grand passion of the lovers in troubadour songs?

But on this particular night, she had more on her mind than the carnal pleasures which the Church said were sinful if not undertaken for the purpose of procreation. She was resentful that William had not come to her bed last week, when she'd been at her most fertile. It was every wife's duty to provide her husband with heirs, a duty all the more urgent when a kingdom was at stake. Joanna's yearning for a baby was much more than a marital obligation, though. It was an ache that never went away, hers the pained hunger of a mother who'd buried a child.

She still grieved for the beautiful little boy whose life had been measured in days, and did not understand why she'd not conceived again in the eight years since Bohemund's death. She'd been worried enough to consult the female doctors at the famed medical school in Salerno, and had been told that a woman's womb was most receptive to her husband's seed immediately after her monthly flux ended. Joanna had relayed that information to William, but he did not always come to her at these critical times, and when that happened, she could only fret and fume in silence, angry and frustrated.

It seemed unfair that he should have complete control over conduct that mattered so much to them both. But she could not come to him unbidden. The few times that she'd done so, he'd obviously been displeased by her boldness. Although this passive role did not come easily to her, she'd done her best to play by his rules, for it would have been humiliating to go to his private chamber and find him in bed with one of his Saracen concubines. The Church might preach that husbands and wives owed a "marital debt" to each other, but how was a wife to collect it when her husband had a *harim* of seductive slaves at his beck and call?

She still remembered how shocked she'd been to learn of his *harim*, a year or so after her arrival in Sicily. As young as she was, she already knew that fidelity was thought to be a mandate for women, not men; her father's affair with Rosamund Clifford had been an open secret for years. But this was different. How could a Christian king embrace such a debauched, infidel practice? Why would he want to live like an Arab emir?

When she'd confronted William with her newfound knowledge, he'd been amused by her forthrightness, explaining nonchalantly that he was merely following in the ways of his father and grandfather. Sicily had its own customs, its own traditions, and his *harim* had nothing to do with her or their marriage, which he was sure she'd understand once she was older. Even at age twelve, Joanna had known she was being patronized. She'd consoled herself that surely he'd put these women aside after she was old enough to share his bed.

But he hadn't. They'd consummated their marriage once she turned fourteen, yet nothing changed. By then Joanna fancied herself in love with him, and that had been a painful time for her. Looking back now, she felt a wry sympathy for that young girl, so innocent and starry-eyed. How could she not have been bedazzled by William, who'd seemed like one of the heroes in those troubadour tales she so enjoyed? He was tall and graceful, with long fair hair, compelling dark eyes, and an easy, engaging smile; he was also courteous, good-natured, and well educated. She'd felt herself so blessed, so fortunate that it seemed churlish to object to a few snakes in her Eden, even if they were alluring, dusky-skinned temptresses who were sleeping with her husband.

Joanna was not sure when she'd fallen out of love with William, assuming it had been love and not youthful infatuation. It may have begun after they'd lost their son, for they were both devastated by his death and yet they grieved alone. She'd turned to him for comfort, but he'd withdrawn into his own sorrow, and instead of coming closer together, they'd drifted further apart.

But a good marriage did not need love to flourish, and people did not enter into matrimony with expectations of finding their romantic soul mates. Joanna had many reasons to be thankful that she was William's wife, and she knew she was much luckier than the vast majority of women, including those secluded slave girls in her husband's *harim*.

It was true that as she matured, she began to have misgivings about William's prudence and his political judgments. He pursued a very aggressive foreign policy, one motivated as much by revenge as ambition, for he bore a bitter grudge against the emperor of the Greek Empire, who'd betrothed his daughter to William and then changed his mind, leaving William waiting in vain for her arrival at Taranto. William never forgot that public humiliation, and never forgave. He'd bided his time and saw his chance midst the chaos that followed the emperor's sudden death. He dispatched the Sicilian fleet and a large army to capture Constantinople, but the result was a costly, embarrassing defeat.

Joanna had been troubled by his determination to conquer the Greek Empire, for it did not seem likely to succeed. In that, she was her father's daughter, a pragmatist at heart. She was even more troubled by the marriage that William made to pave the way for his war. There had long been great enmity between the Kingdom of Sicily and the Holy Roman Empire, but when Emperor Frederick Barbarossa had unexpectedly offered a marital alliance, William accepted, for that would free him to devote all his efforts to the conquest of the Greek Empire. And so he'd wed his aunt Constance to Heinrich von Hohenstaufen, the King of Germany and the emperor's eldest son and heir. The marriage created an uproar in Sicily, for it raised a frightening specter. If William were to die without a son or daughter to succeed him, Constance would be the heiress to the Sicilian throne, and the Sicilians would rather have the Devil himself rule over them than Constance's hated German husband.

Joanna had shared the public distaste for this alliance, for the Holy Roman Emperor had long been a foe of her family's House. Moreover, she hated to see Constance, whom she'd grown to love, sent off to exile in Germany, a cold, harsh land to a woman accustomed to the sun-splashed warmth of Palermo. Heinrich was only twenty at the time of the marriage, eleven years younger than Constance, but he'd already earned a reputation for brutality, and Joanna doubted whether even an empress's crown would compensate Constance for the life she'd lead with Heinrich. William had brushed aside her misgivings, though, just as he ignored the impassioned, panicky objections of his subjects. He was young and healthy, after all, and Joanna had proven herself capable of bearing a son, so he was confident that Heinrich would never be able to claim Sicily on Constance's behalf, and it irked him that others remained so adamantly opposed to their union.

Joanna had kept her qualms to herself after Constance's marriage, for what was done was done. Nor did she blame William for not heeding her advice. Unlike her mother, who'd ruled Aquitaine in her own right, she was merely William's consort and the power was his, not hers. She'd done her best to comfort him after his army's devastating defeat by the Greeks, for that was a wife's duty, but to her dismay, he vowed to continue the war at a later date. She was greatly relieved when he had to put his Greek ambitions aside, even if the cause was the disastrous news out of Outremer. The King of Jerusalem's army had been destroyed by the forces of Salah al-Dīn, and before the year was out, he'd taken the Holy City itself. William was horrified, and he'd immediately dispatched the Sicilian fleet to the aid of Tyre, the last bastion of Christian control, while offering his harbors, riches, and armed forces to the kings who'd taken the cross and sworn to recapture Jerusalem from the Saracens.

Joanna felt some guilt that the catastrophic loss of Jerusalem should be the cause of joy, but the crusade would mean that she'd get to see her father and her brother Richard, for they'd both taken the cross. It had been thirteen years since she'd left her home and family, and she was elated at the prospect of their reunion. When word trickled across the Alps and into Italy of fresh discord between Henry and Richard, she'd refused to let it discourage her. Her father and Richard were often at odds, for they were both stubborn, strong-willed men and Richard remained embittered by the continuing confinement of their mother. She had no trouble convincing herself that they'd patch up this latest squabble, too, as they'd done in the past, and she continued to lay plans for their arrival, for she wanted their welcome to be truly spectacular. She wanted to show them that they'd made the right decision in wedding her to William.

She'd even entertained the notion of accompanying them to the Holy Land. Her mother had done so while wed to the French king Louis, had risked her life and reputation by taking part in a crusade that was an abysmal failure, one that eventually led to the end of her marriage to Louis and remarriage to Joanna's father. Joanna would gladly have followed in her mother's footsteps, for it would be the experience of a lifetime. But she could not be sure that William meant to join the crusaders. He'd been very generous in the help he offered. Would he actually leave Sicily, though? He never had done so in the past. He'd launched military expeditions to Egypt, North Africa, Greece, and Spain, but not once had he taken a personal role in one of his campaigns. And this was Joanna's secret fear, one she could not even acknowledge to herself, that William would again stay safely at home while he sent men out to die in his name.

His *harim* and faulty political judgment were minor matters compared to this dark shadow. Theirs was a world in which a king was expected to lead his men into war. Her father had done so since the age of sixteen. So had all her brothers and her mother's male relatives. Even Philippe Capet, the French king, who had a known distaste for war, still commanded his own armies. So had William's grandfather and his father. Joanna could think of no other ruler in Christendom who'd never bloodied his sword in combat. Only William.

Joanna had not allowed herself to venture any farther along this dangerous road. She was by nature both an optimist and a realist, believed in making the best of what she had rather than yearning for what might have been. She could be happy with William even if she did not love him. But she did not think she could find contentment in marriage to a man she did not respect, and so she kept that door tightly shut and barred. Of course William would accompany her father and brother to the Holy Land. He'd been deeply grieved by Jerusalem's fall, had withdrawn for days to mourn its loss, even donning sackcloth. It was true he'd not yet taken the cross himself, but surely he would do so when the time came. She firmly believed that. She had to believe that.

She finally fell asleep, but her rest was not a peaceful one, for she was awakened several times by her husband's tossing and turning. They both slept later than usual in consequence, and when Joanna opened her eyes, the chamber was filled with light. William was stirring, too. His hair had tumbled onto his forehead, giving him a youthful, disheveled look that she found very appealing. He still retained his summer tan, his skin bronzed wherever it had been exposed to the hot Sicilian sun, and as he started to sit up, she found herself watching the play of muscles across his chest. She could feel her body warming to desire, thinking that she was indeed lucky compared to those countless wives who shared their beds with men potbellied, balding, and foul-smelling. William had an eastern appreciation for bathing and she enjoyed breathing in the clean, seductive smell of male sweat.

"God's Blessings upon you, O *Musta'z*," she murmured throatily, playfully using one of his Arabic titles, which they'd turned into a private joke, for it meant "The Glorious One." Sliding over, she nestled against his body, trailing her hand across his stomach to let him know her intentions were erotic, not merely affectionate.

His response stunned her. "Do not do that!" he snapped, pushing her hand away. Sitting up, he grimaced and then glanced over, saw the stricken look on her face. "Ah, Joanna . . . I am sorry, darling," he said quickly. "I did not mean to growl at you like that. But that ache in my belly has gotten much worse since yesterday and even your light touch caused pain."

Joanna had never known anyone as concerned with his health as her husband. He insisted that his physicians live in the palace and when he heard of the new arrival of a doctor of renown, he would make it worth the man's while to remain in Sicily and enter his service. Because he rarely seemed sick, Joanna had learned to view his preoccupation as an endearing quirk. She remembered now that he had been complaining last night of soreness in his abdomen, and when he revealed that he'd slept poorly and the pain had moved down into the lower right side of his belly, she showed the proper wifely sympathy, feeling his forehead for fever and asking if he wanted her to summon one of his physicians straightaway.

"No . . . I think not," he decided. "I'll see Jamal al-Dīn later if I do not feel better." He offered amends then for his earlier rudeness with a lingering kiss and, peace made between them, they rose to begin their day.

———

JOANNA HAD PROMISED to take Alicia to see Zisa, their nearby summer palace in the vast park called the Genoard, and after making sure that her husband had consulted his chief physician, Jamal al-Dīn, she saw no reason not to keep her promise. Accompanied by several of her younger attendants and household knights, they made a leisurely progress down the Via Marmorea, acknowledging the cheers of the market crowds and throwing handfuls of copper *follari* to the shrieking children who sprinted alongside their horses.

Joanna's obvious popularity with her subjects was a source of great pleasure to Alicia. She was already in high spirits, for Joanna's favorite Sicilian hound had whelped and she'd been promised one of the puppies for her own. She'd spent the morning with a tutor, for Joanna was determined that she learn to read and write, and feeling like a bird freed from its cage, she was talking nonstop, pointing out sights that caught her eye and blushing happily when the queen complimented her riding style, for that was another of her lessons.

Joanna was gratified to see the difference that the past few months had made; this cheerful chatterbox could not have been more unlike that mute, terrified child she'd first encountered in the abbey infirmary. Upon their arrival at Zisa, she enjoyed taking Alicia on a tour of the palace's remarkable hall, where a marble fountain cascaded water into a channel that flowed across the hall and then outside into a small reflecting pool. Alicia was awestruck, kneeling to study the mosaic fish that seemed to be swimming in the ripples generated by a hidden pump, and giggling in polite disbelief when Joanna told her that during special feasts, tiny amphorae of wine were borne along by the water to the waiting guests.

As fascinated as Alicia was with the indoor fountain, she was even more interested in the royal menagerie, home to lions, leopards, peacocks, a giraffe, and elegant cheetahs which Joanna swore could be trained to walk on leashes. Afterward, they took advantage of the warm spell known as St Martin's summer and had a light meal by the large artificial lake, sitting on blankets and rooting in the wicker baskets packed by palace cooks with savory wafers, cheese, sugar plums, and oranges. Joanna would later look back upon this sunlit November afternoon as a final gift from the Almighty, one last treasured memory of the privileged life that had been hers in the island kingdom of Sicily. But at the time, it seemed only a pleasant interlude, a favor to an orphaned child in need of days like this.

Joanna's knights were flirting with her ladies, her dogs chasing unseen prey in the orchards behind them. Finding herself briefly alone with the queen, Alicia seized her chance and bravely broached the subject that had been haunting her for weeks. "May I ask you a question, Madame? The Lady Mariam . . ." She hesitated and then asked bluntly, "Is she truly a Christian?"

"Yes, she is, Alicia. Her mother died when Mariam was very young, just as your mother did. Mariam was brought up in the palace and naturally she was raised in the Truth Faith, for it would have been cruel indeed to deny her salvation." Joanna finished peeling an orange before saying, "I know why you are confused. You've heard the talk, the gossip that the Saracens who've converted are not true Christians, that they continue to practice their infidel faith in secret . . . have you not?"

When Alicia nodded shyly, Joanna handed a section of fruit to the girl. "That is most likely true," she admitted composedly. "The Palace Saracens take Christian names and attend Mass, but I am sure many of them do cling to the old ways. My husband and his father and grandfather before him believed that this is a matter between a man and his God. People ought not to be converted by force, for that renders their conversion meaningless. I've heard men accuse us of turning a blind eye, and I suppose we do, but it is for the best. Judge the results for yourself, child. Where else in Christendom do members of differing faiths live in relative peace?"

"But . . . but my brother said that nothing was more important than recovering the Holy City from the infidels," Alicia whispered, relieved when Joanna nodded vigorously.

"Your brother was right. The Saracens in Outremer are our enemies. But that does not mean the Saracens in Sicily must be our enemies, too. Think of old Hamid, who tends to the royal kennels. Remember how patiently he talks to you about the dogs, promising to help you teach your puppy. Do you think of him as an enemy?"

"No," Alicia said slowly, after a long pause. "I suppose I do not. . . ."

"Exactly," Joanna said, pleased that Alicia was such a quick study. "Let me tell you a story, lass, one that was told to me by my husband. Twenty years ago, a dreadful earthquake struck our island. Thousands died at Catania, but Palermo was luckier and the damage was less here. The people were still very fearful and William heard nothing but cries and prayers to Allah and His Prophet from those who had supposedly embraced the Christian faith. He did not rebuke them, though, instead told them that each one should invoke the God he worships, for those who have faith would be comforted."

Alicia was still bewildered, but if Joanna and William did not believe all Saracens were the spawn of the Devil, she would try to believe it, too, she decided. "And Lady Mariam . . . she is a true Christian, not a pretend one?"

Joanna laughed, assured her that Mariam was indeed a "worshipper of the Cross," as the Muslims called those of the Christian faith, and then rose to her feet, brushing off her skirts, for she saw one of the palace servants hastening up the pathway toward them.

"Madame." He prostrated himself at her feet in the eastern fashion, waiting for her permission to rise. When he did, she caught her breath, for his eyes were filled with fear. "You must return to the palace, my lady. It is most urgent. Your lord husband the king has been stricken with great pain and is asking for you."

"Of course. Alicia, fetch the others." Joanna studied the man's face intently. "What do his doctors say, Pietro?"

He looked down, veiling his eyes. "They say that you must hurry, my lady."

CHAPTER 3

NOVEMBER 1189

Palermo, Sicily

s the Lady Mariam approached the king's private quarters in the Joharia, she saw the vice chancellor, Matthew of Ajello, hobbling toward her. For more than thirty years, he'd been a powerful force in Sicilian politics. Ambitious, ruthless, shrewd, and farseeing, he'd been an effective ally and a dangerous foe, but he was now in the winter of his life, suffering from the relentless ailments of age, and some of his enemies believed his influence was waning. Mariam thought they were fools, for those heavy-lidded dark eyes still blazed with intelligence and vitality. She smiled at the sight of that stooped, wizened figure, for she had a fondness for the old man, rogue though he may be.

He greeted her with a courtly flourish, but when she asked if there had been any change in the king's condition, he slowly shook his head. "My poor William," he said sadly, "my poor Sicily . . ."

Mariam felt a chill, for he seemed to be offering an epitaph both for her brother and his kingdom. Seeing how his words had affected her, Matthew sought to sound more cheerful, saying with a surprisingly youthful grin, "A pity you were not here at noon, my dear, for that pompous ass, the Archbishop of Palermo, made a ridiculous spectacle of himself—again. He actually began to argue with the Archbishop of Monreale about where the king ought to be buried, insisting that his cathedral was the proper site even though we all know the king founded Monreale as his family's mausoleum. The Archbishop of Monreale was understandably horrified that he'd bring up such a subject at such a time and tried to silence him ere the queen overheard. But Archbishop Walter plunged ahead unheedingly and ran straight into a royal tempest."

"Joanna heard?" Mariam said and winced when he nodded.

"I met her mother once . . . did I ever tell you, my dear? The incomparable Elea-nor of Aquitaine. It was more than forty years ago, but the memory is still green. She and her husband—it was the French king then—were on their way home from the Holy Land when their ships were set upon by pirates in the pay of the Greek emperor. Fortunately, our King Roger's fleet was in the area and came to the rescue. But the queen's ship was blown off course and by the time it dropped anchor in Palermo's harbor, she was quite ill. Once she'd recovered, I was given the honor of escorting her to Potenza, where her husband and King Roger were await-ing her. She was a remarkable woman, very beautiful, of course," he said, with a nostalgic sigh. "But she did have a temper. I saw today that she passed it on to her daughter. Our bombastic archbishop wilted before the Lady Joanna's fury, shed his dignity like a snake shedding its skin, and bolted, his robes flapping in the breeze."

Mariam could not share his satisfaction, even though she did share his dislike of Archbishop Walter. What must it have been like for Joanna, keeping vigil by her husband's sickbed and hearing the prelates squabble over where he was to be buried? Bidding the vice chancellor farewell, she continued on her way. When she glanced back, she saw Matthew was almost out of sight, moving with surprising speed for a man so crippled by gout. He would never be as inept as the arch-bishop, but he'd been bitterly opposed to Constance's German marriage, and she was sure he was already plotting how best to thwart Heinrich should William die.

Mariam was no more eager than the vast majority of William's subjects to see Sicily swallowed up by the Holy Roman Empire. She loved Constance as much as Joanna did, but she loved her Sicilian homeland, too, and had no doubts that the kingdom would suffer under Heinrich's iron yoke. Damn William's stubbornness for refusing to see what a great risk he was taking! This spurt of anger shamed her. How could she be wrathful with her brother when he could well be dying?

Two of William's African bodyguards moved aside respectfully as she ap-proached the door to his bedchamber. It was then that she saw the reddish-brown creature huddled on the floor. Recognizing Ahmer, her brother's favorite Sicil-ian hound, she frowned. But her disapproval was directed at William's Saracen doctors, not Ahmer. Muslims looked upon dogs as dirty animals, and she knew they were responsible for banishing Ahmer from his master's bedside. The hound whimpered as she scratched his head, and she found herself smiling as a memory surfaced, one of William debating his chief physician, Jamal al-Dīn, about the status of dogs. Jamal had insisted that they were ritually unclean and were to be shunned by Believers, and William, whose Arabic was fluent enough to allow him to read their holy book, had pounced gleefully, pointing out that there was only one reference to dogs in the *Qur'an* and it was a positive one, citing the Companion in the Cave *sura* as proof. Her smile faded then, for she could not help wondering if they'd ever be able to engage in such good-natured arguments again. Each time she saw William, he seemed to be losing more ground.

Opening the door, she let Ahmer squeeze in ahead of her. She had a moment of concern, fretting that he'd jump onto the bed, but he seemed to sense the gravity of the situation and sat down sedately at Joanna's feet, his almond-shaped eyes never straying from William's motionless form. Joanna's drawn face and slumping shoulders bespoke her utter exhaustion, but she mustered up a smile, saying, "Your sister is here, my love."

Mariam sat in a chair by the bed, reaching for William's hand as she tried to conceal her dismay at the deterioration in his appearance. Her handsome brother looked like an ashen, spectral version of himself, his eyes sunken and his cheeks gaunt. He'd lost an alarming amount of weight in so brief a time, and his skin felt cold and clammy to her touch. "*Zahrah*," he said hoarsely, bringing tears to Mariam's eyes with the use of this Arabic childhood endearment. He was obviously in great pain. He seemed pleased, though, when she told him she'd sneaked his dog in, and dangled his fingers over the edge of the bed for Ahmer to lick.

The physicians had been conferring in a corner, studying a vial of liquid that Mariam assumed was William's urine. Glancing over, Jamal al-Dīn noticed the dog and glared at Mariam, who favored him with an innocent smile. When he approached the bed to take his patient's pulse, Mariam took advantage of the distraction to implore Joanna to get some sleep, but the other woman stubbornly shook her head.

"He is calmer when I am here," she said before lowering her voice still further to whisper an indignant account of the Archbishop of Palermo's gaffe. "That wretched old man still bears a grudge against William for establishing an archbishopric at Monreale. But I never imagined that his rancor would impel him to contemplate burying William whilst he is still alive!"

Mariam concurred, but all the while she was regarding Joanna with sympathy so sharp it felt like a dagger's edge. Joanna seemed to be the only one blind to the truth, that William's labored breaths were measurable and finite. Barring a miracle, he was dying, and all knew it but his wife. While Jamal al-Dīn spoon-fed his patient an herbal remedy for intestinal pain, Mariam continued to urge Joanna to take a brief nap. When William added his voice to Mariam's, she finally agreed, promising to be back before the bells rang for Vespers.

As soon as she was gone, William beckoned his sister to the bed. "Send for a scribe," he murmured. "I want to list all that I bequeath to the English king for his campaign to recover Jerusalem. Joanna became distraught whenever I mentioned it. . . ." And as their eyes met, Mariam realized that there had been an odd role reversal between her brother and his wife. Joanna had always been the practical partner, William the dreamer, given to impulse and whims. Yet now she was the one in denial and he was looking reality in the face without blinking.

It took William a long time to dictate his letter, for his strength was ebbing and he had to pause frequently to rest. Mariam sat by the bed, holding his hand, half listening as he offered up the riches of Sicily for a crusade he would never see. "A hundred galleys . . . sixty thousand seams of wheat, the same number of barley and wine . . . twenty-four dishes and cups of silver or gold . . ." When he was finally done, she tried to get him to eat some of the soup sent up by the palace cooks in hopes of tempting his fading appetite, but he turned his head aside on the pillow and she put the bowl down on the floor for Ahmer, which earned her a weak smile from William and a look of genuine horror from Jamal al-Dīn.

William's fever was rising and Mariam took a basin from the doctors and put a cool compress upon his hot forehead. "At least . . ." William swallowed with difficulty. "At least I need not worry about Joanna . . . Monte St Angelo is a rich county . . ."

"Indeed it is," Mariam said, her voice muffled. Joanna had been provided with a very generous dowry at the time of her marriage. It was to William's credit that even in the midst of his suffering, he was concerned for his wife's future welfare. Did he spare a thought, too, for his kingdom? Did he regret that foolhardy alliance now that it was too late? Gazing into William's eyes, Mariam could not tell. She found herself hoping that he was not tormented with such regrets. He had been a careless king, but he'd been a kind and loving brother, and she did not want him to bear such a burden in his last hours. What good would it do, after all?

JOANNA JERKED UPRIGHT in the chair, ashamed to have dozed off. Her eyes flew to the bed, but William seemed to be sleeping. He had not looked so peaceful in days and her faltering hopes rekindled. Taking care not to awaken him, she smiled at his doctor. "He appears to be resting comfortably. Surely that is a good sign?"

Jamal al-Dīn regarded her somberly. "I gave him a potion made from the juice of the opium poppy. It eased his pain and helped him to sleep. Alas, it will not cure his ailment, Madame."

Joanna bit her lip. "But he may still recover?"

"*Inshallah*," he said softly, "*Inshallah*."

Physicians were the same, no matter their religion. Joanna knew that when they said "God willing," there was little hope. Leaning over the bed, she kissed her husband gently upon his forehead, his eyelids, and his mouth.

JOANNA PAUSED in the doorway of the palatine chapel, waiting until her eyes adjusted to the shadows. When a priest appeared, she waved him away. Approaching the altar, she sank to her knees on the marble floor, and began to pray to the Almighty and the Blessed Martyr, St Thomas of Canterbury, entreating Them to spare her husband's life, not for her sake or even for William's, but for his island kingdom and all who dwelled there in such peace. Never had she offered up prayers that were so heartfelt, so desperate, or so utterly without hope.

FEW MONARCHS were as mourned as William de Hauteville. His death was greeted with genuine and widespread sorrow by his subjects, for his reign had been a time of prosperity and security, in dramatic contrast to the troubled years when his father had ruled. For three days, they filled the streets of Palermo, lamenting in the Sicilian manner. Women wore black, dressed their servants in sackcloth, their hair unbound and disheveled, wailing to the beat of drums and tambours, their grieving magnified by their fear, for none knew what the future now held.

TAKING ADVANTAGE of her privileged position as Joanna's childhood nurse, Dame Beatrix was reproaching Joanna for "not eating enough to keep a nightingale alive. I know you've no appetite, but you must force yourself lest you fall ill. Indeed, you are much too pale. Should I summon a doctor?"

"There is no need," Joanna said hastily. "I am not ailing, Beatrix. I have not been sleeping well."

Beatrix's brisk, no-nonsense demeanor crumbled. "I know, my lamb, I know. . . ."

"None of it seems real," Joanna confessed. "I cannot count how many times I have awakened in the morning, thinking I'd had a truly dreadful dream. It is almost like reliving that moment of William's death, over and over again. When am I going to accept it? When am I going to be able to weep for him, Beatrix? I feel . . . feel as if there is ice enclosing my heart, freezing my tears . . ."

Beatrix sat beside Joanna on the bed, putting her arm around the younger woman. "I remember my late husband, may God assoil him, telling me about battlefield injuries. He said that sometimes when a man was severely wounded, he did not feel the pain straightaway. He thought it was the body's way of protecting itself."

Joanna leaned into the older woman's embrace even as she said with a rueful smile, "So you are saying I should be patient? That the pain is lurking close at hand, waiting to pounce?"

Beatrix would have sacrificed ten years of her life if by doing so she could spare Joanna sorrow. But she had never lied to Joanna, not to the homesick little girl or the grieving young mother or the bewildered new widow. "Scriptures say for everything there is a season. Your tears will come, child. In time, this will seem all too real to you."

Joanna did not reply and after a few moments she rose, crossing the chamber toward the window. The blue Sicilian sky was smudged with smoke to the west, and she thought reality was to be found out in the streets of Palermo. "The rioting continues," she said bleakly, "with men taking advantage of William's death to pillage the Saracen quarters. Barely a fortnight after his death and his people are already turning upon one another, putting the peace of the kingdom at risk. How he'd have hated that, Beatrix. He was always so proud that there had been no rebellions or plots after he came of age and that Christians, Muslims, and Jews lived in harmony under his rule . . ."

"Saracens make good scapegoats in times of trouble." This new voice came from the doorway, and Joanna turned toward the speaker, nodding in unhappy agreement as Mariam entered the chamber. "The palace seneschal is waiting outside, Joanna. He says the Archbishop of Palermo is here, seeking to speak with you."

Joanna's mouth tightened. Her first impulse was to send him away. She was not sure she trusted herself to be civil to the man who'd defied William's express wish to be buried at Monreale, ordering the royal sarcophagus to be taken to his own cathedral in the city. Faced with the outraged opposition of Joanna, the Archbishop of Monreale, and Matthew of Ajello, Archbishop Walter had eventually backed down and William was interred at Monreale, but he'd spitefully refused to surrender the magnificent porphyry tomb William had commissioned for his final resting place.

Joanna spat out an imprecation that would have done her profane father proud. But then she said, "Tell the seneschal to escort him to William's audience chamber." Seeing their surprise, she said, grimacing, "He is the only one who supports Constance's claim to the crown. I owe it to her to hear what he has to say."

THE AUDIENCE CHAMBER had always been Joanna's favorite room, an elegant vision of gold and green and blue artistry. Now, though, the colors seemed subdued, the designs static and flat. It was as if the archbishop's very presence leeched all the vibrancy and life from the mosaics. Interrupting his diatribe against the other members of the royal inner council, Joanna said impatiently, "So you are saying the council is split over the succession?"

"That vile miscreant and his accursed puppet are up to their necks in the muck, Madame. They began intriguing as soon as the king was stricken, plotting to put Tancred of Lecce on the throne, and they paid us no heed when my brother and I reminded them that all of the kingdom's nobility had sworn their fidelity to the Lady Constance ere she departed the realm to wed Lord Heinrich."

Joanna had no difficulty interpreting his intemperate language; the "vile miscreant" was the vice chancellor, Matthew of Ajello, and the "accursed puppet" the Archbishop of Monreale. She thought it was a sad irony that Constance's adversaries were men far more capable and trustworthy than her advocates, the archbishop and his weak-willed brother, whose service as Bishop of Agrigento had been utterly undistinguished so far. With men of their caliber in her camp, Constance was bound to lose. It was so unfair. Constance was the legal heiress of the House of Hauteville, King Roger's daughter, while Tancred of Lecce was merely an illegitimate son of Roger's eldest son. What greater proof could there be of their desperation that Matthew and the archbishop were willing to embrace a man bastard-born rather than see the crown go to Heinrich? Why had William been so shortsighted? If only he'd chosen another husband for Constance, anyone but a hated German prince! By marrying her off to Heinrich, he'd robbed her of her rightful inheritance.

Joanna did her best to suppress her anger, for there was no undoing William's mistake. "What of the other lords? Do all the noble families support Tancred, too?"

"I regret to say most do, my lady. Naturally I am not privy to their conspiracy, but I have my own ears and eyes. The Count of Andria has advanced a claim, too, but many feel his blood ties to the Royal House are tenuous, and they have settled upon Tancred as their choice, overlooking his base birth, may God forgive them.

My informants say they wasted no time in sending Matthew's son to Rome to argue Tancred's case with the Holy Father. So our only hope is that Pope Clement will recoil at the thought of crowning a man not lawfully begotten."

"If that is Constance's only hope, then she is well and truly doomed. Nothing frightens the papacy more than the prospect of seeing the Kingdom of Sicily united with the Holy Roman Empire." Not for the first time, Joanna marveled that she must point out something so obvious. "The Pope will gladly overlook Tancred's tainted birth if that will prevent Heinrich from claiming the Sicilian crown. He'll keep his support covert, not daring to openly antagonize the emperor and Heinrich, but covert support will be enough to carry the day for Tancred."

Joanna had begun to pace, wondering if there was any chance England might intercede on Constance's behalf. No, that hawk would not fly. Her father would no more aid the son of the Holy Roman Emperor than he would ally with the Sultan of Egypt. Turning, she saw that Archbishop Walter was looking at her in befuddlement. He seemed surprised that a woman could have any understanding of political matters. Did he think she'd never discussed statecraft with William? She was the daughter of the greatest king in Christendom and Eleanor of Aquitaine, not one of William's secluded *harim* slave girls, and she longed to remind the archbishop of that. No longer able to endure his odious presence, she was about to end the audience when the door burst open and the Archbishop of Monreale strode into the chamber, flanked by her seneschal, Mariam, Beatrix, and a monk clad in the black habit of the Benedictine order.

Joanna was startled by this blatant breach of protocol, but Archbishop Walter was incensed. "How dare you come into the queen's presence unbidden and unannounced! You've the manners of a lowborn churl, a great irony given how often you've maligned my family origins!"

Archbishop Guglielmo responded with the most lethal weapon in his arsenal; he ignored the other prelate entirely, not even deigning to glance in his direction. "My lady queen, I seek your pardon for my abrupt entrance; I mean no disrespect. But it was urgent that I speak with you at once. I bear a message of great import from the English king. I regret to be—"

It had been months since Joanna had heard from either of her parents, and she interrupted eagerly. "A letter from my lord father? Where is it?"

The archbishop hesitated. "No, Madame," he said at last, "a letter from your brother."

"But you said the king..." Joanna's words trailed off. "My father...he is dead?"

"Yes, Madame. He died at Chinon Castle in July, and your brother Richard was crowned in September."

"July? And we are getting word in December?" Archbishop Walter was incredulous. "What sort of scheme are you and the vice chancellor hatching now?"

The Archbishop of Monreale swung around to confront him. "How could I possibly benefit by lying to the queen so cruelly? King Richard sent a messenger several months ago. But the man fell ill on the journey, got no farther than the abbey at Monte Cassino. He was stricken with a raging fever and the monks did not expect him to live. But after some weeks, he regained his senses and confided his mission to the abbot. Since he was too weak to resume his travels, the abbot dispatched Brother Benedict with the letters, one from King Richard and one from Queen Eleanor. He took the overland route, loath to sail during winter storms, and just reached my abbey this morn—"

"Your abbey?" Archbishop Walter was sputtering, so great was his fury. "And why should the letters—assuming they are even genuine—be sent to you? What greater proof of a plot—"

"He sent the letters to me because Monreale is a Benedictine abbey like Monte Cassino and he knew I could be trusted to deliver these letters to the queen!"

By now they were both shouting at each other, but Joanna was no longer listening. William had often told her about the great earthquake that had struck Sicily twenty years ago, describing the sensations in vivid detail, and she felt like that now, as if the very ground were quaking under her feet. Turning aside, she clung gratefully to Beatrix for support as she sought to accept the fact that her world had turned upside down yet again.

WORD HAD SPREAD swiftly through the palace and Joanna's chaplain was awaiting her by the door of the palatine chapel. He'd been in her service since her arrival as a child-bride, and after one look at her face, he knew she did not want his comfort, not yet. "I would have a Requiem Mass for my lord father on the morrow," she said, her voice sounding like a stranger's to him, faint and far away. When he would have followed her into the chapel, she asked to be alone and he positioned himself in the entrance, ready to repel an army if need be to give her privacy to pray and to grieve.

Joanna felt as if she were in a waking dream; nothing seemed familiar or real. How could her father be dead? He had dominated his world like the Colossus of Rhodes, towering above mortal men, stirring awe and fear in his wake for more than thirty years. To imagine him dead was like imagining the sun blotted out. Stumbling slightly, she knelt before the high altar and began to recite the *Pater Noster*. *"Fiat voluntas tua, sicut in caelo et in terra."* She still clutched the letters, not yet ready to read them. She found herself struggling to remember the rest of the prayer, one she'd known by heart since childhood, and then she crumpled to the ground, overwhelmed by a torrent of scalding tears, her body wracked with sobs as she wept for her father, for her husband, and for Sicily, the land she'd come to love.

WILLIAM'S DEATH had destroyed the sense of security that Alicia had gained in the months since the sinking of the *San Niccolò*. Suddenly Sicily had become an alien place again, a dangerous place. She grieved for the young king and for Joanna, who seemed like a lost soul, pallid and frail-looking in her stark black mourning gowns and veils. She was frightened by the outbreaks of street violence and she could tell that the palace's Saracen servants were frightened, too. Almost overnight, everything had changed.

Alicia had seen little of Joanna in the weeks after William's death, and when she did, the queen seemed distant and preoccupied. The royal household was in a state of turmoil. Two of Joanna's ladies-in-waiting had already departed her service, for they were kin to the Countess Sybilla, the wife of Tancred of Lecce. But Alicia knew that several others were talking of leaving, too, hoping that Sybilla might take them on. A reigning queen was a far more attractive mistress than a widowed one.

After finding Alicia crying, Beatrix had reassured the girl that Joanna's future was secure. She held the Honour of Monte St Angelo, with the revenues from all its cities and towns, Beatrix explained, thinking it best not to mention that Monte St Angelo was on the mainland, far from Palermo. Alicia took comfort from that, for her trust in Joanna was absolute and she felt sure that Joanna would take her along when she moved to her dower lands. But then they got word of the English king's death and everything changed yet again.

After the Requiem Mass for her father, Joanna had withdrawn into her bed-chamber, and Alicia sought out Emma d'Aleramici and Bethlem de Greci for answers. The news of the English king's passing seemed to have alarmed everyone and she wanted to know why.

She found them in the process of packing their belongings, obviously planning to leave Joanna's service. Last week she'd overheard them discussing their chances of entering Sybilla's household once she was crowned, reluctantly concluding that she was not likely to accept them and it was better to remain with Joanna than to return to the tedium of their own homes. So what had changed their minds?

They were quite willing to tell her, always welcoming an opportunity to gossip. Joanna's influence had died with William, they said bluntly. It would have been different if she'd given William a son, for then she'd have been regent until he came of age. She had still been more fortunate than most barren, widowed queens, though, for she was the daughter of a great and powerful king, a man known to be very protective of his children, at least the females in the family. All knew how he'd come to the aid of his daughter Matilda when her husband, the Duke of Saxony and Bavaria, had been driven into exile by the Holy Roman Emperor, giving them refuge at his court whilst he maneuvered to get their banishment edict revoked.

But once he died, Joanna was vulnerable, fair game for those who might want to abduct her and force her into marriage. She was a valuable prize, they told the horrified Alicia, for she was beautiful and her dower lands were rich enough to tempt any man. So they were looking after their own interests whilst they still could.

"But . . . but Lady Joanna still has a royal protector," Alicia stammered. "Her brother is the English king now. Surely he'd come to her aid if—" She broke off in bewilderment, for they'd begun to laugh at her.

"You are such a child, know nothing of the ways of the world. Brothers rarely show much concern for sisters sent off to distant lands. That is especially true when the needed alliance died with a sister's foreign husband. If you want proof of that, consider the sad history of Agnes Capet, the French king's little sister."

Alicia sensed that she did not want to know Agnes's story, but she made herself ask, not wanting to display timidity before these women she disliked. "What happened to her?"

Bethlem hesitated, suddenly realizing that Alicia was too young to hear of these horrors. Emma had no such qualms, however. "Agnes was betrothed to Alexius, the son of the Emperor of the Greeks, sent off to Constantinople at age eight and wed to the boy the following year when she was only nine. That was well below the canonical age for marriage, of course, but the Greeks are barbarians and care little for such niceties. That same year the emperor died and Agnes and Alexius, who was ten, ascended the throne. But two years later a cousin named Andronicus Comnenus seized control of the government. Shall I tell you what happened next?"

By now Alicia was positive she did not want to know, already feeling great pity for the little French princess sent to live amongst barbarians. She shook her head mutely, but Emma was enjoying herself and forged ahead.

"When Andronicus took power, he began to get rid of anyone he saw as a threat. He poisoned Alexius's sister Maria and her husband, the very same Maria who was to wed our King William until the emperor changed his mind. He then forced Alexius to sign his own mother's death warrant and had her strangled. The next year he had himself crowned co-emperor with Alexius. You can guess what he did then. He murdered Alexius and had the boy's body thrown into the River Bosphorus. Poor Agnes found herself widowed at age twelve, but the worst was still to come. Andronicus forced her to marry him. Can you imagine wedding your husband's murderer?

"He was more than fifty years older than Agnes, too," Emma said with a fastidious shudder. "The thought of bedding a man so aged is enough to make me want to take a vow of chastity! Andronicus soon revealed himself to be a monster, began a reign of terror, and within two years, the people of Constantinople rose up against him. He fled with Agnes and his favorite concubine, but they were captured and brought back to the city, where he was subjected to torture and then turned over to the mob. He was doused with boiling water, had his eyes gouged out, his hand cut off—"

"Stop!" Alicia cried in a strangled voice, fighting back nausea.

Emma cocked a finely plucked brow. "I hope Agnes is not as squeamish as you, Alicia, given all she has had to endure. Surely you want to know what became of her? Sadly, we do not know. That was four years ago and her fate remains a mystery. I assume she is still alive, still dwelling in Constantinople, unless her ordeal drove her mad. But the point of my story is that Agnes is the full sister of Philippe Capet, the powerful King of France, and he did nothing whatsoever on her behalf. Brothers cannot be relied upon, Alicia, and that is why Bethlem and I are leaving your beloved queen's service. A woman's lot is not an easy one, and once she has no husband or father to protect her—"

"That is enough!" They all spun around as Mariam stalked toward them. Alicia shrank back, but then realized that she was not the target of Mariam's wrath. "The two of you ought to be ashamed," she said scathingly, "scaring the child with such ghastly tales. What do you plan to do next, torture Alicia's new puppy or poison the garden songbirds?"

"It was not me!" Bethlem protested, her voice rising in a squeak. Emma attempted to stand her ground, but she was soon squirming under the heat in Mariam's blazing brown eyes, and when Mariam told them to get out, neither woman argued. Once they'd fled the chamber, Mariam took Alicia's hand and led the trembling child over to the window-seat.

"You must not pay any heed to those spiteful cats, Alicia. They have not a single brain between the two of them, just more malice than the law ought to allow."

"Was . . . was it true, though?"

"Alas, what she said about Agnes was true. But her tragedy has naught to do with Joanna, who is in no peril. This is Palermo, not Constantinople. Ours is a more civilized society. And Joanna is far from friendless. Have you forgotten that her brother rules the greatest empire in Christendom?"

"Yes, but . . . but the French king—"

"Philippe and Richard are as unlike as chalk and cheese. I know Joanna has told you stories of her brother. He is a brilliant battle commander, utterly without fear, so courageous that men call him the Lionheart. No one would ever call Philippe that, trust me. Mayhap Rabbitheart," Mariam added, and succeeded in coaxing a smile. "Now do you feel better?"

Alicia nodded, realizing to her surprise that she did indeed trust Mariam. "But what will happen when this Tancred becomes king? Emma and Bethlem said he is bastard-born, that he rebelled against King William's father and spent years in gaol, that he is so ugly men call him the 'monkey,' that—"

"Alicia, by now you ought to know better than to believe anything Emma or Bethlem says. Yes, Tancred was born out of wedlock, but he is of good blood; his mother was the daughter of a lord. And yes, he did rebel against William's father. But he was pardoned by Queen Margarita and served William loyally during his minority and afterward. He is a brave soldier and a capable administrator and I believe he truly cares about Sicily. He is not a man to maltreat a woman, least of all Joanna, his cousin's widow."

"Thank you, Lady Mariam," Alicia said gratefully. "But . . . but you did not deny that Tancred looks like a monkey?"

"Well, there you have me," Mariam admitted, "for poor Tancred has been cursed with a face that would scare a gargoyle," and they both laughed, a moment that would mark a turning point for Alicia. From then on, she viewed the Lady Mariam as an ally, and she jettisoned the last of her brother Arnaud's values, adopting the beliefs of Joanna's Sicily as her own.

THE RAINY SEASON began in the autumn and when Tancred of Lecce's ship dropped anchor in Palermo's harbor at dawn on December 11, a steady, chill rain had been falling for days. Undaunted by the winter weather, he hastened to a council meeting with Matthew of Ajello, the Archbishop of Monreale, and the highborn lords of the realm. Despite the dynastic nature of the Sicilian kingship, Tancred was elected king by unanimous consent, for those who disapproved, such as the Archbishop of Palermo and his brother, had not been invited. That evening Tancred, his fourteen-year-old son Roger, and a military escort rode to the royal palace for a task that was both necessary and unpleasant. Tancred was not looking forward to it, but he refused to delegate it to others, for honor demanded that he be the one to tell the queen; he owed her that much.

As they approached the Joharia, Tancred noticed that Roger's steps were lagging, and he found himself torn between amusement and impatience, for he understood Roger's reluctance. The boy was totally besotted with Joanna, could not speak to her without blushing, squirming, and stammering.

"Roger," Tancred said, putting his hand on the boy's shoulder. When Roger met his eyes, he felt a surge of parental pride, for his son was all that he was not: tall and well formed. "Would you rather wait here whilst I speak with the queen?" He thought it was only fair to offer Roger that choice, for Matthew of Ajello had also begged off from accompanying them, using his gout as an excuse to avoid facing Joanna, whom he'd always liked.

Roger was silent for a few moments and then shook his head resolutely. "No, Papa, I will come with you." Tancred smiled and they continued on.

JOANNA WAS AWAITING THEM in the royal audience chamber, accompanied by her seneschal, her chaplain, several of her household knights, and her ladies Beatrix and Mariam. She had already heard of the day's events, and while she was not happy that Tancred should claim the crown that belonged to Constance, she knew there was nothing she could do about it. She did not know Tancred very well, but what she did know was to his credit: He'd served William loyally and had distinguished himself in William's disastrous military campaign against the Greeks. She could only pray that he was up to the challenge and would be able to restore peace to their island kingdom.

Refusing Joanna's polite offer of wine and fruit, Tancred wasted no time in getting to the heart of the matter. "Madame, I have come to tell you that I have been chosen by the lords of this realm to rule as king. The election was held this afternoon, and the coronation will take place after Epiphany, at which time I shall name my son the Duke of Apulia."

Although Joanna liked Roger, it still hurt to think of him bearing the title that had so briefly belonged to her infant son. "My congratulations, Roger," she said with a smile before turning back to his father. Tancred's cool formality was a change from past occasions when he'd affably chatted with "Cousin William" and his "lovely lady." She wondered if he felt as uncomfortable as she did. Taking her cue from him, she addressed him now as "My lord," saying that she wished him well. To say more would be hypocrisy and they both knew it.

"You say the coronation is set for January? I will be sure to vacate the palace by then," she assured him. "I may choose to rent a house in Palermo until the spring, as I would rather not make the long journey to Monte St Angelo during the winter months." Her smile this time was not as warm as the one she'd bestowed upon Roger, for it was not easy to ask when it had always been hers to command. "I assume that meets with your approval, my Lord Tancred?"

She'd made the request as a mere courtesy, and she was shocked when he said, "I am sorry, Madame. That will not be possible."

Was he so eager to get her out of Palermo? "As you wish," she said coolly. "I will depart as soon as the arrangements can be made."

"I am afraid you do not understand, Madame. Whilst Monte St Angelo is a wealthy province, its greatest importance is strategic. It controls the roads from the Alpine passes, the route that Heinrich von Hohenstaufen will take when he leads an army into Italy. It is imperative that Monte St Angelo remains under royal control. I regret, therefore, that I cannot permit it to be given over to you."

Joanna had never expected this. "I am sure I need not remind you that my dowry is guaranteed both by my marriage contract and the inheritance laws of the realm. So what do you propose to offer in exchange for Monte St Angelo, my lord?"

"I do not deny the truth of what you say, my lady. But I am facing a rebellion. Many Saracens have fled to the hills after the unrest in Palermo and have begun to fortify villages, whilst some of the mainland lords continue to support the Count of Andria's false claim to the crown. An even greater threat is posed by the Germans, for we know Heinrich will wage war on his wife's behalf, with all the resources of his father's empire to draw upon."

Joanna's mouth had gone dry. "Just what are you saying, my lord?"

"I am saying that I cannot afford to compensate you for the loss of your dowry lands," he said bluntly, and Joanna's knights began to mutter among themselves, their anger all the greater for their sense of helplessness. Roger was no longer looking at Joanna, and Tancred wished he were elsewhere, too. He'd known it would not be easy, and was hoping she'd not burst into tears, for he felt awkward and ill at ease with weeping women. He saw now that he needn't have worried, for she'd raised her chin and was staring at him defiantly.

"So you plan to turn me out penniless? Or do you have some other surprises in store for me, my lord?"

Tancred did not try to sweeten the brew; it was bound to go down hard. "I will speak candidly with you, Madame. You and your lord husband were well loved by the people, and I am sure there will be much sympathy for your . . . situation. Your own sympathy for the Lady Constance is well known, too. Should you fall into Heinrich's hands, either by choice or by chance, he would make good use of you to advance his wife's cause. I think it best, therefore, that you remain here in Palermo."

By now there were outraged protests by Joanna's knights and gasps from her women. She was stunned, too. But she'd not give this man the satisfaction of seeing how shaken she was. She knew how her mother would have reacted to such a threat and she responded accordingly. "So I am under arrest? Is it to be the palace dungeon, or have you someplace else in mind?"

Tancred had dreaded female hysteria. Now, though, he found himself irked by her icy composure. "Of course not!" he snapped. "You will be lodged in comfortable quarters and will be treated with courtesy and respect; upon that, you have my word. And once I am secure upon my throne, I hope to be able to review your circumstances. But for now, you may consider yourself a guest of the Crown."

"I consider myself a hostage, my lord," Joanna snapped back. "It is obvious that there is no point in arguing with you. But this I will say, and I hope you heed it. You think I am utterly defenseless now that my lord husband and my father the English king are dead. That is a great mistake, and you will answer dearly for it."

"I believe the Almighty will understand, my lady."

Joanna's lips curved in an angry, mocking smile. "The Almighty may, but my brother, the Lionheart, will not."

Tancred was not a vindictive winner and was willing to concede her the last word. He bowed stiffly and withdrew, leaving her standing in the wreckage of the life that just a month ago had seemed well-nigh perfect.

CHAPTER 4

MARCH 1190

Nonancourt Castle, Normandy

fter William Marshal's young wife had been presented to the Queen of England, Will guided Isabel toward the relative privacy of a window-seat, for he knew she'd be eager to discuss it with him. And, indeed, as soon as they were seated, she turned toward him, cheeks flushed with excitement.

"She is not as beautiful as I'd heard, Will. I suppose that is because she is so old now. You said she was nigh on sixty-and-six." Isabel paused to marvel at that vast age, for both of her parents had died in their forties. "Are you sure the king is not here yet?" She sat up straight, her eyes sweeping the crowded hall. "What does he look like?"

"Richard is taller than most men, two fingers above six feet, with curly hair betwixt red and gold. Trust me, lass, he is not one to pass unnoticed. If he were here, you'd need none to point him out to you."

"Well, I hope he comes soon, for I must be the only one at court who has not even laid eyes upon the king." Isabel looked around, then, for Richard's brother, but could find no one who matched the king's description. "Count John is not here, either?"

"John is over there, the one talking to the Lady Alys, in the green gown." Will started to identify Alys as the French king's sister, Richard's neglected, long-suffering betrothed, then remembered that Isabel knew Alys better than he did, for prior to their marriage she'd resided at the Tower of London with Alys and another rich heiress, Denise de Deols.

"John does not look at all like Richard, does he? He is as dark as a Spaniard, and nowhere near as tall as you, Will." Isabel gave her husband a fond glance from the corner of her eye. "He is handsome, though, I must admit. In fact, I've never seen so many comely men gathered in one place. Look at that youth with the fair hair and sky-blue eyes, just like a Norse raider! And there is another beautiful lad—can you use the word 'beautiful' for men? The one laughing, with chestnut-colored hair."

Will took her teasing in stride, for he was amused by her lively, playful personality and was too sure of his manhood to deny his young bride the fun of flirting. He'd never hoped to be given such a prize—a great heiress like Isabel—for he was just a younger son of a minor baron, a man whose worth had been measured by the strength and accuracy of his sword arm. He still remembered his astonishment when the old king had promised Isabel de Clare to him, a deathbed reward for years of steadfast loyalty. He'd been sure that his bright future was lost when King Henry's life ebbed away at Chinon Castle. But the new king, Richard, had confirmed Henry's dying promise and, at that moment, Will had begun to believe in miracles.

"You truly are a king's granddaughter," he said, "for you've singled out men with royal blood flowing in their veins. Your 'Norse raider' is Henri of the House of Blois, the Count of Champagne, nephew to two kings—Richard and Philippe of France. And your 'beautiful lad' is Richard's Welsh kinsman, Morgan ap Ranulf. His father was the old king's favorite uncle, and Morgan served Richard's brother Geoffrey until his death, then joined Henry's household."

"Life at court is going to be rather dull with so many gallant young lords off to fight the Saracens," Isabel said with a mock sigh, still bent upon mischief. It was a safe game, for Will wasn't tiresomely jealous like so many husbands. Her friend and Tower companion, Denise de Deols, had recently been wed to King Richard's cousin, André de Chauvigny, and he was so possessive she had to conduct herself as circumspectly as a nun.

"They have not all taken the cross. John is not going to the Holy Land."

Isabel's pert, vivacious demeanor sometimes led others to underestimate her; she had a quick brain and was a surprisingly good judge of character for a girl of eighteen. She caught the unspoken undertones in her husband's voice, and eyed him curiously. "You do not like Count John, do you, Will?"

"No," he said tersely, "I do not."

Seeing that he did not want to discuss the king's brother, she obligingly steered the conversation in a more agreeable direction, asking the identity of the woman talking with Morgan ap Ranulf. When Will told her that was Constance, the Duchess of Brittany, Isabel studied the older woman with heightened interest. She knew Constance had been betrothed to Richard's brother Geoffrey in childhood, wed to him at twenty, widowed five years later. Will had told her King Henry had then compelled Constance to marry his cousin, the Earl of Chester, wanting to be sure her husband would be loyal to the English Crown. She'd reluctantly agreed to the marriage in order to retain wardship of her two young children, but one of Richard's first acts after his coronation had been to demand that she turn her daughter over to his custody.

Gazing at the Breton duchess, Isabel felt a pang of sympathy, and moved her hand protectively to her abdomen. She knew, of course, that children of the highborn were usually sent off to other noble households for their education. Constance's daughter had been just five, though, taken against her mother's will. Isabel had been taught that a wife's first duty was to her husband, not her children, but she'd often wondered if a woman's maternal instincts could be stifled so easily. She was only in the early months of her first pregnancy and already she felt that she'd defend the tiny entity in her womb with her last breath.

"Will you introduce me to the duchess, Will?" Receiving an affirmation, she continued her scrutiny of the hall. "Is that the Archbishop of York? And my heavens, who is *that* man?"

"Yes, that is the Archbishop of York, Richard's half-brother," William said, then followed her gaze to see who had provoked her outburst. "Ah . . . that is Guillaume Longchamp, the Bishop of Ely, the king's chancellor and most trusted adviser. At first sight, he seems a pitiful figure, small and ugly and crippled in the bargain. But do not be misled by his paltry size or his lameness, for his intelligence is exceeded only by his arrogance."

"No, not him. *That* man over there, the one who looks like he escaped from Hell!"

Once Will identified the object of her interest, he smiled grimly. "That is Mercadier. I assume he must have a given name, but I've never heard it. His past is a mystery, too. I know only that he entered Richard's service about seven years ago as a routier—that is the term used for men like Mercadier, men who sell their swords to the highest bidder. He has been loyal to Richard, I'll grant him that much, and he is as fearless in battle as Richard himself. But he knows no more of mercy than a starving wolf, and when he walks by, other men step back, instinctively making the sign of the cross."

Isabel was staring openly at the routier captain, mesmerized by his sinister appearance—lanky black hair, cold pale eyes, and the worst facial scar she'd ever seen, slashing across his cheek to his chin like a diabolical brand, twisting the corner of his mouth into a mockery of a smile. "If ever there was a man who had a rendezvous with the hangman, that is the one," she declared, suppressing a shiver. Suddenly the great hall lost some of its appeal. "I am tired, Will. May we retire to our chamber?"

"Of course, Isabel." Will's natural courtliness had been greatly enhanced by Isabel's pregnancy, so much so that she had to remind herself not to take advantage of his solicitude. "We'll have to bid the queen good night first," he said, helping her to rise. As they headed toward the dais, he identified the woman who'd just joined Eleanor.

"That is the Lady Hawisa, the Countess of Aumale. She'd been wed to one of King Henry's friends, the Earl of Essex, but he died in December and Richard ordered her to marry a Poitevin lord, William de Forz. The Lady Hawisa balked, though, actually dared to defy the king. You great heiresses tend to be a stubborn lot," he murmured, showing that when it came to teasing, he could give as good as he got. "But Richard is a stubborn one, too, and he seized her estates until she yielded. She accompanied Queen Eleanor from England, and most likely will be wed once Lent is done."

Isabel came to a sudden stop. Her eyes shifted from the Lady Hawisa, soon to marry a man not of her choosing, to the queen, held prisoner by her own husband for sixteen years, and then over to the Duchess of Brittany, another unwilling wife, in conversation now with a woman who asked only to be wed, the unfortunate French princess Alys, a bride-to-be who'd become a hostage instead. Isabel was too well bred to make a public display of affection, but she reached out, grasped her husband's hand so tightly that he looked at her in surprise. "Oh, Will," she whispered, "how lucky I am, how very lucky. . . ."

As THEY EMERGED into the castle bailey, darkness was falling and clouds hid the moon. Clinging to Will's arm, Isabel raised her skirts so they'd not trail in the mud, wrinkling her nose at the rank odor of horse manure. Riders were coming in and she and Will paused to watch, for the new arrivals were creating a stir. Men were running along the battlements, dogs were barking, and torches flaring. Isabel found herself staring at the lead rider. He was mounted astride a splendid grey stallion, and although his travel cloak was splattered with mud, she could see the material was a fine wool, dyed a deep shade of blue; his saddle was ornamented with ivory plates, the pommel and cantle decorated with gemstones, and his spurs shone like silver even in the encroaching shadows. As she watched, he pulled back his hood, revealing a handsome head of bright coppery hair, piercing grey eyes, and the whitest, cockiest smile Isabel had ever seen. As he swung from the saddle into a circle of light cast by the flaming torches, Isabel squeezed her husband's arm. "You were right, Will. Only a blind man would not know he was looking at a king."

ELEANOR'S CHAMBER was a cheerful scene. A harpist was playing for their pleasure as the women chatted and stitched, for even the highborn were not exempt from the needlework that was a woman's lot. Denise de Deols was trading gossip with Isabel Marshal as they embroidered, and Eleanor's attendants were occupied with an altar cloth intended as a gift for the castle chaplain. But not all of the women were engaged in such decorous activities. The Countess of Aumale was playing a tavern dice game with Eleanor's granddaughter, Richenza, and Eleanor herself was flipping idly through a book on her lap, for sewing had always bored her. She was finding it difficult to concentrate, and finally set the book aside, getting to her feet. She was at once the focus of all eyes, and when she reached for her mantle, the other women started to rise, too.

She waved them back into their seats. She was in no mood for company, but she knew they'd consider it highly unseemly for a queen to venture out on her own. Eleanor had never given a fig for what other people thought. She'd learned many lessons, though, in those long years of confinement, one of which was that a wise woman picked her battles, and she relented at the last moment, allowing her granddaughter to accompany her.

She'd become quite fond of Richenza, who'd remained behind with her youngest brother when her father's exile had ended and her parents returned to Germany. She was now eighteen, newly a bride, already displaying an independent streak that endeared her to Eleanor, who'd learned long ago that a woman without inner resources would not thrive in their world. Richenza's name had been deemed too exotic for English or French ears and she'd been rechristened Matilda, but once her parents departed, she sought to reclaim her German name, clinging to it as a tangible remembrance of her former life. To most people, she was the Lady Matilda, future Countess of Perche, but to her indulgent family, she was once again Richenza. Even her husband proved willing to overlook the alien sound of her name, for while Richenza had not inherited her mother's fair coloring—she had her father's dark hair and eyes—she had been blessed in full measure with Tilda's beauty.

Eleanor glanced at the girl from time to time as they crossed the bailey, drawing comfort from Richenza's presence, for although she did not physically resemble her mother, she was still Tilda's flesh-and-blood, evoking memories with the familiar tilt of her head, the sudden flash of dimples. She had Tilda's tact, too, for she waited until they'd reached the castle gardens and were out of earshot of curious onlookers before voicing her concern.

"Grandame, forgive me if I am being intrusive. But you've seemed restless and out of sorts in these recent weeks. Would it help to talk about your worries?"

"No, child, but I bless you for your keen eye and your loving heart."

Richenza revealed then how keen her eye really was. "Are you anxious about Uncle Richard's safety in the Holy Land? I know I am."

Eleanor regarded the girl in surprise. She hadn't realized her granddaughter was so perceptive. "I have been melancholy of late," she admitted, "but it will pass, Richenza. It always does."

"God willing," Richenza said softly. She wished that her grandmother was less guarded, for in sharing Eleanor's sorrows, they could have shared hers, too. She still mourned her mother fiercely, and she suspected that Eleanor's "melancholy" was a belated mourning for her own dead, all taken during last year's fateful summer. A daughter dying in a foreign land. The woman who'd been her closest friend. And the husband who'd been partner, lover, enemy, and gaoler. Richenza had seen Henry and Eleanor together often enough to realize that theirs had been a complicated, volatile, and contradictory bond, one few others could understand. But to Richenza, it seemed quite natural that Eleanor could have rejoiced in the death that set her free while grieving for the man himself.

Eleanor reached out, stroking her granddaughter's cheek. "You are very dear to me," she said, adding briskly, "now I am going to speak with the castle chaplain about that altar cloth we've promised him. And you, my dearest, are going to bid your husband welcome."

Following Eleanor's gaze, Richenza saw that Jaufre had indeed ridden into the castle bailey, and a smile flitted across her lips, for she'd found marriage to her liking and when she offered up prayers for her uncle Richard, she prayed even more fervently that the Almighty would safeguard Jaufre, too, in that blood-soaked land where the Lord Christ had once walked. She waved to Jaufre before turning back to her grandmother. But Eleanor had gone.

ELEANOR HAD MENTIONED the altar cloth as a pretext, not wanting to continue the conversation. She had never found it easy to open her heart, especially to those of her own sex. She'd only had two female confidantes—her sister Petronilla and Henry's cousin Maud, Countess of Chester. Petronilla had been dead for a number of years, but Maud's loss was still raw, as she'd died barely six months ago. Glancing over her shoulder, Eleanor saw that Richenza was hastening to greet her husband. Turning away, she headed toward the chapel.

It was deserted at that hour and she found the stillness soothing. Pausing to dip her fingers in a holy water font reserved for clerics and the highborn—for even in church class differences were recognized—she moved up the nave. Kneeling before the altar, she offered prayers for lost loved ones. William, the first of her children to die, the image of that heartbreakingly tiny coffin still burned into her brain. Hal, the golden son, a wasted life. Geoffrey, called to God too soon. Tilda, a gentle soul surely spared the rigors of Purgatory. Maud, missed as much as Eleanor's blood sister. And Harry, whose name had so often been both a caress and a curse. "*Requiescat in pace*," she murmured and rose stiffly to her feet.

It had taken her by surprise, this quiet despondency. It was not dramatic or despairing, more like a low fever, but it had lingered in the weeks following the Christmas festivities. And because Eleanor the prisoner had mastered one skill that had often eluded Eleanor the queen and duchess—the art of introspection—she'd been giving some thought to this change in mood. Could Richenza be correct? Was it a mother's anxiety that was fueling her unease?

There was justification for such fears, God knows. How many of the men who took the cross ever saw their homes again? Outremer had become a burial ground for thousands of foreign-born crusaders. And since she'd regained her freedom, she'd made a startling discovery about her eldest surviving son. Richard had won battlefield laurels at an early age, earning himself a well-deserved reputation for what their world most admired—military prowess. But his health was not as robust as his appearance would indicate; she'd learned that he was subject to recurrent attacks of quartan fever, contracted during one of his campaigns in the Limousin. And more men were killed by the noxious diseases and hellish heat of the Holy Land than by Saracen swords.

Or was it memories of last summer? So much had happened, so fast. On the day her husband had drawn his last, tortured breath, she'd been a royal captive. By nightfall, she was the most powerful woman in Christendom, the one person who had the complete trust of England's new king. The news of Maud's death had reached her soon after Richard's coronation; it had taken longer for word of Tilda's death to come from Germany. But there'd been little time to mourn, for in those early weeks of Richard's kingship, they'd been riding the whirlwind.

The more she thought about her flagging spirits, the more it made sense to her. She was grieving for the dead and fearing for the living, for the son who'd always been closest to her heart. And because she was a political being to the very marrow of her bones, she feared, too, for her duchy and their kingdom should evil befall Richard in the Holy Land. She'd have given a great deal if only she could have convinced him to abandon his quest, or at least delay it until he was firmly established upon his throne. But she knew that was a hope as easily extinguished as a candle's flame. Richard would gladly sacrifice his life, if in so doing he could free Jerusalem from the infidels.

Eleanor leaned against the altar. "Ah, Harry," she said softly, "if only Richard shared your sense of practicality. You were satisfied to be a king, not the savior of Christendom."

"Madame."

Eleanor spun around, her cheeks burning. She wasn't easily flustered, but being caught talking to her dead husband was embarrassing. Her eyes narrowed as she recognized the intruder. Constance of Brittany was once her daughter by marriage, but Eleanor regarded her now without warmth. "Lady Constance," she said coolly as the younger woman dropped a rather perfunctory curtsy.

"My lady queen, may I speak with you?" Taking Eleanor's consent for granted, Constance approached the altar. "I have come to ask a favor," she said, although there was nothing of the supplicant in either her voice or her posture; Constance had learned at an early age to use pride as a shield. "It is my hope that you will speak with the king on my behalf. He claimed the custody of my daughter last autumn and sent her off to England despite the agreement I'd struck with his lord father. King Henry promised that he'd permit me to keep Aenor with me if I agreed to wed the Earl of Chester. I held to my side of the bargain, but now my daughter is gone and I've not seen her in nigh on six months. Where is the fairness in that?"

"Your deal was with Henry, not Richard. Does it truly surprise you that Richard regards you with suspicion? How many times did you ally yourself with his enemies? How many times did Geoffrey lead a Breton army into Aquitaine?"

"I've sought only to protect Brittany, to safeguard my duchy. I would think that you of all women would understand that, for Aquitaine has been the lodestar of your life. You even sacrificed your marriage for it. So how can you judge me?"

"I am not judging you for your devotion to your duchy," Eleanor said icily. "I am faulting you for your inability to learn from your mistakes. You have never made a secret of your antipathy—"

"Are you saying I had no reason for resentment? Have you forgotten that Henry forced my father to abdicate and sent him into exile? I was five years old when I was torn from the only home I'd ever known and betrothed to his son. Yes, I bore him a grudge. I was not a saint."

"Or a good wife to my son!"

Constance gasped, for she'd not seen that coming. "I do not know what you mean, Madame."

"I mean that you did all you could to estrange Geoffrey from his family. Again and again you urged him to make war upon Richard, and then you convinced him to disavow his father and ally himself with our greatest enemy, the French king."

"That is not true! I never encouraged Geoffrey to do that. It was his decision to seek out Philippe in Paris."

Eleanor did not bother to hide her disbelief. "I am not saying you bear all the blame. Geoffrey must bear some, too, as must my husband. But this I do know for certes. If Geoffrey had not gone over to the French king, he'd not have been taking part in that tournament, and he'd still be alive today."

The manifest unfairness of that left Constance momentarily speechless. "How dare you blame me for his death? I loved Geoffrey!"

"Did you, indeed?" Eleanor said skeptically. "I will grant you this much, Constance. I do believe you love your children. But you are putting their future in peril by your stubborn hostility toward Richard. If you were half as clever as you think you are, you'd see that. Richard will be facing daily dangers in the Holy Land, and if he dies there, he leaves no heir of his body, only his brother and his nephew—your son, Arthur. Any other woman would be doing whatever she could to gain Richard's goodwill, to convince him that he should name Arthur as his successor in case he dies without a son of his own. But just as your desire for vengeance was stronger than your so-called love for Geoffrey, it is stronger than your responsibilities as a mother and as a duchess, for you cannot be such a fool as to believe Brittany would fare better under French rule."

When Constance would have protested, Eleanor raised her hand in an imperious gesture. "There is nothing more for you to say. I will not intercede with

Richard on your behalf—not until you prove that you can be trusted." Brushing past the Breton duchess, she walked swiftly toward the door. Her outward calm was deceiving, for the accusations she'd made against Constance had ripped open a wound that had never fully healed. She'd had to accept the fact that Hal had brought about his own doom. But Geoffrey . . . surely Geoffrey could have been saved. If only Harry had not been so stubborn, if only Geoffrey had not been so proud. If only his wife had not been so vengeful and filled with malice.

Constance had begun to shake, so great was her fury and her pain. She was almost as angry with herself as she was with Eleanor, for she realized how badly she'd botched things. She'd made an enemy of the only woman who could have helped her. She'd ruined her one chance of getting her daughter back. *I loved Geoffrey!* The irony of her outburst did not escape her—that she'd admitted to Geoffrey's mother what she'd never said to him.

She sank down on the step leading into the choir, wrapping her arms around her drawn-up knees to stop her trembling. How dare Eleanor accuse her of being a bad mother? Geoffrey's parents had failed their children in so many ways, above all in having favorites. For Henry, it had been Hal and then John, and for Eleanor, Richard. Geoffrey had been the forgotten son. He'd always sworn that he'd never make that mistake with his children, that he would be a better father than his own. But he'd had so little time with Aenor and had never even seen his son, for Arthur had been born seven months after his death.

Tears had begun to burn Constance's eyes, but she blinked them back, for what good would crying do? She could fling herself onto the floor of this church and weep and wail until she had no more tears, until her cries would echo unto Heaven. But Geoffrey would still be dead. She'd still be yoked to a man she could not abide. Her son would still face a precarious future, her daughter would still be a hostage, and Brittany would remain trapped between England and France, a rabbit hunted by wolves.

Constance hadn't heard the soft footsteps approaching and her head came up sharply at the sound of her name. Angrily swiping the back of her hand against her wet cheeks, she frowned at the sight of the woman coming toward her. Since her arrival at Nonancourt, Alys Capet had been seeking her out at every opportunity, eager to reminisce about their shared past. It was true that Constance and Alys and Joanna had passed several years at the queen's court in Poitiers, but friendship needed more than proximity to flourish. The fact was that Joanna had been too young, and Constance and Alys, while the same age, had never liked each other. Constance remembered even if Alys apparently did not, and she'd been hard put to be civil, as Alys insisted upon making their time together sound like an idyllic childhood. Now before she could get to her feet, Alys sat beside her upon the altar step.

"Constance, you've been weeping! What is wrong? May I be of any help?"

Her concern seemed genuine and, much to Constance's dismay, she heard herself blurt out that she'd just sought Eleanor's aid in recovering her daughter, to no avail. It was almost as if the words had escaped of their own will, for she'd never have chosen Alys as a confidante. But there was no calling them back, and Alys responded with such sympathy and indignation that Constance told her how Richard's men had swooped down upon Brittany and carried Aenor off to England within a fortnight of his coronation. "They have been keeping her at Winchester," she concluded bleakly, "and I have no idea when I'll be able to see her again...."

Alys had insisted upon putting a consoling arm around Constance's shoulders, much to the latter's discomfort. But at the mention of Winchester, Alys forgot about offering solace and looked at Constance in surprise. "Aenor is not at Winchester. She is in Normandy now. She traveled upon the queen's own ship. Once we landed at Barfleur, the rest of us headed south toward Nonancourt to meet Richard whilst Aenor was sent to Rouen. You did not know?"

"Obviously not," Constance snapped, her brain racing as she sought to process this new and startling bit of information. She was furious that no one had thought to inform her, but the mere fact that Aenor was no longer in England was surely a reason for rejoicing. At the least, visits would be much easier. Would Richard permit it, though? If she approached him in public, midst a hall filled with eyewitnesses, and asked for permission to see her daughter, how could he dare say no? He'd be shamed into agreeing. But she could not make the same mistake with him that she'd done with Eleanor. God help her, she must assume the role of a humble petitioner, swallow her pride even if she choked on it.

Alys had continued to talk, but Constance was so caught up in her own thoughts that she was no longer listening. It was only when she heard her mother's name that she turned back to the other woman. "My mother?"

Alys nodded. "Yes, the Lady Margaret was permitted to visit Aenor at Winchester." Doing her best to ease Constance's worries, she said earnestly, "Aenor is being well treated, Constance, truly she is. At Winchester, she often played with the Lady Richenza's little brother, and the queen made sure that well-bred palfreys were provided for her escort. She was sent off to Rouen in fine style, as befitting a child of her high birth."

Constance had never doubted that Aenor would be comfortably housed or given solicitous servants, so she was not appeased to hear it confirmed. It was some comfort, though, that her mother had spent time with Aenor. Margaret had wed an English baron after the death of Constance's father, and Constance had hoped she'd be able to keep an eye upon Aenor. Alys had a pleasant voice, but it was grating now on Constance's nerves, for she needed time alone to marshal her thoughts and plan how best to approach Richard. She paid the other woman no heed until Alys said something so startling that she whipped her head around to stare at the French princess. "What did you say?"

By now they were both on their feet, brushing off their skirts. "I said that I can be of little assistance to you now, Constance. But once I am queen, I promise that I will do all in my power to have Aenor returned to you."

Constance was dumbfounded. Did Alys truly believe that Richard was going to marry her? If so, she was more naïve than a novice nun and more forgiving than the Blessed Mother Mary. If she'd been treated as shabbily as Alys, Constance would have prayed every day for the demise of her tormentor. Where was Alys's indignation, her spine?

But as she gazed into the other woman's face, Constance was struck by Alys's wide-eyed, girlish mien. Alys was the elder of the two by six months, would be thirty come October. At that age, she ought to have been in charge of her own household, presiding over her highborn husband's domains in his absence, a mother and wife, mayhap even a queen. Instead, she'd spent these formative years in pampered, secluded confinement, with no duties or responsibilities, denied the chance to mature, denied her womanhood. And Constance suddenly understood why Alys had been so eager to claim a friendship that had existed only in her own imagination, why—despite all evidence to the contrary—she still clung to the romantic belief that she would marry the man to whom she'd been betrothed since the age of nine. Looked upon in that light, it was not even surprising. Who would expect a tame bird to fend for itself if it were set free after a lifetime of gilded captivity?

With this realization, Constance found herself faced with an uncomfortable dilemma. Should she be the one to shatter Alys's illusions? Constance had little patience with fools, yet there was no cruelty in her nature. To tell Alys the truth was akin to pulling the wings off a butterfly. But someone had to tell her. Surely it would be less painful coming here and now. The alternative would be to hear it from Richard himself, and Constance did not trust him to be tactful as he trampled Alys's dreams underfoot.

"Alys . . . there is something you must know, and better you hear it from me than from Richard. He has no intention of marrying you."

Color flamed into Alys's face and then ebbed, leaving her white and shaken. "That is not true! It was his father who kept delaying our marriage, not Richard."

"Alys, you need to face the truth. Richard has been king for over six months. If he'd wanted to marry you, it would have happened by now. He has never had any interest in making you his wife, at first because your marriage portion was so meager and then because he no longer trusts your brother, the French king. None of this is your doing but you must—"

"No!" Alys shook her head vehemently, began to back away. "You have not changed at all, Constance, you are still as sharp-tongued and jealous as you always were!"

Constance blinked. "Jealous?"

"Yes, jealous! Joanna and I were raised to be queens, but you had to settle for less and you still resent me for it."

Constance experienced the righteous resentment of a Good Samaritan not only rebuffed but accused of unworthy motives. She started to defend herself, but Alys had whirled and was halfway up the nave, making her escape in a swirl of silken skirts. Constance made no attempt to call her back. She'd done what she could. It was now up to Alys. She could accept the truth or continue to dwell in her fantasy world. Suddenly Constance felt very tired. Watching Alys retreat, she faced a bitter truth of her own—that she'd rather have been Geoffrey's duchess than the queen of any kingdom under God's sky.

CHAPTER 5

MARCH 1190

Nonancourt Castle, Normandy

In order to have a private conversation without fear of eavesdroppers, Eleanor had retreated to her bedchamber with her son. After dismissing her attendants, Richard joked that they ought to plug the keyhole with candle wax to thwart any French spies. Taking the wine cup he was holding out, Eleanor raised an eyebrow. "Is your news as incendiary as that?"

Richard had seated himself by the fire, stretching long legs toward its welcome warmth—for spring came later to Normandy than it did to their beloved Aquitaine—and regarded her enigmatically over the rim of his wine cup. "Let's just say it is news that Philippe would pay dearly to have, news I do not intend to share with him when we meet at Dreux on Friday."

"May I hope that you do intend to share it with me . . . eventually?" But Eleanor's impatience was feigned, for she was accustomed to this sort of teasing. Henry had been a master of suspense, too. It struck her how alike her husband and son were, doubtless one of the main reasons why they'd so often been at odds.

"You know I was in Aquitaine last month. I spent several days in Gascony at La Réole, and during that time I had a very private meeting with trusted agents of the King of Navarre."

"Did you now?" Eleanor sat back in her chair, a smile playing about the corners of her mouth. They'd talked about this before, the possibility of a marital alliance with the Navarrese king, and were in agreement as to its potential. "I know you've raised the matter with Sancho in the past. I take it he is still interested."

"Why would he not be? We still do have some issues to agree upon. So when

I'm back in the south later this spring, I will meet again with his envoys, mayhap his son. What do they say about marriage contracts, Maman—that the Devil is in the details? But I am confident that we have an understanding, for it will be a good deal for both sides. I gain a valuable alliance, and God knows I'll need a reliable ally to safeguard my southern borders from that whoreson in Toulouse. It is not by chance that Count Raimon is the only lord of note who has not taken the cross. He thinks this will be a rare opportunity to wreak havoc whilst I am occupied in the Holy Land. I'd wager he is already laying plans to invade Quercy even as we speak. But between Sancho and Alfonso," he said, referring to the King of Aragon, a friend since boyhood, "I think they can keep him in check until I return."

"Yes, it would be an advantageous match," Eleanor agreed. Neither bothered to mention what Navarre was gaining from it, for that was obvious. Sancho's daughter would become Queen of England, a lofty elevation for a young woman from a small Spanish kingdom. Sipping her wine contentedly, she studied her son, thinking he was taking pleasure, too, in outwitting the French king, for their friendship had been one of expediency, and once Henry had been defeated, the erstwhile allies were soon regarding each other with suspicion and hostility.

"Does . . ." She paused, prodding her memory to recall the girl's name. "Does Berengaria speak French? The native tongue of Navarre is Romance, is it not?"

"When I visited her father's court six years ago, her grasp of French was somewhat tenuous, but Sancho assured me that she has studied it diligently since then." Richard's smile was complacent. "The chance of a crown proved to be a powerful inducement. And she knows our *lenga romana* quite well, for it is spoken in many parts of Navarre." He was pleased by that, for like Eleanor, he was fluent in both French and the language of Aquitaine. "I write most of my poetry in *lenga romana* and I'd prefer not to have to translate it for her."

Eleanor was pleased, too, that Berengaria spoke the *lenga romana,* for that indicated she was well educated and familiar with the troubadour culture of the south. While compatibility was not a consideration in royal marriages, it did make marital harmony more likely, and Eleanor, like any mother, wanted her son to be content with the bride he chose. "When we've discussed this in the past, Richard, we spoke of political concerns, not personal ones. But after the marriage contract has been signed and the vows said, you'll be sharing your life with a flesh-and-blood woman. What are you seeking in a wife?"

"Fertility," he quipped, but then, seeing that she really wanted to know, he paused to give it some thought. "I'd want her to be sensible, not flighty or needy.

Not overly pious, for no man wants to bed a nun. What else? A queen must be educated and worldly, of course . . ."

He almost added "loyal" but caught himself in time, for his mother's loyalty to his father had been neither unconditional nor enduring. In his eyes, she could do no wrong. But he preferred a more conventional wife for himself, just as he did not want the tempest that had been his parents' marriage. Civility seemed a much safer foundation for a royal union than wanton lust or love that burned so fiercely it became indistinguishable from hatred.

Almost as if she'd read his mind, Eleanor startled him by saying dryly, "The best marriages are based upon benign indifference or detached goodwill. That was the advice Harry's father gave him ere we wed. Looking back, I suspect he may have been right." She knew she would not have given up the passion, though, for she had not been born for safe harbors. "It sounds as if you have a realistic grasp of matrimony, Richard, which bodes well for you and your bride, and you seem satisfied with the girl herself. But I can only marvel at your powers of persuasion, even with a crown in the offing. Not many fathers would agree to wed a daughter to a man already betrothed to another woman for more than twenty years. How did you get Sancho to overlook your plight-troth to Philippe's sister?"

"Sancho knows that marriage will never take place."

"But does Philippe?"

"Well, not yet," he conceded. "I cannot very well renounce the betrothal now, for Philippe would seize upon that as an excuse to forswear his holy vow. He never wanted to take the cross, was shamed into doing so by the Archbishop of Tyre's fiery public sermon. And if Philippe does not go to Outremer, I dare not go myself." Richard's mouth twisted, as if the French king's very name tasted foul. "As soon as I was gone, he'd overrun Normandy, making war upon my subjects instead of the Saracens, damn his craven soul to Hell."

"I am not arguing with you, Richard. I can see the logic in waiting until Philippe has committed himself too fully to back out. But whether you reject Alys now or when you reach the Holy Land, Philippe is going to take it very badly. Not that he cares a whit for Alys herself. He cares a great deal, though, about his pride, and he will try to hold you to the betrothal, claiming that you have no legal grounds for breaking it."

"Ah, but that is the beauty of it, Maman," Richard said, his eyes gleaming. "Philippe has given me the grounds. Two years ago, when he was desperate to turn me against my father, he sent the Count of Flanders to me with a story likely to do that. You remember the meeting we had at Bonsmoulins?"

"All too well." It was then that Richard had given Henry one last chance to acknowledge him publicly as his heir. When Henry balked, he'd unwittingly confirmed Richard's darkest suspicions—that he meant to crown John—and Richard had reacted with a dramatic renunciation, kneeling and doing homage to Philippe for Aquitaine and Normandy and his "other fiefs on this side of the sea." Henry had been stunned, and when she heard, Eleanor had wept, knowing there would be no going back. The bitter struggle between father and son could end only in defeat or death for one of them.

"Well, ere we met him at Bonsmoulins, I had a secret conclave with Philippe at Mantes. Philippe had been claiming for some time that I was in danger of being disinherited. But to make sure I had grievances enough to hold firm, he sent the Count of Flanders to me with a rather remarkable tale—that my father was swiving my betrothed."

"Jesu!" But once the shock ebbed, she shook her head emphatically. "I do not believe that. Harry had his flaws. God alone knows how many women he bedded over the years. He was accused of any number of sins, some true, some not. But no one ever called him a fool, and seducing his son's betrothed, the sister of the King of France, no less, would have been more than foolhardy. It would have been utter madness."

Richard grinned, for his mother had unknowingly used almost exactly the same words to refute the accusation as his chancellor, Guillaume Longchamp, had once done. "I know," he said. "I never gave it any credence, either. Philippe's weakness is that he tends to hold his foes too cheaply. I suppose he thought I'd be so outraged that I'd not see the great gaps in the story."

"Well, many men would have reacted like that. But not anyone who knew Harry. He would never have jeopardized so much for so little."

Richard was amused that they were defending Henry on grounds of pragmatism, not morality. He doubted that a priest would approve of such a cynical argument, but it rang more true to him than any claims of virtue. "So you see," he said, "Philippe has given me the key to unlock the chains binding me to Alys. I will be appalled that he'd expect me to wed a woman who'd lain with my father, truly appalled."

Eleanor began to laugh, for what could be more satisfying than turning an enemy's own weapon against him? Neither she nor Richard gave much thought to Alys, the innocent pawn, for when kingdoms were at stake, it was easy to justify almost any action in the name of a greater good.

Rising, Richard held out his hand. "I just wish you could be there to see

Philippe's face when I tell him, Maman. Now I want you to accompany me to the castle solar. I have made some changes in my plans to safeguard the governance of my realm whilst I am away, will reveal them at the great council meeting tomorrow. Since not all will be pleased, I thought it only fair to warn several of them beforehand, giving them time to come to terms with these changes. They are awaiting me now in the solar."

Eleanor rose and took his arm, gratified that he always included her in matters of state, that he truly valued her opinions and her political instincts. She wondered occasionally if things might have been different had her husband only showed her the same trust and respect that her son did. But she also knew that the intimate bond she had with Richard was what Henry had desperately wanted, too, not understanding why the sons he'd so loved had become his enemies—and that was a regret she'd take to her grave, her awareness of the part she'd played in their family's tragic disintegration. As they moved toward the door, she asked whom they'd be meeting and stopped in her tracks when Richard told her.

"Is that a jest? You've put your brothers and the Bishop of Durham and Long-champ together in one chamber and left them alone? Good Lord, Richard, you'd be hard pressed to find four men who loathe one another more than that lot does! Geoff will never forgive John for abandoning Harry as he lay dying, and John cannot abide him, either. Durham was adamantly opposed to Geoff's elevation to the archbishopric of York, and they all despise your chancellor. We're likely to find the solar knee-deep in blood."

"I know. It will be even better than a bearbaiting."

She eyed him dubiously, thinking that she'd never fully understand the male sense of humor. "But who is the bear and who are the hounds?"

"We'll soon find out," he said and opened the door.

———

GEOFFREY FITZ ROY considered himself blessed to have been the son of Henry Fitz Empress. He'd not been so lucky in the circumstances of his birth, for his mother had been one of Henry's passing fancies, and even a royal bastard began life at a distinct disadvantage. Henry had been determined that Geoff would not suffer from the stigma of illegitimacy, though, and had sought a career in the Church for his eldest son, ignoring the obvious—that Geoff was utterly unsuited for the priesthood. He'd named Geoff to the bishopric of Lincoln when he was only twenty-one, much to Geoff's dismay. Because he was under the canonical age for such an elevated post, Geoff had persuaded Henry to delay his ordination

60 © SHARON PENMAN

and years later, when the Pope demanded that he either accept consecration or resign, Geoff had chosen the latter, for he was much more at home on the battlefield than at the altar. He'd become his father's chancellor then, fiercely loyal to Henry and bitterly resentful of the half-brothers who'd caused his sire so much grief.

But Henry had expressed a deathbed hope that Geoff be given the archbishopric of York, and Richard declared that he would carry out his father's wishes. Knowing the ill will between Richard and Geoff, many people had been surprised, speculating that Richard must be feeling guilty for having gone to war against his father. Geoff was highly skeptical of that theory, convinced that none of his half-brothers were capable of remorse or regret. He was sure that Richard had forced him to take a priest's vows because that would bar him from laying any claims to the English crown. While he did not doubt that he'd have made a good king, a better one than any of his faithless brothers, he'd known it would never come to pass. It was true that William the Bastard had claimed his father's duchy of Normandy and then used it to launch a successful invasion of England. But that was well over a hundred years ago, and the Holy Church would no longer sanction the coronation of one born out of wedlock. Some churchmen did not think a bastard ought to be a bishop, either, and Geoff was one of them, for all the good it did him.

Shifting in his seat, Geoff glowered at the other inhabitants of Nonancourt's solar, thinking he'd rather have been trapped in a badger den than here with this unholy trinity. Guillaume Longchamp had once been Geoff's own clerk, but with a fine eye for the main chance, he was soon serving Richard, and he'd benefited lavishly once Richard became king. Now he and the Bishop of Durham were joint justiciars, set to rule England during Richard's prolonged absence in Outremer, and Geoff thought only the Almighty's Divine Mercy could save his homeland from utter ruination. With that prideful pair at the helm, they'd run the ship of state onto the rocks in no time at all.

Geoff did not trust Longchamp, but he had a greater grudge against Hugh de Puiset, the Bishop of Durham, for the latter had sabotaged his attempts to regain royal favor. After they'd clashed over the appointment of Hugh de Puiset's nephew as treasurer of York, Richard had seized Geoff's castles and Episcopal estates, and Geoff had to promise to pay two thousand pounds to get them back. But the Bishop of Durham would not relinquish custody of these manors, refusing to allow Geoff to collect their revenues, thus making it impossible for him to pay that large fine. Richard had then confiscated his estates again and increased the fine, brushing aside Geoff's attempts to lay the blame at Hugh de Puiset's door.

So Geoff would have freely conceded that he disliked Longchamp and loathed the Bishop of Durham. But even de Puiset's treachery paled in comparison with the sins of Geoff's half-brother John, the Count of Mortain, who'd betrayed his dying father, breaking Henry's spirits and his heart in the last days of his life. Geoff's gaze moved coldly now past the diminutive chancellor and the tall, elegant bishop, shooting daggers at the young man standing by the window.

John sensed Geoff's eyes boring into his back, and his jaw muscles tightened, his fists clenching and unclenching as he sought to control his fury. He'd had enough of Geoff's self-righteous censure, was bone-weary of being treated as if he bore the Mark of Cain. He'd done no more than countless other men had done, swimming away from a sinking ship. He'd never fought against his father as Hal, Geoffrey, and Richard had done. He was not the one who'd dragged Henry from his sickbed to make a humiliating surrender at Colombières; Richard and Philippe bore the blame for that. He'd been loyal to his sire almost to the last, which was more than his brothers could say. Yes, Geoff had been loyal, too, but what other choice had he? He was a king's bastard, utterly dependent upon the man who'd sired him whilst rutting with a whore.

John could feel the heat rising in his face. It was so unfair. Yes, he'd made a secret peace with Richard and the French king, but he had not wanted it to be that way. He'd not forsaken his father until the waves were beginning to break over the deck. He was sure Henry would not have wanted them both to drown.

And in the weeks after his father's death, it seemed as if he'd been vindicated, for he had been welcomed by Richard, shown a generosity that he'd not truly expected, for his brothers had usually treated him either with indifference or annoyance. Eleven, nine, and eight years younger than Hal, Richard, and Geoffrey, fifteen years younger than Geoff, he'd always felt like the foundling, the afterthought, John Lackland. He was finally given his just due, though, once Richard became king. He was wed at long last to a great heiress, Avisa of Gloucester, a marriage that his father had promised but never delivered. He was given vast estates in six English shires, lands with income worth four thousand pounds a year. He was someone of importance, no longer the insignificant little brother. He was the heir to the English throne.

But that triumphant flush had soon faded. Geoff was not the only one who scorned him for doing what any sensible man would have done. Most were not as outspoken as Geoff, but he could see it in their eyes—their silent disdain. Will Marshal, that Welsh whelp Morgan, Baldwin de Bethune, all those who'd stayed with his father till the last, daring to judge him. He would not defend himself, for he was a prince of the blood royal, mayhap one day a king, and kings were accountable only to the Almighty. But he could not brush aside their implied condemnation as he knew Richard would have done. Their disapproval shadowed his days and bad dreams disrupted his nights, for Henry came to him in those lonely hours before dawn, a mute, reproachful ghost haunting his sleep. John would wager the surety of his soul that Richard was never stalked by that unrelenting spirit, never troubled by vain regrets. Everything was always so easy for Richard.

No longer able to abide Geoff's unspoken accusations, John swung around, staring defiantly at the older man. "If you have something to say, Geoff, say it then," he challenged, a gauntlet the reluctant archbishop was quick to pick up.

"Right gladly," he growled, rising to his formidable height, angry color staining his cheeks.

"It will serve for naught to squabble amongst ourselves," the Bishop of Durham interceded smoothly. "My lord archbishop, my lord count. I realize that nerves are on the raw, that we have had disputes in the past that are not easy to put aside. But we owe it to the king to do so, for he will depend upon us to cooperate with one another, to govern in a spirit of harmony whilst he is overseas, fighting the godless infidels who've captured the holiest city in Christendom."

As unlike as they were, a remarkably similar expression crossed the faces of the estranged brothers, the look of men marveling at such blatant, shameless sanctimony. Guillaume Longchamp stifled a smile, preferring to maintain the dignified bearing of one who was above the fray. He thought the Archbishop of York was a dangerous hothead and the Count of Mortain an even more dangerous adversary, for John had few if any scruples and a newly awakened appetite for power. But he reserved his greatest contempt for Hugh de Puiset. The Bishop of Durham was the epitome of all that Longchamp most despised—an arrogant, smug hypocrite, who'd traded upon his high birth, good looks, and glib tongue to advance himself in the Church and at the royal court.

Longchamp was Hugh's opposite in all particulars, for he'd risen by merit alone, overcoming his modest family background, his small stature, and unprepossessing appearance, no easy task in a world in which people saw physical deformity as an outer manifestation of inner evil. He'd realized early in life that he was much more intelligent than most, and took pride in his intellectual abilities, burning to prove himself to all who'd dismissed him as a "lowborn cripple" or an "ugly dwarf." Once he'd entered the Duke of Aquitaine's service and rose rapidly in Richard's favor, he was no longer treated with ridicule. His detractors became enemies, and he gloried in their hostility. The ambition he'd always kept hidden now came to the fore, and he dared to dream of what had once been unthinkable—a bishopric. And indeed, when Richard became king, he rewarded Longchamp with the bishopric of Ely and the chancellorship. In turn, Longchamp rewarded Richard with the sort of loyalty that was beyond value, almost spiritual in its selfless intensity, rooted as much in Richard's acceptance of his physical flaws as in the tangible benefits of royal favor.

Longchamp's ambitions were no longer earthbound, soared higher and higher with each elevation: chancellor, bishop, and then justiciar. He'd even begun to think of the pinnacle of Church power. The Archbishop of Canterbury was going to the Holy Land, too, and he was not a young man. A vacancy might well occur in the next year or two, and what would be more natural than that the king should look to the one man he knew he could trust.

But what Longchamp's enemies did not understand was that he was also a man of piety. He was not a worldly prince of the Church like the Bishop of Durham, who lived as lavishly as any king, claimed an earldom, and flaunted a mistress by whom he'd had at least four children. Longchamp was offended by such a blatant disregard for a priest's holy vows, and he meant to punish Hugh de Puiset for his carnal sins as well as for his political machinations and unabashed greed. Looking now at the bishop, so graceful and urbane and haughty, Longchamp smiled to himself, sure that a day of reckoning was coming.

They all jumped to their feet then as the door opened and the king and his mother swept into the chamber; Richard could no more make an unobtrusive entrance than he could have understood his brother John's crippling insecurities. "I trust you've been able to entertain yourselves whilst I was delayed," he said blandly, giving himself away by the amused glint in his eyes.

After they'd all greeted Eleanor, Richard wasted no time getting to the heart of the meeting. "Tomorrow I will be announcing to the great council that I have decided to change my original arrangements for governing the realm whilst I am away. Instead of acting as co-justiciars, you, my lord," he said to the Bishop of Durham, "will be justiciar north of the River Humber, and my chancellor will act as justiciar for the rest of England."

Hugh de Puiset drew a sharp breath, then swung around to glare accusingly at Longchamp. The chancellor had not yet mastered the art of inscrutability, and one glance told Hugh that his suspicions were right; Longchamp had known this was coming. It was an easy step from that to the next—that he had planted this noxious seed and then watered it till it took root in Richard's mind. "My lord king, surely you do not doubt my loyalty? I've had far more experience than the Bishop of Ely, know the barons of the kingdom as he does not—"

"The decision has been made, my lord bishop," Richard interrupted. "I am not disrespecting you, merely doing what is best for England." Hugh would have continued his protest, but Richard was already turning his attention upon his brother Geoff.

"I do not have the money to pay that fine," Geoff said morosely before Richard could speak.

"That can be discussed later. What I've come to tell you now is that I will require you to swear a solemn oath that you will not set foot in England for the next three years." Geoff's mouth dropped open, and then his eyes flashed. Richard gave him no chance to object, though. "I will be requiring the same oath from you, Johnny," he told John, whose response was more guarded than Geoff's. He stiffened, but said nothing, slanting his gaze from Richard to Eleanor, back to Richard again.

Richard let the silence stretch out, smothering any embers of rebellion, and then got to his feet. "I shall see you at the great council tomorrow," he said, and after beckoning to his chancellor, he kissed his mother on the cheek and sauntered out, Longchamp hurrying to catch up. Geoff was the next to go, fuming helplessly. The Bishop of Durham would have lingered to argue his case with Eleanor, but she was not receptive and he soon departed, too, followed by John.

Welcoming this rare chance to be alone, Eleanor sat down in the window-seat. She approved of Richard's move to circumscribe the Bishop of Durham's authority, for he'd never impressed her, a courtier cloaked in the garb of a cleric. But there were risks, too, in the road Richard had chosen. Longchamp was now chancellor and chief justiciar, in possession of the king's great seal and the Tower of London. If Richard's request to make him a papal legate was granted by the Holy Father, he'd have a formidable arsenal of weapons, both religious and secular. Was it wise to give any one man that much power?

A soft knock interrupted her musings. "Enter," she said with a sigh; she should have known her solitude would be fleeting. To her surprise, it was John. "May I speak with you, Madame?" he asked formally. "It is a matter of importance."

"Come in, John." When she gestured toward the window-seat, he declined with a quick shake of his head, keeping some distance between them by leaning against the table. Of all her children, he alone had inherited her coloring, dark hair and hazel eyes. He did not speak immediately and she regarded him pensively. How could she feel so detached from a child of her womb, her flesh-and-blood?

She supposed it was not truly so surprising, though, for he'd been six when she'd been captured and turned over to her wrathful husband. She had not been denied access to her daughter Joanna and eventually Henry had relented, allowing her older sons to visit her, too. But she'd not seen John again until he was twelve and then rarely, even after Henry had dramatically eased the terms of her confinement. He'd been Henry's, never hers. As she gazed into the greenish-gold eyes so like her own, a memory flickered of an afternoon soon after Hal's death. She'd confessed to Geoffrey that she did not really know John, and Geoffrey had proven once again that he was the family seer, predicting that Henry did not really know John, either.

"Mother . . . I fear that Richard may be making a mistake in investing so much royal authority in his chancellor."

"Oh? Do you have reason to doubt Longchamp's loyalty?"

"No, I do not. But loyalty is not the only consideration. There are men who function quite well as second in command, yet do not thrive when given absolute authority, and it can be argued that Longchamp will be acting as a *de facto* king with Richard away in the Holy Land for who knows how long. Especially if he is named a papal legate, as the rumors go."

Eleanor was surprised that he knew about the papal legateship, for that was not common knowledge. But she was intrigued that John was showing such interest in political matters. He was twenty-three now. At that age, their eldest son had cared only for tournaments. Her face shadowed, for memories of Hal were always painful, their beautiful golden boy who'd had more charm than the law ought to allow and barely a brain in his head.

"I do not think Longchamp will be able to meet Richard's expectations," John said, choosing his words with care. "Our English barons are likely to balk at taking commands from a man of obscure birth. Yes, I know," he said when Eleanor started to speak. "He is not the grandson of a peasant, as the Bishop of Coventry claims. But neither is he highborn, not like the men he must rule over. Mayhap if he were more tactful . . . but his arrogance beggars belief. He makes enemies easily."

"So what are you asking of me, John? You want me to convince Richard not to leave the government in Longchamp's hands? He'd not heed me."

"I know. But he might listen to you if you argued against exiling me for three years."

"I see," she said noncommittally, and John moved closer, trying to read her face without success.

"I ought to be there, Mother. My presence might temper Longchamp's more overweening inclinations. And then, too . . ." John paused, meeting his mother's gaze steadily. "If evil befalls Richard in the Holy Land, would you want me in England, able to take control of the realm? Or hundreds of miles away in Normandy or Anjou?"

He knew he'd gambled with such blunt talk, but he saw that he'd won when she smiled ever so faintly. "I will give it some thought," she said, and then, "I think I am beginning to see what Harry saw in you, John." And when John flinched, that told her, too, much about this stranger, her son.

CHAPTER 6

MARCH 1190

Dreux Castle, France

I t was customary for the kings of England and France to hold their conclaves out in the open to preclude treachery; a favorite site had been the Peace Elm near Gisors, until Philippe had lost his temper after an unproductive encounter with Henry and ordered the tree cut down. But because Richard and Philippe were purportedly allies, united in a sacred quest to recover Jerusalem, they'd chosen Dreux Castle for their meeting, a French fortress just eight miles from Richard's stronghold at Nonancourt. Henri, the young Count of Champagne, was glad of it, for the sixteenth had been stormy, not a day to be huddled in a muddy field at the mercy of slashing March winds.

The great hall was crowded with dignitaries—barons of the two kings and princes of the church. Richard and Philippe had formally sworn to serve each other faithfully and to defend the other's lands as if they were his own. Their lords also agreed to honor the peace, and the prelates then vowed to excommunicate any man who broke this covenant.

But there were still issues to be hammered out, and Richard, Philippe, and their most trusted advisers were seated at a long trestle table in the center of the hall, discussing those matters with tight smiles and barbed courtesy. Henri was watching them with keen interest, for he was uniquely bound to both kings. When he was in a mischievous mood, Henri liked to boast of his convoluted family tree, explaining that his mother, Countess Marie, was the child of Queen Eleanor's first marriage to Louis of France, and thus a half-sister to Richard on her maternal side and half-sister to Philippe on the paternal side. Moreover, Henri would continue gleefully, his father was the brother of Philippe's mother, thus making him nephew to Philippe twice over. By then his listeners' heads would be spinning and Henri would be laughing so hard he rarely got to reveal that his mother and his aunt Alix were sisters by blood and marriage, for they'd wed brothers, his father and his uncle Thibault, who were therefore also brothers and brothers-in-law. Or what Henri considered the greatest oddity of all, that his grandfather had been both father-in-law and brother-in-law to the same men, for Louis had wed his two daughters by Eleanor to the brothers of his third wife, Philippe's mother.

Not only was Henri blood-kin to Philippe, the French king was his liege lord; he held Champagne from the French Crown. And he and Philippe were of an age, twenty-three and twenty-four, respectively. But Henri had ridden into Dreux in Richard's entourage, not Philippe's, even though he knew the French king would not be pleased by his presence in the enemy camp. Henri was young enough, though, to delight in tweaking the lion's tail. And he enjoyed his uncle Richard's company, whereas his idea of Purgatory was more than an hour alone with his uncle Philippe, for they had nothing whatsoever in common as far as Henri could tell.

Like most young men, Henri loved the hunt, tournaments, horses, gambling, troubadour songs, wine, women, and war. Philippe was bored by hunting, had banned tournaments in France, disliked horses and only rode the most docile mounts, never gambled or swore, cared nothing for music, and saw war as the means to an end, not as a way to test his manhood. He did like wine and women, although he'd been wed since he was fifteen, and if he strayed from his queen's marital bed, he was discreet about it. Moreover, Philippe was of a nervous disposition; he was known to flinch at sudden loud noises and was rarely without bodyguards. Henri much preferred spending time with Richard, who swore like a sailor, loved spirited stallions, wrote both courtly and bawdy poetry, had done his share of youthful carousing, and gloried in the challenges of the battlefield.

Above all, Henri admired Richard for being one of the first to take the cross. Philippe was a reluctant crusader, and that alone was enough to damn him in the eyes of his nephew, for Henri's own father had taken the cross twice. He'd participated in the disastrous second crusade led by Louis of France, and then made another pilgrimage to the Holy Land with the Count of Flanders; on his way home, he'd been captured and held for ransom, dying soon after his release, his health broken by that stint in a Turkish prison. Henri had been fourteen at the time, and he saw the coming crusade as a sacred quest to honor his father's memory.

Richard and Philippe were exchanging gritted-teeth smiles, and it looked to Henri as if they'd be at this for the foreseeable future. He was turning away to find a wine bearer when he was waylaid by his uncle Thibault. "It is one thing to go hunting or drinking with Richard, Henri. But when you rode into Dreux at his side, you risked stirring up suspicions about where your true loyalties lie. Please tell me you are not now planning to travel with him to the Holy Land."

Henri had adored his father, his uncle not so much. But Thibault was the head of the House of Blois and Henri had been raised to respect his elders. So instead of responding as he'd have liked—telling Thibault that he and Philippe could both piss in a leaking pot—he said mildly, "You need not fret, Uncle. I still intend to accompany you and my uncle Etienne and the Count of Clermont." That had been an easy decision, for they'd be able to depart after Easter, whilst he thought they might see the Second Coming ere Richard and Philippe finally got under way. "I know it is no easy task to transport an army," he conceded. "Richard told me that he had to order fifty thousand horseshoes from an iron mine in Devon and he expects to bring at least ten thousand horses." Henri shook his head, marveling at the magnitude of such an undertaking. "Fortunately, it is much easier for us; we need only hire ships in Marseille and, God willing, we'll reach Tyre ere it falls to the Saracens."

Henri stopped, seeing that his uncle was not listening. Following Thibault's gaze, he saw that Philippe was no longer at the table, nowhere in the hall, and the English did not look very happy. *What now?* he wondered, and headed toward Richard to find out what was going on.

Richard didn't know much more than Henri, though, saying that Philippe had been called away by the castle steward. "I am guessing a courier has ridden in," he said, "but I cannot see what would be important enough to interrupt these discussions. Unless we get these matters settled, we'll have to delay our departure yet again. We've lost enough time as it is. It has been over two years since I took the cross, Henri, two years!"

Richard signaled to a wine bearer, and Henri stayed to commiserate with Richard and Will Marshal and Hubert Walter, the newly named Bishop of Salisbury, who'd be accompanying Richard to the Holy Land. But the longer Philippe was gone, the more impatient Richard became, and by the time the French king finally returned to the hall, the English king's temper, never dormant, was beginning to smolder. Striding over to confront Philippe, he said, with pointed politeness, "Are you ready to resume our talks now, my lord?"

"No, I am not. We'll have to address these matters at a later time."

Richard's mouth tightened. But his protest never left his lips, for he was becoming aware that something was not quite right with Philippe. The younger man had a naturally ruddy complexion, but now his face had taken on a sickly ashen hue, and his voice sounded oddly hoarse, as if his words had been forced from a throat swollen and raw. "Are you ailing?" Richard asked abruptly, dispensing with court etiquette, but Philippe merely looked at him stonily.

"We are done here," he said curtly. "We'll meet at Vézelay in July as previously agreed upon. Any remaining matters can be resolved then." And to the astonishment of Richard and the others within earshot, he then turned on his heel without another word and walked away.

No one knew what to make of this, and speculative murmurs swept the hall. Richard was angry, but puzzled, too. Drawing Henri aside, he said quietly, "If he is playing some damnable game to delay our departure yet again, he'll regret it. Can you find out what he's up to, Henri?"

"If I have to sneak into his chapel and overhear his confession," Henri promised cheerfully, and when Richard departed soon afterward, the Count of Champagne remained behind in Dreux, eagerly embracing this new role—that of royal spy.

MOST PEOPLE ARRANGED their lives around the cycles of the sun, rising at dawn and going to bed once darkness descended, for candles and lamps were expensive, and few could afford the vast numbers of tapers, torches, and rushlights needed to keep night at bay. As kings did not have that concern, Richard and Eleanor felt free to follow their own inner clocks. After a late supper upon his return to Nonancourt, Richard was holding court in the great hall. A minstrel and musicians had entertained, followed by a jape in which a motley-clad fool juggled balls and knives, accompanied by a small dog that danced on her hind legs, turned cartwheels, and balanced on a beam set between wooden trestles.

Richard had enjoyed the minstrel's songs, but he soon lost interest in the antics of the fool and his dog, and withdrew to a window-seat for a low-voiced conversation with his chancellor and Will Marshal. From her seat upon the dais, Eleanor glanced his way from time to time, knowing he was trying to anticipate any crisis that might arise in his absence. The coordination of a crusade of this size was more than daunting. While lords and knights would provide their own weapons and armor, infantrymen would have to be outfitted. The army would need horses and fodder, crossbow bolts, beans and cheese and salt and dried meat, blankets, wine, barrels of silver pennies for expenses abroad, medical supplies—the list was endless. Richard was doing what no other crusading king had dared—assembling and equipping his own fleet of more than a hundred ships, and the cost of these ships and wages for the crews was likely to reach fourteen thousand pounds, more than half the royal revenue from England. Richard had raised huge sums by methods that sometimes verged upon extortion, dismissing all his sheriffs and making them buy their posts back, levying heavy fines, offering town charters, forest rights, earldoms, lordships, and bishoprics for cash, recognizing Scotland's independence in return for ten thousand marks. Men joked, some bitterly, that it was a wonder he'd not taken bids on the very air the English breathed, and Richard himself had jested that he'd have sold London if only he could have found a buyer.

Eleanor was uneasy about such massive expenditures, wondering how the royal treasury could ever be replenished, for she'd been spared the crusading fever that had infected her son and so many others. But she took comfort in Richard's strategic sense, his impressive grasp of logistics. Her French husband's crusade had been a catastrophe of inept organization and shortsighted mistakes. If Richard must do this, she wanted the odds to be in his favor, and she was grateful that he seemed to be so adept at comprehensive planning.

She was dreading his departure as she'd dreaded few events in her life, well aware that he'd be wagering with Death on a daily basis. And each morning she would awaken not knowing if he'd survived another day in that earthly Hell. Could the Almighty take yet another of her sons? She knew the answer to that, knew the cemeteries of Christendom were filled with the children of grieving mothers. And if Richard was slain on a distant, desert battlefield, the empire his father had forged at such great personal cost might well die with him.

"Grandame?" Richenza had reached out to touch her hand, concerned by the faraway look in her grandmother's eyes, sure that whatever Eleanor was seeing, it was not the great hall at Nonancourt Castle. Relieved when Eleanor blinked and then summoned up a smile, she asked if it would be permissible to seek out Alys, a forlorn figure hovering on the edge of the festivities.

"She looks so lonely, Grandame," she said forthrightly. She knew, of course, that Alys would never be her uncle Richard's queen. So, too, did everyone else at court and they preferred to keep Alys at a distance, either because they found her presence uncomfortable or because they did not want to risk royal disfavor. It had not been so awkward, Richenza thought, whilst the Lady Denise, the Duchess of Brittany, and Isabel Marshal had been present, for they'd been Alys's friends. But

Constance and her Breton lords had ridden off that morn, having gotten permission from Richard to visit her daughter in Rouen; Denise and André had departed, too, and Isabel was absent from the hall tonight, suffering from the queasiness of early pregnancy. Now that Alys was alone with her ladies-in-waiting, Richenza could not stand by and watch her be politely shunned for no sin of her own.

Eleanor glanced toward Alys, then back at her granddaughter. "Of course you may, child. You need not seek my permission to perform a kindness," she assured the girl, thinking that it would be best for all concerned, including Alys, when she was settled at Rouen Castle. "Richenza . . . first tell your uncle John that I wish to speak with him."

Richenza fulfilled her errand with her usual dispatch, and John was soon approaching the dais, looking pleased but wary, too. Once he'd seated himself beside her, Eleanor said, pitching her voice for his ear alone, "You were at Dreux this afternoon. What do you think happened?" When he admitted that he did not know, she divulged the real reason why she'd summoned him. "I have never met the French king," she said regretfully, "so I have to rely upon the opinions of others. Richard believes Philippe to be a coward, so that naturally colors his judgment."

"Naturally," John echoed, thinking that Richard's sole measure of a man was his willingness to bleed. "So . . . you want to know what I think of Philippe?" His question was a delaying tactic, for he sensed that she was testing him, and he wanted to be sure that he did not disappoint. "I agree that Philippe is a cautious sort," he said carefully, "but I do not know if that makes him craven. Most men are more familiar with fear than my brother. I do think Philippe is more dangerous than Richard does, for he is clever and ruthless and utterly single-minded. And he loathes Richard with the sort of passion that burns to the bone."

"Indeed?" Eleanor studied her youngest son intently. He'd never shown much political acumen, unless deserting the losing side in his father's last war qualified. The one time he'd been entrusted with authority, when Henry sent him to govern Ireland, he'd made an utter botch of it, allowing his young knights to mock and ridicule the Irish lords, spending money so lavishly that he'd been unable to pay his routiers, who'd then defected to the Irish. It was true he'd been just eighteen then. Of course Richard and Geoffrey had been leading successful campaigns in Aquitaine and Brittany at that age. But she wanted very much to believe that John was maturing, that he was capable of learning from his mistakes, for if he was another Hal, their dynasty might well be doomed.

"Why do you believe Philippe bears such a grudge against your brother?

Richard has never had a serious falling-out with Philippe." *Not yet,* she amended silently, thinking of Alys and Berengaria.

John was surprised that the question even needed to be asked. "Richard is all that Philippe is not," he said candidly. "He overshadows most men without even trying. But kings do not expect to be overshadowed and take it rather badly. Philippe does not seem to me like one given to self-doubts. I think it grievously wounds his pride, though, that he will always be the moon to Richard's sun. And now they are going off together to the Holy Land, where he must look forward to being eclipsed by Richard at every opportunity, knowing he cannot hope to compete with Richard's battlefield heroics." John flashed a sudden, sardonic smile. "I could almost pity poor Philippe, if only he did not have a stone where his heart ought to be."

"I suspect there is much truth in what you say," Eleanor said thoughtfully, although she could not help wondering if John could discern Philippe's envy so easily because he shared it. But when she smiled, John decided that if this had indeed been a test, he'd passed it.

Just then there was a stir at the end of the hall and Henri of Champagne and his men entered. Eleanor was instantly alert, for Henri would not have ridden back after dark unless he'd found out something of importance. Richard had the same thought, for he was already moving to intercept the young count.

Henri offered a graceful obeisance. "My liege, Madame. I bring sad news from Dreux. Queen Isabelle died in childbed yesterday in Paris, after giving birth to stillborn twin sons."

His revelation was met with an unnatural silence. For an uneasy moment, every woman of childbearing age found herself identifying with the young French queen, and every husband was reminded how dangerous childbirth could be. People began to make the sign of the cross, to murmur conventional expressions of piety and sympathy for the bereaved French king; some of them even meant it. A pall had settled over the hall, for Isabelle's death was an unwelcome proof of their own mortality, of the Church's insistent teachings that flesh was corrupt, the body but an empty husk for the soul, and death came for them all, even the highborn.

Richard joined Eleanor and John on the dais, and after a few moments, so did Richenza. Seeing how pale she was, Eleanor rose and slipped her arm around the girl's slender waist. "That is so sad," Richenza said, "so very sad. . . ."

"Yes, it is," Eleanor agreed. "But you must not take Isabelle's tragic death too much to heart, Richenza. There are some women who are more suited for the cloisters than the marriage bed, and Isabelle was one of them. Within five years, she had at least five pregnancies, only one of which produced a live baby, and Louis is said to be a sickly little lad. Another son died within hours, and she suffered several miscarriages, too. Most women do not have such difficulty in the birthing chamber. I had ten healthy children myself, after all. We have no reason to think that your pregnancy will not be as easy as mine were."

Richard looked from his mother to his niece. "Are you with child, lass?"

Richenza blushed and nodded, marveling that her grandmother had somehow divined her secret, for she'd told no one but her husband so far. She found herself enfolded then in her uncle Richard's arms as he offered her his hearty congratulations. John kissed her, too, and their pleasure helped to dispel the chill cast by the French queen's death. Henri was waiting patiently to speak with Richard, but the king detoured to slap Richenza's husband jovially on the back before joining his nephew. Richenza then hastened over to explain to Jaufre how the king knew of her pregnancy, for they'd agreed to keep it private until she'd passed the risky first months.

Glancing at her youngest son, Eleanor found herself thinking that she'd not been entirely honest with Richenza, for John's birth had been a very difficult and dangerous one. He'd come early, on a snowy December night, soon after she'd confirmed Henry's affair with Rosamund Clifford, a girl young enough to have been her daughter, and the bitter circumstances of his birth had kept her from bonding with him as she had with her other children. Years later, this would come to be one of her greatest regrets, but by then it was too late. Looking pensively at John now, she wondered if she'd been wrong about that. The mistakes she and Henry had made with Hal and Geoffrey could never be made right. But John was still alive. Was it truly too late?

ELEANOR HAD RETIRED for the night soon afterward, dismissing all of her ladies-in-waiting but Amaria, who'd served her so loyally during those long years of confinement. When she began to tell Amaria of the French queen's death, she was surprised to find tears welling in her eyes. How fragile life was, how fleeting their days on earth, and how fickle was Death, claiming the young as often as the old, the healthy as often as the ailing, cruelly stealing away a baby's first breath, a mother's fading heartbeat. And if he showed so little mercy in the birthing chamber, what pity could he be expected to display on the bloody battlefields of Outremer?

Sensing Eleanor's dark mood, Amaria did not try to engage her mistress in their usual nightly conversation. As she moved unobtrusively about the chamber, there was a sudden rap on the door, startling both women. Eleanor came quickly to her feet as soon as she saw her sons standing in the doorway, a premonition of trouble prickling down her spine.

After assuring Amaria that she need not withdraw, Richard crossed the chamber to his mother, with John trailing a few feet behind. "It was not the news of the French queen's death that brought Henri back to Nonancourt tonight, Maman; that could have waited till the morrow. Whilst he was at Dreux, another courier arrived, bearing papal letters for Philippe and for me. After talking with the messenger, Henri took the liberty of opening my letter to confirm what the man said. He thought it best to confide its contents to me in private first, ere announcing it in the great hall. The King of Sicily is dead."

Eleanor sat down upon the bed, biting her lip to keep from crying out at the unfairness of the Almighty. Was it not enough that Joanna had been denied the child she so desperately wanted? Must she lose her husband, too, be widowed at the age of twenty-four? "My poor girl . . ."

"I could scarcely credit the news," Richard confessed. Like his mother, he ached for Joanna's pain. However little love there'd been between him and his brothers, he'd always cared for his sisters, especially Joanna, the youngest, the family favorite. But he did not have the luxury of responding merely as a brother, for William de Hauteville's unexpected death could have dire consequences for the king. William had offered Sicily's ports and riches and its formidable fleet to aid in the recovery of Jerusalem. Losing him as an ally was a setback of monumental proportions. And the silence surrounding his death held sinister implications of its own.

"When did he die, Richard?" At his answer, she stared at him incredulously. "November eighteenth? And we are only hearing of it now?"

"I know," he said. "It makes no sense. If a courier can travel from England to Rome in one month's time, why would it take four months for us to receive news of such magnitude?"

"Well . . . the roads south of Rome are dreadful, little better than goat tracks in places," Eleanor said, the memories of her Italian sojourn still vivid despite the passage of forty years. "And they were even more deplorable in Sicily. But why was the letter sent by the Pope? Why have we not heard from Joanna?"

"I was wondering that myself. Henri had the wit to bring the courier back to Nonancourt, and from him I learned that this was the second papal messenger. The first one mysteriously vanished en route. The Pope was too wary to commit his suspicions into writing, but he entrusted his man with a verbal message, too. He suspects that the Germans may have intercepted his first courier."

John had so far been a silent witness. During his childhood, he'd been either ignored or bullied by his brothers, and he'd never been one to forgive and forget. His two oldest sisters had been sent off to foreign lands when he was too young to remember them, but Joanna had been his companion and playmate and fellow pupil at Fontevrault Abbey, and he'd missed her very much after her departure for Sicily. John's family feelings were ambivalent at best, but not where Joanna was concerned, and he was genuinely distressed on her behalf.

"Germans?" he interjected before he could think better of it. "You mean the Holy Roman Emperor? I thought Frederick set out for the Holy Land months ago."

"He did, Johnny," Richard said with uncharacteristic patience. "But his eldest son remained in Germany and William's death would be of great interest to Heinrich, for his wife is the rightful heiress to the Sicilian crown. The Pope says that Heinrich and Constance learned that William was dead not long after Christmas. He thinks Heinrich may have wanted to delay word reaching England until he'd been able to secure his claim to Sicily. I'd like it not if Sicily fell into Heinrich's hands, no more than the Pope would, and Heinrich well knows it. If Heinrich seizes the Sicilian throne, how likely is it that he'd honor William's promises of supplies and the use of his ports and ships?"

Eleanor understood Richard's concern about losing his Sicilian alliance, but at the moment, her own concern was for her daughter. "Even if Heinrich did waylay the missing papal courier," she pointed out, "that still does not explain why there has been no word from Joanna. I do not like her silence, Richard, not at all."

Richard hesitated, but he'd never lied to her and was not about to start now. "I do not like it, either, Maman."

John was cursing himself for not having paid more attention to Italian and German matters and vowed to remedy that in the future, for he was learning that knowledge was power. As much as he disliked revealing his ignorance, especially to Eleanor and Richard, his anxiety for Joanna prevailed over pride.

"You think, then, that Heinrich would have led an army into Italy as soon as he learned of William's death. How would he treat Joanna?" Adding quickly, "He would have no reason to look kindly upon one of our family," for he did not want them to think he was uninformed about the hostility between the Angevins and the House of Hohenstaufen, a political rivalry that had become personal when Henry wed his daughter Tilda to the Emperor Frederick's most recalcitrant vassal, the Duke of Saxony.

It was Eleanor who addressed his concern. "Heinrich's wife was very close to Joanna ere her marriage. Although from what I've heard about Heinrich, I have trouble imagining him as an uxorious husband."

That masterly understatement earned her a smile from Richard. "It is by no means certain that Heinrich will prevail. The Sicilians quite sensibly are balking at the prospect of a German master, and the Pope says that several of William's lords are advancing claims of their own to his crown."

A silence greeted this revelation, as they considered what that might mean for Joanna. John at last gave voice to what they were all thinking. "So Joanna could be caught up in the midst of a war."

"Yes," Eleanor said reluctantly, "that could well explain why we've not heard from her." It was only natural that she should fear for her soldier son's life in far-off Outremer, a land convulsed by war. But how could she have been expected to see danger for her daughter, ruling over a sunlit island paradise? It would seem that the Almighty possessed a perverse sense of humor.

CHAPTER 7

JUNE 1190

Chinon, Touraine

The Count of Perche's son had escorted his young wife to Chinon Castle so that she might spend time with her grandmother and bid her uncle farewell before Richard departed for the Holy Land. Jaufre and Richenza reached Chinon in midmonth. Three days later, Richard arrived with a large entourage of barons, knights, and bishops, after a successful mission into his southern domains to punish the Lord of Chis, a lawless vassal who'd been robbing pilgrims on their way to the Spanish shrine at Santiago de Compostela.

The next morning Jaufre found the English king holding informal court in the great hall. The men seemed in high spirits, their laughter wafting toward him even as he crossed the threshold. Richard was engaging in a good-natured argument with a young man who looked vaguely familiar to Jaufre; as he drew closer, he recognized the king's Welsh cousin, Morgan ap Ranulf. Edging inconspicuously into the circle of men, he murmured a discreet query to another of Richard's cousins, the Poitevin lord, André de Chauvigny. Morgan was boasting of the prowess of Welsh archers, André replied, sounding as skeptical as Richard looked.

"So you are saying that the arrows penetrated an oaken door that was four fingers thick?" Richard shook his head, grinning. "Why do I doubt that, Morgan?"

"Because you're not Welsh," Morgan shot back cheekily. "If you doubt me, my liege, you need only consult some of your Marcher barons. Ask the Lord of Brecon, William de Braose, to tell you what happened to one of his knights in a skirmish with the Welsh. He was struck with an arrow that pierced his hauberk and thigh, pinning him to his saddle. And when he swung his stallion around, a second arrow impaled him on the other leg!"

That evoked another wave of incredulous laughter. "And the reason why Welsh arrows have such magical power? Are they blessed by Merlin?"

Morgan took the teasing in stride. "No, my lord king. Welsh archers have no need for Merlin's blessings as long as they are shooting Welsh bows, which are more deadly than crossbows, God's Truth."

"And why is that, Cousin?" Richard asked, no longer joking, for few subjects interested him more than weaponry. "The crossbows are baneful enough for the Pope to ban their use against all but infidels. What makes your Welsh bows so dangerous?"

"Welsh bows are nigh on a foot longer than the bows known in England or France."

Some of the other men continued to joke about the "magical Welsh bows." Richard was not one of them. "Yes," he said thoughtfully, "that makes sense. The greater the length of the stave, the greater the force of the bow. So they have more power than the crossbows. What other advantages, Morgan?"

"An archer can shoot four or five arrows in the time that it will take a crossbowman to reset his weapon to shoot again. But they do have one great disadvantage, my lord. It does not take much skill to learn to shoot a crossbow, nor does it take much strength. That is not so for the Welsh bow, which needs much time and effort to master it."

"A pity," Richard said, for he had neither the time to hire some of those elite Welsh archers nor to teach other men their lethal skill. He'd have to make do with his contingent of crossbowmen. His gaze happened to alight then upon Jaufre of Perche. "I hope you've brought my niece with you?" Getting a confirmation, he welcomed the younger man with an easy smile. "So . . . are you planning to sail with us to the Holy Land?"

Jaufre hesitated, wishing he could do so. It ought to have been acceptable, for Richard was his uncle by marriage, after all. He knew better, though, knew that the French king would have seen it as an act of disloyalty, and while Richard was his kinsman by marriage, Philippe was his liege lord. "King Philippe requested that I accompany him, my lord," he said, relieved when Richard did not seem offended. He'd leaped at the chance to wed the English monarch's niece and blessed his luck from the moment he first laid eyes upon his bride-to-be, but he'd not anticipated how challenging it would be to keep both kings contented. Eager to change the subject, he said quickly, "What happened with the Lord of Chis? I'd wager he soon repented his crimes, no?"

"I daresay he did," Richard agreed, "up until the moment when I hanged him."

Jaufre blinked, not sure if the English king were jesting or not, for lords were rarely if ever held to the same standard of justice as those of lesser birth. But as he met Richard's eyes, he saw that Richenza's uncle was serious—dead serious—and he wondered if Saladin knew the mettle of the foe he'd soon be facing. He wondered, too, if Philippe knew.

THERE WERE FEW DAYS more perfect than a summer afternoon in the Loire Valley, and after their noontime dinner, Richard had chosen to savor its pleasures out in the castle gardens. He'd ordered chairs to be fetched for Eleanor, Richenza, and the Countess of Aumale, but he and Jaufre made themselves comfortable on the grassy mead, tossing a wineskin back and forth. The women were more decorous and sipped from silver-gilt wine cups, so ornate that Richard joked he ought to sell them, for when it came to financing his campaign, every denier counted. He had been surprised to find the Countess of Aumale in his mother's household, but he bore her no grudge now that Hawisa had yielded to his will and wed William de Forz, and to show that bygones were bygones, he favored her with a smile, saying, "I have some good news for you, my lady. I am naming your husband as one of my fleet commanders."

"An honor, indeed," Hawisa said, for such a response was expected of a wife, even one who fervently hoped that her new husband would never return from the Holy Land. She was too shrewd to continue fighting a battle already lost, though, and shared such heretical thoughts with no one. "My liege . . . I recently received a troubling letter from my steward at Skipton-in-Craven, regarding the unrest in Yorkshire since the slaughter of the Jews in the city of York. Men are concerned that violence will break out again once you have left for Outremer. Can you assure me that measures have been taken to keep the King's Peace?"

Her bluntness raised a royal eyebrow, but did not kindle the royal temper, for Richard was in a good mood now that the time for his crusade was finally nigh. Reminding himself that this irksome female was also a great landholder and she therefore had a legitimate concern, he said, "You may rest easy, my lady countess. As soon as I got word of the York massacre, I dispatched my chancellor to England to restore order and punish the guilty. Bishop Longchamp led an armed force to York, where he discovered that the culprits had fled into Scotland. He took strong measures, though, to make sure such an outrage will never happen again in my domains, dismissing the Yorkshire sheriff and the castellan, imposing heavy fines, and taking one hundred hostages from the city."

"I am gladdened to hear that, my lord." Hawisa still feared for England's peace in Richard's absence, but she knew better than to raise these doubts with the king. She could only hope that Longchamp's swift action would put the fear of God into Yorkshire's lawless and masterless men.

Jaufre glanced uneasily toward his wife, for he knew she'd not heard of the York massacre and he preferred to keep it that way, believing that a pregnant woman needed to be sheltered from strong emotions. Moreover, he did not trust Richard to give Richenza a suitably censored account of the York atrocity, for no son of Eleanor of Aquitaine could fully understand the fragility of the female sex. And as he feared, Richenza was quick to ask, "What happened in York, Uncle? Was the Jewry attacked?"

"That was the least of it, lass." Richard sat up, scowling. "There are times when I think most men have less brains than God gave to sheep. I thought we'd quenched the fires after the London rioting, but apparently some embers still smoldered."

"When was there rioting in London?"

"On my coronation day. You did not hear of that?"

"On your coronation day," Richenza reminded him with a smile, "Jaufre and I were being married in Rouen."

"Ah, yes, so you were." Richard returned her smile, but it soon faded as he called up memories of the ugly incident that had marred what should have been a sacred event, the day when he'd been consecrated with the holy chrism, crowned as England's king and God's Anointed. "In the past when campaigns were proclaimed against the Saracens, they often stirred up hatred against the Jews, the 'infidels in our midst,' as I've heard them called. I'd hoped to avoid any such outbursts by forbidding Jews to attend my coronation. But two affluent Jews, Benedict and Josce of York made the journey anyway. They came bearing gifts in hopes of winning royal favor. Instead they unwittingly caused a riot. A crowd had gathered outside the palace gates, and some of them fell upon the Jews, began to beat and curse them. Josce was able to escape, but Benedict was grievously wounded and then terrorized into accepting baptism. The mob was now drunk with blood lust and they surged back into London, where they attacked any Jews they found, killing at least thirty, and setting the Jewry afire."

Richenza was frowning. "It is shameful when men commit murder in God's

Name. Scriptures say plainly that Jews are not to be killed, ordering us to 'Slay them not,' for it is ordained that they will one day come to salvation through Our Lord Christ and bring about the Second Coming. Were you able to punish the guilty ones, Uncle?"

"We arrested some, hanged three, but it is almost impossible to identify members of a mob. The Archbishop of Canterbury and I interviewed the Jew Benedict, who recanted his conversion. The archbishop was wroth with him for that, unable to understand why he'd rather be 'the Devil's man instead of God's,' but a baptism done at knifepoint surely cannot please the Almighty. My main concern was making sure this did not happen elsewhere, and I sent writs throughout the realm, commanding my subjects to leave the Jews in peace. And indeed they did . . . as long as I remained in England. But after I crossed over to Normandy in December, trouble was not long in breaking out again."

"Was that when the York Jews were attacked?"

"No, it began in East Anglia, at Lynn and Norwich, and then spread like the pox to Stamford, St Edmundsbury, and Lincoln. Men who'd taken the cross were eager to fight infidels, and the Jews were closer at hand than the Saracens. Drunken mobs were soon pillaging the Jewish quarters in those towns, forcing the Jews to take refuge in the royal castles."

The echoes of anger in Richard's voice did not surprise his audience, for the rioters had dared to disobey his royal writ and to threaten the King's Peace. No king could tolerate such lawless defiance, especially one about to depart on crusade. "Eventually, the madness reached York." By now Richard was on his feet, heedlessly trampling daisies underfoot as he paced. "But there it was different. At York, the mob was urged on by men of rank, men who owed money to the Jews. First they set a fire to distract the Watch, then broke into Benedict's house, killed his family, and stripped it bare. Most of the city's Jews fled to the royal castle for safety, but the mob continued to roam the streets. They attacked the house of the other moneylender, Josce, beat any Jews they found, and forced them to accept baptism. York had become a place without law, a city in my realm!" Richard's voice cracked like a whip, sending several nesting birds fluttering from trees up into the sky.

By now Jaufre was squirming, unable to think of a way to spare his wife a ghastly story sure to trouble her soft heart, for he knew most women hated to hear of the deaths of children, even if they were infidels. Unaware of his husband's discomfort, Richenza was regarding Richard with a puzzled expression. "But if the York Jews took shelter in the castle, why were they not safe from the mob?"

"Because the castellan left the castle and whilst he was gone, the fools panicked and decided they could not trust him. So when he returned, they overpowered the garrison and refused to let him back in."

Jaufre was trying to catch the other man's eye in hopes of sending a mute message, but Richard never noticed. "That was the first mistake. The second was made by the idiot castellan, who then panicked in his turn and summoned the sheriff of the shire. He was the one who made the third, fatal mistake, deciding to assault the castle and drive the Jews out." Richard paused, using an extremely vivid obscenity to describe the sheriff, but since he habitually swore in *lenga romana*, only Eleanor understood. "The drunken louts happily joined in, of course, and by the time the sheriff realized how grievously he'd erred and tried to call the attack off, it was too late. By then the mob was utterly in control, spurred on by a demented hermit who'd convinced them they were doing God's Work. The Jews managed to defend themselves for two days, but when siege engines were brought out, they realized they were doomed."

Richard paused again, reliving the rage he'd felt upon hearing of the massacre in York. "Rather than be butchered by the mob, the Jews chose to die by their own hands. Husbands slit the throats of their wives and children, Josce being the first to slay his family. The men were then slain by Josce and their rabbi, what they call their priests. I've been told nigh on a hundred and fifty Jews took refuge in the castle, and most of them chose to die. By morning—the eve of Palm Sunday, it was, too—there were only a score or so still alive."

Richenza was staring at him in horror. "God in Heaven," she whispered, as Jaufre got hastily to his feet and crossed to her side. She ignored his attempt at consolation, keeping her eyes upon her uncle, almost as if she sensed the worst was still to come. "What happened to those Jews?"

"The survivors appealed for mercy, offering to accept Christian baptism, and they were promised that their lives would be spared. But when they emerged from the castle with their families, the mob seized them and murdered them all."

Richenza shuddered, instinctively bringing her hands up as if to shelter her unborn baby from such a world. "Even the children, Uncle Richard?"

"Yes, lass, even the children." To Richard, this was the cruelest twist of all, that the mob had treacherously slain people seeking God's Grace. He'd been taught that the Almighty held His Breath over every Jew, waiting to see if he would choose Christ as his Saviour. He understood that the surviving Jews most likely sought baptism out of fear, but what if their ordeal had awakened them to the Divine Truth? Not only had they been shamefully betrayed, they'd been denied salvation.

"What happened next revealed the real reason for the rioting," he said. And now his anger was that of a king, not a man of faith. "The leaders of the mob forced their way into York Minster, where the Jews had kept their debt bonds. They terrified the monks into giving up the bonds, and then burned them right there in the nave of the church."

Richard had begun to pace again. In destroying the bonds, the rioters had struck a blow at the Crown itself, for the debts of Jews were also the debts of the king. The Jews were an important source of royal revenue and they were under royal protection. So this had been an act of political defiance as well as an outrage against the Church and the laws of the realm. And justice would not be done. The citizens of York had sworn that they'd played no part in the assault on the castle, blaming strangers and soldiers who'd taken the cross, and the few men identified— those who'd burned the bonds—had long since fled the city by the time Long- champ arrived. His action in punishing the sheriff and castellan would strike fear into others of rank, men unaccustomed to being held to account for their sins or their blunders. Their fall from favor ought to be enough to prevent another York. But Richard could take little satisfaction from that. When men defied the Crown, they deserved to hang.

"The stupidity of men never fails to amaze me," he said. "How does killing defenseless Jews aid in the rescue of the Holy City? Only in Winchester did reason prevail. Some fools accused the local Jews of ritual murder when a Christian child died, a charge dismissed by the royal justices as being without merit. A pity they could not have shown such sense in the other towns."

"The poor and the uneducated are most likely to believe such tales," Eleanor observed, reaching out to squeeze her granddaughter's hand. "They think the Jews practice the Black Arts, fear what they do not understand. Fortunately, men of rank are not as susceptible to such superstitions, nor are the princes of the Church. You all know I was no friend to the sainted Bernard of Clairvaux," she said with a thin smile, remembering the abbot's oft-quoted declaration that the Angevins came from the Devil and to the Devil they would go. "But when a Cistercian monk began preaching that German Jews must be slain ere war could be made upon the Saracens, Bernard hastened to Germany and single-handedly kept violence from breaking out."

Richard demurred at that, saying, "Not all men of rank are so rational, though. The French king once told me about a Christian child supposedly killed by the Jews in Pontoise. Even though this took place ere Philippe was born, he harbored no doubts whatsoever that the boy had been sacrificed in some vile Jewish ritual.

When I reminded Philippe that his lord father had never believed such tales, he bristled like a hedgehog, claiming that Louis had been easily led astray, and then babbled some nonsense about the Jews meeting secretly in caves beneath Paris to sacrifice Christian children. Philippe Capet," he said, in a voice dripping with scorn, "may be the greatest fool ever to sit on the French throne, and considering that they once had a king known as Charles the Simple, that is saying quite a lot."

Jaufre now found himself in an extremely awkward position, not wanting to offend his wife's uncle, but feeling obligated to defend his liege lord. "King Philippe is not the only one to give credence to those accusations against the Jews. I was just a lad when it happened, but I remember my father telling me that the Count of Blois once executed a number of Jews for killing a Christian child."

"When was this?" Richard demanded, and when Jaufre said he thought it had occured nigh on twenty years ago, he gave a dismissive shrug. "I was only about thirteen then, know nothing of this."

"But I do," Eleanor interjected. "I remember the incident well, and the guilt lay with Count Thibault, not the unhappy Jews. Thibault is the uncle of your cousin Henri of Champagne," she added for Richenza's sake, knowing the girl was not yet familiar with the bloodlines of the French nobility. "I hear he has gone to the Holy Land to expiate his sins, as well he should, for he has the blood of innocents upon his hands."

"I do not understand, Madame," Jaufre objected, feeling compelled to continue his half-hearted defense of the French king. "How can the count be responsible for a crime committed by Jews?"

"There was no crime, Jaufre. The charge was particularly outrageous, for there was no body, either, nor even any reports of a missing child. A servingman claimed he saw a Jewish peddler throw a child's body into the River Loire, and the story grew from there, until it was being said the boy had been crucified. Mind you, there was no evidence whatsoever to back up this charge, but Thibault ordered the arrest of all the Jews in Blois, some forty souls. Thirty-one men and women were burned at the stake, the others imprisoned, and their children forced to undergo baptism."

Richard spoke for them all when he asked, "Why? From what you've just told us, Maman, Thibault could not possibly have believed the story. So why did he do it?"

"For the meanest, most unworthy of reasons, Richard—to quell a scandal. You see, Thibault had been imprudent enough to take a local Jewess as his concubine. He was careless, too, and it eventually became known. When it did, he found himself facing the wrath of the Church, the outrage of his fellow Christians, and the fury of his wife—my daughter Alix, from my marriage to the French king," she explained in another aside to Richenza. "So when this charge was made, Thibault seized upon it to prove that he was no longer ensorcelled by his Jewess mistress, sacrificing those thirty-one men and women to regain the goodwill of his subjects and to appease the bishops of Blois."

Richenza had a vivid imagination and could envision all too well the horror the Jews had endured, for surely death by fire was the worst of fates. She shivered and Jaufre slid his arm around her waist, angry with Richard and Eleanor for telling his pregnant wife stories sure to disturb her sleep that night. After a somber silence, Richenza thought to ask about the rest of the Jews, those who'd been imprisoned rather than sent to the stake.

"The other French Jews were horrified at what had befallen their brethren in Blois. They were understandably terrified, too, that the anger against Jews would spread to their cities, and they appealed to the French king. Louis too often showed as much backbone as a hempen rope, but he was always steadfast in his protection of the French Jews, never believing those stories of ritual murder. He at once issued a charter to be published throughout his domains, warning his subjects that the Jews were not to be molested or threatened, and they were not. The Jews also turned to Thibault's brother, the Count of Champagne, for aid. He had already dismissed a similar accusation against the Jews in Epernay, and like Louis, he took measures to see to their safety. Meanwhile, the Jews sought help from the third brother, the Bishop of Sens, and through his mediation, Thibault agreed to release the imprisoned Jews and to return the children who'd been forcibly baptized. Harry heard that Thibault had extorted a hundred pounds from the Jews for that concession, and I cannot say it would surprise me if so. And no," Eleanor said, anticipating their next questions, "I do not know the fate of his Jewess once she was freed from prison. Nor do I know how Thibault managed to placate his wife."

Now it was Eleanor's turn to fall silent, thinking of Alix, the daughter she'd not seen in nigh on forty years, for once their marriage had ended, Louis had banished her from their daughters' lives, had done all he could to blacken her memory. At least Harry had not entirely forbidden her to see their children during her long confinement, and she had to admit he had far more reason than Louis for doing so.

Looking back at the woman she'd once been, Louis's unhappy, bored wife and Harry's reckless, rebel queen, she sometimes felt as if that younger Eleanor was a stranger, one often in need of the guidance she could now have provided. Why was it that wisdom seemed to come only with age, when it no longer mattered as much? No, that was not so. It did matter, and she was determined that her children should benefit from the lessons she'd learned at such great cost in the course of her long and eventful life. Glancing from Richard to Richenza, she tempered her silent vow with a prudent *God willing*, for she finally understood that the race was not to the swift, nor the battle to the strong, but time and chance happened to them all.

JAUFRE HAD SOON CONCOCTED an excuse to take Richenza back to their chamber, treating his wife with the exaggerated care of one handling a rare and exotic flower that could be bruised by a breath. Hawisa watched them wistfully, but then tossed her head, summoning up a brittle smile. "Men are so solicitous, so awe-struck over the first child. Alas, Richenza will find that by her third or fourth pregnancy, he'll be wondering why she must take a full nine months when his favorite greyhound bitch can whelp in two."

Eleanor laughed. Richard was not as amused, but he held his tongue until Hawisa had tactfully excused herself and moved out of earshot. "Passing strange that she'd make such a jest when her first marriage was barren. Nor do I understand why you seem to like the woman's company, Maman. She is as strong-willed as any man, with a tongue sharp enough to slice bread."

"She jests about childbirth, Richard, for the same reason that men use humor to hide their unease ere a battle begins. And yes, I do enjoy her company. She was courageous enough to resist a marriage she did not want, but sensible enough to yield once she saw defeat was inevitable. And in case you've not noticed, I have a mind of my own, too."

He chuckled. "That would be like not noticing the sun rises in the east and sets in the west."

Eleanor emptied her wine cup, setting it down in the grass at her feet. "If my memory serves, Will Marshal's elder brother John was the sheriff of Yorkshire. I thought I saw him in your entourage, and that explains it. He came to beg for his post back?"

Richard nodded. "He can grovel from now till Martinmas, for all the good it will do him. Gross incompetence is the least of his sins. Longchamp suspects him of being hand in glove with the instigators of the rioting, although he admits he has not been able to prove it. That is why he acted so swiftly, dismissing Marshal and appointing his brother, Osbert, as sheriff in his stead."

Eleanor had no problems with the dismissal of John Marshal, who'd shown appallingly poor judgment. But by replacing Marshal with his own brother, Longchamp was playing into his enemies' hands, giving them a means of impugning his motives. "You told me that the Pope agreed to name Longchamp as a papal legate—"

"'Agreed'?" Richard interrupted. "He sold the office plain and simple, extorting fifteen hundred marks from me ere he'd even consider it."

"Be that as it may, Longchamp is now the papal legate, chancellor, justiciar, and Bishop of Ely. You are entrusting great authority to one man, Richard. Do you think that is wise? History shows us that peace is more likely when you have two rivals of equal power. Should the balance tip too far in one direction, war becomes inevitable, as with Athens and Sparta or Rome and Carthage."

Richard claimed one of the vacant seats. "And who are you nominating to play Sparta to Longchamp's Athens? Might it be Johnny, by chance?"

"Yes, John did approach me about that vow you demanded of him. He thinks it would be dangerous if you and he both were absent from England for the next few years. And after giving it some thought, I agree with him. His very presence will reassure those barons who are suspicious of Longchamp's intentions. And Longchamp might well temper his dealings with those same discontented barons if he knows they can turn to your brother with their grievances. As it is, you've denied them any outlet for their complaints."

"There is truth in what you say, Maman. Longchamp would have done better not to thrust his brother into Marshal's place. But if I overruled him, I'd be subverting his authority when he most needs it. I know he is not without flaws. I can trust him, though, with no misgivings whatsoever. Can I say as much for Johnny?"

"I raised this very question last summer at Winchester. I was somewhat surprised by your lavish generosity to John since you'd shown no favor to the other men who'd abandoned Harry, whilst rewarding men who'd stayed loyal to him. Do you remember what you told me? You said John deserves a chance to show he can be trusted. Has he given you any reason to exile him from England?"

"No," Richard admitted, "he has not." Picking up the cup Richenza had left behind, he drained the last of the wine before saying, "Who am I to argue with myself? Or with you, Maman. Tell Johnny I free him from his oath."

Eleanor smiled, but she was not as confident as she'd have Richard believe, for her youngest was still a mystery to her. She could only hope John would prove her right.

"If I am releasing Johnny, I suppose I'll have to open the door of Geoff's cage, too," Richard said, rolling his eyes. "Actually I'd been giving that some thought, for had he been in York, he might have been able to keep Marshal from panicking. Say what you will about Geoff, he does not lack for courage and would have thought nothing of plunging into the midst of that mob, swinging his crozier like a battle-axe!"

That image amused them both. Eleanor was becoming puzzled, though, that he'd not yet brought up the subject of his bride-to-be. He'd told her last night that while he was in Bayonne, he'd been able to slip across the border for a secret meeting with the King of Navarre, settling the last issues of the marriage contract. Now that they were alone, why was he not sharing with her what had been decided? Surely Sancho could not have been dissatisfied with the generous dower Richard was offering? Berengaria was to receive Gascony and, after Eleanor's death, lands in Normandy and Anjou as well. So why was Richard suddenly so tight-lipped about the deal he'd struck with Sancho?

At last losing patience, Eleanor said, "So . . . tell me of the meeting with Sancho and his son. I assume he was contented with the dower?"

"Indeed he was. No, there was but one obstacle to overcome. Sancho was unwilling to delay the marriage until my return from the Holy Land. Quite understandable," Richard said with a sudden grin, "since neither he nor his daughter would benefit if I were inconveniently slain in Outremer. Nor did I want to delay the marriage, either. My wife's father would make a more reliable ally than the father of my betrothed. And if it is my destiny to die in the Holy Land, I'd rather not entrust my empire to either Johnny or Arthur, so the quicker Berengaria can give me a son, the better."

Eleanor frowned, for she did not like him to discuss his death so nonchalantly. She already knew the odds were not in his favor for a safe return, did not need to be reminded of that in casual conversation. "But you cannot wed the girl ere you leave or you'll be leaving without Philippe. So how did you resolve it?"

"We could think of only one way—have Berengaria join me in Sicily and marry me there or, if she arrives during Lent, then once we reach Outremer."

"And you actually got her father to agree to this?" Eleanor was incredulous. "I know you can be convincing when you put your mind to it, Richard, but with a tongue as agile as that, you could lick honey off thorns!"

"Well, Sancho did impose one condition. To show my good faith and to safeguard his daughter's honor, I told him that you would travel to Navarre and bring Berengaria to me in Sicily."

Eleanor's eyes widened. "Did you now? Richard, you do remember that this will be my sixty-sixth summer on God's Earth? Most women of that age do not stir from their hearths, but you want me to traverse the Pyrenees and then make a winter crossing of the Alps? Would you like me to make a side trip to Cathay, too?"

Richard could not hide his dismay, for he'd taken his mother's consent for granted, and if she balked now, the marriage itself might be put at risk. "Maman . . . I ought to have consulted with you first. I just assumed you'd agree, but if you do not want to—" He stopped then, for Eleanor had begun to laugh. Letting out a sigh of relief, he confessed, "Jesu, but you gave me a bad moment there! I thought you truly did not want to go."

"Not want to go? Do you know me as little as that, Richard? I've always loved to travel, have always been eager to see new places and sights, one of the reasons why I found Harry's confinement so hard to bear. I never expected to visit a Spanish kingdom, nor to see Sicily again. You are offering me a rare gift, a chance to see my son wed and to have one last adventure."

"I knew I could rely upon you, Maman, be it to bring me a bride or keep England at peace whilst I am gone." It had been disconcerting to be reminded that she was only four years removed from her biblical three-score and ten, a great age for a woman who'd always seemed ageless to him. It was an unwelcome thought and he was quick to push it away, for midst the turmoil and chaos that had roiled their family life as long as he could remember, his mother had been the one constant, the only island in a turbulent sea. Leaning over, he kissed her exuberantly on both cheeks, calling her his lodestar and his luck.

He would have escorted her back into the castle then, but she chose to remain in the gardens, for the sun had begun its slow slide toward the horizon and the sky had taken on a golden glow. Agreeing to let him send her ladies out to her, Eleanor leaned back in her chair, watching as he strode off. He could no more amble than he could fly, was always rushing from one moment to the next, eager to seize the day. "Just like you, Harry," she murmured, wondering what he'd have thought of her latest quest.

It would never have occurred to her to tell Richard no. She had sixteen years' worth of energy stored up. What better way to expend it than to bring her favorite son a wife? It was true that she was facing a journey that would have daunted a woman half her age. But Richard needed her. And it would indeed be an adventure, ending where she most wanted to be—in Sicily, reunited with her daughter. They'd learned by now that a bastard cousin of William de Hauteville had seized the crown, and Heinrich was said to be planning a military response. But they still knew nothing of Joanna, not even her whereabouts. Richard had promised that he would find her, though, and whatever had gone wrong for her, he would make right. If she had been forced into marriage with one of Tancred's lords, as was too often the case with young widows and heiresses, he would free her from it, he vowed. He sounded so sure of himself that it was easy for Eleanor to believe, too. Only death could defeat his resolve, and Eleanor refused even to acknowledge the possibility that her daughter's silence could have such a simple and sinister explanation. Richard would restore Joanna to them. He would not fail.

CHAPTER 8

R ichard met Philippe at Vézelay in early July, where, forty-five years earlier, Richard's mother and Philippe's father had taken the cross. The two kings made a solemn pact to "share equally whatever they conquered together," and the third crusade got under way. Most of Philippe's lords had already departed for the Holy Land, so he had a much smaller force than Richard, who had almost seven thousand men under his command. With such a large infantry, they could manage less than fifteen miles a day, and did not reach the city of Lyon until the thirteenth.

AFTER RICHARD AND PHILIPPE and their households had crossed the wooden bridge spanning the Rhone, they set up their tents on high ground overlooking the river. Dismounting, Philippe handed the reins to his squire and then accepted a wineskin, for his mouth was so dry he could barely swallow. He felt as if he'd been bathing in dust, for smothering clouds had been churned up by horses, carts, and thousands of marching feet. The sun was a fiery white sphere in a sky bleached of all blue, beating down upon them with brutal intensity. It was hard to imagine that Outremer could be as hot, and yet he'd heard it claimed that summers there were a foretaste of Hell. Wherever Eden had been, surely it could not have been located in the Holy Land, where dust storms turned day into night and rivers trickled away into cracked, parched earth and mysterious, lethal maladies struck men down without warning, more dying from plagues and fevers than from Saracen swords.

Philippe could not admit even to his confessor how loath he was to make this perilous journey, leaving his realm and his sickly little son behind. It ought to be enough that he was a good Christian, a good king, and yet he knew it was not, at least not in the eyes of other men. The only one who'd shared his reluctance to take the cross had been the man he'd done so much to destroy, and he supposed that Henry was laughing now from the depths of Hell. Henry had appreciated irony—all those accursed Angevins did—so most likely he'd also found it ironic that the youth he'd aided again and again had become the instrument of his doom. But Philippe had no regrets. He'd done what he must, for it was his destiny to restore France to greatness, as it had been in the days of Charlemagne.

"Why so doleful, Philippe?" The question—sudden, intrusive—caught the young French king by surprise, and he frowned as Richard reined in beside him, stepping back as the stallion's pawing hooves kicked up yet more dust. The older man was grinning down at him, odiously cheerful, as he'd been every blessed day since their departure from Vézelay. "Damn me if you do not look like a poor wretch on his way to the gallows. It could be worse, much worse. You could be the only one leaving for the Holy Land whilst I remained behind to look after your lands for you."

Richard laughed then, while Philippe forced a sour smile. He would never understand why the English king took pleasure in telling awkward truths in the guise of jests. But Richard's perverse sense of humor was just one more burden he had to bear. Why could Richard not have been the one to die of the bloody flux instead of Hal? Life would have been so much easier had Henry's amiable eldest son succeeded him. He'd have made a fine king—for France—easily bored, frivolous, and fickle. But Hal was seven years dead, and his grieving widow—Philippe's older sister Marguerite—long since wed to the King of Hungary. And Hal's brother Geoffrey, the only man Philippe had ever respected, was dead, too.

Even now, thinking of Geoffrey stirred faint echoes of loss, for he had been the ideal ally, mayhap even a friend, whereas Richard embodied all that Philippe most despised in other men—swaggering, arrogant, reckless. Their day of reckoning would eventually come and he did not doubt that when it did, his brains would prevail over Richard's brawn. It was vexing, though, to have to watch as a man inferior to him in all the ways that truly mattered was lavished with praise, acclaim, and renown. And the Holy Land would be the perfect stage for Richard, a never-ending circus of bloodshed and posturing and battlefield heroics.

Below them, soldiers were moving out onto the bridge. It would take forever and a day to get them all across, Philippe thought gloomily. At least then he'd be spared Richard's irksome company for a while, as they'd agreed to separate once they'd crossed the Rhone, Philippe and his men heading overland for Genoa, where he'd hired ships to transport the French to Sicily, and Richard riding south to Marseille, where his fleet would be awaiting his arrival. Cheered up somewhat by the thought of their impending separation, Philippe was turning toward his tent when the screams began.

Whirling around, he gasped at the sight meeting his eyes. Several arches of the wooden bridge had collapsed under the weight of so many men, flinging them into the river. Some were clinging desperately to the bridge pilings and wreckage, while others were struggling in the water, all of them calling upon the Almighty and their fellows for aid.

Richard had already galloped his stallion down the hill, shouting commands. Men were throwing ropes out into the river, extending lances for the drowning to catch on to, and several knights were bravely urging their mounts into the turbulent current. Philippe was not surprised when one horse balked at the water's edge, sending his rider splashing into the river, for it had been his experience that horses were as flighty and unpredictable as women. He was surprised, though, by the speed and success of the rescue effort. Soon most of the floundering men had been pulled to safety; they lost only two to the Rhone's flood tide. But their armies were now cut off from their commanders, trapped on opposite sides of the surging river.

PHILIPPE'S TENT OFFERED welcome shelter from the noonday heat, but it was rather crowded, for he'd been joined by his cousins, the Duke of Burgundy, the Count of Nevers, and the Archbishop of Chartres, the Count of Perche's son, Jaufre, and several other lords and knights. Guillaume des Barres alone took up enough space for any two men; he was as sturdy as an oak and almost as tall. He was one of the most popular members of Philippe's entourage, for he'd never let his battle renown go to his head, and was adroit at using humor to prevent minor squabbles from flaring into more serious confrontations. Keeping their men from turning their tempers upon one another before they could fight the Saracens was a serious concern. Richard had issued a strict code of conduct for the sailors, with severe penalties for murder, brawling, theft, gambling, and blasphemy. But these prohibitions were not aimed at maintaining the peace between highborn lords accustomed to getting their own way, and Guillaume des Barres had taken it upon himself to make their journey as free of strife as he could.

Guillaume wished that he could ease his king's mind, too, for Philippe was obviously troubled. He'd dispatched couriers back to Paris, bearing letters to his mother and uncle with further instructions for governing in his absence, but after that he'd lapsed into a brooding silence, paying no heed to the conversations swirling about him. When Guillaume challenged him to a game of chess now, he seemed tempted, for that was a pastime that played to his strengths, requiring a strategic sense and patience. But that brief flicker of interest did not catch fire.

Instead, he signaled for a small coffer to be brought to him, and read again the last report of his son's health. Louis was just three, and often ailing. Philippe's greatest dread was that he would die in the Holy Land and Louis would not live to reach manhood. Why had the Almighty taken the twin boys born in March? Had they lived, he could have left France with far fewer fears for the future of his dynasty. Instead, Isabelle had bled to death, never seeing or holding the pitiful little bodies expelled from her womb, and Philippe's destiny rested upon the thinnest of threads, the fragile life of his only surviving son.

Philippe did not understand why Richard seemed so unconcerned about his own lack of an heir of his body. He was fortunate enough to have a brother full grown, it was true, and a young nephew who had been blessed with the robust good health denied to Philippe's own son. Was he content to have the crown pass to John or Arthur? Or was he utterly and blasphemously confident that he'd not die in the Holy Land? Knowing Richard, it was most likely the latter, Philippe thought morosely. The Angevins were notorious for confusing the Almighty's Will with their own.

"Sire!" The flap was ripped aside and Mathieu de Montmorency plunged into the tent. Mathieu was highborn, blood-kin to Philippe's queen, but his presence was proving to be another irritant to the French king's raw nerves, for Mathieu was just sixteen and so enthusiastic about their crusade that he seemed drunk on excitement alone. Now his face was flushed and his smile so euphoric that Philippe knew he was not going to enjoy whatever the boy had come to tell him.

"I have wondrous news, my liege! Our problems are over, thanks to the English king. Richard has come up with a truly brilliant idea. He wants to build a bridge of small boats, lashing them together so our soldiers may cross the river. His men are already searching the shorelines and commandeering whatever boats they find . . ."

Mathieu belatedly became aware of the silence. He'd expected the men to share in his delight, but they showed no such joy, their expressions wary and guarded. Mathieu looked from them to Philippe in dismay, realizing he'd somehow incurred his king's disfavor.

"I am surprised Richard is bothering with a bridge," Philippe snapped. "Why does he not simply smite the waters, the way Moses parted the Red Sea?"

RICHARD REACHED the port of Marseille on the last day of July, but his fleet was not there. He would later learn the delay was due to a riotous stopover at Lisbon, where the sailors got roaring drunk, attacking Jews and Muslims and accosting women, whether they were prostitutes or respectable wives. The enraged King of Portugal ordered the city gates shut, trapping hundreds of sailors, who were then tossed into prison until they sobered up and their leaders made amends for their offenses. As a result, they were three weeks late in getting to Marseille, and by then Richard was already gone. After waiting a week, he hired two large vessels known as busses and twenty galleys, leaving word for his fleet to catch up with him in Italy.

Six days later, Richard's ships dropped anchor at Genoa, where Philippe was lying ill. The French king requested the loan of five of Richard's rented galleys. When Richard offered three, Philippe reacted with anger and refused any. It occurred to many of their men that this was probably not a good omen for a future harmonious partnership between the two kings.

MORGAN AP RANULF sometimes wondered if it was sinful to be enjoying a holy quest as much as he was enjoying their sojourn in Italy. He'd been nervous at first, for the Welsh were not a nation of seafarers. But the voyage had been easy on even the most delicate of stomachs so far. They cruised along the Italian coast, rarely out of sight of land, often putting ashore so the men could stretch their legs and visit local sites, for Richard shared Morgan's interest in sightseeing.

Every day brought fresh delights for educated and inquisitive travelers. Morgan hoped he'd remember enough to regale his family once he was back in Wales—a pirate castle on the summit of Cape Circeo, the volcanic island of Ischia, the Roman baths at Baia. They tarried for ten days at Naples, so interesting did they find the sights there. Morgan accompanied Richard to visit the crypt at San Gennaro, where the four mummified sons of a legendary French hero were proudly displayed, and he then went to see Virgil's tomb, the ruins of a pagan Greek temple, and the isle of the Sirens where Ulysses had nearly been lured to his doom.

Morgan was even more intrigued by the exotic sea life of the Mediterranean.

He'd befriended a helmsman from Brittany, for Breton and Welsh were similar enough for mutual understanding, and Kavan was happy to share his knowledge, pointing out seals basking in the sun on the rocky shoreline, flying fish that arced through the air like silver arrows, the fin of a shark shadowing their fleet, and once a whale with oddly wrinkled skin that was almost as long as their galley; watching in awe, Morgan no longer doubted the scriptural story of Jonah. It was the dolphins, though, that won his heart. They would splash playfully in the wake of the galleys, and then swim boldly alongside the ships, making loud clicking sounds as if they were trying to talk to the men peering at them over the gunwales, and Morgan marveled that he was actually looking upon the legendary creatures seen by Caesar and Alexander.

He'd had only one disappointment so far. When they landed at the mouth of the Tiber River, the cardinal bishop of Ostia was waiting to invite Richard to visit His Holiness the Pope at Rome, just sixteen miles away. The king was having none of that, though, and subjected the cardinal to a caustic lecture on the sins of simony, accusing Pope Clement of extorting large sums from the English Crown in return for naming Longchamp as a papal legate and approving the consecration of the Bishop of Le Mans.

So they never got to Rome. Instead, Morgan got his first glimpse of the English king's fabled, fiery temper. He had entered Richard's service with some reluctance, for he'd been devoted to the king's brother Geoffrey, and had then served his father, an anguished eyewitness to the wretched death of the old king at Chinon. But Morgan was a realist and Richard was now king, so he'd attempted to put the past behind him. He was still getting to know Richard, and he'd been unnerved by the intensity of his royal cousin's rage at Ostia. Henry had been notorious for his own bursts of temper, said to be hot enough to blister paint off walls. Morgan had soon concluded, however, that there was a calculated element in Henry's rages, just one more weapon in a king's arsenal. But as Richard verbally flayed the discomfited cardinal, Morgan felt as if he were watching a fire at full blaze, one that could easily have gotten out of control, and that had never been true of Richard's father.

Aside from missing Rome, though, Morgan had no complaints, and he had to admit Richard had gone out of his way to treat him as a kinsman, which did much to elevate his status in the royal household. So he put aside any lingering misgivings, determined to make the most of these carefree, pleasant days in Italy, knowing life would be neither carefree nor pleasant once they reached Outremer.

Their leisurely progress down the Italian peninsula would soon come to an end. Upon leaving Naples, they'd ridden to Salerno so Richard could consult with the city's famed doctors about his recurrent bouts of quartan fever. While there, he finally got word that his missing ships had been spotted near Messina, and he at once picked up their pace, no longer having time to spare for sightseeing. Richard had heard troubling rumors in Naples that Joanna had not been seen in nigh on a year. Now that they'd soon be rendezvousing with the royal fleet, he was hopeful that he'd finally get reliable news about his sister's circumstances.

BY SEPTEMBER 21, Richard had reached Mileto in Calabria, where he was offered the hospitality of the Benedictine abbey of Holy Trinity. Like many of the other knights, Morgan had found lodgings in the town, and the next morning, he strolled back to the abbey in hopes of breaking his night's fast in the guest hall. There he found the king in a volcanic rage, stalking about the hall like a great cat on the prowl, spitting out curses under the awed eyes of Mileto's bishop, abbot, and monks.

Morgan sidled up to a friend, the Fleming Baldwin de Bethune, who'd been with him in the old king's service. "What has happened? Why is the king so wrathful?"

"He learned that his sister has been grievously maltreated by the usurper. Not only did Tancred seize the dower lands that were rightfully hers, he has been holding her prisoner in Palermo, keeping her isolated from the rest of the world so she could not appeal to Richard or to the rightful Queen of Sicily, the Lady Constance. Richard," Baldwin said dryly, "took the news rather badly."

"This Tancred must be a fool!"

"According to the bishop, Tancred had more immediate worries than the anger of a distant English king, for he was facing a rebellion of the island Saracens and fearing a German invasion. I suppose he hoped that political turmoil would keep Richard in his own domains or that he'd be as indifferent a brother as the French king. Those were two serious miscalculations."

"Indeed," Morgan agreed, wondering if they'd be shedding blood in Sicily ere they even reached the Holy Land. Not that he blamed Richard for reacting with such fury, for he had a sister, too, back in Wales. He thought it likely that the news of Joanna's imprisonment had also lacerated an old wound, for all knew how bitterly Richard had resented his mother's long confinement. He suspected that Tancred might be about to pay a debt twice over, both for Joanna and Queen Eleanor.

Richard had gotten his temper under control long enough to bid his Benedictine hosts and the bishop a courteous farewell, making a generous donation to
the abbey coffers before giving the command to move out. They'd planned to
return to their ships for the final leg of their journey, but Richard changed his
mind once he was in the saddle. "The rest of you go ahead," he ordered. "I need
some time to myself. Have my galley meet me at Bagnara."

His knights and lords raised an immediate protest. Richard's habit of going off
on his own without a thought to his personal safety had given them more than
one sleepless night. He usually paid no heed to their fears, annoyed that they
thought he, of all men, had need of a nursemaid, but this morning he made a
grudging concession and agreed to take a knight with him. His gaze falling upon
his cousin, he decided Morgan would do as well as any, and told the Welshman he
could come along.

Morgan was less than thrilled to be accompanying Richard in his present dark
mood, but he hastened to mount and follow the king as they rode out of the
abbey precincts. Once they were on the road, some of Richard's anger seemed to
dissipate in the open air, and by the time they stopped to water their horses, he
was telling Morgan about the plans for his entry into Messina.

"Philippe arrived last week, in a single ship if you can believe that, with all the
fanfare of a merchant returning home from a day at the market." Richard shook
his head in mock sorrow at the French king's lack of majesty. "There is more to
power, Morgan, than the exercise of it. There is also the demonstration of it, as I
shall show Philippe and the citizens of Messina on the morrow."

Morgan was not fully in agreement with Richard, for Henry had been utterly
indifferent to the trappings of power, needing no props to display his mastery
over other men. He was not about to argue with the king, though. Instead, he
offered his sympathy for the Lady Joanna's plight, which Richard acknowledged
with a nod, saying ominously, "God help Tancred if he has laid so much as a finger on her."

They'd dismounted beside a small stream so their horses could drink, and they
soon began to attract the attention of the inhabitants of nearby houses, who
shared the curiosity of villagers worldwide about strangers in their midst. Eventually, a matronly woman approached, speaking a tongue that was alien to them
both, though Richard guessed it was an odd dialect of Greek. She made it clear
by gestures that she had food and drink for sale, and after Morgan fumbled in
his scrip for a few Sicilian coins—kings rarely bothered to carry money—she
returned with slices of freshly baked bread smeared with olive oil, and two clay

cups of a strong red wine. She'd been followed by her daughter, and Morgan could not resist flirting a bit, exchanging complicit smiles with the girl until her mother noticed and shooed her back toward their house.

"I'd take care if I were you, Morgan," Richard said, amused by the byplay. "I hear they are right protective of their womenfolk in Sicily, and a wink or a lingering gaze can cost a man dearly. So unless you have peculiar yearnings to become a gelding, I suggest we ride on." He stopped, though, in the act of mounting his stallion, his head cocked. "Did you hear that?"

Morgan nodded. "It sounded like a hawk." When it came again, he was taken aback by Richard's next action. Tossing his reins to Morgan, he strode off toward a nearby house. The woman's pretty daughter had ventured out again and was removing laundry from a line of rope tied between two trees, watching Morgan all the while. He was tempted to go over and help but, mindful of Richard's warning, he stayed with the horses, giving her a regretful smile and a shrug.

It was a tranquil scene, people going about their daily chores, dogs sleeping in the sun, children interrupting a game with wooden weapons to stare at Morgan's real sword. He was about to toss them a few coins when the village peace was suddenly shattered by angry voices and the piercing cry of a hawk. Morgan tensed as several men hurried toward the house, for by now he recognized one of the raised voices as Richard's. He couldn't make out the words, but there was no mistaking the belligerent tone. He hastily swung up into the saddle just as the door burst open and Richard backed out, using a knife to keep the furious villagers at bay.

"Morgan!" he yelled, not daring to take his gaze from the threatening crowd, for by now other villagers had been drawn into the fray, several carrying pitchforks and hammers. They scattered as Morgan rode into their midst, giving Richard the time he needed to mount his own stallion. Spurring their horses, they soon outdistanced the curses, barking dogs, and a few poorly thrown rocks.

When they at last drew rein on the crest of a hill, Morgan turned in the saddle to stare at the other man. "What in Christ's Name was that all about?"

"The hawk," Richard said, as if that were self-explanatory, busying himself in brushing a powdery substance from his tunic. It looked like flour to Morgan and that only deepened the mystery.

"What about the hawk?"

"It was a fine goshawk, obviously stolen." Richard paused, having discovered a cut on his wrist. "But when I seized it, they protested vigorously and tried to stop me from leaving with it." Seeing the incredulous expression on his cousin's face, he said impatiently, "Rustics are not allowed to own hawks. You know that, Morgan."

Morgan opened his mouth, about to point out the obvious. *That may be true enough in England or France, but this is Sicily!* He caught himself in time, and then said in measured tones, "Under the circumstances, would it not have been easier just to give them back their blasted hawk?"

"Why? They were in the wrong, not me. At first they were just cursing me; at least that is what I assume all that shouting meant. But then one hothead lunged at me with a knife. I was not about to spill a peasant's guts in front of the fool's family, so I hit him with the flat of my sword. But damned if the blade did not snap in two!" Richard sounded astonished and indignant. "When I think how much I paid for it. . . . Then they were all flailing at me, even the women. I snatched up whatever I could, pelting them with apples and eggs until I could wrest the knife away and reach the door."

Looking over his shoulder at the village below them, Richard frowned. "And they still have the goshawk."

"I do hope you are not thinking of going back." Morgan was trying very hard to act as if Richard's insanity was normal behavior for a king, but it was not easy. He could not imagine Geoffrey or Henry ever getting themselves into such a ludicrous predicament. "You do know you are bleeding?"

"My head?" Richard explored the gash, looked at his bloodied fingers, and shrugged. "That must have happened when the man's wife hit me with her broom. She was buzzing about like a maddened hornet. I am probably lucky she was not the one wielding the knife!"

The image of the King of England under assault by an outraged Sicilian housewife was too much for Morgan, and he nearly strangled as he tried to choke back his mirth. Fortunately for him, Richard was also beginning to see the humor in his mishap. His mouth twitched and soon both men were laughing so hard that they had to dismount, leaning against their horses as they sought to get their hilarity under control. When Richard admitted that one greybeard had swung at him with a crutch, Morgan lost it altogether and sank to his knees, gasping for breath.

Richard reached down, pulling Morgan to his feet, and then unhooked a wineskin from his saddle. They took turns drinking from it, not caring that the wine was warm and overly spiced. Realizing that they'd best be on their way if they hoped to reach Bagnara in time to cross the straits, they remounted and Richard tossed the empty wineskin into the grass. After a moment, he glanced over at Morgan with a grin. "I ought to send you back to retrieve the goshawk," he joked and learned a new swear word from his Welsh cousin.

WHEN THEY GOT to Bagnara, they found Richard's private galley waiting for them. So was the royal fleet, having at last caught up with the king, and Morgan thought it was an astounding and magnificent sight: over a hundred ships riding at anchor, so many masts reaching skyward that it was like gazing upon a floating forest. They crossed the straits without difficulty and set up tents upon the beach a few miles from Messina. At supper that night, Richard had his companions in hysterics as he related the day's misadventure, comically describing the goshawk, the enraged rustics, and the woman armed with a deadly broom. It was an amusing story and Morgan conceded that Richard told it well; too well, for the men were laughing so much that they did not seem to realize what a narrow escape their king had in that little village near Mileto. He could have been killed or severely wounded by one of those understandably irate peasants, and what would have befallen their holy quest then? It was a question that would trouble Morgan's peace in the days and weeks to come.

THE CITIZENS OF MESSINA had been disappointed by the French king's inconspicuous entry into their city, for they'd become accustomed to splendor and pageantry from their royalty. But Philippe had no interest in impressing Sicilian merchants and burghers. He'd been suffering from seasickness brought on by a storm so violent they'd had to jettison some of their supplies to stay afloat, and he'd wanted only to set his feet on firm land again. Moreover, he was shrewd enough to realize that Tancred, an insecure king of dubious bloodlines, would not appreciate being outshone by foreign monarchs. And he was rewarded for his modest arrival, being welcomed warmly on Tancred's behalf by Jordan Lapin, the new Governor of Messina, who turned the royal palace over to the French for their stay in Sicily.

PHILIPPE WAS ENTERTAINING a delegation of Sicilian lords and prelates, including Jordan Lapin; Margaritis of Brindisi, the highly respected admiral of Tancred's fleet; and Richard Palmer, an Englishman who'd managed to become the Archbishop of Messina. Attendants padded in and out, bringing dishes of ripe fruit and refilling wine cups. They were, Philippe thought, the perfect servants, invisible and deferential. It was unsettling, though, to be waited upon by men of the same blood as those he'd be fighting in Outremer. Sicily was a strange land, and while he admired its riches, he could not help wondering if it was truly a Christian kingdom. In his brief stay, he'd seen indications of indolence and moral laxity, the same corrupt influences that had tainted society in Aquitaine and Toulouse. He would be glad when he could depart for the Holy Land and was disheartened to be told that the season for sailing was all but past, that winter storms would make it too dangerous to venture out onto the open sea.

"And so, my lord," the archbishop was saying with a genial smile, "it is our hope that you'll give consideration to our king's offer of an alliance between the kingdoms of France and Sicily. Lord Tancred has several lovely daughters, any one of whom would make a fine queen for you or mayhap a bride for your young son."

"I am honored by the offer," Philippe said with a noncommittal smile of his own, wondering if Tancred really thought he'd jeopardize his friendship with the Holy Roman Emperor for an alliance with a bastard-born usurper as likely to be overthrown by his own subjects as by the Germans. "I have indeed heard of the beauty of your king's daughters."

"We want to make your stay in Sicily as pleasant as possible, my lord king. I hope you will not hesitate to ask if I may be of any service whatsoever," Jordan Lapin was declaring when one of the admiral's men entered and murmured a few words in his ear.

Margaritis rose at once. "I ask your pardon, my liege, but we must depart. Richard of England's fleet is entering the harbor."

Philippe did not believe in delaying unpleasant tasks, preferring to get them over with as soon as possible. "We will accompany you," he said, rising, too. "I am eager to see the English king, who is my former brother by marriage and a valued ally."

THE WHARVES, DOCKS, AND BEACHES were crowded with spectators by the time Philippe and the Sicilian officials arrived. Coming to a halt, they gaped at the drama being played out before them. As far as the eye could see were brightly painted warships, shields hanging over the gunwales of the galleys, banners and pennons flying from their mastheads, as the oarsmen rowed in time to the beat of drums. Trumpets were blaring and horns blasting. The sun glittered on metallic hauberks and helmets, the turquoise waters of the harbor churning with frothy waves. And with an unerring instinct for stagecraft, Richard was standing erect in the prow of the lead galley, bareheaded, the wind tousling his red-gold hair, regal and proud, the very essence of what a king ought to be, all that Philippe Capet was not.

For that was the thought, however unkind, that crossed the minds of those witnessing Richard's spectacular entry into Messina. It crossed Philippe's mind, too, as he made ready to welcome his "brother by marriage and valued ally."

AFTER RICHARD'S ARRIVAL, Philippe made a rash decision quite out of character for him, announcing that he would leave at once for the Holy Land although the sailing season was rapidly coming to a close. But even nature seemed to be conspiring against him, for no sooner had he left the harbor than contrary winds sprang up, forcing him to abandon his impulsive plan. For better or worse, he would be wintering in Sicily with the English king.

MATTHEW OF AJELLO, the new chancellor of Sicily, arrived at the royal palace in Catania several hours after Compline. He was not in a cheerful frame of mind, for it had been raining for most of the day and wet weather aggravated his gout. He knew why he'd been summoned at such an hour. Tancred had heard of the English king's arrival in Messina.

He was escorted at once up to Tancred's private chamber, where he found the king, his wife Sybilla, her brother Riccardo, the Count of Acerra, and their eldest son, Roger. So this was to be a family conference, was it? Matthew did not blame Tancred for taking his troubles to heart. God knows, he had enough of them. They'd finally put down the Saracen rebellion, and a German force led by the Bishop of Mainz had been repelled that past May. But the Saracens did not have the same loyalty to Tancred that they had to William. It was only a matter of time until Heinrich launched a full-scale invasion. And now they had the English king to deal with, a man with the Devil's own temper, and a genuine grievance against Tancred. No, Matthew understood why Tancred had so many wakeful nights and uneasy days. What he did not understand was why Tancred was suddenly balking at taking his advice. Who'd have thought that it would be so much easier to make him king than to keep him one?

Matthew took a seat as close as he could get to the brazier of smoldering sea coals, for at his age, the cold and damp seemed to penetrate into his very bones. He smiled gratefully when Roger hurried over with a stool so he could prop up his throbbing foot. He was a good lad, Roger, would make a good king one day—if they made no foolish mistakes now, if he could get Tancred to listen to reason.

Sybilla, a conscientious hostess even in the midst of a crisis, had seen to it that a cup of his favorite wine was waiting for Matthew. Before he could touch it, Tancred leaned across the table and thrust a letter toward him. "A message from the English king," he said. "Read it."

Matthew had barely scanned the letter before Tancred erupted. "He demands that I send his sister to him in Messina with an escort to see to her safety, that I restore all of her dower lands to her, and for good measure, that I compensate her for the 'suffering' she endured at my hands. From the hostile tone of this letter, you'd think I'd been holding the woman in an underground dungeon instead of at the Zisa Palace!"

"For all we know, he may have been told that she was being maltreated," Matthew said, reading the letter again, more deliberately this time.

"I do not care if he thinks I sold her to the Caliph of Baghdad! You've read the letter, Matthew. This is not the language that one king uses to another king."

"No . . . it is the language of an angry brother, one with a formidable fleet at his command and the largest army ever to set foot on Sicilian soil."

Tancred gave Matthew a sharp look. "I do not want to have that argument again, Matthew. You made it quite clear that you think we'd do better in seeking an alliance with England, not France. But I will not be treated as if I am of no consequence. I am an anointed king, and by God, he will acknowledge me as one!"

Glancing around the chamber, Matthew saw that Tancred had the full support of his brother-in-law. That did not surprise him, for Riccardo was a man of action, not given to contemplation. Sybilla looked worried, though, and he took hope from that, for he knew how much influence she wielded with Tancred. Roger had withdrawn into the shadows filling the corners of the room, but Matthew knew he'd do whatever his father wanted, even if he had doubts himself. Matthew decided it was time to call for reinforcements; on the morrow he'd summon the Archbishop of Monreale to Catania.

Taking the letter back, Tancred was reading it again, heat rising in his face and neck. "The English king does not seem to realize that he is not in a position to make threats. This is my kingdom, not his. And his sister is in my hands, not his. Suppose I hold her as a hostage for his good behavior?"

There was an involuntary movement from Roger, quickly stilled. Matthew suppressed a sigh, wondering why Tancred did not see that one man's hostage was another man's pretext for a war of conquest. "I would advise against that, my liege," he said quietly. "I would advise very strongly against that."

"What a surprise," Riccardo said sarcastically. But Tancred did not reply. Instead, he crumpled the parchment in his hand, then crossed to the brazier and dropped it onto the coals. As the acrid odor of burning sheepskin filled the chamber, he stood without moving until the letter had been reduced to ashes.

CHAPTER 9

ixteen years. Those two words had become Joanna's lifeline, for whenever she despaired, she reminded herself that her mother had survived sixteen years of confinement, and had suffered far greater deprivations and indignities. At least she still had a few of her ladies for company—the faithful Beatrix, the young widow Hélène, little Alicia, and Mariam, as loyal as any blood sister could be—whereas Eleanor had lacked any companionship whatsoever in her first two years of captivity. Joanna's jewelry had been confiscated so she could not use it to bribe servants, but she did have access to her own clothes, her dogs, her books, all of which had been denied her mother in the beginning.

Where had Maman found the strength to face those endless days? How could she have borne the inactivity, she who'd always been occupied from dawn till dusk? How had she abided the isolation, not knowing what was happening in the world beyond those castle walls? That was what Joanna found most difficult—the lack of news. Was Richard on the way to Outremer? Or had he been detained by another war with France? Did he still intend to stop over in Sicily? Did he even know of her plight? Had Tancred denied him the use of Sicilian ports? How secure was Tancred's throne? When would Heinrich lead a German army into Sicily to claim Constance's crown?

Joanna had no illusions, did not see Heinrich von Hohenstaufen as her savior. Constance would do all she could, but would Heinrich pay her any heed? Joanna doubted it. A man known to be cold-hearted and vengeful, he would be sorely tempted to punish Richard by continuing her captivity or forcing her to make a deliberately demeaning marriage to a German lord of low rank. That was the fate

Joanna most feared, being wed against her will to a husband of Tancred or Heinrich's choosing. Tancred had implied that he might reconsider her position once he'd defeated his enemies. Joanna doubted that, too. Most likely he'd marry her off to a man he could trust, just as her father had done with her brother Geoffrey's widow, Constance of Brittany.

Putting up a brave front before the other women, Joanna acted as if she was certain that she'd regain her freedom. She'd not lost faith in her brother, was sure that Richard would do all in his power to rescue her. But she'd learned some painful lessons in the mysterious Ways of the Almighty, which were so often beyond the understanding of mortal men. Why had God taken William so suddenly? Their infant son? Hal and Geoffrey and Tilda? Those were questions she could not answer, so how could she know what He intended for her?

As September drew to a close, Joanna found it harder and harder to maintain her confident pose, for she was dreading the days to come. In less than a fortnight, she would mark her twenty-fifth birthday. In November, it would be a year since her husband's death. And in December, she'd begin her second year of confinement. She resorted to her talisman, whispering, *Sixteen years*, in those lonely hours when sleep would not come, but it was losing its potency. *How, Maman? How did you endure it?*

JOANNA WAS STARTLED by the unexpected appearance of her gaoler, Hugh Lapin, as church bells were summoning the faithful to Compline. Hugh had always treated her with respect, but he'd also made sure that she was kept secluded, in adherence to his new king's command. He and his brother Jordan had profited handsomely from their support of Tancred; Hugh was now Count of Conversano and justiciar of Apulia, while Jordan fared even better, as Count of Bovino and Governor of Messina. She acknowledged Hugh's greeting courteously, for it made no sense to antagonize her warden, but her women were not as prudent. Gathering around her protectively, they glared at him with open hostility. William's dog had become Joanna's shadow after his master's death and, sensitive to the sudden tension in the chamber, Ahmer growled low in his throat. Resting her hand reassuringly upon the hound's head, Joanna sought to appear unconcerned. But all the while her mind was racing. Why was he here at such an hour? What did he want?

"My lady queen, I ask your pardon for giving you so little warning, but I had none myself. A ship is waiting in the harbor for you, ready to sail tonight. Will your women be able to pack your belongings within the hour? If not, I will send servants to be of assistance."

Joanna's breath hissed through her teeth. "Where am I going, my lord?"

Looking uncomfortable, he shook his head apologetically. "I am sorry, Madame, but I am not able to tell you." If it were up to him, he'd have answered what was a very reasonable question under the circumstances. But he was not about to risk offending his king, for Tancred's terse command had been smoldering with barely suppressed fury.

Joanna stared at him in dismay. The secrecy was alarming, as was the fact that she was being hurried out of the city under cover of night, so the citizens of Palermo would not know of her departure. What would be awaiting her at the end of this ominous voyage? A less comfortable prison than the Zisa? An unwanted husband? "I am taking my dogs," she said, raising her chin defiantly.

The count was glad that he could accommodate her wishes, since he'd had no orders to the contrary. "As you will, my lady." His gaze shifting then to Beatrix, he said, "Be sure to pack all of the queen's possessions. She will not be returning to Palermo."

THEIR SHIP STAYED CLOSE to the coast, and by the eve of Michaelmas, it was approaching the Straits of Messina. Joanna had retreated into the canvas tent set up to shelter the women, saying that she needed to comfort Alicia as they entered the turbulent waters of the Faro, where her brother had drowned. Mariam knew that Joanna had another reason for her withdrawal; she did not want the crew or the arrogant ship's master as witnesses if she became queasy. She was no longer that little girl who'd suffered so much from seasickness that she'd had to continue her marital journey by land but, like Alicia, she would take to her grave a deep-rooted fear of the sea. Mariam preferred to stay out in the open air, and she was leaning over the gunwale, watching seagulls swoop and circle overhead when the ships came into view.

During the last year of William's reign, he'd sent the Sicilian fleet to cruise the waters of Outremer, keeping the Saracens from blockading Tyre. But Mariam was not surprised that it would have been recalled by Tancred, given his precarious grasp on power. The fleet was under the command of the renowned admiral, Margaritis of Brindisi, who happened to be Mariam's brother-in-law, for he was wed to her half-sister Marina, another of the out-of-wedlock daughters sired by the first King William. For a fleeting moment, Mariam wondered if she could coax Margaritis into speaking up for Joanna, then laughed at her own foolishness. The admiral was a man of many talents, a born sailor who'd been a highly successful pirate before he'd won royal favor, but he was more likely to sprout wings than to be swayed by an appeal to sentiment. Moreover, Mariam had not been close to Marina. Like her other half-sisters, one of whom was wed to the Emperor of Cyprus, they were all much older than Mariam, who'd been born in the last year of her father's life.

As their galley began to maneuver among the anchored ships, Mariam was pleased when Joanna joined her on deck. "Margaritis is back from the Holy Land, Joanna. I did not realize the Sicilian fleet was so numerous, did you?"

"That is not the Sicilian fleet." Joanna's voice sounded so oddly muffled that Mariam swung around to face her. Joanna was smiling, though, one of the most blindingly radiant smiles Mariam had ever seen. "Look," she said, pointing. Following her gesture, Mariam gazed upward and saw, for the first time, the gold and scarlet banner flying from mastheads, silhouetted against the brilliant blue of the September sky—the royal lion of England.

THE SHIP'S MASTER HAD BEGUN to regret that Messina was a deepwater port, with ships able to dock at the city wharves. If he'd anchored out in the harbor, he'd not be arguing with this troublesome woman; he knew she was a queen, but since he was not Sicilian, he wasn't impressed by her status. "As I have explained, Madame," he said impatiently, "my orders are very clear. I am to hand you over to the governor, and he will then escort you to the English king's camp."

Joanna scowled, not liking the image conjured up by the phrase "hand you over," as if she were a sack of flour to be delivered to a local baker. "And how long do you expect me to wait? It has already—" When her frown vanished, replaced by a triumphant smile, the master had an unpleasant premonition. She was looking past him, and he turned, already suspecting what he would see. People on the wharves were clearing a path for approaching riders. They were clad in mail, the sun reflecting off the metal links of their hauberks, the man in the lead astride a snorting grey stallion that seemed bred for the battlefield, not the city streets of Messina. Realizing that he was staring defeat in the face, the master brusquely ordered his crew to lower the gangplank.

JOANNA WANTED TO GREET Richard in a dignified fashion; after all, she was no longer the cheeky little sister he remembered, but a wife, mother, widow, and queen. Her resolve lasted until she set foot on the dock. Swinging from the saddle, Richard tossed the reins to one of his men and strode toward her, smiling. Picking up her skirts then, she ran into his arms. They'd attracted a crowd and people were jostling to get closer, having recognized their queen. The arrival of the large English army had not been welcomed by the citizens of Messina, and already there'd been some hostile clashes between the locals and soldiers. But for now, all of those watching were beaming, touched by this dramatic reunion of brother and sister.

When Richard released her, Joanna felt as if the air had been squeezed from her lungs, so tightly had he hugged her, and her eyes were brimming with tears, she who'd cried so rarely during those miserable months of captivity. "Oh, Richard . . . I have never been so happy in all of my born days!"

"Me, too, *irlanda*," he said, and that forgotten pet name caused her tears to fall in earnest. Her brothers had delighted in finding teasing and affectionate endearments for their baby sister; Hal had called her "imp" and Geoffrey "kitten," but Richard had preferred "swallow" and "lark" and "little bird," always in the *lenga romana* of their mother's homeland.

"Joanna . . . you must tell me the truth." Richard was no longer smiling. "Have you been hurt?"

The tight line of his mouth and the grim tone told her what he was asking, and she hastened to shake her head. "No, Richard, no. My honor is quite intact, I promise you. To give the Devil his due, Tancred saw to it that I was always treated with respect. My confinement was a comfortable one," she insisted, thinking again of their mother's captivity, and then she grinned. "Mind you, the wretched man did hold me hostage and steal my dower lands, so I'd not want to praise him too much!"

Richard put his arm around her shoulders again, saying, "Well, you're safe now, lass." And in the security of her brother's embrace, Joanna could finally admit to herself just how frightened she'd been.

RICHARD HAD TAKEN JOANNA to the nunnery of St Mary's, for he was lodging in a house on the outskirts of the city, the royal palace having been given over to the French king and his entourage. After a celebratory meal in the guest hall, the other women had retired for the evening, while Joanna and Richard sought to fill in the gaps of the past fourteen years. Only Mariam had not gone to bed. Sometime after midnight, she'd dozed off, awakening with a start to find Joanna leaning over her.

"I told you not to wait up for me," she chided, as Mariam sat up, yawning.

"And when do I ever listen to you? What time is it? Is it dawn yet?"

"Soon," Joanna said, climbing onto the bed beside her. "There was so much to say, Mariam! I wanted to tell him about William and my life in Sicily, and I wanted to know about the strife that tore our family apart. But Richard had few answers for me, not when it came to our father and brothers." Joanna pulled off her veil and shifted so Mariam could free her hair from its pins. "It is almost as if some evil spell was cast upon them all. . . ."

"And is your brother as you remembered him?"

"Indeed—confident, prideful, amusing, and stubborn," Joanna joked, leaning back with a contented sigh as Mariam began to brush out her hair. "He says we cannot stay in Messina, that it is not safe. There have already been fights between his men and the townspeople and he fears it will only get worse, so he means to find us a secure lodging across the Faro. I told him I wanted to remain here in Messina with him, but he would not heed me. As I said," she smiled, "stubborn!"

"I'd say that was a family trait," Mariam teased, and Joanna gave the other woman a quick, heartfelt hug.

"You are as dear to me as my own sisters," she proclaimed, "and I will never forget your loyalty in my time of need. To prove it, I am going to divulge a secret. But you must promise not to speak of it to anyone else."

"Of course I promise. What is it?" Mariam prodded, for she shared Joanna's love of mysteries.

"I've told you about Richard's long-standing plight-troth with the French king's sister. Well, it will never come to pass. I know, hardly a surprise, for it is obvious to all but the French king that Richard has no intention whatsoever of marrying Alys. That is not the secret. This is—that Richard has agreed to wed Berengaria, the daughter of Sancho, the King of Navarre, and she is coming to join him in Sicily."

Mariam knew more of Navarre than most people, for William's mother had been a princess of that Spanish kingdom, Sancho's sister. "Then you'll be getting a cousin as well as a sister by marriage," she said, "since her father was William's uncle." The Navarrese connection made the news more interesting than it would otherwise have been, but she was still surprised that Joanna seemed so excited about the arrival of a woman she did not know—until Joanna told her the rest, the heart of her secret.

"And guess who is bringing her to Richard? My mother! Yesterday I was not sure that I'd ever see any of my family again and now . . . now I have not only been reunited with my brother, but my mother is on her way to Sicily, too." Stretching out on the bed, Joanna confided, "I never dared hope for so much. . . ."

Mariam was more eager to meet the legendary Eleanor of Aquitaine than Sancho's daughter, and she was delighted that Joanna would be given this rare opportunity to see her mother again; a foreign marriage usually meant lifelong exile for highborn young women like Joanna. Rising, she crossed the chamber to pour two cups of the night wine sent over by the abbess. "I am so pleased for you, dearest. Fortune's Wheel has truly turned with a vengeance, has it not?"

When Joanna did not answer, Mariam glanced over her shoulder, and then smiled, for the young queen had fallen asleep in the time it had taken to lay her head upon her pillow. Returning to the bed, Mariam covered her with a blanket. "Sleep well," she murmured, "and God bless your brother for justifying your faith in him."

RICHARD RETURNED to the nunnery the next day, bringing two kinsmen for Joanna to meet: their maternal cousin, André de Chauvigny, and their paternal cousin, Morgan ap Ranulf. But Richard and Joanna had soon withdrawn to the nunnery's parlor for more private conversation, as they'd just scratched the surface the day before. Left to amuse themselves, André began a dice game with several of their knights and Morgan took Joanna's dog out into the cloisters.

He was intrigued by Ahmer's appearance, for the Sicilian cirneco had ears like a rabbit and fur as red as a fox. Sicily was an unusual land in all respects, so it seemed only natural that even its dogs would be unlike dogs elsewhere. Morgan had never seen palm trees before, or birds that looked like feathered jewels, or churches that had once been mosques, giving the city an exotic aura all its own. The women were exotic, too, sashaying about the streets in silks and fluttering veils, bejeweled fingers decorated with henna, wellborn Christian ladies choosing to dress like Saracens. Morgan wondered if it was Sicily's alien aspects that seemed to unsettle so many of Richard's men. It did not help that the Messinians were overwhelmingly of Greek heritage, followers of the Greek Orthodox Church. Were they even true Christians? All knew that Rome was God's City, after all, not Constantinople.

As a Welshman, Morgan had an outsider's perspective, so he was willing to give the Messinians the benefit of the doubt, at least until they proved him wrong. But in less than a week, most of his comrades and fellow crusaders had become convinced that the citizens of Messina were bandits in the guise of merchants, vintners, and shopkeepers. Seated on a bench under a fragrant citrus tree in the convent's guest cloisters, within sight of the turquoise waters of the straits, Morgan thought he'd rarely looked upon a scene so lovely or so tranquil, although he suspected that the tranquility was an illusion, a candle soon to be guttered out by the storms gathering along the horizon—the growing hostility between the townspeople and the crusaders.

Several of their knights had entered the cloisters, plucked an orange from a nearby tree, and began a boisterous game of catch. They paused, though, at sight of the woman gliding up the walkway. She attracted Morgan's eye, too, for she was a vision in embroidered gold silk, with jangling bracelets, gilt slippers, and a delicately woven veil the color of a sunset sky. He'd been throwing sticks for Ahmer to chase, and he reached now for another one, meaning to toss it into the vision's path, saying softly, "Go get it, boy. Act as my lure." But one of the knights was quicker, swaggering across the mead to intercept the woman as she passed. Morgan shook his head, marveling that men could be such fools. Her elegant garb proclaimed that she was of high rank, either a nunnery guest or a member of the queen's own household, definitely not someone to be accosted as if she were a street whore. "Come on, Ahmer," he said. "Let's go rescue a damsel in distress."

He soon saw there was no need of that. She turned upon the would-be lothario with such outrage that none could doubt her privileged status. Morgan was still out of hearing range, but he could see the knight wilting under her scorn. By the time Morgan reached them, the man was in full retreat, his friends were roaring with laughter, and the woman was threatening him with the fate that all males most dreaded. To the Welshman's astonishment, she switched then from fluent, colloquial French to an alien tongue, so foreign that he decided it could only be Arabic.

At the sound of Morgan's footsteps on the pathway, she spun about, ready to take on another antagonist, and he hastily raised his hands in playful surrender. "I come in peace, my lady. My dog and I thought—erroneously—that you might be in need of our assistance. But I soon saw the poor fellow was the one needing help!"

She was taller than many women, with more curves than was fashionable, at least in France and England, her face half hidden by her veil. He was fascinated by what he could see, though, for her eyes were so light a shade of brown that they appeared golden in the sun. She'd glanced down at the dog, saying, "What strange company are you keeping these days, Ahmer?" But then she turned those mesmerizing eyes upon him, and he found he could not look away. "I must thank you then," she said, "for your good manners, since so many men have no manners at all."

"I'll give you no argument about that," he said cheerfully. "May I pose a question, though? I could not help overhearing some of the tongue-lashing you gave that fool. Was the tongue Arabic?"

Those almond-shaped eyes seemed to narrow, ever so slightly. "Yes," she said, "it was Arabic. No other language can match its creative insults or its colorful curses."

"Mayhap you could teach me one or two of them, then?" Morgan gave her his most beguiling smile. "In return, I will gladly teach you a few of mine."

"I rather doubt that you know any I do not."

"Ah, but do you speak Welsh, my lady? Or English?"

"No, I cannot say that I do. In fact, I've never even heard either of those tongues spoken."

"The pleasure is mine, then. *Beth yw eich enw? Thou may me blisse bringe.*"

"Judging from your honeyed tone, I do not think those are curses, sir knight."

"You've caught me out, my lady. I asked your name and then I dared to hope that you may bring me bliss. A smile would do it."

"You are easily satisfied, then." But as she reached down to pat Ahmer, her veil slipped, as if by chance, and his pulse quickened, for she had skin as golden as her eyes and a full, ripe mouth made for a man's kisses. She did not attempt to replace the veil, instead saying coolly, "Staring like that may not be rude in your homeland, but it is very rude in mine."

"*Mea culpa, demoiselle.* But I could not help myself. For you are truly the most beautiful woman I've ever laid eyes upon."

"Indeed?" She sounded very skeptical. "I assume you are one of King Richard's men. So surely you've met his sister, the queen."

"Yes, I had that honor this morn."

"Then either your vision is flawed or you are a liar, for the Lady Joanna is far more beautiful than I am." Drawing the veil across her face again, she moved around him and began to walk away.

Morgan was not about to give up yet. "Yes," he called after her, "but can the Lady Joanna swear in Arabic?"

She didn't pause, nor did she answer him. But Morgan watched her go with a grin, for he was sure he'd heard a soft murmur of laughter floating back on the breeze.

JOANNA HAD NO TROUBLE reconciling her memories with reality; the nineteen-year-old brother who'd escorted her to Marseille and the waiting Sicilian envoys was recognizable in the thirty-three-year-old man who'd pried open the door of her gilded prison. But for Richard, those fourteen years had wrought dramatic changes in the little girl he'd remembered with such affection. "Are you sure you're my sister?" he joked. "I have never seen such a remarkable transformation. Well, not since I last saw a butterfly burst from its cocoon!"

"Are you calling me a caterpillar?" Joanna feigned indignation, jabbing him in the ribs with her elbow, so easily had they slipped back into their familiar family roles. "I was an adorable child!"

"You were spoiled rotten, *irlanda,* for you took shameless advantage of your position as the baby of the family. You managed the lot of us like so many puppets." Richard paused for comic effect. "Though I suppose that was good training for marriage."

"Indeed it was," she agreed, for she believed that a woman with brothers had a decided advantage over other women when it came to understanding the male mind. "But I was not the baby of the family. That was Johnny."

Richard did not want to talk about John, for he knew that would inevitably lead to further conversation about Hal and Geoffrey and then their father. So far he'd been successful in avoiding a serious discussion of their family feuding, but he knew sooner or later he'd have to answer her questions. Just not yet. He sensed she'd be hurt by the truth—that he'd detested Hal and Geoffrey—for she'd had an inexplicable fondness for the pair of them. She did not know how Hal had plotted with rebel lords in Aquitaine to overthrow him, how Geoffrey had twice led armies into his duchy, once with Hal and then with Johnny. He held no grudge against Johnny, for he'd been only seventeen at the time. But he was not sorry that Hal and Geoffrey were dead. Nor was he sorry that their father was dead, although he did regret that the ending had been so bitter. He'd not wanted it to be that way, had been given no choice. How could he expect Joanna to understand all this, though? A pity their mother would not be here for months. It would have been so much easier if he could have left the explanations to her.

To deflect any questions about their family's internal warfare, he said quickly, "When I warned Tancred that you must be released straightaway, I demanded the return of your dower lands, too. Moreover, I told him to include a generous sum as recompense for your ordeal."

"Did you truly, Richard? Very good!" By Joanna's reckoning, Tancred owed her a huge debt, and she thought it was wonderful that she had so formidable a debt collector in Richard. "Tancred owes you a debt, too."

Richard was immediately interested. "What do you mean?"

"William died without a will. But he meant to leave our father a vast legacy, to be used in freeing Jerusalem from the infidels. He would have wanted that legacy to pass to you now that Papa is dead, for the fate of the Holy City mattered greatly to him."

"Do you know what he intended to bequeath, Joanna?"

"Indeed I do. A twelve-foot table of solid gold, twenty-four gold cups and plates, a silk tent large enough to hold two hundred men, sixty thousand measures of wheat, barley, and wine, and one hundred armed galleys, with enough provisions to feed their crews for two years."

"Bless you, lass!" Richard swept her up into a jubilant embrace. "I bled England white for this holy quest, would have pawned the crown jewels if Maman had let me. A bequest like this is worth more than I can begin to tell you, and might well make your husband the savior of Outremer."

"William would have been so pleased to hear you say that." Tilting her head so she could look up into his face, she gave him a smile that somehow managed to hold sadness, satisfaction, mischief, and even a hint of malice. "And if Tancred balks at honoring the legacy, I might remember other items that William wanted to bestow upon you. Be sure to tell him that, Richard."

Richard was laughing, delighted to discover that his little sister shared the family flair for revenge. But just then they were interrupted by one of his men with surprising news. The French king had arrived to pay his respects to Joanna.

PHILIPPE WAS NOT looking forward to his courtesy call upon Joanna, for he found it stressful to spend any time in Richard's company. Moreover, he was bone-weary of the fuss Richard had made over his sister's predicament, for he was convinced that the English king had an ulterior motive for his most innocent act. Since he found it hard to believe that Richard could still be so fond of a woman he had not seen for fourteen years, he'd concluded that the other man was using Joanna in a subtle attempt to make him look bad, wanting people to contrast Richard's concern for Joanna with his own lack of concern for his youngest sister,

Agnes. He found it very irritating. What was he supposed to have done—launched a war against the Greek Empire? Led an army to lay siege to Constantinople?

But like it or not, he felt obligated to welcome Richard's sister to Messina, knowing that failure to do so would have made him seem petty and discourteous; she was a queen, after all. Accompanied by his cousin Hugh, the Duke of Burgundy, Jaufre of Perche, and Mathieu de Montmorency, he was in a better mood by the time they reached the convent, for they'd been cheered in the streets by the townspeople. The Messinians were showing far more friendliness to the French than to their English allies, and Philippe was gratified that they had not been seduced by Richard's usual theatrics.

The abbess herself escorted them into the guest hall. The irrepressible young Mathieu came to an abrupt halt at sight of the woman standing by Richard's side. "My God, she's gorgeous!" Jaufre had taken the teenager under his wing, having seen how easily he irked Philippe, and he gave the boy a reproachful look, for lavishing praise on Richard's sister was no way to regain the French king's favor. But when he glanced toward Philippe, Jaufre was astonished to see that he was staring at Joanna with the same rapt expression as Mathieu. He was even more astonished when Philippe strode forward to greet Richard with impeccable courtesy and Joanna with outright enthusiasm.

"I am honored to make your acquaintance, Madame. I do have a bone to pick with your lord brother, though, for he never told me how very beautiful you were."

This was familiar ground to Joanna, who was an accomplished flirt. "My brother has indeed been remiss, my lord king, for he did not tell me how gallant you were, either." And when Philippe offered his arm, she allowed him to escort her toward a window-seat so they could converse in greater privacy.

This was a side of Philippe that none had ever seen before, not even his own men, and they watched in amazed amusement as the dour French king was suddenly transformed into a courtier, ordering wine to be brought for Joanna, displaying so much animation that he seemed to shed years before their eyes, reminding them that he was but twenty-five and in need of a new queen to grace his throne and his bed.

Richard showed no obvious reaction to the French king's unexpected interest in his sister, for he'd long ago mastered that most valuable of kingly skills—showing the world only what he wanted it to see. But those who knew him well were not deceived, and the Duke of Burgundy could not resist sauntering over to make mischief. "Our king and your sister seem right taken with each other, even smitten. Passing strange, the ways of fate. Who knows, mayhap there might be a double wedding in the future, you and the Lady Alys and my cousin Philippe and the Lady Joanna."

Richard had long borne the Duke of Burgundy a legitimate grievance, for Hugh and the Count of Toulouse had joined forces with Hal in his attempt to lay claim to Aquitaine, hastily abandoning that sinking ship once Hal had been stricken with a mortal ailment. Richard had not called the duke to account, but he rarely forgave a wrong and never forgot one. He was not about to give Hugh the satisfaction of seeing his barb had drawn blood, though, and refused to take the bait, saying only, "Passing strange, indeed. Life is filled with turns and twists and we never know what lies around the next bend in the road." All the while thinking that Hugh would one day find an unpleasant surprise awaiting him on that road, and thinking, too, that he'd see Joanna wed to Lucifer himself ere he'd let her marry Philippe Capet.

"JOANNA, WE NEED TO TALK. I think it is only fair to tell you that under no circumstances would I consent to a union between you and the French king. The man is sly, craven, and untrustworthy—" Richard got no further, for Joanna had begun to laugh.

"Philippe and me? Good Heavens, Richard, the thought never crossed my mind!"

Richard felt a surge of relief. "I am very glad to hear that, lass! The way he was doting upon you, I half expected him to make an offer for you then and there, and I was not the only one who thought that. But if you had no interest in him, why were you encouraging his courtship?"

"I was flirting with him, Richard, not inviting him into my bed! What was I supposed to do—publicly humiliate him by rejecting his overtures? Not only would that have been the height of bad manners, it would have been foolish, too. Offending a king is never a wise move, especially when that king is supposed to be my brother's ally."

He looked at her in surprise, for few people dared to speak so forthrightly to him. "You are right, of course," he conceded. "Since Philippe can vex me merely by breathing, you can imagine how much I enjoyed watching him pant over you like a lovesick calf. I'd not trust him with the lowliest of sumpter horses, much less my sister!"

"I am glad that you value me more than a sumpter horse," she said, seeking to match his playful tone, although she'd not been misled by it. She found it troubling that he was trapped in an alliance with a man he scorned; that did not bode well for their success in the Holy Land. But there was naught she could do about it. Even if Philippe was truly smitten with her—and she very much doubted that—it would change nothing. According to Richard, their father had saved Philippe's kingship repeatedly in the early years of his reign, protecting him from his mistakes of youth and inexperience. And yet he had turned upon Henry without hesitation when the opportunity arose, hounding him to that wretched end at Chinon. A man so utterly incapable of gratitude was not one to be swayed by lust.

"You need not worry, Richard. Philippe let his guard down this afternoon, and I daresay he is already regretting it. I am sure he quickly realized that my charms could not compensate for the misery of having you as his brother-in-law."

Richard blinked and then it was his turn to laugh. By God, she *was* her mother's daughter. "I hope you are right. It would be awkward if he actually made an offer for you. To save his pride, I'd have to tell him you were already spoken for, and then I'd need to find a husband for you in such haste that any fool with a pulse would do."

"It is reassuring to know you'll have my best interests at heart, Brother," Joanna said wryly. "But I'd rather you not be in such a hurry to marry me off. I do not know what the future holds for me. I am eager to find out, though."

"I want to talk with you about that, Joanna. It is my hope that you'd be willing to accompany me to Outremer. I think your presence would be a comfort to Berengaria."

He was asking a great deal, for life was not easy for women in the Holy Land, not even for queens. Just getting there would mean severe hardships and danger—and a daunting sea voyage. But Joanna did not hesitate, for how could she refuse him? If not for Richard, she'd have had no future at all. And she found it rather touching that he'd realized Berengaria would be in need of comfort; she would not have expected that of him.

"Yes," she said, "of course I am willing, Richard. I owe you so much, welcome a chance to do something for you in return. Besides, it will be a great adventure!"

"Yes, it will," he said, pleased that she understood that. "You are indeed a sister to be proud of, Joanna. And who knows," he added with a grin, "mayhap we'll find you a husband in the Holy Land!"

"So you think Saladin may be in need of another wife?" she riposted and they both laughed, for they were finding in each other what had often been lacking for the Angevins: a sense of family solidarity.

———

THE FOLLOWING DAY, Richard crossed the Faro, took possession of the town of Bagnara, and installed Joanna and her household in the Augustinian priory of St Mary, with a strong guard of knights and men-at-arms to see to her safety. Returning to Messina the next morning, he then seized the Greek Orthodox monastery of the Holy Saviour, located on a strategic spit of land outside the harbor; summarily evicting the monks, he turned the abbey into a storage facility for his siege engines, provisions, and horses. The citizens of Messina were enraged by his high-handed action, but alarmed, too, for now that he held both Bagnara and the monastery, he controlled the straits, and they began to wonder what his intentions were. So did Tancred.

CHAPTER 10

OCTOBER 1190

Messina, Sicily

It began innocently enough, with a dispute between one of Richard's soldiers and a woman selling loaves of bread. When he accused her of cheating him, she became enraged, and he was set upon by her friends and neighbors, badly beaten by citizens very resentful of these insolent foreigners in their midst. They then shut the gates of Messina to the English and put up chains to bar the inner harbor to their ships. Infuriated that crusaders should be treated so shabbily, the English were all for forcing their way into the city. Only Richard's appearance upon the scene prevented a riot. After dispersing his angry men with some difficulty, he summoned the French king and the Sicilian officials to an urgent meeting the next day at his lodgings, in hopes of resolving these grievances through diplomacy.

THE MESSINIANS WERE REPRESENTED by their governor, Jordan Lapin, Admiral Margaritis, and the archbishops of Messina, Monreale, and Reggio. The French king was accompanied by the Duke of Burgundy, the counts of Nevers and Louvain, Jaufre of Perche, and the bishops of Chartres and Langres. Richard's companions included the archbishops of Rouen and Auch, and the bishops of Bayonne and Evreux. But before the conference began, he drew the French king aside for a private word.

"We cannot sail for Outremer until the favorable winds return in the spring. Since we're going to be stuck here all winter, we cannot allow these stupid squabbles to continue. It will help immeasurably if you and I present a united front, Philippe. I assume I can count upon your support in these negotiations."

"My men have encountered no troubles with the Messinians. The strife did not begin until your army arrived, so I'd look to them as the source of contention, not the local people."

"How many men do you have with you—less than a thousand? I doubt that the French would be such welcome guests if they numbered as many as mine."

"Or mayhap it is simpler than that, Richard. Mayhap your men are not as well disciplined as mine."

"Need I remind you that Saladin is the enemy, not me?"

"And need I remind you that your men took the cross to fight the Saracens, not the Sicilians?"

And on that sour note, the peace conference began.

THE DISCUSSIONS WERE going better than Richard had expected, solely due to the diplomatic efforts of one man, the Archbishop of Monreale. Jordan Lapin and Admiral Margaritis were openly hostile, complaining angrily about the bad behavior of the English. Philippe declared that the French were impartial and offered to mediate, but he also agreed with all of the Sicilian accusations, much to Richard's fury. Only the archbishop seemed willing to concede that there were wrongs on both sides; he alone did not reject Richard's proposal to set fixed prices for bread and wine, and did his best to calm rising tempers.

Jordan Lapin was not as conciliatory. "Prices have risen because the demand for food has increased dramatically, not because our people are seeking to cheat your men. I should think that would be obvious to anyone with a brain in his head!"

"What is obvious," Richard said curtly, "is that something is amiss when a loaf of bread suddenly costs more than three chickens, or the price of wine triples from one day to the next. Your king, may God assoil him, often said that nothing was more important than the recovery of Jerusalem. He would have been appalled that his subjects are seeking to defraud Christian pilgrims, men who've taken the cross."

Jordan glared across the table at the English king. "My lord William would have been appalled to see those 'Christian pilgrims' behaving like barbarians in a city of his realm. And your lords do nothing to rein them in. When I complained to one of your barons about the way his men were accosting our women, he laughed. He laughed and said they were not trying to seduce the wives, just to annoy the husbands!"

Richard hastily brought his wine cup to his mouth, but not in time to hide a grin. "They are soldiers, not saints. Yes, some of them are going to flirt with women and get drunk and brawl in your taverns. But I can control my army as long as they do not think they are being gulled or duped. That is why it is so important to fix prices. Nor are your people blameless in this. I've heard them cursing my men in the marketplace, jeering and calling them 'long-tailed English.'"

The governor interrupted to point out that the English were just as offensive, using the insulting term "Griffon" to refer to citizens of Greek heritage. Richard ignored him, turning his attention to Margaritis. "I've been told that your crews roam the streets, my lord admiral, seeking to start fights with any English they find."

Margaritis shrugged. "They are sailors, not saints." As their eyes met, the Greek admiral and the English king shared a brief moment of understanding, one soldier to another. It did not last, though. The governor reclaimed control of the conversation, insisting that Richard pay for property damages and threatening to declare Messina off-limits to all of his men. The Archbishop of Monreale again stepped into the breach, and was attempting to find common ground when the door burst open.

"My liege, you must come at once!" Baldwin de Bethune was flushed and out of breath. "Hugh de Lusignan's lodging is under attack!"

The de Lusignans were some of Richard's most troublesome vassals, but they *were* his vassals. Jumping to his feet, he started toward the door, pausing only when the governor demanded to know what he meant to do. "I mean to do what you are either unable or unwilling to do, my lord count," he said sharply. "I am going to restore order in Messina."

<hr />

TURNING AT THE SOUND of his name, Morgan saw a friend, Warin Fitz Gerald, coming toward him. "I just heard about the attack on de Lusignan's house. The king chased the mob off?"

Morgan nodded. "They fled when he rode up with some of his knights. But he has run out of patience, Warin, and he returned to his lodgings to arm himself. I think he means to take the city."

"About time! The lot of them are worse than vultures, eager to pluck our bones clean, and if one of our men dares to venture off on his own, he's likely to end up dead in an alley or floating facedown in the harbor." Warin paused, giving the younger man a quizzical look. "So why are you not happier about it, Morgan? We get to teach those grasping louts a much-needed lesson and have some fun doing it. Yet you look about as cheerful as a Martinmas stoat." Warin was genuinely puzzled, for he knew the Welshman was no battle virgin; he'd bloodied his sword in the service of both the old king and Richard's brother Geoffrey. "Why are you loath to punish the Griffons as they deserve?"

"I am not." Morgan hesitated, not sure he could make Warin understand. "When the king ordered the townsmen to disperse, they defied him at first, jeering and cursing and even daring to make that evil-eye gesture of theirs. He was infuriated by their defiance, angrier than I've ever seen him, and I've seen him as hot as molten lead."

"So? Kings do not take well to mockery. What of it?"

Morgan paused again. How could he admit that he had misgivings about Richard's judgment, that he feared Richard's temper might lead him into doing something rash? He was spared the need to respond, though, for Richard had just ridden into the camp. The knights of his household were gathering around him, and Morgan and Warin hastened to join them. By the time they reached him, Richard had just chosen André de Chauvigny to lead the assault upon the town gates.

André was delighted, but surprised, too, for he'd never known Richard not to be the first one into the breach. "We will need time to make a battering ram, though—"

Richard was already shaking his head. "No . . . take axes and strike at the gate hinges. That will keep them occupied whilst I lead some of our men around to the west. There is a postern gate in the wall there and the approach is so steep that it is not well guarded. We ought to be able to force an entry easily enough, and once we're inside, we can open the gates for the rest of you whilst our galleys attack the city from the sea."

That met with enthusiastic approval. Morgan felt a rush of relief, realizing his qualms had been needless. There was nothing haphazard or impulsive about the battle plan Richard had just proposed; it was well conceived and tactically sound. But he had to ask. "How do you know about that postern gate, sire?"

"The day after my arrival in Messina, I went out and inspected the city's defenses."

Morgan wasn't sure what surprised him the most—that Richard had the foresight to anticipate trouble with the townspeople, or that he sounded so coolly matter-of-fact now. It was as if the liquid fire of Sicily's great volcano had suddenly iced over, he marveled, so dramatic had been this transformation from enraged king to calculating battle commander, and when Richard began to select men for that covert assault upon the postern gate, he was among the first to volunteer.

THE ASCENT WAS A STEEP ONE, but once they reached the postern gate, they discovered that Richard was right and it was unguarded. A startled sentry did not appear until their axes had smashed it open, and his cry of alarm was choked off by a crossbow bolt to the throat. Scrambling through the shattered timbers, they followed Richard into a ghost city, for at first it seemed like one. The street was deserted, and the few civilians they encountered fled before them. They advanced cautiously, knowing word would quickly spread of their intrusion, and people were soon shouting and cursing from open windows. Before long, rocks and crockery and arrows were raining down upon them, but they fended off the aerial onslaught with their shields. One bold householder flung the contents of a chamber pot and drenched an unlucky soldier, much to his outrage and the amusement of the others. He wanted to exact vengeance then and there, but was sternly reminded that they had more pressing matters. He was still arguing about it, though, when one of Richard's scouts came racing back, warning that a large group of men were gathering ahead.

Richard dispatched some of his knights toward a nearby alley, saying it led into a street that ran parallel to their own. Morgan was one of the men chosen for this diversion and they took off at a run, hoping to cover as much distance as possible while they still had the element of surprise. Impressed by the thoroughness of their king's reconnaissance, for the alley had indeed opened into a narrow lane, they hastened along it until they came to a wider cross street. By now they could hear the unmistakable clamor of conflict and they followed the sound, soon coming onto a chaotic scene.

Several carts had been overturned to form an impromptu barricade. The townsmen crouching behind it outnumbered Richard's knights and crossbowmen, but they were mismatched against battle-seasoned, mail-clad warriors and were already giving ground by the time Morgan and his companions assailed them from the rear. Within moments the skirmish was over, the burghers in flight.

Hurrying to keep pace with their king, the men followed him into another alley, barely a sword's length in depth, and saw ahead of them one of the city gates.

Here they encountered fierce resistance from the guards, and in the bloody street battle that ensued, men on both sides began to die. Morgan was caught up in the emotional maelstrom peculiar to combat, a familiar surge of raw sensation in which excitement was indistinguishable from fear. A soldier was lunging forward, shouting in Greek. Morgan was yelling, too, Welsh curses interspersed with the battle cry of the English Royal House, *"Dex aie!"*

His foe's sword was already raised high. It swept down before Morgan could get his shield up to block the blow and he took the hit on his shoulder. A sword could slice through mail with lethal force, but only if it was a direct strike. Morgan was blessed that day, for the aim was off and the blade's edge skipped over the metal links instead of cutting into flesh and bone. He staggered under the impact, somehow kept his balance, and slashed at his adversary's leg. There was a spurt of blood and a scream. As the man's knee buckled, Morgan slammed him with his shield, then hurdled his crumpled body and went to the aid of Baldwin de Bethune, whose sword blade had just broken against an enemy axe.

Baldwin's foe turned swiftly upon Morgan, swinging his axe to hook the edge of the Welshman's shield. But Morgan had been trained to thwart just such a gambit. Instead of instinctively resisting, he let himself be pulled toward his opponent and counterthrust, his sword cutting through the other man's mail coif and slicing off his ear before the blade bit into his neck. As the man fell, Baldwin snatched up his axe, giving Morgan a grateful grin before the tide of battle swept them apart.

Some of Morgan's companions were already starting to loot bodies, but there were still several pockets of fighting, as savage as any drunken alehouse brawl. Morgan caught sight of his king then, just in time to see Richard perform a classic maneuver known as a "Cut of Wrath," making a powerful, downward diagonal strike that severed his attacker's arm at the elbow. Without even pausing for breath, he whirled to take on a new opponent, this one wielding a spear. Morgan started toward them in alarm, for he'd never seen a spear so long. It looked almost like a lance, and he thought it could be difficult for a swordsman to counter its greater reach. But as the man charged him, Richard leaped aside and then brought his sword down upon the weapon, chopping off the spearhead before the man could react. He gaped at his demolished spear, then spun around and fled. Morgan was no less astonished, for the shaft had been reinforced with strips of metal and yet Richard had sliced through it as if it were butter.

As he reached Richard, a cheer went up, for their men had taken control of the gate. As they flung it open, their troops streamed into the city, and they raised another cheer, knowing that Messina was theirs.

RICHARD HAD PICKED UP the broken spear. "Look at this, Morgan. Have you ever seen such a weapon?"

Morgan hadn't. Instead of a spearhead, a hooked blade had been attached to the haft. It was undeniably interesting, but it seemed neither the time nor the place to have a casual conversation about Sicilian innovations in weaponry. Richard had not waited for him to respond, though, and was already beckoning to André de Chauvigny. "Send some of our knights to guard the royal palace. If our lads go looking for booty there, Philippe will have a stark raving fit. There's likely to be more fighting, too, so make sure that our men do not start celebrating until it's safe to do so."

"I'll see to it," André promised. "But afterward . . . they can have their sport?"

Richard nodded. "Yes, but do not let it get out of hand, André. Remind them that we're going to have to spend the winter here. Our men can have their fun, but keep it within reason. No slaughtering the citizens if they're not offering resistance."

Morgan was impressed by Richard's composure in the midst of madness. His own emotions were still in turmoil. He'd killed at least one man and had nearly been killed himself, good reasons to get drunk, he decided. But then he had a better idea and hurried after Richard, who was heading toward the harbor, where smoke had begun to spiral up into the sky.

"My liege, someone ought to bring word to your sister that the city has been captured. She'll be able to see the smoke from Bagnara and will be fearing the worst."

"That is true," Richard conceded. "Good thinking, Cousin. Are you volunteering for the mission?" When Morgan nodded eagerly, Richard slapped him playfully on the shoulder. "You'd best wash up first, then. Women tend to be squeamish about blood and gore."

By the time they reached the harbor, the smoke had become so thick that an early dusk seemed to have settled over the city, the sun utterly obscured by those billowing black clouds. Richard was relieved to discover that the town was not on fire; it was the Sicilian fleet that was burning. Several of his admirals were already on the scene and they began complaining to him about the actions of the French, declaring they'd assisted the townspeople in keeping their ships from entering the inner harbor.

Seeing that Richard would be occupied for some time to come, Morgan sank down on a nearby mounting block. All around him was bedlam. Soldiers were looting shops and houses, gleefully carrying off the riches of Messina—candlesticks, furs, jewelry, bolts of expensive cloth, spices. They were also helping themselves to sides of bacon, sacks of flour, and baskets of eggs, claiming livestock, chickens, and horses. Some were helping themselves to local women, too, for screams were echoing from houses and alleyways. From where he sat, Morgan could see bodies sprawled in the street. He hoped he'd not lost any friends in the fighting. He was more shaken than he was willing to admit, and he decided to find a tavern, a public bathhouse, and a boat to ferry him across the Faro, in that order.

JOANNA HAD WATCHED in dismay as smoke darkened the sky above Messina. She was not surprised when the English lion was soon flying over the city, for Richard was the most celebrated soldier in Christendom. His sister rejoiced in his victory. But the queen could take no pleasure in the sight of a foreign flag on Sicilian soil. She did not doubt that the townspeople of Messina had been vexing, belligerent, and eager for profit, for they were known to be like that with their fellow citizens. They were still William's subjects, her subjects, however, and she grieved that it had come to this.

She'd never expected that she'd have to choose between her two lives, her two worlds. But her precarious position was brought home to her by the Bishop of Bagnara, who'd demanded that she intercede on behalf of the Messinians and berated her as he'd not have dared to berate Richard. He was so incensed that he'd inflamed her own temper; she found herself fiercely defending her brother, burning yet another of her Sicilian bridges. After his angry departure, she'd remained at a window in her bedchamber, staring out across the straits at Messina for hours, her eyes blurring with tears.

Morgan's arrival was the only flicker of light in a very dark day. Heedless of convention, she had him brought to her private chamber, greeting him so warmly that he actually blushed, for he was somewhat in awe of this beautiful cousin whom he'd known for less than a week. Joanna's common sense told her that Morgan could not tell her what she yearned to hear. He could not deny that Messina had fallen to Richard's troops. But she hoped that he might be able to explain the bloodshed in a way that would enable her to accept it as inevitable and thus reconcile her divided loyalties.

It had not occurred to Morgan that she might not see Messina's fall in the same light that he did—as a triumph. The aftermath of battle could be intoxicating, and his senses were still reeling from the sweetness of his reprieve, as well as from several flagons of spiced Messinian wine. The sight of Joanna reminded him of the feats her brother had performed that day, and he launched into an enthusiastic account of the battle, lavishly praising the courage of their men and boasting of the ease with which they'd captured the city.

"Your brother's strategy was brilliant, my lady. He is by far the best battle commander I've ever seen, leading the assault himself, always in the very thick of the fighting." He started to tell her that more than twenty of Richard's own household troops had died in the attack but decided it was better she not know that. "The king is utterly without fear and I understand now why his men vow they'd follow him to Hell and back. So would I, for he is doing God's Work, destined to regain Jerusalem from the infidels."

"You believe that, Morgan . . . truly?" And when he assured her earnestly that he did, Joanna discovered there was comfort in that thought, in the reminder that nothing mattered more than the recovery of the Holy Land. "If Richard is doing God's Work, does that mean the Messinians were heeding the Devil's whispers? Were many of them slain, Cousin?"

"Not so many." He almost added, "Not as many deaths as they deserved," but thought better of it, remembering Richard's warning that women were distressed by violence. "There was plundering, of course, for that is a soldier's right. But the king took measures to make sure there'd be no widespread slaughter."

"I am glad to hear that." She was silent for a few moments before saying softly, "Did . . . did my brother give any orders to protect the women of the city?"

Morgan found himself at a rare loss for words, suddenly realizing that she had come to consider Sicily as her home. He supposed it was to be expected that she'd pity the wives and maidens of Messina, for rape was likely to be a fear ingrained in every woman's soul, even one as highborn as Joanna. He wondered if he ought to lie to her, decided she'd not believe him if he did. "My lady . . . men see that as a soldier's right, too."

She said nothing, but he'd begun to notice the signs of stress—her pallor, the dark hollows under her eyes. "It was not as brutal as it could have been, Madame," he said, and Joanna gave him a wan smile, thinking that was a meager comfort to Messina, yet recognizing the uncompromising truth of it, too.

"It was good of you to bring me word yourself, Cousin Morgan. You'll not be wanting to cross the Faro after dark, so I'll see that a comfortable bed is made ready for you."

"Thank you, Madame." Morgan glanced toward Joanna's attendants, who'd withdrawn across the chamber to give them privacy. The woman he'd wanted to see was not among them. "I was hoping I might pay my respects to the Lady Mariam."

Joanna gave him a surprised look and, then, her first real smile of the day. "Mariam mentioned that she'd met one of Richard's knights at the nunnery, a 'cocky, silver-tongued rogue,' she said, 'with a great interest in learning Arabic.' So that was you, Cousin?"

Morgan grinned, pleased beyond measure that Mariam had discussed him with Joanna; that was surely a good sign. "Do you think she might see me?" But when Joanna hesitated, some of his confidence waned.

"It might be better to wait for another time, Morgan. This has been a difficult day for her."

Morgan was disappointed, but it made sense that Mariam would mourn the fall of Messina, for the blood of a Sicilian king ran in her veins. After taking his leave of Joanna, he was escorted to the priory guest hall. Richard had garrisoned Bagnara with a large number of knights sworn to see to Joanna's safety, and the hall was crowded. Upon learning that Morgan had taken part in the assault upon the town, they were eager to hear his account, and he was quite willing to accommodate them. Eventually, men unrolled blankets and made ready to bed down. Morgan's nerves were still vibrating like a taut bowstring and he knew sleep would not come for hours yet. Helping himself to a wineskin, he wound his way midst the bodies and bedrolls, and then slipped out a side door.

The night was mild, the sky spangled with remote pinpoints of light. On this October evening, his Welsh homeland seemed as distant as those glittering stars. It was a pleasure to inhale air untainted by the coppery smell of blood or the stench of gutted entrails. He would, he decided, find the priory church and offer up prayers for the men who'd died that day. For Joanna's sake, he would pray, too, for Messina's dead.

The church was scented with incense, shadowed and still. Morgan knelt at the high altar and felt a calm descending upon his soul, God's Peace entering his heart. After praying for those who'd died on this October Thursday, he prayed for his dead liege lords, for Geoffrey and Henry, hoping they would not see it as a betrayal—that he'd pledged his loyalty to Richard. He rose with some difficulty, for his body had stiffened in the hours since the battle, his muscles cramping and his shoulder throbbing with the slightest movement. It was already turning the color of summer plums, the bruises seeming to reach into the very marrow of his bones. But the injury could have been worse, could have been fatal. God willing, he would live out his biblical three-score years and ten. If not, better to die before the walls of Jerusalem than in the dusty streets of Messina.

He was about to depart when a gleam of light drew his attention. The windows were encased in glass, yet more proof of the affluence of Sicily, and he could see a faint glow coming from the cloisters. He peered through the cloudy glass, and then he smiled, for a woman was sitting on a bench in one of the carrels, a lantern beside her, a familiar red dog lounging at her feet.

She glanced up at the sound of his footsteps on the walkway, a flicker of recognition crossing her face, followed by a frown. Before she could speak, he said quickly, "Lady Mariam, forgive me for disturbing you. I'd been in the church, praying for those who'd died today." When she did not speak, he moved closer, oddly pleased when Ahmer wagged his tail in a lazy welcome. "I came to tell the queen about the strife in Messina. I can tell you, too, if that be your wish."

She was not wearing a face veil tonight, but her silver bracelets and bright silken gown still gave her an exotic appearance; he was near enough now to catch the faint fragrance of sandalwood, to see the graceful fingers clasped in her lap, decorated with henna in the Saracen fashion. But there was no light in those golden eyes, and he knew at once that this woman was in no mood for playful flirtation or teasing banter.

"What makes you think I'd want to hear about it?"

Her tone was challenging, but he took encouragement from it, nonetheless; at least she was not telling him to go away. "Messina is a Sicilian city," he said, choosing his words with care, "and you are the daughter of a Sicilian king. If the bloodshed brought distress to the Lady Joanna, it must be even more distressing for you."

"Actually, it was not," she said coolly, much to his surprise. "I have no reason to grieve for Messina. Shall I tell you why? Because it is not Palermo."

"I am not sure I understand."

"Why should you?" She'd been curled up on the bench like a sleek, elegant cat, her feet tucked under her skirts, but the tension in her body belied her casual pose. "The inhabitants of Messina are Greek. I believe you call them Griffons. Your men distrust them because they heed the Patriarch of Constantinople and not the Holy Father in Rome. But it is not their religious beliefs that I find objectionable. It is their loathing for those of Saracen blood. Aside from the ones who serve the king, few Saracens dare to dwell in Messina. So I do not mourn that the Messinians have reaped what they have too often sown."

Morgan decided that it would take a lifetime to understand the crosscurrents and rivalries in this strange land called Sicily. "I am not sorry to hear you say that, my lady. I'd feared that you might see me as one of those 'long-tailed Englishmen' who'd wreaked havoc upon the innocent citizens of Messina, that you'd not believe we were provoked into taking control of the city."

He knelt by the bench, ostensibly to pet Ahmer, and looked up intently into her face. "But it is obvious that you are greatly troubled this night. If it is not the bloodshed in Messina, what causes you such sadness? I know it is presumptuous of me to ask such a question. I have found, though, that sometimes it is easier to confide in a stranger, doubtless why so many drunken confessions are exchanged in taverns and alehouses."

She ducked her head, but not in time. Catching that fleeting smile, he felt a triumphant flush, as warming as wine. "Take up my offer, Lady Mariam. I can be a good listener, and surprisingly perceptive for one of those long-tailed English. Although I ought to say at the outset that being called 'English' is a mortal insult to a Welshman."

She gave him a speculative, sidelong glance. "I do not remember telling you my name. How did you learn it?"

"I was not only smitten, I was resourceful, too," he said with a grin. "I befriended some of the abbey servants, asking about the lovely lady with amber-colored eyes who was likely a member of the queen's household. They knew at once whom I meant, told me that my heart had been stolen by King William's sister."

She turned her head to look him full in the face. "They told you, then, that my mother was a Saracen?"

He started to joke that they may have mentioned it, but caught himself in time, sensing that his answer mattered. Dropping his teasing tone, he said only, "Yes, they did."

He saw it was the right answer, saw, too, that she seemed to be wavering. "No," she said, after a long silence. "You would not understand. You know nothing of dual loyalties, of the whispers of the blood."

"Did you not hear me say I am Welsh, *cariad*? Who would know better than a Welshman in the service of an English king?"

Her gaze was searching. "What would you do, then, if your English king led an invasion into Wales?"

"If it were Gwynedd, my loyalty to my family and my homeland would prevail over my loyalty to the king. If he attacked South Wales, it would depend upon the justness of his cause, upon whether I felt that he was in the right."

"You answered that very quickly," she observed. "So quickly that I think you must have given it some thought."

"I have," he admitted, "for there is no love lost between the Welsh and the English. Not that Richard thinks of himself as English. He enjoys ruling over them, but does not see himself as one of them, being a true son of Aquitaine. So you see, my lady, our loyalties are almost as murky as those of you Sicilians." Starting to rise, he found that he had to steady himself with a hand on the bench. "Jesu, I think I aged ten years in the streets of Messina. So . . . now that you know how I would deal with a crisis of conscience, shall we discuss yours?"

Mariam's face was guarded, but her fingers had begun to clench and unclench in her lap. He was willing to wait, and at last she said, "Richard wants Joanna to accompany him to Outremer and she has asked me to come with her."

"May I?" he asked, gesturing toward the bench. When she nodded, he sat down beside her, expelling an audible sigh that had more to do with his aching bones than the proximity of this desirable female body. "We are very enlightened in Wales, allow children born out of wedlock to inherit if they are recognized by their fathers. I would guess that Sicily is as backward as England and France in that regard, but since you're the daughter of a king, I'm guessing, too, that you've been provided for. So you are not dependent upon the queen's bounty and could remain in Palermo if you wish."

Taking her silence as assent, he shifted gingerly on the bench before continuing. "Those helpful abbey servants told me you'd been with Lady Joanna since her arrival in Sicily, so clearly there is a deep affection between you. Why would you balk, then? I can think of only two reasons. Many women would shrink from the hardships and dangers of such a voyage—but not you, Lady Mariam. That leaves those 'whispers of the blood.' You feel a kinship with the Saracens of Sicily, and fear that you may feel kinship, too, with the Saracens of Syria."

She stared at him in astonishment. "You do not know me. As you said, we are strangers. So however did you guess that?"

"We Welsh have second sight."

"I think you do. What is your name—Merlin?"

"Ah, so Lady Joanna has introduced you to the legend of King Arthur, who was Welsh, by the way." Getting stiffly to his feet, he reached for her hand and brushed a kiss across those hennaed fingers. "Ask your queen to tell you about her Welsh cousin. Good night, my lady, and God keep you safe."

"Wait—I have not solved my 'crisis of conscience' yet!"

"Yes, you have. You just were not asking yourself the right question."

Mariam did not know whether to be annoyed or intrigued, finally deciding she was both. "At least tell me what '*cariad*' means."

"You can safely assume it is not a Welsh curse, my lady." Although he'd already moved from the moonlight into the shadows, she could hear the smile in his voice and could not help smiling in return.

Once he'd gone, she slipped off the bench and began to pace the cloisters pathway, Ahmer trailing loyally at her heels. What was the right question, then? She'd been raised at the royal court, but "Merlin" was right; she'd always felt a kinship to her mother's people, the "Saracens of Sicily." Even though most of them still practiced the faith of Islam and she was a Christian, she'd heard those whispers of the blood. Just as "Merlin" had heard the whispers from . . . Gwynedd, was it? What had he said about the other Welsh, though? Ah, yes, that his loyalty would depend upon the justness of the cause.

She came to an abrupt halt, and then bent down and put her arms around the dog. "He was right, Ahmer. I *was* asking the wrong question. Do I believe that Jerusalem should be retaken from the Syrian Saracens? Yes, I do." Hugging the puzzled dog, she began to laugh, so great was her relief. "Of course I do!"

THE ARCHBISHOP OF MONREALE was not sure what sort of reception to expect in Catania. He knew that he and Chancellor Matthew had not been in the king's good graces lately, for they'd been telling him what he did not want to hear—that an alliance with the English would better serve Sicily's interests than one with the French. Now that the English king had dared to seize the second city of his realm, whose voices was Tancred more likely to heed—those demanding vengeance or those urging moderation and restraint?

Before he could make his presence known to the king, he was intercepted by the chancellor. Following Matthew into the chapel, he said dryly, "I assume we are not here to pray?"

Matthew smiled. "Given my sinful past, I have need of all the prayers I can get. But I wanted to speak with you ere you see the king. Jordan Lapin and the admiral got here first, and as you'd expect, they were in a rage, the killing kind. Not only did the city fall whilst they looked on, their houses were amongst those plundered by the English. So quite understandably, they are hell-bent upon war. As are Tancred's brother-in-law and most of his council, especially after they learned of the French king's offer."

"What offer, Matthew?"

"You'd almost think Messina was a French city, so great was Philippe's fury. Some of it is wounded pride. The Messinians had appealed to him for protection, and then he had to stand by and watch whilst Richard captured the city in less time than it would take a priest to chant Matins. But much of it seems to be pure and honest hatred. If I were a gambling man, I'd be giving odds that the English and the French turn upon each other long ere they ever reach the Holy Land."

"The offer, Matthew," the archbishop prodded. "What was the offer?"

"Philippe sent the Duke of Burgundy to Tancred, suggesting that they form an alliance against Richard, promising the use of French troops in an attack upon the English."

The archbishop's jaw dropped. "What does the king say to this?"

"His head is at war with his heart. He knows that Heinrich von Hohenstaufen is our true enemy, but Richard's arrogance is a bitter brew to swallow. I'd still hoped to be able to convince him that Richard would make a more useful ally than Philippe. But now I fear that this offer from the French might tip the scales in favor of war with the English."

"I think I'd best see the king straightaway, then," the archbishop said, "for I have information about the French king that he needs to know."

TANCRED LOOKED HAGGARD, his sallow complexion and red-rimmed eyes testifying to anxious days and sleepless nights. "Sit down, my lord archbishop," he said wearily. "But do not waste your breath arguing that the English king's enmity toward Hohenstaufen matters more than his outrageous seizure of Messina. I've already heard enough of that from the chancellor."

"You well know that the English king is no friend to the Holy Roman Emperor, my liege, so there is no need to remind you of it. I would rather talk with you about the French king."

"Matthew told you of the Duke of Burgundy's message? I admit I was taken by surprise. But the duke brought a letter in Philippe's own hand, apparently written whilst the city was still under attack, for it is splattered with ink blots as if he were gripping his pen like a sword. Show him the letter, Matthew. Let him see for himself."

"I do not doubt the sincerity of the French king's rage, sire. But his actions after the fall of the city do raise doubts about the sincerity of his offer. As angered as he was by Richard's attack upon Messina, he was even angrier to see the English flag flying over the city afterward. He demanded that the French flag be flown instead, reminding Richard of a pact they'd made at Vézelay to share equally all spoils during their campaign."

Tancred stiffened. "You are sure of this?"

"I am, my lord. As you'd expect, Richard did not take kindly to the demand. I heard that his first impulse was to tell Philippe exactly where he could fly those French flags, in vivid and rather obscene detail. But when he calmed down, he agreed to replace his banners with those of the Hospitallers and the Templars, putting the city in their custody until he could come to terms with you."

Tancred slumped back in his chair as the other men exchanged troubled glances. Richard was not going to be satisfied until Tancred turned over Joanna's dower and William's legacy. But once this was done, he'd be more amenable than Philippe to an alliance against the Holy Roman Empire. Tancred knew this, for he was far from a fool. But would he be willing to put Sicily's welfare above his lacerated pride?

RICHARD ARRIVED in Bagnara bearing gifts—casks of wine for his knights and a beautiful chestnut mare for his sister, white mules for her ladies. He brought word, too, that peace reigned in Messina now that the dead had been buried, hostages taken for the citizens' good behavior in the future, prices set for bread and wine, and some of the plundered goods returned. He was in such high spirits that Joanna suspected he had more to tell her, and that would prove to be true.

"I AM SORRY I could not come over sooner, Joanna, but for the past few days I've been having secret negotiations with the Archbishop of Monreale and the chancellor's son; the old man's health did not allow him to make the trip from Catania."

"There is no need to apologize, Richard. I know there were not enough hours in the day to get everything sorted out. Besides, Morgan has been very conscientious about keeping us informed of developments in Messina. Hardly a day has passed without him paying us a visit."

"Yes, I'd noticed the lad was spending much of his time here in Bagnara this week. Need I remind him that you and he are cousins, *irlanda*?"

"I do enjoy his company, for I suspect he is a bit of a rake, and women always find men like that irresistible," she said with a laugh. "But it is not my charms that are luring him across the Faro. He is very taken with Mariam."

Richard was not sure who Mariam was, had no real interest in finding out. "Are you not going to ask how the negotiations with Tancred are going?"

"Since you have that cat-in-the-cream look about you, Brother, I'm guessing they are going well."

"Better than that, lass. Tancred and I have made peace, and he has agreed to compensate you for the loss of your dower lands. How does twenty thousand ounces of gold sound to you?"

To Joanna, that sounded very good, indeed. "That is wonderful, Richard!" she cried, and flung herself into his arms. "And what of William's legacy?"

"Another twenty thousand ounces in gold," Richard said, sounding very pleased with himself. "Officially it is to be an advance payment for the marriage of his daughter to my heir, and is to be paid to the girl when the marriage takes place . . . if it ever does. It is a satisfactory arrangement, saving Tancred's pride and giving me the use of the money in the Holy Land. I might well need to draw upon your share, too, Joanna, depending upon how long we're in Outremer. Would you have any objections to this?"

"Of course not, Richard! I'd not begrudge you my last copper *follaris*," she promised, generously and a little recklessly. "You said there is to be a marriage? Tancred's daughters are very young, but is he willing to wait until you have a son? He does not know about Berengaria, after all."

"No, Tancred preferred a flesh-and-blood heir for his girl. So I had to provide one for him."

"But Johnny already has a wife. You told me you'd permitted him to wed the Gloucester heiress."

"I did. Since they'd not been granted a dispensation for their marriage—they are cousins—I suppose it might have been possible to have it annulled. But I was not about to pay the Pope's price for a favor like that. Fortunately I had another prospect, this one happily free of any marital entanglements—my little nephew Arthur."

"Good Heavens, Richard!" Joanna was shocked that he seemed so casual about the succession to the English Crown, switching heirs as if it were of no greater matter than switching saddles. But then she realized why; he did not expect either John or Arthur to succeed him. And God willing, Berengaria would give him a son; she fervently hoped so. What of Johnny, though? How would he take this?

"I was very fond of Johnny once," she said. "We were the two youngest, together at Fontevrault Abbey, and it was only natural that we'd form a bond. Granted, I have not seen him since I was ten and he was nine, so I know naught about the man he's become. But you indicated that he sees himself and not Arthur as your heir. Will he not be very disappointed when he hears of this treaty with Tancred?"

"I suppose," he said and shrugged. "But I never formally named him as my heir. He must have realized that it is likely I'd wed and sire a son of my own and, if not, that is his misfortune, not mine. I have already dispatched Hugh de Bardolf to England; he sailed this morning. With luck, he'll bring the news to my justiciar, Longchamp, ere Johnny gets wind of it. If you're right and Johnny does take it badly, Longchamp will make sure that he does no more than sulk."

Joanna hoped that would be so. "I am glad that you've come to terms with Tancred, Richard. As dearly as I love Constance, I would not have wanted to see Heinrich ruling over Sicily. From what I've heard of the man, he is one to nurse a grievance to the grave. I do not know about Johnny, but I am sure you've made an enemy of Heinrich. He is going to be utterly enraged when he learns that Tancred's kingship has been formally recognized by England. With this treaty, you may have earned his undying enmity."

"I would hope so!" he said and laughed, sounding so carefree and confident that she could not help laughing with him.

WHEN PHILIPPE LEARNED that Tancred had agreed to pay Richard forty thousand ounces of gold, he was infuriated and claimed half of that amount as his share. Richard was no less infuriated by this demand, pointing out that Joanna's dower could not possibly be considered spoils of war. The French king remained adamant, though, and Richard eventually and very grudgingly agreed to give Philippe a third, for he feared that the French might desert the crusade if he did not. After they'd patched up this latest dispute, they settled down to pass the winter in Messina and to await the return of favorable winds in the spring. But unbeknownst to Philippe, Richard was also awaiting the arrival of his mother and betrothed.

CHAPTER 11

amplona was an ancient city, founded by the Roman general Pompey. Located on the pilgrim road to the holy shrine of San Juan Compostela, it was the Navarrese city best known to the world beyond the Pyrenees, and at one time Navarre had even been called the Kingdom of Pamplona. But Sancho de Jimenez spent little time there, for it was an Episcopal city, and his relationship with its bishop was a tense one. So the impending arrival of the English queen posed a dilemma for him. He'd have preferred to entertain her at Tudela, yet it seemed very inhospitable to expect her to travel another sixty miles after such a long journey; even his palace at Olite was still almost thirty miles farther south. He'd been building a residence in Pamplona, but it was not completed. He'd finally decided that Eleanor's comfort mattered more than his reluctance to request a favor from a man he disliked. The bishop was quite willing to play host to his king and his royal guest, relishing an opportunity to have Sancho in his debt and curious, too, to meet the woman who'd been the subject of so much gossip for more than half a century.

ELEANOR'S WELCOME had been lavish enough to please all concerned: a princely feast meant to show her that Pamplona could match the splendors of Poitiers and Paris. The guests had not departed to their lodgings in the bishop's palace or within the city until long after darkness had descended upon the Arga River valley. But not all were ready for their beds, and Sancho's eldest son and namesake was walking in the gardens with his sister.

"So . . . what did you think of your future mother-in-law, little one?"

"I found her to be gracious, charming, and rather formidable," Berengaria said and then paused. "As long as she lives, there will be two Queens of England."

"For some brides, that would be one queen too many. But not you?" Sancho asked, even though he was sure he already knew the answer.

"She is Richard's mother. I will be Richard's wife. I do not see why we must be rivals, much less adversaries. I am sure we can both carve out our own domains, hers in the council chamber and mine in the bedchamber. Besides," she said, with a faint smile, "I would be foolish, indeed, to begin a war I could not hope to win."

Sancho smiled, too. "How did one so young become so wise?" he teased before saying, on a more serious note, "You'll need to keep your wits about you in that family, for they are not like us, little one."

"The Devil's Brood?"

"Ah, so you heard that, did you? You know I count Richard as a friend, but he and his brothers could have taught Cain and Abel about brotherly strife. And his war with his sire was proof to many that St Bernard was right when he said the Angevins came from the Devil and to the Devil they'd go. It will not be easy for you to understand them, coming from a family as tightly knit as ours."

"But their family is not utterly lacking in love, Sancho. Richard is fond of his sisters, and all know he and his mother are like spokes on the same wheel."

Sancho knew how deeply Berengaria missed their own mother, who'd died in childbirth when she was nine, and he was not surprised that she sounded wistful of Richard's close bond with Eleanor. He hoped she had no illusions about Eleanor filling that void for her. Fortunately, his sister had always been sensible, for he suspected that a starry-eyed romantic would not have fared well as Richard's wife. He knew Berengaria's delicate appearance and serene demeanor belied an inner will as strong as his own. He was protective of her, nonetheless, and found himself asking now, even though it was too late, "You are content with this match . . . truly?"

"Of course I am, Sancho," she said at once, wanting to put his mind at ease. She was scrupulously honest, though, and felt compelled to confide, "I confess it is not the destiny I'd expected for myself. I have always yearned for tranquility and I suspect life with Richard will be anything but tranquil."

Coming from anyone else, he'd have taken that for a droll understatement. But his sister lacked any sense of the absurd and would not see the irony in it—that a young woman who'd once thought of becoming a nun, craving neither attention nor influence and comfortable in the shadows, was about to wed the most renowned king in Christendom, a man who gloried in his fame and wielded power as zestfully as he handled a sword.

Berengaria read faces well and saw the shadow that crossed his. "But it is the destiny that the Almighty and our father chose for me, Sancho, and I do not question it. It is flattering, too, that Richard should have picked me, for he has seen me and knows that I am no great beauty." When he would have protested, she stopped him with a smile. "Bless you, dearest, but I possess a mirror. Mind you, I am not saying I am plain or drab. I think my eyes are my best feature, and I've been told I have a pleasing smile. But I am not a beauty as Richard's mother was, or as his sisters are said to be. So it is good that we've already met and I need not worry that he might be disappointed."

Sancho was touched by her matter-of-fact appraisal of her attributes. "Richard is a lucky man," he said and snatched her up in his arms, whirling her around while she protested this was not seemly, but laughing, too.

Neither one had heard the footsteps on the path or realized that their father was watching with a fond smile. As always he was amused by the contrast they presented. Berengaria was barely five feet and Sancho towered above her like a vast oak, for he was said to be the tallest man in all of Navarre, more than seven feet in height, one reason why he'd become known as Sancho el Fuerte—Sancho the Strong. Sancho senior had been given an accolade of his own, Sancho el Sabio—Sancho the Wise—a tribute to his shrewdness in dealing with his powerful, predatory neighbors in Castile and Aragon. Berengaria's marriage had further enhanced his reputation in the eyes of his subjects, for what better ally could Navarre have than the redoubtable Lionheart?

But on this moonlit October night in the Bishop of Pamplona's garden, the king found himself beset with a father's misgivings. He loved all five of his children, even more fiercely since the tragic loss of his wife, but Berengaria had always been his secret favorite. He knew he was being foolish, for she was nigh on twenty-one, well past the age when princesses were wed. It was time for her to try her wings. Yet how empty the nest would be without her.

"Papa!" Berengaria blushed at being caught in such tomfoolery and made Sancho put her down. Coming toward him, she turned her cheek for his kiss. "The revelries were truly spectacular. People will be talking of it for weeks to come."

"I daresay even the most illustrious Queen of England was duly impressed," Sancho said with a grin, for their father's admiration of Eleanor of Aquitaine had long been a family joke. He'd met her in Limoges nigh on twenty years ago, and had returned to Navarre singing her praises so enthusiastically that his own queen had feigned jealousy. He'd even interceded on Eleanor's behalf after her ill-fated rebellion, asking Henry to show her mercy, a gallant gesture that had pleased Sancho's wife and irked the English king. In welcoming Richard's mother to Pamplona, he was also entertaining a glamorous ghost from his past, and the obvious pleasure he'd taken in the reunion gave his children pleasure, too.

"Yes, it did go well," he agreed modestly, as if he'd not fretted over every detail beforehand. "Our esteemed bishop is claiming full credit, of course. But at least he is no longer grumbling about being a member of your escort, Berenguela. He is finally seeing it as the honor it is." He glanced questioningly then at Sancho. "Have you told her yet, lad?"

Sancho shook his head, for he'd known their father would want to do it. He watched, still smiling, as their sire took Berengaria's hands in his. "Your brother and I have been discussing it, sweetheart, and we've decided that he will accompany you on your bridal journey."

Berengaria's delight was revealing, showing how much she was dreading that final farewell. For once utterly oblivious to her dignity, she embraced her father with a squeal of joy, and then pulled her brother's head down so she could scatter haphazard kisses into his beard. Laughing, Sancho warned that he could not escort her all the way to Messina, not daring to spare so much time away from Navarre. But he would see her safely across France and through the alpine passes into Italy, he promised, and saw that he could not have given her a more welcome wedding gift.

Berengaria soon retired for the evening, but before returning to the great hall to collect her duennas, she bade them good night with a smile radiant enough to rival the silvered Spanish moonlight. They watched her go in silence, and as soon as she was out of earshot, Sancho's father said softly, almost as if to himself, "Am I doing right by her?"

Sancho looked at him in surprise. "Papa, you've arranged a brilliant future for her!"

"Yes . . . but will she be happy?"

Sancho doubted that there was another king under God's sky who'd have asked a question like that. But his parents' marriage had been that rarest of rarities, a political union that had evolved into a genuine love match. He was sure that his father had never been unfaithful to his mother, and he was still faithful to her memory. In the eleven years since her death, he'd taken concubines from time to time, but he'd not taken another wife, and Sancho did not think he ever would.

"Yes, Papa," he said, with all the conviction at his command, "I do think Berenguela will be happy as Richard's queen."

He could see that his father took comfort from his certainty, and he was glad of it. It was not as if he'd lied, after all. Why would Berenguela and Richard not find contentment together? The ideal wife was one who was chaste, obedient, and loyal. Berenguela would come to her marriage bed a virgin and would never commit the sin of adultery. She believed it was a wife's duty to be guided by her husband. And she would be loyal to Richard until her last mortal breath—whether he deserved it or not.

RICHARD'S FATHER had been renowned for the speed of his campaigns; Henry had once covered two hundred miles in just four days. Most travelers set a more measured pace and would be very pleased to manage thirty miles a day in summer and twenty in winter. Traveling with a large retinue slowed the rate of speed, however, and Eleanor and Berengaria were averaging only about fifteen miles a day, for they were accompanied by Poitevin bishops and barons, Navarrese prelates and lords, ladies-in-waiting, grooms, servants, knights, and enough soldiers to guarantee their safety. The presence of women inevitably slowed them down, for they had to ride sidesaddle or in horse litters. But so far they'd not encountered any severe storms and Eleanor remained confident that they would be able to reach Naples by mid-February, where Richard's ships would be waiting to convey them to Messina.

Within a month of departing Pamplona, they'd reached the city of Avignon, where they crossed the River Rhone over the splendid new St Benezet Bridge, and then followed the old Roman road north along the River Durance. As they'd traveled through southern France, they'd accepted the hospitality of the local nobility—the Trencavels of Carcassonne, Viscountess Ermengard of Narbonne, the ailing Lord of Montpelier—although they'd detoured around Toulouse, whose count was no friend to the Angevins. When castles were not available, they stayed at monasteries, but rarely for more than a night, as Eleanor was determined to get to Sicily before February 27 and the start of Lent, when marriages would be banned.

That was the only intimate confidence she'd shared with Berengaria so far—her confession that she very much wanted to attend Richard's wedding. She was quite willing to discuss politics and statecraft with her son's betrothed, and she was willing, too, to indulge Berengaria's curiosity and tell her stories of Richard's boyhood. But she revealed nothing of herself, to Berengaria's disappointment, for the younger woman hoped that they might forge a bond during their long journey.

Berengaria did form an unexpected friendship, though, with one of Eleanor's ladies, the Countess of Aumale. Wary initially of the countess's sarcastic asides, she was gradually won over by Hawisa's often startling candor. Hawisa had proven to be a good source of information, too, for her first husband had been a close friend of the old king. From her, Berengaria learned that Nicholas de Chauvigny, the courtly middle-aged knight in charge of Eleanor's household, had been with her when she was captured by Henry's men and had been imprisoned for his loyalty to the queen. She pointed out one of the notorious de Lusignan clan and shocked Berengaria by telling her how they'd dared to ambush Eleanor in a fool-hardy abduction attempt after Henry had seized their major stronghold. A young knight, William Marshal, had held them at bay long enough for the queen to escape, thus beginning his illustrious career in the service of the English Crown.

Berengaria thought the de Lusignans sounded more like brigands than vassals, yet she had to admit their history could have come straight from a troubadour's tale. After numerous rebellions, several brothers from the unruly family had sought their fortunes in Outremer, where Guy de Lusignan had unexpectedly made a brilliant marriage with Sybilla, the elder sister of Baldwin, the Leper King. After Baldwin's death, the crown had eventually passed to Sybilla and Guy, and this highly unpopular knight, a younger son with limited prospects, found him-self the King of Jerusalem. His reign had been a disaster, for he'd rashly led his army against Salah al-Dīn at the Horns of Ḥaṭṭīn and suffered a devastating defeat, one which led to the capture of the Holy City. Freed by Salah al-Dīn, who'd said that kings did not kill kings, he'd returned to Tyre, the only city still in Christian hands. But Tyre was now under the control of Conrad d'Aleramici, son of the Marquis of Montferrat, an Italian-German aristocrat and adventurer who'd won the gratitude of the citizens by staving off a Saracen attack, and Conrad not only refused to acknowledge Guy as his king, he'd refused Guy entry into the city. Guy had no political skills or sense, but he'd never lacked for courage and he'd ridden off to lay siege to Acre. To the surprise of Saracens and Christians alike, this gallant, foolhardy gesture inspired others; and as the siege dragged on, more and more men joined Guy before the walls of Acre. He was still a king without a kingdom, though, his fierce rivalry with Conrad yet another problem confronting Richard and Philippe upon their arrival in the Holy Land.

The winter had been mild so far, but it was snowing when they reached the town of Sisteron, situated on both sides of the Durance in a narrow gap between two mountain ranges. Here they hired the local guides known as *"marons"* and encountered travelers who'd trekked from Italy into France and were eager to share their stories of hardship and peril, dramatic tales of deadly avalanches and steep alpine paths and dangers so great that it was easy to conclude Hell was an icy, frigid wasteland, not the fiery pits of flame proclaimed by priests.

Their progress slowed dramatically; on some days, they only covered three or four miles. The *marons* led the way, using long staves to test the snow's depth, setting out wooden stakes to mark the path. It was bitterly cold now, their breaths lingering in the air like wisps of pallid smoke, men's beards stiff with hoarfrost, tears freezing in the time it took to trickle down chapped, reddened skin. The cloud-shrouded jagged peaks sometimes blotted out the sun, and the winds roared relentlessly through the ravines, the eerie echoes reminding them that dragons were said to dwell in ice caves on the barren slopes. The routier Mercadier scoffed at these legends, though, wanting to know why any sensible dragon would choose to freeze its bleeding ballocks off instead of flying away to warmer climes.

Berengaria disapproved of his crude language, but appreciated his pointing out the obvious to their men; there was enough to fear in the Alps without adding dragons and monsters to the list. She had very ambivalent feelings about Mercadier, for Hawisa had acquainted her with his fearsome past. This dark-haired man with the sinister scar had an even more sinister reputation, one of the most notorious of the routiers who sold their swords to the highest bidder. It was said that grass withered where he'd walked, Hawisa murmured, eyeing Mercadier with fascinated horror. But he'd served Richard faithfully for the past seven years, she assured Berengaria, and his presence here showed the king's concern for the safety of his mother and his betrothed. Berengaria agreed that Mercadier's very appearance would be enough to frighten off most bandits, for he looked like one of Lucifer's own. She found it disquieting, though, that Richard would admit an ungodly routier into his inner circle, and she realized how little she really knew about the man she'd soon wed.

The women had to ride astride now, for sidesaddles were too dangerous. They'd been forced to leave their carts behind in Sisteron, transferring the contents to pack mules and bearers, men who made their living as the *marons* did, by braving the mountain passes in all but the worst weather. The air was so thin that some were suffering headaches, queasiness, and shortness of breath, common complaints of those unaccustomed to such heights, according to the *marons*.

They spent Christmas in the village of Briançon, just a few miles from the Mont-genèvre Pass, but a storm blew in soon afterward, trapping them for more than a week, and they were not able to continue their journey until the approach of Epiphany.

They passed the night at a travelers hospice and departed at first light, after kneeling in the snow as one of the bishops prayed to the "Holy Lord, Almighty Father, and Eternal God," entreating Him to send His angels of peace to show His servants the way and to let the Holy Spirit accompany them in their time of need. And then they began their trek up Montgenèvre.

The sky was a blanched blue-ice that seemed as bloodless and frozen as the lifeless, empty landscape, and the surrounding drifts of snow were so blindingly bright that they had to squint and shade their eyes. They were vastly relieved to reach the summit of the pass, only to realize that the worst still lay ahead of them. The men would have to dismount and lead their horses, the *marons* directed, and the queen and her ladies must be strapped into ox hides so they could be slid down the slope. None bridled at the *marons'* assertiveness, for on the alpine heights of Montgenèvre, theirs was the command of kings. Seeing the dismay on so many faces, the *marons* tried to reassure these novice mountaineers that it could have been much worse. There had been journeys when the horses had to be lowered on ropes, their legs bound. This time they need only blindfold the more fearful of the animals, they said cheerfully. After an oppressive silence, Hawisa stirred nervous laughter when she said, as if ordering a cup of wine, "I'll take a blindfold, too, if you please."

Eleanor had crossed the Alps once before; she'd been much younger then, though. "I never expected to be sledding down a mountain at my age," she mut-tered to Hawisa, but she was the first to allow herself to be wrapped in an ox hide, for queens led by example. It was a rough, bumpy ride, but she made only one concession to the brittle bones and physical frailties of a woman of sixty-six, clos-ing her eyes during the most perilous part of the descent. She could hear horses whinnying in fright, could hear men's muffled oaths as they edged along the trail, sometimes on their hands and knees, and then, hysterical sobbing. She was thank-ful when the cries were abruptly cut off, for they'd been warned that even loud talking could bring on an avalanche. She wondered if that terrified woman was one of her ladies or one of Berengaria's. She wondered, too, if any queen had ever been swallowed up in an alpine crevice. Was Harry watching from Purgatory and laughing? And how in God's Name had the Carthaginian general Hannibal ever gotten elephants across the Alps?

A hospice was nestled at the foot of the pass, its monks waiting to welcome the shaken, shivering travelers with mulled wine and the promise of food and beds for the night; they knew from experience that even highborn guests would not complain if the wine was weak, the blankets frayed, and the straw mattresses infested with fleas, so thankful would they be to have survived their pilgrimage through the Montgenèvre Pass. The women were escorted to safety first; it would be hours before the pack mules and the last of the bearers trudged into the hospice. They huddled in front of the open hearth, seeking to thaw frozen fingers and feet, expressing their heartfelt relief that the worst was over. Until they had to return in the spring, Hawisa reminded them darkly, and it would be almost as dangerous then, for the *marons* claimed avalanches were more common when the snows began to melt. "I may well start life anew in Sicily," she declared, so dramatically that Eleanor could not help smiling, and held out her wine cup for Hawisa to share, a gesture of royal favor that caused some of the other women to look askance at the countess.

Hawisa drank deeply, sighing with pleasure as the wine's warmth flowed into her veins. "Did you hear that Spanish girl, Uracca?" she asked the queen. "She was on the verge of panic, and it might well have spread. But Mercadier strode over and stopped her screams by clamping his hand over her mouth. She was quiet as a mouse after that!"

"I daresay she was," Eleanor said dryly, for she'd noticed Mercadier's unsettling affect upon women; they were either appalled or secretly attracted in spite of themselves. When she said as much to Hawisa, the countess laughed, saying she'd never confess which response was hers, and Eleanor laughed, too, for the younger woman's blithe insouciance stirred echoes of a dearly missed friend, Maud, the Countess of Chester.

"Of course, once we were safe, Uracca went off in a fury to Berengaria, complaining that a 'lowborn routier' had dared to lay his hands upon her. But Berengaria surprised me. She gave the girl a right sharp talking to, saying that she'd put us all at risk. She then told her, more kindly, that it is only natural to be afraid, but a gentlewoman must not give in to it."

Eleanor glanced across the chamber, where Berengaria was conversing quietly with her brother; she missed no opportunities to spend time with Sancho, for he'd soon be leaving them, planning to go no farther than Milan. "Blood does tell," she agreed. "Berengaria has shown commendable courage so far. I am sure she has not endured hardships like these, but she never complains. I think she will make Richard a good wife."

"Mayhap you ought to tell her that, Madame."

Eleanor was taken by surprise. "Mayhap I will," she said at last, and Hawisa hoped that she would, knowing how much her praise would mean to Berengaria. She'd not expected to like Richard's young bride as much as she did, and she wished the girl well, even though she was certain that a wife would always be incidental to a military man like Richard. But that did not mean their marriage would not be a success. All that truly mattered was that Berengaria fulfilled her duties as a queen—that she provide Richard with a son and heir.

ALL OF THEM were thankful to leave the Alps behind, but Eleanor was particularly happy to cross into Italy, for she hoped now to be able to reestablish contact with Richard. She hoped, too, to learn the reason for her daughter's disquieting silence. As soon as they reached Turin, where they accepted the hospitality of the young Count of Savoy, she immediately dispatched a courier with instructions to ride with all possible speed to Genoa and there take ship for Messina, carrying a letter to her son. The teenage count knew nothing of the events in Sicily, though. She had somewhat better luck at Milan, where the bishop had heard of a peace made between Richard and the Sicilian king, Tancred. But he could tell her nothing of Joanna. Eleanor consoled herself with common sense; surely word would have gotten out if evil had befallen Joanna? She was not surprised by the lack of information, for Sicily must seem as remote to the people of the Piedmont region as the moon in the heavens. At least she'd learn more in Rome, for the papacy had a vested interest in the fate of the Sicilian kingdom.

Bishop Milo insisted upon accompanying them through Piedmont, an act of commendable courtesy in light of the fact that their next stop would be Lodi, which had long been a bitter rival of Milan. Eleanor had already contacted the bishop of that riverside town to arrange for accommodations, and they departed Milan before dawn, for Lodi was more than twenty miles away. They set a faster pace than usual, but darkness had long since fallen by the time they saw the city walls in the distance. Cursing the weakness of age, Eleanor had been forced to ride the last part of the journey in her horse litter, and she leaned out the window at the sound of shouting. The young knight who'd ridden on ahead to let the Bishop of Lodi know of their impending arrival was back. His mount was lathered, evidence of haste, and Eleanor beckoned to him. "Is something amiss? The bishop is still expecting us?"

"Yes, Madame, he is. But he is as flustered as a rabbit in a fox den," the youth said and then grinned. "He did not expect to be entertaining the Queen of England and the King and Queen of Germany at the same time, but that is what he's facing. Heinrich von Hohenstaufen and the Lady Constance arrived this morn with a vast entourage—a baker's dozen of bishops, several German counts, Lord Boniface of Montferrat, and so many knights and men-at-arms it would take half a day to count them all."

Eleanor sat back against the cushions as she processed this startling news. "So his war against Tancred has begun. Passing strange that he'd not have waited until the spring. Few campaigns are fought in winter."

"He has a pressing need to get to Rome, Madame—to be crowned by the Holy Father without delay."

Eleanor drew a sharp breath. "His father is dead?"

"Yes, my lady, he is. According to the bishop, the Emperor Frederick Barbarossa drowned last summer whilst trying to cross a river in Armenia. His younger son led their army on to the Holy Land, but most of them died or deserted along the way. Heinrich did not learn of his father's death until last month, and set out for Rome as soon as he could. The bishop says that once he is crowned as emperor, he'll lead his army into Sicily to claim the throne."

Frederick's death would be a blow to Richard and the other crusaders, for Heinrich was not likely to take the cross, at least not until he'd been crowned as King of Sicily. It would be an even greater blow to Tancred, for now Heinrich could draw upon all the resources of the Holy Roman Empire to win his war. The ramifications of Frederick's death would be felt throughout Christendom. But it would begin in Lodi, with this chance meeting of Richard's mother and an avowed enemy of their House.

"Well," Eleanor said, after several moments of silence, "this ought to be interesting."

BECAUSE HEINRICH WAS AN ALLY of the French king, they decided that it would be best if Berengaria's true identity was not made known to him, and she agreed to pose as one of Eleanor's ladies. The Bishop of Milan already knew that she was the Navarrese king's daughter, but he was quite willing to honor Eleanor's request for secrecy. Although it was almost thirty years since Heinrich's father had deliberately reduced the city of Milan to rubble and charred timbers, the Milanese had long memories.

Berengaria's parting from her brother had been painful, for she did not know when they'd meet again. She kept her grieving to herself, though, and prepared to follow Eleanor's lead when they met the new Holy Roman Emperor and his consort. She was not sure what to expect, given Heinrich's hostility toward the English Crown. But when she broached the subject with Eleanor, the older woman laughed, saying that she and Heinrich would be poisonously polite, scrupulously observe all the proprieties, and then studiously avoid each other for the balance of their joint stay in Lodi. She even sounded grimly amused at the prospect, and to Berengaria, that was further proof that she'd never fully understand the enigmatic English queen. *They are not like us, little one.*

HEINRICH VON HOHENSTAUFEN was not as Berengaria had envisioned him. He was of moderate height, but seemed shorter because of his slight, almost frail physique. His face would have been handsome if it was not so thin, and his fine blond hair and patchy beard made him seem even younger than his twenty-five years. He could not have been more unlike her brother Sancho or her betrothed, the Lionheart, and her first impression was that he was not at all kingly. But she changed her mind as soon as she looked into those piercing pale eyes, for what she saw in their depths sent an involuntary shiver up her spine.

Thinking that she'd not have wanted to be wed to this man, Berengaria had glanced toward his wife with both sympathy and curiosity, for her father's sister Margarita had often written to them about life at the Sicilian court. Constance de Hauteville was as tall as her husband, very elegant in a lilac gown embroidered with gold threads and tiny seed pearls. Her veil and wimple hid her hair, but Berengaria was sure she'd been blessed with the flaxen tresses so praised by troubadours, for her skin was very white and her eyes were an extraordinary shade of blue, star sapphires framed by thick golden lashes. Berengaria had expected her to be fair, for the de Hautevilles were as acclaimed for their good looks as Henry and Eleanor's brood. Time or marriage had not been kind to Constance, though; in her mid-thirties now, she was almost painfully thin, and what remained of her beauty had become a brittle court mask. Her manners were flawless, her bearing regal. But Berengaria could see in this aloof, self-possessed woman no traces of the girl in her aunt Margarita's letters, the fey free spirit who'd been privileged to grow up in Eden.

Just as Eleanor had predicted, the conversation was coldly correct. She'd offered her condolences for the death of Heinrich's father and received an appropriate response in return. They then talked of the weather and their respective journeys through the Alps, both agreeing that his had been the easier route, for the Brenner Pass was at a much lower altitude than Montgenèvre. The stilted dialogue was rendered even more awkward by their language barrier, and long pauses ensued while Heinrich's German was translated into French for Eleanor's benefit and her replies were then repeated in his native tongue. The visibly nervous Bishop of Lodi had finally begun to relax, thinking this unsettling encounter was almost over, when Heinrich chose to veer off the road paved with platitudes.

His translator gave him a startled look, and then lowered his eyes discreetly as he relayed the message to Eleanor. "My lord king says that he was pleased to hear of your arrival, Madame, for he is sure that you could not have reached such a venerable age without acquiring the prudence and wisdom that your son so obviously lacks. It is his hope that you will exert your influence with the King of the English ere it is too late. His rash decision to embrace that bastard Tancred and even to sanctify their unholy alliance by wedding his heir, Arthur of Brittany, to the usurper's daughter is one that will cost England dearly—unless you can convince him that he has made a monumental blunder."

Berengaria was grateful that no eyes were upon her, for she could not suppress a gasp. When she looked toward Eleanor, she felt a flicker of admiration, for the queen did not even blink at the astonishing news that her son John had been disinherited in favor of a Breton child who was not yet four years old. "Tell Lord Heinrich," she said, with a smile barbed enough to draw blood, "that I have the utmost confidence in the judgment of my son, the English king. I will overlook his blatant bad manners, though, as reaching such a 'venerable age' has given me a greater understanding of the human heart. It must be unbearably humiliating and humbling for him—being rejected by the lords and citizens of Sicily in favor of a man born out of wedlock."

The translator looked as if he'd swallowed his tongue. "Madame, I . . . I cannot tell him that!"

"Of course you cannot," the Bishop of Milan interceded smoothly. "Let me do it." And Milo gleefully proceeded to do just that, in fluent Latin. By the time he was done, Heinrich's pale skin was blotched with hot color. He spat out something in German, then turned on his heel and stalked away, as the counts of Eppan and Shaumberg and the Bishop of Trent jettisoned their dignity and scurried to catch up with him.

Constance did not follow. Instead she accepted a wine cup from a passing servant and smiled blandly at Eleanor. "I'd rather not translate that last remark, if you do not mind, my lady." Eleanor smiled just as blandly, saying that sometimes translations were unnecessary and, to Berengaria's amazement, the two women then began to chat nonchalantly, as if nothing out of the ordinary had occurred. Listening as they discussed benign topics of interest to neither of them, Berengaria wondered if she'd ever achieve that sort of icy aplomb. How did they learn to immerse the woman in the queen? Could she learn to do that, too? Did she even want to learn?

The conversation soon turned to music, for Boniface of Montferrat was a noted patron of troubadours, with one of the best known in his entourage here at Lodi: Gaucelm Faidit. Gaucelm was native to Eleanor's world, a son of the Limousin, and she assured Constance that they could look forward to an evening of exceptional entertainment. "Gaucelm Faidit was often at my son Geoffrey's court in Brittany and with Richard in Poitou ere he became king. I've been told that Gaucelm and Geoffrey once composed a tenso together, and I would dearly love to hear it."

"I'm sure that can be arranged. I know your son Richard is a poet. Geoffrey was one, too, then?"

"He turned his hand to poetry from time to time, but not as often as Richard, who derives great pleasure from music. If you'll overlook a mother's pride, I can honestly say that several of his sirventes are as sardonic and witty as any composed by Bertran de Born."

"Does he write in French or in *lenga romana*?" Constance asked, sounding genuinely curious, and nodded thoughtfully when Eleanor said he composed in both languages but preferred the *lenga romana* of Aquitaine. "My lord husband is a poet, too ... did you know that, Madame? Heinrich could easily compose in Latin, or even French. But like your son, he prefers his native tongue, and has written several songs of courtly love that are quite good—if you'll overlook a wife's pride."

"Indeed? Most interesting. Lord Heinrich is a man of hidden talents," Eleanor murmured, all the while seeking to decipher the message cloaked in those seemingly casual words. Constance had just alerted her—and with a subtlety that Eleanor could appreciate—that she should guard her speech in Heinrich's hearing, for if he understood enough French to compose in it, he'd had no need of a translator. What she did not understand was why the other woman was giving her this warning.

She soon had her answer, though. Constance glanced about the hall, saw that they were no longer attracting attention, their conversation too banal to stir suspicions, and lowered her voice, pitching it for Eleanor's ears alone. "You said that you were traveling to Rome, Madame. Since you've come so far, I assume you'll continue on to see your son in Messina. If I give you a letter for your daughter, will you deliver it to Joanna for me?"

Eleanor did not hesitate, instinctively sure that the other woman was acting for herself, not for Heinrich. "Of course I will. Joanna often mentioned you in her letters, saying you'd done much to ease her loneliness when she arrived in Palermo."

For the first time, Eleanor saw a genuine smile light Constance's face. It had a transforming effect, shedding years and cares and calling up the ghost of the carefree young girl she'd once been. "I always thought of Joanna as if she were my flesh-and-blood. Mayhap not a daughter since there were only eleven years between us, but most definitely a little sister. During our stay in Lodi, I would be pleased to share with you stories of Joanna's girlhood at William's court."

"That would give me great pleasure, Lady Constance." Eleanor proved then that Constance had won her trust by saying with unguarded candor, "Do you know what has befallen my daughter? William's death was followed by a strange and ominous silence. She did not write and I very much fear it was because she was unable to do so. I'd hoped to learn more in Rome, but I am guessing that your lord husband hears of it as soon as a tree falls in a Sicilian forest."

"Indeed, he does. You had reason for concern, Madame, for Joanna was ill treated by Tancred. He seized her dower lands and then held her prisoner in Palermo, fearing her popularity with the people and her fondness for me. But she is safe now, has been free since last September. Have you ever heard of a *scirocco*? It is the name we use for a wind that comes out of the African desert and rages across the sea to Sicily, where it wreaks great havoc. Well, your Richard swept into Messina like a *scirocco*, and Tancred not only set Joanna at liberty, he soon settled her dower claims, too. I daresay his sudden change of heart had something to do with the fact that Richard had seized control of Messina. It is called negotiating from a position of strength, I believe."

Eleanor paid Constance a rare compliment, allowing the younger woman to see the vast relief that flooded through her soul. "Thank you," she said simply, and they exchanged a look of silent understanding, the mutual recognition that women like them, however high of birth and resolute of will, would always be birds with clipped wings, unable to soar in a world ruled by men.

DESPITE THE PRESENCE of a king and two queens, the center of attention soon proved to be the younger son of an Italian marquis. Boniface of Montferrat was a magnet for all eyes, for he was strikingly handsome, with curly fair hair, vivid blue eyes, and the easy smile of a man who well knew the potent appeal of his own charm. He had a reputation for battlefield heroics and reckless gallantry, his exploits often celebrated by the troubadours who frequented his court, and, unlike his German cousin Heinrich, he was outgoing and affable. Fluent in four languages, one of which was the *lenga romana* of Aquitaine, he and Eleanor were soon chatting like old and intimate friends. He continued to hold sway over the high table during their elaborate meal, flattering Heinrich, flirting with Constance, jesting with Eleanor and Bishop Milo. But when the talk turned to the struggle with the Saracens, he related a story about his brother Conrad that caused an astonished silence to settle over the hall.

For the benefit of those unfamiliar with his family history, he explained that his eldest brother William had been wed to the Lady Sybilla, sister of Baldwin, the Leper King, but he'd died soon afterward, and Sybilla had then made that accursed marriage to Guy de Lusignan, which resulted in the loss of the Holy Land to the infidels. "My lord father was amongst those taken prisoner at the Battle of Ḥaṭṭīn. When my brother Conrad took command of Tyre, Saladin brought our father to the siege, demanding that Conrad yield the city or our sire would be put to death before his very eyes. He did not know my brother, though. Conrad shouted down from the walls that he'd never surrender Tyre, that his father had lived a long life and Saladin should go ahead and kill him!"

Boniface paused then for dramatic effect, and burst out laughing at the dumbfounded expressions on the faces turned toward him. "Conrad does not lack for filial devotion, I assure you. But he would never surrender the only city still under Christian control, and if the price of Tyre's survival was our father's death, so be it."

Most of those listening were greatly impressed by Conrad's piety. Only Eleanor thought to ask what had happened to his father. Boniface's answer was somewhat anticlimactic. "Oh, Saladin eventually freed him, and he was allowed to join Conrad in Tyre."

Boniface then diplomatically shifted attention back to his royal cousin, asking Heinrich about his Sicilian campaign. Eleanor was no longer listening, for Boniface's offhand revelation had stirred an old memory from the waning years of England's civil war. At the age of five, Will Marshal had been offered up by his father as a hostage, a pledge of John Marshal's good faith. But Marshal had broken his oath, and when the outraged King Stephen had warned that his son would die if he did not surrender Newbury Castle as he'd promised, his ice-blooded reply had passed into legend. Go ahead and hang Will, he'd said, for he had the hammer and anvil with which to forge other and better sons. John Marshal had gambled the life of his son upon his understanding of his foe, sure that Stephen could not bring himself to hang a child—and indeed, Will had been spared. Eleanor wondered now if Conrad had been wagering, too, upon an enemy's honor.

THEIR HOST HAD ENGAGED harpists to play while his guests dined. Afterward, Boniface's renowned troubadour took center stage. Gaucelm's repertoire was an extensive one, offering cansos of love and the dawn songs known as albas, interspersed with the stinging political satire of the sirvente. When he retired to thunderous applause, several of Boniface's joglars were summoned next. They began with a tactful tribute to Boniface's liege lord, performing one of Heinrich's songs of courtly love, although only the members of the royal retinue understood German. They then accepted audience requests, and the hall was soon echoing with popular songs of past troubadour stars like Bertran de Born, Jaufre Rudel, and a female trobairitz who'd composed under the name Comtessa de Diá.

As the evening progressed, the songs became increasingly bawdy, culminating in Heinrich's request for a song by Eleanor's grandfather, Duke William of Aquitaine, a man often called "the first troubadour," who'd delighted in outraging the Church both in his life and in his songs. The one chosen by Heinrich was surely his most ribald, the rollicking tale of a knight who'd pretended to be mute so two highborn ladies would think it safe to dally with him. After testing him by letting a savage tomcat rake its claws along his bare back, they'd taken him to bed, where he boasted that he'd sinned so often that he'd been left in a woeful state "with harness torn and broken blade." When he'd recovered from his amorous ordeal, he'd sent his squire back to the women, requesting that, in his memory, they "Kill that cat!"

The song was a carnal celebration of sin, but if Heinrich had hoped to embarrass the English queen, he'd misread his adversary. Eleanor was proud of her incorrigible, scandalous grandfather, and she laughed as loudly as anyone in the hall at his amatory antics. It was her son's betrothed who was embarrassed by the blunt language and immoral message. Berengaria had listened with discomfort as the songs became more and more unseemly. She'd been particularly offended that a woman could have written the lascivious lines penned by the Comtessa de Diá, "I'd give him reason to suppose he was in Heaven, if I deigned to be his pillow," for the comtessa's song was a lament for an adulterous lover. Berengaria kept her disapproval to herself, sipping her wine in silence as the hall rocked with laughter, but she'd not yet mastered one of the subtleties of queenship: the art of subterfuge. Her face was still the mirror to her soul and her unease was noticed.

As the evening revelries drew to an end, Hawisa seized the first opportunity to draw her aside. "You seemed disquieted earlier," she said with her usual forthrightness. "Is something preying upon your mind?"

By now Berengaria had become accustomed to the countess's disregard for propriety. Sancho's departure had left her feeling dispirited and forlorn, her loneliness exacerbated by her inability to join in the evening's merriment, and she welcomed Hawisa's concern, for tonight she was in need of a friend. "I was downcast," she admitted shyly. "I miss Sancho already. And the entertainment was not to my liking."

Hawisa's plucked blond brows shot upward. "You do not fancy troubadour poetry?"

"No, not really. It has not flourished in Navarre, not as it has in Aragon or Aquitaine. And to be honest, I find much of it distasteful. I can understand why the Church disapproves of the troubadours, for some of their songs glorify infidelity." Berengaria did not think she'd said anything out of the ordinary and she was surprised to see an expression of dismay cross the other woman's face.

"Because you speak their *lenga romana*, the queen and Richard took it for granted that you'd take pleasure in their music. You do know that Richard composes troubadour poetry himself?" After a moment to reflect, though, Hawisa shrugged. "Well, no matter as long as you've been forewarned. We'll just keep this as our secret and no harm done."

Now it was Berengaria's turn to stare in dismay. "Are you saying I should lie to Richard? I could not do that, Lady Hawisa, for I believe there ought to be truth between a husband and wife."

"Good heavens, child, marriages are made of lies!" Hawisa said, laughing. "They can no more withstand the truth than a bat could endure the full light of day. I am simply suggesting that you practice a harmless deception. If the husband is content, most often the wife will be content, too, for he'll be less likely to take out his bad moods on her. I assure you that other women weave these small falsehoods into the daily fabric of their lives, be it feigning pleasure in the bedchamber or feigning interest in the great hall, and they see no need to confide such falsehoods to their confessors!" Hawisa beamed at the younger woman, pleased to be able to instruct her in the intricacies of wedlock, oblivious to the fact that she'd never applied any of these lessons in either of her marriages.

Berengaria was too well mannered to admit that she found Hawisa's advice to be cynical and demeaning. So she merely smiled politely. But then she stiffened, for she'd just noticed the woman standing a few feet away. When heat flamed into Berengaria's face, Hawisa was touched by her innocence, thinking she'd been embarrassed by the talk of marital sex. But she was mistaken. Berengaria's consternation was due to the alarming realization that Heinrich's wife had overheard them discussing her marriage to his enemy, the English king.

Berengaria was horrified by her blunder. How could she have been so careless? The queen had cautioned them that her identity must remain secret from Heinrich, lest he warn Philippe of Richard's intention of repudiating Alys. And now her secret had been delivered into the hands of Heinrich's queen. She was utterly at a loss, not knowing how to remedy her mistake. She shrank from the thought of confessing to Eleanor, her pride rebelling at the very notion, for she did not want Richard's mother to think less of her, to know that she'd failed in so simple a task. Nor did she want to implicate Hawisa, and how could she confess without admitting the part the countess had played in their heedless conversation? Yet Eleanor must be alerted to the danger, so how could she stay silent?

In the end, desperation drove her to approach Constance. The other woman listened impassively as she made a halting request for a private word. It was only when the queen murmured in German and her ladies withdrew that Berengaria knew her plea had been granted. As their eyes met, Berengaria felt dwarfed in comparison to Constance, who was so much taller, so much older, and so much more experienced in the ways of statecraft. Not knowing what else to do, she fell back upon candor, saying quietly, "I believe you may have overheard my conversation with the Countess of Aumale, Madame."

It occurred to her that it would be easy for Constance to deny she'd heard anything, and what would she do then? But to her relief, the German queen nodded, almost imperceptibly. "I was not intending to eavesdrop," she said, with the faintest hint of a smile, "but yes, I did hear some of your conversation. Am I correct in assuming you are the King of Navarre's daughter?" She did smile then, at Berengaria's unguarded amazement, saying, "I do not have second sight, I assure you. Bishop Milo mentioned that King Sancho's son had accompanied Queen Eleanor as far as Milan. Since he is known to be friendly with the English king, I thought his escort was a courtesy to Richard. But once I overheard the countess extolling the advantages of marital ambiguity, I saw Lord Sancho's presence in another light."

That Constance de Hauteville was so clever only increased Berengaria's despondency. She could never outwit this woman. "I am Berengaria de Jimenez," she said, "the daughter of King Sancho, sixth of that name to rule the kingdom of Navarre. It is my earnest hope, Madame, that you will consider keeping my identity to yourself. My betrothal to King Richard has not been made public yet and . . ." She could go no further, overcome by the futility of her entreaty. Why would Constance agree to assist Richard, the man who'd allied himself with Tancred, who'd usurped her throne? But Constance was waiting expectantly, and she said drearily, "It was a foolish idea. Why would you want to do a service for the English king?"

"You are right," Constance said. "I have no reason whatsoever to oblige the English king, nor would I do so. But I am willing to keep silent for the King of Navarre's daughter."

Berengaria's brown eyes widened. "You—you mean that?" she stammered. "You will say nothing to your lord husband?"

"Nary a word. Consider it a favor from one foreign bride to another."

Overwhelmed with gratitude, Berengaria watched as Constance turned away then, crossing the hall to join her husband. It was ridiculous to feel pity for a woman so blessed by fortune. She knew that. But she knew, too, that she'd never seen anyone as profoundly unhappy as Constance de Hauteville, on her way to Rome to be crowned Empress of the Holy Roman Empire.

CHAPTER 12

FEBRUARY 1191

Messina, Sicily

I n the span of one week, Richard received two messages from his mother, dispatched from Turin and Lodi, a letter from Chancellor Longchamp's cojusticiars in England, complaining of his arrogance and refusal to heed any opinion but his own, and a warning from Longchamp himself, reporting that Count John had recently returned to England in a disgruntled frame of mind, having learned of Arthur's designation as Richard's heir. But these messages were eclipsed by the one that arrived on February 1 from Outremer, an urgent appeal for aid from Guy de Lusignan, his desperation proven as much by the timing of his letter as by his words themselves, for few ships ventured from Mediterranean ports during the stormy winter months.

RICHARD HAD RIDDEN OFF after getting Guy's message, heading for the royal palace to inform Philippe of the latest developments in Outremer. André de Chauvigny had been privy to the letter's contents, and he was soon surrounded by Baldwin de Bethune, Morgan ap Ranulf, and Robert Beaumont, the new Earl of Leicester. Robert had been given the earldom by Richard that very morning, word having reached them in the past week of his father's death. The elder Beaumont had chosen a land route to Outremer, and it had proven to be as unlucky for him as it had been for Frederick Barbarossa; he'd died in Romania that past September.

André glanced from face to face, then nodded. "The king will be announcing the news soon enough, so I see no reason to make you wait. The word from

Outremer was not good. There have been many deaths, more from sickness than Saracen swords, and they are suffering from famine as well as plague. Amongst those who've died at Acre are Thibault, the Count of Blois, and his brother, the Count of Sancerre. The Archbishop of Canterbury was also taken ill, dying on November nineteenth. But the most significant death was that of the Queen of Jerusalem. The Lady Sybilla died of the plague in October, a few days after her two young daughters were called home by God."

The other men exchanged troubled glances, understanding now why Richard had seemed so grim as he'd ridden out of camp. Guy de Lusignan's hold upon power had always been precarious, given his widespread unpopularity, but with the death of his queen and daughters, he was rendered truly superfluous, for the bloodright to the throne had been vested in Sybilla.

"Who does the crown pass to now, then?" Leicester asked, for he was quite unlike his late, unlamented father and, having no false pride, was willing to ask if he did not know. "Does Sybilla have any other kin?"

"Yes, a younger half-sister, Isabella. But she was wed to a man even less respected than Guy de Lusignan, a lord named Humphrey de Toron who'd long been regarded as a weakling and milksop. Knowing that none wanted to see Humphrey crowned, Conrad of Montferrat saw his chance and seized it. Conspiring with the Bishop of Beauvais and Isabella's mother, Queen Maria, who is now wed to one of the powerful Ibelin family, he argued that Isabella's marriage to Humphrey was invalid because she'd been only eight when the marriage was arranged and eleven when it took place."

"And how did Conrad benefit from this?"

André smiled. "Ah, Morgan, you Welsh do get right to the heart of the matter. Conrad offered to wed Isabella himself once she was free of Humphrey—for the good of the kingdom, of course. I daresay he'd have taken her if she'd been a misshapen, poxed hag, but Conrad has always had the Devil's own luck, for the girl is just eighteen and said to be a beauty. Humphrey balked, though, and so did Isabella, saying she'd freely given her consent. There was some sympathy for Humphrey at first, but he lost it all when one of Conrad's men challenged him to a duel to settle the matter and he refused. Isabella showed more backbone, insisting she loved her husband and did not want to be parted from him. But Conrad and her mother eventually bullied her into going along with it, arguing that only a strong king could save Outremer from Saladin. The Archbishop of Canterbury was made of sterner stuff, though, and flatly refused to annul the marriage, saying it was valid in the Eyes of God. But then he was stricken with the plague. As soon as he died, Conrad got the Archbishop of Pisa to annul Isabella's marriage and they were quickly wed by Philippe's cousin, the Bishop of Beauvais. So now Conrad is claiming the crown as Isabella's husband and Guy de Lusignan is entreating Richard to come to his aid as soon as possible, arguing that he is the rightful king."

There was silence after he was done speaking, for they understood the implications of Guy's plea. Conrad was cousin both to the French king and the new Holy Roman Emperor, while Guy was Richard's vassal, with the right to claim his liege lord's protection. They could well end up fighting one another instead of the Saracens.

RICHARD WAS STILL in a foul mood the next day, infuriated that these political rivalries were putting the crusade at risk. Rather than brooding about it, he decided to exercise his stallion, setting out along the coastal road with his cousins and some of his household knights. It was remarkably mild for Candlemas, the sea shimmering like blue-green glass, the sun warm on their faces, their horses eager to run, and by the time they headed back toward Messina, Richard was in better spirits.

"Guy says that Conrad bribed the archbishop and others to gain their support," he told André and Morgan, "and he claims Conrad was not even free to wed, having left a wife back in Montferrat and another one in Constantinople. Of course Conrad swore that they both were dead," he said, with such obvious skepticism that Morgan saw he'd already made up his mind. He was going to support his vassal, just as Philippe would surely support Conrad, his cousin. As he glanced over at the English king, a Welsh proverb popped into Morgan's head. *Nid da y peth ni phlyco* warned it was a bad bow that would not bend. From what he'd so far seen in Sicily, neither Richard nor Philippe were ones for bending.

"As if you did not have troubles in abundance," André sympathized, "now you must quickly act to fill the vacancy at Canterbury. Lord knows who those fool monks would elect if left to their own devices."

"Actually, I've been thinking about that for some time," Richard admitted. "Archbishop Baldwin was elderly, not in good health, and likely to die in the Holy Land. So I already have a man in mind—the Archbishop of Monreale." Richard grinned then, for he enjoyed catching others by surprise. "During our negotiations over Messina, he impressed me with his intelligence and integrity. He has taken the cross, too, unlike so many of his fellow prelates who were loath to give up the comforts of home. The Canterbury monks are as stubborn as mules, so

they might well balk at electing one they consider a foreigner. But I'll soon—"
Breaking off suddenly, he reined in his horse. "What is happening up ahead?"

The road was blocked, men on horseback milling about, others dismounted,
all of them watching a bohort, an informal tournament taking place in an adja-
cent field. Some of the bystanders were English, but most were French, and they
were laughing and shouting rude advice as knights engaged one another with
long reeds called sugar canes by the Sicilians. At the sight of his wife's uncle, Jaufre
swung his mount around to greet the English king. "We came upon a peasant
taking his canes to market," he said, pointing toward an elderly farmer; holding
the reins of his donkey, he was watching with bemusement as these foreigners
wielded his canes like lances. He did not seem indignant, but Richard still asked
if he'd been paid for his crop, for he wanted no more trouble with the townspeople during the remainder of their stay.

"We kept handing over coins until he smiled," Jaufre assured Richard, for
Philippe was just as adamant that the Messinians not be cheated. "Why not join
in, my liege? We have more than enough canes. Unless of course your men fear
defeat?"

The challenge was good-natured, given with a grin, and Richard saw that his
knights were eager to accept it. "Go on," he said indulgently, and most of them
quickly dismounted, squabbling with one another over the longest, sturdiest
canes. Richard had no interest in joining them, for he had no need to hone his
own skills and dismissed tournaments as mere rehearsals for the real event. But
then the young Mathieu de Montmorency noticed the new arrivals.

"My lord king," he cried out gleefully, "you are just in time! Surely you are not
going to pass up a chance to knock a French knight on his arse? You can have my
own cane to smite them!"

Mathieu offered it then with a dramatic flourish, and to the surprise of Richard's men, he reached out and took it. They knew Richard deliberately encouraged the boy's hero worship because it obviously annoyed Philippe. But they
knew, too, his indifference to tourneys. "He must be as just as bored as we are,"
André murmured to Morgan. As he followed the direction of Richard's gaze,
though, he drew a sharp breath. "Ballocks!"

Morgan and Baldwin looked, too, saw nothing out of the ordinary. When they
turned questioningly to him, André said softly, "There's the reason for his sudden
interest, the man on that bay stallion—Guillaume des Barres."

They both knew of the French knight, of course, for he was almost as celebrated for his martial skills as William Marshal. It made sense to them that

Richard should want to test himself against such a worthy foe, and they saw no cause for concern; it was only a bohort, after all. But then André quietly told them of Richard's history with the other man.

"It happened the year ere the old king died. Richard had not yet forged an alliance with Philippe, and when he got word that the French king was at Mantes, he made a raid into the surrounding countryside. There was a skirmish with the French and he captured Guillaume des Barres. Because he was a knight, Richard accepted his pledge, and continued the fight. But des Barres broke his parole and escaped by stealing a sumpter horse."

Seeing their surprise, André shrugged. "I do not know why he dishonored himself like that. Mayhap he acted impulsively when he saw a chance to flee. Mayhap he feared he'd not be able to pay the ransom Richard would demand. I can only tell you that Richard was outraged when he learned of it and has borne des Barres a grudge ever since."

Baldwin and Morgan agreed that Richard had a legitimate grievance. They did not share André's unease, though, for when had a man ever been run through with a sugar cane? And surely des Barres would have the sense to keep out of Richard's way.

Now that there was to be a French–English clash, the impromptu bohort seemed more like a genuine tournament, and Richard's unusual participation ratcheted up the excitement. The knights lined up on opposite sides of the field, and since no one had a trumpet, the signal was the battle cry of the first crusade. *"Deus vult!"* "God wills it!" Their stallions kicking up clouds of dust, the men charged toward one another as the spectators shouted and cheered.

Just as André had suspected, Richard headed straight for Guillaume des Barres, his path as true as an arrow. Guillaume urged his mount forward and they came together in the center of the field. Richard got the worst of the exchange, for his cane broke when Guillaume parried the blow. He was circling around to get another cane from one of his squires when he saw the triumphant smile on the other man's face. Disregarding the outstretched cane, he spurred his stallion forward as if they were on the battlefield, slamming into Guillaume's bay with such force that he stumbled and Guillaume would have gone sailing over his head had he not grabbed the mane. But Richard had not emerged unscathed, for the impact loosened his cinch and his saddle started to slip. He swiftly dismounted, snatched the reins of the nearest horse, and vaulted up into the saddle to continue the attack.

By now they had attracted the attention of the spectators and even some of the men on the field, who'd lowered their canes to watch. Guillaume had managed to regain his balance. When Richard's stallion charged him again, his bay shied and only his skilled horsemanship kept him from falling. Before he could right himself, Richard grabbed his arm and yanked, expecting to pull him from the saddle. He had not often encountered a foe with his physical strength, but now he found himself unable to dislodge the other man. Guillaume clutched his horse's neck, clasping his knees tightly against the animal's sides, and when Richard angrily demanded that he yield, he stubbornly refused, resisting the English king's attempts to unseat him as if his very life depended upon the outcome.

All eyes were riveted upon them, the French dismayed to see one of their own in danger of being publicly humiliated, the English cheering their king on. But gradually the spectators fell silent, worried by the ferocity of the struggle, so utterly out of place in the midst of a bohort. It was the newly titled Earl of Leicester who sought to break the impasse. Impulsively spurring his stallion forward, he reined in beside Guillaume and reached out to grab the French knight. He had good intentions, wanting only to help his king. He did not know Richard that well, though. Those who did, winced.

"Get away!" Richard snarled. "This is between the two of us!" By now their exertion had begun to take a toll. Both men were flushed and panting, their chests heaving and their tunics soaked in sweat, their faces smeared with dust. After Leicester's brutal rebuff, none dared to intervene. They could only hope that neither man would draw his sword and turn this bizarre duel of wills into a combat to the death.

"Yield, you misbegotten son of a whore!" Again and again Richard pulled with all of his considerable strength, but to no avail. The other man clung to his horse like a barnacle, refusing to admit defeat. At last Richard released his grip and drew back. Feeling as if his arm had been wrenched from its socket, Guillaume straightened up in the saddle, keeping his eyes warily upon the English king, for Richard's fury showed no sign of abating. To the contrary, he was staring at Guillaume with such utter and implacable hatred that the Frenchman felt a chill, for now that the red haze of battle was subsiding, he was realizing how grievously his pride had led him astray.

He had no chance to offer an olive branch, though. "Get yourself from my sight," Richard said, his words all the more alarming for the flat, measured tone in which they were uttered, "and take care never to come before me again. From now on, you are my enemy and there is no place for you in our army."

Guillaume gasped, for that sounded ominously like a sentence of banishment.

That was how the other men took it, too, and an uneasy silence fell, no one quite understanding how a friendly game with canes could end in an ultimatum and exile.

GUILLAUME DES BARRES was too edgy to sit and was pacing back and forth. When Jaufre walked over to offer a wine cup, he shook his head. "You think our king will be able to make him see reason?"

"I do," Jaufre said, hiding his doubts with a display of hearty confidence. "Once Richard's anger cools, he'll see the unfairness of it."

"But what if he does not?" This mournful query came from the window-seat where Mathieu de Montmorency was huddled, knees drawn up to his chest. Jaufre felt a twinge of pity, for the boy had been even more shaken than Guillaume by Richard's threat. Jaufre had not liked this glimpse of Richard's dark side, either, but unlike Mathieu, he'd never seen the English king as the living embodiment of the chivalric code. He was about to offer Mathieu the same assurances he'd just given Guillaume when the youth twisted sideways on the seat and leaned out the open window. "The king is back! But he looks so grim! Do you think that means . . ."

"He always looks grim, lad," Jaufre said, thinking that Philippe doled out smiles the way a miser doled out coins. Within moments, Philippe strode into the hall. One glance at his narrowed eyes and thinned mouth told them that his mission had been a failure. He was trailed by the Duke of Burgundy, who shook his head and grimaced.

"He would not heed you, my liege?" Now that he was facing the worst, Guillaume's nervousness had ebbed, and he sounded quite calm, his the sangfroid of a man who'd spent most of his life soldiering.

"No." Philippe bit off the word so tersely that they could see the muscles clenching along his jawline. "He remains adamant, insisting that you be dismissed from my service. He dared to give orders to me, an anointed king and his liege lord!"

"So be it," Guillaume said softly, and then raised his head, squaring his shoulders. "I will leave Messina as he demands, for I do not want to jeopardize our quest. Nothing matters more than the recovery of the Holy Land. But I will not abandon my vow. If I cannot accompany you to Outremer, my liege, I will go on my own."

"No, you are going nowhere!" Philippe said sharply, and Guillaume looked to the other men for guidance.

Seeing that the Duke of Burgundy was not going to intercede, Jaufre suppressed a sigh. "Sire . . . Guillaume is right. Ours is a sacred quest, one that requires sacrifices."

Philippe's lip curled disdainfully. "Sacrifices? What sacrifices has Richard made?"

"Mayhap it was the wrong choice of words. I ought to have said 'compromises.' I am not defending Richard. He is in the wrong, not Guillaume. But he has been the one to compromise in the past."

Philippe's gaze was so piercing that Jaufre took an involuntary step backward. But farther than that he would not go. "You may not want to hear it, my lord king. It has to be said, though. After Richard seized Messina, you demanded that he lower his banners and replace them with yours. Even though you'd taken no part in the capture of the city, he agreed to fly the flags of the Templars and Hospitallers instead of his own. He compromised. And when he got that gold from Tancred, he gave you a third, even though you had no claim to Queen Joanna's dower. Again, he compromised. Now . . . now it is your turn."

To Jaufre's relief, he got support then from an unexpected source—from Hugh of Burgundy. "As much as it pains me to say it, Cousin, Jaufre is right. You do need to compromise, however unjust Richard's demand. Humor him for now, if that will keep the peace between you. Mark it down as a debt owed, one to be repaid when the time is right."

Philippe did not have much regard for Jaufre's opinion, suspicious of his marriage to Richard's niece, but he did respect Hugh's judgment. After a long, labored silence, he beckoned to Guillaume. "I will ask Tancred to give you shelter at Catania. But this I promise you—that when I sail for Outremer, you will sail with me."

———

PHILIPPE'S ANGER BURNED all the hotter that Guillaume had behaved so honorably, offering no protests, no complaints about the injustice of the banishment. He was still fuming hours later when a messenger arrived, bearing a letter from Heinrich von Hohenstaufen. Breaking the seal, he scowled to see it was in Latin, for he had no knowledge of the language that was the voice of the Church, a verbal bridge linking the countries of Christendom. Rather than summoning a scribe or clerk, he handed the letter to his cousin. "You know Latin, Hugh. What does it say?"

Hugh scanned the contents, then looked up at the others in genuine surprise. "He says that Richard's mother is in Italy! They crossed paths at Lodi last month." After a moment to reflect, he said, "That is one mystery solved, then. At least now we know how Richard learned of Frederick Barbarossa's death ere we did."

Philippe shook his head impatiently. "That does not matter. What does is the reason for that witch's presence in Italy. What could be important enough to justify such a long and difficult journey at her age?" He was looking at Hugh, but it was obvious to the others that he was no longer seeing the duke, his gaze turning inward. "Why did he send for her?" he muttered, as if to himself. "What is that swine up to now?"

AT ROME, Eleanor had another chance meeting, this time with Philip d'Alsace, the Count of Flanders, who'd also taken the cross and was on his way to Outremer. He decided to accompany them south to Naples, and as she watched Eleanor conversing composedly with the count, Berengaria could only marvel at the older woman's self-possession, for Hawisa had confided that the queen had good reason to detest Philip. He'd been wed to Eleanor's niece, her sister's daughter, Hawisa revealed, and after some years of a childless marriage, he'd accused her of adultery. The man said to be her lover had been brutally murdered, but Philip had not divorced his wife; instead he'd compelled her to turn her inheritance, the rich county of Vermandois, over to him. According to Hawisa, many people felt the charges were false; the alleged lover's brothers were so outraged that they'd rebelled. And yet Eleanor made sure that the count saw only the queen, never the angry aunt, still more proof to Berengaria that she was entering an alien world where statecraft seemed to matter more than family feelings or even the teachings of the Holy Church.

In Naples, Aliernus Cottone, the city's *compalatius*, welcomed them effusively, hosting a lavish feast in their honor and turning one of Tancred's castles over to them for the duration of their stay in his city, a stone fortress on a small island in the harbor. They then settled down to await the arrival of Richard's ships. Now that she was within days of her reunion with her son, Eleanor's spirits soared, but Hawisa's plummeted, for she was not eager to see her new husband, William de Forz.

Berengaria's emotions were more ambivalent; she was excited to meet Richard again, but she was nervous, too, now that her new life was about to begin, for she was starting to realize how much would be demanded of her as England's queen.

RICHARD'S GALLEYS ENTERED the city harbor at nightfall. Richard had sent one of his admirals, William de Forz, and two of his kinsmen, André de Chauvigny and Morgan ap Ranulf, to escort his mother and betrothed to Messina. The men were tired, dirty, and hungry after their voyage, and they were grateful when Eleanor sent them off to their sleeping quarters, where baths and food awaited them. De Forz departed at once, insisting that his wife personally tend to his needs. André and Morgan soon followed, after giving Eleanor letters from Richard and Joanna.

Eleanor picked up an oil lamp and sat down to read the letters. But as she was about to break the seal on the first one, she glanced up and saw the forlorn look on Berengaria's face. After spending more than three months together, she'd concluded that the girl would make a suitable wife for her son; her quiet courage and common sense were qualities he'd appreciate. She'd been pleased that Berengaria had shown no signs of the "neediness" that Richard had fretted about, but she could understand why the young woman was disappointed that there'd been no letter for her, and so she said, with a wry smile,

"Even the most intelligent of men can lack a woman's perception or insight, child. That was surely true of Richard's father, who had not a spark of romance in his soul. When we were first wed, he bestowed compliments so sparingly that I finally complained. He said he saw no point in flattery, for if a woman was a beauty, she already knew it, and if she was not, she'd know he lied."

While Berengaria was slightly embarrassed that Eleanor had seen her chagrin, it was the first time that Richard's mother had spoken to her like this, woman to woman, and she reveled in the intimacy. "Is Richard like his father?"

Eleanor started to speak, then realized, somewhat to her surprise, that she did not know how her son was with a woman. She'd been cheated of so much during her years of captivity, losing time with her children that could never be gotten back. But one lesson she'd learned long ago was that regrets served for naught. And so she smiled at Berengaria, saying, "Yes, they were more alike than either one would admit. So I can speak from my own experience when I tell you that life with Richard will not always be peaceful. But it will never be dull."

Berengaria returned Eleanor's smile, remembering a dinner conversation they'd had in Rome with an Italian countess. She'd asked playfully what quality they most valued in a husband, offering wealth as her own criterion. Hawisa had quipped that the ideal husband was one who was absent, while Eleanor had chosen one with wit, a man who could make her laugh. Berengaria would have picked kindness, thinking of her father and the tenderness he'd always shown her mother. She'd not spoken her thoughts aloud, though, not wanting them to think her naïve. She wished now that she could ask Eleanor if her son was kind. But she would have to find that out for herself.

BERENGARIA DID NOT LIKE Hawisa's new husband. William de Forz dominated the conversation at dinner the next day, not even letting the Count of Flanders get a word in edgewise. He dwelt upon his command of Richard's fleet at
interminable length, making ocean voyages sound so perilous that Berengaria
shivered, thinking of the turbulent, untamed sea that lay between Italy and Outremer. But what followed was even worse, for he began to tell the women about the
great perils awaiting their army in the Holy Land.

"Plague and famine haunt that unhappy kingdom," he proclaimed theatrically,
"posing far greater threats than the most bloodthirsty of Saracen infidels. During
the winter when ships could not reach the camp at Acre, food became so scarce
that a penny loaf of bread sold for as much as forty shillings, a single egg cost six
deniers, and a sack of corn one hundred pieces of gold. Horses were worth more
dead than alive, and men were reduced to eating grass to survive. If the bishops of
Salisbury and Verona had not raised money to feed the poor, the Good Lord
alone knows how many might have died."

André and Morgan exchanged amused glances, for de Forz's posturing made
it sound as if he'd been present at the siege of Acre instead of getting the news
secondhand from Guy de Lusignan's letter to Richard. "The arrival of three supply ships eased the famine," he continued, "but there was no protection against
the plague. Death relentlessly stalks that bloody ground, and high birth is no
defense. The Queen of Jerusalem and her young daughters died at Acre. So did
the Count of Blois and his brother. The Archbishop of Canterbury. The Grand
Master of the Templars. And your grandson, Madame, the young Count of
Champagne. . . ."

When Eleanor gasped, de Forz belatedly hastened to reassure her. "Nay, he is
not dead. But he was struck down by the same illness that killed his uncles, and
for a time they despaired of his life. They say the very air of Outremer is noxious
to newcomers, for how else to explain why so many are stricken so soon after their
arrival?"

Morgan noticed Eleanor's sudden pallor. Glancing over, he saw that Berengaria was looking distressed, too, and he frowned, marveling that de Forz could
be such a lack-wit. Did he truly think Richard's mother and betrothed wanted to
hear of all those deaths, of all the dangers the king wald be facing in Outremer?
"The king built a wooden castle on the hill above Messina," he said abruptly,
determined to banish the fearful images de Forz had been conjuring up, "and he

had all the sections marked so it can be taken apart and packed up when he departs for Outremer. He has done the same for his siege engines, too, so they can be easily reassembled at Acre."

The women seemed interested in that, but de Forz was not ready to relinquish control of the conversation. "Tell them what he calls the castle, Morgan," he said with a grin. "Mate-Griffon, or Kill the Greeks!" He then launched into a melodramatic account of Richard's seizure of Messina before returning to his favorite subject, the killing fields of the Holy Land.

By now André had also noticed the effect de Forz's blustering was having upon Eleanor and Berengaria. Leaning forward, he interrupted smoothly, "I think the queen and the Lady Berengaria would rather hear about the king's meeting with the prophet, Joachim of Corazzo."

"Indeed I would." Eleanor turned toward Berengaria, intending to explain that Joachim was a celebrated holy man, renowned for his knowledge of Scriptures and his interpretations of the Book of Revelations. But Berengaria needed no such tutoring.

"I've heard of him!" she exclaimed, her eyes shining. "He says that there are three ages, that of the Father, the Son, and the Spirit, and that the Last Days are nigh, which will precede the Last Judgment."

"Exactly so, my lady," André confirmed. "The king wanted to hear his prophesies for himself, as he'd heard that Joachim identifies Saladin as the sixth of the seven great enemies of the True Faith. We were much heartened by what he told us—that Saladin will be driven from the Kingdom of Jerusalem and slain, and it will be King Richard who brings this about."

Berengaria felt a thrill of pride, greatly honored that her betrothed was the man chosen by God to fulfill these holy prophesies and vanquish such a deadly foe of the Church. She found it very encouraging, too, that Richard had sought the mystic out, for that showed his faith had deeper roots than his worldly demeanor might indicate.

"Joachim claimed that the Antichrist, the last of Holy Church's seven tormentors, is already born," André resumed, "and dwelling in Rome. According to Joachim, he will seize the apostolic throne and proclaim himself Pope ere being destroyed by the Coming of the Lord Christ."

De Forz cut in again, chuckling. "The king disputed Joachim on that point, suggesting that the Antichrist was already on the apostolic throne, the current Pope, Clement III!"

That evoked laughter, for they all knew how much Richard disliked Clement.

But to Berengaria, Richard's sardonic gibe skirted uncomfortably close to blasphemy, and she could manage only a flicker of a smile. She forgot her discomfort, though, with de Forz's next revelation.

"Soon thereafter, the king made a dramatic act of penance, summoning his bishops to the chapel where he knelt half naked at their feet and confessed to a sinful, shameful past in which he'd yielded to the prickings of lust. He abjured his sin and gladly accepted the penance imposed upon him by the bishops, who commended him for his repentance and bade him live henceforth as a man who feared God."

Berengaria caught her breath and then smiled, suffused with such utter and pure joy that she seemed to glow and, for that moment, she looked radiantly beautiful. "How courageous of him," she murmured, more impressed by that one act of devout contrition than by all the tales she'd heard of Richard's battlefield heroics. "Scriptures say that 'God resisteth the proud, but giveth grace unto the humble.'"

Eleanor murmured a conventional piety, but, unlike Berengaria, she was more puzzled than gratified by Richard's spectacular atonement. She was convinced that her husband's equally spectacular penance at the martyred Thomas Becket's tomb in Canterbury had been more an act of desperation than one of contrition. She knew, though, that Richard was more emotional and impulsive than his father. Moreover, he had a flair for high drama that Henry had utterly lacked. Was that enough to explain his *mea culpa* in Messina? Were his sins so great that he felt the need for a public expiation?

Once the meal was over, a harpist was summoned to play and the guests broke into small groups. William de Forz withdrew to a window-seat with the Count of Flanders for a spirited discussion of recent political developments in Outremer. Morgan was flirting with Berengaria and several of her ladies. Eleanor could not help noting that Hawisa stayed as far away from de Forz as she could get, and she felt a flicker of sympathy, for she'd become fond of the outspoken countess and she knew what it was like to be yoked to an unwanted husband. She chatted for a time with the Navarrese envoys and then seized her chance to draw her kinsman aside for a private word.

"You know Richard as well as any man alive," she said quietly, "for you've fought beside him for years. Tell me, André . . . what impelled him to make an act of atonement like that?"

"I think it was because of what Joachim told him, Madame. He said that the king is destined to fulfill those prophesies, that Almighty God will grant him victory over his enemies and glorify his name for all eternity. Naturally, such a prophesy gladdened the king's heart, but I believe it caused him to search his soul, too. To be told that his deeds could bring about the salvation of mankind is both a great honor and a great burden. I think he wanted to be sure that he was worthy, and so he felt the need to cleanse himself of past sins."

Eleanor was glad that she'd asked André, for his explanation made perfect sense to her. "Well," she said with a smile, "he surely emerged as pure as one of the Almighty's own lambs after such a public scourging of his soul."

"Indeed, Madame." André's answering smile was bland, for not for the surety of his own soul would he have discussed Richard's sins with his mother, even a mother as worldly as this one. Theirs was a friendship that went deeper than blood, for it had been forged on the battlefield, and he thought it likely that only Richard's confessor knew more about his cousin's vices than he did, for some he had witnessed, some he had shared, a few he had suspected, and others neither he nor Richard considered to be sins at all.

Turning away then to fetch Eleanor more wine, André found himself dwelling upon those questions that all true Christians must grapple with. He believed that he was a good son of the Church. But he did not understand why lust was so great a sin. Why must his faith be constantly at war with his flesh? He listened dutifully when priests warned that he must not lie with his wife in forbidden positions or on holy days or Sundays or during Lent, Advent, or Pentecost. He did not always follow those prohibitions, though, and this was a source of dissention in his marriage. But why was it a sin if Denise mounted him or if they made love in the daylight? Why was a man guilty of adultery if he burned with excessive love for his own wife?

It sometimes seemed to him that the Church Fathers knew little of the daily struggles of ordinary men and women. In his world, fornication was not a vice, at least not for men, and it was his secret belief that adultery ought to be a conditional sin, too. What of married men who'd taken the cross? Were they supposed to live as chastely as saints until they could be reunited with their wives? Even the worst sins, those held to be against nature, any sex act that was not procreative, seemed less wicked under certain circumstances. If a poor couple could not afford another child, was it truly so evil to try to avoid pregnancy? He thought the sin of sodomy was more understandable, more forgivable, when committed by soldiers, for what did clerics know of the solidarity of men at war or the sudden, burning urges that followed a battle, a narrow escape from death? All knew that was a vice of the monastery, and surely the Almighty would judge soldiers less harshly than easy-living, privileged monks? No, it seemed to him that there were greater sins than those of the flesh, and no sermons about the Devil's wiles and eternal damnation had explained to his satisfaction why the Lord God would have made carnal intercourse so pleasurable if such pleasure was a pathway to Hell. Certain that celibacy was an unattainable goal for most men and women, he'd found himself a confessor who'd lay light penances and he took communion before battles so he'd die in a state of grace. More than that, he was convinced, a man could not do.

He'd just returned to Eleanor with a goblet of sweet red wine from Cyprus when his cousin Nicholas de Chauvigny hastened toward them. "Madame, the *compalatius* has just ridden in and is requesting to speak with you."

As they awaited his entry, Eleanor commented to André that Aliernus Cottone had doubtless heard of their arrival and wanted to bid them welcome on King Tancred's behalf. That seemed likely to André. But he changed his mind as soon as the *compalatius* was ushered into the hall, for his discomfort was obvious to all with eyes to see.

Eleanor noticed it, too, and she began to assess the man at Aliernus's side. His costly garments proclaimed him to be a lord of rank, as did the sword at his hip, and unlike his companion, he seemed utterly at ease, with the smug complacency of one who enjoyed being the bearer of bad tidings.

The Count of Flanders had sauntered over to join them, his nonchalant smile belied by his narrowed gaze, for Philip read men as well as Eleanor did. After exchanging greetings, Aliernus introduced the stranger as Count Bernard Gentilis of Lesina, Captain and Master Justiciar of Terra de Lavoro, and then said, with the resolve of one determined to get an unpleasant task over with, "The count brings unwelcome news, Madame. I will let him speak for himself, though."

Eleanor realized then that Aliernus's disquiet was actually the embarrassment of a man confronted with a duty he did not like. "My lord count?" she asked silkily. "I assume you come from King Tancred. Since he is allied with my son, the English king, I cannot imagine that any news from him would be unwelcome."

"I have been instructed to tell you, Madame, that you may not sail from Naples. My lord king has decided that your entourage is too large to be accommodated in Messina, and you must continue your journey by land."

There was a moment of shocked silence before the hall erupted in angry protest, William de Forz identifying himself grandly as the king's admiral and André dismissing the count's explanation as utter rubbish. It was Philip d'Alsace, though, who shouted the others down, demanding to know if this idiotic order applied to him, too.

The Count of Lesina seemed unperturbed by the hornet's nest he'd stirred up. "No, my lord Count of Flanders, you may go wherever you will," he said with insulting indifference. "My orders apply only to the English queen."

By now Berengaria had moved to Eleanor's side, looking bewildered but resolute, and the older woman gave her a quick glance of reassurance. The quarrel was heating up and Eleanor interrupted before it could get out of control. Drawing Philip and Richard's men aside, she said in a voice pitched for their ears alone, "We accomplish nothing by arguing with this man. We need to learn why Tancred has issued such an inexplicable order, and only my son can do that. I think you ought to return to Messina on the morrow and let Richard know what has happened."

This delay meant that they would arrive in Messina after the start of Lent and she would not be able to see Richard and Berengaria wed. It was a great disappointment, but she was not about to let anyone see that, for she'd had much practice at hiding her heart's wounds. Instead of raging as she yearned to do, she said calmly, "Tell Richard that we are well and will continue our journey south whilst he resolves this matter with Tancred."

RICHARD'S ASTONISHMENT gave way almost at once to outrage. He resisted his first impulse, which was to berate the Count of Flanders for not remaining with his mother and Berengaria; he could not blame Philip for his eagerness to reach the Holy Land and an overland passage would add another month to his journey. Instead he said, "How would you like to meet the King of Sicily, Cousin?" Not waiting for Philip's reply, he beckoned to one of his knights. "Ride to Catania with all due speed, and tell Tancred that the King of England will be there by week's end, if not sooner."

CHAPTER 13

MARCH 1191

Catania, Sicily

acing Tancred across a wooden trestle table was not the same as facing him across a battlefield, but the hostility in the chamber was unmistakable. Richard's gaze flicked from the Sicilian king to his teenage son, Roger, and then to his counselors, the aged Matthew of Ajello and his two grown sons, Tancred's brother-in-law, the Count of Acerra, the Archbishop of Monreale, the pirate-admiral Margaritis, and Jordan Lapin. While he'd arrived with a large escort, Richard had been accompanied into the council chamber only by his cousins, the Count of Flanders and André de Chauvigny, and by Gautier de Coutances, the Archbishop of Rouen. They'd so far remained silent, content to let Richard speak for himself. With Tancred, it was just the opposite; his advisers were doing all the talking, while he said very little, studying Richard through opaque, heavy-lidded eyes. While they were obviously on the defensive—it was difficult to mount a convincing argument for the claim that Messina could not have accommodated Eleanor's entourage—they were not giving any ground, insisting that their king must act in the best interests of his own subjects. And Richard's patience, always as ephemeral as morning mist, soon evaporated in a surge of exasperation.

"I have a suggestion," he said abruptly. "At this rate, Easter will have come and gone ere we've made any progress whatsoever. Counselors always seem to have time to waste; kings do not. So it would be in our mutual interest, my lord Tancred, if you and I threshed out the wheat from the chaff by ourselves. Unless, of course, you feel more comfortable here in the council chamber. . . ."

It was a challenge few kings could have refused and Tancred was quick to accept it. Shoving back his chair, he got to his feet and said tersely, "Follow me."

As THE MONARCHS APPROACHED the gardens, they were watched with curiosity and some amusement by the palace guards, for the two men could not have presented a more dramatic contrast. Even Richard's enemies acknowledged that he looked like a king out of legend, tall and athletic and golden, whereas even Tancred's most devoted supporters would admit that there was nothing regal about his appearance, for he was of small stature and very ill favored. But there was affection, not derision, in the smiles of the guards, for in the fourteen months since he'd claimed the crown, Tancred had displayed qualities that men-at-arms valued more than a handsome face and a royal bearing: courage and energy and tenacity.

Tancred would have been greatly surprised had he known the English king agreed with his soldiers. Richard had devoted most of his life to perfecting the martial skills that had won him such fame, but he did realize that he'd been blessed by the Almighty with physical advantages not given to all—uncommon height and strength and cat-quick reflexes. It was obvious to him that Tancred's military prowess had been earned by sheer force of will, by his refusal to accept his body's limitations and his willingness to risk all on the field of battle. To Richard, that made him a man deserving of respect, and he stopped as soon as they came to a marble fountain so Tancred would not have to struggle to keep pace, for his shorter legs required him to take two steps for every one of Richard's.

Perching on the edge of the fountain, Richard regarded the other man thoughtfully. "We are both kings. But we are both soldiers, too, and I cannot believe that you fancy these diplomatic dances any more than I do. So let's speak candidly. Unless I know your real reason for refusing to permit my mother to sail from Naples, we do not have a prayer in Hell of reaching any sort of understanding."

Tancred continued to pace back and forth, keeping his eyes upon Richard all the while. "Do you truly want to reach an understanding?"

Richard blinked. "Why would I not? We are allies, after all."

"Allies of expediency," Tancred said bluntly, "dictated by circumstances. But who is to say what will happen if those circumstances change? And the death of Frederick Barbarossa is a great change indeed."

"So you feel the need to take greater precautions now that Heinrich is stepping into his father's shoes. You want to protect your borders. I understand that. But surely you do not see my aging lady mother as a threat, Tancred?"

Tancred was quick to respond with sarcasm of his own. "Come now, Richard.

Your 'aging lady mother' is no matronly widow in her sunset years, content to embroider by the hearth and dote upon her grandchildren. In the game of state-craft, Eleanor of Aquitaine has been a high-stakes player for more than fifty years. You could not have chosen a better agent to confer with Heinrich. Did they reach an accord at Lodi? Or did she merely open the door so you could then pass through?"

Richard was more astonished than angry. "Is that what this is about? You think my mother was scheming with Heinrich? Their meeting at Lodi was happen-stance, no more than that, and to hear my mother tell it, it was awkward for both of them."

"Happenstance is like charity in that it covers a multitude of sins. Suppose I accept what you say—that their meeting at Lodi was by chance—however unlikely that seems. But that still does not explain your mother's presence in Italy. She is well past the age to be crossing the Alps in winter unless she had an urgent reason for doing so. Why is she here, Richard, if not to strike a deal with Heinrich?"

Before Richard could reply, Tancred flung up his hand, for there was a relief in being able to confront the English king with the suspicions that had been so dam-aging to his peace of mind. "If you are about to remind me of the hostility between the Angevins and the von Hohenstaufens, spare your breath. Mutual interests can bridge the greatest of gaps, as we both know. At one time, you were considering a marriage with one of Frederick's daughters, were you not? So is it so far-fetched that you and Heinrich could reach an accord at my expense? I have been told that he has offered you enough gold to buy an entire fleet and has promised to send German troops to the Holy Land, whilst your own mother has suddenly turned up in Lodi with that treacherous two-legged snake. Why should I not believe that I am about to be stabbed in the back?"

Richard was quiet for several moments, considering his options. "So you think Heinrich has bribed me to abandon our alliance? You are a brave man to say that to my face. But I will not take offense, for I think someone is playing a very dan-gerous game with us both. I am no man's pawn, though, and neither are you. Let's prove it by making a bargain here and now. I will tell you the true reason for my mother's arrival in Italy if you then tell me who has been pouring this poison into your ear."

Tancred's mistrust was still obvious, yet he did not hesitate. "Fair enough."

"My mother is bringing me a bride, the Lady Berengaria, daughter of King Sancho of Navarre."

"I thought you were plight-trothed to Philippe's sister."

"For more than twenty years, surely the world's longest march to the altar. I have valid grounds for refusing the marriage, grounds the Church will recognize. But that is between Philippe and me."

"It is none of my concern, and I'll be the first to admit that. Yet would it not have been easier to disavow the plight-troth and wed the Spanish princess whilst you were still in your own lands?"

"I dared not do that, for Philippe had not wanted to take the cross. In fairness, neither did my father, but they were both shamed into it by the Archbishop of Tyre. I knew that Philippe would seize upon any excuse to forswear his oath, and I would have given him a silver-gilt one had I revealed my intention to marry Sancho's daughter. He would have refused to sail for Outremer, using my action as his pretext, for he cares naught for the future of the Holy Land. And then I'd have been faced with an impossible choice—to break my blood oath to liberate Jerusalem in order to defend my own lands, or to honor it, knowing that my domains would be overrun by French forces as soon as we sailed from Marseille. I chose the lesser of evils, and whilst I do not deny it was underhanded, I have no regrets."

"You have even less reasons for regret than you think, Richard. Philippe is the one who has been 'pouring poison' into my ear. He insisted that you and Heinrich were conspiring against me, claiming that Heinrich has bought your support, and using the Lodi meeting to lend credibility to his accusations." Tancred paused then, mustering up a small, abashed smile. "I suppose I was a fool to heed him. But he was very convincing."

"I daresay he was," Richard said grimly. "He has proven himself to be diabolically adept at taking advantage of other men's vulnerabilities, using my brothers against my father with a puppeteer's sure touch. In my case, I was using him as much as he was using me, and he had a rude awakening once he realized that. In truth, I think that is one reason why he harbors such animosity toward me."

Tancred thought it was probably simpler than that; the two men seemed like fire and ice to him, so utterly unlike in every way that conflict was inevitable. The tragedy was that their bitter rivalry would continue to rage in Outremer, and that did not bode well for the rescue of Jerusalem.

TO THE SURPRISE OF ALL, including the two kings, Richard and Tancred discovered they found pleasure in each other's company, and the brief confrontational visit stretched into a five-day sojourn, with excursions to Mount Etna and the holy shrine of St Agatha, with feasting as lavish as Lenten rules allowed, and an exchange of royal largesse. Richard presented the Sicilian king with Excalibur, the sword of the fabled King Arthur, discovered at Glastonbury Abbey. Tancred offered a more practical gift: fifteen galleys and four horse transports for the crusade.

THE NIGHT BEFORE Richard's departure, a messenger had arrived from Philippe announcing his intention to meet him at Taormina, halfway between Catania and Messina. This came as no surprise, for Richard and Tancred did not doubt that his prolonged stay must be a source of growing unease for the French king, wondering what secrets were being revealed, what confidences exchanged. Tancred then decided to accompany Richard as far as Taormina, knowing such a gesture of royal goodwill would cause Philippe even greater disquiet. Before they rode out the next morning, though, he took Richard into his private solar, saying he had another gift for the English king.

Richard insisted that no further gifts were necessary, pointing out that nothing could be more welcome than those fifteen galleys. But Tancred merely smiled and produced a key, which he used to unlock an ivory coffer. Removing a rolled parchment, he held it out, still with that enigmatic half-smile. "You need to read this, Richard."

Taking the letter, Richard moved into the morning light streaming through the window. He'd read only a few lines before he spun around to stare at the Sicilian king. "Jesu! Where did you get this, Tancred?"

"From the Duke of Burgundy. He brought it to me last October, just after you'd taken Messina. The seal is broken, of course, but it is written in Philippe's own hand. Keep reading, for it soon gets very interesting indeed. Your fellow Christian king and sworn ally offers to fight with me if I decide to make war upon you."

By the time Richard had finished reading, his hand had clenched into an involuntary fist. He eased his grip, then, not wanting to damage the parchment, for he understood what a lethal weapon he'd just been given. "I did not think that faithless weasel could surprise me, but even I did not expect a betrayal of such magnitude. If any proof was needed of his indifference to Jerusalem's fate, here it is for all the world to see." After rereading the letter, he glanced back at the Sicilian king, his gaze searching. "Why did you show me this, Tancred?"

"Because I do care about the fate of Jerusalem, and I thought you ought to know you'll have more enemies than Saladin in Outremer."

Their eyes met and held, and Richard found himself admiring the Sicilian king's subtle vengeance. He did not doubt that Tancred was sincere in his desire to aid in the delivery of the Holy City. But Tancred was not a man to leave a debt unpaid, and with this damning letter he would be paying Philippe back in the coin of his choosing.

THE FRENCH KING returned to Messina in a cold fury, for he'd ridden all the way to Taormina only to discover that Richard had already departed via another road. Tancred was no help at all, blandly shrugging off Philippe's questions and insisting he did not know why Richard had not waited for his arrival. Philippe usually set a moderate pace due to his dislike of horses, but spurred on by anger, he reached Messina not long after Compline had begun to ring. The next morning, he rose early and after hearing Mass, he headed out of the city for a confrontation with the English king.

RICHARD HAD CONTINUED to reside in a house on the outskirts of Messina, using Mate-Griffon only for entertaining. As Philippe dismounted in the court-yard, his eyes fell upon the Count of Flanders and his mouth thinned. Philip was his godfather and his uncle by wedlock, for he'd arranged Philippe's marriage to his niece Isabelle. That was back in the early days of Philippe's reign, when the Flemish count had believed the young French king was malleable, easily led. When Philip discovered the steel in the boy's soul, their clash of wills had soon led to armed conflict. Twice the old English king had intervened on Philippe's behalf, patching up an uneasy peace between Flanders and France, but the French king had a long memory. After exchanging acerbic greetings with Philip, he followed the Flemish count into the great hall.

There he received an equally icy welcome by Richard. When he demanded to know why Richard had not waited at Taormina, the other man stared at him for so long that he began to bristle, thinking he was not going to get an answer. But then Richard said curtly, "We need to talk about this in more private surroundings." And without waiting for Philippe to agree, he led the way toward the family chapel that adjoined the hall. Philip of Flanders, the Archbishop of Rouen, and

André de Chauvigny trailed after him without a word being said, as if they'd been expecting just such a move.

Philippe was followed by his own retinue—the bishops of Chartres and Langres, his cousins, the Count of Nevers and Hugh of Burgundy, Jaufre of Perche, and Druon de Mello. The chapel was a small one and the men had to jockey for space, finding it a challenge not to tread on toes or jab elbows into ribs. Breathing in the pungent scents of incense, sweat, and tallow-dipped rushlights sputtering in wall sconces, Philippe looked around in distaste. The church seemed dingy to him; the whitewashed walls were streaked with smoke, the floor rushes matted and rank, and the magnificent reliquary of rock crystal and gold on the altar seemed utterly out of place in such shabby surroundings. Moreover, this chapel had been the scene of Richard's spectacular Christmas penance. Philippe was convinced that Richard got as drunk on fame as some men did on wine, and he saw that dramatic act of expiation as just one more example of the English king's constant craving for attention, although he never doubted that Richard had as many sins to atone for as Judas Iscariot.

"This is ridiculous," he said. "There are not even any prayer cushions to sit upon. You may not want us to dine with you, my lord king, but surely you can spare some wine in your solar."

His men chuckled at that; Richard did not. "I chose to have this talk here because I would never shed blood in God's House."

Philippe was staring at him in shock. Before he could recover, Richard moved to the altar and picked up the parchment he'd placed next to the reliquary. "I'd planned to demand an explanation from you. But what would be the point? Your own words speak for themselves."

Watching intently as the French king took the letter, Richard gave the younger man credit for his self-control. Not a muscle flickered and he showed no emotion even after he'd recognized what he was reading; he could not keep heat from rising in his face and throat, though, a sudden surge of color noticeable even in the subdued lighting of the chapel. Philippe's men were watching in obvious confusion, and Richard turned toward them. "Since I doubt that your king is going to read his letter aloud, let me enlighten you. It is a message that he sent to King Tancred, offering to fight alongside him should Tancred declare war upon his English allies."

There was a stifled sound, like a collective catch of breath. As Richard had expected, the only one who did not seem stunned was Hugh of Burgundy. Philippe's head jerked up and he flung the letter down into the floor rushes. "This is a clumsy forgery."

"And why would Tancred bother to forge a letter? How would he benefit from setting us at odds?"

"How would I know?" Philippe snapped. "I can only tell you that it is not mine."

"Tancred says the letter was delivered by the Duke of Burgundy. Are you also going to disclaim any knowledge of it, Hugh?"

"Indeed I am," the other man said coolly. "I know nothing about it."

"Then you ought to be willing to prove it." Before Hugh guessed what Richard had in mind, he'd snatched up the reliquary. "This contains a splinter of the True Cross. Swear upon it, Hugh, swear that your king is right and this is a damnable forgery."

Hugh was not easily disconcerted, but Richard had managed it now. His eyes cut toward Philippe, back to the holy relic. He made no move to take it, though, and Richard's mouth twisted into a mockery of a smile. "Well, at least you'll not lie to God. What about you, Philippe? Dare you to swear upon the True Cross?"

Philippe ignored the challenge. "I am beginning to understand now. This is not that bastard Tancred's doing. The two of you are in collusion. You've hatched this ludicrous plot to provoke a breach between us, to put me in the wrong."

"And why would I want to do that?"

"So you'd have an excuse not to marry my sister!" Philippe almost spat the words, and this time Richard's smile was like an unsheathed dagger.

"You are half right. I have no intention of marrying your sister. But I need no excuse or pretext, for our union is prohibited by the Holy Church."

"What are you claiming, Richard? That you've suddenly discovered you and Alys are related within the forbidden degree? Do you truly expect the Pope to believe such drivel? After a betrothal of more than twenty years?"

Philippe had regained his balance by now and his voice throbbed with such scornful indignation that his men found themselves nodding in agreement.

"I am not talking of consanguinity. That can be remedied if a dispensation is granted. This is a far more serious impediment." Richard's eyes swept the chapel before coming to rest upon the Archbishop of Rouen. "Is it not true, my lord archbishop, that Holy Scriptures say it is a mortal sin for a man to have carnal knowledge of his father's wife?" Getting a solemn affirmation of that from the prelate, Richard swung around to confront Philippe. "Would it be any less of a sin for a man to bed his father's concubine?"

All the color had drained from Philippe's face. "Damn you, what are you saying?"

"I am saying that I was told my father took your sister as his leman, that she may have borne him a child, and their liaison was notorious enough for it to become known at the French court—"

"Enough!" Philippe took a quick step forward, his hand dropping instinctively to the hilt of his sword. "You'll rot in Hell for this!"

"Me?" Richard feigned surprise. "Most people would say that I'm the one wronged. If my father seduced my betrothed, then surely he is the one burning in Hell. And if the story is false, if it was contrived for political advantage, then the one responsible will be judged even more harshly—by the Almighty and by all of Christendom once his perfidy is exposed."

"My lord Richard." The Bishop of Chartres had stepped forward, saying gravely, "Can you provide proof of this most serious accusation?"

"I can provide witnesses who heard that he'd bedded her. And I can give you the name of the man who told me—Philip d'Alsace, the lord Count of Flanders."

All heads turned toward Philip, who seemed untroubled to find himself the center of attention. For a moment, he studied the French king, who returned his gaze with a hawk's unblinking intensity, saying in a dangerously soft voice, "You'd best think ere you speak, my lord count, for your heedless words could have consequences you cannot even begin to imagine."

"Surely you're not threatening him, Philippe?" Richard jeered, earning himself a look from the French king that was truly murderous.

"Not at all." Philip dismissed Richard's accusation with a casual wave of his hand, as nonchalantly as if they'd been exchanging social pleasantries. "I am sure my nephew by marriage merely meant to remind me how much was at stake. You need not worry, Philippe; I understand quite well. What Richard has said . . . it is true. I did seek him out at Mantes not long after Martinmas in God's Year 1188 and told him of the troubling gossip I'd heard about his father and the Lady Alys. Can I swear upon yonder holy relic that the rumors were true? Of course not. But I felt that he had a right to know of these rumors since he was betrothed to the lady. In his place, I would have wanted to know. Any man would," he said, with a sudden, sardonic smile that both acknowledged his own sordid marital history and dared anyone to mention it.

With all eyes now upon him, awaiting his response, Philippe drew several bracing breaths as he sought to get his rage under control. As he looked around the chapel, he could see that even his men had been won over by Richard's argument; how could he be expected to wed a woman who may have been his own father's bedmate? "I do not believe these malicious reports," he said fiercely. "They are vile lies meant to tarnish the honor of the French Crown, and I will not permit my sister's reputation to be besmirched like this."

"I see no reason to do that, either," Richard said, for he could afford to be magnanimous now that victory was within reach. "I have never blamed the lass. We know women are weak and easily led into sin, and we know, too, that kings are ones for getting their own way. Release me from my promise to wed Alys and I am content. I will gladly return her to your custody and that will end it."

Until that moment, Philippe would not have thought it possible to loathe another man as much as he now loathed Richard. "And are you going to return Gisors Castle and the Vexin, too?" he snarled. "A fine bargain you want me to make. You get to keep her dowry and I get back a woman whose value on the marriage market is—"

"My liege, this serves for naught." The Bishop of Chartres was regarding Philippe somberly. "We are in agreement that the plight-troth is no longer binding upon the English king. I would suggest that we select trustworthy men to conduct the necessary negotiations, but this is neither the time nor the place."

Philippe opened his mouth, closed it again. If Bishop Renaud, who was his cousin as well as one of his prelates, saw Richard as the wronged party, then this was a war he'd already lost. "So be it," he said through gritted teeth and turned on his heel, shoving aside anyone in his path as he stalked from the chapel.

As the other men exited the church, Richard leaned over and retrieved Philippe's letter from the floor rushes. He'd been confident he would prevail, having the bishops and Leviticus on his side. But the letter had undoubtedly made his task easier, for Philippe's men were more receptive to his argument after seeing their king's treachery laid bare like this. What Philippe failed to understand was that many of his vassals had been proud to take the cross and they did not think Christian kings should be fighting each other instead of the infidels. Richard rolled the parchment up, tucking it into his belt. He was free of Alys at long last and he still held Gisors and the Vexin. Not a bad day's work.

He glanced up at the sound of footsteps. Not everyone had left, for the Count of Flanders was several feet away. Sauntering toward the altar, Philip ran his hand admiringly over the reliquary. "It was clever to confront Philippe here. Does this truly contain a sliver of the True Cross?"

"Of course it does. I borrowed it from the Archbishop of Messina." Richard had been surprised when Philip had indicated his willingness to speak honestly about their meeting at Mantes. Now that the count had proven true to his word, he was grateful. But he was also puzzled by the other man's motivation, for self-interest had been the guiding force of Philip's life, and he did not see how his cousin had benefited from his candor. To the contrary, he'd just made a mortal enemy of the French king.

"I'd be hard put to decide which one of us Philippe hates more at the moment," he said, and Philip laughed softly.

"If it were a horse race, I'd wager that I win by a nose," he said, "for he felt the prick of my blade at his throat. But then I unexpectedly showed mercy and he'll never forgive me for that."

Richard laughed, too, for he thought that was an astute assessment of the French king's character. "By not revealing that Philippe was the one who'd told you about the seduction rumors? No, that is something Philippe would not have wanted known. I've often wondered about that. Think you that he invented the story out of whole cloth?"

"I've thought about that, too. It is true that he feared you'd reconcile again with your father, as you'd done so often in the past, and that would be far less likely if you believed your father had been swiving your betrothed. But I doubt that he was the source of the story, for Philippe is too protective of his own honor. I think he probably heard it from one of his spies, who'd picked it up from any of your father's legion of enemies. To hear some of them tell it, Harry was like a stag in rut, always on the prowl. I remember a similar accusation made against him some years earlier, that he'd deflowered the daughter of a rebellious baron in Brittany, so it might be the Alys tale had its roots in that charge. Any truth to that Breton story, you think?"

"Your guess is as good as mine," Richard said with a shrug. "From what I've heard, he preferred knowing bedmates, not skittish virgins." He thought that showed his father's common sense, for he'd never understood why so many men prided themselves upon luring coy or chaste women into their beds. Why bother with smiles and songs when it was so much easier and quicker to buy a bedmate with coins?

While Richard had little interest in discussing his father's carnal conquests, he did want to know why Philip had taken such a risk. "You're going to pay a price for your honesty, as you well know. Not many men would have dared to defy Philippe like that, for he's one to nurse a grudge to the end of his earthly days. Yet that does not seem to trouble you."

"And you want to know why." Philip leaned back against the altar and was silent for a moment. "Ah, hellfire, Cousin, I'd think the answer would be obvious.

I am nigh on fifty and there are mornings when I feel every one of those fifty years, thanks to aging and the joint-evil. I can no longer ride from dawn till dusk without aching bones, find the pleasures of the flesh are losing their allure, and I've had to face the fact that I'll not be siring a son to follow after me. At this point in my life, I do not much care about disappointing Philippe Capet. What matters is not disappointing the Almighty. This is the second time I've taken the cross. The first time I had less worthy motives, for I had it in mind to meddle in Outremer's politics, hoping to see the Leper King's sisters wed to men of my choosing. As you know, that did not happen. Now I've been given another chance, and I mean to make the most of it. Most likely I'll die in the Holy Land, but to die fighting for Jerusalem is not such a bad fate, is it?"

Richard had never expected to feel such a sense of solidarity with Philip, for they'd been rivals for as long as he could remember. Now he found himself looking at his cousin through new eyes. "No, it is not such a bad fate at all," he agreed, although he did not share the older man's fatalism. He was confident that he would return safely from Outremer, for surely it was not God's Will that he die in a failed quest.

THE COUNT OF FLANDERS gave Philippe another reason to despise him by hammering out an agreement that handed Richard virtually all that he sought, for the French king's bargaining position had been crippled by the exposure of his double-dealing, the disapproval of his own vassals, and the Church's rigid code governing sexual relations. Richard was released from his promise to wed Alys in return for a face-saving payment of ten thousand silver marks to Philippe. He was to retain the great stronghold of Gisors and the Vexin; it would revert to the French king only if he died without a male heir. The other lands in dispute were disposed of according to which king held them at the present time. And Alys was to be returned to Philippe's custody upon the conclusion of the crusade.

ELEANOR AND BERENGARIA reached the ancient seacoast city of Reggio on the twenty-ninth of March, where they were welcomed by its archbishop and installed in the royal castle. Berengaria was anxious now that she could see Messina from the window of her bedchamber, and she had a restless night. As a result, she slept past dawn, and when she was awakened later that morning, she was startled to see a blaze of sunlight filling the room. "Why did you not wake me, Uracca?" she said reproachfully, for she could not remember the last time she'd missed Morrow Mass.

"My lady, you must get up! The English king is here!"

Berengaria sat bolt upright in the bed. "Are you sure? We were not expecting him till late this afternoon!"

"He is with the queen, and they have requested that you join them in the solar." The girl's eyes were round. "I see why they call him Coeur de Lion, my lady, for he is as golden as a lion and just as large!"

She continued to burble on, but Berengaria was no longer listening. Fumbling for her bedrobe, she flung the coverlets back. "Fetch my clothes!" Her ladies obeyed, pulling her linen chemise over her head and then helping with her gown, lacing it up with fingers made clumsy by their haste, and then fastening a braided silk belt around her hips. She sat on the bed as they gartered her stockings at the knees, while Uracca undid her night plait and tried to brush out the tangles. When they brought over a polished metal mirror, Berengaria felt a pang of disappointment, for she'd planned to wear her best gown for her first meeting with Richard, not this rather plain one of blue wool. She was debating with herself whether she had time to change into the green silk with the violet sleeves when a knock sounded on the door.

As one of the women hurried over to open it, Berengaria reached for a wimple and veil. "Tell the servant that I will be ready soon, Loretta." This was not how it was supposed to be, she thought, a flicker of resentment beginning to smolder. But at that moment, Loretta cried out that the queen herself was at the door. Berengaria gasped, forewarned by a sudden premonition. There was no time for the wimple, but she managed to cover her hair decently with a veil before Loretta opened the door and Eleanor entered, with Richard right behind her.

"You must forgive my son's bad manners, child. If I did not know better, I'd think he had been raised by wolves."

Eleanor's reprimand was nullified by her indulgent tone. Later, Berengaria would remember and realize that Richard could do no wrong in his mother's eyes. Now she had no thoughts for anyone but the man striding toward her. She quickly sank down in a deep curtsy, lowering her gaze modestly, for well-bred young women were expected to be demure and self-effacing in the company of men. But then that rebellious glimmer sparked again, and, as Richard raised her up, she lifted her chin and looked him full in the face.

If he thought her boldness displeasing, as men in her country would have done, he hid it well, for he was smiling. "My mother is right," he said lightly, "but for once I have an excuse for my bad manners. What man would not be eager to see his bride?" He kissed her fingers with a courtly flourish, and then pressed a kiss into the palm of her hand.

His breath was warm on her skin and Berengaria felt an odd frisson go up her back. He was as handsome as she remembered, but she did not remember being as intensely aware of his physical presence as she was now. How tall he was! She had to tilt her head to look up into his face, and as their eyes met, she found she could not tear her gaze away. His beard was closely trimmed, his teeth even, his lips thin but well shaped, his eyes the color of smoke. But a crescent-shaped scar slanted from one eyebrow into his hairline, and the hand still clasping hers bore another scar, this one zigzagging along his thumb and disappearing into the tight cuff of his sleeve. She wondered how many other battle scars were hidden underneath his tunic, and then blushed hotly, shocked by her own unseemly thoughts.

"I'd forgotten what a little bit of a lass you were," Richard said, and she gave him a quick sidelong glance. He did not seem disappointed, though, for he was still smiling.

"And I'd forgotten how tall you were," she said, returning his smile shyly. "Not as tall as my brother, of course, but then no men are . . ." Worrying that she was babbling like Uracca, she let the rest of her sentence trail off. Richard had turned toward his mother, saying that he'd never seen another man as tall as Sancho, and she took advantage of his distraction to take a backward step, for she was finding his close physical proximity to be rather unsettling. It seemed safer to concentrate upon his conversation with his mother instead of her own wayward thoughts, and she glanced toward Eleanor. What she heard was disappointing, for Richard wanted them to leave Reggio as quickly as possible, and she'd hoped to have time to change her gown. But it would never have occurred to her to object, and she murmured her assent when Richard asked if she'd soon be ready to depart.

Eleanor had reassured Richard that little unpacking had been done because of their late arrival in Reggio the night before, and a glance around the chamber confirmed that for him. "Good," he said. "Why don't you let the others know we're leaving, Maman? I'll be with you as soon as I've had a private word with my bride." He was both amused and annoyed by the reaction of Berengaria's duennas, for they looked as horrified as if he'd just announced that he planned to drag the girl off to a bawdy house. But he left the matter in his mother's capable hands, watching with a grin as she ushered the women out. *Like so many clucking hens,* he thought, and turned back to Berengaria as soon as the door closed behind them.

To his surprise, she looked as flustered as her duennas. So it was true that Spanish women were kept almost as sequestered as Saracen wives. Well, the lass would just have to adapt to Angevin ways, for Navarre was part of her past now. "You need to explain to your women, little dove, that I do not always have ravishment in mind when I seek some privacy with you."

Berengaria blushed again, her lashes fluttering downward as she explained softly that she'd never been alone with a man before, for that would cause a great scandal. "Other than family, of course," she added and then her breath quickened, for Richard had reached for the long, dangling ends of her silk belt and was playfully pulling her toward him.

"So . . ." he said, and there was a low, intimate tone to his voice now that she found both mesmerizing and disquieting. "Sancho's little sister is all grown up. . . ." There was no longer space between them, and she could feel the heat of his hands through the thin wool of her gown as he slid them down to her waist. "I am going to take a wild guess and venture that you've never been kissed?"

"Not yet," she whispered, shivering when his fingers moved caressingly along her throat. But she did not protest when he tilted her chin up and then brought his head down, his mouth covering hers. The kisses were gentle at first, awakening sensations that were unfamiliar but not unpleasant. When his arms tightened around her, she followed his lead, dimly aware that this was surely sinful but paying more heed to the messages her body was sending to her brain—that she liked what he was doing to her. When he at last ended the embrace, she felt lightheaded and out of breath, relieved that he meant to take it no further, and understanding for the first time why men and women put their immortal souls at risk for the carnal pleasures of the flesh.

"Well," he said, "now you've been kissed, Berenguela. But I promised *irlanda* that we'd get to Bagnara by noon, and if we do not, she'll put some vile Sicilian curses on my head."

Berengaria did not find it as easy as Richard to return to the real world. She could still taste his mouth, feel his hands on her waist, and she had no idea who Irlanda was or where Bagnara was, either. But when he took her hand and propelled her toward the door, she followed obediently for several steps. Stopping abruptly then, she looked up at him in delighted surprise. "You called me Berenguela!"

"Why not? It is your name, after all."

"Yes, but for the past five months, I've heard only Berengaria, the French version, for I was told it was more fitting for your queen. Berenguela is my real name, what I am called in Navarre. And you remembered!"

"I like the musical sound of it," he said, reminding her that he was a poet, too. "I find it more pleasing to the ear than Berengaria. But it does make sense for you to have a French name when the majority of my subjects speak French. So we'll compromise. You can be Berengaria at court, Berenguela in bed."

Not waiting for her response, he opened the door and started swiftly down the stairs, towing Berengaria behind him. Feeling as if she had been caught up in a whirlwind, she let herself be swept along, for what else could she do?

JOANNA HAD MANAGED to lay out an impressive dinner, given that it was Lent and she'd had only one day's notice. The priory guest hall was filled with linen-draped trestle tables for all the people accompanying Eleanor, Berengaria, and Richard. But she'd reserved the high table for her family, not willing to share her mother with any others, however briefly.

Berengaria found herself forgotten in the jubilation of the Angevin family reunion, but she didn't mind. She'd been deeply touched by Joanna's joy, and slightly envious, too, for she'd have given almost anything to see her own mother again. They'd been talking nonstop during the meal and she was content to listen and to learn, although she did not catch all of their words. She'd spoken the *lenga romana* with Eleanor and Richard, but apparently Joanna's grasp of that language had waned during her years in Sicily, and they were conversing in French, at times too rapidly for Berengaria, whose own French was adequate but not yet fully fluent. There was no mistaking their pleasure, though, and after all the stories she'd heard of the Devil's Brood, it was reassuring to see such obvious family affection. She did not understand how Richard could have hated his own father and brothers, but there could be no doubt that he loved his mother and sister, and she took heart from that.

Richard remembered her from time to time; occasionally he smiled and once he winked. But for most of the meal, he was focused upon his mother, for he and Joanna were competing for Eleanor's attention. Joanna wanted to talk of family, the one she'd left behind and the one she'd found in Sicily. But Richard was intent upon political matters, and as soon as the last course was done, he shoved his chair back and rose to his feet.

"I need to borrow Maman for a while, *irlanda*, but I promise to have her back at Bagnara tonight."

"Richard, no!" Joanna flung her napkin down and jumped to her feet, too. "It has only been nine months since you've last seen Maman, but we've been separated for nigh on fifteen years!"

Berengaria was astonished that Joanna should dare to challenge Richard like that. She enjoyed a free and easy relationship with her own brother, but Richard seemed much more formidable than Sancho; moreover, she'd not have disputed Sancho in public. Richard showed no signs of anger, though. Leaning down, he kissed his sister on the cheek, saying with a coaxing smile, "I know how much you've missed Maman. However, it cannot be helped. We've got to talk about the news from Rome."

Joanna was not won over and continued to argue until Eleanor intervened, saying she'd make sure that Richard brought her back from Messina by Vespers. Watching wide-eyed, Berengaria found herself hoping that Richard would not forget to bid her farewell, for it was obvious to her that his mind was very much on that "news from Rome." Her worry was needless, for he took the time to kiss her hand and to tell Joanna to look after her before he escorted his mother from the hall.

Berengaria had assumed that she and Richard would spend their first day together. Glancing toward Joanna, she saw that the other woman was frowning and she wondered if Richard's sister found this as awkward as she did. While Joanna had welcomed her warmly, they were still strangers, after all. Richard had mentioned casually that Joanna would be accompanying them to the Holy Land, and Berengaria wasn't sure how she felt about that. She found Joanna somewhat intimidating, for she was extremely beautiful and worldly and self-confident, all the things that Berengaria knew she herself was not.

"Did you ever want to throttle your brother, Berengaria?" Joanna made a wry face. "I ought to have known he'd pull a sneaky trick like this, for he has not enough patience to fill a thimble."

"Is he always so . . . so sudden?" Berengaria asked, and Joanna grinned.

"All the males in my family are like that. My father was the worst of the lot, unable to be still even during Mass. At least Richard can get through Prime or Vespers without squirming. But once he gets an idea into his head, he wants to act upon it straightaway."

Berengaria was disarmed by Joanna's easy bantering and ventured to confide, "Things seem to happen so fast with him. That will take getting used to, I think."

"You'll have to," Joanna said, "for he's not likely to slow down. I'd say the secret of marriage to Richard is just to hold on tight and enjoy the ride!"

Berengaria flushed, for as innocent as she was, she still could recognize a double entendre when she heard one. As she met Joanna's eyes, she saw in them amusement and a glint of mischief. But she saw, too, genuine friendliness and, in that moment, she decided she was glad that Joanna would be coming with them. As she entered this new and alien Angevin world, what better guide could she have than Richard's favorite sister?

CHAPTER 14

leanor leaned back in her chair, regarding her son with affectionate, faintly suspicious hazel eyes. Richard had explained
why he'd—as he put it—switched horses in midgallop, des-
ignating his little nephew Arthur as his heir instead of his
brother John. He'd been candid about his troubles with the recalcitrant citizens
of Messina, and he'd surprised her by speaking well of Tancred, insisting that he'd
made sufficient restitution for his ill treatment of Joanna. But so far he'd not said
a word about the "news from Rome," and she was wondering why. Before she
could ask him, though, he launched into a scathing account of the French king's
duplicity, and she listened with interest, marveling that Philippe could have been
a son of the mild-mannered Louis's loins.

"So Philippe is the one responsible for making me miss your wedding. I owe
him a debt for that, and will look forward to repaying it."

Richard smiled, thinking that he'd have loved to witness his mother's retribution. "Alas, it will have to wait, for Philippe is no longer in Messina. He sailed for
Outremer this morning at dawn, in such haste I could almost believe he did not
want to meet you and my bride, Maman."

"I am sorry to hear that," Eleanor said truthfully; she'd wanted to judge for
herself the danger that the French king posed to her son. "Meeting Heinrich was
quite interesting, for I now know that if he were cut, he'd bleed pure ice. I was
hoping to have an opportunity to take Philippe's measure, too."

"Philippe is more of an annoyance than a threat," Richard said derisively. "If he
were cut, he'd most likely faint, since I doubt that he's ever seen blood up close,
for certes not on the battlefield."

"You still have not told me why we must confer in private like this. If I were not the trusting sort, Richard, I'd think that you have something to tell me that I'll not want to hear."

A flicker of surprise crossed his face, followed by a fond smile. "You know me far too well, Maman." Rising, he busied himself in fetching her a cup of wine, such an obvious delaying tactic that she did not bother to point it out. "Last night a messenger arrived from Rome," he said after he'd resumed his seat. "The Pope has been called home to God—or the Devil, depending upon which master he served. Clement died on March twentieth."

"And . . . ?" Eleanor prompted. "Have they chosen his successor yet?"

"Not officially, but I have it on good authority that they'll select one of the Orsini family, Cardinal Giacinto of Santa Maria in Scola Greca. I believe you've met him, Maman?"

"I did," she confirmed, "many years ago. An odd choice, for he must be well into his eighties by now."

"Eighty-five, I'm told." Richard leaned forward, his eyes probing hers. "As little as I liked Clement, at least I knew whom I was dealing with. And he was receptive to English needs as long as I made it worth his while. So his death is inconvenient, for I'd recently put several requests before the papal curia, one of them to confirm Longchamp again as his papal legate."

She raised an eyebrow, for she'd heard in Rome of the growing complaints about Longchamp's heavy-handed rule. "Is that wise, Richard?"

"I know," he conceded, "I know. . . . He has been collecting enemies as hungrily as a squirrel hoarding acorns. I'm not happy about it, but his loyalty is not in question. He needs to be reined in ere he goes too far, though, so I am sending the Archbishop of Rouen back to England to do just that. Between the two of you, you ought to be able to keep Longchamp from getting too besotted with his own importance."

Eleanor thought the Archbishop of Rouen was a good choice. "I still do not see why we could not have discussed this at Bagnara."

"Because I need you to be in Rome for the new Pope's consecration, and Joanna will not be happy about that."

"Neither am I, Richard. I've been here less than a day!"

"I know how much I ask of you, Maman. But we must make sure that the new Pope is friendly to English interests, and to do that, we need to get to him ere Philippe and Heinrich do." Seeing her frown, he said before she could refuse, "There is no one better than you at such diplomacy. Moreover, you already know the man and none would doubt your authority to speak for me."

Eleanor's eyes searched his face intently. After a silence that he found ominous, she said with a sigh, "Very well. But it will be up to you to reconcile Joanna to our abrupt departure. I am sure she'd expected to have some time to get to know Berengaria."

Richard looked uncomfortable. "Joanna will not be returning with you, Maman. I want her to accompany us to Outremer. It will not be easy for Berenguela in the Holy Land, and I thought she'd feel less homesick if she had Joanna for company. That is even more true now that we cannot wed until the end of Lent, for her reputation will suffer if she does not have a woman of high rank to act as her . . . duenna, as the Spanish call it."

Eleanor bit her lip to keep from protesting. As little as she liked it, his reasoning made sense. "I will not be rushing off on the morrow," she warned. "I'll act as your envoy at the papal court, but I want some time with my daughter first."

"Of course," he agreed hastily and leaned over to graze her cheek with a grateful kiss before holding out his hand to assist her to her feet. "I am truly sorry that we cannot wed whilst you're here, Maman. You missed so many family events during those years of confinement. It does not seem fair that you'll be deprived of my wedding, too."

Eleanor was both surprised and touched that he understood how much it had meant to her. "So . . ." she said with a warm smile, "what do you think of your bride?"

"She seems quite suitable," he said with an easy smile of his own. "From all you've told me, she acquitted herself well during the hardships of your journey. I think she'll make a good queen."

Eleanor thought so, too. But for a moment, she felt an unexpected pang of regret, for she was in her twilight while Berengaria's sun was just rising. Almost at once, she rejected that twinge of envy, for she'd not have traded her past for her daughter-in-law's youth. She'd experienced so much that Berengaria never would, that few women had, and she smiled, thinking that no man would ever have dismissed her with Richard's casual "quite suitable." She'd wanted more, and if her memories were bittersweet now, they still testified to a life lived to the fullest, a life that had not lacked for passion or adventure or the élan of her beloved Aquitaine.

Richard was looking at her curiously. "You've an odd expression, Maman. If you were a cat, you'd be licking cream from your whiskers. What were you thinking?"

She gave him a half-truth. "Of my marriage and yours. Have you given any thought to how awkward it will be for Philippe, having to bear witness as you wed the woman who replaced his sister?"

"Why? You think I ought to ask Philippe to give the bride away?" He laughed down at her, stirring memories of the mischievous boy he'd once been, and she stilled the voice whispering that he took his enemies too lightly, for she knew he'd not have heeded her words of warning.

ELEANOR DID NOT DEPART for another four days, despite Richard's coaxing. It was not until the afternoon of April 4 that her ship's oarsmen began to maneuver their way out into the harbor. Richard, Joanna, and Berengaria stood on the quay, and Eleanor continued to return their farewell waves until Messina began to recede into the distance. A northwest wind had robbed the sun of much of its warmth, but Hawisa stayed loyally beside the queen instead of withdrawing to the shelter of their canvas tent. She knew that this parting was painful for Eleanor, so she'd done her best to hide her own elation, her joy that she'd not have to lay eyes again upon her husband for many months, if ever. Men died so easily in the Holy Land, after all.

Eleanor remained on deck, indifferent to the spray splashing over the gunwale. "I knew Richard would be facing daily danger in Outremer," she said at last. "But I'd not expected to have to fear for my daughter's safety, too."

Hawisa glanced at the queen's profile, wishing she could say there was no cause for anxiety. She couldn't, of course, for the deadly miasmas and maladies of those eastern climes did not discriminate between men and women. But she wanted to offer some comfort, for she greatly admired the aging queen. "I understand your concern, Madame. I feel confident, though, that the Lady Joanna will come to no harm, not with the king to protect her. I'd wager that even Death himself would think twice ere he took Richard on," she said lightly, "for I've never met a man who was so invincible."

Her attempt at humor failed. "Richard is not invincible," Eleanor said sharply. After a long, uncomfortable silence, she added, so softly Hawisa barely heard her, "He just thinks he is. . . ."

MORGAN WAS VERY PLEASED to be one of the knights chosen to accompany Richard to Bagnara. Life had gotten hectic in Messina now that their departure date was so close, and he welcomed this brief respite from his supervisory duties at the waterfront. He welcomed, too, the chance to renew his flirtation with the Lady Mariam and to visit with his cousin Joanna. After Richard went off to see Berengaria, Morgan strolled over to the guest hall with Warin Fitz Gerald, Baldwin de Bethune, and the Préaux brothers, Pierre, Guilhem, and Jean.

They were in high spirits, anticipating a pleasant supper with Joanna and her ladies, joking that they might even get to spend the night, for plight-troths were almost as binding as actual marriage vows and they all knew Richard was not one for waiting. While they were excited to be leaving Sicily at long last and eager to reach the siege of Acre, they were also uneasy, dreading the dangerous sea voyage that lay ahead of them, and so their laughter was loud and their badinage caustic. They mocked Pierre, whose recent run of bad luck carried over into several dice games, they threatened to tell Mariam of Morgan's frequent visits to a dockside tavern and a buxom, black-eyed servingmaid, and they tormented Guilhem, who'd unwisely confessed to a fear of the sea, with tales of shipwrecks and savage storms. But when Richard suddenly strode into the hall and tersely announced that they were returning to Messina, they got hastily to their feet, keeping their faces carefully blank and their tongues bridled. They nodded dutifully when he told them to fetch their ship's crew from the town tavern, and it was only after he'd gone to find Joanna that they dared to exchange knowing grins.

Joanna was in the priory gardens, teaching Alicia how to play chess. She was taken by surprise when Richard appeared without warning, announced he was going back to Messina, and turned on his heel before she could respond. She caught up with him in a few strides, though, grasping his arm while she looked up into his face. "Why are you leaving so soon? You just got here—" Comprehension dawning, she tried unsuccessfully to hide a smile. "Oh . . . she turned you down?"

It was one of the few times she'd seen her brother off balance. He stared at her in open astonishment. "What are you, a witch?"

"It hardly took second sight to figure that out." She glanced around to make sure Alicia was out of earshot, pleased to see the girl was already making a discreet exit. "You are obviously in a temper, and you have not been here long enough to quarrel with anyone but Berengaria. I'm surprised, though, that she was bold enough to tell you no."

Richard had been surprised, too. "I had no idea she could be so stubborn. The plight-troth is binding upon us, the marriage but a formality—"

"Not to Berengaria."

"Even if we'd not been plight-trothed, it is no great sin, venial at most."

Joanna was not going to be sidetracked by a discussion of fornication. She didn't doubt that most men shared Richard's view, and many women, too. What mattered, though, was that Richard's betrothed did not. "This is an argument you do not need—or even want—to win, Brother. I'm sure you've not been living like a monk whilst waiting for her arrival. If you've an itch, you can get it easily scratched in Messina. But if you coax or coerce Berengaria into doing something she sees as a grievous sin, you could make her skittish of the marriage bed. And Morgan and André say you never commit your troops to battle without first weighing the consequences and assessing the risks."

Richard wasn't sure if he was annoyed or amused. "Well, this I can say for certes, that I never expected to be lectured on carnal matters by my little sister."

"Your 'little sister' is a woman grown, in case you've not noticed. For a number of years, I presided over a court as worldly as any in Christendom, and that includes Maman's court at Poitiers." There was an edge to her smile. Yes, Maman had been forced to overlook Papa's infidelities, but at least he'd not kept a *harim* of Saracen slave girls. She was not about to discuss that with her brother, though. Instead she linked her arm through his and then gave him a playful push, telling him to go back to Messina whilst she comforted his bashful bride.

Joanna was as good as her word, and soon thereafter, she knocked upon the door of Berengaria's guest cottage. It opened so quickly she knew the other woman must have been expecting Richard to return, an inference confirmed by the conflicted emotions that chased across Berengaria's face: hope, disappointment, and relief. She stepped aside, politely opening the door wider when Joanna asked to enter.

Joanna was glad to see she was still alone, not having called her duennas back yet, for a delicate discussion like this required privacy. She was glad, too, that Berengaria did not seem overly distraught; she'd half expected to find her in hysterics, weeping and apprehensive. But her pallor was the only sign of distress; Berengaria's brown eyes were dry. Joanna suddenly wished she'd thought out what she wanted to say beforehand. Too late to retreat now, though. "I thought you might feel like talking, Berengaria. I remember my first argument with William—"

Berengaria gasped. "Richard told you?"

"No, he did not," Joanna said hastily. "I guessed, which was easy enough to do, since he looked like a storm cloud. Also, I know how eager men are to plant their flags and claim their territory."

Berengaria raised her chin. "If you've come to counsel me to yield—"

"Indeed not! You must follow the dictates of your conscience, not Richard's. Assuming he has one," Joanna added with a grin. "Actually, I think it was good that you stood up to him. It never hurts to remind a man that he cannot always have his own way. I wanted to make sure that you were not overly troubled by the quarrel. You need not fear that he'll nurse a grudge or that he is well and truly wroth with you, for he is not."

Berengaria surprised her then by saying, "I know. I could see that he was more vexed than outraged." Sitting down on a coffer chest, she studied the other woman, trying to make up her mind. It would be wonderful to have a confidante, to be able to talk about the confusing feelings and urges that were preying on her peace. But did she dare to confide in Richard's sister? When Joanna moved to the table and poured wine for them both, she said before she could repent of it, "I wish Richard and I had not quarreled. But I am not so sheltered that I do not know husbands and wives will disagree. It is something else that is troubling me, a serious sin. . . ."

Joanna did not like the sound of that. Summoning up what she hoped was a reassuring smile, she seated herself beside Berengaria on the coffer. "Can you tell me about it?"

Berengaria wavered before saying in a low voice, no longer meeting Joanna's eyes. "Padre Domingo, my confessor, cautioned me that I must be vigilant in protecting my virtue. He said . . . said Richard might want to lie with me ere we were wed, but I must not permit it. So I was prepared when he . . ." She let her words trail off, but then she stiffened her spine and said resolutely, "I did not expect, though, to like it so much when Richard kisses me. I was too prideful, Joanna, sure that I could not be tempted by the sin of lust. . . ."

"I see," Joanna murmured, trying to conceal her relief. She'd feared Berengaria was going to confess that she believed sexual intercourse was always a sin, even in the marriage bed, for she knew some women took to heart the Church's teaching that no fruitfulness of the flesh could be compared to holy virginity, the highest form of spiritual purity. She watched color stain Berengaria's cheeks and she suddenly realized that Padre Domingo was probably her only source of information about carnal desires. Her mother had died when she was just nine, and her sisters were younger than she. Joanna was convinced that there was not a father ever born willing to discuss lust with his daughter, and she doubted that Berengaria's brother would have been willing, either. She doubted, too, that Berengaria, reserved and proud, would have turned for advice to her attendants, for they were all flighty young girls, and if one was not a virgin, she'd never have admitted it.

Joanna felt a surge of sympathy for her brother's young bride, thinking how lucky she herself had been. Her mother had always been candid and comfortable about sexual matters, and Joanna had concluded at an early age that the marriage bed must be a place of great pleasure since her parents spent so much time in theirs. Wed at eleven, she'd had years to get to know her husband before she was old enough to consummate their marriage, and she'd had trusted female confidantes in Beatrix, Mariam, and Constance. Poor Berengaria, with only Padre Domingo to show her the way, the blind leading the blind! Well, it was not too late, thankfully.

"When Padre Domingo was warning you of the dangers of lust, did he happen to mention that marital sex is not a sin?"

"Yes . . . but only if it is done for procreation."

"Not so," Joanna said triumphantly. "The Church teaches that there are four reasons for a husband to have carnal knowledge of his wife, and only one is a sin. As you said, it is never sinful when it is done in hopes of having a child. But it is not sinful either if it is to pay the marital debt."

Berengaria looked puzzled, but interested. "What is the marital debt?"

"Padre Domingo forgot to tell you about that, did he? According to St Paul's teaching, the husband must render the conjugal debt to the wife and the wife to the husband, for he has power over her body and she over his. The Church position on this is so uncompromising that even if a husband or wife contracts leprosy, the partner still owes the marital debt."

Berengaria's eyes were wide with amazement. "You mean that I could demand this 'debt' from Richard and he'd have to oblige me?" And when Joanna confirmed that he would, that idea was so improbable to Berengaria that she began to giggle. Joanna joined in her merriment, and their shared laughter did much to diffuse any awkwardness between them.

"The third permissible reason for having marital sex," Joanna resumed, "is one of the reasons for getting married, to avoid the sin of fornication." She almost added that most people parted company with the Church on that, agreeing with Richard that fornication was harmless as long as the participants weren't married or had not taken holy vows, but she thought better of it. "The only time that a married couple sin is if they are so driven by lust that satisfying their carnal needs is all that matters to them."

"Oh. . . ." Berengaria was quiet for a moment, considering what she'd just been told, and then she smiled. "Joanna, thank you! You see . . . I told Richard that we could not lie together until we were properly wed. Yet I did not dare remind him that even married couples are supposed to abstain during Lent. After he left, I realized that this would pose a problem in our marriage, for there are so many days when the Church prohibits carnal union—Sundays and Wednesdays and Fridays and during Pentecost and Advent or when the wife is with child. . . . Somehow I could not envision Richard taking all these restrictions in good grace. And as his wife, I could not refuse him, which would mean that I'd be sharing his sin. But now I see that I would not be sinning, that I'd merely be satisfying the marital debt!"

She laughed, almost giddy with relief. But then her face shadowed again. "You said it was still a sin to be 'driven by lust.' I feel reasonably sure that I feel lust when Richard kisses me, Joanna, or touches me . . ." She was blushing hotly now, and Joanna felt a protective urge that was almost maternal.

"You feel desire," she corrected, "the natural desire that a woman is supposed to feel for her husband. And that is not a sin. It is part of the Almighty's Plan, for many doctors believe that a woman cannot conceive unless she experiences pleasure."

This was a day of surprises for Berengaria. "Is that truly so?"

Joanna hesitated, but Berengaria had been very candid. It seemed only fair to be candid in return. "Richard told you that my son died soon after birth." She had to blink rapidly, for there were some wounds that never fully healed. "I was unable to conceive again after that. Eventually, I had William take me to Salerno, which has some of the best doctors in Christendom, and a few of them are female. I consulted several of these women physicians, hoping they could help. They told me when a woman was most fertile and gave me herbs and assured me that I was more fortunate than many wives, for I enjoyed making love with William. That would improve my chances of getting pregnant, they said. . . ." She managed a flickering smile, a slight shrug.

Berengaria found herself blinking back tears, too, for the pain on Joanna's face was so naked that she felt as if it struck at her own heart. "I cannot even imagine what it would be like to lose a baby," she confessed. "But it must be of some comfort to know that he is in God's Keeping, blessed and safe for all eternity." When Joanna nodded, Berengaria overcame her natural reticence and squeezed her sister-in-law's hand. "I am very glad that you are coming with us," she confided. After a few moments of companionable silence, though, she said, "But what of a woman who is raped and then gets with child? That happened to a milkmaid at our palace in Olite. She was forced by a drunken lout, so I am sure she got no pleasure from it. Yet she became pregnant."

"That same thought occurred to me, too," Joanna admitted, "and I asked the Salerno doctors and midwives about it. Most likely a male physician would have insisted pregnancy was proof of pleasure. Women know better, of course. So, yes, a woman can sometimes conceive even if she was unwilling. But they assured me it is true more often than not, and it made sense to me that a husband's seed would be more likely to take root if his wife was relaxed and receptive."

Berengaria thought that made sense, too. "I am grateful we had this talk," she said, smiling at the older woman. "You are much more knowledgeable about carnal matters than Padre Domingo!"

"Consulting a priest about carnal matters is like asking a blind man to describe a sunset," Joanna said teasingly, and was gratified when Berengaria joined in her laughter, for even a few days ago, she was sure the young Spanish woman would have seen such flippancy as blasphemous. She began to relate a story she'd heard some years ago, one meant to reinforce in Berengaria's mind the link between sexual pleasure and conception: that the French king had been persuaded to divorce Eleanor only after his advisers convinced him that she'd never bear him a son now that their marriage was irretrievably broken and she was unlikely to find satisfaction in his bed.

Joanna was very pleased with herself, confident that she'd done much this afternoon to make sure her brother's marriage would be a successful one. It might be a good idea, though, to suggest to Richard that Padre Domingo be sent back to Navarre and a more open-minded confessor found for his bride. A pity Richard would never know how much he owed her. But she could not tell him without violating Berengaria's trust, and she had no intention of doing that. She thought they'd planted the seeds this day of something worth nurturing—a genuine friendship.

RICHARD HAD HIS wooden castle dismantled and the sections were marked before being stowed in ships to be reassembled in Outremer. The same was done for his numerous siege engines. As his army made ready for departure, huge crowds gathered upon the docks to watch. The Messinians were awed by the magnitude of the undertaking. The cargo vessels were gradually filled with tuns of wine, sacks of flour and cheese and dried fruit and beans and salted meat; rumors spread that these long-tailed Englishmen were taking more than ten thousand slabs of cured pork alone. They were fascinated by the endless procession of provisions being lugged onto the gangplanks: huge barrels of water, grain and hay, arrows, crossbow bolts, armor, saddles, blankets, tents, and coffers filled with silver pennies, gold plate, and jewels, an astonishing mix of the mundane and the precious.

Daily life in Messina came to a halt, and even the markets were deserted as people gathered to watch hundreds of horses being loaded upon transport galleys called "taride." These vessels were backed onto the beaches instead of the wharves, and port doors were opened in their sterns. Then the stallions were blindfolded and led up ramps into the ships, where they'd be separated by wooden hurdles and held upright by canvas slings that slid under their bellies and were attached to overhead iron rings. A tarida usually accommodated forty horses, and once they were stabled below deck, the vertical inner door was barred and the outer door caulked to make it watertight. The loading of so many high-strung destriers did not always go smoothly. Sometimes the horses balked and men's tempers flared, and the spectators agreed it was almost as entertaining as a troupe of traveling players.

It was not until Wednesday in Holy Week that the royal fleet was ready to sail, and most of the city turned out for the event, thankful that this foreign army was finally departing but also delighting in this extraordinary spectacle. More than two hundred ships and seventeen thousand soldiers and sailors. Large transport vessels called busses. Naves that relied only upon sails. And the ships that drew all eyes and evoked admiring murmurs from the townspeople—the sleek, deadly war galleys, painted in bright colors, their gunwales hung with shields, the red and gold banners of the English king streaming from their mastheads. The crusade of Richard Coeur de Lion was at last under way.

AFTER SUCH a dramatic departure from Messina, what followed was anticlimactic. The wind died and the fleet found itself becalmed off the coast of Calabria. They were forced to drop anchor and wait. After the sun had set in a blood-red haze, many took comfort from the glow of the lantern placed aloft in Richard's galley. He'd promised to light it each and every night, a guiding beacon for his ships, reassuring proof of his presence in the midst of the dark, ominous Greek Sea. The next day the winds picked up, but they remained weak and variable, and not much progress was made. Yet so far the voyage had been calm and for that, seventeen thousand souls were utterly thankful.

RICHARD HAD CHOSEN one of the largest busses for Joanna and Berengaria; it was a heavy, cumbersome vessel, but safer than the low-riding galleys. As Good Friday dawned, the fleet sailed on, the swift galleys holding back to keep pace with the slower craft. Determined to keep them all together, Richard kept a sharp eye out for any stragglers—like a sheepdog nipping at the heels of its flock, his men joked. But they welcomed the sound of trumpets echoing from one ship to another, and took heart from the sight of the royal galley cleaving the waves like a battle sword as it led the way toward the Holy Land.

By midmorning, the winds shifted, coming now from the south, and the sea grew choppy. As their buss wallowed in the heavy swells, most of the women were soon stricken with seasickness. To her dismay, Joanna discovered that she was still as susceptible to *mal de mer* as she'd been during her initial sea voyage at the age of eleven. As her suffering intensified, she was groggily grateful to her future sister-in-law; Berengaria never left her side, holding a basin when she had to vomit, wiping the perspiration from her face with a cool, wet cloth, fetching a vial of ginger syrup herself and gently persevering until Joanna had choked it down. The atmosphere in their tent was stifling, the stench enough to roil heaving stomachs, their coffers and trundle beds pitching every time the ship did. Joanna's dogs were whimpering softly, and she could hear the sobbing of one of Berengaria's ladies. When she realized that Alicia was huddled by her bed, she tried to put a comforting arm around the girl's trembling shoulders. But it was then that the deck dropped so steeply that several of the women screamed and Joanna would have been thrown from the bed had Berengaria not grasped her arm and held tight. None of them breathed until the ship righted itself, sure for a terrifying moment that they were plummeting down to their deaths.

"Joanna!" A gust of salt air swept in as Mariam stumbled into the tent. Her face was blanched of all color, and she clutched her pater noster beads so tightly the string had frayed. "The ship's master . . . he says a bad storm is nigh."

THE SKY DARKENED long before the rain arrived. It was as if night had come, hours before its time. The crew of Richard's galley was rushing to lower the sails, tugging on the pulleys that controlled the halyard. All the day's light had been smothered by sinister storm clouds as black as pitch, and as Richard and his men watched in awe, lightning blazed overhead, casting an eerie green glow over their ship. The sea was tossing and bucking like an unbroken horse, and each time the galley plunged into a trough, it took an eternity until it struggled back up again. Most of Richard's companions fled to the dubious shelter of their tent, but he had always faced his foes head-on and he remained on deck, clinging for support to the gunwale as the sailors struggled to pull in the oars.

The hours that followed were the most frightening of his life. The waves flung their ship about as if it were a child's toy; never had he felt so helpless, so at the mercy of forces beyond his control. The helmsman remained at the tiller, jerking it with all of his strength, but it was obvious to Richard that the rudder was not responding. Rain was soon pelting down, stinging with needle-sharpness against his skin; within moments, he was utterly drenched. Water was splashing over the gunwale and the deck was awash. Each time a wave smashed into the hull, it sounded as if millstones were raining down upon them, and the wind was keening like the souls of the damned. Distant peals of thunder were much closer now, and when lightning stabbed through the clouds, he was horrified to see it strike the mast of a nearby galley, half blinding him with a searing flash of blue-white fire. Flames illuminated the doomed ship for a harrowing moment, and then it was gone, swept away into the black void of sea and sky, the drowning men's screams muffled by the howling wind. Richard did not dare release his hold on the gunwale to make the sign of the cross; closing his eyes, he entreated the Almighty to spare his fleet and his men, offering up a despairing prayer that he not be punished for past sins ere he had the chance to redeem himself in the Holy Land.

The squall was as swift-moving as it was savage, and by evening the wind's force began to ease and the sea gradually quieted. The sailors recovered first, for they were accustomed to gambling with Death and winning. For those experiencing their first storm at sea, it was not as easy. Richard's men, their bodies bruised and battered, their stomachs still churning, were too shaken to sleep, and slumped, glassy-eyed and mute, on their soaked bedding, not yet believing their reprieve.

Richard could not sleep, either. He did his best to appear composed, for a battle commander must not show fear before his soldiers. But he did not think his appetite would ever come back, and he found he had no more control over his brain than he'd had over the tempest. He could not forget the faces of the men on that burning galley. Two hundred and nineteen ships. How many of them had survived the storm? How many men had he lost? What of his sister? Berenguela? Surely their buss was sturdy enough to have ridden out the gale? How could it be God's Will that they perish at sea, alone and afraid?

ALMOST AS IF NATURE were making amends for the Good Friday storm, the winds were favorable the next morning and on the four days that followed. By Wednesday, April 17, a dawn flight of birds and seaweed in the water alerted the sailors that they were approaching land. When the ship's master informed Richard that the island of Crete lay ahead, Richard gave the order to put ashore there.

The southwest coast of Crete was exposed to southerly winds and sudden squalls sweeping down from the mountains, so the fleet had to seek shelter on the island's northwest coast, finally dropping anchor in the Gulf of Chandax. Richard then dispatched Guilhem de Préaux in a small galley called a "sagitta," with orders to count their ships as they straggled in, to see if any were missing and if any were in need of storm repairs. After that, he settled down to do what he found most difficult—wait.

The sun was flaming out in spectacular fashion when Jaufre of Perche was rowed over to the king's galley. He found Richard studying maps of Rhodes and Cyprus, which had been designated as rendezvous ports in case the fleet was scattered at sea. Refusing an offer of cheese and bread, Jaufre confessed that the mere sight of food would be enough to make him sprint for the gunwale and begin feeding the fish. He did accept a cup of wine, though, saying, only half in jest, that he'd heard Crete was a fine place, and if his men began to desert, he'd be sorely tempted to join them.

"I was told that the mountain we saw as we approached the coast is midway between Messina and Acre," Richard said. "But if I thought the second half of the journey would be as accursed as the first half, I might consider starting life anew in Crete myself. You may have been better off sailing with Philippe, Jaufre. At the least, you'd be approaching the Holy Land by now, with the worst of the voyage behind you."

"I've no regrets about that," Jaufre said noncommittally. He'd never discussed with Richard the reasons for his defection, but the English king had not been surprised by his decision, for he'd seen the look of shock on Jaufre's face during that chapel confrontation with Philippe. It had taken courage, though, to defy his king, and Richard intended to bestow enough favors upon Jaufre and Richenza to compensate for Philippe's hostility.

"Besides," Jaufre added with a smile, "if I'd sailed with Philippe, I'd not have been in Messina for your lady mother's arrival and I'd not have gotten her news— that my wife gave birth to a healthy son last September. My father will be overjoyed when he hears, for this is his first grandchild."

Jaufre's father had been at the siege of Acre for the past year. Seeing the genuine pleasure on the young man's face, Richard was surprised to find himself envying the bond that obviously existed between the count and his son. He did not often think of his turbulent relationship with his own father, for he'd never been one to dwell upon past regrets. Mayhap it was because he'd come so close to death during that Good Friday storm, he decided. He'd certainly had his share of narrow escapes on the battlefield, but a man fighting for his life did not have time for fear. "My father liked to boast that he'd never gotten seasick in all those Channel crossings, but I wonder how he'd have fared—" He broke off, then, for he'd heard the shouting that heralded Guilhem de Préaux's return.

Plunging from the tent, with Jaufre right at his heels, Richard was waiting on deck as a ladder was lowered into Guilhem's smaller vessel. Scrambling aboard, he gave the king a look of such misery that Richard's mouth went suddenly dry.

"My news is not good, my lord. Twenty-five of our ships are missing."

There were gasps from the men gathered around to hear Guilhem's report. Richard spat out a savage oath, profane enough to impress even the tough-talking sailors. But when Guilhem looked away, no longer meeting his eyes, Richard knew worse was to come. "What else?" he said hoarsely. "Hold nothing back."

"I am so sorry, my liege. But one of the missing ships is the buss carrying Queen Joanna and the Lady Berengaria."

CHAPTER 15

MAY 1191

Off the Coast of Cyprus

ll of the passengers of the buss had crowded to the gunwales, so hungry were they for their first glimpse of land in more than two weeks. The Good Friday storm had swept their vessel far out to sea, almost to the African coast, where they'd then been becalmed for some nerve-wracking days, dreading both pirates and Saracen ships. Then their attempt to sail to the fleet's first rendezvous, Rhodes, had been defeated by contrary winds. The buss's master had finally decided to head for the next gathering point at Cyprus, charting his course by the sun's position in the heavens and a floating magnetized needle that pointed toward the pole star. As a courtesy, he'd first consulted Stephen de Turnham, the English baron charged to see to the safety of Richard's women. Stephen was wise enough to defer to the master's far greater knowledge of the sea, and his faith was justified on the first of May when a sailor up in the rigging called out the sweetest words any of them had ever heard: "Land on the larboard side!"

At first, the passengers could see nothing. But then the smudged shadows along the horizon slowly began to take shape. In the distance, the sea was changing color, shading from deep blue to turquoise as the water grew shallower. "Is that Cyprus?" Berengaria asked, and when the master said it was, her murmured *"Gracias a Dios"* needed no translation, found echoes in every heart. She turned then, intending to thank the master, too, for they'd survived because of his seamanship. But at that moment, Joanna appeared on deck.

It was the first time she'd left the tent in days, and she blinked and squinted in the blaze of midday sun. As much as they'd all suffered during their ordeal, none had been as desperately ill as Joanna. She'd lost so much weight that she seemed alarmingly frail, her collarbones thrown into sudden prominence, her gown gaping at the neckline, and her chalky-white pallor made the dark shadows under her eyes look like bruises. Berengaria started toward her, but Stephen de Turnham and Mariam reached her first. She was too unsteady on her feet for false pride, and allowed them to guide her toward the gunwale. She was soon swallowing convulsively and when Berengaria took her hand, it was clammy to the touch. But she kept her eyes upon the horizon, watching with a painful intensity as the coast of Cyprus gradually came into view.

"Oh, no!" Joanna's murmur reached no farther than Berengaria's ears, more like a broken breath than a cry. They looked at each other in dismay and then back at the beautiful, blue-green, empty sea. For by now they ought to have seen a floating forest of timber masts, sails furled as the ships rode at anchor offshore. An involuntary groan burst from dozens of throats, so sure had they all been that they'd find the royal fleet awaiting them in Cyprus. None voiced their fears aloud, though, for the knights did not want to alarm the women, and Joanna and Berengaria's ladies-in-waiting dared not speak out, for their mistresses had entered into a conspiracy of silence, refusing to acknowledge the possibility that Richard's ship might have gone down in that Good Friday gale.

The silence that settled over the deck was a strangled one, therefore, fraught with all that they dare not say. When she saw Uracca struggling to stifle a sob, Berengaria forced a smile and offered the only comfort she could, saying with false heartiness, "How wonderful it will be to set foot on land again."

She was taken aback by Joanna's vehement reaction to that innocuous comment. "No!" Seeing Berengaria's lack of comprehension, Joanna drew a bracing breath before saying, more calmly, "Cyprus is ruled by a man unworthy of trust. Isaac Comnenus seized power six years ago and dares to call himself emperor. But he has no honor, no scruples, and no mercy. We cannot go ashore."

"The queen is right," Stephen de Turnham said, swiftly and very firmly, wanting to head off any arguments. "Ere we left Messina, we were told to sail for Cyprus if our ships became separated. But the king said that if we arrived first, under no circumstances were we to land. We must await the arrival of the fleet." Another silence fell at that. But while none were willing to say it aloud, the same thought was in all their minds. *The fleet ought to have been here by now. What if it never comes?*

THE REALIZATION that her brother was still missing seemed to have sapped the last of Joanna's strength and she asked Stephen to escort her back to the tent.

Berengaria would have liked to escape the scrutiny of the others, too, but she sensed that Joanna needed some time to herself. Instead, she drew Mariam aside. "Can you tell me more of this man? Joanna called him Isaac Comnenus. Is he a member of the Royal House of Constantinople?"

"Yes, he was a kinsman of the old emperor. He has good bloodlines, but a dubious past. Cyprus was a possession of the Greek Empire, and seven years ago, Isaac showed up on the island, claiming to be its new governor. I've heard it said that his documents were forged; be that as it may, his claim was accepted. The following year, that monster Andronicus was overthrown and slain, and Isaac took advantage of the chaos in Constantinople to declare himself the Emperor of Cyprus. Actually, he just calls himself the emperor, so his ambitions may well extend to the Greek Empire itself. But he has Cyprus in a stranglehold, maintaining power by hiring Armenian routiers and terrorizing the local population. He is loathed and feared by the Cypriots for arbitrarily seizing their property and imposing high taxes. And he has a truly vile reputation where women are concerned; even respectable wives and daughters are not safe from his lustful attentions."

Berengaria glanced toward the rolling hills now silhouetted against the sky. After so long at sea, Cyprus looked like a veritable Eden, but the snake in this Eden sounded more lethal than any viper. She was puzzled that this was the first she'd heard of Isaac Comnenus, given that his island was a rendezvous point for their fleet. "I am surprised," she confessed, "that Joanna did not mention this man to me."

"She was ashamed to do so," Mariam said bluntly, "for Isaac Comnenus was her husband's ally." She smiled, somewhat sadly, at Berengaria's shocked expression. "My brother had a good heart, but his judgment was flawed. So great was his hatred of the Greek Empire that he'd have allied himself with Lucifer himself to bring Constantinople down. As for Isaac, he realized the new Greek emperor would seek to reclaim Cyprus, so he made overtures to all of the empire's enemies. He benefited far more from this alliance than Sicily did, for when Constantinople sent an invasion force, the fleet of William's admiral, Margaritis, easily scattered them. After stories began to trickle back to Palermo of Isaac's cruelties, I think William had second thoughts, but he was too stubborn to admit it. And by then it was too late for my half-sister Sophia, who'd been packed off to Cyprus as Isaac's bride. Fortunately for me, I was wed when Isaac proposed that marital pact. But Sophia fancied the idea of being an empress. . . ." Mariam suppressed a sigh. Did a crown truly matter if she reigned in Hell?

Berengaria blinked in surprise. "I did not know you'd been married. Did your husband . . . ?"

Mariam was amused by that delicate pause. "My husband died after four years of marriage. He was a good man, albeit old enough to be my father, and I had no complaints as his wife. But widowhood is the only time when a woman is not under a man's thumb, first as daughter and then as wife, and I like the freedom—"

Mariam cut herself off so abruptly that Berengaria instinctively turned to see what had caught the other woman's attention. And then she, too, gasped, clasping her hand to her mouth as she looked toward the Cypriot coast.

As soon as she was alone, Joanna slumped down onto her bed, keeping her eyes tightly shut so no tears could squeeze through her lashes. She would not cry for her brother; that would be a betrayal of faith, an admission that he could be dead. But where was he? Surely the fleet would not have sailed on to Outremer? Did he think they'd perished in that accursed storm? No, he would not give up hope that easily, not Richard. When Star, her favorite hound, put a paw on the bed and whined, she rolled over and gathered the dog into her arms. "Sweet girl, you hate the sea, too. How dreadful it must be for the poor horses. . . ."

"Joanna!" Mariam pulled the tent flap aside. "You need to come back out on deck."

With Mariam's help, Joanna got to her feet. She asked no questions, already sure she'd not like the answers. They were well into the bay by now, and the hills seemed beautiful beyond words after endless vistas of nothing but sky and sea. A ship was anchored not far from shore, a buss like theirs. Its deck was filled with waving, shouting men, but the passengers on Joanna's ship were staring past them at the shredded sails, broken masts, and shattered timbers scattered along the beach, skeletal remains partially buried in the sand, washed by the waves, a scene of destruction and death looking eerily peaceful in the bright May sunlight.

"Dear God . . ." Joanna made the sign of the cross with a hand that shook. "How . . . how many?"

Stephen de Turnham shook his head, unwilling even to hazard a guess, but after studying the wreckage with a grim, practiced eye, the master said, "Two ships, mayhap three."

The other buss had erupted into frantic activity, and their longboat was soon launched, men straining at the oars to close the gap between the two vessels. The master gave the command to drop their anchors, and as his sailors hastened to obey, a ladder was flung over the side. Joanna recognized Hugh de Neville, one of Richard's household knights, as he scrambled up the ladder, and felt comforted by the sight of a familiar face in this alien, inhospitable environment.

Hugh seemed just as glad to see her. "Lady Joanna, thank God you're safe!" Ever the gallant, he insisted upon kissing her hand before answering the questions bombarding him from all sides. "When the great storm hit," he said, pausing to take deep, grateful gulps from a proffered wineskin, "our ship and three others managed to stay together. It was a week ago today that we were approaching Cyprus. A sudden squall came up and drove us toward the shore. Our ship's anchors held, but theirs did not and they were swept onto the rocks and broke apart. Many drowned, may the Almighty have mercy upon their souls. Some clung to the floating debris and managed to reach the beach, battered and half-naked from the waves. We could only watch as the local people—God-cursed Griffons—came out and took them away."

Hugh paused to drain the wineskin. "King Richard had warned us that Cyprus was ruled by a tyrant, an ungodly man who preys upon pilgrims, extorting ransoms from the wealthy and enslaving the poor. So we feared for the survivors and sent a small landing party ashore at dawn, hoping to discover their whereabouts. By the Grace of God, the first one we encountered was an elderly priest. None of us spoke Greek, but he had a smattering of French. He managed to convey to us that our comrades had been taken prisoner. His agitation and his gestures made it clear that we were in great danger, so we retreated back to our ship. After that, all we could do was wait . . . and pray."

"You acted wisely," Stephen said, catching the undertones of remorse in the other man's voice. "It would have served for naught to join them in their prison. One of our sailors is from Messina and Greek is his mother tongue. We'll send him ashore after dark to see if he can learn where they're being held. Once we know that, we can decide what to do next."

Hugh's face was sunburned and gaunt, a raw, red welt slashing across his forehead into his hairline. But his smile was radiant with relief. "When we saw your sail, we dropped to our knees and gave thanks to God for answering our prayers. Where is the fleet? When will the king get here?" His smile fading as his words were met with averted eyes and utter silence.

JOANNA'S COMPANIONS were convinced that her weakened state was due in large measure to her inability to keep fluids down or to get the rest her ailing body needed. Mariam had brought along a store of useful herbs and persuaded her friend to take a sleeping draught after drinking a cup of seawater, which was said to aid those suffering from *mal de mer*. Whether it was because they were now anchored in the relative calm of the bay or because she'd reached her breaking point, the draught worked and Joanna fell into a deep, dreamless sleep that lasted almost eighteen hours. When she finally awakened, she was surprised to discover it was now late afternoon on the following day and even more astonished to learn that she'd slept through a gaol break and a rescue mission.

Much to Joanna's relief, she found that she needed a chamber pot for its proper purpose and not because she was overcome by nausea again. Beatrix and the young widow Hélène helped her to dress as Mariam perched on their clothes coffer and told her of the day's eventful happenings.

"Whilst it was still dark and there were no sentries on the beach, Stephen had Petros rowed ashore. He seemed remarkably cocky for one going alone into the lion's den, but young men ofttimes seem to have more courage than common sense. It was arranged to pick him up at nightfall, but he suddenly appeared on the beach in midmorning, astride a mule. He rode it right past the startled guards and out into the bay! At that point he and the mule had a difference of opinion, the mule wanting to return to shore and Petros to continue on. The mule won. But Petros slid off into the water and swam like a fish toward Hugh's ship, which was closer than ours. I do like that lad's style," Mariam said with a grin before continuing.

"When he was pulled onboard, he said that he'd found our men being held in a house on the outskirts of Amathus, that village off the beach. It did not seem to him as if they were well guarded, and when he saw several of them at an upper window, he said he acted on impulse, yelling out in French that a second buss had dropped anchor offshore. Soon thereafter, he heard shouting and thumping and realized they were trying to overpower their captors, so he raced back to the beach, 'borrowing' the mule along the way. Stephen and Hugh at once ordered their knights and crossbowmen into our longboats and they rowed for shore, where they found the prisoners had broken out and were being chased by the villagers. Their arrival tipped the scales in our favor, and after some fighting which we could actually see from our buss, our men reached safety on our ships. That noise you hear is the victory celebration. It was," Mariam concluded, eyes sparkling, "well done, Joanna, well done, indeed!"

Joanna agreed that it was, hoping that this bold sortie would raise morale. She did not ask about the missing fleet, for Mariam's silence on that issue was an answer in itself. Instead, she managed to swallow a little wine and even a few bites of bread, the first solid food she'd had in days, and then ventured out onto the deck with Mariam unobtrusively bracing her on one side and Beatrix on the other.

Her appearance was welcomed with boisterous enthusiasm, and she had to listen again to an account of the day's events, this one offered by the participants themselves. Petros was the hero of the hour, obviously enjoying his well-earned turn on center stage, and much praise was also lavished upon Roger de Harcourt, a Norman knight who'd managed to seize a local man's mare, charging into the crowd of pursuers and riding down those who were not agile enough to jump out of the way. Now that they had an audience of highborn women, the men were only too happy to gloss over the very real dangers they'd faced and the blood spilled on both sides, dwelling instead upon the sweet taste of their triumph and the individual heroics of men like Petros and Roger. Joanna and Berengaria and their ladies played their part, too, with sincere exclamations of admiration and approbation and, for a time, all were able to ignore the realities of their plight, stranded in the domains of a man said to surpass Judas in faithlessness and Ganelon, the betrayer of Roland, in treachery.

The respite soon came to an end. While the men were laughing and teasing Roger for having ridden a mare, a mount deemed unmanly for knights, Stephen quietly drew Joanna and Berengaria aside. "Isaac knew of your presence in the fleet, and when the shipwrecked men were interrogated, they were asked many questions about you both. You can be sure he now knows that it is your ship out in the bay, for the people on shore will have told him they've seen women aboard. I daresay Isaac can scarce believe his good luck, and like as not, he is already wondering how much ransom to demand."

Joanna was expecting news like this, but Berengaria was shocked. "Surely he could not be that foolhardy? He must know that even if Richard paid to get us safely back, he'd then wreak a terrible vengeance upon Isaac and Cyprus."

"From what I've heard, Isaac Comnenus is both arrogant and stupid, a dangerous combination." Stephen hesitated before deciding that they deserved to know the full extent of the danger they were facing. "I am sure he has heard what happened in Messina and he must be uneasy about the arrival of an army led by a soldier king. He may well be thinking that you ladies could prove to be very useful hostages. There have been rumors for years of Isaac's clandestine contacts with the Saracens. What would King Richard do if Isaac threatened to turn you over to Saladin?"

Berengaria's face was suddenly ashen. Joanna had not considered a threat like that, either. But she soon rallied her defenses and said briskly, "That will never happen. I have no desire to end up in a Saracen *harim*, which is likely even worse than a Sicilian one. Moreover, I would die ere I let Isaac use us as weapons against my brother like that. It is unthinkable that Richard should have to choose between rescuing us and recovering the Holy City."

"I agree," Berengaria said resolutely, and Stephen gave the women a tight smile that was both admiring and grim, assuring them that his men would fight to the death in defense of the king's sister and betrothed. But after they were left alone by the gunwale, Berengaria said softly, "What now, Joanna?"

"We do what Hugh de Neville did. We wait and we pray that Richard arrives ere Isaac does."

JOANNA'S PRAYER was not to be answered. The next day, the men and women on the two busses spent hours staring out to sea, but no sails appeared on the distant horizon. In the afternoon, though, there was a sudden commotion on the beach. Riders were being greeted by the sentries, and so much deference was paid to a richly clad man on a spirited dun stallion that few doubted they were looking upon the self-proclaimed Emperor of Cyprus.

Hugh had rowed over to Stephen's ship, and when they saw a small boat launched from the beach, he said bleakly, "Here is trouble on the way."

It drew so close to the buss that some of the crossbowmen had itchy trigger fingers and exchanged looks of resignation and longing. As soon as it had dropped anchor, a man rose and made his way to the prow. His clothing and sword proclaimed him to be a person of rank, as did the fact that he addressed them in French. It was so heavily accented, though, that they did not find him easy to understand, and Stephen beckoned Petros to join them at the gunwale.

Delighted to be the center of attention again, Petros called out in Greek. The man looked both surprised and relieved, and the two engaged in a conversation that was utterly incomprehensible to those listening; the only words they could make out was the name "Isaakios Doukas Komnenos."

Stepping back from the rail, Petros rolled his eyes. "What a pile of—" Remembering that the queen and queen-to-be were listening, he censored himself and said with a shake of his head, "He was amazed that there would be one amongst the barbarians who could speak Greek. He claims to be some highborn local lord, but I think he is one of Isaac's lackeys, so I paid no heed to his name or title. This is his message from his august emperor; Christ keep me if he did not call

Isaac *Kosmokrator*!" Seeing the blank looks, he said with a chuckle, "It means 'master of the world.' Anyway, Isaac wants us to believe that he knew nothing about the imprisonment and deaths of our men. He says he was greatly displeased to hear of it and will punish the culprits severely. I was hard put to keep a straight face at that point, God's Truth!"

But when Stephen prompted him to relay the rest of the message, Petros lost his jaunty demeanor. "He wants you to come ashore, my lady," he told Joanna. "You and the 'Damsel of Navarre.' He says he will put his palace at Limassol at your disposal and do all in his power to make your stay in Cyprus a pleasant one. It was like watching a wolf trying to coax lambs into his cave, but this wolf is not going away."

"Tell him," Joanna said, "that we are greatly honored by his kind invitation. But we are awaiting the arrival any day now of my brother the English king and his fleet. King Richard, known throughout Christendom as the Lionheart in recognition of his great prowess on the battlefield, will gladly accept the emperor's hospitality once he reaches Cyprus. Whilst we wait, we wish to send some of our men ashore to replenish our water supply. As we are pilgrims on our way to the Holy Land, I am sure that one as celebrated for his Christian faith and generous spirit as the illustrious Emperor Isaac will gladly grant our small request."

Petros had listened intently, committing her words to memory, and then nodded, giving her an approving grin. "Well said, my lady." Leaning over the gunwale, he spoke at some length and with considerable animation. The other man's face was grim by the time he was done speaking and his own response was terse. As his boat headed toward the beach, Petros turned back to his attentive audience. "I told him what you said, my lady, throwing in a few sweeteners by calling Isaac all the high-flown titles I could think of. The lackey was not pleased, as you could see. He said he'd tell Isaac of your request for water. He also said that he hoped you'd reconsider, for his emperor might well take your refusal as an insult. I got the sense," Petros said somberly, "that he was speaking for himself then. I'd wager Isaac is not one for rewarding failure."

It was quiet for a time after that. Hugh made a point of telling Joanna that he thought she'd refused Isaac's offer very tactfully, and with luck, that might well be the end of it. They both knew better, though.

———

ISAAC'S MAN WAS BACK the next morning, this time requesting permission to come aboard their buss. He was conspicuously ill at ease, obviously fearing that

he might be held hostage by these alien barbarians. Stephen would have considered it had he thought Isaac actually cared about the welfare of anyone but himself. But when Isaac had defied the Greek emperor Andronicus, the two kinsmen
who'd stood surety for his good faith had been put to a gruesome death by impal-
ing, and there was no evidence that their fate had weighed upon Isaac's conscience.
His messenger was bringing gifts from the emperor for Joanna and Berengaria:
Cypriot wine and bread and ram's meat.

Joanna had to stifle a hysterical giggle. *Beware of Greeks bearing gifts.* When
he again urged the women to come ashore, she told him that they dared not,
for they could not leave the ship without the permission of her brother the
king. No man had ever looked at her as he did now, with utter and implacable
hatred. Even though she knew he dreaded returning to Isaac with another refusal,
she found it unsettling, nonetheless. He did get the last word, though, telling
them brusquely that his emperor had refused to give them permission to replenish their water supplies, saying there would be water in plenitude in the royal
palace.

After his departure, there was nothing to do but stare out to sea. But in late
afternoon, a flurry of activity began on the beach. Men rowed out to the wrecked
ships and began chopping at the broken masts. Others were bringing carts from
the direction of Limassol, the nearest town, and whipping heavily laden small
donkeys. As those on the ships watched, the doors of houses and shutters and
planks were piled onto the sand, soon joined by barrels and fence rails and large
shields, even benches. A barrier was being constructed out of whatever materials
the Cypriots could lay their hands upon. Their barricade might be makeshift, but
there was no mistaking the intent. These were preparations for war.

THEIR FIFTH MORNING at Cyprus dawned in a sunrise of breathtaking beauty,
pale gold along the horizon, and a rich, deep red above as clouds drifted into the
sun's flaming path; for a timeless moment, it looked as if the earth itself were
afire. Then as if by magical sleight of hand, the vivid colors disappeared and the
sky took on the same brilliant blue as the foam-crested waves below, the clouds
now gliding along like fleecy white swans in a celestial sea. Enticing scents wafted
out into the bay, the fragrances of flowers and oranges and sandalwood, the sweet
balm of land, almost irresistible to people trapped in seagoing gaols, ships they'd
come to hate for the fetid smells and lack of privacy and constant rolling and
pitching, even at anchor. This Sunday gave promise of being a day of surpassing

loveliness and Joanna hated it, caught up in a sense of foreboding so strong that she could almost taste it. Something terrible was going to happen today.

She had not long to wait before her premonition took tangible shape and form: five large ebony galleys. At first some of the others had been excited by the lookout's shout, but they soon realized that these galleys came from the wrong direction, from the east. They anchored close to shore and several armor-clad men embarked in small boats, on their way to confer with the man who commanded these deadly instruments of war.

Within the hour, Isaac's envoy was making his by-now familiar voyage out to their ship. This time, his little boat did not anchor, the men resting on their oars as he shouted across the water. Petros chewed on his lower lip, mumbling the message, as if that could somehow make it less than what it was—an ultimatum. "He says the emperor is done with waiting. He insists that you come ashore today. The lackey added the usual blather about hospitality, but he did not even try to make it sound convincing. What do I tell him, my lady?"

Joanna plucked at Stephen's sleeve and they drew away from the rail, joined after a moment by the ship's master. "Tell me the truth," she said. "It is obvious they mean to take us by force if we do not agree. Can they do that?"

While her question was ostensibly directed at Stephen, it was really for the master to answer. Staring across the bay at those predatory beaked galleys, he said glumly, "Yes, I fear that they can. We do not have enough water to venture out into the open sea. And even if we did, the winds today are light and variable. We'd not be able to outrun them. I am not saying they'd have an easy time of it. A lot of men would die. But they'd likely be able to take the ship."

Joanna looked from one man to the other. "So we yield or we fight and lose. I do not like either of those choices. Find me another one," she said tautly, and they stared at her in wary surprise, suddenly remembering that this woman was the daughter of Eleanor of Aquitaine, the sister of the Lionheart. Turning away, she returned to the rail. "Tell him, Petros, that we will be honored to accept the emperor's kind offer of shelter. We will have need of a doctor, for the Lady Berengaria is ill. But I think she will be well enough on the morrow for us to leave the ship for the emperor's palace in Limassol."

The man in the boat frowned, insisting that the emperor wanted them to come ashore today, claiming that a storm was brewing and they'd be safer on land. But when Joanna repeated her promise to disembark the next morning, he was forced to settle for that. The ship's passengers watched in silence as he was rowed back toward the beach. Joanna closed her eyes for a moment, blocking out the sinister sight of those galleys, their sails as red as blood. Looking over then at Stephen and the master, she said, "I've bought us some time. Now it is up to you to make the most of it."

They eventually came up with a third option, although it, too, was fraught with peril. They would try to slip out of the bay under cover of darkness that night and head for the island's northern coast. There were sheltered coves where they could take refuge, and with luck, it might take Isaac a while to track them down. The winds would have to be favorable, though. And even if they succeeded in slipping out of this trap, they risked another danger. What if the king's fleet arrived and found them gone? Limassol was the designated port; he'd not think to look for them on the other side of the island. Since it was still a better choice than surrendering, it was agreed upon, and Stephen sent their boat over to Hugh's buss to let them know what was planned. Meanwhile, men continued to work on the beach barricade, more armed guards appeared to keep watch on the two ships, and the five galleys rode easily at anchor, sea wolves awaiting the word to attack.

Never had a day passed so slowly. The men occupied themselves with their weapons, sharpening their swords on whetstones and replacing the strings of their crossbows. But for the women, there was nothing to do but gaze out hopelessly at that vast, empty sea. When Joanna found Alicia weeping soundlessly in a corner of the tent, she felt remorse stab her as sharply as any dagger's blade. Gathering the girl to her, she dried Alicia's tears with her sleeve. "I am so sorry, Alicia. I ought to have insisted that you remain in Sicily, I ought to . . ."

"No." Alicia clung tightly, but her voice had steadied. "I want to be with you."

Joanna did the only thing she could and sat with the child, stroking her blond braids as she tried not to think what might befall Alicia and the other women if they ended up in Isaac Comnenus's power. She thought she and Berengaria could reasonably expect to be safe from molestation; damaged goods were worthless in trade. But who would protect Mariam and Beatrix and Hélène and Alicia?

The sun was slowly sliding into the sea when Berengaria found Joanna standing at the rail, watching as the waves took on delicate tints of rose and lavender. For a time they stood in silence. "When we were in Bagnara," Joanna said at last, "my mother told me something my father had once said to her, that kings play chess with the lives of other men. So do queens, Berengaria, so do queens. . . ."

"I have faith that all will be well for us, Joanna." Berengaria was not sure if she still believed that, for this terrible sea voyage had not been what she'd expected when her father promised her to the English king. So much had gone wrong. It was almost as if the Almighty had turned His Face away from them. But true faith did not waver when tested. If she yielded to despair, she'd be failing her God, herself, and the man she'd pledged to wed. "I am sure of that," she said, with all the conviction at her command, and Joanna managed a shadowy smile, thankful that her brother had chosen a woman of courage for his wife.

A sudden shout turned all eyes toward the rigging, where a sailor had been perched all day. Straddling the mizzenmast, he leaned over so far that he seemed in danger of losing his balance. "I see a sail to the west!"

It seemed to take forever before those on deck could see it, too, a large ship skimming the waves, its sails billowing out like canvas clouds. When the lookout yelled that there were two ships, excitement swept the buss, for with these rein-forcements, surely they could fend off Isaac's galleys? Men were laughing and slapping one another on the back, sailors scrambling up into the rigging to get a better view, and Joanna's dogs began to bark, hoarsely, as if they'd forgotten how. "You see," Berengaria said, with a beatific smile. "God does hear our prayers."

"Yes, He does," Joanna agreed, for it would have been churlish to quibble with salvation. But she could not banish the question from her mind as she could from her lips. *Where was the fleet? Where was Richard?*

It happened with such suddenness that men were not sure at first if they could trust their senses. There was nothing to the west but sea and sky and those two ships tacking against the wind. And then the horizon was filled with sails, stretch-ing as far as the eye could see. A moment of stunned disbelief gave way almost at once to pandemonium, and for the rest of their lives, there would be men who vowed they'd never experienced an emotion as overwhelming as the joy of deliv-erance on a May Sunday off the coast of Cyprus.

The sharp-eyed sailors spotted it first. "The *Sea-Cleaver*! The king's galley!" But Richard's women needed to see it for themselves, scarcely breathing until it came into focus, looking like a Norse long-ship, its hull as red as the sunset, its sails catching the wind, and streaming from its masthead the banner emblazoned with the royal lion of England.

Berengaria found it hard to tear her gaze away from the sight of that blessed galley. "It is like a miracle, Joanna," she said in awe, "that he should reach us in our hour of greatest need."

Joanna gave a shaken laugh. "Richard has always had a talent for making a dramatic entrance, but he has outdone himself with this one!"

As soon as Richard swung himself up onto the deck, Joanna took a backward step to make sure the first one he greeted was Berengaria. She needn't have worried, though. For once, the younger woman's Spanish reserve was forgotten and she flung herself into Richard's arms. He embraced Joanna next, and then Berengaria again, this time bending her backward in a kiss that seared like a brand and left her flushed and breathless. But when he really looked at Joanna, his own breath hissed through his teeth and his hand clamped onto her arm hard enough to hurt. "Jesu, Joanna!"

"I do not feel as wretched as I look," she assured him hastily. "Truly I am on the mend. But where were you, Richard? We were half out of our minds with worry!"

"We ended up having to spend ten days in Rhodes, waiting for the missing ships to straggle in. I sent out galleys to look for our lost sheep, and that took time," he said with a quick smile. He'd also been stricken with a recurrence of the malarial fever that had plagued him for years, but he saw no reason to mention that since he preferred to deal with his illnesses by ignoring them if possible. "We finally sailed on last Wednesday and would have been here earlier had we not encountered a storm in the Gulf of Satalea. We were actually blown backward by the winds."

Even as he was speaking, his gaze had shifted past the women to the barricaded beach and the stark evidence that ships had run aground. "Not all of my fleet is with me, but it looks as if I got here just in time. What is going on?"

He'd directed that last question toward Stephen de Turnham, but Stephen had taken Joanna's measure by now and he deferred politely to her. "Three of our ships sank after being blown onto the rocks, and one of the men drowned was your vice chancellor," Joanna said sadly, knowing that would grieve him. "That buss is Hugh de Neville's. He and Stephen have been a godsend, Richard, doing all they could to keep us safe under very difficult circumstances."

His eyes had narrowed. "Tell me about those 'difficult circumstances.'"

They did, Joanna now the one to defer to Stephen when it came to describing the struggle to free their men. Richard listened in ominous silence, then summoned Roger de Harcourt to get a firsthand account of their imprisonment. He even called Petros over to question him about what he'd seen in Amathus. And then he moved over to the gunwale, stood for a time staring at the beach and those low-riding Greek galleys. When he turned back to the other men, there was a universal sense of relief that this lethal rage was not directed at any of them.

"It takes great courage to maltreat half-drowned shipwreck survivors and to threaten defenseless women. But now we will see how Isaac likes dealing with me."

CHAPTER 16

Т he women's buss dared to venture closer to shore after the arrival of the royal fleet. Blessed with calmer waters and no longer fearful of the Cypriot emperor's treacherous intentions, they enjoyed their first night's peaceful sleep since the Good Friday storm. So they were still abed the next morning when Alicia darted into their tent, exclaiming that they must come out on deck straightaway. Making themselves presentable in record haste, they emerged into the white-gold sunlight, only to halt in shock, for the bay was afloat with small boats, all heading toward the barricaded beach.

Stephen de Turnham's knights were lined up along the gunwale, watching and cheering as if they were spectators at a game of camp-ball. Stephen himself was in a far more somber mood. He turned at once, though, to greet Joanna and Berengaria with deference and, in response to their alarmed questions, he answered concisely and candidly.

"The king sent two of his knights and an armed escort ashore at dawn, along with a man fluent in Greek, for he'd prudently thought to ask Tancred for a translator. They carried a message to Isaac, seeking redress for the harm done to his shipwrecked men, who'd been robbed as well as imprisoned. They soon returned, reporting that they thought Isaac must be mad, for his response was an amazingly rash one to make to a justly aggrieved king with an army at his command. They said he blustered and ranted, insisting that a mere king had no right to make demands upon an emperor. When they asked if that was truly his reply, he spat out a one-word Greek oath. Tancred's man was not sure how to translate it into

French, but he said it was highly insulting. When this was told to our king, he showed that he could be just as terse as Isaac. His response: 'To arms!'"

Joanna and Berengaria shared the same conflicted emotion, pride in Richard warring with concern for his safety. Joining Stephen at the gunwale, Joanna soon noticed his tension; he'd kept his eyes on the shore even while answering their questions, one hand clasping and unclasping the sword hilt at his hip, almost as if acting of its own volition. "It must be hard for you," she said sympathetically, "having to stand guard over us instead of taking part in the invasion."

He acknowledged her perception with a crooked smile. "I cannot deny, Madame, that if I'd had my choice, I'd be at my king's side, especially here, especially now."

"Is this so dangerous, then?" she asked in a low voice and when he nodded, she felt a chill that not even the sun's sultry heat could vanquish. "Can you tell me why, Sir Stephen? And please, treat me as you would a man and answer me truthfully."

"No one would ever mistake you for a man, my lady," he said, with a surprise flash of gallantry. "But I will honor your courage with the honesty you seek. The king is attempting one of the most dangerous and difficult of military actions—landing upon an unfamiliar beach occupied by an enemy army on their own ground. Our men are not at their best, not after so much time at sea, and those skiffs and snekas offer little protection from the Cypriot crossbowmen."

"Are you saying that they will be defeated?"

"Indeed not, my lady!" He sounded genuinely affronted. "We will prevail, for I trust in the Almighty and King Richard. But men will die this day and there will be sights not suitable for female eyes. It might be best if you and your ladies retire to the tent until the fighting is over."

Joanna took him at his word and bade Hélène take Alicia back into the tent, much to the girl's distress. But she did not follow, for she could not believe that an All-Merciful God would allow her brother to die before her eyes. While there was a corner of her mind that recognized the lack of logic in such a conviction, she did not let herself acknowledge it. If she stayed out on deck, she'd be assuring his safety.

Her throat closed up, though, when she saw the Cypriot galleys raise anchor, for how could the small landing craft fend off those sinister sea wolves? Stephen seemed to read her mind, for he pointed out that the first rows of their boats were filled with crossbowmen and archers. She saw that he was right, and as soon as the enemy galleys went on the attack, Richard's arbalesters unleashed a withering fire.

Joanna had often heard men claim that they'd seen the sky darken as arrows took flight, but she'd always dismissed it as hyperbole—until now. The men on the galleys were shooting back, and she watched in horror as bodies fell into the bay, the bright blue water taking on a red tinge where they splashed and sank. But the crossbowmen in the skiffs were coordinating their attacks; as men loosed their bolts, they ducked down to reload while the second row rose to take aim. The result was that arrows and bolts were smashing into the galleys in waves, one right after another, giving the men no chance to reload their own weapons. The knights on Joanna's ship were cheering wildly now. She was slower to understand. It was not until several men jumped into the sea to evade the lethal bolts raining down upon them that she realized the galleys had been effectively taken out of the action.

For a moment she forgot that men were dying, feeling only a fierce surge of pride. "Stephen, they are winning!" Getting a more measured response from him, a "Not yet. But we will."

There was such confusion and dismay on the beach that it was obvious its defenders had been expecting the galleys to wreak havoc with the small boats of the invading force. But when Richard's crossbowmen and archers now turned their fire upon them, they hastily retreated to their wooden barricade and began to shoot back. Once again the sun seemed to dim behind clouds of shafted death. Even to Joanna's untutored eye, it appeared as if the men in boats were making no progress toward shore, the skiffs wallowing in the surf. Turning toward Stephen, she saw her own apprehension mirrored on his face. Gripping the gunwale until his knuckles whitened, he leaned forward, his body rigid, and she realized that victory hung in the balance.

"Stephen, what if . . . what if they cannot land?"

"He'll not let that happen," he insisted, just as the knights began to shout and pump their fists in the air. Joanna squinted to see, half blinded by the glare of sun on water. One of the snekas had shot through a gap between boats, its crew straining at the oars as it headed straight for the beach. Joanna gasped, her eyes locking upon the armed and helmeted figure standing in the prow, unable to choke back a muffled protest as he jumped from the boat into the water and began to wade through the shallows toward shore. All around her, men were yelling, cursing, laughing. Her courage finally failing her, she spun around and buried her face in Stephen's shoulder, not even aware of what she did, knowing only that she could not bear to watch her brother die.

"You need not fear, my lady. They are following him. Look for yourself!"

Stephen had expected to see tears streaking her face. When she raised her head, though, her eyes were dry. But they were still filled with fear as she turned back toward the beach. "Blessed Mother Mary," she breathed, for Stephen was right; dozens of knights had leapt from their skiffs, heedless of their armor, and were splashing after their king. Richard had already reached the shore. If he was aware of his vulnerability in that moment, he gave no indication of it, raising his shield to deflect arrows and then swinging around to confront the armed rider bearing down upon him. Joanna's mouth was too dry for speech. She heard a woman's scream behind her, and for an anguished moment, her eyes and Berengaria's caught and held. When she dared to look again, a riderless horse was rearing up, a body lay crumpled at Richard's feet, and the sand was rapidly turning red. By now his knights were scrambling onto the beach, and when Richard charged toward the barricades, they raced to catch up with him, flashes of light reflecting off raised swords and shields, shouting like madmen.

Stephen glanced at Berengaria, who was clinging to the rail as if her knees could no longer support her, and he blamed himself for not insisting that she retreat to the tent, for he thought she would have been more biddable than Joanna, more likely to have heeded him. Women were not meant to see bloodshed. As little as he liked to criticize his king, they ought not to be here at all. "The worst is over now," he said calmly. "The king won his victory as soon as he set foot upon the beach."

"How can you be so sure? They have much larger numbers. Even I can see that."

He was surprised by the steadiness of Berengaria's voice, but pleased, too, for he knew she'd have need in Outremer for all the strength she could muster. "It matters for naught if we're outnumbered, my lady. We know more of war than they do."

Stephen proved to be an accurate seer. The hand-to-hand combat on the beach was fierce but brief, and the emperor's men were soon in flight, with Richard's knights in close pursuit. The rest of his boats were landing now, some of the soldiers pausing to loot the bodies of the slain before climbing over the broken barricade and disappearing from sight. Several ships had already corralled the drifting Cypriot galleys, sailors nimbly leaping onto the bloodied decks and flinging anchors over the side. Joanna averted her gaze as they began to dump bodies overboard, and Berengaria shuddered.

"Will it be like this in the Holy Land?" she asked, and Joanna had no answer for her.

In midafternoon, Richard sent word to Stephen that he was to bring the women ashore. They discovered, though, that it was much more difficult to leave the ship than it had been to board it, for they'd been able to cross a gangplank from the dock to the deck in Messina and now they had to be lowered into a sagitta, which rode so low in the water that they were soon drenched with spray and Joanna had to fight off a recurrence of nausea in the pitching, rolling waves. They were not rowed toward the beach at Amathus, Stephen explaining that Limassol lay a few miles to the east, and it was there that they'd find shelter. Even though it meant a longer trip in that accursed small galley, the women were glad to be spared the sight of Amathus, where the fighting had occurred. They'd already seen more bodies in one day than they'd expected to see in their entire lifetimes.

Limassol was a small town of undistinguished appearance—houses of sundried brick, dusty, deserted streets, no signs of life. It looked forlorn, abandoned, and above all, vulnerable, for it lacked walls, although it did have a paltry, neglected citadel at the mouth of the River Garyllis. But Limassol also looked peaceful, and for that they were thankful. Isaac's self-proclaimed palace could not begin to compare with the royal palaces in Palermo and Messina. After almost four weeks at sea, it still seemed like paradise to the women, and they set about exploring it with zest, laughing at the antics of the dogs, for they had yet to regain their landlegs, and exclaiming in delight when they discovered fruit trees in the courtyard. They also found two servants cowering behind a wall hanging. Fortunately, Joanna had thought to bring Petros along. He'd been sulking, unhappy that Richard had chosen to rely upon Tancred's interpreter. Being asked to communicate with these terrified girls cheered him up considerably, and he was successful in reassuring them that these "barbarian women" would treat them well. They scurried away and returned with flagons of wine, bread, figs, olives, dates, goat cheese, and oranges. Joanna's appetite had yet to return, but the others fell upon the food with gusto, marveling that their prospects could have improved so dramatically in just one day.

A twilight sky had shaded from violet to plum when Jaufre and Morgan arrived, sent by Richard to make sure the women were safely settled in. They were in high spirits, eager to share stories of the day's events. By now Joanna understood that men were often euphoric in the aftermath of battle, but it was a learning experience for Berengaria, who was bewildered that they could shrug off death and bloodshed with such apparent ease.

Isaac's men had scattered like chickens when a hawk flies overhead, they reported gleefully, and Richard had turned Amathus over to his soldiers as their reward. Not that there was much worth taking; Amathus had once been an important city back when the Persians and the Romans ruled Cyprus, yet it was a pitiful place today, a ghost of its former greatness. Some of the knights had hoped to find better pickings in Limassol, they admitted. But there were large communities here of foreign merchants from the Italian city-states of Genoa and Venice, and they'd greeted the king like a liberator. So Richard had ordered that it not be sacked.

Neither man could remember when he'd last eaten, so they finished the food as they told the women how they'd pursued the fleeing Griffons through Amathus and into the hills beyond. At one point the king had even encountered Isaac himself and challenged him to combat. But the tyrant had run for his life, they chortled, whilst Richard fumed that he had no horse to give chase. Then he spotted a pack horse and vaulted onto its back. It did not even have proper stirrups, just hemp cords, and he had no chance of catching Isaac, who was mounted upon a handsome dun stallion, said to be faster than a lightning bolt. When they continued to dwell upon the attributes of this wonderful horse, Joanna finally had to interrupt, asking the one question that mattered. Where was Richard and could they expect to see him that evening?

Jaufre and Morgan glanced at each other and shrugged. The king had gone back to the beach whilst more of his men came ashore, giving orders to tend to the wounded and bury the dead, then met with the merchants again to assure them that their families and property would be safe, and sent out scouts to discover the whereabouts of Isaac's army. At this point, Joanna raised a hand to cut off their recital, for their meaning was clear enough. Richard would get to them when he could; at the moment, they were not a high priority.

Morgan then redeemed himself by making a suggestion that was both intriguing and vaguely scandalous. Would they like to make use of the public baths? The women looked at one another, seriously tempted. But none of them had ever been to a public bath before. Was it something that respectable, well-bred women did? As a queen, Joanna had greater liberty to defy conventions. She knew, though, that she was too exhausted to take another step, and started to shake her head when she remembered that Isaac was said to love luxury. Surely he'd have a bath somewhere in his palace? The little Greek servingmaids quickly confirmed that it

was so, and after that, the women could not wait for their guests to leave, so eager
were they to wash away the grime of their voyage in perfumed, warm water.

By the time they'd gotten some of their guards to haul and heat water and then
took turns soaking in Isaac's large copper bathing tub, it was full dark. Wrapped
in bedrobes, Joanna and Berengaria towel-dried and brushed out each other's hair,
the easy familiarity reminding them both of their childhood and sisters they might
never see again. It was Berengaria who gave voice to their shared nostalgia, confiding, "I do not think I could have endured this voyage without you, Joanna."

"You do not give yourself enough credit, for you are stronger than you think."
Joanna could not help adding, then, with a rueful smile, "If you'd known what
lay ahead, I daresay you'd have run for the nearest nunnery when your father
broached the matter of marriage with my brother. And who could blame you?"

Berengaria wondered if she'd ever get used to Angevin candor. Richard and
Joanna were constantly saying aloud what other people did not even dare to whisper. There had indeed been times when she'd yearned for her tranquil, lost world
of Navarre, not sure if a crown was truly worth so much misery. "I admit I did not
bargain on an Isaac Comnenus. But till the day I draw my last breath, I will
remember the sight of Richard's galley against that sunset sky, like the champion
in a minstrel's chanson. What woman would not be proud to have such a man for
her husband?"

She'd inadvertently touched upon a tender spot. As she'd grown into womanhood, Joanna had done her best to deny her qualms about a husband who sent
other men out to die without ever putting himself at risk. But Richard's flashy
heroics had done much to tarnish William's memory, casting a sad shadow over
her marriage, reminding her that her father had always led his troops into battle,
as had her brothers. Even Philippe did so. Only William had stayed at home, William who'd yoked Constance to a hateful husband so he could pursue his foolish
dreams of destiny, willing to spill any blood but his own to lay claim to Constantinople. She lowered her head, hiding the tears that suddenly burned her eyes.
Was that all her life in Sicily had amounted to—a husband she could not respect
and a son whose tiny tomb she might never see again?

Berengaria sensed that something was wrong. She was not sure what to do,
though, for she was developing with Joanna something she'd never had before—a
friendship between equals—and she fretted that questions borne of empathy
might be taken as intrusive. She was not given the chance to make up her mind,
for at that moment Richard made one of his typical entrances, unexpected and
unannounced.

Joanna's ladies were amused by his brash invasion of the women's quarters; Berengaria's were horrified. Midst laughter and shrieks, they retreated into the inner sanctum, the bedchamber set aside for their mistresses. Joanna was already on her feet. She was about to embrace him when she realized that he was still wearing his hauberk. Her eyes drawn irresistibly to the dried blood caked on some of the iron links, she said, as calmly as she could, "I trust none of that is yours?"

"From a skirmish like that? I've not so much as a scratch." Putting his hands on her shoulders, he gazed down intently into her face. "Well, at least you are not as pale as yesterday. You gave me quite a scare, you know."

"I gave *you* a scare? How do you think we felt, Richard, watching you take on all of Isaac's army by yourself?"

"I knew my men would follow," he said, dismissing the danger with a negligent gesture. "And I knew, too, that Isaac's men were likely to be ill-trained, poorly paid, and not eager to die on his behalf."

Joanna was not won over by that argument and was about to remind him that it would have taken only one well-aimed arrow. But he was already turning his attention toward his betrothed.

While he'd been greeting Joanna, Berengaria had belted her bedrobe. Remembering then that her hair was tumbling down her back, she looked around hastily for her veil. When she would have snatched it up, Richard reached out and caught her hand. "Do not cover your hair, Berenguela. I like it loose like this."

Berengaria let the veil flutter to the floor at her feet. She knew it was not seemly that he should see her like this until they were wed. But as their eyes met, she realized that if he meant to share her bed this night, it would not be easy to deny him. Moreover, she was not sure that she'd want to say no. Shocked by her own thoughts, she forced herself to wrench her gaze away from his. Because of her discussions with Joanna, she no longer worried that she'd be imperiling her soul by finding pleasure in her husband's embrace. But she knew that what she was contemplating now was most definitely a sin.

He still held her hand and she found herself staring at their entwined fingers, imaging his clasped around a sword hilt. What he'd done this day was both exhilarating and terrifying. As much as she'd feared for his life, she'd been thrilled, too, for would Almighty God have blessed him with such lethal skills if he were not destined to be the savior of Jerusalem?

"I am truly sorry that you both had to endure so much," he said, glancing from one woman to the other. "But I promise you that you'll never face danger like this again."

While Joanna did not doubt his sincerity, that was not a promise he could keep. Not even Richard could exert royal control over the forces of nature, over another Good Friday storm or a plague stalking the siege camp at Acre. She would never point that out to him, though, and said lightly, "As long as you keep riding to our rescue in the nick of time, we will have no complaints."

Spying a flagon of wine, Richard strode over and poured wine for them. "My little sister is too modest," he said to Berengaria. "I'd wager that she'd have been more than a match for Isaac. For certes, she had Stephen de Turnham quaking in his boots." Seeing her lack of comprehension, he grinned. "Ah, she did not tell you about that?"

Returning with the wine, he took obvious pride in relating Joanna's ultimatum to Stephen. He brushed aside their questions about the fight on the beach, insisting that it was more of a brawl than a genuine battle, an argument that would have been more persuasive had they not been eyewitnesses. He told them that Philippe had safely arrived in Outremer, for they'd encountered a dromon from Acre after they'd left Rhodes, and he expressed concern that the city might fall ere he reached the siege, saying, "God forbid that Acre should be won in my absence, for it has been besieged for so long, and the triumph, God willing, will be so glorious." And when they asked him why only part of the fleet was with him, he said he'd sailed against the wind after hearing that a large buss had been spotted off the coast of Cyprus, revealing how seriously he'd taken the threat posed by Isaac Comnenus. But he asked few questions about their own ordeal. They were glad of it, though, not wanting to add to his burdens.

When he suddenly rose and bade them good night, they were caught by surprise. Joanna protested, sure that he'd not had a proper meal all day, and he allowed that was true. "But I cannot spare the time. My scouts told me that Isaac has committed yet another astonishing blunder and his army is camped just a few miles to the west of Limassol. The fool thinks he is safe there, for he also thinks that we have no horses. So I plan to unload some of them tonight and pay him a visit on the morrow."

Leaning over, he dropped a playful kiss on the top of Joanna's head, then pulled Berengaria to her feet. But while his mouth was warm on hers and he took care to not to embrace her too tightly, murmuring he did not want her to be scratched by his hauberk, she sensed his distraction; his mind was already upon that moonlit beach and the surprise he had in store for the Cypriot emperor.

And then he was gone, as quickly as he'd come, leaving the two women to look at each other in bemusement. Berengaria wasn't sure whether she was relieved or disappointed; some of both, she decided. "I know," she told Joanna, with a rueful smile of her own. "I know . . . hold tight and enjoy the ride."

UNDER RICHARD'S SUPERVISION, fifty horses were unloaded from a tarida and exercised upon the beach to ease their stiffness and cramped muscles. He then returned to the army camp they'd pitched on the outskirts of Limassol and got a few hours' sleep. Early the next morning, he inspected their defenses, wanting to make sure that they were safe from enemy attack in his absence. Since he thought a clash was likely, he ordered a number of knights and men-at-arms to follow on foot. And then he rode out with more than forty knights and a few clerks to see Isaac's army for himself.

His scouts had reported that the emperor was camped some eight miles east of Limassol, near the village of Kolossi. The countryside was deserted, no travelers on the roads, no farmers tending to their fields, for most of the people had fled to the hills with their livestock and what belongings they could carry away. Richard and his knights kept their mounts to an easy canter, wanting to spare their sea-battered horses as much as possible. Despite the taut anticipation of battle, the men found themselves enjoying the warmth of the sun, a wind that carried the fragrance of flowers and myrtle rather than the salt tang of the sea, and the familiar movement of their stallions between their legs instead of the alarming pitching and rolling of galley decks slick with foam. Soon afterward, as they passed through an olive grove, they encountered a few of Isaac's soldiers.

The Greek horsemen at once retreated. Richard and his men followed, and before long they could see the Cypriot encampment in the distance. Their approach caused a commotion, and as they reached the mouth of the valley, they saw Isaac's men massing behind the stream that separated the two forces. The emperor's pavilion was visible behind the army lines, a splendid structure that irresistibly drew the eyes of Richard's knights, wondering what riches lay within. Isaac himself was nowhere in sight and they joked among themselves that he must be sleeping late this morn.

Richard paid no heed to their edgy banter, studying the enemy with a growing sense of disgust. When André drew rein beside him, he said, "Have you ever seen such a pitiful sight? Where are their sentries? Where are their captains? Look at the way they are milling around, more like a mob than an army. Isaac ought to be ashamed to put men such as this in the field. Whilst we were in Rhodes, I was told that he has to rely upon Armenian routiers from the Kingdom of Cilicia, and it is obvious he has hired the dregs. No surprise there, for would you sell your sword to a man like Isaac if you could find service elsewhere?"

Some of the others saw only the size of the army, not its lack of discipline. Hugh de la Mare, one of Richard's clerks, nudged his mount to the king's side. "Come away, sire," he entreated. "Their numbers are too overwhelming."

The knights close enough to hear grinned and looked at Hugh with sardonic pity, knowing what was coming. Richard turned in the saddle and, for a long moment, stared at the other man as if he could not believe his own ears. "Tend to your books and Scriptures, sir clerk," he said icily, "and leave the fighting to us."

As Hugh hastily fell back, André laughed. "Say what you will of clerks, Cousin, they can count. He is right that we're greatly outnumbered."

Richard took no offense, for he knew that an experienced soldier like André would not see numbers as the only factor that mattered. "But look at them," he said, gesturing scornfully toward their agitated foes. "Are they making ready to charge? Lining up in battle array? No, they are huddling behind that shallow stream as if it were a raging torrent, wasting arrows since we're out of range, whilst shouting and cursing as if we could be slain by their insults alone. And where is their noble commander? Watching from yonder hill instead of being down there with his men."

Following the direction of Richard's gaze, André and the Earl of Leicester saw that he was right. Horsemen were gathered on a nearby slope, and one of the riders was mounted on a magnificent dun stallion. As he snorted and pawed the earth, Richard said, "At least Isaac's destrier is eager to fight. But he looks to be the only one." And with that, he gave the signal his men had been expecting. Shifting his lance from its fautré, he couched it under his right arm and spurred his horse forward, shouting the battle cry of the English Royal House, *"Dex aie!"*

There were few sights more impressive or more daunting than a cavalry charge of armed knights, especially to men unaccustomed to this form of warfare. The ground trembled under the hooves of their stallions, such thick clouds of dust kicked up in their wake that they seemed to be trailing smoke. Archers watched in dismay as their arrows bounced off shields or embedded themselves harmlessly in mail hauberks. There was disbelief at first, shock that these lunatic barbarians would actually dare to attack when they were vastly outnumbered. Even as some of their equally astonished captains rallied and began to shout orders, most of the routiers continued to gape at the oncoming wave and then, self-preservation prevailing over training, they scattered to avoid being trampled underfoot.

Richard had already selected his opponent, a man on a raw-boned chestnut, and leveled his lance as he braced himself for the impact. It struck the other rider in the chest, flinging him backward in a spray of crimson. Dropping his shattered lance, Richard slid his left arm through the straps of his shield and unsheathed his sword. A soldier ran at him, axe raised high. He smashed his attacker in the face with his shield and, as he went down, Richard's destrier rode right over him, screaming in rage at the sight of another stallion. This horseman was swinging a sword with a curved blade. He missed. Richard did not.

All around him, his knights were either closing with foes or looking for men to attack, for the ragged Cypriot line had broken just as he'd expected it would. Once they discovered that staving off these battle-seasoned veterans was not as enjoyable as terrorizing defenseless civilians, many of Isaac's routiers lost interest in fighting and fled. His crossbowmen had already sensibly faded away, as had the local men forced to fight for the emperor. Ahead of Richard loomed the emperor's luxurious pavilion, but that was not his target. Spurring his destrier, he struck down the banner-bearer who'd courageously held his ground in defense of the imperial standard. Reining in before the wooden cart that anchored it, Richard grasped the staff, jerked, and cast the flag to the ground as nearby knights cheered.

Guilhem de Préaux appeared beside him. He was drenched in other men's blood; even the nasal guard of his helmet was splattered. But his smile was jubilant. "Well done, sire! We've got them on the run. Can we claim our rewards now?"

Richard's gaze swept the Cypriot camp, by now empty of all but bodies, trampled tents, smoldering fires, a few riderless horses, and dropped or discarded shields, swords, and slings. At the head of the valley, rising puffs of dust signaled the imminent arrival of the rest of their men. "Yes, you've earned it, Guilhem, all of you. But not the standard. That is mine, so guard it well."

"I will, my liege," Guilhem promised. "You were right about Isaac's hired men— a worthless lot. No tears will be shed for them—" But Richard was no longer there, for he'd spotted the small band of riders cutting across the battlefield, protectively surrounding a man on a tall dun stallion. With a defiant yell, Richard took off after them, his destrier responding gallantly to his urging, and at first the distance seemed to be narrowing. But after that one brief spurt, his mount faltered, shortening stride, and he was forced to ease up, realizing the horse was in no condition for an all-out pursuit after a month at sea. Reaching over to stroke the animal's lathered neck, he watched and cursed as Isaac's destrier bore him to safety, his hooves skimming the ground so smoothly he seemed to be flying.

"Sire?" The Earl of Leicester had ridden after Richard, and now pulled up alongside him. "Is that the emperor?"

"Yes, God rot him," Richard said savagely. "If I'd just seen him sooner . . ."

Leicester didn't think the king had any reason to reproach himself, not after winning two such spectacular victories in the span of one day. "Our men have never been so happy," he said, gesturing around the camp, "for never have they found such rich booty. Horses, oxen, cows, sheep, goats, weapons, armor, wine, food, and in Isaac's tent, gold and silver plate, fine clothes, silken bedding. I had no idea that Cyprus was so wealthy."

"My liege!" This time it was Baldwin de Bethune and Morgan. Coming from the direction of Isaac's plundered tent, they were prodding a man forward with their swords. Reaching Richard, they forced their prisoner to his knees. "This one claims to be a *magistros*, one of Isaac's court officials, so we thought he'd be worth more alive than dead."

Richard looked down at their new hostage. "He speaks French?"

"A little, lord king," the man said quickly; having decided that he was not willing to die for the fugitive emperor, his only other choice was to ingratiate himself with the barbarians and hope they'd find him useful enough to spare his life.

"Take him back with us," Richard said, and dispatched Leicester to find out how many casualties they'd suffered. All around him, his soldiers were enthusiastically looting the camp. He found himself unable to share their elation, not when he'd come so close to ending it here and now. He should have known that Isaac would be too craven to fight like a man. "You," he said curtly, pointing to the prisoner. "You know the emperor's dun stallion?"

"Yes, lord." The man nodded vigorously. "That is Fauvel. Very fast. None catch him."

"Fauvel," Richard repeated. Isaac did not deserve a horse like that. Nor did he deserve a crown. And God willing, he'd soon lose both.

⁎

"STOP SQUIRMING, LAMB." Beatrix's voice sounded muffled, for she was holding pins in her mouth as she marked where the seams of Joanna's bodice would have to be taken in.

"I still do not think this is necessary," Joanna complained. "Now that I'm on the mend, surely I'll gain back the weight I lost."

"And until then walk around in gowns that fit you like tents? I do not think so," Beatrix said firmly, hers the self-assurance of one who'd been tending to Joanna since the cradle.

Joanna sighed, feeling like an unruly child instead of a grown woman, wife, and widow. Casting a mischievous glance toward her future sister-in-law, she said, "I was thinking, Berengaria, that we ought to visit a public bath this afternoon. Donna Catarina—the wife of that Venetian merchant—says this particular one is delightfully decadent, like the bathhouses in Constantinople, with scented oils and pools of hot and cold water. I suppose I can go with Mariam if you think your duennas would not approve . . . ?"

Berengaria had been frowning over a parchment, trying to compose a letter to her family that would be honest without giving her father an apoplectic seizure; it was too delicate a task to entrust to Joanna's clerk. She glanced up quickly, but realized that she was being teased, and said composedly, "I am beginning to think you're more in need of duennas than I am, Joanna. As for Mariam, she appears to have other matters on her mind than public baths. It certainly sounds that way."

As laughter was floating into the open window from the courtyard, Joanna could not argue with that. Tilting her head to listen, she said with a smile, "For years I've watched men flirt with Mariam, but I've never known her to flirt back—until now. Of course if he were not my cousin, I might be tempted to flirt with Morgan, too."

Alicia was kneeling in the window-seat, playing with the dogs. Looking out, she reported, "Lady Mariam and Sir Morgan are seated together on a bench. I think he is teaching her a game, for they are throwing dice." She giggled then, saying, "She just accused him of cheating." Twisting around on the window-seat, she said, "I like it here in Cyprus, my lady. Do you think we will be staying long?"

"I do not know, Alicia," Joanna admitted. "But I will ask my brother when I see him next—whenever that may be." She at once regretted that mild sarcasm, for she was not being fair to Richard. It was true they'd seen him only once in the past three days, but that was hardly his fault. After defeating Isaac at Kolossi, he'd put out an edict by public crier that the local people who wanted peace had nothing to fear, that his quarrel was only with Isaac. Since then, Cypriots had been flocking to his camp, many with stories to tell of the emperor's cruelties and grasping ways. Cyprus had a surprising number of bishoprics for such a small island—fourteen in all—and several of these prelates had come to seek assurances from Richard, too. And she knew he continued to be occupied with military matters, sending out scouts to keep track of Isaac's whereabouts, and meeting with the Knights Hospitaller, a martial order of warrior monks almost as celebrated as the Templars, who'd established a presence in Cyprus before Isaac's usurpation. It was still frustrating, though, to know so little about what was occurring, and she worried lest Berengaria feel neglected, for a bride-to-be might reasonably expect more attention than a sister would.

Alicia was still spying on Mariam and Morgan, and she informed them now, "I think he is going to kiss her. But she— Oh! The king is here!" In her excitement, she almost tumbled out the window, for Richard's rescue had convinced her that he was the greatest knight in all of Christendom. Joanna hastened over to put a steadying hand on the girl's shoulder and to see for herself.

"Alicia is right. Richard has just arrived, with a few bishops and some of his knights. But he is talking to Mariam, so he will not be up straightaway," she said, letting Berengaria know she'd have a few moments to adjust her veil or rub perfume onto her wrists. "Mariam is probably asking him if he has heard anything about her sister. Sophia is unlucky enough to be wed to the Cypriot emperor," she explained to Alicia, who shivered and crossed herself for, if she now believed Richard could walk upon water, she was no less sure that Isaac was the Antichrist.

When Richard strolled into the chamber, Beatrix had already made a discreet departure, taking the reluctant Alicia with her, Joanna was removing the last of the pins from her bodice, and Berengaria was biting her lips surreptitiously to give them color. He shook his head at the sight of the dogs, saying, "Whenever I see those strange beasts, I think I've stumbled into a fox burrow."

"I'll have you know cirnecos are greatly valued in Sicily," Joanna said, coming over to give him a quick hug and a critical appraisal. "Well, you do not appear to have suffered any injuries since we saw you last. Does that mean you've had no more 'skirmishes' with Isaac?"

"Nary a one," he said, crossing the chamber to give Berengaria a casual kiss. "In fact, that is one reason why I stopped by—to tell you that the Hospitallers have brought me a message from Isaac. He is asking for peace, promising to meet whatever demands I make of him." Richard's smile was skeptical. "I put as much store in his sworn word as I would in Philippe's. But we shall see."

Both women were delighted, and Joanna moved to a table, pouring wine so they could celebrate Richard's victory. They knew they would be fearing for his life day and night once they reached the Holy Land, but at least they could enjoy a brief respite until they left Cyprus. Sipping Isaac's excellent red wine, Joanna realized that this truce would allow them to see some of the island, an appealing prospect after being stranded in Limassol for the past four days.

"The wives of the Venetian and Genoese merchants have been coming by to pay their respects and to tell us how happy their husbands were with your arrival; apparently the only thing that would make them happier would be if you dispatched Isaac to the Devil forthwith. They were telling us about a place called Kourion, a few miles east of Kolossi. It was once the site of an ancient city and there are many ruins still there, including a large amphitheater and a sanctuary for the pagan god Apollo. Could you take us to visit Kourion, Richard? I've seen an amphitheater in Sicily but Berengaria has not, and you've always been interested in history . . ."

Joanna halted then, for her brother was shaking his head, saying he did not think it would be possible. She was not willing to give up so easily, though. "If you cannot spare the time, then surely Stephen could accompany us? Or is it that you do not think we'd be safe even with his knights?"

"Most likely you would, but I'd as soon not take the risk."

Joanna fell silent, suddenly realizing what life would be like for her and Berengaria in Outremer—as sequestered as William's *harim* girls, under guard as if they were prisoners or hostages. At least her mother had gotten to see the great city of Antioch during her pilgrimage to the Holy Land. Almost at once, though, she chided herself for her lack of faith. Their seclusion would be a small price to pay for the opportunity to walk the hallowed streets of Jerusalem, to follow in the footsteps of the Blessed Lord Christ.

Setting his wine cup down, Richard looked from one woman to the other. "I have something else to tell you. I think Berenguela and I should get married on Sunday."

They stared at him, eyes wide, mouths open. "Are you serious?" Joanna said incredulously.

"Very. Lent is over, so we are free to wed. And there are some compelling reasons for not waiting until we get to Acre. Do we really want Philippe lurking in the shadows, looking like a disgruntled vulture eager to pick my bones? And an army encampment is not the ideal site for a royal wedding. I could probably think of a few more reasons for wedding here and now," he added playfully, amused by how easily he could make Berenguela blush. "But more to the point, I cannot think of any reasons why we should not wed in Cyprus."

"Well, I can." Joanna was regarding her brother in dismayed astonishment. "That is two days hence, Richard! How could we possibly prepare for a royal wedding in so little time?"

"How hard could it be? I assume Berenguela did not intend to get married stark naked, so she must have a suitable gown in her coffers. I thought we'd have her coronation at the same time." Richard glanced over at his mute betrothed and smiled. "I daresay you'll be the first and the last Queen of England ever to be crowned in Cyprus, little dove."

"But what about food? And entertainment? And—"

"I have complete confidence in you, *irlanda*, am sure you'll do just fine. But it is only fair that we let the bride decide." They'd been conversing in French. Richard switched now to *lenga romana*, a language more familiar to Berengaria. "So . . . what say you, Berenguela? Do you want to marry me on Sunday?"

Berengaria well knew what response was expected of her. For twenty-one years, she'd been taught that a highborn young woman must be demure and dutiful in the presence of men. She must keep her eyes cast down and not speak out of turn. Above all, she must be chaste and modest and guard against impure thoughts. The proper answer would be to defer to Richard as her lord and husband, to say she'd be guided by his wishes in this, as in all matters. But Joanna and Queen Eleanor were not at all demure or submissive, and it was obvious that he loved them dearly. She hesitated, sensing that she was at a crossroads, and then, disregarding the lessons of a lifetime, she followed her heart. Looking up into his face, she said, softly but clearly, "I would very much like to wed you on Sunday, Richard."

CHAPTER 17

erengaria was astonished by how much Joanna had been able to accomplish in so little time. She'd had the inspired idea to seek the assistance of the wives of the Italian merchants, who were delighted by the prospect of a royal wedding and eagerly volunteered the services of their cooks and household servants. After their shipboard ordeal, the women took particular pleasure in appropriating the Cypriot emperor's personal effects. Isaac's reputation for luxurious living was borne out by the contents of coffers and cupboards: finely woven linen tablecloths, gold and silver plate, gem-encrusted cups, ivory salt cellars, Venetian glassware, a silk baldequin canopy, silver-gilt candlesticks, and costly, exotic spices, all of which would be put to good use. It had been decided that the wedding ceremony and coronation would be held in the chapel of St George, and the guests would then return to Isaac's palace for the revelries. The floor of the great hall was now covered with fragrant rushes, and scarlet flowers were everywhere, garlanding the doors and windows, floating in the ewers of scented water that would be provided for guests to wash their hands between courses.

Berengaria had no false pride, well aware that her experience in Navarre could not compare to Joanna's, for the lavish hospitality of the Sicilian court had been famed far beyond its borders. She was thankful, therefore, that the other woman had taken over the wedding preparations. She was touched, too, that Joanna took care to consult her on every decision. There would be three courses, each with five dishes; did Berengaria think that would be adequate? One of the Venetian cooks suggested a risotto of rice and chicken baked in pomegranate juice; did Berengaria agree? Did she want a Lombard stew of pork, onions, wine, and spices?

What about a fruit pottage with strawberries and cherries? Berengaria gratefully approved the bountiful menu: oysters, roast venison, sturgeon eggs which Isaac had imported from the Black Sea, haunches of the native sheep called *agrinon*, egg custard, blancmange, fried eels, and salmon in jelly. She also approved Joanna's selection of wines from Isaac's buttery: an Italian vernage, a wine named after the city of Tyre, sweet wines from Greece, local red wines, and the costly spiced wine known as hippocras.

When she fretted, though, that Joanna might be undertaking too much in light of her recent illness, the Sicilian queen brushed her qualms aside, saying staunchly, "I am not going to let my sister-by-marriage be wed in a cursory manner. Now . . . how does this sound to you? In addition to our own minstrels, we will have harpists and other musicians who can play the rebec and the lute. Also tumblers and a man who can juggle torches—or so he says. I suppose we can have pails of water on hand, just in case. And one of the Genoese merchants will provide a trumpeter to introduce the courses."

Glancing around, then, to make sure the other women were not within hearing, Joanna lowered her voice. "How are you bearing up? Are you nervous? Most brides are," she said quickly, lest Berengaria take the question as an implied criticism.

"Yes . . . a little. But not as much as I expected to be," Berengaria confided. She was about to thank Joanna again, this time for her counseling about the marriage bed, when they were informed that André de Chauvigny had just arrived.

"Have you noticed how often André has been stopping by?" Joanna asked as they made their way toward the great hall. "He's been paying court to Hélène, who told him forthrightly that he is very charming and very married. Apparently he is also very stubborn."

But as soon as they reached the hall, they discovered that Joanna's cousin had more on his mind than a casual dalliance. "Three sails were sighted on the horizon," André reported even before greetings had been exchanged. "As these galleys were coming from the east, we thought they might be bringing word of the siege of Acre. The king, bless him, was not willing to wait patiently on shore, and went out to meet them in a small boat. He was soon back, sending me to tell you there will be highborn guests for dinner—Guy de Lusignan, his brother Joffroi, Humphrey de Toron, whose wife was stolen so shamefully by Conrad of Montferrat, the Prince of Antioch, the Count of Tripoli, and the brother of the Prince of Armenia."

Joanna stared at him, and then looked at Berengaria, the same dismayed thought in both their minds: As if they did not have enough to do, with the wedding scheduled for the morrow! "The de Lusignans," Joanna said wearily, "have always had a deplorable sense of timing."

GUY DE LUSIGNAN was quite handsome, tall and well formed, with curly brown hair and hazel eyes, clean-shaven in the fashion of Outremer. And he was young to have gained and lost a kingdom and a queen, not that much older than Richard. He was very attentive to Joanna and Berengaria, flirtatious and lavish with the practiced charm that had served him so well in the past. Neither woman liked him at all.

They both felt some sympathy for Humphrey de Toron, Queen Isabella's discarded husband. He, too, was very handsome, but without Guy's swagger, his dark eyes filled with intelligence and sadness, a poet in a land that venerated soldiers. They felt even more sympathy for his young wife, though, pulled from his gentle embrace and thrust against her will into the arms of Conrad of Montferrat, a man as unlike Humphrey as a sword blade was unlike a lute. How alone and abandoned she must have felt, a young girl of eighteen confronted with Conrad's iron will, with an ally in her own mother. But Humphrey had failed her, too. A husband unwilling or unable to fight for his wife was not a husband either of them would want. The world was too dangerous a place to depend upon the protection of poets.

After the meal was done, the conversation turned to politics. Richard was infuriated to learn that Philippe had arbitrarily recognized Conrad as King of Jerusalem, and he agreed to aid Guy in reclaiming the crown, giving the destitute king without a kingdom the sum of two thousand silver marks, for Guy had expended the last of his resources upon the siege of Acre. Watching as Guy, his brother, Humphrey, and one hundred sixty of their knights knelt and did homage to Richard, Joanna was grimly amused by the irony inherent in that dramatic scene, for the de Lusignans had long been a burr under the Angevin saddle.

Berengaria was shocked by Joanna's sotto voce account of de Lusignan sins; not only had they rebelled repeatedly against Richard's father and against Richard himself when he was Count of Poitou, they'd even dared to ambush Queen Eleanor, who'd been saved from capture by the courage of the young Will Marshal. By an absurd twist of fate, Joanna revealed, it was his family's perfidy that had gotten Guy a crown. His older brother Amaury had fled to the Holy Land to evade the king's wrath, and eventually summoned Guy to join him. The de Lusignans were as surprised as everyone else when Guy snared the Leper King's sister. Lowering her voice even further, Joanna said, "When his brother Joffroi learned of Guy's good fortune, he is said to have commented, 'If they'd make Guy a king, they'd have made me a god.' Joffroi later joined his brothers when Richard forced him to take the cross after one rebellion too many, and he and Amaury won respect for their military skills. But Guy was the feckless little brother, not taken seriously by anyone until Sybilla took him as her husband."

Joanna smiled. "The lords of Outremer would not recognize her as queen after her brother's death unless she first divorced Guy. But as soon as she was crowned, she announced that she had the right to pick her own consort and put the crown herself upon Guy's handsome head. She was clever, was Sybilla. A poor judge of men, though, for Guy's flawed leadership would result in the disaster at Ḥaṭṭīn. Richard says that was one of the most inept and inexcusable military blunders since the dawn of time. He gets angry every time he talks about it. He grudgingly gives Guy credit for courage, but says he has not the sense God gave a goat!"

"Then how can he be so friendly to Guy?" Berengaria said, looking across the hall where Richard was engaged in amiable conversation with the de Lusignans.

Joanna blinked in surprise. "Because he is a king, dearest. Because the de Lusignans, whatever their manifest failings, are still his vassals and he owes them his protection." Honesty then compelling her to add, "And because Philippe has chosen to back Conrad."

To Berengaria, Outremer was beginning to sound more and more like a labyrinth. Once Richard got in, could he ever get out? She did not understand how Christians could feud so fiercely with their fellow Christians whilst the Saracens laid claim to the Holy City. No one's motives seemed utterly pure or untainted by political considerations. Even Richard was influenced by his rivalry with the French king, and she feared that Philippe saw Richard as the enemy, not Saladin. But then she banished these disquieting thoughts, determined not to let forebodings cast a shadow over the most important day of her life. On the morrow she would become Richard's wife, would be crowned as his queen. Nothing mattered more than that.

FROM THE TWELFTH-CENTURY chronicle *Itinerarium Peregrinorum et Gesta Regis Ricardi*: "On the following day, a Sunday, on the Feast of St Pancras, King Richard and Berengaria, daughter of the King of Navarre, were married at Limassol. The young woman was very wise and of good character. She was there crowned queen.

The Archbishop of Bordeaux was present at the ceremony, as was the Bishop of Evreux, and the Bishop of Bayonne, and many other magnates and nobles. The king was merry and full of delight, pleasant and agreeable to everyone."

RICHARD COULD NOT even remember the last time he'd bedded a virgin, for he'd long ago concluded that coy or skittish maidens were more trouble than they were worth. He'd always taken a very matter-of-fact, pragmatic approach to his body's needs. When he was tired, he slept. When he was hungry, he ate. And when he felt lustful, he looked around for a bedmate, with convenience and proximity being important considerations. He was amused when his friends became besotted with concubines or light o' loves, knowing it would not last; fevers of the flesh never did. A flame fed by lust was bound to burn out once the craving was satisfied, and for that, one woman would usually do as well as another. Although he enjoyed writing courtly poetry, he had no great interest in the workings of the female brain, for women were too often lacking in logic or backbone, either overly headstrong or weak-willed and timid. Like Sybilla, who'd well nigh doomed her kingdom because she'd wanted Guy de Lusignan in her bed. Or her sister Isabella, who'd let herself be bullied into marrying Conrad.

Thankfully, the women in his own family were not like most of their sex. His mother could think like a man, and rule better than most kings. And his sisters had been blessed with courage and common sense, especially Joanna, Marie, and Tilda, may God assoil her sweet soul. He had hopes for her daughter, too, as Richenza did not seem prone to feminine whims or foolishness. And so far, what he'd seen of Berenguela was encouraging. She might look as fragile and unsubstantial as a feather floating on the wind, but she'd showed fortitude and bravery when faced with hardships and outright danger.

Nor was she a casual bedmate, to be forgotten come dawn. She was his queen, his wife, and he owed it to her to make her first time as easy as he could. Moreover, he liked the lass, he truly did. So he'd limited his wine during the evening, wanting to be clear-headed, for he was not accustomed to pacing himself, to hold back when his every urge was to plunge ahead. He'd also told his squires to sleep elsewhere that night, in deference to his bride's modesty, and had done what he could to keep the bedside revelries brief, knowing this would be her first exposure to bawdy male humor. So by the time he slid into bed beside her, he was feeling rather proud of himself for being more sensitive to her needs than most men would have been.

He'd occasionally heard stories of brides who'd gone to the marriage bed as if to a sacrificial altar, so convinced they were committing a mortal sin that they were trembling with fear or rigid with disgust. He had no such concerns about Berenguela, though, and she justified his faith by smiling shyly when he drew her into his arms. Reminding himself of her inexperience, he kept his kisses gentle at first, murmuring endearments and reassurances in *lenga romana* as his caresses grew more intimate. She did not reciprocate, but she did not protest as he explored her body. Her breath quickening, she closed her eyes, letting him do what he wanted, and he decided that bedding a virgin was not so burdensome after all.

Despite his good intentions, he realized that he'd risk spilling his seed too soon if he waited much longer, and reached for a pillow, sliding it under her hips before he mounted her. "I will try not to hurt you, Berenguela," he promised, parting her thighs. Her arms were tightly wrapped around his neck, and he barely heard her response, soft as a breath against his ear. "I know the first time will hurt," she whispered. "But . . . but will it fit?" He gave a sputter of surprised laughter, delighted by her unexpected spark of humor, and then stopped listening to his brain, let his body take control. She stiffened at his first thrust, but she did not cry out, not until after he'd found satisfaction and collapsed on top of her.

"Richard, I cannot breathe," she gasped, sounding panicky, and he supported himself on his elbows until he was ready to withdraw, joking that she was too delicate a filly to bear a rider's full weight. Her eyes were tightly shut, but he could see tears trickling through her lashes. Had it been that painful for her, then? He had no experience in comforting tearful bedmates, and no interest in acquiring any. But this was his wife, and she had the right to expect soothing words, an affectionate embrace. Shifting onto his side, he reached over to stroke her wet cheek. It was then that he saw all the blood. "Christ Jesus!"

Her eyes flew open. "What? Did I . . . did I do something wrong, Richard?"

"Good God, woman, you're bleeding like a stuck pig!" He started to swing his legs over the side of the bed, trying to decide if a doctor or a midwife should be summoned. Better a midwife, since they were accustomed to dealing with female ailments.

Before he could rise, though, she reached out and caught his arm. "I think this is natural, Richard," she said, sounding remarkably calm to him for a woman who might well be bleeding to death. "Because I knew so little about carnal matters, I spoke to Joanna beforehand. She said that the first time is different for each woman. It can be quite painful or hardly hurt at all, and bleeding can be very meager or a flood. Yes, it hurt when my maidenhead was breached, but no more than it was supposed to, I'm sure. Otherwise, I'd still be bleeding and I am not."

Richard exhaled an audible, uneven breath, so great was his relief. "For a moment, I was afraid I'd ruptured you," he admitted. "You are such a little bit of a lass. . . ."

He still looked dubious as he glanced down at the blood-soaked sheet, and she said quickly, "I would rather I bled a lot than not at all. At least now I have provided you with indisputable proof that I came to my marriage bed a maiden."

Richard was beginning to see the humor in it, that she should be the one reassuring him. "I harbored no misgivings whatsoever about your virtue," he said, hiding a smile as he attempted to match her serious tone. "Even had you not bled a drop, I would never have doubted you."

"Thank you," she said, sounding as if he'd paid her a great compliment.

"You're very welcome." Getting to his feet, he stood by the bed, frowning at what he saw. The women had done their best to transform the chamber into a bridal bower. It was aglow with white wax candles. The floor rushes were fresh and fragrant with the sweet scent of myrtle, its bright green leaves and delicate white flowers scattered about with a lavish hand. Cinnamon and cloves had been burned to perfume the air. A gleaming gold wine flagon and two crystal cups had been set upon a linen-draped table, next to a platter of wafers, figs, and candied orange peels. There was even a silver bowl filled with ripe pomegranates and hazelnuts, both of which were thought to be aphrodisiacs; Richard saw his sister's fine hand in that playful touch. But they'd forgotten to set out one of a bedchamber's basic needs; there was no washing basin or any towels.

When he finally came back to the bed, he was carrying the wine flagon, a napkin, and a richly embroidered silk mantle that he'd found in one of the coffers. Setting them down, he slipped his arms under Berengaria's shoulders and knees and picked her up before she'd realized what he meant to do. "Hold on to me," he directed, and when she did, he shifted her weight to one arm and with his free hand spread the mantle over the wet, stained sheet. "I hope this is Isaac's favorite cloak," he said, and deposited her back onto the bed while she was still marveling that he'd been able to lift her with such obvious ease. "This is the best I can do," he explained, pouring wine onto the napkin. "I suppose we can consider it a baptism of sorts."

She blushed when he began to wipe the blood from her thighs, but when he joined her in bed, she slid over until their bodies touched. It was only then that he realized how tired he was and he laughed softly; who knew that deflowering virgins was such hard work? When she gave him an inquiring look, he kissed her on the forehead. "Sleep well, little dove."

"You, too, my lord husband," she whispered. He was soon asleep, but she lay awake beside him, watching the candles twinkle in the shadows like indoor stars as she thought about their love-making. It had hurt more than she'd expected and she'd derived no pleasure from it. The intimacy of the act would take getting used to; she'd been shocked when he'd touched her in places she'd never even touched herself. And what he'd taken as a jest had been a genuine concern, for she'd never seen a naked man until tonight. But she was very grateful that he'd tried to be gentle with her, and she would never forget that this man who'd seen so much blood had been so dismayed at the sight of hers. Richard had placed her crown on the table, joking that she could wear it to bed if she wished. She could see it now, catching the candlelight in a glimmer of gold and silver. But it was her wedding band that held her gaze. She was Richard's queen. Tonight, though, it mattered more that she was his wife.

TWO DAYS LATER, Richard met the Cypriot emperor in a fig orchard between the sea and the Limassol road. Determined to awe Isaac with the power of the English Crown, Richard was mounted on a white Spanish stallion as handsome and spir- ited as Isaac's Fauvel, the cantle of his saddle decorated with snarling golden lions, his spurs and sword hilt gilded with gold, his scabbard indented with silver. He wore a tunic of rose samite, a mantle woven with silver half-moons and shining suns, and a scarlet cap embroidered in gold thread. A large crowd had gathered to witness the remarkable spectacle: Richard's knights and men, the Italian mer- chants, and local people daring their emperor's wrath for the rare pleasure of seeing him publicly humiliated. Richard's appearance created quite a stir, daz- zling the citizens and causing much amusement among his soldiers, who'd so often seen him soaked in blood, sweat, and mud. By the time the Cypriot emperor arrived, he was already at a disadvantage, just as Richard had hoped.

At a distance, he was very regal, astride Fauvel, his saddle and trappings just as gaudy as Richard's. His purple silk mantle was studded with precious gems, and his long, fair hair was graced by a golden crown. The English were surprised by his youth, for he appeared to be about Richard's age, in his early thirties. At closer range he was not quite so impressive, for he was sharp-featured, with darting pale eyes and a thin slash of a mouth unfamiliar with smiles. Richard's knights had long ago learned how deceptive appearances could be, for sometimes the most ignoble souls were camouflaged by attractive exteriors. Staring at the Cypriot emperor, they exchanged knowing glances, agreeing that this was one pirate ship not flying false colors; Isaac Dukos Comnenus looked to be exactly what he was, a man doomed to burn for aye in Hell everlasting.

Garnier de Nablus, the Grand Master of the Knights Hospitaller of Jerusalem, had brokered the peace conference and he acted now as intermediary, making use of one of his Cypriot Hospitallers to translate French into Greek. They met in the center of the field, Richard's Spanish destrier and the fiery Fauvel eyeing each other with as much suspicion as their riders. The spectators nudged one another and grinned, agreeing that it was fortunate the English king and the Cypriot emperor were both skilled horsemen or else their stallions might have taken it upon themselves to end this parley here and now.

Richard was willing to follow the protocol for such surrenders, but not to waste much time doing it. So while he greeted Isaac with cold courtesy, he soon laid out his terms for peace. When they were translated for Isaac's benefit, the Greek speakers in the audience gasped, murmuring among themselves that this would be too bitter a brew for Isaac to swallow. Richard demanded that Isaac swear fealty to him, that he take the cross and accompany the English to the Holy Land, provide one hundred knights, five hundred horsemen, and five hundred foot soldiers for the service of God and the Holy City, and pay thirty-five hundred marks in compensation for the injuries inflicted upon Richard's men. As a pledge of his good faith, he would be required to surrender all of his castles to the English king and to offer his only daughter and heir as a hostage. There was great astonishment, therefore, among those who knew Isaac when he indicated to Garnier de Nablus that he was willing to accept Richard's terms.

Once agreement had been reached, Richard and Isaac dismounted, and after the emperor had sworn an oath of fealty, they exchanged the ritual kiss of peace. As a gesture of goodwill, Richard then offered to return Isaac's tent and the silver plate plundered from it at the battle of Kolossi. Isaac at once ordered it set up in the open field, announcing he preferred to camp there rather than to enter Limassol, where there might not be adequate accommodations for his men. Since Richard had appropriated his palace and the fortress of St George, no objections were raised. Richard gave orders for wine and food to be sent out to the emperor's encampment, and they agreed to meet on the morrow to arrange for the transfer of Isaac's castles to castellans of Richard's choosing, and to make plans for their joint departure for Acre. The conference ended with an exchange of courtesies that was impeccably correct and utterly unconvincing.

As they rode back toward Limassol, Jaufre spurred his horse to catch up with Richard and André. Richard seemed in good spirits, talking about the arrival that morning of the remainder of his galleys from Rhodes. He said nothing, though, about the peace he'd just concluded with the Cypriot emperor, not until Jaufre expressed his concern. "My liege, those are harsh terms you imposed upon him."

"Yes, they are," Richard agreed, tracking with his eyes the graceful flight of a hawk, soaring on the wind high above their heads.

"I think it was wise to demand sureties for his good faith. But will even that be enough? His entire history is one of deceit and betrayal. Do you truly expect him to honor the pact?"

Richard shrugged. "That is up to him. The choice is his."

"I find it suspicious that he would agree so readily," Jaufre confessed, but then he caught the look of amusement that passed between Richard and André and he understood. Reassured, he said no more and they rode on in silence.

As RICHARD CROSSED the chamber, Berengaria watched him through her lashes. Few big men could move with such easy grace. She knew he was called Lionheart in tribute to his reckless courage, but she thought the name fit in more ways than one, for he was as quick as a cat, too, a very large, tawny cat. It was a revelation to her, this realization that the male body could be beautiful.

He handed her the wine cup before getting back into bed, saying, "How many women have a king at their beck and call?" She smiled, taking several swallows of Isaac's sweet white wine. But when she passed it back, he didn't drink himself. Settling against the pillows, he regarded her with an expression she could not read. "If you are still sore, Berenguela, I am sure the other women could advise you about herbs or ointments that would help the healing."

So he'd noticed! She'd not expected that. She took another sip of wine to cover her confusion. "It is still new to me," she admitted. "This is just our third night together. Based on my experience so far, I am sure I will not begrudge paying the marriage debt." She gave him a smile, then, that belied the formal, stilted phrasing of her words. "But there is something we need to talk about, Richard. I am just not sure how to begin. . . ."

He reached over and took the wine cup, setting it down in the rushes. "Say it straight out. That saves a lot of time."

He made it sound so easy. She sighed. "Very well. I would never want to offend or insult you, Richard, truly I would not. But your . . . your male member is so large that—" She got no further, for her husband was roaring with laughter. This was not the response she'd expected and she stared at him in bewilderment.

"I am not laughing at you, little dove," he said, once he'd gotten his breath back. "But your innocence is downright endearing at times!" Leaning over, he gave her a quick kiss. "Trust me on this. There is not a man born of woman who'd ever take it as an insult to be told that his 'male member' was too large."

She did not understand his hilarity, but then she was often puzzled by male humor. And despite his denial, she did think he was laughing at her. His amusement was far preferable, though, to the other reactions she'd imagined. She'd been unable to approach Joanna, for this was too intimate a topic to discuss with his sister. And so she'd nerved herself to confide in Mariam, greatly relieved to be told there was a simple solution to her problem. But as awkward as that conversation had been, this one with Richard was even worse. There was no going back now, though.

"It is the moment of entry that is painful," she said, startling herself by her own bluntness. "After that, it does not hurt much at all. I am indeed an 'innocent,' as you've often reminded me, so I sought advice from someone more knowledge-able about such matters, one of Joanna's ladies. She said there would be no dis-comfort if we used a scented oil first. . . ."

She paused, hoping there was no need to be more explicit. But his expression was quizzical, expectant. "Yes?" he prompted. "A scented oil. And then what?"

She blushed, acutely embarrassed. She was bracing herself to blurt it out when she noticed that the corner of his mouth was curving, ever so slightly. Suddenly suspicious, she sat up in bed, heedless of her nudity. "You know what I am talking about," she accused. "You are just teasing me!"

That set him off again. But he sought to get his laughter under control once he saw that she was genuinely upset. "You are right," he confessed. "I was teasing you. I am sorry, Berenguela. I have always teased my sisters—they'd say 'tormented'— and I forget that you are not as accustomed to Angevin humor."

He sounded contrite, but she was not entirely mollified. "You must remember, Richard," she said with as much dignity as she could muster, "that I am still learn-ing to be a wife, and Pamplona is a far different world than Poitiers."

"You are right," he said again, "absolutely right. I cannot promise to mend my wicked ways overnight, but I will try, Berenguela."

There was still a teasing undertone to his apology, but she did not mind as much now, for he'd drawn her into his arms. She cradled her head against his chest, listening to the lulling beat of his heart against her ear. "So," he said, "ask your confidante for some of that oil and we will try it tomorrow night." When she smiled and nodded, he slid his fingers under her chin and tilted her face up to his. "Of course, if I am going to be basted with oil like a Michaelmas goose, it is only fair that my wife be the one to do the basting."

As he expected, color surged into her face again, even giving her throat a rose-colored glow. But she surprised him by bravely agreeing that it was indeed only fair. Taking pity on her, he said, "We'll see, little dove. You are just learning to . . . cook, after all."

He retrieved the wine cup from the floor and they took turns drinking from it. When he yawned, she knew she'd have to make a decision soon. Joanna had warned her that it was not a good idea to have a serious conversation after love-making, for men usually wanted to roll over and go to sleep. But the only time she seemed to have Richard's undivided attention was in bed. When he shifted his position, she knew it was now or never, for she'd observed that he liked to sleep on his side. "Richard . . . I need to talk to you."

He propped himself up on his elbow, and she drew the sheet against her breasts, nervously twisting her wedding ring as she tried to think of a way to ease into it. Not finding any, she took his earlier advice to say it straight out. "Joanna told me that you have a young son."

"Did she, now?" Richard's voice was even, giving nothing away. But she was learning to read the subtle signs behind that guarded court mask, and she knew he was not pleased.

"Please do not be angry with her, Richard. She only told me because she did not want me to hear it through gossip. She did not see it as breaking a confidence since so many others know about him."

Richard had to grudgingly concede the truth in that. "Yes," he said, "I have a son. Philip is ten, and lives in Poitiers."

"Does he live with his mother?"

"No. I assumed responsibility for him when he was very young."

From the terseness of his answers, she knew that he was not happy having this conversation. If the boy was ten now, that would mean he'd been conceived when Richard was young himself, only about twenty-two or so. She thought it was to his credit that he'd acknowledged Philip as his, for she knew not all men of high birth bothered about the consequences of their carnal exploits. She was very proud of her brother Sancho for taking his own bastard sons under his care and making sure they wanted for nothing.

"Is there a reason why you are asking about the lad, Berenguela?"

"Yes, there is. I thought that when we return from Outremer, you might want him to live with us. I wanted to assure you that I would do all in my power to make him most welcome."

"Indeed?" He did not try to hide his surprise. "You are not troubled that he was born out of wedlock?"

"Why would I blame him for a sin that was yours, Richard? That would be unjust."

He did not consider it a sin at all, but he saw no point in arguing that with her. "By the time we get back, Philip will be old enough to begin his training as a squire, so he'd not be living in our household. But I will want him to visit, of course, and it gladdens me that you would welcome him, Berenguela."

"My father is a man of deep faith, and he often spoke to us about the power of Divine Mercy, pointing out that if the Almighty is willing to forgive us our trespasses, how can mortal man do less? He is a great admirer of St Augustine, and one of his favorite quotations is *'Cum dilectione hominum et odio vitiorum.'* I do not know Latin but I've heard him quote it so often that it took root in my memory. He said it meant 'Love the sinner and hate the sin.'"

Like all of Henry and Eleanor's sons, Richard had been well grounded in Latin. "The actual translation is 'With love for mankind and hatred of sins,' but I'd say that is close enough." His own favorite quotation from St Augustine was a prayer to "Give me chastity and continence, but do not give it yet." He suspected, though, that his wife would not find it as amusing as he did. Leaning over again, he gave her a lingering kiss before saying, "This has been a most interesting evening, little dove. But I am supposed to meet again with Isaac in the morn and if I do not get some sleep, I'll be in no shape to fend off his excuses and lies. Whilst he claimed today that he was willing to accept my terms, I'll not be surprised if he tries to weasel out of the more onerous ones."

She thought that was a tactful way to let her know he was done talking for the night. The rhythm of his breathing soon told her that he slept. She was still wide awake, but she did not mind, for she had much to think about. She knew she'd pleased him tonight. That last kiss had been somehow different; in the past they'd either been casual or demanding and passionate. But this one had been tender. Their bed hangings were drawn back as he'd agreed to let his squires sleep elsewhere for a few more days, and the chamber was silvered with moonlight, for they'd left a window open to the mild May air. After such a frightening introduction to Cyprus, she'd never have expected to feel any affection for the island, but she was collecting memories that she'd cherish till the end of her earthly days.

Watching Richard as he slept, she remembered the uncertainty of her journey to Sicily, wondering what manner of man he was, wondering if he would prove kind. She thought she could answer that now; no, he was not. That was as it ought to be, though, for kindness would avail him naught in his battle to save the Holy Land. Yet he *was* kind to her, at least so far, and she felt grateful to see a side of his nature that no one else did. Her feelings about marrying Richard had been more ambivalent than she'd been willing to admit, even to herself. Refusal was out of the question, for she'd known how much her father and brother had wanted this alliance. Marriage to the King of England was a great honor for Navarre, some of Richard's luster sure to spill over onto her father's court. It was an honor for her, too, that he'd chosen her when he could have had any woman he wanted as his queen.

But she'd realized that her life would never be the same, that she would be surrendering to forces utterly beyond her control, and there had been times when she'd feared the unknown future awaiting her, times when she'd felt as if she'd been swept up in an Angevin riptide, carried far from all that was familiar and safe. She'd been determined to do her duty as queen, wife, and mother, determined not to disappoint Richard or shame her father. So far nothing had turned out as she'd expected, though. She'd not envisioned a friend like Joanna or an enemy like Isaac Comnenus. And nothing had prepared her for Richard Coeur de Lion.

Her long hair had caught under her hip and she tugged to free it, wishing she could put it in a night plait. But Richard liked it loose, had wrapped it around his throat during their love-making. In the morning she would ask Mariam for the scented oil. Mariam had hinted that there were other erotic uses for it, and she decided that she would ask about them, too. Innocence was an admirable attribute for a virgin maid, not so much for a wedded wife. She drifted off to sleep with a smile, wondering if she would dream of Michaelmas geese.

BERENGARIA JERKED UPRIGHT, torn from sleep so abruptly that she felt disoriented. It was not yet dawn, for the sky visible from the window still glimmered with a scattering of stars. Someone was pounding on the door and she could hear raised voices. Richard was already out of bed, sliding his sword from its scabbard. Striding to the door, he apparently heard enough to be satisfied there was no imminent danger, for he lifted the latch. Clutching the sheet modestly to her throat, Berengaria waited anxiously as he exchanged a few words with someone on the other side of the door, her imagination taking flight as she tried to guess what was wrong.

"Tell them I'll be there straightaway," Richard directed his unseen audience.

"And send my squires in to help me arm myself." Closing the door, he moved to a coffer and began to select clothes at random. "Isaac seems to have had a change of heart," he said as he pulled his braies up over his hips. "He fled his camp in the middle of the night, leaving all of his belongings behind."

"That wicked, deceitful man!" Berengaria was highly indignant, but alarmed, too. She'd thought that Isaac was part of their past, and suddenly here he was again, posing a new danger to Richard, threatening to disrupt their departure for Outremer. "Surely the Almighty will punish him as he deserves for this latest treachery!"

"From your lips to God's ear, little dove," Richard said, pulling a shirt over his head. "Have you seen my boots?"

"Over there, under the table." Berengaria sat up, watching him in growing puzzlement. He did not seem surprised by Isaac's flight. He did not even sound angry. "Were you expecting him to do this, Richard?"

"Well, I had hopes," he said, sitting down to attach his chausses to his braies. "But it was hard to believe that even Isaac could be so foolhardy. Of course," he said with a sudden grin, "he may have been tempted by the ease of it. Had he been lodged in Limassol midst my men, it would have been more difficult to sneak away in the night like that."

By now she was thoroughly confused. "I do not understand. You want to fight him? Why?"

"It is quite simple, Berenguela. With favorable winds, a ship can sail from the port at Famagusta to the Syrian coast in just a day." He could see that she still did not comprehend, and said with rare patience, "It is not enough to retake Acre or even Jerusalem. Then we have to hold them in a land where we are vastly out-numbered, and we cannot do that unless we can keep the kingdom supplied with food, weapons, and soldiers. That means relying upon other Christian countries for such aid. As soon as I looked at a map, I saw that Cyprus would make an ideal supply base for the Holy Land. It would be an invaluable ally—if it were not ruled by a renegade, a man suspected of conniving with Saladin."

She was staring at him. "Are you saying you planned to take Cyprus?"

"Well, the thought did cross my mind. How could it not? Its strategic im-portance was obvious to any man with eyes to see. And the more I heard about Isaac—a man so hated that he'd not be likely to have the support of the Cypriots—the more convinced I became that Cyprus would benefit as much as Outremer if he were deposed. Whilst I did not sail from Messina with the intent of taking Cyprus from him, I did mean to seize the opportunity if one presented itself."

Berengaria was dumbfounded. "Is that why you chose Cyprus as a rendezvous point for the fleet? And why you asked Tancred for a Greek interpreter?"

"No to your first question, yes to your second. Cyprus was the logical choice, indeed the only choice, for there were no other islands beyond Rhodes. Of course I did not expect the fleet to be scattered and for certes I did not expect your ship to reach Limassol on its own."

"But . . . but why did you agree to make peace with Isaac, then?"

"Because it seemed like I might get what I wanted without having to fight for it. He agreed to swear fealty to me and pledged his full support to recapture Jerusalem. If he honored the terms, we'd have gotten a thousand men, the promise of Cypriot harvests, and money I could put toward the cost of the campaign. Naturally, I trusted him about as much as I'd trust a viper, so I demanded his daughter as a hostage and the surrender of his castles. If he'd kept faith, I'd have been satisfied with that."

"Did you think he would keep faith?"

He smiled without answering and went to the door to admit his squires. Jehan and Saer were so excited they could barely contain themselves, seeming so young and eager to Berengaria that she felt a pang. "I'll wait to arm myself until after I meet with my commanders," Richard decided, but when the boys objected, protesting that Isaac might well seek to win by treachery what he could not win on the field, he agreed to wear his hauberk. Berengaria had not even considered the dangers of a hidden crossbowman and she reached for the coverlets, pulling them up around her shoulders to combat a sudden chill.

His squires had assisted Richard with his hauberk and he was buckling his scabbard. She was still trying to come to terms with this new knowledge, that Richard had been two steps ahead of the Cypriot emperor from the very first. If Isaac were not such a monster, she might have felt a twinge of pity for him. But she did not doubt he deserved whatever Richard had in mind for him, and now that it had been explained to her, she could see that holding Cyprus would be very beneficial to the Holy Land. Yet how could Richard spare the time to defeat Isaac when they were awaiting him at the siege of Acre?

Coming back to the bed, Richard leaned over and kissed her. "Keep that oil handy," he said. "I'll send your women in so you can dress."

"What of the men at Acre, Richard? Will they not be upset by this delay?"

"It will not take that long."

"How long would it take to conquer an entire country?" She'd not realized she'd spoken the words aloud, not until Richard paused on his way to the door.

"Well," he said, "I wagered André that we could do it in a fortnight." And then he was gone, leaving her alone in their marriage bed, a bride of four days, staring at that closing door.

CHAPTER 18

MAY 1191

Famagusta, Cyprus

Jaufre did not know what to expect as their army approached the town called Ammokhostos by the Greek-speaking Cypriots and Famagusta by the "Latins," the term for those who adhered to the Pope in Rome rather than the Patriarch in Constantinople. Richard had quickly learned that Isaac had fled toward Famagusta, for the Cypriot emperor was now reaping the hatred he'd sown for the past seven years, and his long-suffering subjects were willing, even eager, to provide information that might mean his downfall. Leaving Berengaria and Joanna in Limassol under the protection of the Prince of Antioch and the Armenian prince Leo, Richard entrusted Guy and Joffroi de Lusignan to lead his army overland while he sailed along the coast to Famagusta with some of his fastest galleys.

So Jaufre was sure that the king would already have reached Famagusta. But what sight would await them? A city under siege? Charred houses and still smoldering ruins? Instead they came upon a scene of surprising tranquility. Richard's galleys rode at anchor in the harbor, and his army was encamped upon the beach, soldiers strolling about as if they hadn't any fears for their safety. The town itself seemed no less peaceful. It looked like a mere village to Jaufre, with narrow streets and alleys and small houses with flat, tiled roofs. He could not imagine how Isaac had hoped to hold it, for it lacked walls like Limassol, and the buildings he could see were simple structures; he was truly amazed to be told that one of them was the residence of the Archbishop of Cyprus.

Despite the apparent serenity of this Cypriot seaport, the English camp was well guarded. They were saluted cheerfully by men glad to have been spared that long, dusty journey, and the de Lusignans and Jaufre were escorted to Richard's large pavilion. Once greetings had been exchanged, Richard explained that Isaac had retreated inland as soon as he'd gotten word of the fleet's approach. Some of the citizens had fled, too, but others flocked to the harbor to welcome the invaders, reassured by what they'd heard about the treatment of Cypriots who'd offered no resistance.

"You'd best get a good night's sleep," Richard told the new arrivals. "We march at dawn for the interior of the island." He had a map spread out upon the table, and showed them his intended target, the town called Lefkosia by the Greeks and Nicosia by the Latins. "We've had reports that Isaac is lurking in the vicinity of Nicosia, about forty miles east of here. So on the morrow, we go to find him."

Peering over Richard's shoulder at the map, Jaufre asked if Nicosia was walled; he'd been astonished that the Cypriot towns were so vulnerable to attack. "I thought the man was foolhardy beyond belief when he dared to defy you as he did. But now that I know his so-called empire is so defenseless, I think he must be mad."

"According to what I've been told, there is a small fortress at Nicosia, but the town itself has no walls, so it is not likely that Isaac will try to make a stand there. My guess is that he will seek to ambush us on the road, and when that fails—as of course it will—he will then retreat to one of his citadels along the north coast. Apparently he does have several well-fortified castles there. The strongest is the one at Kyrenia." Richard gestured toward a spot on the map. "Supposedly this is where he keeps his treasure and the local people say he sent his wife and daughter there for safety. He also has castles at Deudamour, Buffavento, and Kantara."

Richard was interrupted then when one of his knights entered the tent to announce that some monks had ridden into the camp and were seeking an audience. "One says he is the abbot of . . . Mahera or Makera?"

Richard glanced toward one of Famagusta's Venetian merchants for enlightenment. He was not disappointed, for the mercer was already nodding knowledgeably. "Makheras Monastery. That would be Abbot Nilus. You ought to see him, my lord king, for he is highly respected. Next to the archbishop and a revered hermit who lives in a cave near Paphos, Abbot Nilus wields great influence, even more so than most bishops."

When Richard indicated he would see the abbot, his knight went to fetch him. As he ushered the monks through the camp, their long, bushy beards raised some English eyebrows, for this Greek fashion seemed bizarre to most of the soldiers, who were either clean-shaven or had closely trimmed beards like Richard. They were careful not to show any overt amusement, though, for the king had given orders not to harass the locals. But Abbot Nilus was aware of the disrespectful stares, the murmured jests about "Griffons," and he hoped he'd not made a mistake in approaching the barbarians like this. At first he'd held back even as other bishops and abbots sought to make peace with these English invaders, for he'd known how vengeful Isaac would be once they were gone. It was only when it began to look as if the emperor might truly be deposed that he'd dared to seek English protection for his abbey. Now he was not so sure he'd made the right decision.

Some of his misgivings waned as he entered the king's tent and saw so many familiar faces: Italian merchants who'd resided for years in Famagusta, the bishops of Kition and Tremetousha, and several highborn defectors from Isaac's court. His pride was soothed, too, by his courteous reception, and when the English reassured him that they meant no harm to monasteries or churches, Nilus decided to trust this Latin warrior-king, at least enough to relay information that might hasten Isaac's defeat. He'd been relying upon a Venetian merchant to act as translator, and he told the man now to ask the English king if he knew why Isaac had fled like a thief in the night.

"I do not think he ever meant to keep faith with our pact," Richard said candidly, "though he hoped to fool us into believing he would. I admit I was surprised that he bolted within hours. I suppose he found the terms too humiliating even if he did not intend to abide by them."

"That may well be. But I heard that he was warned to flee by one of your own."

Richard frowned as he glanced from the abbot to the interpreter. "Ask him what he means by that. Is he accusing one of my men of treachery?"

After a murmured exchange with Abbot Nilus, the merchant shook his head. "He meant a Latin, my liege. He says a lord from Outremer sailed for Cyprus as soon as they learned of your clash with Isaac. This man told Isaac that you meant to seize him come morning and this is why he ran as he did." Anticipating Richard's next question, he turned again to Nilus. "He says the name of this evil adviser is Pagan, the Lord of Haifa."

The name meant nothing to Richard or his knights, but the de Lusignans and Humphrey de Toron reacted as if they'd been told Judas was in their midst. Pagan de Haifa, they told him, was a close ally of Conrad of Montferrat and a bitter enemy of the de Lusignans. It was obvious what Pagan hoped to do, Guy sputtered. He wanted Richard's war with Isaac to drag on, keeping him occupied on Cyprus long enough for Conrad to seize Acre and gain all the glory for himself, thus making sure that few could oppose his claim to the Kingdom of Jerusalem.

Glancing around, Nilus saw that most of the men shared Guy's indignation. Richard alone looked amused. "If that is true," he said, "it is indeed proof that the Almighty has a sense of humor, for by running away, Isaac provided me with the justification for taking Cyprus from him. I really ought to send Pagan and Conrad some of Isaac's wine in appreciation for their help."

That stirred some amusement among his knights, but the de Lusignans continued to fume, fearing that this delay could prove fatal to Guy's hopes of regaining his crown. Jaufre also worried that Richard may have bitten off more than he could chew. He did not doubt that Isaac would be defeated. Yet if Conrad took Acre whilst Richard took Cyprus, would it be worth it? "Are you sure, my liege," he said, "that you can conquer the entire country ere Acre falls?"

Richard's mouth quirked. "Well, it is a small country." After the laughter subsided, he said, no longer joking, "Tell me this, Jaufre. How many men do you think are willing to die for Isaac Comnenus?" And when this was translated for Nilus's benefit, the abbot smiled grimly, thinking that could well serve as the hated despot's epitaph.

THE ELDERLY ARCHBISHOP BARNABAS shared the views of his compatriots— eager to see Isaac deposed, but eager, too, to see the English army sail for the Holy Land. So far Famagusta had been spared the usual misery that befell occupied towns and he meant to keep it that way, hosting an elaborate feast that evening in honor of his unwelcome guests. The meal had just ended when Richard got word that a galley had been spotted approaching the harbor, flying the flag of the Kingdom of Jerusalem.

As the news rippled across the hall, Richard found himself struggling with conflicting emotions. He knew that as a Christian, he ought to be praying that Acre had fallen. But he dreaded to hear it, for he could not bear that the siege should have ended before he got there to take part in the assault. "Do you think it is a sin to hope that Acre holds out for another few weeks?" he asked his companions with a tight smile, and then crossed the hall to tell the archbishop and Abbot Nilus about the approaching ship.

His audience—Morgan, Baldwin de Bethune, and Jaufre—were equally ambivalent, especially after learning of Pagan of Haifa's meddling. As they glanced around, they could see that the de Lusignans and Humphrey de Toron and their knights were making no attempt to hide their consternation. It seemed to take forever before one of Richard's men hurried into the hall to announce that envoys from the French king had arrived. Realizing what they all were thinking, he shook his head emphatically, letting them know the siege of Acre continued.

Morgan recognized one of the lead knights, for Druon de Mello had been a member of the French king's household during their stay in Messina. He did not know Druon's companion, a stocky, powerfully built man in his early thirties who strode into the hall with the swagger of one accustomed to getting deference from others. He was clad in an obviously expensive hauberk, which was partially covered by an equally expensive surcote emblazoned with a coat of arms unfamiliar to Morgan. He was surprised that the stranger would come armed into the hall, for most men preferred to eschew the weight of their hauberks unless they expected to be in physical danger. And so he instinctively sensed that this man was bringing trouble into their midst even before he heard Jaufre's dismayed hiss of breath.

"I cannot believe Philippe sent *him*!" Lowering his voice, Jaufre said, "That is Philip de Dreux, the Bishop of Beauvais and Philippe's first cousin. He is also the man loathed by the de Lusignans almost as much as Conrad, for he connived with Conrad to steal Isabella from Humphrey de Toron and then performed the marriage ceremony himself."

Morgan had heard of the bishop, who was said to love battles more than books and had won himself a reputation for being utterly fearless in combat. It astonished him that the French king would entrust a message to a man whose very presence was a provocation to the de Lusignans. Remembering, then, that there was said to be bad blood between Richard and Beauvais, too, he started hastily toward the newcomers. Jaufre and Baldwin and a number of Richard's other knights were already in motion.

Richard's greeting had been icy enough to put the bishop at risk for frostbite, and the latter's response was so terse as to be downright rude. It was left to Druon de Mello to try to pass over the awkwardness with strained courtesy. Because he respected the older man, Richard thawed somewhat, but he pointedly addressed himself to Druon, all the while staring at Beauvais with a hawk's predatory appraisal. The bishop glared back, conveying defiance with no need of words. It was then that Guy de Lusignan pushed his way through the crowd.

"First Pagan de Haifa and now Conrad's tame bishop," Guy said with a sneer. "Conrad must truly be desperate to keep us here in Cyprus."

"I do not know what you are babbling about," Beauvais said disdainfully. "I do indeed respect Conrad of Montferrat, but I do not do his bidding. I answer only to Almighty God."

Guy feigned surprise. "God told you to marry Isabella to a man who already had a wife?"

"Conrad's Greek wife was dead, so there was no impediment to his marriage with Queen Isabella."

"The 'Greek wife' you dismiss so easily has a name and an identity of her own—the Lady Theodora, sister to the Emperor of the Greeks. Nor is she dead, as you so conveniently claim. She is well and living in Constantinople." This challenge came from a new speaker, Humphrey de Toron, who was staring at the bishop with the frustrated fury of a man who realized that his words would be neither heard nor heeded.

Just as he feared, Beauvais did not even bother to deny his charge, for they both knew that the truth of it was irrelevant. "I am not here to argue a matter that was decided months ago. I bear a message from the king of the French." His gaze flicking from Guy and Humphrey as if they were negligible, he turned his attention back to Richard, "He wants to know why you are tarrying here in Cyprus when there is such an urgent need for your presence at the siege of Acre."

"'Tarrying here in Cyprus'?" Richard echoed incredulously. "What do you fools think—that we've been lolling about on the beach, taking our ease with their wine and their women? It does not surprise me, my lord bishop, that you apparently cannot read a map, but I expected better of your king. Cyprus is an ideal supply base for the Holy Land, or it was until Isaac Comnenus seized power. It is too dangerous to leave so strategic an island in the hands of a man hostile to the Kingdom of Jerusalem."

"And why is he 'hostile' to us? Because you were intent upon its conquest from the day you sailed from Messina!"

There were angry protests at that from many of Richard's men. Richard was as outraged as his knights. "Isaac Comnenus has refused for years to send supplies to the Holy Land. He would not even permit ships from Outremer to dock in Cypriot harbors. And whilst he plotted with Saladin, men died at Acre—not from battle wounds, but from hunger!"

"My lord king knew you'd have excuses for your irresponsible actions; he says you always do." At that, Druon de Mello, who'd been looking increasingly uncomfortable, sought to intervene, but the bishop ignored him. "I suppose we must be thankful that you confined yourself to Cyprus and did not go off on a whim to assault Constantinople. But the irrefutable fact is that good Christian knights are dying at Acre because settling a grudge matters more to you than the success of the siege."

"Since you are so free with your advice, let me give you some, Beauvais. It is always better to let men think you're one of God's great fools than to open your mouth and remove all doubt. It is obvious that you know as little about siege warfare as you do about the spiritual duties of a bishop. I have already arranged to send ships to Acre loaded with grain and—"

"And are you sending, too, the Cypriot treasury? I admit that this has been a right profitable digression for you. But it might cost you what you value most, my lord Lionheart—that reputation you've so carefully cultivated for demented courage. The longer you remain in Cyprus, killing fellow Christians instead of God's true enemies, the Saracens, the more likely it is that men will begin to wonder if it is cowardice that keeps you here."

Richard had been standing on the dais. He came down the steps so fast now that the alarmed French knights clustered protectively around the bishop. "I'll tell you what cowardice is," Richard spat. "It is hiding behind your holy vows, using them as your shield. You know full well that I'd kill any man who dared to call me a coward. But you know, too, that I'd not be likely to strike down a prince of the Church."

"Now why would I think that? After all, your family has a history of ill-treating princes of the Church. If my memory serves, your grandfather, Geoffrey of Anjou, once ordered a bishop to be gelded. And it is barely twenty years since your father's knights left a saint bleeding to death on the floor of his own cathedral."

The expression on Richard's face was one that his men had often seen—on the battlefield—and hands instinctively dropped to sword hilts. He surprised them, though, by not lunging for Beauvais's throat as they expected. "You're right," he said, with a very dangerous smile. "My father was exonerated by the Pope for the part he played in a holy martyr's murder. So why should I worry about dispatching a luxury-loving, godless pretend-priest to Hell?"

Beauvais's lips peeled back in a snarling smile of his own. But Guy de Lusignan gave him no chance to respond. He'd been seething at the other man's contemptuous dismissal, and now he said menacingly, "Well, I have no qualms whatsoever about shedding the blood of a bishop. You'd best bear that in mind, Beauvais, for I doubt you're in a state of grace to meet your Maker. Where would you ever find a priest corrupt enough or drunk enough to absolve you of all your sins?"

Richard laughed, a chilling sound. Beauvais did not appear at all intimidated by either king, though. "It would give me great pleasure to put the anathema of excommunication upon any man rash enough to lay hands upon a consecrated bishop. You'd best bear *that* in mind, de Lusignan. As for you, my lord Lionheart—"

He got no further, for Guy took a threatening step forward. "Call me by my rightful title, you son of a whore!"

The bishop's eyes gleamed. "Which title is that? Surely not the one you earned in Sybilla's bed? Or mayhap you mean 'hero of Ḥaṭṭīn.' No, that will not do, either, for that was the battle in which the entire army of the Kingdom of Jerusalem was destroyed by Saladin, destroyed because of your unforgivable, idiotic blunders!"

When Guy lunged at him, the bishop started to draw his sword. It never cleared the scabbard, though, for Joffroi de Lusignan grabbed his brother just as Jaufre darted forward and interposed himself between the two men. "You are shaming yourself, my lord bishop," he said, "and worse, you are shaming our king. I cannot believe Philippe sent you here to shed blood in the Archbishop of Cyprus's house."

"No, he did not!" Druon de Mello seized his chance and said loudly, "Our lord king bade us tell King Richard to stop wasting time and make haste to reach Acre, for he has been delaying a full assault upon the city as a courtesy to the English king—" Druon stopped in astonishment, for the hall was rocking with derisive laughter. He scowled, angry that they dared to mock his king like this. But after a moment to reflect, he decided their mockery was a small price to pay for the dispersal of this dangerous tension. He knew, even if he feared his king did not, that their hopes of recovering Jerusalem rested upon the military expertise of the English king, and for that, Druon was willing to overlook Richard's arrogance and bravado, even his regrettable alliance with Guy de Lusignan.

Richard raised a hand for silence. "Go back to Philippe, Sir Druon, and tell him that I will not leave for Acre until I have secured Cyprus for the Holy Land. Remind him that a king does not give orders to another king. Now return to your ship and pass the night. But at dawn, set sail for Outremer, for I want this man gone from here by the time I rise from my bed tomorrow." And with that, he deliberately turned his back on the bishop and walked away.

Joffroi de Lusignan had pulled his raging brother aside, and although the bishop seemed inclined to continue the confrontation, Druon and the French knights were already withdrawing, giving him no choice but to follow. Jaufre took it upon himself to make sure Beauvais would actually return to his galley and hastened after them. Richard was still infuriated and was giving voice to his wrath before a very receptive audience. But slowly calm began to settle over the hall again.

The aged Archbishop of Cyprus and Abbot Nilus had been dumbfounded witnesses from their seats upon the dais. As they exchanged glances now, the archbishop suggested that they summon one of the Greek-speaking Italian merchants so they could find out what had caused this ugly scene. Nilus shrugged, shaking his head in bemusement. "Does it truly matter? If I were the Sultan of Egypt, I'd be sleeping soundly at night, knowing that the Christians will never be able to retake Jerusalem, for they would rather fight one another than the Turks."

Barnabas sadly concurred. "Well, at least some good has come out of this. Whatever happens in Outremer, Cyprus has been freed of a tyrant, and for that we must thank the God of our Fathers, His only-begotten Son, and the holy *Theotokos* and Ever-Virgin Mary."

Abbot Nilus murmured his agreement. But as grateful as he was to be rid of Isaac Comnenus, he would reserve judgment as to the future of Cyprus under the Latins. His was a sorrowfully cynical view of his fellow men and he knew sometimes the cure could be as bad as the disease.

THEY'D BEEN TOLD the flat, bleak plain was called the Mesaoria, a Greek term meaning "between the mountains." Warned that it would be desolate, Richard had ordered his men to carry enough rations for several days, and they were glad of it, for it was soon apparent that no army could live off this land. They passed an occasional deserted hamlet, its inhabitants gone into hiding. Even before they'd left Famagusta, they'd gotten reports from locals that Isaac had gathered a force of seven hundred lightly armed horsemen called *turcopoles*, and so Richard insisted that they maintain a tight formation as they marched, entrusting the vanguard to the de Lusignans and taking the rear guard himself, for he thought that would be the likely target of an ambush.

It was hot and dusty, the road little more than a narrow mule track, and the few streams they found were dried up; it was hard for Richard and his knights to believe this arid area would be transformed into vast, marshy quagmires by heavy winter rains. There were no trees in sight, and the only signs of life were several hawks lazily circling in a sky as empty as the plain below them. The men were uniformly glad when they reached the abandoned village of Kalopsyda, for there the road veered toward the northwest, and the tedious monotony of the landscape gave way to an occasional gully carved out by winter floods. If Isaac meant an ambush, it would be in one of these deep, dry riverbeds, and they found themselves almost looking forward to the prospect, for at least some action would ease the boredom of the march.

Off to the east, they could see mud-brick buildings far in the distance. Shading his eyes against the sun's merciless glare, Richard decided this must be

Tremetousha. He'd met its bishop in Famagusta, and he marveled now that this isolated village could be the seat of a prelate of the Greek Orthodox Church. "There is a monastery there," he told Jaufre, "and we can halt to rest awhile." He eased his Spanish stallion so he could unhook his wineskin from the saddle pommel, grimacing at the taste of the warm liquid as it trickled down his throat.

"Your cool head was useful last night, Jaufre. Whilst I cannot imagine anyone mourning that misbegotten hellspawn, I suspect the new pontiff would not have been happy if I'd sent one of his bishops to eternal damnation. For certes, my mother would not have been pleased with me. After all, I'd asked her to get to Rome with all haste so she could gain the new Pope's favor."

"Well, my 'cool head' did not avail me much later, Uncle. When Beauvais berated me for sailing with you instead of Philippe, I was sorely tempted to push him over the side of his galley." Jaufre glanced at Richard with a grin. "A dislike of the good bishop seems to run in our family. Druon de Mello told me that my father and Beauvais almost came to blows at Acre when the bishop told him he ought to be ashamed to have a son like me!"

But he no longer had Richard's attention. The other man was gazing toward the gully looming ahead of them. "If I were planning to entrap Isaac, that is where I'd do it, for yonder hollow offers the best cover we've so far seen. You think Isaac is clever enough to figure that out?"

The words were no sooner out of his mouth than they heard the sound so familiar to them all, the battle cries of men on the attack. Richard began to curse. "Bleeding Christ! I was so sure that craven swine would hit us from the rear! Take over, Jaufre!" And with that, he was off in a cloud of dust as Jaufre began to shout commands to the men left in his charge.

By the time Richard caught up with his vanguard, the attack had been repulsed. A seasoned soldier like Joffroi de Lusignan had no difficulty in keeping his troops in formation, and once they'd broken out of the ravine, he turned them upon Isaac's *turcopoles*. When Richard came upon the scene, some individual clashes were still taking place, but the thrust of Isaac's assault had been blunted, and his lightly armed horsemen were retreating before the charging knights.

Midst the confusion on the field, Richard detected a flash of purple, the color worn only by Greek royalty. Isaac had donned a silk surcote over his hauberk to proclaim his imperial rank, and it drew the English king now like a beacon in the dark. The emperor was armed with a Damascus bow, and if Richard had not been so set upon running him through, he might have admired the other man's dexterity with the weapon, for shooting from horseback was a skill few Latins had mastered. Isaac was shouting in rage, obviously urging his troops to regroup, when he suddenly sensed danger and turned in the saddle to see Richard bearing down upon him.

As soon as he was within range to strike, Richard rose in the stirrups, leveling his lance at the emperor's chest. He was too close to miss and so he was stunned when he did. But Isaac jerked on the reins and Fauvel responded like a great, graceful cat, swerving out of harm's way just in the nick of time. When Richard swung his horse about for another run, Isaac was almost a bowshot length away. So sure was he of Fauvel's superior speed that he dared to slow down and shoot two arrows in quick succession. The first one bounced off Richard's shield; the second sailed over his head. As he spurred his steed forward, Isaac gave Fauvel his head and the dun stallion once again showed that he was as fast as he was agile, pulling away from Richard's horse with infuriating ease.

The Spanish destrier was as frustrated as his rider, eager to close with the other stallion, and it took Richard several moments to bring the lathered animal to a full stop. By then, Isaac was disappearing into the distance and, as at Kolossi, all Richard could do was watch and indulge in some creative cursing.

"Richard!" André reined in beside him. "You were not hit by those arrows?"

"No . . . why? Even if his aim had been better, I doubt the arrows would have penetrated my hauberk." Richard shifted in the saddle to look at his friend. "Why the sudden concern for what would have been a minor wound at most, André?"

"Because one of the captured *turcopoles* told de Lusignan that Isaac is known to use arrows tipped in poison."

"Isaac is beginning to annoy me exceedingly." Richard was still staring after the dust trail churned up by the fleeing emperor as Joffroi and Guy de Lusignan rode over to him. When they asked if he wanted to continue pursuit, he shook his head. "What would be the point? He's astride Fauvel."

IT HAD NOT BEEN an easy time for Berengaria and Joanna, left behind in Limassol waiting for word. They'd learned that there had been no fighting at Famagusta, but after that, there was only silence. Joanna now understood that this was a foretaste of their life in the Holy Land; she was not sure if Berengaria had realized it yet, too. So Guilhem de Préaux's arrival was eagerly welcomed by both women, for he bore a message from Richard.

He told them about Isaac's thwarted ambush outside Tremetousha. Editing his account to be suitable for a female audience, he neglected to mention that the emperor had shot poisoned arrows at Richard, instead stressing the low casualties and the ease of their victory. "Nicosia surrendered at once," he reported exuberantly. "The king received them in peace, but ordered the men to shave their beards as a symbol of their change of lordship. People continue to seek out the king and disavow their allegiance to Isaac, much to his distress and fury. So it will be over soon. The king has sent Guy de Lusignan to besiege the castle at Kyrenia, which holds the emperor's treasure and his family, and he has set Stephen de Turnham's brother Robert to patrolling the coast in case Isaac tries to flee to the mainland—"

"Why?"

"My lady?" Guilhem regarded Joanna so innocently that he confirmed all of her suspicions.

"Why has Richard entrusted Guy with the assault upon Kyrenia? Why is he not leading it himself?"

Guilhem had hoped the women would not pick up on that. "The king has been unwell, so he remained at Nicosia whilst he recovers." He tried then to divert the conversation into more innocuous channels, but they were having none of it, and he reluctantly admitted that upon his arrival in Nicosia, Richard had come down with a sudden fever. Despite his best efforts to make it sound like a minor matter, Joanna and Berengaria knew that Richard must have been afire with fever for him to have taken to a sickbed instead of pursuing Isaac, and they immediately began to lay plans to hasten to Nicosia.

"You cannot do that!" Guilhem cried, shaking his head vehemently. "The king forbids you to leave Limassol." They did not look at all pleased and Joanna seemed on the verge of mutiny, so he hastily explained that Richard felt it would be too dangerous to undertake an inland journey as long as Isaac remained on the loose. "The king is not seriously ill, my lady queens, and it is better that he recovers on his own. Men are notoriously poor patients," he joked, "and the king is not taking this disruption of his plans with good grace. Indeed, he has been so bad-tempered that you'd surely want to smother him with a pillow, and think what a scandal that would cause!"

His attempt at humor fell flat. "Do you swear he is not gravely ill?" Berengaria demanded, and when he offered an eloquent avowal upon his very soul, she and Joanna conceded defeat. Guilhem had no time to savor his victory, though, for after thanking him for being honest with them, Berengaria then asked, "Did my lord husband give you a letter for me?"

Guilhem opened his mouth, shut it again. He knew it was safest for him if he simply told the truth, but he could not bring himself to do it, for he thought her brown eyes were as soft and trusting as a fawn's. "Of course he did, Madame. A long one it was, too, and he wrote it in his own hand instead of dictating it to a scribe, since it was meant for your eyes only. But . . . and I hope you can forgive me . . . I no longer have it. We had a mishap fording a river. The water was much deeper than we'd expected and I was drenched to the skin. To my dismay, I later discovered that the king's letter had gotten soaked, too, and the ink had run so badly that it was totally unreadable. I am indeed sorry for my clumsiness."

Berengaria's good manners prevailed over her disappointment and she assured him that he had no cause for reproach. She soon excused herself, saying that she wanted to offer up prayers for Richard's quick recovery and victory over the Cypriot emperor. Guilhem escorted her to the door and then returned to bow over Joanna's hand in his most courtly fashion. But as their eyes met, she said, too softly for her ladies across the chamber to hear, "You are a gallant liar."

"What do you mean, Madame?"

"I've been here long enough now to learn something about Cyprus. Did you know it has no navigable rivers? And whilst they are prone to flooding during the rainy season, they dry up into mudholes during the summer months. So any rivers you encountered between Nicosia and Limassol would have been too shallow to drown a snake."

Guilhem was stricken into silence, not knowing what to say. His relief was considerable, therefore, when she smiled. "Moreover, I know my brother, know how single-minded he is when he is in the midst of a campaign. I wish he'd spared a thought for his new bride, but in fairness to Richard, he is a battle commander, not a court poet."

Guilhem returned her smile, pleased that she understood. "I am grateful that you are not angry with me for lying, my lady." He hesitated a moment. "Do you think she believed me?"

"I do not know," Joanna confessed. "I hope so."

UPON HIS RETURN to Nicosia, Guilhem was delighted to find his king much improved and very flattered when Richard interrupted a strategy session to question him about his trip to Limassol. "Thank God," he said candidly, after Guilhem explained that he'd been able to persuade the women that they could not come to nurse him back to health. He took the letters from his wife and sister and tucked them into his belt to be read when he had the time. He was turning away when Guilhem asked for a moment more. He dreaded telling Richard about that river-soaked letter, but he figured it would go worse for him if the king was ambushed and caught unaware by his queen, so he began to stammer out the story, watching nervously for any signs of Angevin anger. To his surprise, he caught an expression upon Richard's face that he'd never seen before—guilt.

"God's Blood," Richard muttered. "I did not even think. . . . Were you able to make her understand?"

"Well . . . I did not try, my lord. I . . . I lied." He saw Richard's eyebrows shoot upward and said a silent prayer that he'd not done something his king would not forgive. But by the time he was done with his awkward confession, Richard was looking amused and—much to his relief—approving.

"That was quick thinking, Guilhem. Sometimes a kind falsehood is better than a hurtful truth. My queen does not yet know much about war or its demands. She'll have to learn, of course. . . ." Just when Guilhem thought he'd been forgotten, the king smiled and said, "Come in. We are going over the latest reports by my scouts."

Following Richard into his chamber, Guilhem felt a flush of excitement at the sight of the men gathered around a table littered with maps, for these were lords of rank and privilege: André de Chauvigny, the Earl of Leicester, Joffroi de Lusignan, Baldwin de Bethune, William de Forz, and Richard's nephew, Jaufre of Perche. Thinking these were high-flying hawks for a Norman knight, Guilhem eagerly approached the table when Richard beckoned. "This is Deudamour," he said, "which overlooks the road between Kyrenia and Nicosia. But now that we've taken Kyrenia, it cannot hold out for long."

"Kyrenia has fallen?" Guilhem was pleasantly shocked, for the local people had been insisting it was impregnable.

Richard nodded. "Two days after you left for Limassol, the castle yielded to Guy de Lusignan."

Guilhem whistled softly, rapidly reassessing his opinion of Guy. If the man could have captured a stronghold like Kyrenia with such ease, he was a better soldier than people thought. "I kept hearing that it could withstand a siege from now till Judgment Day!"

"Well, mayhap it could—if the garrison had offered any real resistance. I'd wager it fell into Guy's lap like a ripe pear. How else explain his quick success?"

Guilhem was startled, not so much by that caustic appraisal of Guy's military skills, as by the source—it had come from his own brother, Joffroi. He was not surprised that Richard seemed untroubled by Joffroi's sarcasm, for he knew there had been no love lost between the king and his brothers. But Guilhem and his brothers had always been as close as peas in a pod, and he found himself feeling an unexpected flicker of sympathy for Guy de Lusignan. "So we have captured Isaac's treasury?"

Richard confirmed it with a coolly complacent smile. "And whilst that loss probably pains Isaac the most, we now have his wife and daughter, too. The way his luck is going, Isaac may well end up with just enough Cypriot land for a burial plot."

AFTER KYRENIA HAD SURRENDERED, Guy laid siege to the nearby castle at Deudamour, but so far he'd made no progress. Richard was not surprised, for this was one of the most formidable mountain citadels he'd ever seen; its north, west, and south sides were made inaccessible by sheer cliffs, and its eastern approach was protected by three walled baileys, with two towers perched even higher up. After consulting with Guy's captains, Richard left some of his men to assist in the siege and rode the few miles to Kyrenia.

Richard's first sight of Isaac's seacoast stronghold convinced him that Guy could never have taken it so rapidly had its garrison not been too disheartened to offer resistance. Situated between two small bays, the castle reminded him of English shell keeps: high walls enclosed a large inner bailey, with sturdy corner towers, a barbican, and two-story gatehouse. He was pleased to see his royal lion flying from the highest tower rather than the golden crosses of the Kingdom of Jerusalem, a diplomatic gesture he'd not have expected from Guy.

Guy was waiting to welcome them as soon as they emerged from the barbican, and as he escorted them toward the great hall nestled along the west wall, he boasted of his triumph with an almost boyish glee. But Richard was willing to indulge him, for however he'd done it, the capture of Kyrenia had dealt Isaac Comnenus a mortal blow: How could he hope to continue the fight now that his treasury was in his enemy's hands?

Guy wasted no time giving a report on the riches stored in Kyrenia's coffers. Almost as an afterthought, he revealed that Isaac's wife and daughter and their women were being held in the southwest tower, where they could be comfortably but securely guarded. Isaac had intended for them to flee to the mainland of Cilicia if it looked as if the castle might fall but, like so many of Isaac's plans this May, that one had been thwarted by the arrival of Richard's galleys, which had easily bottled up the harbor, making a sea escape impossible. Richard was not looking forward to his audience with them for, like most men, he was not comfortable dealing with hysterical women. A pity, he thought, that Joanna and Berenguela were not here to assure them that they were in no danger.

Wine was served in Isaac's goblets of silver studded with gems, and the wine itself was excellent, more than justifying the reputation of Cypriot vineyards. After savoring the taste, Richard asked if Sophia knew anything useful about her husband's whereabouts. Guy seemed surprised by the question, reminding the English king that he'd had no Greek translators with his army. Now it was Richard's turn to be surprised. "Why did you not try French?"

Among the disadvantages Guy labored under, he'd been cursed with a transparent face, his thoughts easily read by friends and foes alike. It was obvious now that he was perplexed by this question. "Why would she speak French? She is an Armenian princess."

Richard was beginning to understand why Joffroi de Lusignan held his youngest brother in so little regard. "No, Guy, she is not. Isaac's first wife was the Armenian princess. His current wife is a bastard daughter of the Sicilian king William I, so we can safely assume that she speaks French as well as we do."

Guy did not seem convinced, and was arguing that she'd spoken only Greek at Kyrenia's surrender when the women were ushered into the hall. Rising to his feet, Richard started toward them, wondering how Guy could ever have imagined they were blood-kin. Sophia was short and dark and plump, whereas her stepdaughter, although only about thirteen, was already the taller of the two, slender and willowy, with white-blond braids that reached to her hips. They embarrassed him by sinking down in deep, submissive curtsys, and he hastily took Sophia's hand to raise her up; he did not offer assistance to the girl, thinking she might shun the touch of her father's conqueror.

When Richard politely addressed Sophia by her title, she inclined her head and then gestured toward her stepdaughter. "This is Anna," she said, and Guy scowled, demanding to know why she'd not told him she spoke French. He was not pleased when she said dryly, "You did not ask me."

"I imagine the empress preferred to assess the terrain before committing her troops," Richard said, and she gave him a sidelong, amused glance that told him this woman was not to be underestimated, not if she could face calamity with such aplomb. Seating them in high-backed chairs, he looked from her to the girl. Upon reflection, Sophia's poise was not so surprising, for she'd known of Joanna's presence and could assume she'd have a protector in her brother's widow. But while he was grateful for Anna's almost eerie composure, he was puzzled by it, too; he'd not have thought one so young would display such self-control. "Does your stepdaughter speak French, Madame?"

"Well, I taught her to swear in French. So, yes, she speaks a little, but not enough to follow our conversation."

"Does she have any questions for me?" After a quick exchange in Greek, Sophia shook her head, and he marveled anew at the enigma that was Anna Comnena. "She is showing remarkable courage for one so young."

Sophia gave Anna a fond look that told him much about their relationship. "She has been compelled, of necessity, to learn how to deal with adversity, for she has not had an easy life. Isaac was a prisoner of the Armenians during her first years, and her mother died when she was just six. Isaac was then turned over to the Prince of Antioch and managed to convince the Emperor of the Greeks to pay part of his ransom. When he did not pay the remainder, Anna and her brother were held as hostages in Antioch for two years. When they were finally permitted to join Isaac in Cyprus, her brother took ill and died soon afterward. So Anna learned at an early age how fickle fortune can be."

Sophia took a sip of wine. "I daresay you've heard the grisly stories about Isaac's crimes. Most of them are true, but not all. He did not poison his first wife, as his enemies in Armenia allege, and he most certainly did not kill his own son in a fit of fury, as others have claimed."

"I was told that when one of his nobles advised him to make peace with me, he had the man's nose cut off," Richard said, curious to see if she'd defend Isaac from this charge, too.

Sophia did not even blink. "Now that does sound like Isaac." A castle servant was approaching with a tray of sugared comfits, and she helped herself to several, as if there was nothing strange about her circumstances, to have gone from mistress of Kyrenia to a prisoner in her own chambers in the span of days. "May I ask what you intend for Anna once Isaac is defeated?"

"Well, I do not think it would be safe to leave her in Cyprus, where her father is so hated. So I am going to entrust her to my wife and sister. They will care for her and instruct her in our customs, and I can assure you that they will welcome her most lovingly. What of you, Lady Sophia? Do you wish to accompany Anna to Outremer? Or would you rather return to your homeland? If so, I can arrange for your safe journey to Sicily."

"Thank you for giving me a choice. I prefer to remain with Anna." Sophia drank more wine, as if this was a social occasion, and when Richard asked if she had any knowledge of Isaac's whereabouts, she answered readily, saying that he had only one lair left, his castle at Kantara. As she leaned over to tell Anna that they would be sailing with the queens of England and Sicily to Outremer, Guy gave voice to his growing disapproval.

"How do we know we can trust what she says?" he asked in a low voice. "She does not seem very loyal to Isaac, after all." He was vexed when they did not appear to take his concern seriously; Richard and André were looking at him as if he'd suddenly started to speak a foreign tongue and Joffroi heaved an exaggerated sigh.

Turning back to them, Sophia looked quizzically from one man to the other. "What is it? Do you have other questions for me?" Richard shook his head, impressed by how observant she was; he supposed that was how she'd survived six years of marriage to a man like Isaac Comnenus. "There is something else you need to know," she said. "As soon as Kyrenia surrendered, you won your war. You see, Isaac is a man with many sins on his soul and much blood on his hands. But he has one redeeming quality. He truly loves his daughter."

Had anyone else said that, Richard would have laughed aloud. He felt that Sophia deserved courtesy, though, after all she'd been through. He was framing a politely skeptical response when he had an ugly thought. Among the many accusations made against Isaac was that he was a despoiler of virgins. Richard's gaze shifted to Anna, who was very young and very pretty. Glancing around, he saw that André and Joffroi and even Guy shared this sudden suspicion.

Sophia saw it, too, and her black eyes blazed. "No," she said sharply, "whatever his sins, Isaac is not guilty of that one. Anna is his blood, the one pure corner of his soul. He would never abuse her like that. Nor would I ever have allowed it."

"And how would you have stopped him?" Guy challenged.

"I would have cut his throat whilst he slept," Sophia snapped, and Guy laughed in disbelief.

Not Richard, though. He did not doubt that she meant exactly what she said, and he decided he could learn to like this shrewd, forthright woman who'd sensibly given her loyalty to the stepdaughter who needed it rather than to the husband who did not deserve it. "Even if you are right, Madame, that only means that Isaac is grieving for his daughter's capture. Why is that something we need to know?"

"Because Isaac expects other men to act as he does. He will be terrified, sure that you will maltreat Anna the way he would have maltreated an enemy's daughter. You might want to consider making use of that fear."

This time none of the men were able to disguise their disbelief. They carefully avoided one another's eyes, lest they laugh at Sophia's ludicrous suggestion—that a man like Isaac would ever sacrifice his own selfish skin for anyone else's welfare. Richard changed the subject then by telling Sophia that her half-sister Mariam was with Joanna in Limassol. She seemed pleased, saying she ought to have known Mariam would never have been able to resist such an adventure. From time to time, she glanced over at Anna, smiling reassuringly. Anna always smiled back. But none of the men knew what she was truly thinking.

DEUDAMOUR SOON YIELDED, its garrison unwilling to die for a lost cause. Richard was laying siege to Buffavento, the most inaccessible of Isaac's mountain-top strongholds, when a messenger rode in under a flag of truce. To the utter astonishment of everyone except Sophia, Isaac offered to surrender unconditionally to the English king in return for a guarantee of his daughter's safety. He asked only that his imperial rank be respected and he not be placed in irons like a common felon.

A HUGE CROWD had assembled to watch Isaac's surrender at his former castle of Deudamour. The contrast with his earlier appearance could not have been more dramatic. Accompanied by a small band of his dwindling supporters, he was clad in mourning garb, his hair and beard unkempt, his fingers stripped of his jeweled rings, his head bare. Dismounting, he knelt at Richard's feet and spoke in a hoarse voice, keeping his eyes downcast as an interpreter conveyed his plea for mercy.

The Cypriots began to jeer and curse, enraged when Richard allowed Isaac to rise instead of making him grovel in the dust as he deserved. Their threats echoed after Isaac as he was escorted by Richard's soldiers into the safety of the castle, their fury the final verdict upon his wretched reign, and Richard wondered if he'd really surrendered because he knew what would have befallen him if he'd been captured by his own subjects.

But that cynical suspicion was soon dispelled. Once they'd entered the hall, Richard gestured for Isaac to sit beside him upon the dais and then had Anna brought out to show that she'd not been harmed. At the sight of his daughter, Isaac amazed his audience by bursting into tears. He leaped to his feet and hastened to her side, embracing her with such obvious joy and relief that those watching no longer doubted the sincerity of the tyrant's affection for his child.

Exchanging bemused looks with André, Richard shrugged. "I suppose," he said, "even a wolf can care for his cubs." And André nodded, for that seemed as good an explanation as any for this unexpected and unlikely end to their Cyprus campaign.

———

SINCE GIRLHOOD, Joanna had sought to vanquish fear or worries by shaming herself into letting them go. Upon their arrival in Famagusta, she was trying it again, mentally enumerating all that she had to be thankful for. Glancing about the sunlit courtyard of the Archbishop of Cyprus's residence, she added a sisterly reunion to the list, for Mariam and Sophia seemed genuinely delighted to see each other. Anna was seated beside them on a marble bench, and the sight of the girl stirred Joanna's maternal instincts anew. Anna's rescue was surely cause for gratitude, too. Joanna had no doubts whatsoever that Isaac's daughter would be better off away from his baneful influence, and she meant to do all in her power to make sure Anna thrived in her new world.

Richard was the center of attention, as usual. But Joanna was pleased to see that he'd drawn Berengaria into the circle, an arm draped possessively around her shoulders as he bantered with André and Jaufre. Richard was being properly attentive to his new wife and her dark eyes never left his face. Joanna had overheard him murmuring to her about a Michaelmas goose, and while that meant nothing to her, it obviously did to Berengaria, who'd blushed and then laughed. Joanna thought it was a very encouraging sign that they already shared private jokes, for she took it as an indication that their marriage was getting off to a good start.

Continuing to tally up her reasons for gratitude, she added the capture of Cyprus, for Outremer would benefit greatly, now and in years to come; some of their ships were already loaded with wheat, sheep, chickens, and wine. Richard's soldiers were also contented with their Cypriot campaign, for Richard was always generous about sharing booty with his men. And she thought the Cypriots had reason for rejoicing, too, freed from Isaac's yoke. Richard had chosen two trusted castellans to govern the island until he could make long-term provisions for its future, and he'd agreed to issue a charter confirming the laws and rights as they'd been in the days before Isaac's seizure of power, although he'd exacted a steep price for this privilege; he'd imposed a levy of half of the possessions of the Cypriots to help finance the crusade. Joanna had enough experience with governing to know this would be highly unpopular with the local people, but she still felt that her brother was leaving Cyprus better off than he'd found it.

So she had much to be thankful for and she ought to be counting her blessings. But the lecture did nothing to ease the hollow, icy feeling in the pit of her stomach. The voyage from Limassol to Famagusta had been tolerable, for they'd hugged the shore. But on the morrow their fleet would head out into the open sea. Berengaria and Mariam kept reassuring her that this would be a much quicker passage, for ships could sail from Cyprus to the Syrian coast in just a day. But Joanna knew better. Storms could strike at any time, blowing them far off course, and she knew that she would suffer grievously again in heavy seas; her memories were still so graphically vivid that she found herself shivering under a hot Cypriot sun.

"Whatever you are thinking about, stop." Richard was standing over her. "You look positively greensick, Little Sister." Holding out his hand, he said, "I've something to show you and Berenguela."

Berengaria shrugged her shoulders, indicating she did not know what he had in mind, and Joanna let Richard steer them across the courtyard, several of their knights protectively trailing at a discreet distance. He led them into the archbishop's gardens, a shaded refuge from the summer heat, and then out a postern gate, refusing to reveal where they were going. When Berengaria congratulated him upon winning his wager with André, he made a mock grimace and said he'd lost, for the campaign had actually taken fifteen days. He'd already alerted them that he would be remaining in Cyprus for a few days after the fleet sailed, as he had arrangements still to work out with Stephen de Turnham's brother Robert, one of the men he'd entrusted with the governance of Cyprus. He explained now that he also wanted to oversee Isaac's departure for the Syrian castle at Margat, where he'd be turned over to the Knights Hospitaller for safe-keeping.

As they walked, Richard told them about Isaac's surprisingly touching reunion with Anna and that the erstwhile emperor had not even raised the question of ransom, asking only that he not be placed in iron chains or fetters. This caused protests from the local people, Richard said, for they'd wanted him to suffer the punishment that would have been meted out in Constantinople—blinding or maiming. "So I ordered chains to be made for Isaac of solid silver."

"You are jesting . . . no?" Berengaria asked uncertainly. But Joanna laughed, assuring her new sister-in-law that he was quite serious, saying the men in her family could teach the Devil a trick or two about slyness. Berengaria was not sure she approved of this; it seemed somewhat guileful to her. She kept her opinion to herself, though, for she did not think it was a wife's place to meddle in such matters.

"Ah, here we are," Richard said, and they saw he'd led them to an enclosure next to the archbishop's stables. As they approached, the stallion came over to the fence, curious but wary. Both women exclaimed admiringly, for he was a beautiful animal, high-shouldered, with a long neck and broad chest, a coat that gleamed like pale gold.

Richard was beaming. "This is Fauvel," he said proudly.

JOANNA HAD TRIED to hide her anxiety with jests, joking that Richard had not come to see them off, that he really wanted to make sure Fauvel had enough esparto grass for bedding and secure ringbolts for his underbelly sling. But as soon as their buss hoisted its sails and left the harbor behind, she'd gone ashen and hastily retreated to their tent, followed by most of the other women.

Berengaria remained on deck, committing to memory her last view of Richard, waving from the dock. She told herself she was being foolish, that they'd soon be reunited at Acre. But she was beginning to realize that her husband was as elusive as quicksilver, his eyes always on the horizon, inhabiting a world she would find difficult to share. None of the usual rules of marriage seemed to apply to Richard. How many royal wives had to live like camp followers? What sort of home life could they establish for themselves in the midst of a holy war?

"Ah, Papa," she whispered, "did you truly think this through?" But watching the sea change color as they headed into deep water, she knew she had no regrets. At least not yet. Becoming aware then that she was no longer alone, she turned and was surprised to find her companion was the girl they were calling the Damsel of Cyprus, Anna Comnena. She smiled to let Anna know her company was welcome, for she had enormous sympathy for the girl. How could a flower uprooted so rudely flourish in foreign soil?

Anna seemed to want to ask a question. Her French was very tentative, strongly accented, and Berengaria was not sure she understood. "My . . . my husband?" she asked, and Anna smiled and nodded. She soon frowned, though, fumbling in vain for the phrase she wanted. She repeated "*mari,*" pointing toward Berengaria, back toward Famagusta, and then placed her hand upon her own heart. Her frustration was obvious when Berengaria still did not understand. She did the pantomime again, and then gave a lilting, triumphant laugh, saying "*aimer,*" so pleased she'd remembered the right word that she did not even notice the older woman's recoil.

Berengaria was so nonplused because she'd never expected to be asked this question. A marriage was a legal union, recognized by the Church and the Crown as a means of begetting children and transferring property in an orderly fashion from one generation to the next. Love was not a component of marriage, especially royal marriages. It was true there had been love in her parents' marriage, but that had been an unexpected blessing, a mutual devotion that had developed over time. She had harbored no such expectations once she'd agreed to wed Richard, would have been content if they could forge a bond of respect and consideration and possibly affection. But with this innocent question, Anna had forced her to look into her heart.

"So you, too, are bedazzled by Richard, child," she said, with a rueful smile. "He does seem to have that effect upon people. . . ." Anna was looking puzzled, for she'd spoken in her native Romance, and she reached over, patted the girl's arm. "You do not understand what I am saying, do you?" She hesitated, feeling as if she'd reached another crossroads and, as she'd done then, she embraced the truth. "Oui," she said, nodding and mimicking Anna's gesture by placing her hand over her heart. Anna smiled, obviously approving, and they remained together on deck, watching until the island of Cyprus had vanished into the low-lying clouds cloaking the horizon.

CHAPTER 19

JUNE 1191

Tyre, Outremer

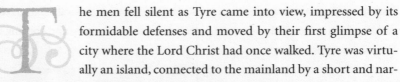

he men fell silent as Tyre came into view, impressed by its
formidable defenses and moved by their first glimpse of a
city where the Lord Christ had once walked. Tyre was virtually an island, connected to the mainland by a short and nar-
row causeway. A protective breakwater or mole extended out into the sea, a heavy
chain stretching from a high tower on its eastern edge to a second tower on land,
barring entry to the harbor. Richard was surprised to find his eyes misting as he
gazed upon the ancient stone walls of this legendary biblical city. It had been
more than three years since he'd taken the cross upon hearing of Jerusalem's fall,
years in which his holy quest had often seemed like a tantalizing dream, glimmer-
ing on the horizon just out of reach. At long last, it was about to take tangible
form.

André joined him in the prow of their galley, frowning at the sight of that taut
chain, for they'd sent Baldwin de Bethune and Pierre and Guilhem de Préaux
ahead in a small sagitta to announce Richard's arrival. "Why have they not lowered the barrier so we can enter the harbor?"

That pragmatic query brought Richard back to reality and he frowned, too. He
signaled to Alan Trenchmer, his galley's master, and as soon as they were within
hailing distance, Trenchmer demanded entry for the English king's fleet. But
there was no response from either guard tower, although they were close enough
now to see men upon the battlements. Trenchmer was about to shout again when
they saw their sagitta coming back.

The smaller ship's oarsmen skillfully angled it alongside the royal galley. Even
before Baldwin and the Préaux brothers scrambled onto the deck, the men knew

that something was greatly amiss. Richard could not recall ever seeing the phleg-matic Fleming so agitated. Baldwin's fair skin was mottled with hot color, his blue eyes narrowed to slits, and he was cursing under his breath as he swung himself over the gunwale. Richard did not speak a word of Flemish, but there was no need of translation.

"The whoresons refuse to let us into the harbor!"

There was a moment of shocked silence and then exclamations of outrage. Richard was incredulous. "Conrad dared to say that I am not welcome in Tyre?"

"He was not there. He is at Acre, taking part in the siege. But his men said that he'd given them explicit orders that the English king was not to be admitted to his city. To their credit, they looked ashamed at turning away men who'd taken the cross." Baldwin grimaced, as if tasting something sour. "Apparently Conrad's father is now dead, for his men were referring to him as 'the marquis.' And it seems he has laid formal claim to the crown, for they also called him 'the King-elect of Jerusalem.'" He punctuated that sentence by turning and spitting over the side of the gunwale.

André glanced toward a nearby galley, flying the yellow crosses of Outremer. "That will not please Guy," he said, in a masterful understatement.

It did not please Richard, either. Raising a hand to silence the indignant pro-tests of his men, he gave Alan Trenchmer a terse command to anchor the fleet in the lee of the breakwater. Glancing back at Tyre, looking deceptively tranquil in the golden dusk, he shook his head in disgust. "What does it say," he said causti-cally, "when our enemy, an infidel Saracen, is a man of greater honor than our Christian ally?"

THE FOLLOWING MORNING their fleet cruised south, the twenty-five galleys staying within sight of the coast. Richard had invited Guy and Joffroi de Lusignan to join him on the *Sea-Cleaver*, for he wanted to discuss the siege with men who'd been there since the beginning. Ironically, the attack upon Acre was the result of a rebuff like the one Richard had just experienced. After the defeat at Ḥaṭṭīn, Guy had been held prisoner by Salah al-Dīn for more than a year. Freed after swearing not to bear arms against the sultan, Guy had found a bishop willing to absolve him of his oath and then headed to the only city still under Christian control— Tyre. Its savior, though, was not about to turn it over to the man he blamed for the catastrophe at Ḥaṭṭīn, and Conrad refused to allow Guy into the city. In des-peration, Guy had gone off with a small force to besiege Acre, and it slowly became the focal point of resistance to Salah al-Dīn; even Conrad had been compelled by public opinion to join in. Nearly two years later, the Saracen garrison was in dire straits, and Richard's greatest fear was that Acre might fall before he got there.

Richard, the de Lusignans, and several of their knights had retreated to his tent to escape the sun's burning heat and were studying a map of Acre. Like Tyre, it was a coastal city, protected to the west and south by the sea, and to the north and east by a strong wall, numerous towers, and a deep ditch. Using his dagger to point, Joffroi scratched marks in the parchment to show the alignment of the besiegers.

"Walking through the camp, you'll hear almost every language spoken in Christendom, for there are Genoese, Pisans, English, French, Flemings, Danes, Frisians, Armenians, Germans, and Hungarians. Your nephew Henri of Champagne took command upon his arrival last summer." Joffroi's face was impassive, as if unaware of what a telling commentary that was upon the scant confidence men had in his brother, a crowned king supplanted by a young count of twenty-four. "Here is where Saladin's army is camped, in the hills behind us." He gestured again with the dagger. "Whenever we launch an attack upon the city, Saladin's men try to draw us off by raiding our camp. They've never been able to break through our ditches and fortifications. But we had a rough time of it this winter when bad weather kept ships in port and food well nigh ran out; I daresay you heard about that."

Richard nodded and Joffroi turned his attention back to the map. "Since the French king arrived, he's been concentrating his siege engines upon the Accursed Tower in the northeast corner of the city." Anticipating the question, he said with a slight smile, "Supposedly it is where Judas's thirty pieces of silver were minted. With all the trebuchets that you've brought, my lord king, we ought to be able to batter their walls into dust by Midsummer Eve."

"God willing," Richard agreed, and when he revealed that some of his trebuchets were operated by counterweights rather than ropes and were therefore more powerful than traction trebuchets, he and Joffroi were soon deep in a technical discussion of siege engines that Guy found quite boring. He welcomed, therefore, an interruption by one of Richard's knights.

"What is it, Morgan?"

"My liege, there is a ship ahead, the likes of which we've never seen!"

Richard, the de Lusignans, and the knights hastened onto the deck, only to halt in amazement, for none of them had ever seen such a ship, either. It was huge, more than twice the size of their largest buss, with no less than three tall masts. Its sides were draped in green and yellow tarpaulins, giving it an odd, exotic look, and to Richard, a suspicious one, for it flew no banners. Calling to the master of a nearby galley, he instructed them to find out the mystery ship's identity. It was soon back, the master reporting that it claimed to be French, on its way from Antioch to Acre.

Richard was quick to shake his head. "I do not believe Philippe has any ships like that."

The others were dubious, too. It was then that one of the sailors pushed his way over to the English king. "My lord, that is a Turkish ship."

Richard glanced from the man's tanned, weathered face to the enormous buss. "Are you sure?"

"Aye, I am. It looks verily like one I once saw in Beirut harbor. And I can prove it. Send another galley after them. Only do not hail them or offer a greeting. See what they do then."

That made sense to Richard and he gave the order. They crowded to the gunwales, watching tensely as the galley caught up again with the towering buss. This time its sailors did not salute the other ship and they were immediately fired upon.

"Prepare to attack," Richard commanded and hurried back to his tent to arm himself. The others were quick to do the same as trumpets blared from galley to galley, signaling that battle was about to be joined with the massive Saracen ship.

It ought to have been able to outrun the English galleys. But the wind had dropped suddenly and its sails hung limply, slowing it enough so that they could keep pace. As soon as they overtook it, they swarmed the great ship like dogs set loose at a bearbaiting. Their oarsmen laboring at their posts, the galleys circled the buss. Each time they tried to get close enough to force a boarding, though, the Saracen sailors and soldiers drove them off with an unrelenting hail of arrows and bolts. Even when the more daring sailors braved the fire and reached the buss, they were thwarted by its steep, high sides, their low-riding galleys dwarfed by the sheer size of the Saracen ship, their grappling hooks and ropes falling short.

Most of Richard's knights were facing their first sea battle, and were willing to defer to the sailors, who were as comfortable on a pitching deck as the knights were on horseback. Morgan had never doubted his own courage, but he was awed now by the bravery of the crewmen, willing to scale those cliffsides while coming under heavy fire. He was worried, too, about Richard's safety, fearful the king would join in that hazardous assault, clad in full armor that could drag him down like an anchor. It would have been sheer madness for Richard to try it—and unforgivably irresponsible, for his death could well doom the crusade. And yet Morgan knew Richard well enough by now to be sure he would seek to board the buss if given half a chance. He was greatly relieved, therefore, when he realized that others shared his concern. Richard was so busy shouting encouragement and firing a crossbow whenever a Saracen came into sight that he didn't notice how adroitly the helmsman steered their galley, keeping it in the midst of the action but never quite close enough to attempt a boarding.

Exhausted and disheartened, the crews of the galleys finally drew back out of bowshot, at a loss what to do next, for the Saracen ship was proving to be as impregnable as a heavily fortified castle. Several of the galleys rowed over to the *Sea-Cleaver* to consult with the king, their masters asking Richard if they should continue with the attack.

Richard was astonished that the question would even be raised. "Are you serious? This is a Turkish ship, loaded with soldiers, weapons, and supplies. If it reaches Acre, God alone knows how much longer the garrison can hold out. Are the lot of you turning into cowards? If you let them escape, you all deserve to be hanged!"

Morgan gaped at the king, then sidled over to André, who was reloading a crossbow. "He would not really do that, would he?"

André seemed grimly amused. "Richard is given to bloodcurdling threats whenever defeat looms. He has never carried any of them out, though, and his men know that. But they'd best find a way to board that ship, for we cannot let it get away, not with so much at stake."

The sailors had reached the same conclusion, and despair now gave way to inspiration, for they came up with a scheme that was as daring as it was imaginative. Returning to the attack, they distracted the crew of the Saracen ship while several men stripped to their braies and plunged into the sea, clutching coils of rope. Diving under the buss, they came up sputtering and swam back to their galleys. Richard leaned over the gunwale, never taking his eyes from the swimmers, and then burst out laughing. "Clever lads, they tied up the rudder!"

His guess proved to be correct, and the knights began to cheer as the buss listed suddenly to starboard. No longer responding to the tiller, the ship wallowed in the waves, turning in a circle as the helmsman sought desperately to regain control. Taking advantage of the confusion onboard, some of the oarsmen rowed toward the stern, flung their grappling hooks into the tarpaulin hanging over the sides, and managed to scramble up onto the deck.

What followed was the most vicious hand-to-hand fighting that Morgan had ever seen. The Saracen crew might be infidels doomed to eternal damnation, but he thought that none could fault their courage. The deck was soon slick with blood and men fell overboard or were pushed, some splashing to the surface midst spreading pools of crimson, others sinking like stones. The galleys hovered as close to the buss as they could get, the crews leaning over the gunwales to rescue their own men while their crossbowmen aimed at the Turks floundering in the water. More sailors had managed to climb over the bulwarks, and for a time it seemed as if they would prevail. But then other Saracens burst out of the ship's hold, charging at the invaders with the reckless boldness of men who had nothing left to lose. Swords flashed, cutting off arms, hands, even heads, and eventually Richard's men were forced to retreat toward the stern, jumping into nearby galleys or diving into the sea and grabbing at oars to keep themselves afloat. Shouting defiance and curses, the Saracens reached for their bows again and began to heave bodies over the side. But their victory was ephemeral and they knew it, for they were trapped on a crippled ship, surrounded by sea wolves.

Knights were accustomed to fighting with swords or lances, and few of them were able to follow Richard's example. But he could handle a crossbow as skillfully as he did other weapons, and even when some of the crossbowmen stopped firing, afraid of hitting their own during the assault, he'd continued to shoot, confident of his aim. He did not put his crossbow down until all of his galleys were out of Saracen arrow range. His knights kept their distance, for they could feel the fury radiating from him, the black-bile rage that was the accursed legacy of the Angevins, giving rise to those legends that the counts of Anjou traced their descent from Lucifer himself.

He surprised them, though, when some of the galleys made ready to return to the attack, for he called them back. "I'd hoped to capture it," he said angrily, "for its hold is likely to be filled with weapons and food, mayhap even Greek fire. But there are too many of them and they are not going to surrender. Enough good Christians have died this day already. No more." He paused to cough, for his throat was sore from shouting orders and curses, and then he said hoarsely, "Sink it."

Though they'd never have admitted it, most of his men were relieved to be spared another assault upon the Saracen ship. But they also wanted revenge for the deaths of their comrades, and they responded eagerly to this new command. The galleys once more encircled the buss, waiting for the signal. A trumpet blasted, and when the drums began to sound, the sailors strained at their oars, seeking to gain as much speed as possible before their iron spurs slammed into the hull. The impact flung men to their knees, even those who'd been braced for the collision, and they shouted in triumph when the vessel was gashed open in several places. They were preparing to ram the wounded ship again when it seemed to shudder and then began to sink.

The death throes of the huge Saracen ship were astonishingly swift, baffling the watching sailors. They'd barely gotten safely away from the undertow when the buss tilted and slid, prow first, under the waves. Most of its crew drowned; others died at the hands of their Christian enemies. The knights unsheathed their swords to strike at any Saracens within reach and the crossbowmen found such easy targets for their bolts that the sea was soon streaked with blood. Richard decided to save some, wanting to interrogate them about the siege weapons they'd carried, and the thirty-five men pulled into the galleys would be the only survivors.

Emotions were raw and overlapping for most of the men; relief that they were alive mingled with grief for dead friends and a surging sense of triumph. Morgan was still shaken several hours after the battle, unable to join the other knights on the *Sea-Cleaver* in celebration of their victory. He was not sure why he felt so unsettled, finally deciding that there was something particularly frightening about death by drowning. He'd asked one of the sailors why the Saracens had died in silence, not even crying out to their God as they disappeared beneath the waves. He was soon sorry he did, for the sailor related his own near-drowning experience in gruesome detail, explaining that a drowning man rarely called for help, too caught up in a panicked struggle to get air into his lungs. He also volunteered that a drowning victim sank at once, unlike a man who was already dead when he hit the water, although he admitted he did not know why this was so. Having been told more than he'd wanted to know, Morgan consoled himself with the wry reminder that he need not fear such a fate in the desert sands of Outremer.

Two of the rescued Saracens had been taken aboard the *Sea-Cleaver* for questioning. Richard was already short-tempered, bitterly disappointed that he'd not been able to capture the cargo, and his mood was not improved by the delay in finding a translator. Finally Guy remembered that his former brother-in-law, Humphrey de Toron, was fluent in Arabic, and he was hastily summoned to the king's galley.

One of the captives was a man in his middle years, and he remained stubbornly silent, his dark eyes filled with defiance and hate. The other prisoner was younger, about Morgan's age. He seemed in shock, not so much fearful as stunned, as Morgan imagined he'd feel if he'd just witnessed the deaths of so many of his own companions. He could not suppress an unexpected twinge of pity for the youth, even if he was an infidel pagan, and when Humphrey squatted down beside the prisoner, he remained to hear what this Saracen survivor would say.

Humphrey had a low, pleasant voice and his interrogation sounded almost lyrical as he put questions to the prisoner in a language few of them had heard before. The answers were given readily, but indifferently, as if nothing mattered anymore. Getting to his feet, Humphrey raised some eyebrows by giving the Saracen a sympathetic pat on the shoulder before turning toward Richard.

"He says they were to reinforce the garrison at Acre, that their ship held six hundred and fifty soldiers, and had been fitted out at Beirut with one hundred camel-loads of weapons: siege engines, spears, swords, frame-mounted crossbows, flasks of Greek fire, and two hundred deadly snakes. They'd made one attempt to run our blockade and planned to try again at dark. He also says that when they realized they were facing defeat, their captain gave the command to scuttle the ship, determined to deny us their cargo. When we rammed it, they were already chopping holes in the hull so it would quickly sink."

"What was their captain's name?" Richard asked, and when told it was Ya'qūb al-Halabī of Aleppo, he repeated it, saying that such a brave man deserved to be remembered. He looked then toward the buss's watery graveyard. The blood had been washed away and the bodies were gone, too, claimed by the sea. The only evidence of carnage was a broken timber from the mizzenmast, a few floating barrels, and the fins of several sharks, drawn by the scent of death. But Richard was not thinking of all the men who'd died, Christian and Muslim. He was thinking of six hundred and fifty soldiers and a cargo hold filled with weapons. His lips moving silently, he made the sign of the cross, and then said huskily, "What if we'd not encountered them? God truly was on our side this day."

There were murmurings of heartfelt agreement from those listening. Humphrey nodded, but then he smiled sadly. "Men always think God favors their cause. I am sure Ya'qūb of Aleppo never doubted it, either."

That did not go down well with some of the knights, who thought such a remark bordered upon blasphemy. Richard gave the younger man an appraising look before saying dryly, "But Ya'qūb of Aleppo is dead, is he not?"

IT HAD BEEN seven weeks since Philippe's arrival at Acre, seven of the most wretched weeks of his life. He'd hated the Holy Land from the first day, hated the oppressive heat, the noxious climate that was so dangerous to newcomers, the stark, treeless landscape so different from France, the poisonous snakes and scorpions that slithered into tents as soon as the sun went down. He worried about his health, a king with only a sickly three-year-old child as his heir, trapped in a land of miasmas and plague where a fit, robust man could be stricken one morn and dead ere the week was out. More men had been killed by illness than by the Turks, men of high birth and rank, some of them his own kin. It was just seven days since Philip, the Count of Flanders, had died of Arnaldia, a painful malady that was very contagious and often lethal. Philippe kept his doctor, Master John of St Albans, close by, but his nerves had become so ragged that he found himself wondering if the man was truly trustworthy, for he was an Englishman, after all. If Richard had poisoning in mind, who better to do it than the king's own physician?

Philippe would normally have welcomed the death of Philip d'Alsace, seeing it as divine retribution for his treacherous alliance with Richard at Messina. But in his current doom-ridden frame of mind, he could focus only upon the political hornet's nest stirred up by Philip's demise. He'd had no son, bequeathing Flanders to his sister Margaret and her husband, Baudouin, Count of Hainaut, the parents of Philippe's late queen, Isabelle. Philippe feared that Baudouin would contest his claim to the rich province of Artois, which had been Isabelle's marriage portion, and Baudouin was in an ideal position to stake his own claims, for he'd been one of the few lords not to have taken the cross. Philippe had no intention of losing Artois, and he even had hopes of annexing all of Flanders to the French Crown. But he was at a great disadvantage as long as he was anchored here in Acre, nigh on two thousand miles from Paris.

He'd spent huge sums so far on siege engines and sapping equipment; he had teams working diligently to undermine the walls of Acre. But as he lay awake at night, for he'd been sleeping poorly since his arrival in the camp, he found himself doubting that they could succeed. Acre had held out for nigh on two years, after all. What if the siege dragged on for months? And even if they managed to take Acre, what then? Was he the only one to harbor such misgivings? Many of the men had convinced themselves that victory would be assured once the English king reached Acre. But to Philippe, that meant only that if Acre was captured, Richard would hog all the credit for its fall. He well knew that the Angevin was not one for sharing glory, and he could foresee a future in which he would be utterly overshadowed by the other man, the King of France diminished by one of his own vassals, a prospect he found intolerable.

He'd been troubled all afternoon by a throbbing headache, and even though darkness was still hours away, he decided to lie down. It had not been a good day. One of their siege engines had been bombarded with Greek fire and destroyed; fortunately, it had not been his. His miners had encountered another setback, a cave-in that slowed their progress toward the walls. And he was still brooding over his failure to recover his favorite falcon. While he did not enjoy hunting, he did find hawking relaxing and had been exercising a large white gyrfalcon when it had suddenly taken flight toward the city. Determined to recover it, he had offered a huge reward of one thousand *dinars*. But the gyrfalcon had been captured and smuggled out of the city, judged to be a worthy gift for Saladin himself. Philippe's household knights were surprised by the depths of his disappointment. They did not realize that he saw the falcon's loss as one more evil omen, yet another portent of ill fortune in this unhappy, accursed land.

It was too hot to draw the bed hangings, and Philippe could hear his squires moving around the tent. Knights came and went, trying to keep their voices low when they were warned the king was resting. He tossed and turned and finally fell into a fretful sleep. He awoke to find one of his squires leaning over the bed, looking apologetic. "I am sorry to disturb you, sire, but the Marquis of Montferrat is here and he says it cannot wait."

Philippe scowled, although his annoyance was directed at Conrad, not the youth. He'd supported the marquis because they were cousins, because he believed Conrad would make a more competent king than Guy, a proven failure, and because he'd known Richard would back Guy's claim. But the more time he spent with the marquis, the less he liked him, concluding that Conrad and Richard were two sides of the same coin, both of them arrogant and hot-tempered and hungry for public acclaim.

Swinging his legs over the side of the bed, he was not surprised to find Conrad standing there, for the man had no sense of boundaries. "Are you ailing, Cousin?" Conrad's query could have indicated concern; Philippe took it to convey surprise that he'd be abed at such an hour, an implied rebuke.

"What is it, Conrad?" he said, gesturing to his squire to pull on his boots, watching to make sure the boy shook them first to dislodge any spiders, scorpions, or other desert vermin.

"Sorry to awaken you, but I thought you'd want to know that Hannibal is at the gates."

Philippe assumed that was some sort of classical allusion since he vaguely recalled Hannibal had been an enemy of Rome. While Conrad had earned fame for his military exploits, he'd won admiration for his eloquence, too. He was fluent in several languages, often flavored his speech with Latin epigrams, and liked to quote from ancient Roman and Greek poets. In that, he reminded Philippe of Richard, another one who prided himself on being well read and knowledgeable about bygone civilizations. Philippe suspected that both men deliberately flaunted their superior education as a subtle means of demeaning him. Yes, his book-learning had been cut short, but a king of fifteen had little time for tutors or the study of Latin, not when statecraft and survival occupied all of his waking hours. He never doubted that he was as capable and quick-witted as Conrad or Richard, and was convinced that he was more formidable than either, for he had a quality they both lacked—patience.

Standing up, he regarded the marquis with cold eyes. He was sure that the Almighty intended great things for him, sure that he was destined to restore France to its former glory. So why had God not bestowed upon him the sort of grace that Conrad and Richard had in abundance? The marquis was no longer young, in his mid-forties, but he was still a handsome man; his fair hair camouflaged any traces of grey and he moved with the lithe step of a man half his age. Philippe was honest enough with himself to admit he'd have attracted no attention had he not been born the son of Louis Capet. But Conrad, like Richard, would never have gone unnoticed. Philippe had wondered occasionally if Conrad's cockiness had come from his physical blessings, but that seemed unlikely. Guy de Lusignan had been equally blessed, after all, yet his center was hollow and that had doomed his kingship. Power was in its own way as mysterious as alchemy, a conclusion Philippe had reached years ago, comparing his good-hearted, weak-willed father with the whirlwind that was Henry Fitz Empress and vowing never to follow in Louis's faltering footsteps. Henry had not seen him as a serious threat, not until it was too late. God willing, that would also hold true for his boastful, reckless son.

"Cousin?"

Conrad was looking at him quizzically, and Philippe brought his thoughts back to the here and now. He knew he was expected to respond to Conrad's cryptic comment about Hannibal, but he was unwilling to admit its meaning had escaped him. Taking his scabbard from his squire, he buckled it and was settling his sword on his hip when Guillaume des Barres spoke up, confessing that he hadn't understood the "Hannibal at the gates" remark. Conrad was happy to enlighten him, explaining that it had been a popular Roman proverb, warning of danger by referring to the man who'd once been Rome's greatest enemy, and Guillaume thanked him politely.

Philippe felt a flicker of affection for the knight, appreciating his adroit inter-
cession. But the sight of Guillaume reminded him of all the just grievances he had
against that accursed Angevin, one of which was the shameful way Richard had
treated the knight in Messina. Guillaume had not been allowed to rejoin Philippe's
household until they'd been ready to sail for Acre, and although he appeared to
have forgiven Richard for that petty fit of temper, Philippe had not. "You mean
Richard has finally deigned to put in an appearance?"

"His fleet has been sighted approaching the harbor." Conrad grinned then, looking rather pleased with himself. "And I'd wager he is not in the best of humors, for I
gave orders to turn him away from Tyre."

By now the tent was crowded with French lords and knights, including the
young Mathieu de Montmorency, Philippe's cousin, the Bishop of Beauvais, and
his marshal, Aubrey Clement. Beauvais laughed loudly, but the other men looked
shocked at Conrad's lèse-majesté.

Philippe did not approve of Conrad's action, either. Unlike Guy, Richard was
not a counterfeit king, and kings were entitled to the respect due them as God's
Anointed. Moreover, it seemed needlessly provocative, guaranteeing Richard's
enmity ere he even laid eyes upon Conrad. Until now, Richard's opposition to the
marquis had been political. After this, it would be personal, very personal. Marveling that men of obvious intelligence could be so foolhardy, Philippe said
brusquely, "Let's get this over with."

As they emerged from Philippe's pavilion, they paused in surprise, for the
entire camp seemed to be in motion. Men were hurrying toward the beach, jostling one another in their haste to secure a good vantage point. There were a
number of noncombatants at the siege—wives of soldiers and their children, the
prostitutes drawn to an army encampment like bears to honey, servants, pilgrims,
local vendors and peddlers. They were all running, too, eager to witness the English king's arrival.

Watching in bemusement as this throng surged toward the sea, Conrad said
scornfully, "Will you look at those fools? You'd think they hope to witness the
Second Coming of the Lord Christ! What is there to see, for God's Sake? Just some
ships dropping anchor offshore."

Philippe gave the older man a tight, mirthless smile, thinking that Conrad was
about to get his first lesson in Ricardian drama. As some of their knights cleared
a path through the crowd for them, he continued on at a measured pace, taking
care to detour around occasional piles of horse manure. "Do you have troupes of
traveling players in Montferrat, Conrad?"

The marquis was obviously puzzled by this non sequitur. "Of course we do. Why?"

Philippe ignored the question. "I imagine they are the same everywhere. As they approach a town, they do what they can to attract as much attention as possible. If there are tumblers or jugglers in their company, they'll lead the way, turning cartwheels and juggling balls or even knives. They'll blow their trumpets to draw a crowd, bang on drums, sing and banter with spectators, trot out dancing dogs or trained monkeys. Once I even saw a dancing bear. The bigger the spectacle they can make, the larger the audience for their performance."

Conrad was making no attempt to hide his bafflement. "Cousin, whatever are you going on about?" But he got no answer, merely that odd, enigmatic smile again. Shaking his head, he followed after Philippe.

By the time they reached the beach, it looked as if every man, woman, and child in camp had gathered at the shoreline. To the west, the sun was setting in a blaze of fiery color, the sky and sea taking on vivid shades of gold and red, drifting purple clouds haloed in shimmering lilac light. The ships entering the bay were backlit by this spectacular sunset, and Philippe wondered if Richard had timed his landing for maximum impact. The sleek war galleys were slicing through the waves like the deadly weapons they were, the royal banners of England and Outremer catching each gust of wind, the oarsmen rowing in time to the thudding drumbeats, the air vibrating with the cacophony of trumpets, pipes, and horns. And just as he'd done at Messina, Richard was standing on a raised platform in the prow of his galley, a magnet for all eyes. When the crowds erupted in wild cheering, he acknowledged their tribute by raising a lance over his head and the noise level reached painful proportions, loud enough to reach the Saracen soldiers lining the walls of the city as they, too, watched, spellbound, the arrival of the legendary Lionheart.

Conrad was staring at the spectacle in disbelief, eyes wide and mouth open. When he finally tore his gaze away from the scene playing out in the harbor, he saw that the French king was watching him with a mordant, cynical smile, one that he now understood. "All that is lacking," Philippe said, "is the dancing bear."

CHAPTER 20

Morgan had taken part in sieges before, but he'd never seen anything like the encampment at Acre. Two years had transformed it into a good-sized city, with tents and pavilions as far as the eye could see. It had an odd air of permanence, for cook-shops and baking ovens had been set up, as had public baths; bathing was an important aspect of daily life in the sultry climate of Outremer. There were even several hospitals, operated by the Knights Hospitaller. Like all the towns Morgan had known, this one was crowded and chaotic, its makeshift streets thronged with off-duty soldiers and their women. Morgan was accustomed to seeing females in an army camp, but they were always whores. Here there were wives, too, and even children, darting between tents as they played or ran errands, their youthful laughter somehow jarring in this place where men lived so intimately with Death.

Vendors wandered about, hawking their wares. Pigs rooted in the piles of garbage and chickens fluttered underfoot, for the winter's famine was long past. Dogs once more roamed the camp. Men were lining up before the laundresses' tents to be deloused, having their wounds treated by physicians and surgeons, heading for the latrine trenches, being waylaid by prostitutes, and scolded by priests fighting a losing battle to keep sin at bay. The siege had its own markets, stables for horses, pens for livestock, a large cemetery where so many crusading hopes had ended. But something was missing, something integral to city life and, after a moment, Morgan realized what it was. Bells normally chimed the canonical hours, pealing to call Christ's Faithful to Mass and to elicit prayers for the dying, to celebrate births and marriages and festivals, the days echoing with shimmering, melodic sound from dawn till dark. Here at the siege of Acre, Mass was held in tents or in the open air, and with no churches, there were no bells.

The camp was far from quiet, though. Each time the siege engines sent rocks thudding toward Acre, men cheered. There were exchanges of insults and catcalls between the besiegers and the Saracen garrison up on the city walls. Raucous songs drifted from open tents, where some were still celebrating Richard's arrival the night before. Voices carried on the wind, laughter and curses and the shrill cries of hawks; Morgan would later learn that the Turks used pigeons to convey messages to Saladin, and the crusaders unleashed hawks to try to bring them down.

To Morgan, the strangest aspect of Acre's siege was that the enemy was only three miles away, camped in the nearby hills at Tell al-'Ayyāḍiyya. Whenever the crusaders launched an assault upon the city, the garrison beat drums to alert Saladin, who would then attack the camp to draw them off. But the besiegers were well protected by fortifications and double ditches, and so far the Saracens had been unable to break through their defenses. Men were sure, though, that the stalemate would end now that Richard was here, and his welcome had been a jubilant one, lasting well into the early hours of dawn.

Morgan bought a handful of dates from a vendor and was heading for Richard's royal pavilion when he heard his name called. Smiling, he reversed course. He'd met the Count of Champagne during his service with Richard's brother Geoffrey, and a mutual liking had developed. Henri of Champagne was standing with a tall man in his middle years, whom he introduced now as Hubert Walter, the Bishop of Salisbury. Morgan was pleased to meet the prelate, for he'd emerged as one of the heroes of the siege, and he was flattered, too, to be addressed as "Cousin" by Henri; they were not really kinsmen, being linked to Richard on his father's and mother's side, respectively. As they exchanged banter now, Morgan found himself studying the other man in puzzlement; something seemed unfamiliar about Henri, but he was not sure what it was.

The young count caught his scrutiny and grinned. "I look different, I know. Whilst I am still a handsome devil, I did not have these ringlets when you last saw me. I lost my hair after a bout with Arnaldia last winter, and when it grew back, it was as curly as a lamb's fleece!"

Morgan resisted the impulse to tease Henri about his "lamb's fleece" and asked instead about Arnaldia, for he'd never heard of this ailment. Henri's smile faded. "I was stricken with a high fever, every bone in my body wracked with pain. I recovered, by God's Grace, but many others were not as fortunate. It struck down the Count of

Flanders just a week ago, and it looks likely now to claim my uncle, the Count of Perche."

"I am indeed sorry to hear that," Morgan said, for he'd become friendly with the count's son Jaufre during their time in Sicily. As he fell in step beside Henri and the bishop, he hoped the Count of Perche was still lucid, able to be told that Jaufre's wife Richenza had made him a grandfather. Henri was telling him of others who'd died during the siege, a bleak litany, and he dutifully made the sign of the cross. By now they were approaching Richard's pavilion, and he came to a sudden stop, staring at the huge crowd milling about the tent. "What in the world . . . ?"

"They are waiting to pay their respects to the king," Henri explained, "and to offer their services. They'll have a long wait, though, for Richard is not within. When he finally went off to bed, he quite sensibly chose his queen's bed and is still in her tent."

"Some of the men have already approached the king," Bishop Hubert added. "Last night both the Genoese and the Pisans sought him out. He accepted the Pisans, but not the Genoese, as they'd pledged themselves to the French king."

"The French king will not be happy to hear that the Genoese tried to defect," Morgan said cheerfully, remembering Philippe's grimacing smile as he'd bade Richard welcome.

"No, indeed he was not," Henri confirmed. "But he is far more wroth with me for my defection."

"You will be fighting under King Richard's banner?" When Henri nodded, Morgan grinned, delighted to have the count and his men in their ranks. "It could not have been easy for you, though, being Philippe's blood-kin and his vassal."

"Actually, I rather enjoyed telling him," Henri said, with a cool smile. "You see, I was in danger of running out of money, for my expenses have been considerable since my arrival at the siege. I paid fifteen hundred bezants alone for a trebuchet, only to have it burned by the Saracens within days."

"You were very generous, too, in helping me to feed the common soldiers, those most in danger of starving during the famine," the bishop interjected, and Henri shrugged, accepting the praise with his usual nonchalance.

"I went to Philippe last month, asking him for a loan so I could pay my men. My loving uncle agreed to lend me one hundred marks, provided that I pledge Champagne as collateral for the debt." Henri's mouth twisted. "I daresay I could have gotten better terms if I'd approached Saladin. Last night I asked my other uncle for aid. Richard at once promised me four thousand pounds of silver, four thousand bushels of wheat, and four thousand salted pigs for my men. In truth, I would have gone over to Richard even had he not been so generous, for no man knows war better than he does. But Philippe made it very easy for me."

Glancing over at the throng of men gathered before Richard's tent, Henri smiled slyly. "That's a sight sure to spoil Philippe's day. And wait till word gets out how much Richard is paying. Even the Saracens will be clamoring to enter his service." Seeing that neither Bishop Hubert nor Morgan understood, he grinned broadly. "Last night Richard asked me what Philippe was paying his knights. When I said three bezants a week, he decided to offer four."

Morgan laughed, but the bishop shook his head. "Mayhap I can get him to change his mind, for that would be provoking Philippe needlessly."

Henri's eyes held a mischievous blue-green glint. "Actually, my uncle Richard is doing him a favor. Now when knights begin to desert Philippe in droves, he can save face by claiming it is merely a matter of money and not because men would rather fight under Richard's command."

"I rather doubt," the bishop said dryly, "that Philippe will see it that way."

As HENRI MADE HIS WAY toward Richard's pavilion, he gazed up gratefully at the starlit sky, as the day had been one of searing summer heat. Although darkness had fallen, the siege engines were still being manned by torchlight, for Richard had his men working shifts of eight hours, enabling the trebuchets to be operated around the clock and giving the beleaguered enemy garrison no respite. His uncle had been at Acre only five days, yet Henri could feel a new energy in the camp, a rejuvenated sense of confidence. He'd watched with amusement as Richard easily assumed command of the siege; even Conrad of Montferrat had felt compelled to offer a perfunctory apology for turning the English king away from Tyre, blaming it on a miscommunication, an excuse that no one believed, least of all Richard. Henri regretted the hostility between the two men, for he thought that Conrad would make a much more effective king than Guy de Lusignan, even if he had acquired his claim by that highly dubious marriage. He wondered now if he might be able to bring his uncle around to his way of thinking, then smiled at the very notion, knowing how unlikely that was.

When he was ushered into Richard's tent, he saw that they were just finishing their evening meal. Richard had quickly adopted the local custom of dining at low tables while seated upon cushions. His wife did not look as comfortable as he did, sitting upright, her skirts carefully tucked around her ankles. She smiled at the sight of Henri, for he was a favorite with all of the women. Joanna smiled, too, and Richard beckoned him over, signaling for Henri to be served wine and a dish of syrup mixed with snow. Henri was happy to lounge on the cushions and display his greater familiarity with the Holy Land, explaining that this was a delicacy of Saracen origin; the snow was brought down from the mountains in carts covered with straw.

The final course was a platter heaped with figs, carobs, and clusters of a local fruit that few of them had ever seen before—its soft flesh encased in a greenish-yellow skin. They were known as "apples of paradise," Henri said, gallantly peeling one for Joanna and then for Berengaria. Because of its suggestive shape and size, it had another name among the soldiers, "Saracen's cock," but he refrained from sharing that bit of bawdy army humor, sensing that Richard's queen would not find it amusing. Instead, he leaned over and asked, low-voiced, if the rumors were true.

"You mean about my squabble with Philippe this afternoon? So word is already out?"

"Well, apparently you were shouting at each other loudly enough to be heard back in Cyprus."

"I suppose we were," Richard conceded, with a tight smile. "Philippe wants us to launch a full attack on the morrow. I reminded him that some of my ships are still at Tyre, waiting for favorable winds, and they are carrying most of my siege engines. It makes sense to wait until they reach Acre. Why risk men's lives today when victory seems more assured on the morrow? But of course he would not heed me, for if I say 'saint,' he has to say 'sinner.' So he's going ahead with his plan, the damned fool. I'll set my soldiers to guarding the camp, but I am not letting them fight under his command. Not that they'd want to—most men would not follow Philippe out of a burning building."

That evoked a burst of laughter from his audience, save only the Bishop of Salisbury, who suppressed a sigh, knowing it was inevitable that Richard's quip would reach Philippe's ears. Richard noticed Hubert's disapproval and elbowed him playfully in the ribs. "I know, my lord bishop, I know. You're thinking I ought to be more circumspect. You may be right, but what fun would that be?" Midst another wave of laughter, he rose to his feet, remembering in time to kiss Berengaria's hand before inviting Henri along on his final circuit of the camp that night.

They were accompanied by André and a number of the knights; others soon tagged along, so that their walk began to resemble a procession. Richard kept up a rapid fire of questions aimed at Henri. Had he heard that Jaufre's father had been given the Sacrament of the Faithful? Had he been told that Baldwin de Bethune's father was also grievously ill? Did Henri know that he'd been bequeathed Philip of Flanders's trebuchet, much to Philippe's vexation? Henri soon stopped trying to answer, for they were constantly being interrupted by men eager to greet the king, seek a favor, report a breach of discipline, or bring an act of bravery to Richard's notice.

They spent over an hour observing the trebuchets in action. This was a new weapon in siege warfare, in which a long beam pivoted on an axle, the shorter arm holding a heavy counterweight, the longer arm, or verge, attached to a sling. Richard watched with a critical eye as the verge was winched down and huge rocks were loaded into the sling, telling Henri that he'd brought stones from Sicily which were much harder than the softer limestone found in the Holy Land. He was hands-on in all that he did, and he could not resist the temptation to release the hook himself. As the counterweight plunged downward, the verge shot up and the sling cracked like a whip, emitting a high-pitched humming sound. All the men followed its trajectory intently as the rocks hurtled toward the city, cheering when they slammed into the walls in a cloud of dust and rubble. Told that Philippe had named his primary trebuchet "Bad Neighbor," Richard joked that they ought to call his "Worse Neighbor," laughing when his soldiers suggested other, more obscene names.

Next they went to inspect the huge belfry that was being constructed for an assault upon the walls. Richard had spared no expense and it would be over one hundred feet high when completed, with three stories, inner stairs, and wheels, covered in ox hides soaked in vinegar as protection against fire arrows. Eventually, Richard drew Henri aside for a private word, as private as any exchange could be in the midst of thousands.

"Tell me about Saladin," he said, and Henri obliged, confirming the general view that the sultan was a man of honor even if he was an infidel. To prove it, he recounted one of the best-known stories of Saladin's gallantry. The Lord of Nablus, Balian d'Ibelin, had been one of the few to escape capture at Ḥaṭṭīn, having fought his way free. His wife and children had taken refuge in Jerusalem, and when Saladin lay siege to the Holy City, Balian asked him for a safe conduct so he could rescue his family. Saladin agreed, upon condition that he passed but one night in the city. Upon Balian's arrival, though, he was entreated by the desperate townspeople to take command, for there were no lords of rank left. Balian felt honor bound to stay and help defend Jerusalem, but he was ashamed of breaking his oath and wrote to Saladin, explaining the circumstances. Saladin not only forgave Balian, he dispatched men to escort Balian's wife, children, and household to safety at Tyre.

Henri liked Balian very much and was tempted to praise his friend's success in saving the citizens, for he'd been able to convince Saladin to spare them from the sort of bloody massacre that had occurred when the crusaders had first taken Jerusalem in 1099. But Balian was an ally of Conrad of Montferrat, and thus already suspect in Richard's eyes. Henri chose, instead, to relate a more recent occurrence.

"Our defensive ditches have so far kept Saladin's army out, but not thieves, I am sorry to say. An unguarded tent is an irresistible target, and about a fortnight ago, a woman's infant was stolen. She was distraught, and came to us, weeping. We could do little, of course, so I told her that Saladin had a merciful heart and she had our permission to seek his help. I had a dragoman escort her to the Saracen lines, where he translated her plea. Mayhap moved by her tears, they took her to see Saladin. After hearing her story, he sent men to search for the baby. Upon learning that it had been sold in a local market, he ordered the purchase price to be paid to the buyer and he himself handed the child over to its mother, then saw that she was safely returned to our camp."

"He is indeed a worthy foe," Richard said approvingly. They'd paused near the belfry, their companions following at a discreet distance at the king's orders. Raising his hand to keep them out of hearing range, Richard reached over and grasped his nephew's arm. "I want to get a message to Saladin, Henri. Can you arrange that?"

He was pleased when Henri merely nodded, showing no surprise, for Philippe had reacted as if he'd proposed a colloquy with the Devil himself. "Good. Now can you recommend an interpreter? Someone I can wholeheartedly trust?"

"Well, Balian speaks some Arabic, but I suppose his friendship with Conrad disqualifies him," Henri said wryly. "I would suggest that you use Humphrey de Toron, for his Arabic is excellent, and you need have no fears about his loyalties. I daresay he loathes Conrad even more than Guy does."

"He seemed rather soft-hearted to me and weak-willed, too, for what man would let his wife be stolen away with such ease? But if you trust him, Henri, then that is enough for me. Send him to Saladin on the morrow with this message— that I seek a face-to-face meeting with him."

"I will make the arrangements as soon as possible. I assume you want to take the measure of the sultan for yourself?"

"Of course. To judge a man's true nature, you need to look him in the eye. I admit I am curious, too, for there are almost as many legends circulating about Saladin as there are about me," Richard said with a grin. "And who knows? Mayhap we could reach an understanding. If he is willing to compromise, we could get what we seek without a war."

Henri was startled. "You'd bargain with Saladin?"

"Why not? You yourself said he is a man of honor, so we ought to be able to trust him to hold to the terms of a peace treaty."

"I am sure he would. But many men in this camp would think the mere suggestion of negotiations with the Saracens is rank heresy."

"But not you," Richard murmured, and when Henri echoed, "No, not me," he surprised the younger man by saying, "A pity you are my nephew and not my brother, lad. I'd worry far less about England if you and not Johnny or Arthur were my heir."

"Well, mayhap you could adopt me," Henri jested, using humor to conceal his pride at being paid such a great compliment. "Uncle . . . I may be borrowing trouble, and God knows we have more than enough of that already. But whenever I've spoken with Philippe in the past week, he seems more concerned about the future of Flanders than he does about the recovery of Jerusalem. Do you think that he would dare to abandon the siege and return to France so he could claim Philip's domains?"

Now it was Richard's turn to be startled. "No," he said, after a long pause. "Philippe took the cross, swore a solemn oath to reclaim the Holy City. Not even he would betray such a sacred vow."

While Henri was relieved by Richard's certainty, he realized that he was not utterly convinced. "I am sure you are right," he said, solemnly and not entirely truthfully, adding a "God willing" under his breath, for the French king's defection could deal a death blow to their chances of regaining control of the Holy Land.

PHILIPPE INSISTED UPON launching an attack upon Acre on June 14. Not only were his men repulsed, Salah al-Dīn's brother Malik al-'Ādil, called Saphadin by the crusaders, almost succeeded in breaking through their defensive fortifications. They were driven back with heavy losses on both sides. Guy de Lusignan's brother Joffroi enhanced his reputation as a "man of prowess" by leading a counterattack upon the Saracens, killing ten men with his own hand. Three days later,

Philippe's siege engines were destroyed by the Acre garrison's Greek fire. The trebuchets had been poorly guarded, many of the crew having defected to Richard,
and Philippe blamed Richard for the loss. He was so enraged that he made
another attack the next day, but this one, too, ended in failure. Camp morale was
boosted, however, by the arrival of the rest of Richard's ships, bringing reinforcements and siege engines, and a grudging peace was patched up between the
French and English kings.

PHILIPPE WAS NOT the only one unhappy to be at the siege. Berengaria was
utterly miserable. At first it had been a great relief to escape the close confines of
their ship, to be back on firm ground again. Separate tents were set up for Joanna
and her women, for Berengaria and her household, for Sophia, Anna, and their
attendants, and they settled in to await Richard's arrival. These round pavilions
were very spacious compared to the canvas tent that had sheltered them on their
buss; they were decorated in bright stripes of red and gold, with costly carpets,
cushions, and screens that gave an illusion of privacy. After their accommodations on the buss, they were a vast improvement, but a tent was still a comedown
for a young woman who'd grown up in palaces. And beyond the fragile boundaries of her pavilion, reality had never been so raw, so immediate.

As soon as she stepped outside, she was assailed by noise, by dust, stifling heat,
swarming insects, and the fetid odors wafting from the latrine pits. She knew, of
course, of those women who bartered their bodies for coins or bread, but she'd
never expected to see their sinning at such close range. It seemed to her that the
camp was filled with whores, some of them surprisingly pretty. Drunkards, beggars, men loud and quarrelsome—they'd all been part of life in Navarre, but she'd
been insulated by stone walls, by her father's knights, by her privileged status.
There were no such protective barriers at the siege of Acre.

She had only to emerge from her tent to become the cynosure of all eyes. And
while she was accustomed to the attention guaranteed by her high birth, this was
somehow different. All were avidly curious about the Lionheart's Spanish bride,
and if not for the efforts of her household knights, she'd have been in danger of
being mobbed, for people were eager to see her close at hand, to admire her fine
silk gowns and soft skin untouched by the hot Outremer sun, to ask for alms.
While they seemed friendly enough, she still felt as if she were on constant display, like the royal cheetahs paraded on jeweled leashes in Joanna's stories about
life in the palaces of Palermo.

Her ladies were even more discontented, complaining constantly that the soldiers were too familiar, that they could not sleep at night because of the bombardment of the trebuchets, that the camp was infested with lice and fleas and terrifying, huge, hairy spiders. While Berengaria soon grew tired of their whining, she could not blame them for their misery. They'd never expected to hear the screams of wounded or dying men, the wailing of their grieving wives and bedmates. Not a day passed without sad processions to the cemetery. Soldiers were struck by rocks launched from Saracen trebuchets and pierced by the arrows of Saracen bowmen. They died in vain assaults upon the city walls, coughed up blood in the hospital tents, burned with fever that blistered their skin and lips, crying out to God or absent loved ones as their lives ebbed away, far from the hallowed walls of Jerusalem. Nor were women and children spared when Death stalked the siege. They, too, died of the bloody flux and tertian fevers and Arnaldia, and Berengaria had seen the bodies of a woman and infant unlucky enough to be in the wrong place at the wrong time, crushed under plummeting stones hurled by the enemy's trebuchets. While she knew that her life was in God's Hands, she was beginning to realize how much Richard had put her safety at risk by taking her with him to the Holy Land.

She'd hoped that his presence would banish some of her qualms, for his supreme self-confidence was contagious. But that had not proved to be the case, mainly because she'd seen so little of him. She'd known that they'd not be lodged in the same tent; even in palaces, kings and queens had their own quarters. She'd expected, though, that he'd want to share her bed as often as possible; they were newlyweds, after all. And she'd hoped that they could have evening meals together, establishing a small island of calm midst the turmoil of this alien sea. Yet in the sixteen days since Richard's arrival at Acre, she'd found herself relegated to the perimeters of his world, treated as an afterthought. He'd come occasionally to her bed, but rarely met her for meals, and usually seemed distracted, focused upon the siege to the exclusion of all else, including his lonely young bride.

She'd tried to be understanding, telling herself that her needs were unimportant when compared to the fate of Acre and Jerusalem. Then he'd stopped coming to her tent at all; it had been four days now without even a message from him. She'd have suffered in silence. That was not her sister-in-law's way, though, and Joanna had insisted that they go to him if he would not come to her, pointing out that she was his wife and queen, not a concubine to be ignored with impunity. Berengaria had allowed herself to be persuaded, for Joanna could be as forceful as her brother, albeit with more finesse.

A glorious sunset was flaming into the sea, and the sky seemed streaked with fire as they made their way toward Richard's pavilion. They were welcomed enthusiastically by his household knights, who were happy to put aside their worries and flirt with Joanna and Berengaria's ladies; despite her youth, Anna had quickly become a camp favorite. But Richard was obviously not pleased to see them, his greeting so terse that Morgan took it upon himself to confide quietly to Berengaria that the king had gotten bad news that day. There had been a rebellion in Cyprus, led by a monk claiming to be kin to Isaac Comnenus. It had been quickly put down, the would-be emperor summarily hanged, but that it had happened at all was troubling, evidence that their occupation of the island would not be as easy as first thought. And this afternoon a message had arrived from Saladin, refusing Richard's request for a personal meeting.

"Saladin replied that kings do not meet unless an agreement has been reached, saying it is not good for them to fight after meeting and eating together. He said an agreement must be made first, and of course that is impossible. King Richard was sorely disappointed, for he very much wanted to judge the sultan for himself."

Berengaria glanced over at her husband, who was sprawled on cushions, studying a map of Outremer. Feeling guilty for imposing her petty concerns upon a man who bore the burdens of a holy war upon his shoulders, she stopped in front of him, saying with a smile, "I can see this is not a good time for a visit, my lord husband, so we'll not tarry." She hesitated, then, for such boldness did not come easily to her. But according to what Joanna had told her, she was at her most fertile now that her flux was past, and she was sure Richard was as eager as she to beget a child. "Will you . . . will you be coming to me tonight?"

He glanced up, his grey eyes appearing so dark and opaque that she felt as if she were gazing upon a stranger. "No," he said, "I think not," and turned back to the map.

Berengaria felt as if she'd been slapped. Mortified, she called to her attendants, not daring to look around for fear that she'd see pity on the faces of those close enough to have heard his rebuff. Actually, few had heard their low-voiced exchange. But one who did was enraged. "You go on, dearest," Joanna said. "I'll follow shortly."

Berengaria's ladies complied at once. Joanna's women were reluctant to leave, enjoying their verbal sparring with Richard's knights. But after looking at their mistress's glittering green eyes, they hastened to obey, too. Only Anna balked and she was quickly nudged toward the tent's entrance by her stepmother and Mariam. Joanna waited until they'd departed, pondering her next move. She could ask to speak to Richard in private, behind one of the screens. But what if he refused?

"Get the men's attention for me, Morgan," she said. Giving her a curious look, he did so, very effectively, by banging upon a drum. Once she was sure all eyes were upon her, Joanna gave them her most engaging smile. "I am sorry to evict you, gentlemen. But I need to speak alone with my lord brother, the king."

There were at least fifty knights and lords present, and few of them looked happy at being so abruptly dismissed. Richard's head had come up sharply; for a moment, Joanna feared that he'd countermand her. Whatever he saw in her face changed his mind, though. Getting to his feet as the men exited, he strode toward Joanna, towering over her and obviously angry.

She was not in the least intimidated. "How dare you treat that sweet girl like one of your camp whores?" she spat, even in her fury remembering to keep her voice pitched for his ears alone.

He seemed taken aback by her vehemence. His own temper still smoldered, though, and he said testily, "I do not know what you are talking about, Joanna. Nor do I have time for this."

"You need not have time for me, Richard. But you owe it to your wife to make time for her. She's not seen you in days! Do you know what it cost her to come to you like this? And then you dismissed her as if she—"

"If I wanted a woman tonight, I'd only have to snap my fingers. But I have more important matters on my mind."

"Oh, yes, that is what men always say. Your 'matters' are so much more consequential than any womanly concerns. I know what you are about to tell me, that you cannot be expected to pay heed to a wife in the midst of a war. But why is she in the midst of it, Richard? Because you put her there!"

Richard was unaccustomed to being called to account and he did not like it in the least. "I had no choice, given the circumstances!"

"You most certainly did! We left Messina on Wednesday in Holy Week. Are you telling me you could not have waited four more days to sail? You could have married Berengaria on Easter, then sent her back to your domains under a safe escort, as you did for Maman. Instead, you chose to take her with you. There are only two explanations for doing so—that you were too besotted with your betrothed to want to be separated from her or that you were keen to get her with child as soon as possible. I think we can safely say that you are not madly in love. So that means you want an heir straightaway. That is certainly reasonable, for Johnny's past record does not inspire great confidence. But Berengaria cannot conceive unless you do your part, Richard."

"What happens between my wife and me does not concern you, Joanna."

"Oh, yes, it does! You were the one who asked me to accompany her, Richard, remember? I did as you bade, have gotten to know her well in these past weeks. She has shown courage in the face of very real dangers and great hardships, and never once has she complained. Even now I daresay she is taking upon herself the blame for your bad manners—"

"That is enough." Even though he kept his voice low, his words resonated with fury. "I've heard you out, but I have no more time for nonsense like this. Stop meddling, Joanna. Do you understand?"

They glared at each other and then she dropped down in a deep, mocking curtsy. "Yes, my lord king, I understand. Have I your leave to withdraw?" He gestured impatiently; waving her away, she thought, as he would brush aside a pesky fly. Raising her chin, she stalked out of the tent without a backward glance.

Her women were gone, but some of her household knights had remained to escort her safely back to her own pavilion. Morgan had stayed behind, too, although after a quick glance at her face, he made no attempt at conversation and they walked on in silence.

Joanna was still furious. It was so unfair. Why did men have so much control and women so little when it came to carnal matters? For all the Church's preaching about the marriage debt, it was a joke, not a claim wives could make, as Berengaria had learned tonight. With each passing month, people would measure her waist with their eyes, and they'd soon be bandying around the one word that every queen dreaded to hear—barren. Joanna knew her mother had been slurred by that accusation for most of her marriage to the French king, even though Eleanor herself had pointed out that she could hardly cultivate soil without seed. Joanna knew, too, that many of her Sicilian subjects had blamed her for failing to give William another son and heir. She'd sometimes wondered what she was supposed to do—hire men to waylay him as he headed for his *harim*? At least Berengaria was spared that humiliation. She was being neglected for a war, not for seductive Saracen slave girls.

Joanna stopped so abruptly that Morgan bumped into her, causing her to stumble. He quickly apologized, but she never heard him. Dear God. Was this about William, not Richard? Yes, he'd been churlish to Berengaria, had hurt her, unwittingly or not. But did his rudeness justify such rage? As soon as she asked the question, she knew the answer. She had overreacted, her anger fueled by memories of a young girl's humiliation years ago, bewildered and resentful and compelled to bury that anger so deep that it only surfaced after William's death.

Morgan was puzzled by her immobility, the distant, inward look in her eyes. Wisely he said nothing, waiting to see what she would do. So did the other knights. Joanna had forgotten their presence entirely. Turning on her heel, she headed back toward her brother's pavilion. She was relieved to find Richard was still alone, although surprised that he'd not summoned his men back after her departure. He was leaning against the cushions, his eyes closed, and for the first time she realized how exhausted he looked, which exacerbated her sense of remorse. With all he had to deal with, he'd not needed to deal with her ghosts, too.

"Richard," she said, and his eyes snapped open, his mouth drawn into a taut line at the sight of her. Before he could order her away, she said quickly, "I come in peace. I still think you were in the wrong. But the greater wrong was mine. I was indeed meddling, just as you charged, and I am very sorry."

She was half expecting him to resume berating her, for she'd given him good reason to be vexed with her. Or else he would react with feigned disbelief, joking that this humble, meek female could not possibly be his willful, sharp-tongued sister. To her dismay, he merely nodded, accepting her apology with an indifferent twitch of his shoulders. She did not want to have to confide in him, to tell him about William's Saracen slave girls. But if she must, she would, and she sat down beside him. "Richard, I truly *am* sorry. Are you that wroth with me?"

"No," he said at last. "You are your mother's daughter, after all."

Relieved to catch a glimmer of a smile, she smiled, too. "I am willing to grovel a bit if that will amuse you," she offered, and leaned over to kiss him on the cheek. She drew back at once, her eyes wide. "Richard, you are burning up!" Ignoring his attempt to pull away, she put her hand upon his forehead; his skin was hot and dry and she was close enough now to see that his eyes had a glazed sheen. "How long have you been ailing? Are you thirsty? Able to eat?"

"I've had no appetite for a few days," he admitted, "and I've not been sleeping well. But it is only a fever, Joanna. Men get them all the time."

She was already on her feet, though. He grabbed for her ankle, missed, and scowled. "I do not need to see a doctor!"

"Yes," she said, "you do!" Pulling the tent flap back, she spoke to someone beyond his range of vision, summoning his chief physician, Master Ralph Besace. He slumped against the cushions in frustration, knowing what he now faced: being poked and prodded and bled and hovered over by his doctors, his wife, his sister, and his friends, all of whom would be underfoot day and night, making bloody nuisances of themselves and flinching if he so much as sneezed.

"Damnation, woman—" He cut himself off, though, when she turned back and he saw the fear on her face. "You need not fret so," he said, more gently. "God did not lead me to Acre only to die of a fever."

She quickly agreed, saying that he was surely right, that such fevers were common. *But this is Outremer, Outremer where fevers are often mortal, where men die with terrifying ease, even kings.*

CHAPTER 21

JUNE 1191

Siege of Acre

The French king was sheltering from the sun under a cercleia, a framework used to protect crossbowmen as they shot at the men up on the walls. Until his arrival at Acre, Philippe had never used a crossbow, for it was not a weapon of the highborn. Much to his surprise, he'd discovered that was not the case in Outremer, and since it could be mastered fairly easily, he'd let himself be tutored by Jacques d'Avesnes, a Flemish lord who'd won considerable renown during the siege. When a Saracen leaned over the battlements to shout taunts, Philippe and Guillaume des Barres both raised their crossbows and fired. The man disappeared from view and Guillaume deferred to his king with a smile, saying, "Your hit, sire."

"For all we know, he merely ducked," Philippe pointed out with a rare flash of humor. He'd been in good spirits since learning that Richard was bedridden with a fever, and that morning the other burr under his saddle had been removed when Conrad had returned to Tyre in high dudgeon after a heated confrontation with Guy de Lusignan's brother Joffroi. Glancing toward Mathieu de Montmorency, he said generously, "You get the next shot, Mathieu."

Jacques had begun teaching the youth and he nodded encouragingly as Mathieu nervously fiddled with the weapon, using a hinged lever to pull the hemp string back to the latch and, once it was cocked, aligning the bolt. But when he pulled the trigger, his aim was off and the bolt soared up harmlessly into the sky. The Duke of Burgundy and the Count of Dreux laughed at the crestfallen boy, joking that the Saracens were their enemy, not any passing birds. Mathieu cheered up, though, when Jacques patted him on the back, saying that he just needed a bit more practice.

Philippe had not noticed this byplay, for he was frowning at the sight of the approaching Count of St Pol. He had no reason to mistrust the man himself, but the count's marital ties were suddenly suspect, for his wife was the sister of Baudouin of Hainaut. Philippe spent more time worrying about Baudouin these days than he did Saladin, for if Baudouin staked a claim to Artois whilst he was trapped here in Outremer, it would be very difficult to make good his own claim upon his return.

The Count of St Pol was accompanied by Philippe's marshal, Aubrey Clement, and Leopold von Babenberg, the Duke of Austria. There was little space in the cercleia, but Leopold still acknowledged the French king with a formal obeisance, for he was punctilious about matters of rank and protocol. There had been a three-hour eclipse of the sun on the Vigil of the Nativity of St John the Baptist, and Leopold asked Philippe now if he believed it was an omen of good or ill fortune. Philippe neither knew nor cared, but he was pleased that the duke did not want to discuss Richard's illness, which was the talk of the camp, and so he politely parried the question, asking Leopold what he thought. The latter at once launched into an enthusiastic discussion about astronomy and divine portents. Only half listening, Philippe kept his gaze upon the battlements in case a Saracen soldier should offer himself as a target.

"My liege!" This stentorian bellow came from Philippe's cousin, the Bishop of Beauvais. He was striding toward them, so quickly that they knew he bore news of importance. But he was smiling broadly, so Philippe felt confident the news would not be unwelcome. Ducking under the cercleia, Beauvais sank down on his haunches next to the French king. "Have you heard? Richard's doctors are now saying that his malady is Arnaldia!"

There were muffled exclamations of dismay from most of his audience. Jacques d'Avesnes, the Count of St Pol, the Duke of Austria, Aubrey Clement, and Mathieu jumped to their feet and hurried off to find out more, leaving the French king alone with Beauvais and his brother, the Count of Dreux, Hugh of Burgundy, and Guillaume des Barres. Reaching for a wineskin hooked at his belt, Beauvais took a swig and grimaced, for the liquid tasted as if it had been heated over a fire. "I suppose it is too much to hope," he drawled, "that Richard's bout with Arnaldia proves fatal."

His brother and Hugh laughed and Philippe permitted himself a small smile— until he saw the shocked expression on Guillaume des Barres's face. Philippe was torn between bafflement and irritation; why would Guillaume of all men care about Richard's plight? Later, on his way back to his tent, he summoned Guillaume to walk at his side and sought an answer to that minor mystery. "You did not approve of the Bishop of Beauvais's jest. I would think you'd be the last one to defend Richard after the shabby way he treated you back in Messina."

Guillaume seemed surprised by the question. "I would be greatly grieved if the English king were to die, my liege, for I see him as our best hope of defeating Saladin. The recovery of the Holy Land is far more important than any rancor between Richard and me."

"Well, you are more magnanimous than Richard would be if your positions were reversed," Philippe said, after some moments of silence. He genuinely liked Guillaume des Barres, but he did not understand the knight's willingness to forgive after such an unfair and public humiliation. Shading his eyes against the dazzling blaze of the noonday sun, he stared up at a sky that was a bleached bone-white, a sky in which there was not even a wisp of cloud, for this was the dry season and there would be no rain for months. Standing there in the midst of the chaotic siege encampment, he finally admitted to himself that his own realm mattered far more to him than the Holy Land ever could, and why not? Outremer had the Almighty to protect it but France only had Philippe Capet, a king far from home with a frail, small son as his heir. There was a certain relief in facing that fact at last. But it was a lonely moment, too, for he knew that none would understand, not even his brash cousin Beauvais. The one man who might have agreed was moldering in a tomb at Fontevrault Abbey.

As Henri made his way toward Richard's pavilion, he was stopped repeatedly by men anxious to hear how the king was faring. To each query, Henri had the same response, one that made it seem as if Richard's illness was of minor concern. Approaching the tent, he was not surprised to find soldiers and knights keeping watch. Before entering, he paused to greet two of the Préaux brothers, Guilhem and Pierre, and when he was asked the inevitable question, he gave them his most reassuring smile.

"Well, it will not surprise you to learn that he is surely the world's worst patient. He has been fuming and fretting at being bedridden, and he's learning to swear in Arabic, so his curses are even more colorful than usual." They grinned and he added lightly, "But he was cheered up to hear that the French king has now been stricken with Arnaldia, too."

As he expected, that evoked laughter, and he moved past them into the tent, thinking bleakly that if lies were sins, his confessor would be laying out penances from now till Michaelmas. Actually, he had indeed hoped Richard would be amused that Philippe was also ailing, surely God's Chastisement for welcoming his rival's ordeal. But Richard had merely grunted, then looked away. Henri had been troubled by that apathetic response, just as he was troubled by Richard's growing lethargy. The temper tantrums that Henri had described for the Préaux brothers had occurred at the onset of his uncle's illness. He'd not pitched a fit for more than a day now, and Henri was not the only one yearning for the return of the Richard they knew best—sardonic, playful, quick to anger, and utterly without self-doubts. It was as if a stranger had suddenly taken over Richard's body, listless and silent and—a word Henri would never have thought to apply to his uncle—vulnerable.

As soon as he entered the pavilion, he was pulled aside by André de Chauvigny. "We had a message from Saladin's brother. He said he'd heard the Franks were not happy about their proposed meeting, saying it endangered the Christian religion, and he asked if Richard had changed his mind because of the protests."

Henri nodded; although Saladin had refused to meet Richard, he'd been willing to have his brother act on his behalf. "That could not have made Richard happy. As if he'd ever be swayed by what other men think!"

"He dictated a response to be sent on the morrow, saying the delay was due to his illness and no other reason. But he took it much too calmly, Henri. He ought to have been outraged by the mere suggestion that he could be overruled by the French king."

"Arnaldia saps a man, André. I remember feeling as weak as a newborn babe. Yet once my fever broke, I was quick to regain my strength, and I am sure Richard will, too. Has he eaten anything since I saw him this morning?"

"Not much," André admitted. "His queen tried to coax him into taking some chicken cooked in white wine, for it's said to be good for the ailing. But he has no appetite. He's about to be bled now. His fool doctors have been arguing all day about the best time to do it. Apparently it depends upon a man's nature, and they could not decide if the king is sanguine or choleric. If he's the former, he ought to be bled at sunrise, at noon if he's the latter. Richard finally just told them to get it done straightaway, which probably proves he's choleric," André said with a faint, sad smile.

The pavilion was a very large one, said to be big enough to hold well over a hundred men, but there was little room, for it was crowded with Richard's household knights, some of his queen and sister's ladies, several bishops, and lords like Jacques d'Avesnes, the Earl of Leicester, and the newly bereaved Jaufre of Perche.

Because André and Henri were known to be members of Richard's inner circle, a path slowly opened, enabling them to reach the screen set up around the king's bed.

Richard was propped up on pillows, his wife and sister watching intently as a physician opened a vein near his elbow. Nervous under their scrutiny, the doctor was talking too much, explaining that this was the basilica vein and lancing here would purge noxious humors from the king's liver, telling them what all already knew, that good health depended upon the proper balance of the four humors— blood, phlegm, white and black bile—and too much blood in the body was one cause of disease. Richard's eyes were closed, but his lashes fluttered when Berengaria leaned over and murmured that his nephew was here.

"Henri," he said, his voice so low that the younger man had to bend down to catch his words. "Take Joanna and Berenguela to dine with you. They've not eaten all day. . . ."

Both women at once protested. Henri was not to be denied, though. "This may not be gallant of me, but the two of you look worse than the king and he's the one who is sick. You need a good night's sleep for certes, but a few hours in my charming company will have to do," he declared, persisting until they grudgingly yielded.

Master Ralph Besace, Richard's chief physician, had been holding his wrist during the bloodletting, and he signaled now for it to cease, saying the king's pulse was dropping too fast. Henri took advantage of the moment to usher the women away and out into the cooling night air. He knew they'd moved into the pavilion, setting up trundle beds behind a screen and taking turns sitting with Richard, but he doubted that either of them had slept more than a few hours in days. He chided them gently as they headed for his tent, pointing out that it would do Richard no good if they fell ill, too. But he did not expect them to heed him, nor did they.

Henri set a better table than most of his fellow crusaders, thanks to his friend Balian, who'd provided him with a cook familiar with Saracen cuisine and spices. Joanna and Berengaria were served a lamb dish called *sikbāj*, roasted scallops, and stuffed dates, but they merely picked at their food, quizzing Henri, instead, about his own experience with Arnaldia. To bring down his fever, Richard had been given ficaria and basil in wine, and when that did not help, the doctors had tried galingale and then black hellebore. Did Henri remember his treatment?

Searching his memory, he recalled taking columbine, pounded and then strained into juice through a thin cloth, and myrrh drunk in warm wine; the women made mental notes to mention this to Richard's doctors. Richard was being given sponge baths with cool water, they related, and bled, of course, although one of the doctors insisted it was dangerous to bleed a man after the twenty-fifth of the month. How, they asked in despair, were they to know which advice to follow?

Henri did his best to console them, talking of the many men, like himself, who'd made a full recovery from Arnaldia, and suggesting prayers to Blasius, the patron saint for diseases of the throat and lungs, as Richard's throat was very sore and he was troubled by painful sores in his mouth. When they were ready to depart, he rummaged around in his coffers until he found a favorite amber ring, for it was said to ward off fevers, and then walked them back to the royal pavilion.

Upon their return, they were initially alarmed to be told the Bishop of Salisbury had shriven Richard of his sins, but André was able to reassure them that this was merely a sensible precaution, not a sign that Richard had taken a turn for the worse. After all, he pointed out, men always confessed their sins ere going into battle. Once Joanna retired behind the women's screen to get a few hours sleep, Berengaria pulled a chair up to the bed. The nights since Richard was stricken had been unusually quiet. She could still hear the thudding of stones as they crashed into the city walls, but otherwise a pall seemed to have settled over the camp. Richard showed no curiosity when she slipped Henri's amber ring onto his finger, and when she brought him a hot beverage brewed from sage leaves, telling him it was said to heal mouth ulcers, he sipped obediently as she held the cup to his blistered lips.

It frightened her that he was suddenly so passive; she much preferred his earlier bad-tempered outbursts, even when they'd been directed at her. As the hours passed, she replaced the wet compresses upon his forehead, gave him wine mixed with the doctors' latest concoction, smoothed ointment upon his blisters, and blinked back tears after he acknowledged her ministrations with the flicker of a smile. She was so exhausted that when Joanna appeared to relieve her vigil, she fell onto her bed fully dressed and was asleep almost at once.

Her transition from uneasy dreams to wretched reality was so abrupt that she awoke with a start, momentarily confused to find Joanna bending over her. "Is it my turn?" she asked, stifling a yawn. But then she saw the tears welling in the other woman's eyes.

FROM THE CHRONICLE of Baha' al-Dīn Ibn Shaddād, a trusted adviser of Salah al-Dīn and an eyewitness to the events at the siege of Acre: "The Franks were at this time so much concerned at the increasing gravity of the King of England's illness that they even discontinued for a while their attack on the city."

RICHARD WAS VERY ILL. But he was aware only of intolerable, searing heat, his body afire with fever that burned ever higher with each passing day, his dreams dragging him into a terrifying world of hallucinatory, demonic visions, shot through with swirling, hot colors of blood and flames. In his delirium, he was haunted by his dead, by his father and brothers, only time seemed oddly fragmented. He was a man grown, then a young boy, calling out for the mother who'd always been his mainstay, but now locked away in a far-distant dungeon, unable to hear his cries for help. Spiraling down into the dark, he was so tired, so very tired that it seemed easier to stop fighting, to let go. He did not, though, instinctively struggling toward a distant, dim light, one that flickered and wavered but promised to lead him home.

When he opened his eyes, he winced, nearly blinded by the sudden brightness. Filtering the light through his lashes, he saw a woman's face, streaked with tears. He wondered why his brain was so muddled. While she looked familiar, it took a heartbeat or two before he recognized his wife. Saying her name, he was shocked by how weak his voice sounded. Holy God, how long had he been ill?

"You're awake!" Berengaria's smile was like a sunrise. She slid her fingers across his forehead, then touched his cheek, above his beard. "Blessed Lady, your fever has broken! Richard, you are going to recover."

"Of course I am. . . ." He wanted to ask who had doubted it, but his throat was too raw and he was grateful when she understood his need and reached for a cup. The wine was warm and soured by medicinal herbs; Richard thought it tasted delicious. Handing it back, he studied her face. "Were you here all the time, Berenguela?" When she nodded, he smiled. "I thought so. I felt your presence. . . ."

Berengaria closed her eyes, feeling truly blessed, so happy was she at that moment. "Richard, we must make a generous offering to the Almighty, for God has been so good to us. Mayhap we could even found a chapel once Acre is yours?"

"I doubt that Philippe is willing to cede all of Acre to me, little dove. How is he? I did not imagine it, that he was stricken, too?"

"No, he was indeed afflicted with Arnaldia. But his was a much milder case, and he is well on the road to recovery. He— Richard, no!"

Richard had already discovered that he was not able to get out of bed; his head was spinning. Shaken by his body's betrayal, he let Berengaria settle him back against the pillows. He was drifting toward sleep again when the screen was jerked aside and then André and Henri were there, looking down at him and laughing.

"We thought we heard your voice!"

Berengaria felt a remorseful pang, starting to explain her own joy had been so intense she'd not thought of anyone else. But the men were not listening to her. They'd pulled up stools beside the bed, wanting to know if Richard was done lolling about and taking his ease, if he was ready to hear what had been happening in the past week. Richard was stunned to learn that he'd lost a week of his life, but he was eager to hear what he'd missed and they were eager to tell him.

Their sappers had been able to undermine a section of the Accursed Tower and French crews had brought down part of the adjoining wall, although they'd not been able to force their way into the city. The garrison commander had ventured out under a flag of truce to discuss terms, but Philippe had received him so disdainfully that he'd returned to Acre in a rage, vowing to fight to the death. Yesterday Philippe had ordered his men to launch another attack, which had ended in failure like the other French attempts. Conrad was back from Tyre, doubtless because he'd heard both Richard and Philippe were ailing. Some of Philippe's sappers had broken into a countertunnel being dug by the Saracens. Both sides pulled back by mutual consent, no rational man wanting to fight underground like weasels trapped in a burrow, but they did manage to rescue some Christian prisoners who were being forced to help dig the tunnel.

Richard was delighted with that story and burst out laughing. Berengaria felt tears burn behind her eyelids, for she'd not been sure she'd ever hear that sound again. The doctors were there now, too, beaming at their patient as if they and not God had brought Richard back from the brink of death. Horrified to realize that Joanna did not yet know, Berengaria hastily sent a man to fetch her; one of Joanna's ladies, her beloved Dame Beatrix, was grievously ill, too, now, and Joanna had begun dividing her time between Beatrix's sickbed and her brother's. After dispatching the knight to Joanna's tent, Berengaria hurried back to her husband. She saw, though, that Richard had not noticed her absence. He was sitting up in bed, looking gaunt and pale, but his eyes were shining, and he was peppering Henri and André with questions about the siege, wanting to know if they thought the Accursed Tower could soon be brought down, if there'd been any messages from Saladin's brother, if the French had suffered many casualties when their assault was repulsed.

Berengaria watched him for a while and then backed away from the bed.

Catching the eye of one of the doctors as she moved around the screen, she beckoned him over. "If the king asks for me," she said quietly, "tell him I have gone to ask the Bishop of Salisbury to say a special Mass tonight in celebration of this miracle."

WHEN BERENGARIA ENTERED Joanna's tent, she was met with so many smiles that she knew Beatrix's crisis must have passed. This was confirmed by her first glimpse of the older woman, who seemed to be sleeping peacefully for the first time in almost a week. Joanna looked exhausted but happy, rising to greet her sister-in-law with a quick hug. "God has indeed been kind to us," she murmured, "sparing Richard and now Beatrix."

As they crossed the camp toward Richard's pavilion, Joanna confided that the best proof of Beatrix's improvement was that she was now fretting about losing her hair and nails. "I told her she need not worry about hair loss yet, for Henri said it did not occur till weeks after he'd been stricken with Arnaldia. Has Richard been fretting about that, too? He is very vain, you know," she said with a fond smile, "for he well knows how much he has benefited from looking like a king out of some minstrel's tale."

"I do not think he has room in his head for nary a thought but the siege," Berengaria said honestly. "He is remarkably single-minded, and now that he is on the mend, he wants only to take part in the fighting. I am hoping that you'll be able to help me keep him occupied this afternoon."

"That is why I brought this along," Joanna said, brandishing a book richly bound in red leather: "Chrétien de Troyes's *Yvain, the Knight of the Lion*. When Richard starts to get restless, I'll insist upon reading it to him." Glancing at Berengaria's serene profile, she sighed softly, for a newlywed wife ought to be able to hold her husband's attention without aid from his sister. They were mismatched, her brother and his Spanish bride, a falcon mated to a dove. But that would not matter as long as she could give him fledglings. Most wives found their joy in their children, not their husbands. She bit her lip, thinking of a small tomb in Monreale Cathedral, and then, shaking off her sadness with a determined effort, she began to tell Berengaria that two of her Sicilian male servants, missing for more than a fortnight, had apparently surfaced in Saladin's camp. "At least that is what Henri heard. So I suppose their conversion to Christianity was not as sincere as I was led to believe," she said ruefully.

By now they'd reached Richard's tent. Their knights were delighted when the women said their services would not be required for the rest of the afternoon, for the Accursed Tower was said to be close to collapse. As they hurried off, Berengaria and Joanna entered the pavilion, only to halt in surprise, for it was deserted except for several men dozing in the July heat. Since solitude was not an attribute of kingship, they exchanged puzzled looks; why would Richard have been left alone like this? Struck by the same premonition, they hastened around the screen, where they found a rumpled, empty bed.

"My ladies?" Spinning around, they saw one of the soldiers, rubbing his eyes sleepily. "May I be of assistance?"

"Where is my lord husband, the king?"

"Last night more of the wall adjoining the Accursed Tower was brought down by our sappers, and the king wanted to be there today when it is breached," he said, so calmly that they both wanted to shake him. "His doctors advised against it, but the king insisted and had himself carried out on a silken quilt so he could take command."

RICHARD HAD HIS CERCLEIA set up near the city's defensive ditch. The crusaders had labored for weeks to fill it, and the camp was still talking about the heroic sacrifice by the wife of a sergeant. She'd been helping to lug rocks to the ditch when she'd been struck by a Saracen arrow. Dying in her husband's arms, she'd begged him to throw her body into the ditch, so that even in death she could contribute to their holy cause. Today, the objective was to clear away some of the rubble from the collapsed section of wall. This was a highly dangerous task, for it exposed men to the fire of the enemy archers above them, yet there was no shortage of soldiers willing to accept this perilous undertaking. As they zigged and zagged toward the breach, they held shields aloft to deflect the arrows and spears raining down upon them.

Richard's arbalesters were providing as much cover as they could, each one flanked by a second man holding a cocked crossbow. As soon as a man shot, he was handed the second crossbow, and by rotating like this, they were able to keep up a steady fire. Richard was doing the same, and when one of his bolts found its target, a Saracen leaning precariously over the wall to shoot down at the men below him, he gave a triumphant laugh, relieved that his lingering illness had not affected his aim. His men glanced over and grinned, for his presence on the front line had greatly boosted morale; they loved it that he was always ready to risk his life with theirs, that he'd been carried out here on a litter since he was not yet strong enough to walk.

Henri handed him a loaded crossbow. "This time aim for that tall one in the green turban."

"What . . . you do not like his taste in clothes?" Richard asked, giving his nephew a curious look as he reached for the weapon.

"The hellspawn is wearing Aubrey Clement's armor."

Richard's eyes flicked from his nephew's grim face to the man up on the battlements. He'd been told of Aubrey's death three days ago during the French assault. The marshal had been the first to reach the walls, but when other knights sought to follow, their ladder broke, flinging them into the ditch. Trapped alone on the battlements, Aubrey had fought fiercely until overwhelmed by sheer numbers, and his friends could only watch helplessly as he was stabbed multiple times.

"Are you sure, Henri?"

"Very sure. He is even wearing Aubrey's surcote. Those dark splotches are his blood. The swine has been taunting us like this for the past two days, daring us to avenge Aubrey. But the man has the Devil's own luck, for none of our bolts have even scratched him."

Richard turned back to the wall and then swore, for the Saracen in the slain marshal's armor was no longer there. "I see what you mean," he said, and gestured toward a nearby flask.

André picked it up and flipped it over to Richard. His royal cousin's pallor was so pronounced that he knew Richard ought to be back in bed. But he knew, too, that there was no point in suggesting it. Instead he reached for his own crossbow and resumed shooting up at the walls.

They were all soaked in sweat by now for the heat had become sweltering as the sun rose higher in the sky. Still, men continued to make that dangerous dash toward the walls, even as others ventured out to drag the wounded back to safety; the dead would have to wait till darkness for their recovery. Just before noon, they were taken by surprise by the arrival upon the scene of Conrad of Montferrat.

"My liege," he said, in casual acknowledgment of Richard's rank. "I'd heard you were out here, had to see for myself." Making himself comfortable next to Richard, he murmured, "Trying to make Philippe look bad for staying in bed?"

Richard gave him a sharp look, but Conrad had already turned toward the Accursed Tower, staring in astonishment at the frantic activity around the breach. "Jesu, look at those crazy fools! In the past, we could not get men to volunteer for death-duty like that. How'd you do it?" His eyes searched Richard's face, half admiring, half envious. "Even when we ordered them, they still balked."

"I did not order them. I offered two gold bezants for every rock they bring back from the breach."

Conrad's jaw dropped and then he gave a shout of laughter. "Now why did we not think of that? Why waste time appealing to men's faith when bribery works so much better?"

"Not bribery. A reward for risking their lives. Do not tell me they do not deserve it, my lord marquis. Not unless you intend to get out there and start clearing away that rubble yourself."

Conrad's eyes glittered even in that subdued light. But Richard was no longer paying him any mind. Snatching up his crossbow, he aimed and fired in one smooth motion. The bolt struck his target in the chest. The Saracen staggered, blood gushing from his mouth, and all around Richard, men began to yell and cheer, pumping their fists and slapping one another on the back, while Conrad looked on in bafflement.

"It was a good shot," he said dryly, "I'll grant you that. But surely all this joy is somewhat excessive? Unless that was Saladin himself you just dispatched to the Devil."

His sarcasm did not go over well with Richard's men, who were beginning to bristle. Richard showed white teeth in what was almost a smile. "You can tell Philippe," he said, "that I just avenged his marshal."

THE FOLLOWING DAY, the French assaulted the city again, taking heavy losses. The Saracen garrison sent a swimmer across the harbor to warn Salah al-Dīn that they must surrender if he could not come to their aid. They then proposed to yield Acre in return for their lives. When this offer was turned down, they offered to free one Christian prisoner for every member of the garrison and to return the fragment of the Holy Cross, captured by Salah al-Dīn after his victory at Ḥaṭṭīn. The Franks, the name used by the Saracens for their foes, insisted upon the return of "all their lands and the release of all their prisoners." This was refused. The crusaders' trebuchets continued to pound away at the walls, and on July 11, Richard's men and the Pisans combined for another attack on the breached wall by the crumbling Accursed Tower. They were eventually beaten back, but they'd come so close to forcing their way into the city that the garrison realized defeat was inevitable.

FRIDAY, JULY 12, dawned hot and humid. Joanna, Berengaria, and their women passed the hours restlessly, unable to concentrate upon anything but the meeting taking place in the pavilion of the Templars, where Acre's commanders, Sayf al-Dīn al-Mashtūb and Bahā' al-Dīn Qarāqūsh, were conferring with Richard, Philippe, Henri, Guy de Lusignan, Conrad of Montferrat, and the other leaders of the crusading army. Berengaria kept picking up her psalter, putting it down again, while Joanna tried to continue Alicia's chess lessons, but her gaze was roaming so often toward the tent entrance that the young girl managed to checkmate her, much to her glee.

"They will yield, yes?" Anna asked at last, giving voice to the question uppermost in all their minds. Her grasp of their language had improved in the six weeks since her world had turned upside down, and she continued in charmingly accented French. "Or they will all die, no?"

"Most likely," Joanna confirmed, too nervous to put a gloss upon the brutal reality of warfare in their world—that a castle or town taken by storm could expect no mercy. Whether there would be survivors depended upon the whims of the victors or upon the ability of the defeated to raise ransom money. There had been a bloodbath after the Christians had seized Jerusalem in 1099, almost all of the Muslims and Jews in the city put to the sword. But Saladin had spared the Christians of Jerusalem four years ago after Balian d'Ibelin persuaded him to let them buy their lives; Joanna was proud that the money her father had sent to the Holy City over the years had kept thousands of men and women from being sold in Saracen slave markets.

Glancing over at Anna, she amended her answer, saying, "That is why they will accept our terms. They know their fate will be a bloody one if our men seize the city. By yielding, they can save themselves and those still living in Acre."

Anna looked from Joanna to Berengaria, back to Joanna. "Why you fret, then, if outcome is certain?" Before either woman could respond, she smiled, dimples deepening in sudden comprehension. "Ah ... I see. You fear for *Malik Ric*." This was how the Saracens referred to Richard, and Anna had begun to use the name, too, much to Richard's amusement. "He would be healed for another ..." She paused, frowning as she sought the right word. "Another attack ... that is it, no?"

"Yes, that is it," Joanna confirmed, exchanging silent sympathy with Berengaria. While Richard was regaining strength with each passing day, he was by no means physically up to taking part in a battle, and yet they feared he would want to do just that; he'd been very frustrated at not being able to join his men in yesterday's assault. Although they felt confident that Henri and the Bishop of Salisbury and Richard's friends would not permit him to risk his life so foolishly, they well knew how stubborn he could be, and so both women were praying that today would end the siege.

They were about to send one of Joanna's household knights back to the Templars' tent to learn how the negotiations were proceeding when they heard it—a sudden roar, as if coming from thousands of throats, even louder than the sound Greek fire made when it streaked toward its target, trailing a flaming tail. Mariam darted toward the entrance and was back in moments, smiling. "Either they've come to terms or the whole camp has gone stark mad, for men are shouting and cheering and all the whores are hurrying out to help them celebrate!"

Joanna and Berengaria were on their feet now, embracing joyfully, determined to ignore the fact that this was but a respite, that Acre's fall was only the first in a series of bloody battles on the road leading to the Holy City.

Within the hour, the noise level suddenly increased, alerting them that Richard must be approaching. He was flanked by Henri and the Earl of Leicester, with friends and lords following jubilantly in his wake. He still looked like what he was, a man recently risen from his sickbed, his cheekbones thrown into prominence by his weight loss, his complexion unnaturally pale for one with such high coloring. But his smile was dazzling and he appeared as happy as either woman had ever seen him.

"It is done," he said huskily. "Acre is ours."

THE ACRE GARRISON agreed to surrender the city and all of their weapons and siege engines, including the seventy galleys of Salah al-Dīn's fleet, anchored out in the harbor. They promised on the sultan's behalf to pay two hundred thousand *dinars*, and to return the Holy Cross. Fifteen hundred Christian prisoners were to be freed, as were one hundred men specifically named. Conrad of Montferrat was to receive ten thousand *dinars* for his help in negotiating the settlement. The garrison was to be held as hostages until the terms were met, and then they and their families would be freed. When the news reached Salah al-Dīn, he was horrified, and after consulting with his council, he determined to send a swimmer back after dark to the beleaguered city, telling the garrison that he could not accept such terms. But he soon learned it was too late, for at noon his men saw the "banners of unbelief" raised over the walls of Acre.

CHAPTER 22

JULY 1191

Acre, Outremer

cre was divided between Richard and Philippe, as were the garrison hostages. This did not please those crusaders who'd been at the siege since the beginning and had expected to benefit when it finally fell. After they'd complained vociferously, the two kings agreed to give them a share of the spoils, but not all trusted in royal promises and some ill will lingered. Nor was Philippe happy with the division, for Richard had insisted upon taking the half of the city that contained the citadel, wanting to lodge his wife and sister there, and Philippe had to make do with the Templars' house. Remembering how he'd been the one to occupy the royal palace in Messina, this seemed like further proof that his status was being deliberately diminished, and he began to nurse yet another grievance against Richard.

Richard paid no heed to these grumblings of discontent and forged ahead, concerned only with making Acre secure as soon as possible, for once the Saracen garrison was ransomed by Salah al-Dīn, he meant to lead his army south. But first the Archbishop of Verona and the other bishops had to reconsecrate the churches, many of which had been used as mosques. Then the streets had to be cleared of the rubble, debris, and garbage that had accumulated during the siege, and habitable houses assigned to crusaders. He'd begun rebuilding the walls at once, but it was nine days before he judged it safe enough to bring Berengaria and Joanna into the city.

ACRE HAD BEEN a notorious seaport prior to its seizure by Salah al-Dīn, known for its diverse population, its raucous vitality, and its multitude of opportunities for bad behavior. As soon as they passed through the gate by the ruins of the Accursed Tower, the women could see that the Acre of old was rapidly reviving, the streets thronged, the markets up and running, taverns, cook-shops, and brothels already open for business. It was bustling and bawdy and they were both fascinated and repelled, but with Richard acting as their escort and guide, they were able to relax and enjoy their tour of this exotic, vibrant, sinful city.

The old boundaries had been restored, the Templars, Hospitallers, and Italian merchants all allotted their own neighborhoods. They barely glanced at the French fleur de lys flying over the Temple to the west, where Philippe was now lodged. But they were intrigued by the Genoese quarter, for they'd never seen a covered street before. It was vaulted, with shaft openings to let in light and air, lined with stalls and stone benches, the air so fragrant with the scents wafting from the soapmakers and perfume shops that they decided they would later return to make purchases, for that simple pleasure had been denied them since they'd sailed from Messina.

They were accustomed to the odd, flat roofs by now, having seen them in Cyprus. But it was surprising to see no buildings of wood, to see so many houses of stone, a luxury back in Europe, and to see canvas awnings stretched across the narrow streets to shelter people from the hot Syrian sun. They were saddened to discover how the Cathedral of the Holy Cross had suffered during the Saracen occupation, and interested to learn that the Templars and Hospitallers had subterranean stables for their horses. Joanna determined to check out the bathhouses for herself after Richard reported that they had rooms with hot and cold pools, with separate accommodations for men and women. And they were delighted by their first sight of a remarkable creature with a humped back and silky, long eyelashes, astonished when it knelt so that its rider could mount. Richard said these beasts were called "camels," able to go long distances without water. He was more interested in the stories he'd heard of lions in the north, declaring that he'd love to hunt a lion ere they returned home. Joanna and Berengaria exchanged glances at that, the same thought in both their minds, that "home" had never seemed so far away.

After exploring the Genoese and Venetian quarters, Richard took them back to the royal citadel, situated along the north wall. The women were eager to see it, for they knew this would be their residence for months to come. It was built like many of the houses in Outremer, around a central courtyard, with corner towers and a great hall; while it could not compare to the luxury of her Palermo palaces, Joanna was so pleased to have a roof over her head after weeks in tents that she was not about to complain. They exclaimed over the courtyard, for it was paved in marble and bordered by fruit trees, with benches, a sundial, and a large fountain, where water was flowing from the mouth of a sculpted stone dragon.

"Wait till you see the great hall," Richard said. "The ceiling is painted to look like a starlit sky." But as they started toward the outside stairway, he was approached by one of his men, and after a brief exchange, he turned back to the women, his smile gone. "The Duke of Austria is here and insisting to speak with me," he said, not sounding happy about it. "Henri will show you the palace and I'll join you as soon as I can."

The women were relieved that the citadel seemed so comfortable. They were impressed, too, by how thoroughly all traces of the former occupants had been erased in such a brief time span, realizing that men must have been laboring day and night to make it ready for them. They admired the painted ceiling in the great hall and its mosaic tile floor, and were delighted by the bedchambers, which were spacious and golden with sunlight, for they had walk-in bay windows that could be opened like doors. One of the chambers had a balcony that overlooked the courtyard, and Berengaria and Joanna immediately began to argue over which one should occupy it; much to Henri's amusement, each woman insisted the other ought to have it.

Stepping out onto the balcony, Berengaria at once beckoned to Henri. "Is that the Duke of Austria below with Richard?"

Henri and Joanna joined her, gazing down at the scene below them in the courtyard. The duke was a compact man in his early thirties, dressed more appropriately for his court in Vienna than the dusty streets of Acre, his tunic of scarlet silk, his cap studded with gemstones, his fingers adorned with gold rings. Both men were keeping their voices low, but it was obvious to their audience that Leopold was very agitated; he was gesturing emphatically, at one point slamming his fist into the palm of his hand, his face so red that he looked sunburned. Richard seemed more impatient than angry, shaking his head and shrugging and then turning away. Leopold's mouth contorted and he lunged forward, grabbing for the other man's arm. The women and Henri winced at that, knowing what was coming. Richard whirled, eyes blazing. Whatever he said was enough to silence Leopold, who was ashen by the time the English king was done berating him. He did not protest this time when Richard stalked off, but the expression on his face was troubling to Berengaria, and as soon as they withdrew from the balcony, she asked Henri why the duke was so wroth with Richard.

"I have no idea," he admitted. "I've had no problems dealing with him. We dined together upon his arrival at Acre this spring, and he was pleasant company, liking troubadour music as much as I do. He is very prideful and concerned about his honor, but what man isn't?"

Henri's favorable impression of Leopold only deepened the mystery for the women. They were still inspecting the chamber, admiring the glazed green and yellow oil lamps and ivory chess figures when Richard strode in. He was still flushed with anger, but he made an effort to conceal it, asking Berengaria what she thought of the room. "I was told the Saracen commander al-Mashtūb occupied this chamber. The carpet is his, and that chess set. You can decorate however you want, of course."

Berengaria assured him that she was very pleased with the chamber. She was quite curious about his quarrel with Leopold, but she did not want him to think she was prying into matters best left to men.

Joanna had no such compunctions. "What was that dispute with the Austrian duke all about?"

Richard grimaced. "He was enraged because some of my men took his banner down from the city walls."

Joanna blinked in surprise. "I assume you assured him that the offenders would be punished. Was that not enough for him?"

"I have no intention of punishing my men. I told them to remove his banner."

Seeing that Berengaria and the other women shared Joanna's puzzlement, Henri took it upon himself to explain, knowing Richard was in no mood to do so. "By flying his banner over Acre, he was claiming a share of the spoils. It is understandable, though, Uncle, that Leopold would be aggrieved about it. He's sensitive to slights, real or imagined. Do you want me to talk to him, see if I can smooth his ruffled feathers?"

"No need to bother." Richard bent over to stroke Joanna's ever-present Sicilian hounds. "Let him stew in his own juices. You'll not believe what he dared to say to me. After I pointed out that *he* was in the wrong, not my men, he accused me of being high-handed and unfair, as when I 'maltreated' Isaac Comnenus! It seems his mother is Isaac's cousin. I told him . . . well, I'll leave that to your imaginations," he said, with a glimmer of his first smile since entering the chamber.

A silence fell, somewhat awkwardly, for both Joanna and Henri felt that Richard ought to have been more diplomatic with the duke; why make enemies needlessly? Berengaria's natural instincts were for conciliation, too, but she was indignant that Leopold would dare to blame Richard for deposing Isaac Comnenus, who still flitted through her dreams on bad nights. Going to her husband's side, she said tartly, "He ought to be ashamed to admit kinship to such a wicked man!"

Richard liked her display of loyalty, and when he slid his arm around her waist, he liked the feel of her soft female curves. His body was still surging with the energy unleashed by his confrontation with Leopold, and he drew her closer, his anger forgotten. "Henri, why don't you show Joanna and Berenguela's duennas the rest of the palace?"

There were gasps from his wife's ladies, scandalized that he meant to claim his marital rights in the middle of the afternoon. Berengaria blushed, a bit flustered that he'd made his intention so plain in front of others. But when he leaned over to whisper in her ear, she laughed softly. Joanna and Henri ushered the women out, both grinning.

SEATED BY RICHARD'S SIDE at the high table, Berengaria felt a sense of satisfaction as she looked around the great hall. It hadn't been easy to prepare a dinner like this on just one day's notice, but she and Joanna had managed it. The linen tablecloths were snowy white, the platters and bowls were brightly glazed, and the rare red glassware she'd found among the Saracen commander's possessions shimmered like rubies whenever the sun struck them. The menu was not as elaborate as she would have wished, but their guests were eating with gusto, the wine was flowing freely, and once the dinner was done, they would be serenaded by minstrels and harpists. This was the first time in her two-month marriage that Berengaria had been able to play her proper role as Richard's queen, entertaining his friends, vassals, and political allies, and she was enjoying this long-overdue taste of normalcy.

The guest list was a distinguished one: the archbishops of Pisa and Verona; the Bishop of Salisbury; the beleaguered King of Jerusalem and his two brothers, Joffroi and Amaury de Lusignan; the Grand Master of the Knights Hospitallers; the Earl of Leicester; Henri of Champagne and Jaufre of Perche; André de Chauvigny; the Flemings, Jacques d'Avesnes and Baldwin de Bethune; Humphrey de Toron; even the master of the Templars, for although Philippe was now residing at their Temple, the new master, Robert de Sablé, was an Angevin baron and one of Richard's most trusted vassals. The women—Joanna, Berengaria, Sophia, Anna, and their ladies-in-waiting—were in the minority and the conversation so far was distinctly male in its tenor.

They discussed the deadly and mysterious weapon, Greek fire, which was so combustible that it could not be extinguished by water, only vinegar. They took turns guessing the identity of an unknown Christian spy, who'd sent them valuable, secret messages from Acre during the course of the siege. Richard revealed that he was negotiating with the Templars, who were eager to buy Cyprus from him. And they drank toasts to the memories of those who'd given their lives that Acre could be taken—the Count of Flanders, Philippe's marshal, Aubrey Clement, the counts of Blois and Sancerre, Guy de Lusignan's queen, and a nameless woman in a long green cloak who'd shot a bow with astonishing accuracy, killing several Saracens before she'd been overwhelmed and slain. They'd begun to talk about Saracen battle tactics when the convivial dinner was interrupted by the unexpected arrival of the Duke of Burgundy and the Bishop of Beauvais.

Richard scowled, for the mere mention of the bishop's name was enough to ignite his temper. Beauvais had earned the undying enmity of the de Lusignans for wedding Conrad to his stolen bride, and he and the duke ran a gauntlet of hostile stares as they were escorted into the hall, followed by Druon de Mello, lagging behind as if he wanted to disassociate himself from their mission. After greeting Richard with very formal courtesy, Hugh apologized for disrupting their dinner and asked if they might speak briefly with him in private, saying that it was a matter of some urgency.

Richard had no intention of accommodating either man, and after a deliberate pause to finish his wine, he said coolly, "I think not. I am amongst friends here, men whom I trust. I assume the French king has a message for me, no? So let them hear it, too."

The duke and the bishop exchanged guarded glances, while Druon de Mello actually took a few steps backward, like a man getting out of the line of fire. It was becoming obvious that neither Hugh nor Beauvais wanted to be the one to speak first, and Richard suddenly realized what they'd come to tell him. He swung around, his eyes seeking his nephew, and he saw his own suspicions confirmed in Henri's grim expression. No one else knew what was coming, though, and they began to mutter among themselves as the silence dragged out.

Hugh outlasted Beauvais, for the bishop had no more patience than Richard did. "Our king has sent us to tell you that he has fulfilled his vow by taking Acre, and so he intends to return to his own lands straightaway."

There was a moment of eerie, utter silence. Then disbelief gave way to outrage and the hall exploded. Men were on their feet, shouting, cushions trampled underfoot and red stains spreading over the tablecloths from spilled wine cups, amid cries of dismay from some of the women as their peaceful dinner turned into chaos. Richard was on his feet, too, raising his hand for quiet. "Shall I send your king a map? He seems to have confused Acre with Jerusalem."

"We've delivered the message," Beauvais said tersely. "Make of it what you will."

"There is but one way to take it, and it does your king no credit. He swore a holy oath to free Jerusalem, and now he just . . . goes home? What do his lords say to that? What do you say? Do you mean to disavow your own oaths, too?"

Both men glared at him. "Indeed not!" Hugh snapped, at the same time that Beauvais pledged to remain in Outremer until it was a Christian kingdom again. They were so clearly insulted by the very question that their indignation gave Richard an idea.

"I have to hear this from your king's own lips," he declared. "Is he at the Temple?"

"When we left, he was about to sit down to dinner." Hugh paused. "He'll take it amiss if you burst in upon his meal without warning." But he did not sound much troubled by that prospect, and Richard was sure now that Philippe had alienated his own men by renouncing his vow.

"I am willing to risk that," he said, very dryly. Glancing around, he saw that there was no need to ask if others wanted to accompany him; most of the guests had risen, too. Reaching down, he squeezed his wife's hand. "I am sorry, Berenguela, but it cannot wait."

"I understand," she said. Settling back upon her cushion, she watched as the hall emptied within moments, even the prelates hastening to catch up with Richard and the de Lusignans. She hadn't lied; she did understand. It was still disappointing to have their first dinner end so abruptly, and she could not help wondering if this would be the pattern for their marriage in years to come, brief moments of domesticity midst the unending demands of war.

Joanna came over and sat down beside her sister-in-law. Her eyes were sparkling with excitement. "Why must women miss all the fun? What I would not have given," she confessed, "to witness their confrontation!"

CONRAD LEANED TOWARD his friend Balian d'Ibelin, Lord of Nablus, speaking in the Piedmontese dialect that was the native tongue of the marquis and Balian's Italian father to deter eavesdroppers. "The last time I enjoyed myself so much," he murmured, "a funeral Mass was being said."

Balian shifted uncomfortably in his chair, wishing that the French king had adopted the Frankish fashion of dining on cushions. "So you noticed it, too—that cloud of gloom and doom hovering over the Temple. Any idea what is going on?"

Conrad shrugged. "God knows Philippe is never the most cheerful of men. But I've not seen his nerves as raw as this. When Leopold dropped his wine cup, I swear Philippe jumped like a scalded cat." Glancing down the table at the Austrian duke, he said softly, "There's another one not exactly bubbling over with joy. I heard he'd had a row of some sort with Richard, but when I asked, he well nigh bit my head off." Poking at the meat on his trencher with his knife, he sighed. "And the food is as dismal as the company. Well, if I am already doing penance for my sins, I might as well add some new ones. You want to check out that bordel in the Venetian quarter tonight? I'm told they have a Greek whore as limber as an eel."

Balian regarded the other man in bemusement. "You do remember that your wife is my stepdaughter?"

Conrad was utterly unperturbed by the implied rebuke. "And I cherish Isabella," he said urbanely. "No man could ask for a better wife. But I'm talking of whores, not wives."

Before Balian could respond, there was a commotion at the end of the table; a nervous servant had dropped a tureen of soup. Philippe's mouth thinned, but he kept his temper under a tight rein, for a boy's clumsiness was a small sin when he was facing such monumental challenges. Absently crumbling a piece of bread into small pellets, he studied his dinner guests. Aside from Conrad of Montferrat, Balian d'Ibelin, and Leopold von Babenberg, they were French lords and bishops, men who'd done homage to him, men he ought to be able to trust. But could he?

His cousin Robert de Dreux had been monopolizing the conversation, but Philippe permitted it because Robert was being highly critical of the English king, implying that there was something very suspicious about Richard's ongoing communications with their Saracen foes. "Look at the way they've been exchanging gifts! Since when does a Christian king court the favor of a Saracen infidel?"

Richard had no friends at that table, but this was too much for Balian to resist, for he had a highly developed sense of mischief. "I heard that Richard sent Saladin a captured Turkish slave," he said in conspiratorial tones. "But is it true that Saladin sent Richard snow and fruit when he was ailing? Snow and fruit—no wonder you are so mistrustful, my lord count."

Robert de Dreux regarded him warily, not sure if he was being mocked or not. Balian seemed to be supporting him, his expression open and earnest. But he was a *poulain*, the vaguely disparaging term used for those Franks born in Outremer, and that was enough to raise doubts in Robert's mind about Balian's sincerity.

Philippe set down his wine cup with a thud, sorely tempted to tell his dolt of a cousin that he was being ridiculed. He did not, though, for he would need Robert's support once word broke of his intent to leave Outremer. But would he get it? Robert's brother Beauvais had reacted much more negatively than he'd expected, for the bishop was the most cynical soul he'd ever met. So had Hugh of Burgundy. He was studying the other men at the table, trying to determine which ones were likely to balk, like Beauvais and Hugh, when there was a stir by the door. A moment later, Philippe was bitterly regretting having agreed to cede security to the Templars, for their white-clad knights were making no attempt whatsoever to stop the English king from barging into the hall, as arrogantly as if he thought all of Acre was his.

Conrad and Balian stiffened at the sight of the de Lusignans, and Leopold shoved back his chair, regarding the English king with frozen fury. The other guests were bewildered by this intrusion, looking to their king for guidance. Philippe half rose, then sank back in his seat, struggling to get his emotions under control, for he knew he must be icy-calm to deal with this crisis. It would not be easy, though; his hands involuntarily clenched into fists as Richard strode toward the high table. He was expecting an immediate verbal onslaught, but Richard had another strategy in mind.

"My lord king." Richard's greeting was gravely courteous, even deferential, as befitting a vassal to his liege lord, a tone he'd rarely if ever adopted in the past with Philippe. After politely acknowledging Conrad, Balian, and the French barons, but not Leopold, he offered an apology for interrupting their dinner. "Alas, this could not wait. We needed to speak with you as soon as possible," he said, gesturing toward the men who'd followed him into the hall. "We've come to ask you to reconsider your decision to return to France, for if you leave, our chances of recovering Jerusalem will be grievously damaged."

The last part of his sentence went unheard, drowned out in the ensuing uproar. All eyes fastened upon Philippe, midst exclamations of shock and anger. Conrad rose so quickly that his chair overturned. "What nonsense is this?" he snarled at Richard. "The French king would never abandon us!" Not all of the French barons were as sure of that as he was, though, unnerved by Philippe's white-lipped silence and the fact that so many highborn lords and prelates had accompanied the English king, backing up his contention by their very presence.

"I would that were true," Richard assured Conrad, managing to sound both sincere and sorrowful. "But the Duke of Burgundy and the Bishop of Beauvais say otherwise. Nothing would give me greater joy than to be told they are mistaken.

Are they, my lord king?" He turned his gaze back to Philippe, his expression hopeful, his eyes gleaming.

Philippe reached for his wine cup and drank, not for courage, but to help him swallow the bile rising in his throat. "I have no choice," he said, very evenly, determined not to let Richard bait him into losing his temper. "My health has been dangerously impaired by my recent illness and my doctors tell me that if I do not return to my own realm for treatment, it might well cost my life."

"Indeed?" Richard's eyebrows rose in surprise. "I was told that your illness was not as serious as my own bout with Arnaldia." He left it for their audience to draw the obvious conclusion—that he'd nearly died and all knew it, yet he was not renouncing their holy cause.

Philippe realized how lame his health excuse would sound. But what else could he offer? He could not very well admit that his concern over securing possession of Artois mattered more than the liberation of Jerusalem or that he'd loathed every moment of every day since his arrival in Outremer and could not abide the prospect of months, even years, in the English king's company. "My doctors insist that I have no choice but to return to France. Lest you forget, my lord Richard, my heir is a young child, often ailing. If I die in the Holy Land, my realm would be thrown into turmoil."

Richard was thoroughly enjoying himself by now. "Your worries about your heir are understandable," he said sympathetically, one king to another. "I have concerns about mine, too." Looking around the hall, he saw that Philippe was utterly isolated; even his own men were staring at him in stunned disbelief. Dropping the pretense of commiseration, then, he went in for the kill, his tone challenging, blade-sharp. "It is no easy thing to take the cross, nor is it meant to be. It is a burden that all true Christians willingly accept, even if they must make the ultimate sacrifice for Our Lord Christ. You took a holy vow to recover Jerusalem from Saladin, not to assist in Acre's fall and then go home once you lost interest. How will you explain your failure to your subjects? To God?"

Philippe's eyes had narrowed to slits, hot color staining his face and throat. "You are not the one to lecture others about holy oaths!" he spat, unable to contain himself any longer. "Time and time again you swore to wed my sister, lying to my face whilst you were conniving behind my back to marry Sancho of Navarre's daughter!"

For the moment, all the others were forgotten, and it was as if they were the only two men in the hall, in the world, so intense was the hostility that scorched between them. "If you want to discuss the reason why I refused to marry your sister, I am quite willing to do so," Richard warned. "But do you truly want to go down that road, Philippe?"

The French king did not, regretting the words as soon as they were out of his mouth. But memories of the bitter confrontation in Messina had come flooding back, memories of that humiliating defeat at this man's hands. He felt like that now, well aware that Richard had their audience on his side, just as he had in that wretched Sicilian chapel. "You want me to stay in Outremer?" he said, his voice thickening, throbbing with fury. "I will disregard my doctors' advice and do so— provided that you honor the agreement we made in Messina. We swore that we would divide equally all that we won, did we not? Yet you have not done so."

"What are you talking about? I even gave you a share of my sister's dower and you had no right whatsoever to that!"

"But not Cyprus!" Philippe was on his feet now, sure that he'd found a way to put Richard in the wrong. "I am entitled to half of Cyprus by the terms of our Messina pact. Dare you deny it?"

"Damned right I do! I took Cyprus only because I was forced to it, because Isaac Comnenus—the Duke of Austria's illustrious kinsman—threatened my sister, my betrothed, and my men. It was never part of our pact, which was to share what we conquered in the Holy Land." Richard paused for breath, and then smiled, the way he did on the battlefield when he saw a foe's vulnerability. "If you want to expand the terms of our agreement, though, so be it. If it will keep you in Outremer, I will give you half of Cyprus." He paused again, this time to savor the expression of shock on Philippe's face. "But that means you must share the lands you inherited from the Count of Flanders. It is only fair—one-half of Cyprus for one-half of Artois."

"Never!"

"Now why does that not surprise me?" Richard jeered. "You care nothing for our holy quest, care for nothing but profit. You may have the blood of kings in your veins, but you have the soul of a merchant, Philippe Capet, and now all know it."

"And what do you care about, my lord Lionheart? Your 'holy quest' is not for God, it is for your own glory and fame! Nothing matters to you but winning renown for yourself on the battlefield. For that you'd sacrifice anything or anyone, as the men foolish enough to follow you will soon find out."

"Shall we put that to the test?" Richard spun around, pointing toward the Bishop of Beauvais and the Duke of Burgundy. "Let's begin with your messengers. It is no secret that there is no love lost between us, and I daresay they also believe that I hunger only for personal glory. But you both told me that you mean to honor your vows. Is that not so?"

Neither man looked pleased to be singled out like this. They did not hesitate, though, each one confirming that he did indeed intend to remain in Outremer. Although inwardly he was seething, Philippe showed no reaction, for he'd been braced for their defection. Yet what happened next caught him off balance. Richard turned to Philippe's guests, the barons, knights, and bishops who owed fealty to the French king.

"What about the rest of you? Are you going to follow your king back to Paris? Or will you follow me to Jerusalem?"

Some glanced toward Philippe, despairing. Some averted their eyes. But when Mathieu de Montmorency shouted out "Jerusalem," the cry burst from other throats, too, sweeping the table and then the hall. One by one, they rose to their feet, as much a public repudiation of Philippe as it was an affirmation of their faith, all orchestrated by the English king. At least that was how Philippe would remember it, till the day he drew his last mortal breath.

BERENGARIA PROPPED HERSELF up on her elbow, regarding her husband quizzically, for he usually fell asleep soon after their love-making. Tonight, though, he was not only wakeful, but talkative, too, and for more than an hour he'd been giving her a dramatic account of his confrontation with the French king, interspersing the narrative with acerbic comments about Philippe's manifold failings, both as a man and monarch. Berengaria was very pleased that he was willing to discuss the day's astounding developments with her, and greatly shocked by Philippe's decision to abandon the crusade, so she was an ideal audience for Richard's tirade, convinced that he was utterly in the right, even if he had not been completely candid about his intentions in Cyprus.

After a while, though, she began to realize that there was more than anger fueling his harangue. Putting her hand on his arm, she could feel the coiled tension in his muscles. "Richard . . . I understand why you are wroth with Philippe. But surely it must be a relief, too, to know that you'll not have to put up with his slyness and ill will, especially since the rest of the French are staying on. So why are you not better pleased that you are now in sole command of the Christian forces?"

"Yes, I will be glad to be rid of Philippe," he admitted. "Having him for an ally made me feel like a cat with a hammer tied to its tail. The problem, Berenguela, is that he is utterly untrustworthy. He is not returning because he is ailing. He is going back to try to wrest Flanders from Baudouin of Hainaut. And then he will start casting covetous eyes toward my domains, toward the Vexin and Normandy."

"But the lands of a man who's taken the cross are inviolable. Surely the Pope would excommunicate him for so great a sin?"

"In a perfect world, yes. In ours, I'm not so sure."

"How could the Holy Father not act, Richard? The Papal See has always given its full protection to men who go on pilgrimage. How shameful it would be if the Church let harm come to their lands or families whilst they are fighting for the Lord Christ in the Holy Land!"

He smiled at her vehemence. "You'll get no argument from me, little dove. I hope the new Pope feels as strongly as you do about the Church's duty to defend those who've taken the cross. All I can do from Acre, though, is send word to my mother and Bishop Longchamp, warning them there'll soon be a French wolf on the prowl."

She looked at him unhappily. It was so unfair that he must worry about Philippe's treachery whilst all of Christendom expected him to be the savior of the Holy City. He seemed to sense her distress, for he reached over and took her hand. But that reassuring gesture brought tears to her eyes. He'd lost his fingernails during his illness, and while he'd acted as if it were a minor matter, the sight of his injured fingers reminded her how very close he'd come to death.

She did her best now to hide her concern, for even her brief experience as a wife had taught her that men did not want to be fussed over. There were several copper-colored hairs on the pillow and she tried to brush them away before he noticed, remembering what Joanna had said about his vanity. She only succeeded in calling his attention to them. "That's odd," he mused. "Henri said he did not begin to lose his hair for nigh on two months after his illness. I wonder if I'm starting early."

She was surprised that he sounded so matter-of-fact. "It does not trouble you, Richard . . . losing your hair?"

"Well, it will if it does not grow back," he said with a smile. "And in all honesty, I'd not have been happy if this happened ere an important event like my coronation or our wedding. I doubt that my crown would have looked quite as impressive if I'd been bald as an egg. But if I have to lose my hair, there is not a better time for it than now. I'm not likely to be looking into any mirrors whilst campaigning."

He laughed then, as if at some private memory. "Soldiers have many vices, but vanity is not amongst them. How could it be? What man is going to worry about his hair when he might lose his head?" Too late, he caught her look of alarm, and to divert her thoughts from the dangers he'd be facing, he said quickly, "It is hard for a woman to understand what campaigning is like, Berenguela. It is a much simpler life we lead. We have to make do without luxuries like this. . . ." He patted their feather mattress. "Or this . . ." he added, cupping her breast. "We eat what can be cooked over campfires. We usually have to bathe in cold water, so it does not take long until we're all stinking like polecats. We'll bring along some laundresses, so at least our clothes will get washed occasionally, and they'll do their best to keep us from getting too lice-ridden. But you can be sure I'll not be looking like that splendid peacock who bedazzled Isaac Comnenus and the Cypriots!"

He laughed again, but Berengaria was dismayed by the image now taking root in her mind. Was it not enough that men must put their lives at risk? Must they endure so much discomfort, too? "Richard, that sounds dreadful!"

"No," he said, "it is not. It is a soldier's life, no more, no less. Do you want the truth, little dove? I love it. It is the world I've known since I was fifteen, the only world I've wanted to know."

She sat up, forgetting to tuck the sheet around her, so intent was she upon what he'd just said. "Why do you love it, Richard?"

"The challenge. I love that, being able to test myself, to prove that I'm the best. Not because I am Henry Fitz Empress's son or because I wear a crown. Because I can wield a sword with greater skill than other men. Because I have worked to perfect those skills for nigh on twenty years. Because when I'm astride Fauvel, I feel as if we're one and he does, too. Because I can see things on the field that other men do not. Sometimes it seems as if I know what a man is going to do ere he does himself. And when the fighting is done, I know that I'm the best because I've earned it."

"Are you never afraid?"

He didn't answer her at once, considering the question. "I suppose so, though it is hard to tell fear from excitement. But I've known for a long time that I do not feel the sort of fear that most do, the sort that can cripple a man. Why, I do not know. I just know that I never feel more alive than I do on the battlefield."

He'd surprised himself by his candor, for this was something he'd rarely talked about, even with other soldiers. "Mind you, it is not just blood and gore," he said, striving for a lighter tone. "It is the companionship, too, the unique bond you forge with men when you fight together, when you know that they'd risk their lives for you and you for them. Jesu, it is so different from the royal court! And since I am being so honest about it, yes, it is for the glory, too. What Philippe cannot understand is that the glory is only part of it."

Berengaria did not know if she'd ever understand fully, either. But she was enthralled by this intimate glimpse into his very soul, for it confirmed what she'd begun to believe, that God had chosen him for this sacred purpose, blessing him with the exceptional abilities he'd need to recover Jerusalem from the infidels. "I would have been ashamed today had I been Philippe's queen," she said at last. "But I am proud to be your wife, Richard, very proud."

He reached out, pulled her down into his arms. "Joanna says I do not deserve you, and she's probably right. I know I'm not the easiest of men to live with. I can promise you this much, little dove. I'll always try to do right by you." He kissed her then, his mouth hot and demanding, and when he rolled on top of her, she wrapped her arms around his back, hoping that the Almighty would smile upon them, that on this special night Richard's seed would take root in her womb. For how fitting that their son should be conceived in Acre, the first of his father's conquests in the Holy Land.

CHAPTER 23

JULY 1191

Acre, Outremer

onrad deliberately kept his distance, for he was sorely tempted to lay rough hands upon the other man. "And that is it? You leave me clinging to the cliff's edge and just walk away?"

Philippe regarded him coldly. "You have not been turned out to beg your bread by the side of the road, Conrad. A sizable French contingent is remaining in Outremer." His jaw clenched at that, for he'd not expected such mass defections. Only his cousins, the Bishop of Chartres and the Count of Nevers, had agreed to return with him to France; the rest were so determined to honor their oaths that they were even willing to fight under Richard's command. "The war goes on," he said tersely, "so I do not see why you have cause for complaint."

"Do you not? With Richard as my sworn enemy, what chance do I have of gaining the crown now?"

"And why is he your 'sworn enemy'? Because you were foolish enough to deny him entry into Tyre. Are you so surprised that you reap what you sow?"

"I would never have done that had I thought you were going to creep away like a thief in the night!"

Philippe's fury was all the greater because he knew this was what others were thinking; Conrad was just the only one who dared to say it to his face. But he had no intention of letting himself be swayed by their condemnation; the sooner he was out of this hellhole and on his way home, the better. "You are right about Richard," he said, with grim satisfaction. "He is not a man to forget a wrong done him. So I would suggest that you waste no time seeking him out. If you humbly beg his pardon for having offended him, he may forgive you—or not. In either case, it is no longer my concern."

Conrad yearned to wrap his hands around the French king's throat and squeeze. He managed to hold on to the last shreds of his self-control as Philippe brushed past him and walked to the door, not once looking back—as if he were already forgotten, of no consequence. After the door closed, he erupted and cleared the table with a wild sweep of his arm, sending goblets, flagon, and tray flying. He could take no pleasure, though, in the damage done, for the costly glassware belonged to the Templars, not Philippe.

THE CITADEL'S GREAT HALL was crowded with men. Conrad's face was stony, his body rigid with rage, but he showed no hesitation, striding toward the dais with a firm step, his head high. As he knelt before Richard, a murmur swept the hall, for few had ever expected to see the proud Marquis of Montferrat abase himself in public. Henri watched with a frown, wishing it had not come to this. He knew Richard was taking satisfaction from Conrad's submission, but as badly as he took losing, he was usually a gracious winner, and his demeanor was regal this day, his expression impossible to read. The de Lusignans were not as diplomatic; Guy and his brothers and his nephew Hugh had gathered by the dais, openly exulting in their enemy's humiliation. Henri found their gloating distasteful. He respected Joffroi and Amaury de Lusignan, even if he did not like them, for they were good soldiers and not as lacking in common sense as Guy. He did not fault Guy's courage, but courage alone did not make a man fit to rule, and in his opinion, Guy could not be forgiven for the debacle at Ḥaṭṭīn.

"I want to talk to you." Balian d'Ibelin materialized at his side and jerked his head toward a side door. Following after him, Henri emerged into a courtyard aglow with sunlight, the morning already promising blazing heat. He perched on the edge of the fountain, but Balian was pacing, unable to keep still. Henri had known few men as easygoing as Balian; he could not remember ever seeing his friend truly angry. He was certainly angry now, though, all but giving off sparks, a banked fire suddenly roaring into full blaze.

"I want you to tell me why," he said, and even his usual lazy drawl was gone, his words sharp enough to cut.

"The de Lusignans are Richard's vassals back in Poitou. He felt obligated to—"

"Ballocks! We both know he supported Guy because the French king supported Conrad. Just as we know Philippe backed Conrad because he was sure Richard would back Guy. No wonder it took them so long to reach Outremer, given how many old grievances they were dragging along. My question was for you, Henri. Why did you switch sides? When you arrived last year, you allied yourself with Conrad, not Guy. What changed your mind?"

"Richard."

Balian studied him. "The money he gave you?"

That brought Henri to his feet; Balian might be a friend but that did not mean he could offer insults with impunity. "You know me better than that, or at least I thought you did. My honor is not for sale. Richard wants Guy as king, not Conrad, and I want what Richard does. It is as simple as that. Nor am I the only one to have a change of heart. The Knights Hospitaller did, too, and for the same reason. Richard is the man with the best chance of defeating Saladin and recapturing the Holy City. Can you deny it?"

"No. He may well retake Jerusalem. But what happens then? He goes home. So do you, Henri. So do all of you, leaving us to hold on to what you've won. Now you tell me this. Who has the best chance of that? Conrad? Or the hero of Ḥaṭṭīn?"

Henri's defensiveness ebbed away. "We forget sometimes," he conceded, "that Outremer is more than the Holy Land. For you, it is home. I'll admit Conrad would make a better king than Guy. But I've already tried to persuade Richard of that, tried and failed. What more would you have me do?"

"On the morrow, Conrad and Guy are to argue their claims before the two kings and the high court of Outremer. Conrad fears that he will not get a fair hearing and Richard may even seek to take Tyre away from him. Men respect you, Henri. God knows why, but they do," Balian added, with a glimmer of his usual humor. "Conrad needs someone to speak up for him. I am asking you to be that man."

Henri started to say that Philippe would surely do so, if only to thwart Richard. Yet who'd listen to him now that he'd besmirched his honor? "I doubt that they'll heed me," he said at last. "But I will do what I can." And Balian had to be content with that, a reluctant promise from a man young enough to have been his son.

———

GUY HAD ARGUED that a crowned and anointed king could not be deposed without offending the Almighty, and Conrad had countered that Guy's claim died with Sybilla, and the rightful Queen of Jerusalem was now his wife, Isabella. They'd then withdrawn reluctantly while their fate was decided by the English and French kings and the lords and prelates of Outremer.

It was now late afternoon and it was obvious to all that they'd reached an impasse, for Richard wanted Guy, and Philippe wanted Conrad, and neither one was willing to compromise. Frustrated and angry, their throats sore from shouting, their tempers just as raw, the men finally agreed to pause in their deliberations, sending out for food and wine. The fruit, bread, and cheese went largely untouched, but the wine was disappearing at an alarming rate. Just what they needed, Henri brooded, for if the debate had been so rancorous whilst they were sober, it might even turn violent once they were in their cups.

Balian had made a passionate speech on Conrad's behalf, but he'd been shouted down by Guy's partisans, as had Renaud, the Lord of Sidon. And when Garnier de Nablus, the Grand Master of the Knights Hospitaller, had spoken up for Guy, Conrad's supporters responded just as rudely. The men had paid the two kings the respect due their rank by hearing their arguments without such heckling, but it was obvious to Henri that neither Richard nor Philippe had changed any minds. And although he'd deliberately not glanced in Balian's direction, he could feel the older man's dark eyes upon him, silently reminding him of his promise.

Setting down his wine cup, he sought out the most respected of the prelates, the Archbishop of Tyre. Joscius was acclaimed for his powers of persuasion, having managed the miracle of getting both Philippe and Richard's father, Henry, to take the cross; Henri wanted to draw upon his eloquence in support of a compromise, assuming he could manage a miracle of his own and turn two balky royal mules into docile beasts of burden. Joscius was one of Conrad's adherents, but he was a realist, too. After getting his assent, Henri squared his shoulders, then crossed the hall and asked for a private word with Richard.

As soon as they'd settled into a window alcove, Henri said bluntly, "Uncle, I suspect that you'll eventually prevail, but it is likely to be a Pyrrhic victory. Conrad is not one to slink away with his tail between his legs. Whatever we agree here, he is not going to put aside his claim to the crown—"

"What claim?" Richard said scornfully. "He abducted Isabella, plain and simple, then forced her to wed him even though he had left a wife behind in Constantinople. But in the eyes of God, she is still wed to Humphrey de Toron. Moreover, the marriage is invalid because it is incestuous as well as adulterous—Conrad's brother was once wed to Isabella's sister Sybilla, and that relationship alone would damn their union under canon law."

Henri waited patiently until Richard paused for breath. "I agree the marriage is dubious at best. But it is a done deed and none of your fuming is going to change that. Have you asked yourself why so many highborn lords and churchmen were willing to swallow such a bitter brew? I know—you'll say some were bribed. Mayhap that is true, but it is also true that they were desperate to pry the crown away from Guy, and who can blame them? Would you want to follow the man who'd led them to the Horns of Ḥaṭṭīn?"

Richard's silence told Henri that he would not. Before he could shift the strategic ground from a defense of Guy to an attack on Conrad, Henri said quickly, "Conrad's friends do not believe your concern for Isabella is genuine. I know it is. They forget that you have more reason than any man in this hall to be protective of Isabella, for she and your father had the same grandfather, Count Fulk of Anjou. But it is too late to save your cousin from a marriage she did not want, Uncle. By seeking to punish Conrad after the fact, you'll only be depriving her of her birthright—the crown of Jerusalem."

Richard frowned, for he'd never considered it in that light. "I cannot just abandon Guy," he said, "for whether I like him or not, I am his liege lord and owe him my protection."

"I know. I also know that the de Lusignans are no more likely than Conrad to accept defeat with goodwill, and nothing could be more disastrous for Outremer than a civil war. We have to find a way to accommodate them both."

Richard grinned. "Good luck with that! Even if I agree—and you've got the Devil's own tongue, lad—what about Philippe? Since when has he ever listened to common sense or reason?"

"He has his moments," Henri said, which evoked a hoot of skeptical laughter from Richard. Then he squared his shoulders again and strode over to beard the other lion in his den.

Philippe's greeting was decidedly cool. "If you are bearing a message from Richard, I have no interest in hearing it."

Henri ignored the suggestion that he was acting as the English king's lackey. "The message is mine, Uncle. I told him what I am now telling you—that we need to find a compromise, a way to accommodate the claims of both Conrad and Guy. Richard is willing to consider that. It is my hope that you will, too."

"No," Philippe said, and would have turned away had Henri not stood his ground.

"I ask you to hear me out, Uncle, if not for my sake, for my lady mother, your sister."

Philippe was not moved by this appeal to their shared blood; he'd never liked his sister Marie, who'd supported the Count of Flanders in one of his rebellions. "It would be a waste of my time and your breath, Henri. I'll never agree to crown Richard's puppet prince. Go back and tell him that."

"As I said, Uncle, I am not doing Richard's bidding in this. I seek only to patch together a peace between Conrad and Guy, for we have no hope of defeating Saladin unless we do. So I am indeed sorry that you remain so adamant—and somewhat surprised, too, that you'd put Conrad's interests ahead of the needs of France."

Philippe's eyes glittered suspiciously. "And just how am I doing that?"

"I should think it would be obvious," Henri said innocently. "Your doctors insist that you return to your own lands straightaway, for they fear it would be the death of you if you do not, no? But you'll be unable to leave Outremer until this is settled. And you know how stubborn Richard is. He'll never agree to crown Conrad, so this dispute may well drag on for weeks, even months." He was about to remind Philippe that if he could not sail before the autumn, he'd be forced to remain in the Holy Land until the following spring. He saw, though, that there was no need. His uncle's expression was inscrutable, for like Richard, he could wield his court mask as a shield if the need arose. But Henri had caught it, that brief, betraying flicker of alarm, and he hid a triumphant smile, sure now that Philippe would rather spend a year in Purgatory than another month in Acre.

WHEN THE RIVAL CLAIMANTS and their supporters were ushered into the hall, there was a marked difference in their demeanors. Conrad and his men looked tense, the de Lusignans smug. Joanna had seized the opportunity to slip in with them and immediately headed for Henri. Linking her arm in his, she teased, "I do not see any blood on the floor. Does this mean you actually reached a decision acceptable to all?"

"To the contrary," he confided. "We reached one sure to infuriate both sides equally, but that was the best we could do."

Before she could interrogate him further, the Archbishop of Tyre rose from his seat upon the dais and signaled for quiet. "I must insist that you remain silent until I am done. It is the decision of the kings of the English and the French and the high court that Guy de Lusignan shall remain king for the remainder of his life. Upon his death, the crown will pass to the Lady Isabella and her husband, the Marquis of Montferrat. Royal revenues are to be shared equally between King Guy and the marquis. Because the marquis kept Tyre from falling to Saladin, he is to be given hereditary possession of Tyre, Sidon, and Beirut. In recognition of his prowess during the siege, Joffroi de Lusignan is to have Jaffa and Ascalon once they, like Sidon and Beirut, are reclaimed from the Saracens. Should it be God's Will that King Guy, the marquis, and his wife all die whilst King Richard is still in

Outremer, he shall have the right to dispose of the kingdom as he sees fit, by virtue of his blood-kinship to the Lady Isabella."

A faint, sardonic smile tugged at the corner of the archbishop's mouth. "Now," he said dryly, "you may express your admiration at the Solomon-like wisdom of our decision."

Conrad's first reaction was relief that he'd not been cut out entirely as he'd feared, followed by frustration, for how likely was it that he'd outlive his younger rival? Guy looked pleased and then puzzled. "But what if I remarry and have children? Surely they'd take precedence over the marquis's questionable claim."

"No," the archbishop said, allowing himself a hint of satisfaction, "they would not."

Guy gasped. "Are you saying I'll have only a life interest in the crown?"

"That's more than you deserve," Renaud of Sidon said with a sneer, and that was all it took. Both sides began to rail at the unfairness of the terms, exchanging insults and threats with a bitterness that did not bode well for acceptance of the decision. Only Joffroi de Lusignan seemed content with the outcome, watching his brother rave and rant with the detached amusement of a future Count of Jaffa.

Richard finally had to intervene and shout the protests down, with some help from Archbishop Joscius. Philippe paid no heed to the turmoil. Instead he beckoned to Conrad, who obeyed, but took his time in doing so. They conferred for a few moments, and then Philippe rose, getting ready to depart.

Balian at once made his way over to Conrad's side. At his low-voiced query, Conrad leaned closer, saying in the Piedmontese dialect, "Philippe is giving me his half of Acre and his share of the ransom for the Saracen hostages."

Balian was surprised, not having expected such a generous gesture from the French king. "You think Philippe is feeling a pang or two of guilt?"

Conrad gave a snort of disbelief. "Since when are you such an innocent? He did it for one reason and one reason only—in hopes that I will make life as difficult as possible for the English king after he's left Outremer." He looked past Balian then, watching Richard with the single-minded intensity of an archer tracking his target. "And by God, I will do my best to oblige him."

Philippe's knights had reached him by now. But as they turned to go, Richard called out in a loud, commanding tone, "My lord king!" When Philippe halted, he said, "We are not yet done. I assume you remain set upon leaving Acre." He got an almost imperceptible nod in grudging response, and then signaled to André, who came forward with an ivory reliquary. "I must ask then that you swear upon these holy relics that you will honor the protection the Church gives men who've taken the cross, and wage no war against my lands whilst I am doing God's Work in Outremer."

Philippe's eyes, always pale, took on the colorless glaze of winter ice. "Indeed I will not! You insult me by even asking for such an oath."

"I am sorry you take it that way. But I must insist." Richard's face was impassive, but his body language conveyed another message altogether, his legs spread apart, his arms folded across his chest, his very posture a challenge in itself. "If you refuse, you raise some very ugly suspicions. Why would you balk if you do not have evil intent?"

"I 'balk' because I find it offensive that you think there is a need for such an oath!" Glancing around the hall, Philippe saw that once again Richard had managed to get public opinion on his side. Well, so be it! He swung around, intending to stalk out, only to find his path blocked by his own lords.

"You'll shame us all if you refuse," Hugh of Burgundy hissed. "For the love of Christ, take the damned oath!"

"The duke is right, my liege," Jaufre said, with an impressive display of quiet courage. "I am sure you'd never invade the English king's domains whilst he is fighting for the Holy City. But it will look bad if you refuse."

"Take the oath, Uncle," Henri urged, as softly as Jaufre but with less deference. "Not for Richard's sake, for your own. Why plant needless seeds of doubt in other men's minds?"

Philippe looked from one man to another, saw the same grim resolve and defiant disapproval on all their faces. "Very well," he snapped. "I'll take his bloody oath. And you, my lord duke, and you, my lord count, may stand surety for my good faith." Neither Hugh nor Henri appeared happy about that, and he took a small measure of satisfaction in their discomfort. But not enough to compensate for yet one more humiliation inflicted upon him by the accursed English king.

Striding over to André, he made no effort to hide his fury as he placed his hand upon the holy reliquary and swore a solemn oath that he'd do no harm to Richard's lands as long as the other monarch remained in Outremer. After announcing that the Duke of Burgundy and Count of Champagne would act as guarantors, he departed immediately thereafter, as did Conrad and his partisans, followed by the French lords, further evidence of the deep divisions still rending the crusading army.

Henri had remained behind. Seeing that Richard had been cornered by the aggrieved Guy de Lusignan, he came to his uncle's rescue with a fabricated message from Guy's brother Amaury. Richard had been listening to Guy's complaints with rapidly dwindling patience, and sighed with relief as the latter reluctantly went off in search of his kinsman. "The more time I spend with Guy," he muttered, "the more I marvel that my cousin Sybilla stayed loyal to him until the day she died. Neither sister had the best of luck with their husbands, did they?"

Accepting a silver-gilt goblet from a wine bearer, he sprawled in the nearest chair. "Jesu, but I am bone-weary of dealing with all these petty squabbles and rivalries. I have no doubts that Conrad and Guy would rather fight each other than the Saracens." Slanting a fond, playful look toward his nephew, he said, "You need not worry, lad, about standing surety for Philippe. I'll not blame you when he breaks his oath. Hellfire, I'll not even blame Hugh of Burgundy, and blaming Hugh is one of my minor pleasures in life!"

"I assumed you'd not hold me to account," Henri said with a smile, "but I am sure Hugh will be relieved to hear that." Taking a swallow from his own wine cup, he regarded the other man pensively. "Are you so sure, Uncle, that Philippe will wage war upon you? He did swear upon holy relics, albeit after some coaxing."

"He vowed, too, to take the cross and what oath could be more sacred than that?" Richard drained his goblet with a grimace that had nothing to do with the taste of the wine. "If he could not keep faith with God, why would he keep faith with me?"

THE LAST DAY OF JULY was not as oppressively hot, for the Arsuf winds had sprung up, blowing from the south. As Henri and Balian and their men rode through the thronged streets, Henri marveled at the resiliency of this coastal city, already rebounding from nearly two years under siege; signs of economic activity were everywhere, and carpenters and masons had more work than they could handle. As he passed the thriving markets, the crowded bathhouses and brothels, Henri thought it was easy to forget that a bloody war was waiting to resume beyond Acre's newly repaired walls. The same illusory sense of peace prevailed at the citadel. As they entered the great hall, they encountered a scene of domestic tranquility, which Henri had rarely, if ever, associated with his uncle.

Richard and a number of lords were gathered around a table covered with maps, but the presence of women kept the hall from resembling a battle council. Anna was holding court in a window-seat, surrounded by young knights eager to improve her French, under her stepmother's vigilant eye. Mariam was playing chess with Morgan, but the looks they were exchanging indicated another game was under way. Joanna and Berengaria were chatting with the Bishop of

Salisbury, while the palace cooks hovered nearby, waiting to discuss the week's menu. There were even dogs underfoot, Joanna's Sicilian cirnecos mingling warily with Jacques d'Avesnes's huge Flemish hounds. All that was lacking were a few wailing babes or shrieking children, Henri thought, feeling an unexpected yearning for the cool greenwoods and lush vineyards of his native Champagne.

To Balian, there was no incongruity between this serene family tableau and the coming brutal campaign, for the *poulains* knew no other way of life; they never forgot the precarious nature of their hold upon this ancient land as sacred to Islam as it was to Christianity. He was more concerned with the unwelcoming expression on the English king's face. "I knew this was a mistake, Henri. I ought not to have let you talk me into it."

"It was not a mistake," Henri insisted. "Give me a moment and I'll prove it." Taking Balian over to introduce him to Joanna and Berengaria, he left his friend exchanging pleasantries with the women and hastened toward Richard, who was moving to intercept him, scowling. Before his uncle could challenge Balian's presence, he took the offensive. "Yes, Balian d'Ibelin is Conrad's adviser and friend. In fact, they are kin by marriage since Isabella is Balian's stepdaughter. But I invited him here because you said you wanted to learn more of Saracen battle tactics and he is the ideal teacher. Not only did he grow to manhood fighting the Turks and often distinguished himself in combat, he was at Ḥaṭṭīn."

"So were Guy and Humphrey de Toron."

"Despite his training as a knight, Humphrey is no soldier. As for Guy, I suppose his experience could be useful—note whatever he advises and then do the opposite."

Richard could not dispute Henri's barbed assessment of Guy and Humphrey. Nor were there that many Ḥaṭṭīn veterans available for questioning, for hundreds had been slain on the field and the best fighters, the Templars and Hospitallers, had all died after the battle, executed by Saladin. "Well, as long as he's here . . ." he said ungraciously and Henri went off, grinning, to fetch Balian.

Several hours later, Richard was glad he'd heeded his nephew. He was still mistrustful of Balian, who was too close to Conrad for his comfort and who was wed to a woman who could teach Cleopatra about conniving, Maria Comnena, a daughter of the Greek Royal House and former Queen of Jerusalem. But he'd forgotten about Balian's dangerous Greek wife once the *poulain* began to talk about war in Outremer.

Balian confirmed all that Richard had been told about Turkish battle tactics. "The Saracens do not fight like the Franks," he said, speaking to Richard as one soldier to another while ignoring the hostile glares he was getting from Guy. "They know they cannot withstand a charge by armed knights, and so they do their best to avoid it. They remain at a distance, for they have mastered a skill unknown to Franks—they can shoot a bow from horseback, on the run. When our knights attack, they retreat and regroup. When Franks are on the march, they swarm us like black flies, bite, and flit out of reach, again and again until our knights are so maddened they can endure it no longer. They break formation and charge, which is what the Saracens have been waiting for. Indeed, they are most dangerous when they appear to be in retreat, for too often our men lose all caution in the excitement of the chase, and by the time they realize they have been lured into an ambush, it is too late."

"I've been told they ride as if they've been born in the saddle."

"You've been told true, my lord king. They are fine horsemen and the horses they breed are as good as any to be found in Christendom. Their steeds are as agile as cats, as swift as greyhounds, and because their armor is lighter than ours, they can outrun us with infuriating ease."

Richard nodded, remembering how Isaac Comnenus had outdistanced them again and again, invincible as long as he was mounted on Fauvel. "If they are not as well armored as our knights, then we'd have the advantage in hand-to-hand combat. So the key to victory would be to hold back until we are sure we can fully engage them."

"Just so," Balian agreed. "But few commanders can exert that sort of control over their men. Even such disciplined warriors as the Templars have been known to break ranks under constant attack by mocking foes who hover just out of range, such tempting targets that they can no longer resist hitting back."

"Tell us more about their armor," Richard directed, and Balian did, thinking that at least this arrogant English king was willing to learn about his foes; all too often, newcomers to Outremer assumed that, just as theirs was the one true religion, so, too, were they inherently superior to infidel Turks on the battlefield.

They stopped to eat when Garnier de Nablus arrived, and then began to study a map of the route Richard intended to take once they rode out of Acre, along the coast south toward Jaffa. Jacques d'Avesnes had been in Outremer long enough to have heard a number of legends and folklore, and when Baldwin de Bethune asked about a river marked on the map, Jacques was only too happy to share one of the more lurid stories. It was called "Crocodile River," he declared, in memory of two knights attacked and eaten by crocodiles when they'd been foolhardy enough to go swimming. The joke was on Jacques, though, for what he'd assumed to be a myth turned out to be true; Balian and Guy confirmed the origin of the name and that there were indeed such creatures lurking in that river. None of Richard's men had ever seen a crocodile, and after hearing a description of these fearsome beasts, they were quite content to keep it that way. Only Richard was intrigued, wondering how one could be killed, and his friends exchanged glances, hoping they'd not be asked to accompany him on his crocodile hunt.

They moved on to a discussion of the man who stood between them and the recovery of Jerusalem. Balian knew the sultan far better than anyone Richard had met until now, and he pelted the *poulain* lord with questions. Was it true Saladin was a Kurd? That he had more than a dozen sons? That Saladin was not really his name? Balian was quite willing to satisfy his curiosity, for he was always pleased when European Franks showed themselves open to learning about his homeland. Saladin was indeed a Kurd, not a Turk or Arab, he confirmed, and Kurdish was his native tongue, although he was also fluent in Arabic. He might well have that many sons, for Muslims had multiple wives and *harims* as well. And Saladin was a misnomer, referring to one of his *laqabs*, or titles, Salah al-Dīn, which translated as "Righteousness of the Faith." In the same way, the Franks called his brother "Saphadin," a contraction of one of his titles. Saif al-Dīn or "The Sword of Religion." But the Saracens knew him as al-Malik al-'Ādil. "Their *isms* or given names, what we'd call their 'Christian names,'" he said with a grin, "are Yusef and Ahmad. So the greatest of all Muslim rulers bears the biblical name of Joseph!"

Richard and his friends were astonished that Saladin shared the name of a revered Christian saint. But when Balian began to explain that Muslims did not consider Christians to be outright pagans, calling them and Jews "People of the Book," Guy could keep quiet no longer. He'd been fuming in silence, deeply offended by Balian's presence in their midst, and now he gave an exclamation of mock surprise, marveling that Balian seemed so knowledgeable about such an accursed religion. "Your good friend Renaud of Sidon speaks Arabic well enough to read that blasphemous book of theirs and men have long suspected him of secretly converting to their vile faith. I wonder now if you, too, were tempted to apostasy during your many visits to Saladin's court."

The other men tensed, for such an insult could well have led to killing back in their homelands. Balian merely smiled. "How kind of you to worry about the state of my soul, my lord Guy. No, I have not embraced Islam. And whilst I have indeed often visited the sultan's court, it was always as an emissary, as when I was seeking to save Jerusalem after your defeat at Ḥaṭṭīn. I must admit that Saladin has never failed to show me great hospitality, as he does to all his foes. He told me that when you were brought to his tent after the battle, he offered you a cool drink and felt the need to reassure you that you would not be harmed, saying that 'Kings do not kill other kings' since you were so obviously distraught and in fear of your life."

That was a memory still haunting Guy's sleep. He jumped to his feet, his hand dropping to the hilt of his sword. But Richard had anticipated that, for Guy's was an easy face to read, and he clamped his hand down on the other man's wrist before he could unsheathe his blade. "I would take it greatly amiss if you were to shed blood in front of my wife and sister," he said, sounding like a host rebuking a guest for a lapse of manners; his fingers, though, were digging into Guy's flesh with enough force to leave bruises.

Balian was on his feet now, too. "I think it is time I departed, my lord," he was saying calmly, when a knight burst into the hall, calling out for the king.

Recognizing one of the Préaux brothers, Richard gestured for him to approach. "What have you come to tell me, Guilhem?"

Guilhem knelt, struggling to catch his breath. "My liege, the French king is gone! He and the marquis sailed for Tyre within the hour."

Good riddance, Richard thought, but he contented himself with saying only that the French king's departure was hardly a surprise. "I did not know he'd planned to leave today, but I suppose he decided to take advantage of the Arsuf winds."

"Sire, you do not understand," Guilhem burst out, his the unhappiness of a man forced to bring his king very unwelcome tidings. "He took with him the most important of his Saracen hostages!"

"He did what?" Richard drew an audible breath, then whirled to face Balian. "Did you know about this treachery?" Balian swore he had not and Richard grudgingly gave him the benefit of the doubt. If the man had known about this latest double-dealing by Philippe and Conrad, he'd hardly have come willingly to the citadel, after all. By now others were clustering around them, all talking at once, but the men parted to allow Richard's queen to pass through.

"My lord husband, what is wrong?"

"Philippe has stolen some of the hostages." Seeing, then, that she did not understand the significance of the French king's action, he added, "I have to be able to turn over all of the hostages to Saladin upon payment of the ransom. I cannot very well do that if they are thirty miles up the coast at Tyre."

Berengaria was loath to believe that a Christian king would deliberately sabotage their pact with Saladin, even one as untrustworthy as Philippe. "Why would he do that, Richard?" she asked softly. Few people had ever awakened his protective instincts, but in the face of such innocence, he found himself wanting to shield her from the wickedness of the world and he made an effort to master his fury, saying that it was doubtless a misunderstanding of some sort.

It was obvious to Berengaria that this was far more serious than a mere "misunderstanding," but she realized that Richard was trying to spare her worry and so she acted as though she believed him. By now Joanna had joined them, and as soon as she was alone with her sister-in-law, she said quietly, "This was done with malice and evil intent, was it not?"

Joanna nodded grimly. "Philippe's parting gift to Richard—a well-placed dagger in the back."

PHILIPPE STAYED IN TYRE only two days and then sailed for home, leaving the hostages in Conrad's custody. Midst all the turmoil over the French king's repudiation of his crusader's vows, few noticed when the Duke of Austria also sailed for Tyre. Unlike Philippe, Leopold had been a fervent crusader; this was his second visit to the Holy Land. But now he turned his back upon Outremer and returned to his own lands, bearing a very bitter grievance.

CHAPTER 24

AUGUST 1191

The Citadel, Acre

ichard ran his hand lightly over the stallion's withers and back, smiling when Fauvel snorted. "You want to run, I know. Mayhap later," he promised, reaching for a curry comb. The horse's coat shone even in the subdued lighting of the stable, shot through with chestnut highlights. It was an outrage to think of Isaac Comnenus astride this magnificent animal. "Of course it could have been worse," he assured the destrier, "for at least Isaac could ride. What if you'd belonged to the French king? Not that he'd have ever had the ballocks to mount you."

"*Malik Ric?*"

He swung around, startled, for he'd not heard those soft footsteps in the straw. He liked Anna, admiring the girl's spirit, and he gave her a smile over his shoulder as he began to comb out Fauvel's mane. She overturned an empty water bucket, perching on it as if it were a throne. "Why not let a groom do that?"

"When I was not much younger than you, lass, I asked a knight named William Marshal that very question, and he told me a man ought to know how to take care of what was his. I suppose it stuck with me." After a comfortable silence, he confided, "Also, it helps to get him familiar with my scent, and takes my mind off my troubles."

"What troubles?"

"The missing hostages, for one. I sent the Bishop of Salisbury and the Count of Dreux to Tyre to bring them back to Acre, but they've not returned yet. Negotiations with Saladin, for another. He has been harder to pin down than a river eel," he added darkly, for the delay in satisfying the terms of the surrender was sowing more and more suspicions in his mind. Setting the comb aside, he looked around for his hoof pick. Finding it on a nearby bench, he turned back toward Fauvel, only to halt in horror, for Anna was no longer sitting at a safe distance; she was in the stall now with the stallion, a battlefield destrier bred for his fiery temperament.

"Anna, do not make any sudden moves. Slowly back out of the stall."

She looked astonished, and then amused. "No danger! Fauvel . . . he knows me," she insisted, and held out her hand. The horse's nostrils quivered and then he plucked the lump of crystallized sugar from her palm, as delicately as a pet dog accepting a treat from a doting mistress.

Richard exhaled a deep breath, for he of all men knew the damage a destrier could inflict upon human flesh and bones. "Do not push your luck, lass," he warned, torn between anger and relief. "Stallions are as unpredictable as women. I'd rather not have to tell my wife and sister that you were trampled into the dust because of my carelessness."

The expression on her face indicated she was clearly humoring him. But after giving Fauvel one last pat, she slipped out of the stall. Taking her place, Richard saw that she'd untied the stallion's halter and he resecured it, swearing under his breath. It was only when she giggled that he realized she'd understood his cursing. "Your French seems to have improved dramatically since we left Cyprus, Anna."

She smiled impishly. "I learn French long ago, when my brother and I are hostages for my papa in Antioch. But after we are set free, he wants us to speak only Greek, so I forget a lot. . . . It comes back now I hear it all the time."

Richard busied himself inspecting Fauvel's legs. When the stallion raised his hoof upon command, he pried manure from the frog with his pick, looking for any cracks or signs of injury. Joanna had told him that Anna occasionally talked about her mother, who'd died when she was six, and her brother, who'd not long survived their arrival on Cyprus, but she never spoke of her father. Richard had no desire whatsoever to discuss Isaac with her. Yet the image of her sneaking into the stables to give treats to her father's stallion was undeniably a poignant one. He supposed he could let her visit Isaac at Margat Castle if it meant so much to her. It would be safe enough to sail up the coast now that Saladin's fleet had been captured at Acre. "Do you miss your father, Anna?" he asked at last, hoping this was not a kindness he'd regret.

"No."

The finality of that answer took him by surprise. He made no comment and, after some moments, she said, "My papa . . . he is good to me. But he is not good to my mama, to Sophia, to others. His anger . . . it scare me sometimes. . . ."

Richard could well imagine it did. What was it Sophia had said at Kyrenia . . . that Anna had not had "an easy life"? His silence was a sympathetic one, but she misread it. "*Malik Ric* . . . you think I am not a . . . a dutiful daughter?"

The incongruity of this conversation was beginning to amuse him. "I'd be the last man in Christendom to lecture you about filial duty, Anna. Ask Joanna sometime about my father and me. As far back as I can remember, we were like flint and tinder."

Pleased that he was not disapproving, she eagerly obeyed when he asked her to hand him a sponge, and watched in fascination as he cleaned around Fauvel's ears and muzzle, for she could not imagine Isaac ever grooming his own horse. "May I ask you, *Malik Ric*? They say you lead your men south. Why not toward Jerusalem?"

"It is too dangerous to head inland from Acre, lass, and too long, more than one hundred fifty miles through the hills of Ephraim. If we march along the coast toward Jaffa, my fleet can sail with us, carrying all the provisions we'll need. Best of all, Saladin cannot be sure what target I am aiming for, Ascalon or Jerusalem."

When one of his knights entered the stables soon afterward, he found Richard kneeling in the dirt outside Fauvel's stall, drawing a map for Anna with his dagger as he explained that Ascalon controlled the road to Egypt. The man didn't even blink, though, for Richard's men were used to his free and easy ways. "The Duke of Burgundy has arrived, my liege, says he needs to see you straightaway."

Grimacing, Richard got to his feet and started toward the door. When Anna didn't move, he stopped and beckoned. "I'm not about to leave you alone with Fauvel, lass. You might get it into your head to take him for a ride." She widened her eyes innocently, and he smiled. But he made sure she followed after him.

THE DUKE OF BURGUNDY was looking without favor at one of Joanna's cirnecos. When a servant brought in wine and fruit, he grabbed a goblet, draining it in several swallows. Richard leaned back in his seat, watching the older man with speculative eyes. He'd known Hugh for years, but this was the first time he'd ever seen the duke fidgeting like this, obviously ill at ease.

Putting his cup down, Hugh wiped his mouth with the back of his hand. "Will we be ready to head south as soon as Saladin honors the surrender terms?"

"Yes. The ships are loaded already."

"We'll have trouble dragging the men out of the bawdy houses and taverns," Hugh prophesied gloomily. "Half of our men have not drawn a sober breath in weeks, and the other half would be drunken sots, too, if they were not so busy whoring the night away."

Richard was not happy, either, with the drunkenness and debauchery that had ensnared his army after the fall of Acre. He'd never worried about the morals of his men, leaving that to the priests to sort out. But this was no ordinary war and it was unseemly for soldiers of Christ to be sinning so blatantly, for surely such brazen behavior was displeasing to the Almighty. Moreover, it would be no easy task to get their minds focused upon the hard campaign ahead, not after weeks of carousing and self-indulgence. Perversely, though, he refused to admit that he shared Hugh's concern, instead saying flippantly, "Soldiers whoring and drinking? Who'd ever have expected that?"

Hugh scowled, first at Richard and then at the hound sniffing his leg. "Do you think it was wise to accede to Saladin's demand, agreeing to let him pay the money due in three installments? He might well take that as a sign of weakness."

Richard set his own cup down with a thud. "If he does," he said coldly, "he'll soon learn how badly he's misread me. If we'd insisted that all two hundred thousand *dinars* be paid when the True Cross and the Christian prisoners are handed over to us, we would have to release the garrison to Saladin then and there. And how am I to do that when so many of them are still in Tyre? By agreeing to this compromise, I gained us the time we need to pry them away from that whoreson Montferrat, and you well know this, Hugh. You raised no objections at the time. So why are you blathering on about it now? Why are you here? Whatever you've come to say, for Christ's sake, spit it out, man!"

Hugh half rose, then sank back in the chair. "I need money to pay my men. Can I get a loan from you to do that? I'll be able to repay it with our share of the two hundred thousand *dinars*."

"You're saying Philippe sailed off without leaving you the funds to provide for your army?" Richard shook his head in disgust. "Why should that surprise me? But I'd not count upon getting much of that ransom if I were you. Philippe gave his half of Acre and the hostages to Conrad, remember?"

Hugh jumped to his feet. "Are you saying you will not lend me the money?"

Richard did not like it much, but he had no choice under the circumstances. "Will five thousand silver marks be enough?"

"Yes." Looking everywhere but at Richard's face, Hugh mumbled a "Thank you" that sounded as if it were torn from his throat.

"My lord king?" Richard and Hugh had been so intent upon each other that they'd not heard the soft knock upon the door. "The Bishop of Salisbury has just returned from Tyre. Will you see him now?"

"Send him in at once. That is the best news I've heard in weeks."

But Richard's pleasure did not survive his first glimpse of Hubert Walter's face. "I am deeply sorry, my liege," the bishop said somberly, "but we failed. The French king had already sailed, and Conrad was determined to thwart us at every turn. He said he will not return to Acre because he does not trust you. Far worse, he refused to turn the hostages over to us. He said he would agree only if he would get half of the True Cross when we recovered it."

For a rare moment, Richard and Hugh were in total accord, both men infuriated by Conrad's effrontery. "And how are we supposed to recover the True Cross without his accursed hostages?" Richard raged. "But if that is how he wants it, so be it. I will go to Tyre myself, see if he is quite so brave face-to-face."

"My lord, I would advise against that," the bishop said hastily. "Saladin would be only too happy to see us fighting amongst ourselves. The French king led us into this labyrinth, so let the French lead us out. I think the Duke of Burgundy ought to be the one to go to Tyre and confront Conrad. You are the commander of the French forces now," he said, turning his steady gaze upon Hugh. "Are you going to allow the marquis to put the war at risk?"

Hugh's jaw jutted out. "I'll go," he said, and then looked toward Richard, in grudging acknowledgment of the English king's authority now that Philippe had left Outremer.

"Very well. See if you can talk some sense into him. But if he still balks, give him this message from me," Richard said, spacing his words out like gravestones. "Tell him that if I have to come to Tyre to collect the hostages, he'll regret it till the end of his earthly days."

AUGUST 11 was the day when Salah al-Dīn was to turn over the True Cross, the 1,600 Christian prisoners, and the first installment of the two hundred thousand *dinars*. Joanna and Berengaria had ambivalent feelings about this momentous occasion. They rejoiced, of course, in the return of the Cross, in infidel hands since the Battle of Ḥaṭṭīn, and they were glad that so many men would regain their freedom. But the day's events would also bring them one step closer to the resumption of the war, and the women were dreading what was to come—being left isolated at Acre, not knowing from one day to the next if Richard still lived.

There was to be a celebratory feast after the exchange had been made, and they'd borrowed Henri's cook to handle the elaborate menu. But as the hours passed without word, both women began to feel uneasy, sensing that something had gone wrong. Their premonitions were soon confirmed. Richard returned to the citadel in a fury, the men with him just as angry. He was in no mood for a meal or for explanations, saying tersely that Saladin had refused to honor the agreed-upon terms before disappearing into the solar for what was obviously a council of war. Berengaria and Joanna hastily looked around the hall for some-one who could tell them what had happened and would also be willing to discuss military matters with women. They finally decided upon Humphrey de Toron, and he soon found himself out in the courtyard as the sun blazed its farewell arc toward the western horizon.

Berengaria let him escort her to a marble bench, but Joanna couldn't wait. "Richard said you were to interpret for the Saracen envoys, Lord Humphrey, so you must have been in the midst of it all. Was Saladin there? What went amiss?"

"We knew Saladin would not attend, but we'd expected his brother, al-'Ādil, to speak for him. He did not come either, though, which was a pity, for we might have been able to reason with him. As it was, the message Saladin sent was an uncompromising one. He sought to impose new conditions ere he'd fulfill his part of the bargain. He wanted us to free the Acre garrison now instead of waiting until the final two payments were made. King Richard refused."

"What else could he do? The Duke of Burgundy has not returned from Tyre with the hostages yet. Do you think Saladin knew this?"

"I am sure he did, Lady Joanna. Both sides have more spies than a dog has fleas. He offered to provide more hostages if the garrison were freed now, but wanted hostages from us if we insisted upon holding on to the garrison, saying he needed proof that we would indeed free them once all the ransom was paid. Your brother refused this, too. He reminded the sultan that Acre had surrendered to the Christian forces and the loser does not get to dictate terms to the winner. When he demanded that Saladin honor the pact as agreed upon, the Saracens went off to consult with their lord. He sent word back that he was not willing to turn over the Cross, the prisoners, or the money unless we either freed the garri-son now or handed over hostages of our own. After that, the meeting ended in acrimony and mutual accusations of bad faith."

"But we already have Saracen hostages—the Acre garrison," Berengaria pointed out. "It does not make sense to release them and then replace them with other hos-tages. I do not see how that benefits Saladin. Do you, Joanna?"

"No, I do not." Joanna had begun to pace. "But a delay would be very much to his benefit. The longer he can keep Richard and our army at Acre, trying to resolve these issues, the more time he has to refortify the coastal cities and castles. Richard thinks that is his real objective. You know the man, Lord Humphrey. Do you agree?"

As she looked intently into his face, Joanna was struck anew by how very handsome this man was; his dark eyes were wide-set, his skin smooth and clean-shaven, his full mouth shaped for smiles and songs. But he would not make a good husband for a queen; his beauty could not compensate for the lack of steel in his spine. He was a *poulain*, though, born and bred in the harsh splendor of the Holy Land, and she thought that made his opinion worth hearing.

Humphrey seemed to be weighing his words, like a man striving to be fair. "Yes, it is indeed in the sultan's interest to delay as long as possible. He knows how desperately we want the True Cross, and he may well think that we will let him drag the negotiations out because there is so much at stake for us."

Joanna's eyes searched his. "Yet you still say he is a man of honor?"

"I do, my lady," he said firmly, but then he gave her a charming, rueful smile. "But it has been my experience that honor is often the first casualty in war. Saladin deserves our respect, is a finer man in some ways than many of my Christian brethren. He is still our enemy, though, and he is pledged to what they call the 'lesser *jihad*,' war against the infidel. I've always found it interesting that their holy men preach that Muslims who fight in the *jihad* will be granted admission to Paradise, just as the Holy Father promises that those who take the cross will be absolved of their sins."

They both were staring at him. "Surely you are not equating Christianity with beliefs offensive to God?" Berengaria said, with unwonted sharpness in her voice.

"No, of course not, Madame." Humphrey was accustomed to having to offer such reassurances, for his was a world in which intellectual curiosity was not viewed as a virtue, not when both Christians and Muslims were convinced that theirs was the only true faith. "I am simply trying to understand Saracen thinking. We are sure we are doing God's bidding, yet Saladin is sure of that, too. He is not by nature a cruel or heartless man. But he will do what he thinks necessary to expel us from the Holy Land."

"Just as my brother will do what he must to recover Jerusalem," Joanna said proudly. "And he will prevail, for God truly *is* on our side."

The women withdrew soon afterward, leaving Humphrey alone in the court-yard. He wished he could share their certainty. But he did not think Joanna and

Berengaria understood how cleverly the sultan was boxing the Christians in. How could the English king give up an opportunity to recover the True Cross? Saladin could have found no better bait than the holiest relic in Christendom. Yet they could not remain in Acre much longer without jeopardizing the entire campaign. Moreover, if the Saracen garrison were not ransomed, what was to be done with them? He sat down on the rim of the fountain, watching as the sky began to redden. He would normally have taken pleasure in such a splendid sunset, for he had an artist's eye as well as a poet's soul. But tonight he could think only of the day's troubling impasse and the danger it posed to his homeland.

THE NEXT DAY, the Duke of Burgundy returned from Tyre with the rest of the Saracen hostages, Conrad having grudgingly yielded to Hugh's angry denunciations and Richard's ominous threats. Two days later, Richard set up camp outside the city walls. Messages continued to go back and forth between the two sides, but their mutual mistrust prevented them from reaching an accommodation, and the stalemate dragged on.

TUESDAY, AUGUST 20, dawned with brilliant blue skies and sweltering summer heat. The men gathered in Richard's pavilion were already sweating despite the early hour. The waiting had begun to wear upon their nerves, and there were several testy exchanges before Richard took command of the council, demanding silence so he could speak.

"We can wait no longer," he said, pitching his voice so all could hear. "Saladin is playing us for fools. He will continue to delay and equivocate and do all in his power to put off a reckoning, because every day we remain at Acre is a day we've lost and he's won. He is using this stolen time to strengthen Jaffa and Arsuf and Caesarea, and could be expecting reinforcements from Egypt for all we know. In two months the rainy season begins, and I've been told campaigning is well nigh impossible then because the roads turn into quagmires. So if we do not move soon, we risk being anchored at Acre until the spring. You know what a setback like that would do to our army. If we let Saladin outwit us like this, they'll say all those deaths in the past two years had been in vain. They'll be loath to trust us again, and who could blame them?" He did not bother to elaborate, sure that his audience already knew what a detrimental effect a winter at Acre would have upon camp morale. How many would have any stomach for fighting after months of gambling, quarreling, whoring, and drinking?

He paused then, waiting for a response. No one disputed him, though, not even the French lords, who'd usually argue with him over the most insignificant trifles. None wanted to lose this God-given opportunity to regain the Holy Cross and free so many Christian prisoners. Nor were they happy to forfeit so much money, for Richard's generosity was almost as legendary as his bravado and they'd been sure the ransom would be shared, enabling them to pay their men and cover their expenses. This was no small consideration, for many a crusader had bankrupted himself by taking the cross. But they were soldiers, too, and like Richard, they could see that remaining at Acre was not an option. Nothing mattered more than the success of the crusade, not even the sacred fragment of the Holy Cross or those unhappy men languishing in Damascus dungeons.

Richard let his gaze move challengingly from Hugh to the Bishop of Beauvais. Beauvais looked as if he were biting his tongue, wanting to protest from sheer force of habit. Hugh's shoulders were slumped, his chin tucked into his chest, his slouching body proclaiming his bitter disappointment over the loss of the ransom. Feeling Richard's eyes upon him, Hugh glanced up and said sarcastically, "Are you asking our opinions? That is a first. Naturally you'd choose the one time when only a half-wit could disagree with you. The fact is that we have no choice, and every man in this tent knows it."

The Germans had either died in the siege or gone home with Duke Leopold. There were numerous Flemings still with the army, though, and Jacques d'Avesnes spoke for them now, agreeing that they could not afford to wait any longer. Guy de Lusignan, his brothers, the Grand Masters of the Templars and Hospitallers, a Hungarian count, and several bishops had their say then, echoing what had already been said, and Richard thought that this was likely the first and last time that they'd all be in such unanimity. He'd not really expected arguments, but was relieved, nonetheless, to be spared the usual rivalries and prideful posturing.

It was Henri who asked the obvious question. "What do we do, then, with the Acre garrison?"

"What can we do?" Richard said grimly. "There are only four choices, none of them good ones. We cannot spare enough men to guard nearly three thousand prisoners, and I am not about to leave them in the same city with my wife and sister unless I could be sure they had no chance of breaking free. Nor can we take them with us on our march south. We do not even have the food to feed several thousand extra mouths, for Saladin has deliberately devastated the countryside to keep us from living off the land. We cannot just turn them loose, not without risking a riot from our own men. Many of them were not happy with the surrender, feeling they'd earned the right to storm the city and take vengeance for the deaths of their friends and fellow soldiers. If we free so many Saracens to fight again without getting so much as a denier, they'll be outraged and, once again, who could blame them? That leaves us but one choice as I see it—we execute them."

None could fault his logic, but not all of them were comfortable with the decision, for the Saracens had fought bravely and surrendered in the belief that their lives would be spared. Henri was the only one to express these regrets aloud, though. "A pity, for they showed great courage during the siege. Had they not been infidels, I'd have been proud to fight alongside any of them."

Some of the other men nodded in agreement, but Guy de Lusignan, the Templars, and the Hospitallers were enraged. Several of them began speaking at once, drowning one another out, until Garnier de Nablus prevailed by sheer lung power. Glaring at Henri, he said wrathfully, "Courage, you say? I'll tell you about courage, about the two hundred and thirty-four Templars and Hospitallers who were butchered by Saladin two days after the battle at Ḥaṭṭīn. Not only did he put these brave Christian knights to death, he set their accursed holy men and Sufis to do it, men who'd never even wielded a sword before. Save your pity for them, my lord count, not for pagans whose hands are wet with the blood of our brethren!"

The vehemence of the Hospitaller Grand Master's attack took Henri by surprise, but he didn't back down. "I mourn those good men, too, my lord Garnier. But courage is worthy of admiration, and I think the Saracens who held Acre for two years deserve to have their bravery acknowledged, especially if they are facing death and eternal damnation."

"I agree with my nephew," Richard interjected before any of the other Templar and Hospitaller knights could chime in. "They are indeed brave men. But they are also our enemies and their lives were forfeit as soon as Saladin refused to honor the terms of the surrender." He glanced then toward Hugh. "Half of these men were claimed by your king, my lord duke. Do you agree that they must be put to death?"

Hugh nodded. "I do not see that we have any other choice. But what of the commanders and the emirs taken when the city fell? Surely we are not going to kill them, too? Some of them might well be rich enough to pay their own ransoms."

"I agree," Richard said. "We will keep those men at Acre, for they can be used, too, to barter for some of our prisoners at a later date."

There was one man present who'd been shocked by the decision to slay the garrison. Humphrey de Toron did not approve of killing men who'd surrendered in good faith, even if it was their own sultan's actions that doomed them. He'd long known he was not suited for warfare, even before he'd taken part in the disaster at Ḥaṭṭīn. It was not that he did not understand the reasons for reaching this decision. But he knew he could never have summoned the ruthlessness to put so many men to death in cold blood.

"We are in agreement, then?" Richard glanced around the tent. "Does anyone have something else to say? If there is another way, speak up now."

Humphrey kept his eyes averted, shamed by his silence even as he told himself none would have heeded him. No one else spoke, either, agreeing it was a military necessity. Some were glad, though, that they did not have to be the ones to make the decision, and were glad, too, that Richard was willing to take that final responsibility and do what must be done. Scriptures might hold that "Blessed are the merciful," but mercy could be a dangerous indulgence in a war against the enemies of God.

SOON AFTER MIDDAY, Richard led his troops out onto the open plain southeast of Acre. Saladin's advance guard had been watching from the hill at Tell al-'Ayyāḍiyya, but they now retreated a safer distance to Tell Kaysān, disturbed and puzzled by this sudden maneuver. Once Richard's knights had lined up in battle formation facing their Saracen foes, the city gates were swung open and the hostages were marched out, bound to one another by ropes. The sight of the garrison caused confusion and alarm in the Saracen ranks, and riders were dispatched to Saladin's camp at Saffaram, for they did not know what the Franks meant to do.

Neither did the captive men of the Acre garrison. That was painfully obvious to Morgan, for he was close enough to see their faces as they were herded out onto the plain. Their emotions ran the gamut from rage to fear to hope, with some bracing for the worst and others believing that a deal had finally been struck for their release. No matter how many times Morgan reminded himself that these were infidels, his sworn enemies, he could not suppress a surge of pity as they passed by; most

Welshmen had an instinctive sympathy for the underdog, being such underdogs themselves. Thankful that the killing would be done by the men-at-arms, he rode over to where Richard, Hugh of Burgundy, and Guy de Lusignan had reined in. "My liege," he said when his cousin glanced his way, "are you sure the Saracens will attack?"

Richard looked from the prisoners to the men watching from the heights of Tell Kaysān. "We would if it were Christians being killed," he said, "and they will, too. But it will be too late."

Morgan marveled that he sounded so dispassionate, so matter-of-fact about the deaths of so many men, but he remembered then that Richard had shown no pity to routiers captured when his brothers Hal and Geoffrey had led an army into Poitou. No one mourned the deaths of mercenaries who sold their swords to the highest bidder. Many had been scandalized, though, when he'd also executed some of Geoffrey's Breton knights. Richard had been indifferent to the criticism and protests, for when he fought, he fought to win. Morgan looked back at the Saracen prisoners, wishing that Saladin had been better informed about the mettle of the man he was now facing.

Morgan tensed then, for Richard had drawn his sword from its scabbard, holding it aloft so that the sun silvered its blade. It was a dramatic scene—the mounted knights with couched lances, the garrison encircled now by shouting and cursing men-at-arms, eager to begin, for there'd been no trouble finding volunteers for this task—and Morgan realized it had been deliberately staged out in the open like this, sending a message to Saladin that his bluff had been called, but not in the way he'd expected. When Richard's sword swept downward, a trumpet blared, and then their soldiers rushed forward, weapons raised. Within moments, the plain resembled a killing field: blood soaking the ground, bodies sprawled in the sun, screams of pain mingling with despairing pleas to *Allah*. Mariam had taught Morgan a few Arabic phrases, so he knew the Saracens were dying with the name of their God on their lips, and he was surprised by the sadness he now felt, sorry these doomed men would be denied salvation and the redeeming love of the Holy Saviour.

Turning in the saddle, he saw that Richard was paying no heed to the slaughter going on behind him, keeping his eyes upon the distant figures of his Saracen foes. They were reacting as expected, with horror, shock, and rage, screaming threats none could hear, brandishing swords and bows, their stallions rearing up as they caught the scent of blood. "Here they come," Richard said suddenly, and Morgan wheeled his horse around to see the Saracen advance guard racing toward them in a desperate rescue mission that would be, as Richard had predicted, too late.

Again and again Saladin's outnumbered men tried to break through the ranks of armor-clad knights. Again and again they were repulsed. The battle raged throughout the afternoon as more Saracens arrived, dispatched from Saladin's camp at Saffaram once he'd learned what was happening. Men died on both sides, and as usual, Richard was in the very thick of the fight. Morgan and his other household knights did their best to stay at his side, often horrified to find him surrounded by the enemy. He always cut his way free, dealing death with each thrust of his sword, now bloody up to the hilt. At last the Saracens abandoned their futile attempts to save men already dead. By then the sun was low in the sky and the plain was strewn with bodies. Richard's men took their own dead and wounded back to Acre, leaving behind the human cost of the miscalculation and mistrust between enemies, twenty-six hundred men bound in ropes and drenched in their own blood.

RICHARD AND HIS KNIGHTS stopped at the city's public baths to wash off the blood and soak their aching bodies in hot water before continuing on to the citadel. Richard was in no hurry to reach the palace, for he did not know what sort of reception he'd get from Berengaria. He thought Joanna would understand why the killings were necessary, as he was sure their mother would have understood. But he knew many women were skittish about bloodshed, and his sheltered wife was more tenderhearted than most. In the aftermath of battle, his blood was usually still racing, for the intoxication of danger was often more potent than the strongest of wines. Tonight, though, he felt only exhaustion and a dulled, dispirited anger that it should have come to this. He was in no mood to justify his actions, and by the time he strode into the great hall, he was already on the defensive.

Nothing went as he'd expected, though. Berengaria was not even there, having gone to attend Vespers at Holy Cross Cathedral. Joanna had not accompanied her sister-in-law, but she seemed oddly subdued, a reticent, silent stranger instead of the supportive sister he'd hoped to find. One of her ladies-in-waiting, the Sicilian Saracen whose name he could never recall, fled the hall as soon as he entered, casting him a burning glance over her shoulder. And the newly elected Bishop of Acre, whom he'd invited to stay at the palace, offered to absolve him of his sins, which he took as an implied criticism of the day's executions. Instead of having a meal in the great hall, he headed for his bedchamber, his squires in tow.

Once Jehan and Saer had removed his hauberk, he finally felt able to draw an unconstricted breath. He was too tired to wonder why the weight of his armor, practically a second skin, should have seemed so heavy tonight. He was usually too impatient to wait while they disarmed him, but now he let them do all the work, remaining immobile as they took off the padded gambeson he'd worn under his hauberk; his legs were already bare for he'd not replaced his mail chausses at the baths. Handing his scabbard and sword to the boys, he was giving them unnecessary instructions about cleaning the blood from the blade when the door burst open and his wife rushed in. Flushed and out of breath, she started to apologize for not having been there when he arrived, but stopped when she realized that he was not really listening to her.

His squires read his moods better than Berengaria, and departed in such haste that they forgot to take his hauberk for cleaning. Finding a towel, Richard sat on the bed and began to rub his thinning hair, still damp from the baths. She hovered beside him uncertainly, at last asking if he was hungry. She was stunned when he lashed out without warning, saying he was surprised she did not want him to fast as penance for his many sins.

"Why would I want that?"

"Why do you think?" he snapped, discovering that there was a relief in finding a target for his unfocused rage. "I know you think what I did today was monstrous. At least have the courage to admit it!"

"Are you a soothsayer now, able to read minds?" she snapped back, and he looked up in surprise, for he'd never seen her lose her temper before. "I do not know why you are seeking to quarrel with me, Richard, but it is manifestly unfair to blame me for something I neither thought nor said!"

"So what are you saying, then?" he said skeptically. "That you are proud of me for this day's work?"

"No, I can take no pride or pleasure in what you call 'this day's work.' Any more than you can. But it would never occur to me to find fault with you over it, for why would I presume to contradict you about a military matter? You know war as I do not, Richard. If you say this had to be done, that is enough for me."

"It did have to be done. Nor do I regret it, for I could see no other way."

"Then you have no reason for regret," she said quietly, and he reached out, catching her wrist and drawing her toward him. Taking that gesture as the closest he'd come to an apology, she sat beside him on the bed. He was clad only in his shirt and braies, and as he pulled the shirt over his head, she caught her breath at the sight of the darkening contusions on his ribs and thighs. In battle, he acted as if he were immortal, but here was proof that his body was as vulnerable as any other man's to a sword thrust or crossbow bolt. Noticing how heavy-lidded his eyes looked, she got to her feet.

"I have some ointment in one of my coffers. I am going to put it on your bruises and then I'll have food sent up." Not waiting for his response, she hastened across the chamber to look for the salve. By the time she found it, he'd lain back on the bed and the slow rise and fall of his chest told her he slept. Sitting beside him, she began to apply the ointment with gentle fingers.

SLIPPING OUT A SIDE DOOR into the courtyard, Joanna headed toward a bench under a flowering orange tree. Even in the shade, the heat was searing, but she'd become accustomed to hot weather during her years in Sicily. She wanted time alone to sort out the confused welter of feelings unleashed by the massacre of the Acre garrison, and she assumed few others would be willing to venture outside when the noonday sun was at its zenith.

She needed to figure out why she was disturbed by the deaths. They were soldiers, after all, enemies of the True Faith. She'd heard Richard and his men talking about the dangers of delaying their march south, and so she understood why he'd done it. Why, then, was she so uncomfortable with it? It would have helped if she could have discussed her feelings openly, but that was not possible. Mariam would have been her usual confidante. Mariam was too distraught, though, to be objective. Joanna knew that they'd only end up quarreling, for she'd feel compelled to defend Richard from Mariam's outrage. The practical Beatrix saw it in starkly simple terms—the garrison's lives were forfeit because Saladin failed to ransom them, so what more was there to say? And Berengaria's loyalties as a devoted wife and devout Christian were so actively engaged that she was unwilling to discuss the deaths at all.

Joanna's expectations of solitude proved to be illusory. No sooner had she settled herself on the bench than Jacques d'Avesnes arrived to see Richard. Detouring across the courtyard, he asked her to look after his Flemish hounds while he was away with the army. Then Guilhem de Préaux came out to offer her a cup of iced fruit juice and syrup, shyly expressing his concern that she risked sunstroke in such heat. Morgan was the next to appear. Looking pleased to find her alone, he hastened over to ask how Mariam was faring.

"She is . . . unwell," Joanna said carefully, for Mariam's position could become precarious if she seemed too sympathetic to the Saracens.

Morgan understood what she was really saying. "Do you think she will see me, Madame? As a Welshman, I also hear the whispers of the blood."

Joanna nodded. "Go to her, Cousin Morgan. It will do her good to unburden her heart to one whom she can trust."

As Morgan went to find Mariam, Joanna heard footsteps and turned to see Henri approaching with Balian d'Ibelin. "Aunt Joanna, you'll be fried to a crisp out here," Henri chided, leaning over to kiss her cheek. She greeted him warmly, Balian coolly, and expressed concern when she saw Henri was limping. He assured her it was a minor matter, confessing sheepishly that a horse had stepped on his foot after the battle. "And the worst of it is that it was my own horse!" Joanna laughed dutifully while Henri and Balian bantered about his injury, relieved when they continued on toward the great hall. Alone at last, she leaned back, closing her eyes.

She had little time for reflection, though. Soon afterward, a shadow fell across her face and she looked up to see Balian standing there. "Are you leaving already?" she asked, summoning up a few shreds of courtesy even though she had no desire to entertain a man so closely allied to Conrad of Montferrat.

"It did not take long to relay my message to the English king—that I am returning to Tyre."

Joanna stiffened, regarding him with sudden suspicion. "You are not going south with the army? Why?"

"Because I am not welcome here, Madame," he said forthrightly. "I've grown weary of fending off the de Lusignans' insults and malice. And your lord brother made his own feelings clear by not inviting me to that council yesterday. I doubt that I could have changed their minds, but I would have liked the opportunity to try."

"You do not approve of the killing of the garrison?"

She bristled, so obviously ready to charge into battle on her brother's behalf that he fought back a smile. "I think it was a mistake, my lady."

"Why?" she asked warily. "My brother felt that it was necessary and I trust his judgment, am sure he was right."

"Yes . . . but you are still not happy about it, are you?"

Her mouth dropped open. How could this man, a stranger, know what she'd confided to no one? "Why do you say that?" she demanded. "You do not know me, after all!"

"I know you came to womanhood in Sicily."

Joanna stared at him. "Why does that matter?"

"It means you grew up with Saracens. You got to know them as people, not just as infidels or enemies. You are not like so many who come here after taking the cross, horrified to find that we have adopted some Saracen customs, that we cooperate with them at times. From what I've heard of Sicily, it is more like Outremer than France or England. So your background practically makes you an honorary *poulaine*, my lady," he said with a smile.

"I'd never thought of it in that light," she admitted. "We had palace servants who were supposedly Christian, though all knew their hearts and souls were still Muslim. My husband looked the other way, saying a good man was a good man, whatever his faith. But few at Acre could understand such a view; they'd have seen his tolerance as the rankest heresy."

"May I?" he asked, gesturing toward the bench. She nodded, for he was very tall and she was getting a crick in her neck, having to look up at him. Sitting down beside her, he said, "We've often encountered this problem with men arriving from the western kingdoms, as eager to kill infidels as they were to visit the holy sites. They took as gospel the words of St Bernard of Clairvaux, who preached that Christians should glory in the death of a pagan, for it glorifies Christ himself. When they discovered that we sometimes lived in peace with Saracens, that friendships were not unknown, that one of our kings consulted physicians in Damascus for his ailing son, they were convinced that we were false Christians, even apostates."

"What you said about St Bernard . . . Richard does not believe that," she insisted and was pleased when he did not dispute her.

"I know, and I confess I was surprised. I'd heard he was the first Christian prince to take the cross, so I'd assumed he was afire with holy zeal. I'd not expected him to be so interested in the Saracens, so genuinely curious. No, I do not doubt that his decision yesterday was a military one. I still regret it."

"What else could Richard have done?" she asked, but without her earlier hostility; she truly wanted to know what he thought.

"He could not stay much longer at Acre; I agree with that. And he was justified to act when Saladin did not pay the ransom. But I think he ought to have sold the men as slaves instead of putting them to death."

Joanna was startled. "That would not have occurred to Richard, for slavery is no longer known in western kingdoms. I remember being shocked by the slave markets in Palermo, for I'd never encountered anything like that before."

"But it is known in the east. The Saracens sell captives into slavery all the time, and that is what they expected Richard to do if it came to that. I am not saying they'd have been happy about it. They'd have understood, though."

Joanna felt a fleeting regret, wondering if things might have been different had Balian taken part in yesterday's council. The sun had shifted and they were losing the shade, but she was not ready to go, for this *poulain* lord was a very interesting man, not at all what she'd expected. What a pity he was so closely allied to Conrad of Montferrat, for he'd have made a much more valuable ally for Richard than those infernal de Lusignans. At least now she understood why she'd been so uncomfortable about the killings of the garrison. Without even realizing it, she'd been seeing these Saracen soldiers as men, too, men who'd surrendered in good faith, men with mothers, wives, children.

"I heard some of Richard's knights saying that Saladin deliberately sacrificed the garrison, that the two hundred thousand *dinars* were worth more to him than the lives of those soldiers, who were not men of rank, after all. Do you believe that?"

"Only Saladin could answer that with certainty, my lady. But based upon my experience with him, I'd say no. Yes, he probably needed the money more than the men to continue the war, and may have had trouble raising so much in such a short time, too. I do not think, though, that he expected your brother to do what he did. You must remember that he does not know Richard yet, is accustomed to facing foes like that dolt de Lusignan. So it is only natural that he'd test this unknown English king, and I daresay he got more than he'd bargained for."

Rising then, he kissed her hand. "It has been a pleasure, my lady Joanna. God keep you safe."

He'd taken only a few steps before she rose, too. "My lord, wait!" As he turned back toward her, she said, "I have one last question for you. I gather your objections to the killing of the garrison are political, not personal, no?"

He looked surprised and then faintly amused. "That is so, Madame. They were brave men, yes. But in my years on God's Earth, I've seen many brave men die, some of them by my sword. Blood does not trouble me. What does is the future of our kingdom. Your brother will be going home eventually. For me, this is home, and so it matters more to me if the wells are poisoned."

"Is that what you think Richard did—poisoned the wells?"

"Only time will tell. I fear that in the long run, the killing of the Acre garrison will be one more grudge borne against the Christians. It is over ninety years since Jerusalem was taken and the Muslims and Jews in the city massacred, yet to hear Saracens speak of it, you'd think it happened yesterday. But in the short run, it might well work to your brother's benefit. After yesterday, how many Saracen garrisons will be willing to hold firm when they hear *Malik Ric* is marching on their castles or towns?" He suspected this had occurred to Richard, too, but kept that suspicion to himself. "If you truly want to aid Outremer, my lady, persuade your brother that Guy de Lusignan could not be trusted to govern a bawdy house or bordel." And having coaxed an answering smile from the English king's sister, he left her alone in the sun-drenched courtyard, marveling that she'd found a kindred spirit in one of Richard's enemies.

FROM THE CHRONICLE of Bahā' al-Dīn, discussing the slaughter of the Acre garrison: "Various motives have been assigned for this massacre. According to some, the prisoners were killed to avenge the deaths of those slain previously by the Muslims. Others say that the King of England, having made up his mind to try and take Ascalon, did not think it prudent to leave so many prisoners behind in Acre. God knows what his reason really was."

FROM A LETTER written by King Richard to the Abbot of Clairvaux: "However, the time having expired, and the stipulation which he had agreed to being utterly disregarded, we put to death about two thousand six hundred of the Saracens whom we held in our hands, as we were bound to do, retaining a few of the more noble ones, in return for whom we trusted to recover the Holy Cross and certain of the Christian captives."

CHAPTER 25

AUGUST 1191

Acre, Outremer

ichard had set up camp outside the city walls and for two days he'd labored to round up reluctant crusaders, men loath to leave the sinful comforts of Acre. Now on this fourth Thursday in August, the army was finally moving out and the women had gathered on the flat roof of the royal citadel so they could watch. It was a stirring sight—the sun slanting off mail hauberks and shields, pennons and Richard's great dragon banner billowing with each gust of the southerly Arsuf winds, dust already rising in clouds as the dry summer soil was dislodged by thousands of marching feet and plodding hooves. All the roofs near the palace were crowded with spectators, too, and people cheered and waved as the columns of cavalry, infantrymen, and supply carts slowly disappeared into the distance.

Some of the rooftop onlookers were soldiers, and Sophia scowled, heaping a few Greek curses upon the heads of these men who'd chosen whores and wine over their vows to liberate the Holy City. Did they suffer no conscience pangs, knowing what their friends and comrades would be facing? Almost eighty miles lay between Acre and Richard's objective—the port city of Jaffa—eighty miles, eight rivers, and the army of the Sultan of Egypt, Salah al-Dīn. A few feet away, Bertrand de Verdun, the new governor of Acre, was doing his best to assuage Berengaria and Anna's fears, and Sophia edged closer to hear.

Berengaria was shading her eyes against the sun, straining to keep the rear guard in view, for Richard was among their ranks. "I am not as ignorant of war as I once was," she said, objecting with quiet dignity to Bertrand's attempts to down-play the dangers. "I've heard my lord husband's men talking, Sir Bertrand, so I know an army is at its most vulnerable when it is on the march in enemy territory."

"That is true, Madame. But King Richard has gone to great lengths to minimize the risks for his men. They will be marching along the coast, so their right flank will be protected by the sea. That is where they will place the baggage carts and wagons. The knights will ride next to them, their left flank shielded by the men-at-arms, who will keep the Saracens at a distance with their crossbow fire. And the king has designated several rendezvous points, where the fleet will be awaiting them to replenish supplies. This is truly a blessing, for it means each man must carry only enough food and firewood for ten days. Moreover, smaller ships will be keeping pace with the army offshore, ready to evacuate the wounded or send messages back to the fleet. Not only is this the largest army ever mustered in the Holy Land, it is the best equipped for victory, led by the greatest battle commander in Christendom."

Richard's queen and Anna murmured their assent to that, but Sophia noticed that Joanna was standing apart from the other women, her expression guarded, and she sidled over. "Bertrand's reassurances seem to be ringing hollow for you," she said, keeping her voice low. "Is he lying to us?"

"No," Joanna said softly, "Richard has indeed done all he could to minimize the risks for 'his men.' But when it comes to his own safety, he can be quite mad at times. You did not hear about the raid on their camp yesterday?" When Sophia shook her head, Joanna drew her aside, out of hearing range of the other women. "Saracen horsemen raced into the camp, shooting and yelling and creating havoc. Richard says they are amazing bowmen, able to fire from a gallop. Some of the knights took off in pursuit, and naturally Richard was in the forefront. It turned out to be a trap, meant to lure them away from the safety of the camp. One of Richard's marshals and a Hungarian nobleman, Count Nicholas of Szatmar, were both captured and borne away. Richard chased after them in a vain rescue attempt. He was very upset afterward that he'd not been able to free them and did not want Berengaria to know, so say nothing to her, Sophia."

Sophia was horrified that Richard had come so close to disaster. "What if he'd been captured instead of Count Nicholas?"

Joanna smiled, though without much humor. "To hear his friends tell it, Richard is all but invincible in close combat, so they sought easier prey. But even Richard's vaunted prowess cannot protect him from a crossbow bolt or a javelin. He well knows that if evil befalls him, the war would be lost. Yet he will continue to gamble his life with reckless abandon . . . until the day his luck runs out."

Sophia glanced over at her stepdaughter, flirting now with several of Joanna's household knights, and felt a protective pang. If the English king was slain or captured, what would happen to the women he'd left behind in Acre?

IN THREE DAYS, the army traveled only four miles, camping near the River Acre as they waited for more men to straggle out of the city and join them. Finally on Sunday, the twenty-fifth, they began their march along the sea, hoping to cover the eleven miles to Haifa. Richard led the vanguard, and the rear guard was entrusted to the Duke of Burgundy and the French. They were shadowed by the sultan's advance guard, for he had instructed his brother al-Malik al-'Ādil to watch for a gap in their ranks. At first they maintained the tight formation ordered by Richard, but as the day wore on, the road narrowed and the rear guard began to lag behind. Late in the afternoon, the sky turned overcast, the first time they'd seen a cloud in three months. They plodded on, casting glances at those ghostly riders occasionally visible in the sand dunes to their left. When fog began to drift in from the sea, it created confusion in the rear guard and they slowed down, losing even more ground. It was then that al-'Ādil struck.

THIS EERIE HAZE was making the men uneasy, for such sudden mists were much more common in early morning. Richard refused to let them slow their pace, though, keeping a sharp eye out for laggards. When André joked that he was like a shepherd with a flock of errant sheep, he summoned up a smile, but he thought there was too much truth in that jest for humor. As accustomed as he was to command, never had he faced such a daunting challenge, for it would not be easy to keep an army like this under control, men of different nationalities and alien tongues, with nothing in common but their Christian faith. He would have to find a way to hold their rivalries in check, to stifle their natural instincts to hit back when they were attacked, for if he did not, they'd not reach Jaffa, much less Ascalon or the holy grail of Jerusalem.

He dropped back to ride beside the Grand Master of the Hospitallers, meaning to share the latest scouting report. But he never got the chance. It was then that the shouting began. Catching the words "the king," he wheeled Fauvel and rode to intercept the rider galloping past the infantrymen on their left flank. The man was close enough now for recognition—an English knight named John Fitz Luke. "Sire, the rear is under attack! They fell behind and the Saracens swept down and cut them off!" He started to tell the king more, but Richard was already gone, his household knights strung out behind him, outrun by the Cypriot stallion.

Fauvel seemed to sense his rider's urgency and pricked his ears as he lengthened stride. Several miles separated the vanguard from the beleaguered rear guard, and Richard and his knights plunged in and out of the swirling sea mist as they rode, loosening swords in scabbards and making sure their aventails were tightly drawn across their throats, for some had unfastened the mail flaps as they marched. Emerging from one last patch of fog, they came upon a scene of utter pandemonium. Several carts had been overturned and looted, others bogged down in the sand, for the Saracens had ridden down the men-at-arms and scattered the knights in their push toward the vulnerable baggage train. It had been a well-coordinated attack, and had come perilously close to surrounding the rear guard and cutting off escape. Some of the French knights had managed to rally in time to prevent their encirclement, and there was fierce fighting on the beach, some of the horses actually knee-deep in water by now.

Richard was not sure his command could be heard above the din of battle, but his household mesnie was composed of knights who'd been with him for years, men who would know what to do without need of words. Just as some of the Saracen soldiers turned and saw them materializing from the mist, they couched their lances and charged. As Richard closed in on a horseman with his bow slung over his shoulder, the startled Saracen tried to raise his shield. But by then Fauvel was upon him, and the lance, with the full weight of Richard's body behind it, drove through the man's *lamellar* armor with such force that the weapon lodged between his ribs. He reeled back in the saddle and then began to vomit blood. As he slid to the ground, still impaled on the lance, Richard unsheathed his sword.

The combat that followed was bloody but brief, for the Saracens were soon in retreat. To Richard, it was not so much a victory as a reprieve, and as he looked around at the crumpled bodies, the plundered wagons, and broken lances, he was infuriated when some of the French knights raised a cheer. "Keep vigilant," he instructed his own knights, "for they may well hit us again if they see us letting down our guard." Spotting a familiar face, he rode over to the Count of St Pol, who had dismounted and was examining his stallion's foreleg.

"I feared he might be lamed," he said as Richard drew rein, "but it seems he just took a misstep—"

"What in Christ's Name happened here, St Pol?"

Bridling at the English king's tone, the count straightened up. "Ask Burgundy. He has the command, not me!"

Another French lord was more forthcoming. Drogo d'Amiens overheard this testy exchange and came over to tell Richard that the Saracens had attacked once they saw the rear guard had fallen behind the rest of the army. "It looked like it would turn into an utter rout," he said soberly. "But thank God for Guillaume des Barres, for he managed to rally his knights and they staved off disaster until your arrival, my liege. It was too close for comfort, though."

Richard was in complete accord with that; had things gone differently, their entire rear guard could have been destroyed on the first day of the march. When he rejoined some of his friends and knights, he was still seething. "One of the Templars told me that the Saracen strategy for victory can be summed up in three words: harass, encircle, annihilate. They might want to add a fourth maxim: Fight the French. Where is Burgundy?" He began to snap out orders then, and his men hastened to obey. But André, Baldwin, and Morgan shared grins, thinking that Hugh of Burgundy's encounter with the Saracens was going to seem downright benign after his confrontation with the English king.

GUILLAUME DES BARRES was so exhausted that it took an effort just to stay upright. He was returning from the surgeon's tent, for toward the end of the fighting, he'd taken a blow to his forearm by a Saracen mace. It throbbed with the slightest movement, but he was greatly relieved that he'd broken no bones. Seeing that his squires were still setting up his tent, he sank down next to one of the supply wagons and braced his aching body against its wheel. He knew he should seek out the duke to learn how many casualties they'd suffered, but he could not muster up the energy to move. From time to time, other men came over and lauded him for his prowess that day. Ordinarily, such acclaim would have been very pleasing; now he was too tired to appreciate it. Despite his uncomfortable position, he was falling asleep when Mathieu de Montmorency squatted beside him.

"You're the talk of the camp," he exclaimed, looking at the older man with bright, admiring eyes. "Men are saying that you saved the day for us, that there'll likely be songs written about your deeds."

"I doubt that Richard will be writing any of them," Guillaume said dryly, smothering a yawn. "Anyway, it was his arrival that tipped the scales in our favor."

"Yes, but it was your action that enabled us to hold on until he got here. Mind you, he did make quite an entrance," Mathieu said, grinning. "He struck the Saracen line like a thunderbolt! Then he . . ." He stopped then, realizing it might not be tactful to be praising the man who'd treated Guillaume so unfairly at Messina.

"I do not mind, lad," Guillaume assured him, for Mathieu's was an easy face to read. "He is indeed a superb fighter—as he'd be the first to tell you."

Mathieu grinned again. "He is over in the duke's tent now, berating Hugh for letting the rear guard lag behind like that. Hugh looked like he'd swallowed a whole lemon!"

"Good," Guillaume muttered, for he'd warned the duke repeatedly that they were courting disaster. Mathieu was still chattering on about the battle, relating a story he'd heard about a sergeant of the Bishop of Salisbury: Supposedly, he'd had his hand cut off by a Turkish blade, but had coolly snatched up his sword in his left hand and continued fighting. Guillaume had often seen limbs severed on the battlefield, had severed a few of them himself, and he very much doubted that a man so maimed would be able to carry on with such sangfroid. He saw no reason to inject reality into Mathieu's account, though. Looking at the teenager through drooping eyelids, he found himself thinking it was miraculous that the lad still retained so much boyish enthusiasm after four months in the killing fields of the Holy Land.

He must have dozed then, for the next thing he knew, Mathieu was jabbing him in the ribs, saying that the English king was leaving. It was that muted twilight hour between day and night and Guillaume was glad the light was fading, glad he'd not chosen to sit by one of the campfires. During their stay in Acre, he'd done his best to keep out of Richard's way, and on the few occasions when their paths had crossed, the other man had stared right through him as if he did not exist. The last thing he wanted tonight was to be called to Richard's attention. But Richard had stopped to speak to one of the crossbowmen and, to Guillaume's dismay, the man nodded and then pointed toward the wagon. Seeing that the English king was heading now in his direction, he struggled to his feet, his heart thudding faster than it had at any time during the battle. He'd taken the cross and that mattered far more than any petty grudge. There was no way he'd disavow such a sacred oath. But what would he do if this accursed, arrogant king banished him from the march?

Mathieu had scrambled to his feet, too, and watched in alarm as the English king bore down upon them. Coming to a halt a sword's length away, Richard regarded the other man, his face inscrutable. Just when the suspense had become intolerable, he said, "You fought very well today."

Guillaume had not realized he'd been holding his breath. "So did you," he said laconically, and thought he saw the corner of Richard's mouth twitch.

"It is passing strange, but the climate of Outremer seems to be affecting my memory. For the life of me, I cannot recall anything that happened between us in bygone days."

"It is indeed odd," Guillaume agreed gravely, "for I am suffering from the same malady."

"Well, then, we'll just have to start anew from this day. Come on back to my tent and we'll eat and refight the battle," Richard said, and this time Guillaume was sure he caught the hint of a smile. He accepted the invitation as casually as it was offered, revealing his relief only in the smile he sent winging Mathieu's way. The youth was beaming, thrilled to see his two heroes reconciling their differences. And when Richard then glanced over his shoulder and said, "You, too, Mathieu," he looked positively beatific as he hurried to catch up with them.

By now they'd drawn a crowd, for Guillaume was well liked by his fellow Frenchmen, and they were smiling, too, gladdened that the English king had acted to make peace with the man he'd wronged. The only two men not caught up in this surge of goodwill were the two standing in the entrance of the duke's command tent. The Bishop of Beauvais shook his head and then spat into the dirt at his feet. "Whatever that whoreson said to des Barres, you can be sure it was no apology. He'd sooner have his tongue cut out with a spoon than admit regret or remorse or, God forbid, a mistake."

"Apologies are for lesser men," Hugh said bitterly. "Not for the likes of Lionheart."

THE ARMY REMAINED at Haifa the next day, where they left piles of belongings behind on the beach, the soldiers jettisoning those possessions that weren't essential. When they resumed the march on Tuesday, the twenty-seventh, they maintained the tight formation that Richard demanded. He would not trust the French again with the rear guard, and from then on, the Templars and Hospitallers rotated that command. He sought, too, to keep morale up by alternating duties for the infantrymen. On one day they guarded the exposed left flank, theirs the daunting and dangerous task of protecting the knights' vulnerable horses from Saracen arrows; on the next, they were allowed to travel with the baggage carts, protected by the sea. The men were finding that the scorching summer heat was as much their enemy as Salah al-Dīn. Richard did what he could to mitigate their misery. They marched only in the mornings, set up camp at noon, and rested every other day, but toiling under that burning sun was taking its toll. Men became ill, and some died from sunstroke. The sick were transported to the small ships, the dead buried where they fell.

It was slow going, for they were following an old Roman road, badly overgrown by scrub, thorns, and myrtle, and the infantry sometimes found themselves wading through chest-high brush. For the four days following the attack on the rear guard, they were spared any skirmishing with the Saracens, for Salah al-Dīn had been forced to lead his army inland as the crusaders made their way around Mount Carmel. But when they reached the deserted town called Merle by the Franks and al-Mallāha by the Saracens, they came under attack again, and Richard was nearly captured when he led a charge to drive the invaders off.

The last day of August found them making a short march from Merle to another town razed by Salah al-Dīn, Caesarea. This was the worst day so far, for the temperatures soared, and the sun claimed as many victims as the Saracens. When they were finally able to pitch their tents on the bank of the River of Crocodiles, they were exhausted, both physically and mentally. But their spirits were bolstered by the arrival of the fleet, which had been delayed by contrary winds, for it brought provisions and fresh troops, men coaxed or coerced from the taverns and brothels of Acre.

The next morning they covered only three miles, camping by a stream so choked with reeds that they called it the Dead River, but they'd had to fight off Saracen attacks for much of the march. They rested there the next day, treating the wounded and sunsick, and wondering how many of them would live to see the Holy City of Jerusalem. Most of them were battle-seasoned soldiers, but they were uneasily aware that they were aliens in an unforgiving land, one that they'd never call home.

They hated the enemy, who'd not fight fairly, swooping in to strike like hawks and then flying out of reach. They loathed the day's heat and dust and bleached-bone skies, and they feared the poisonous snakes, scorpions, and tarantulas that crept out at dark. They tried to chase the latter away with noise, banging on shields and pots and pans, but the racket only kept sleep at bay. Lying wakeful and restive, they found themselves listening for the priest to cry out his nightly blessing, *"Sanctum Sepulcrum Adjuva!"* The comforting chant reverberated throughout the camp, coming from thousands of throats in unison, surely loud enough to reach the Gates of Heaven itself: "Holy Sepulchre, help us!" It would be repeated three times, reminding them that they were in this hellish place to do God's Bidding and if they died on crusade, they'd be shriven of their mortal sins and promised entry into Paradise. As the last echoes of the prayer faded away, they stretched out and tried to sleep, tried not to think about what the morrow could bring.

SALAH AL-DĪN HAD HOPED to goad the Franks into breaking ranks, for then they were at their most vulnerable. But so far he'd been thwarted by their discipline, and by now they were only thirty-four miles from Jaffa. The daily skirmishing continued, with casualties on both sides. Whenever a crusader was captured, he was brought before Salah al-Dīn, interrogated, and then executed; in the past, the sultan had usually shown mercy toward prisoners, but the massacre of the Acre garrison cried out for blood. Entrusting command to his brother, he personally rode out to search for suitable battle sites, for he was determined to force a fight before they could reach the safety of Jaffa.

TUESDAY, SEPTEMBER 3, exposed the crusaders to their greatest danger since departing Acre, for they discovered that the old Roman coastal road had become impassible, an overgrown track that would never support an army of fifteen thousand men, six thousand horses, and heavy baggage carts. For the first time, they were compelled to leave the sea, following the Dead River until they reached an inland road that ran parallel to the coast. They soon found themselves under heavy attack by three divisions of the sultan's army, led by Salah al-Dīn himself.

THE SUN WAS NOT YET high in the sky, but Richard was already fatigued, for he'd been pushing himself without surcease, trying to be everywhere at once. He and his knights galloped up and down their lines, making sure that the army continued on the move, in such a tight formation that it was impossible to throw a stone into their ranks without hitting a man or horse. His crossbowmen did their best to keep the deadly Saracen horse archers at a distance, and when they swooped in for hit-and-run attacks, Richard and his household mesnie raced to the rescue, scattering their foes—until the next time.

Riding back to his standard, Richard swung from the saddle and told his squires to fetch Fauvel, for his Spanish stallion was lathered with sweat. When his cousin Morgan appeared at his side, holding out a flask, he took it gratefully and drank as if it were ambrosia, not warm, stale water. He wished he could pour it over his head, but he dared not remove his helmet with Saracen bowmen within range. He'd entrusted the rear guard to the Hospitallers this day, and he told Morgan now that they'd already lost a score of horses. "It is a strange sight to see knights walking with the men-at-arms, carrying their lances. I've seen men weep over a slain stallion whilst remaining dry-eyed over the deaths of their fellow knights."

"The Count of St Pol has lost a goodly number of horses, too, and has been complaining loudly about it," Morgan said, coughing as he inhaled dust kicked up by so many tramping feet. Unlike their armor-clad riders, the horses had no protection from Turkish arrows. By placing the knights behind a bristling wall of crossbow- and spearmen, they'd hoped to shelter the animals, for they were naturally the first target of every Saracen assault. "This is no fit land for either man or beast," Morgan muttered, suddenly homesick for the green valleys and cooling mists of Wales. But when Richard mounted Fauvel and made ready to resume his patrolling, Morgan still asked to go with him.

They were only about two miles from the Salt River, where they planned to make camp. The vanguard had already begun to pitch its tents when the Saracens launched one last attack upon the rear guard, a desperate attempt to provoke the Hospitallers into a reckless charge. But when Richard and his knights reached the rear, they found the men marching on in close order, even though many of them had so many arrows caught in their armor that they resembled hedgehogs. Richard paused only long enough to shout a "Well done!" to Garnier de Nablus, and then he and his knights set about chasing off their attackers.

When they charged, the Saracens fled, as they'd done before. Only this time they surged back as soon as the knights wheeled their mounts to return to the march. Morgan's lance struck a Saracen shield a glancing blow, but then another Turk was suddenly there, wielding a flanged mace. There was no time to react, not even time for fear. The weapon never completed its downward swing, though. Instead the man's face contorted and he cried out in a foreign tongue, the mace slipping from his fingers. It was only when he toppled from the saddle that Morgan saw the lance that had buried itself between his shoulder blades. "*Diolch yn fawr,*" he whispered, thanking both the Almighty and André de Chauvigny for his reprieve. André had already turned away to find another foe. Spurring his stallion, Morgan followed after him.

Ahead, Richard was pursuing an enemy bowman. Glancing over his shoulder, the man looked shocked to see the king closing fast, and Morgan gave a triumphant shout, as if he were the one riding Fauvel, who could likely outrun the wind. He was startled, then, when the Saracen began to pull away again. Looking over to see what had happened, he saw Fauvel come to an abrupt, shuddering stop, sending sand and dust flying in all directions. He heard André cry out, "Christ Jesus!" But it was only when he reined in his mount next to Richard that he saw the shaft protruding from the king's side.

André, who never showed any fear for himself in battle, was now ashen. "How bad is it?"

Richard shook his head, saying it was nothing. But neither man believed him, knowing he'd not have halted the pursuit for an arrow merely embedded in his hauberk. Morgan was close enough now to see it was a crossbow bolt and his breath caught in his throat, for he knew the fate of the Holy Land and Richard's fate were one and the same, inextricably entwined for better or worse. After a moment of panic, common sense reasserted itself and he realized that the injury could not be lethal, for Richard had managed to stay in the saddle. Unless the wound festered, of course—a thought so unwelcome that he hastily sought to banish it by making the sign of the cross.

André had drawn the same conclusion and expressed his relief in anger, scowling and demanding to know why Richard was fighting without a shield. Richard looked at him as if he'd suddenly gone stark mad. "When I unhorsed a Saracen with my lance, the guige strap broke. What was I supposed to do, André—call a halt to the battle whilst I sent a squire to fetch a new one?"

André's emotions were still roiling, and he was not about to admit he was being unfair or illogical. Richard had diced with Death so often that even if he did not deserve a reprimand this time, he'd earned it for his past recklessness. "The Turks say a cat has seven lives. How many do you think you have, Richard?"

"As many as it takes to free the Holy City," Richard said, managing to sound both flippant and utterly serious, and as usual, he got the last word.

———

"FOR GOD'S SAKE, man, take care with my hauberk!"

Master Ralph Besace was accustomed to dealing with a truculent royal patient; he'd been the king's physician since Richard's coronation. "If you will hold still, sire, you'll make my task much easier." Removing a hauberk was never easy in such circumstances, though. Ignoring Richard's protest, he widened the torn links enough to slide the mail up and over the shaft. Richard would have pulled the hauberk over his head then, but his friends were waiting for just such a move and insisted that they be the ones to remove it. They could see now that the bolt had pierced the padded gambeson, too. Asking for a sharp knife, Master Ralph cut it away around the wound and then stood back while André and Henri helped

Richard peel off the garment. It was soaked with sweat, but no blood; puncture wounds rarely bled much. Holding up an oil lamp, the doctor leaned in to examine the injury.

He was admittedly uneasy about what he might find. Arrow wounds were among those most commonly treated by battlefield surgeons, but they were still among the most challenging, for if the arrow could not easily be extracted, the remaining choices were not good ones. The doctor would have to try to push it through the man's body or else wait a few days until the tissue around the arrow began to putrefy. The first option was not feasible, for he'd risk damaging the king's internal organs, and the second was not doable either, not for a man who'd insist upon fighting on the morrow. But as he studied the wound, he felt a great rush of relief, thinking that Richard's fabled luck had held up once again.

"You were fortunate, my liege. The bolt does not seem to have penetrated too deeply. Your hauberk and gambeson absorbed most of the impact."

"Good. Get it out, then."

Master Ralph signaled for a *tenaille* and clamped the forceps around the shaft. A moment later, he was basking in the grateful approval of the king's friends. The king himself was much more stoic, but then the physician expected just such a reaction, for he knew Richard was determined to make his injury seem as trivial as possible. He was cleansing the wound with vinegar when there was a sudden uproar outside. Richard was all for going to investigate himself, but André was too quick for him. "I'll go, you sit," he insisted and ducked under the tent flap.

Richard was in a foul temper, vexed with his friends for making much ado about nothing and with himself for being so careless. He ungraciously accepted a cup of wine from his nephew, unamused when Henri joked that they'd had to post guards to keep all the well-wishers away. "Guy de Lusignan wanted to see for himself that you're not at Death's door and half the bishops are offering up prayers on your behalf. Even Hugh of Burgundy bestirred himself, sending a man to ask if the rumors were true. I really ought to have a public crier assure the camp that you're not seriously wounded."

"Of course I am not! I suffered worse hurts learning to use the quintain as a lad." Richard finished his wine in several gulps, an indication he did not feel as fine as he claimed, but Henri was not foolish enough to comment on it, merely refilling the cup. And by then André was back.

"Another brawl over dead horses," he said glumly, for this was becoming more and more of a problem. Soldiers quite understandably preferred meat over their daily rations of hard biscuit and a soup of beans and salt pork, so competition was keen to buy the horses slain by the Saracens. But the knights were pricing them beyond the reach of most men, and this was generating resentment and ill will. When André told him how much horsemeat was now selling for, Richard shook his head impatiently.

"I am putting a stop to this now. Get the word out that I will replace any knight's horse slain in combat—provided that he then donates the dead animal to the men-at-arms."

"Even French knights?" Henri asked mischievously. "That is an excellent idea, Uncle, and the soldiers will love you for it. I'll see to it straightaway."

They were interrupted then by the arrival of Guy de Lusignan, followed by the Bishop of Salisbury, Jacques d'Avesnes, the Earl of Leicester, and other visitors too highborn to be turned away. Hours passed before Richard was finally able to get to bed. And there he found himself unable to sleep, for although his body was utterly exhausted, his brain continued to race. After passing through sand dunes and hill country, the terrain was changing. Ahead lay more than twelve miles of oak woods, known as the Forest of Arsuf, and to get back to the coast, they would have to pass through it. It would be an ideal opportunity for an ambush and he thought Saladin would likely take advantage of it. They were locked into a war of wills as well as weapons, the sultan set upon battle and he just as determined to avoid one. So far his men had shown remarkable discipline under constant provocation. But how much longer could their restraint last? He tossed and turned for hours, wincing every time he forgot and rolled onto his side. Did Saladin lie awake, too, this night? Did he also feel overwhelmed at times, knowing how much was at stake?

THE NEXT MORNING Richard was much more stiff and sore than he was willing to admit, and he was glad Wednesday was to be a day of rest. He made a point, though, to be a very visible presence in the camp, reassuring his men that his injury had been a minor one. He soon discovered that they were uneasy about the Forest of Arsuf, too, and when he learned rumors were rampant that the Saracens would set fire to the woods once they'd entered it, he knew he had to act. That afternoon he summoned Humphrey de Toron and instructed him to ride out to the enemy under a flag of truce, telling them that the English king wanted to discuss peace terms with the sultan's brother.

Humphrey was astounded, but he did as he was bidden and carried the message to Salah al-Dīn's advance guard. Their commander, Alam al-Dīn Sulaymān ibn Jandar, wasted no time relaying word to the sultan. Salah al-Dīn was no less startled than Humphrey had been, but he was quite willing to accede to the request, telling his brother, "Try to protract the negotiations with the Franks and keep them where they are until we receive the Turcoman reinforcements we are expecting." It was agreed therefore that Richard and al-'Ādil would meet the following day at dawn.

THE SKY WAS the shade of misty pearl as Richard and Humphrey rode out of camp with only a handful of knights, heading for the designated meeting place with al Malik al-'Ādil. When they saw Saracen riders approaching, Richard told his men to wait, and he and Humphrey slowed their mounts to a walk. "I was surprised that Saladin did not insist upon an interpreter of his own," Richard said, after some moments of silence. "He must consider you very trustworthy, lad."

Humphrey was sorry the English king had brought the subject up, but it never occurred to him to lie. "I was captured at Ḥaṭṭīn, my liege," he said quietly. "My lady mother offered to yield her castles at Kerak and Montreal if Saladin would set me free. He agreed, but the castle garrisons would not obey her command. Since we'd not fulfilled our part of the bargain, I returned and surrendered to the sultan. He said I'd acted honorably and freed me without a ransom a few months later." He looked over at the other man then, bracing for mockery, but Richard was smiling.

"Well done," he said, and Humphrey flushed, so unaccustomed was he to praise.

"Some . . . others insisted that an oath given to an infidel counted for naught," he confided, "and they called me a fool for honoring my pledge."

"They are the fools. Ah, here he comes."

Al-'Ādil was mounted on a chestnut as mettlesome as Fauvel and clad in an elegant tunic of scarlet silk brocade; Richard had been told it was called a *kazaghand* and was lined with mail. He looked to be close in years to Conrad of Montferrat, in his mid-forties. His hair was covered by a mail coif, his skin bronzed by the sun, his dark eyes glittering with intelligence, caution, and curiosity. He was obviously a skilled rider, for he easily handled his spirited stallion, who pinned his ears back at the sight of the other horses. When Humphrey offered a formal greeting, he answered at some length, watching Richard all the while.

"We observed the usual courtesies," Humphrey explained, "but then he said that you and he almost met ten days ago, on the first of *Sha'ban*. The Muslim calendar is different from ours; that would be . . ."

He paused to calculate the date but Richard had already guessed it. "Sunday, August twenty-fifth. So the command was his, then. Tell him he could have made my acquaintance had he only lingered awhile longer."

Although Humphrey spoke fluent French and Arabic, this sort of barbed banter had always eluded him; he'd never learned how to communicate in the sardonic, sometimes cryptic language of men like this. For reasons only the Almighty knew, he'd been born utterly without the swagger, the bravado that seemed essential for survival in their world. Glancing from one man to the other, he felt certain that the English king and the sultan's brother were enjoying this verbal jousting, and that, too, he did not understand. He obediently continued to translate, but he was genuinely puzzled by al-'Ādil's next comment.

"He asks if your stallion is the famous Fauvel, my lord."

Richard's expression remained unrevealing, but his eyes gleamed with amusement. "He is letting me know how much they know about us. Tell him I am flattered that they find my activities so interesting, but I think it is time we speak of peace. Brave men have died on both sides. If we can come to terms, no more need die."

Al-'Ādil's response was brief and to the point. "He wants to know what your terms are."

"Tell him they are simple—that his brother the sultan withdraw from Outremer and return to his own lands in Egypt and Syria."

Humphrey swung around in the saddle to stare at Richard. His obvious astonishment alerted al-'Ādil, but he was still caught off balance when Humphrey slowly translated Richard's demands. He stared at the English king incredulously and then his brown eyes blazed with anger. "He says that if this is Frankish humor, he does not find it amusing."

"Well, mayhap he'll see the humor in it once he has gone home to Cairo or Damascus."

Al-'Ādil wheeled his stallion, flung a terse retort over his shoulder, and galloped off to his waiting men. "Do I want you to translate that?" Richard asked and grinned when Humphrey shook his head. He then turned Fauvel, and Humphrey hastily followed. Catching up to the English king, he did something he'd never done before. He demanded an answer.

"I think I have earned the right to ask, my lord. What was the purpose of that meeting? For certes, it was not to talk peace!"

"I suppose you'd not believe me if I said I was simply curious to meet the man?" Richard gave him a sly smile before saying, "What is the Arabic word for 'diversion,' Humphrey? As soon as we get back to camp, we move out. We're all packed and ready to go. Whilst Saladin's brother goes to report the results of our meeting, we head into the Forest of Arsuf."

SALAH AL-DĪN had not expected the crusaders to set such a slow, deliberate pace, and provisions had become a problem, for he'd not anticipated having to keep an army in the field so long. Continuing to scout for a suitable battle site, he'd gone back and forth with such speed that some of his men became stranded in the Forest of Arsuf and he was forced to wait for them to catch up the next day. He'd ordered his baggage train to head south while he waited to hear about al-'Ādil's meeting with the English king, then changed his mind and called them back, not sure whether his enemy would remain in camp or continue the march south, and Bahā' al-Dīn reported that there was much confusion in their camp all that night.

RICHARD'S PLOY WORKED, the crusaders safely passing through the Forest of Arsuf and halting by the River Rochetaille, where their flank was protected by an impassable swamp. They were now less than twenty miles from Jaffa. They knew, though, that ahead of them lay an open plain, an ideal site for battle. They remained by the river the next day, and when dusk fell, they could see the enemy campfires in the distance. Few men in either army would sleep well that night.

CHAPTER 26

ichard strode to the center of his tent, where his battle commanders had assembled: the Grand Masters and marshals of the Templars and Hospitallers, the de Lusignans and those *poulain* lords who'd not defected to Conrad, his cousins Henri and André, the Préaux brothers, who'd been entrusted with the royal standard, and barons and bishops of England, Normandy, Anjou, Brittany, Flanders, and France. He imagined Saladin and his brother were having a war council this night, too.

"We'll be setting out at dawn," he said, wasting no time upon preliminaries. "It is six miles to Arsuf and we ought to reach it by midday. From Arsuf, it will be just eleven miles or so to Jaffa, so this may well be Saladin's last chance to force a battle. If our roles were reversed, this is where I'd choose to fight—the lay of the land favors an attacking army. There are cliffs between the road and the sea which will keep us from hugging the coast, so there is a danger of being outflanked. And there is a broad plain running parallel to the road and forest, an ideal open space for Saracen horsemen. So we can expect a hellish day on the morrow and courage alone will not get us through safely to Arsuf. Our only chance will be to maintain a tight formation and to keep moving, no matter the provocation."

Richard paused then, but no one spoke. "This will be the order of march. Our army will be organized into twelve squadrons and divided into five battalions. The Templars will have the vanguard. The second battalion will consist of Bretons and Angevins. King Guy and his brothers will lead my Poitevins. The Normans and English will guard the cart with my standard, followed by the French. The Hospitallers will command the rear guard."

He paused again. "The Count of Champagne will guard our left flank." This was a great responsibility for one who'd only recently turned twenty-five, and Henri flushed with pleasure, taking it for the honor it was. Richard's gaze shifted from Henri to the others, to the young Earl of Leicester, his nephew Jaufre, the Fleming Jacques d'Avesnes, and his new ally, Guillaume des Barres, men he liked or respected. His eyes flicked then to those he loathed or mistrusted—the Duke of Burgundy, the Bishop of Beauvais and his brother, the Count of Dreux. A pity they had not skulked back to Paris with Philippe. Given a choice, he'd rather have fought beside al-'Ādil than Beauvais or Robert de Dreux. "You will, of course, lead your own squadrons of knights," he said, "riding with the center and the rear guard. The Duke of Burgundy and I will each take a squadron and ride up and down the line, as I've been doing in past days."

Some of the men began to murmur among themselves once Richard was done. But they fell silent when Jacques d'Avesnes got to his feet, for he'd been at the siege since its start and was that rarity in this maelstrom of fierce national rivalries, a man universally respected and liked by his fellow crusaders. "You say we must 'keep moving, no matter the provocation.' But what if their attacks become too much to bear?"

"I am placing six trumpeters in the vanguard, the center, and the rear guard. If they sound, that will be the signal to charge. But no knight or lord is to do so until I give that signal. The decision will be mine and mine alone."

That answer satisfied Jacques and most of the men. It grated on the nerves of some of the French lords, though, that they should have to take orders from an English king, particularly this one. The Bishop of Beauvais did not even bother to mask his resentment. "Naturally the decision will be yours," he said sarcastically. "If you had your way, all decisions throughout Christendom would be yours. And it will indeed be a 'hellish day.' But our suffering will be much worse if we march on like sheep to the slaughter. Why not hit back? If Saladin wants a battle, why not give him one?"

Richard stared at Beauvais in disgusted disbelief. "Because our scouts and spies say we're outnumbered by nigh on two to one. We may be God's army, but we are also Outremer's only army, and another Ḥaṭṭīn would doom the Kingdom of Jerusalem. Are those enough reasons for you?"

Henri glanced from his uncle to the bishop, half expecting to see the air itself begin to smolder, so searing was the hatred that flared between the two men. Before Beauvais could retort, Henri said quickly, "They are enough reasons for me. But I see no harm in discussing this further if the bishop feels the need." The look he got from Richard would have prickled the hairs on the backs of most men's necks. He ignored it and forged ahead with a quizzical smile. "I was always taught that a battle should be the last resort—unless we had numerical superiority and could choose the site ourselves. Am I wrong?" Sounding as if he were genuinely seeking enlightenment, Henri looked about at the other men crowded into the tent.

As Henri had expected, none of them were willing to embrace the bishop's rash insistence upon combat. Some were shaking their heads; a few seemed vexed that they were wasting time discussing one of the basic tenets of warfare—that pitched battles were too great a risk under most circumstances. Not even Robert de Dreux offered support, and finding himself abandoned by his brother, too, Beauvais lapsed into a sullen silence. Nor was his temper improved when Jacques sought to disperse any lingering tension with a joke. "Well, I'm for fighting on the morrow. After all, we have a two-to-one advantage. . . . Ah, wait, that is Saladin!"

Once the other men had departed and Richard was left alone with his nephew and a handful of friends, he confessed, "For a moment or two, Henri, I was intending to disown you."

Henri grinned. "I could feel your fiery gaze burning into my back, Uncle, but I thought it would be better if I were the one to expose the good bishop for the malcontent we know him to be. If you and Beauvais had gotten into a serious altercation, the other French lords might have felt honor bound to support him. None of them were likely to agree that we ought to seek out a battle on the morrow, though. They know better than that."

"So does that hellspawn," Richard said bitterly. "Our bishop is no battle virgin. No virgin at all, I'd wager," he added, unable to resist a swipe at Beauvais's priestly vows. "The man may be a misbegotten, cankerous viper, but he's spilled his share of blood. So he knows we'd be fools to fight unless forced to it. Nothing matters more to him, though, than making life as difficult for me as he can. And in that, he does not lack for allies—all of them French."

"I am French!" Henri protested, with such mock outrage that the other men laughed and even Richard couldn't help smiling.

"You show so much common sense that we tend to forget your unfortunate origins, Henri. And not all of your countrymen are malicious malcontents. My niece's husband Jaufre is a man of honor." Richard hesitated almost imperceptibly before admitting, "And I never thought to hear myself saying it, but so is Guillaume des Barres."

Richard lay wakeful that night, for he knew how much he was asking of his men. Knights were trained to strike back when hit; to do otherwise was to court shame and dishonor. But a mounted charge was a double-edged sword. If launched at the right time, it guaranteed victory. If it was made too soon, they'd be vulnerable to a Saracen counterattack and the victory would be Saladin's. Propping himself up on his elbow, he listened to the comforting nocturnal chant of their priests, invoking the aid of the Holy Sepulchre. Earlier, he'd heard the *muezzins* summoning Saladin's soldiers to evening prayer, so close were the two army camps. Reminding himself that they were in God's Hands, he finally slept.

THEY MOVED OUT at dawn, but it was already uncomfortably warm for men weighed down by armor, helmets, and padded gambesons. The sky was a pallid blue, as if faded by the sun, and the air was very still. Men tasting the salt of sweat on their lips were soon wishing for a breeze, even a hot one. They drank from wineskins hooked onto their belts, made rude jests as empty of humor as the sky was of clouds, and their breakfast biscuits lay in their bellies like lead, for off to their left, they could see the vast Saracen army arrayed along the plain overlooking the road.

Salah al-Dīn sent his skirmishers in first—the hit-and-run tactics that the crusaders found so frustrating. They kept marching, though, and the sultan committed more of his troops to the attack. The air was soon thick with the dust kicked up by the agile Saracen horses and the sky seemed to be raining Saracen arrows, for their skilled bowmen employed a tactic called "shower shooting." Most of the arrows were deflected by shields or snagged in the links of mail hauberks. But their stallions had no such protection and before long, they began to die.

Still the Franks continued on, transferring their wounded to the baggage carts, marching so closely that men rubbed shoulders and knights rode stirrup to stirrup, only their crossbowmen's lethal fire keeping them from being overrun. But the Saracen attacks grew bolder and more urgent, striking hardest at the beleaguered rear guard.

BY NINE O'CLOCK, Richard's vanguard was approaching the orchards on the outskirts of Arsuf. They were so close, he thought, so damnably close! But he was no longer sure they would make it, for the Saracen onslaught was relentless now, fueled by desperation. They'd made several attempts to outflank the rear guard, and only the marshy ground between the road and the sea cliffs kept the

Hospitallers from being assaulted on three sides. Garnier de Nablus had sent one of his knights to Richard, warning him that they were taking too much punishment. Richard refused to permit them to launch a charge, telling them they must endure it. As the man took that unwelcome message back to the Grand Master, André maneuvered his stallion alongside Fauvel. "Can we reach Arsuf?"

Because André was closer to him than any of his brothers had ever been, Richard gave him an unsparingly honest answer. "In truth, I do not know."

Survivors of the Arsuf march would long remember the heat, the dust, the fear. But above all, they would remember the noise. The Saracen drums kept up an ominous, throbbing beat, and the emirs had in their ranks men whose only duties were to raise a fearsome din with trumpets, clarions, flutes, and cymbals. Assailed by the incessant blaring of horns, the banging of tambours, the screaming of the stallions, and the battle cries of the archers and Salah al-Dīn's elite Mamluks, many of the crusaders found the deafening clamor to be almost as demoralizing as the storm of arrows, crossbow bolts, and javelins. Yet they marched on, clinging to their faith that God and the English king would get them to safety at Arsuf.

Richard had returned to the cart that held his standard, for he'd shattered his lance on a Saracen shield. Waiting for his squire to fetch another one, he found his gaze drawn to the great dragon above his head, said to be the banner of the legendary Arthur. It had been hanging limply from its mast, but as he watched, it caught a vagrant breeze and unfurled in a swirl of red and gold. Taking that as a good omen, he reached for the new lance. It was then that he saw the rider galloping toward him. He recognized the arms on the shield, a silver cross on a black background, and assumed the Grand Master of the Hospitallers was sending him another messenger. But as the man reined in beside him, he was surprised to see a familiar face half shadowed by the wide nasal bar. Garnier de Nablus had come in person to plead his case.

"My lord king, hear me. We're losing so many horses that half my knights will soon be on foot. It has gotten so bad that the crossbowmen have to march backward to protect themselves. We cannot hold on much longer."

"You must."

"My knights are distraught, saying they'll bring eternal dishonor upon themselves if they do not fight back!"

"Tell them I understand. But they must be patient. It is not yet time."

The Grand Master seemed about to argue further. Instead, he agreed tersely and turned his mount. Richard watched him ride off, his expression so grim that André and Baldwin nudged their horses closer. "Will you order a charge, then?"

"I must, André. But not until all of Saladin's army is engaged against us. We have to be sure that they'll bear the full brunt of our charge. If not . . ." Richard didn't bother to finish the sentence, for there was no need. They all knew what would happen to them if their charge failed to sweep the Saracens from the field. They'd be cut off, surrounded, and overwhelmed by sheer numbers.

HENRI WAS PROUD of the fortitude shown by the infantry under his command. They had performed heroically for hours, the crossbowmen doing their best to keep their Saracen foes at a distance, the spearmen defending them while they reloaded their weapons. He and his knights rode between the men-at-arms and the baggage wagons, occasionally making brief forays to chase the enemy away when they got too close. Henri wasn't sure if he ought to admire the valor of infidels, but he did, nonetheless. They may be risking their lives and souls for a false god, yet they did so with courage and conviction. Would that offer any consolation—knowing that he'd die at the hands of brave men? This was such an incongruous thought that he laughed softly, earning himself a sharp glance from Jaufre.

"If you can find any humor in our plight, Henri, tell me—please."

"A private jest, a very perverse one, too. Jaufre, do you think— Jesu!"

Jaufre swung around in the saddle at Henri's exclamation, and his jaw dropped at the sight meeting his eyes. Two knights had leveled their lances and were spurring their stallions toward the Saracens, screaming a defiant battle cry, "Saint George, aid us!" As Henri and Jaufre watched, the Hospitallers wheeled their mounts and followed, nearly trampling their own infantrymen, who had to scramble to get out of the way. The French knights saw the Hospitallers go on the attack and after some confusion, they also joined in.

Henri turned toward Jaufre, his shock evident. "Did you hear the trumpets?" Jaufre shook his head, equally shocked. But Henri was already yelling and their men-at-arms hastily scattered, opening gaps in their ranks for the knights as they, too, charged the Saracens.

RICHARD AND HIS MESNIE had just driven off an attack by Salah al-Dīn's Bedouins when they were alerted by the clouds of dust and screaming. Richard gasped, quick to comprehend what was happening, and shouted for the trumpets to sound. As the knights of the center and vanguard responded to the signal and charged, he raced for the rear guard, his knights spurring their stallions in a vain attempt to keep up with Fauvel.

The sudden charge by the Hospitallers had caught the Saracens by surprise and they took heavy casualties, particularly since some of their bowmen had dismounted to take better aim. By the time Richard got there, Salah al-Dīn's right wing was either dead or in flight. He at once sought to halt the pursuit into the woods, for the Saracens excelled at ambush tactics; he himself had almost fallen into such a trap barely a fortnight ago. It was not easy to rein in soldiers still half drunk on that most potent of brews—an uneasy blend of rage, fear, and excitement—but he managed it, mainly by sheer force of will. The field was strewn with weapons and the bodies of men and horses, but he knew it was not over yet.

Recognizing the rider on a blood-splattered roan stallion, Richard called out and then waited for Henri to reach him. "Who led the charge?"

"Two knights broke ranks, shouting for St George, and then the rest followed after them. I assumed I'd not heard the trumpets midst all the noise, think the others did, too. You did not order the attack, Uncle?"

"I was waiting till Saladin had thrown his reserves into the battle. But when the charge began, of course I committed the rest of our army." Even as he spoke to Henri, Richard's eyes were sweeping the battlefield. "Do you hear that?" When the younger man looked puzzled, Richard pointed behind him, toward the Forest of Arsuf. "The drums. Saladin's drums are still beating. He is trying to rally his men."

"Sire!" Garnier de Nablus drew rein beside them. "Thank the Lord Christ that you changed your mind—" The Grand Master stopped, for he was adept at reading other men's faces; his office required political as well as military skills. "You did not order the attack? But one of the men was William Borrel, our marshal! He would never have done that on his own, for discipline is one of the cornerstones of our order. He must have thought he heard the trumpets."

Richard did not dispute that, for he thought it was possible. But when Garnier continued to defend his marshal, declaring that it did not matter if the charge had been premature since they'd had the victory, Richard felt a flicker of weary anger. "No," he said, "it did matter. Had we waited as I wanted, we could have won our own Ḥaṭṭīn. Instead we had half a victory, for much of Saladin's army is still intact."

The Grand Master was quite willing to settle for half a victory after all they'd endured that morning. He thought it prudent to keep that to himself, however, and was glad when Henri tactfully interceded at that point, gesturing off to the south where their cart with Richard's dragon was coming into view. The standard-bearers had obeyed orders not to join in the battle, for Richard had wanted to hold his

Normans in reserve. They'd followed slowly so they could serve as a rallying point; as long as the king's banner flew, his men would keep fighting. Some of the wounded now headed toward it and other knights began to withdraw from the field and rode in that direction, too.

But Salah al-Dīn had accomplished a miracle of sorts. His army was in a rout, his right wing almost destroyed and his left wing broken. As they fled into the forest, though, they encountered their sultan and his brother. Bahā' al-Dīn, who fought that day, would later write, "All those who saw that the sultan's squadron was still at its post, and who heard the drum beating, were ashamed to go on, and, dreading the consequences if they continued their flight, they came up and joined that body of troops." When they saw the crusaders appearing to retreat toward the king's standard, they seized their chance and surged from the woods, led by al-'Ādil.

The knights who'd been savoring their victory suddenly found themselves embroiled in savage combat. Henri struck down a Turk with long, black braids, but then took a numbing blow on his leg from a man wielding a mace. They were in too close quarters for his lance to be of any use, so he swung his stallion away to give himself time to draw his sword. There was so much dust that it was not easy to tell friend from foe. A horse reared up ahead, screaming as an arrow pierced his throat, and Henri's destrier almost fell when the other animal went down, swerving away in the nick of time. He turned back to help the unhorsed knight, but he was too late; the man had been crushed when his mount fell on him. From the corner of his eye, Henri could see their dragon banner was still aloft, being desperately defended by the Norman standard-bearers. He could not find the king, though. When he finally did locate Richard, he was appalled to see his uncle utterly encircled by Saracens in what looked like a sea of saffron, for he knew those were the colors of Saladin's elite guard. But even as he spurred his horse toward them, he saw Richard break free, decapitating a burly Mamluk and then maiming another one half blinded by the spray of blood.

"Fall back!" Richard's voice was hoarse from shouting, but urgency gave it enough resonance to be heard above the din of battle. "Fall back! To me!"

The men within hearing distance obeyed, fighting their way toward the standard's cart. By now their infantry had reached the cart, too, and as the knights gathered around Richard, the crossbowmen unleashed a devastating fire to keep the Saracens at bay. Richard had broken his lance, but a soldier found one on the field and offered it to him, grinning when Richard tapped him on the shoulder with it as if dubbing a knight. By now the knights had lined up, lances leveled or swords drawn. Off to his left, Richard saw a group of French knights had taken shelter behind their men-at-arms and were also assembling for a countercharge, led by Guillaume des Barres. The battle was still continuing, for not all of the crusaders had been able to join in the retreat. Bodies lay crumpled as far as the eye could see, the dead and the wounded of both sides, and the Saracen drums continued to pound, summoning the sultan's fugitive troops back into the fray. Richard glanced from side to side, making sure that they were ready, and then couched his lance.

"Now!" As their infantry sprang aside with practiced coordination, Richard cried, "Holy Sepulchre, aid us!" and they charged. The Saracens unable to get out of the way were slain when the knights slammed into their ranks, for an armed knight on a galloping destrier had such momentum that a lance could run a man through like a pig on a spit, piercing armor, flesh, and bone with lethal ease. Overwhelmed by this iron onslaught, Salah al-Dīn's soldiers fled back toward the safety of the forest, with the crusaders in close pursuit. Richard halted the chase before they could advance too far into the woods, for a Saracen army was never more dangerous than in retreat.

Leading his men back onto the bloodied battlefield, he gave orders to collect their wounded—the dead would have to wait. Once he was satisfied that his soldiers were on the alert for another Saracen attack, he rode toward the squadron of French knights who'd fought under Guillaume des Barres, and these two former enemies shared a moment that mattered more than grudges or grievances or royal rivalries, for there was a brotherhood of the battlefield that men like Richard and Guillaume honored above all else.

THE BATTERED CRUSADER ARMY resumed its march toward Arsuf. But as they approached the camp already set up by their vanguard, there was another attack upon their rear. Richard, with just fifteen of his own knights, led a third charge that drove them back toward a ridge of hills, and the battle of Arsuf was finally over.

ARSUF WAS SITUATED on a steep sandstone ridge overlooking the sea, but the abandoned town was in ruins, razed by the Saracens, and the crusaders had to camp in the surrounding orchards. They were exhausted but triumphant, all the more thankful when they discovered that their casualties had been only one-tenth that of the Saracen losses. There were many wounded, though, and the surgeons' tents were soon crowded. Before darkness fell, men began to slip away to exercise a soldier's prerogative—plundering the dead.

Richard was in some discomfort, for his exertions on the battlefield had done his wound no good. He still insisted upon making the rounds of the camp himself, confirming that sentinels were on the alert, checking upon the injured, and offering praise to his soldiers, knowing they valued that almost as much as the booty they'd collected from their slain foes. The camp was abuzz with the exploits of Guillaume des Barres, Richard himself, and the young Earl of Leicester, who'd led a charge that had cut off some of Salah al-Dīn's right wing.

"Is it true that Saracens were leaping off the cliffs into the sea to escape Leicester's knights?" the Grand Master of the Templars asked Richard. "I have to admit that I'd not expected Leicester to show such prowess on the field, for he is on the puny side, after all."

Richard shrugged. "Sometimes a man's heart is big enough to overcome his body's shortcomings," he said, thinking of another undersized warrior, Tancred of Sicily. "I've been told that Saladin is only of middling height and slight build, and for certes, he has never lacked for courage." He stopped to banter for a moment with several Angevin crossbowmen and then rejoined Robert de Sablé. "What Saladin did today was remarkable. Once an army breaks and runs, it is well nigh impossible to halt the rout, much less rally them to fight again, and yet he managed it."

The Templar was more interested in discussing the Hospitaller breach of discipline. "Will you punish their marshal for charging on his own?"

Richard found the sharp rivalry between the Templars and the Hospitallers to be yet one more needless complication in his quest to retake Jerusalem. "I talked to William Borrel and the other knight, Baldwin de Carew. They both swear they thought they'd heard the trumpets." Robert de Sablé looked skeptical of that. Richard was skeptical, too, but since there was no way to prove they lied, he had to give them the benefit of the doubt. Despite his frustration that the charge had been launched too soon, he couldn't help admiring their mad courage in making such an assault—two knights against the might of Saladin's army.

He saw his nephew approaching with Guy and Joffroi de Lusignan and he moved to meet them, wanting publicly to commend them for fighting so bravely that day. But then he saw their faces. Henri and Guy looked distraught and even the phlegmatic Joffroi appeared troubled.

"Uncle!" Henri was so close now that Richard could see he was fighting back tears. "Jacques d'Avesnes is missing. No one has seen him since the battle."

THE MAN ON THE BLANKETS was young, blessed with a handsome face and robust body. But he was dying, for his injuries were beyond the healing skills of the Hospitallers' surgeons. Two kings were keeping watch at his deathbed, and so many barons and bishops that there was barely room for them all in the tent, for he'd been recognized as one of Jacques d'Avesnes's household knights, and they hoped that he'd be able to tell them what had befallen his lord.

As they waited, they spoke quietly among themselves. The soldiers who'd gone back to the battlefield in search of booty had reported that they'd encountered some of Saladin's men, come to collect their wounded. Both sides had ignored one another, by common consent, and there'd been no more blood spilled. They'd reported, too, that at least thirty-two emirs had been slain and there were more than seven hundred Saracen bodies. But they'd found no survivors, and Jacques d'Avesnes's fate remained a mystery—unless this mortally wounded Flemish youth could speak in the little time left to him.

Richard and Guy had been summoned when the knight had shown signs of regaining consciousness, and as they watched the shallow rise and fall of his chest, Guy confided how much he owed to Jacques, who'd arrived at Acre soon after the start of the siege. "Not only did he bring desperately needed men and supplies, he did much to raise our spirits. He never doubted that we would prevail and his faith was contagious."

"Do you know if Jacques has a son?" Richard asked, gazing down at the Fleming and finding himself overwhelmed with sadness, even though he knew that a man who died fighting for God would have all his sins remitted as a martyr to the True Faith.

"Yes, four sons," Guy said, "and four daughters, too. He often joked about the difficulty of finding husbands for them—" He stopped abruptly and Richard saw why; the young knight's lashes were fluttering again.

Supported by one of the surgeons, he managed to swallow some wine. His eyes were dulled with pain, but he was lucid, and he wanted to bear witness. He was too weak to summon up his French, gasping in his native Flemish as Baldwin de Bethune leaned over to translate those labored, whispered words.

"He says it happened when the Saracens made that second attack. They were cut off and surrounded. They still hoped to break free, but then his lord's stallion stumbled and threw him. He says Lord Jacques fought with great courage, even though he knew he was doomed. His knights were struck down as they sought to reach him. . . ."

Jacques's friends and fellow crusaders had known the news would be bad and thought they were braced for it. They were discovering now that they were not, and there were tears, a few muffled sobs, and the anguished cursing of men struggling to accept God's Will. The Bishop of Salisbury was about to offer the comfort of prayer when Baldwin leaned over the dying man again. Straightening up, he raised a hand for quiet.

"There is more. He says a lord was nearby, a man Jacques knew well. When he was unhorsed, he cried out to his friend for aid. Instead this man rode away with his own knights, leaving them to be slain by the infidel Turks."

This was a serious accusation, and there was an immediate outcry, demands to know the name of the craven cur who'd abandoned another Christian lord to save his own skin. "He says . . ." Baldwin paused, his eyes searching the tent until he found the one he sought, standing in the rear. "He says it was the Count of Dreux who refused to help his lord."

Robert of Dreux's face flooded with color. "That . . . that is not true! He lies!" His gaze shifted frantically from one man to another, seeking allies, seeking champions. He found none. They all were regarding him with shock and disgust, even Hugh of Burgundy and his own brother, Beauvais. No one spoke as he continued to protest his innocence, swearing that this Flemish whoreson was lying. Seeing their disbelief, he switched tactics, insisting that the man was out of his wits with fever and pain. But their continued, stony silence told him that his frenzied denials were a waste of breath. They believed this dying knight, and they would not forgive such a blatant breach of the code by which they lived. His honor would be tattered and tarnished until the day he drew his last breath.

AT DAWN, the Templars and Hospitallers went out and conducted a thorough search of the battlefield, at last finding the bodies of Jacques d'Avesnes and three of his kinsmen, who'd died with him. His mutilated corpse was washed and prayed over and then buried with great honor in the Minster of Our Holy Lady in Arsuf. Their army remained in camp on that Sunday, which was one of the most sacred holy days in the Christian calendar, the Feast of the Blessed Lady Mary, Mother of God. It was also Richard's thirty-fourth birthday.

FROM THE HISTORY of Bahā' al-Dīn. "God alone knows the depth of grief which filled the sultan's heart after this battle; our men were all wounded, some in their bodies, some in their spirits."

THE CRUSADERS broke camp on Monday, and though they were harried again by Salah al-Dīn's men, Richard kept them in formation and they marched on. The following day they at last reached Jaffa, almost three weeks after leaving Acre.

CHAPTER 27

They huddled together, the flaring torches revealing both their poverty and their fear. Richard assumed that they were a family—an older couple, a young wife or widow, and two small children peering out from behind her skirts. The Templar *turcopole* interpreter beside him looked aggrieved, but the story he'd related was so improbable that Richard wanted confirmation from Humphrey de Toron; he'd come to trust the young *poulain* even though they were as unlike as wine and buttermilk. When Humphrey finally arrived, obviously roused from bed, Richard drew him aside.

"They told one of the *turcopoles* that they've come from Ascalon, that Saladin forced all the townspeople from their homes and set about destroying the city and castle. But I find that hard to believe, for Ascalon is one of the great jewels in the sultan's crown. So I want you to question them for me."

He watched intently as Humphrey interrogated the family, his Arabic so fluent and his manner so courteous that some of their fright appeared to lessen. Even though he didn't speak the language, Richard did read faces well—a king's survival skill—and he soon concluded that they were either speaking the truth or were remarkably skilled liars. But how *could* it be true?

When Humphrey was done, he shook his head, saddened but not surprised by yet more evidence of the suffering that war inflicted, usually upon the innocent and the helpless. "They say that Saladin arrived at Ascalon six days after the battle of Arsuf and personally supervised the destruction of their city. This created a panic, of course, as the townspeople sought desperately to sell what belongings they could not take with them. Their family was lucky enough to have a donkey cart, but many did not and the prices of horses soared, while the prices of household goods and livestock plummeted so low that a man could buy twelve chickens for only one *dirham*. Whilst some sought passage on ships to Egypt, most of the citizens did not know where to go, and there was much weeping and fear. The sultan opened the royal granary to the people, but most lost everything they owned. They had a candlemaking shop which is gone now, burned like much of the city. They say they are Christians, not Muslims, and so they hoped we would take pity on them."

Seeing a question forming on Richard's lips, Humphrey said swiftly, wanting to protect these poor wretches if he could, "I suppose they may be lying, but it could well be true, for it is not unusual to find native-born Christians living in Saracen towns. In fact, Saladin encouraged the Syrian Christians and Jews to remain in Ascalon after he captured it four years ago." Adding reluctantly, "I can find out for certes if you wish, see if they know the *Pater Noster*, the *Ave Maria*, and the *Credo*—"

Richard cut him off impatiently, for he had more pressing concerns than the religious faith of these bedraggled refugees. "What would compel him to sacrifice such an important stronghold?"

"They say Saladin was sorely grieved, so much so that he took sick when he saw the misery of the townspeople, and they heard he'd even said he would rather have lost all of his sons than demolish a single stone of their city. But his soldiers told them that he'd been advised he could not defend both Ascalon and Jerusalem, and he feared that no garrison could be trusted to hold firm after the killing of the men at Acre. So rather than have it fall intact into your hands, he chose to destroy it."

It was obvious to Richard that Humphrey believed them, but he was still not convinced that Saladin had truly taken a measure so desperate. "See that they are fed, Humphrey," he said, and then looked around at the other crusaders, all of them dumbfounded, too, by what they'd just heard. "Take a galley at first light," he told Joffroi de Lusignan, "and see if Ascalon is truly in flames."

As soon as Joffroi de Lusignan had finished speaking, Richard moved to the center of his tent. "Well, we know it is indeed true. But the city is not fully razed to the ground yet, so there is still time. I will take part of the fleet on the morrow whilst the Duke of Burgundy follows along the coast road. It is only thirty miles from Jaffa, so we ought to be able to seize the city ere Saladin can complete its destruction."

"Attack Ascalon?" Hugh of Burgundy was staring at Richard in disbelief. "Why would we want to do that? Now that we hold Jaffa, we can march upon Jerusalem."

Richard was taken by surprise, for the advantages of taking Ascalon seemed so obvious to him that he hadn't expected to have to argue about it. "Ascalon controls the road to Egypt," he said, striving to hide his vexation beneath a matter-of-fact demeanor, "and Egypt is the base of Saladin's power. If we hold Ascalon, we can cut off his communications and supplies from Alexandria. Moreover, Saladin will fear that we mean to strike into Egypt itself, and so we could—"

"Have you lost your mind?" Hugh was on his feet now, but the Bishop of Beauvais was even quicker.

"I cannot speak for the rest of you," he said angrily, "but I did not take the cross to help Lord Lionheart add Egypt to his Angevin empire! Was Cyprus not enough for you, Richard? Are you lusting after the riches of the Nile now, too?"

"I am not seeking to conquer it, you fool! It is enough if Saladin thinks we are, for if he believes his Egyptian domains are threatened, he'll be all the more likely to agree to favorable peace terms—"

"Now we come down to it," Hugh interrupted. "I've been suspicious of your intentions from the first, for you opened talks with Saladin as soon as you arrived at Acre, treating this infidel as respectfully as if he were another Christian prince. But I can assure you that the rest of us did not come to the Holy Land to make peace with the enemies of God. We came to recover the city of Jerusalem!"

"And how do you plan to do that, Hugh? We were able to reach Jaffa because we had the support of my fleet; they kept us supplied. When we head inland toward Jerusalem, we have to bring all our provisions with us. Have you even spared a thought to what a march like that would be like? We cannot put an army in the field to match Saladin's; we cannot even replace the horses we lose!"

"What are you saying, my lord king?" Even though he was from one of the noblest families of France, Mathieu de Montmorency usually kept quiet in such councils, acutely aware that he was only seventeen years old and a battle novice. But he was too distraught now to remain silent. "You mean we have no chance of retaking the Holy City?"

"I am not saying that, Mathieu," Richard assured the boy. "But we must first make sure we can protect our supply lines. If we had marched toward Jerusalem from Acre as some of you wanted, we would likely all be dead by now. We reached Jaffa because you listened to me, not the Bishop of Beauvais and his ilk. So heed me now. Ascalon is the key to Jerusalem, and if you doubt that, why would Saladin destroy it rather than risk its capture? It is not enough to take the Holy City. Then we must hold it. And if we have Ascalon, we just might be able to do that."

Richard had been focusing his attention upon Hugh and Beauvais. Turning toward the others, he was dismayed by what he saw—or did not see. They looked troubled, uncertain, ambivalent, not like men who understood the truth, his truth. Even some of his own lords seemed conflicted. "Listen to me," he urged, in what was as close as he could come to an entreaty. "I cannot stay in Outremer indefinitely. None of us can. You think Saladin does not know that? All he has to do is to outlast us, wait for us to go back to our own lands. This is why we must come to terms with him. And to get him to agree to a peace that both sides can live with, we need leverage. We need Ascalon."

"You are giving the Saracens too much credit and our army too little." Hugh had gotten his temper under control, and his calm certitude was more convincing than his earlier antagonism; even Richard could see that. "This is not just another squabble between the kings of England and France. This is a holy war, sanctioned by Almighty God. Can you not see what a difference that makes? Our Lord Christ died on this hallowed soil. Do you think He has led us this far to fail? You talk of strategy and supplies. But what of God's Will? I say we continue refortifying Jaffa and then use it as a base to recapture Jerusalem."

"The Almighty still expects us to do our part! By your logic, Hugh, Ḥaṭṭīn ought to have been a Christian victory since they had God on their side. Yet even God's Army can be defeated if outmaneuvered and outnumbered."

"I am glad that you recognize it is God's Army, not your own," Beauvais jeered. "If you want to chase off to Ascalon, do so. But the rest of us are going to honor our vows to recover the Holy City."

Richard's eyes glittered, his color rising. Before he could respond, Hugh seized the opportunity the bishop had given him. "Do you remember the question you posed to the French lords at Acre? You asked them whether they were going back to Paris with our king or going on to Jerusalem with you. I say we ask again. How many of you want to follow the English king to Ascalon? And how many of you would rather we lay siege to Jerusalem?"

It was soon apparent that Hugh and Beauvais would win the vote count. Richard was backed up by the Templars, the Hospitallers, Guy de Lusignan and his brothers, the other *poulain* lords, and most of his barons and bishops. But the crusaders from Europe saw Ascalon as a needless detour on the road to Jerusalem. Virtually all of the French, Flemings, Bretons, and some of Richard's own vassals wanted to recover the Holy City as soon as possible, eager to see the sacred Holy

Sepulchre for themselves and to walk in the Lord Christ's blessed footsteps, but eager, too, to fulfill their vows so they could return to their homes and families and the lives they'd left behind.

Richard was shocked, for he'd honestly believed that his argument would carry the day. How could seasoned soldiers like Guillaume des Barres and the counts of St Pol, Chalons, and Clermont fail to see that he was in the right? Yet of the French lords, only Henri had loyally declared in favor of Ascalon; even Jaufre, looking stricken, had mumbled "Jerusalem." For several moments, Richard considered going his own way, leading his men and Outremer's lords south to seize Ascalon whilst letting the others fend for themselves. But that was the Devil whispering in his ear, for what could gladden Saladin more than such a schism in the Christian ranks?

"So be it," he said curtly, for he was damned if he'd be a good sport about it, not when so much was at stake. "But it is a mistake, one we are all going to regret."

HENRI AND ANDRÉ had been searching for Richard in growing concern, unable to understand how a king could suddenly disappear. They finally found him on the beach. The wine-dark sky was spangled with an infinity of shimmering stars, the moon silvering the whitecaps as they churned shoreward, a light, variable wind chasing away the last of the day's heat. But the serenity of the night was at odds with the emotions unleashed by the scene in Richard's command tent. He turned in the saddle as they rode toward him, and for a time they watched without speaking as the waves splashed onto the sand, receded, and surged back.

"How can they be so blind?" Richard asked after a long silence. His mood had swung from fury to frustration to bafflement; now he just sounded tired. "They are not fools, not even those whoresons Burgundy and Beauvais. So why would they not heed me?"

André had no answer for him, but Henri did. Reining in his horse beside Richard's Spanish stallion, he said, "Because Hugh was right. A holy war *is* different. They are listening to their hearts, Uncle, and the heart is not always rational."

"Are you saying that Jerusalem matters more to them than it does to me? God's Bones, Henri, I was one of the first to take the cross!"

"No one doubts your devotion to our quest, Uncle. But you are a soldier, first and foremost, and most of them are now pilgrims, albeit armed ones. You want to win the war and secure a peace that Saladin will honor. They just want to recapture Jerusalem, whatever the cost. Try not to blame them for that."

"I do not," Richard insisted, not altogether truthfully. "But as I told them tonight, this was a mistake, a great mistake."

They agreed, so emphatically that Richard took a small measure of comfort in their loyalty. But he remained convinced that they'd let a rare opportunity slip away, one that might not come again.

THEY CONTINUED WITH the refortification of Jaffa, Richard occasionally taking a hand himself in the repair work, which astonished his barons and endeared him to his soldiers. By Michaelmas, they'd made so much progress that Richard felt he could spare a few hours to go hawking in the low hills south of Jaffa. He'd brought his own gyrfalcons on the crusade; they were used mainly against cranes, though, and required greyhounds for the kill once the falcon had brought down its much larger prey. But Saladin had sent him a saker during his illness at Acre, and he was curious to try it out, having been told it was the main hunting bird of the Saracen falconers. They had a successful hunt, catching partridges and even a red hare. Richard was still restless, and after sending the falcons and their game back to Jaffa, he headed out to do reconnaissance.

This hunt was not as successful; they encountered no Saracen scouts or patrols. By now the enervating heat of midday was upon them, and when they found a small stream by a wild olive grove, they dismounted to water their horses and rest awhile. Bracing his back against a tree, Morgan was grateful to escape the Syrian sun, for he did not think he'd ever adjust to Outremer's torrid climate. Off to his left, he could hear Richard talking with Renier de Maron, telling the *poulain* lord that they'd heard Conrad had been making overtures to Saladin and asking Renier if he thought Conrad was capable of such treachery. Under another tree, Warin Fitz Gerald had produced some dice and was playing a game of raffle with Alan and Lucas L'Etable. Morgan was half tempted to join in, but that would require moving. He was dozing when Guilhem de Préaux plopped down beside him, saying he'd like to learn some more Welsh curses.

Morgan was happy to oblige, for he shared Guilhem's interest in foreign languages; they'd both picked up a few useful Greek phrases in Sicily and Cyprus and were now doing their best to master a bit of the equally challenging Arabic. He taught the other knight a handful of Welsh obscenities, translating *twll din* as arsehole, and *coc oen* as lamb's cock, assuring Guilhem that the latter was highly offensive in Wales. Guilhem repeated the words dutifully, committing them to memory, and then asked for the worst insult a Welshman could utter.

"Well, it is a grievous affront to say that a man is incapable of protecting his wife, for that is a serious slur upon his manhood. But I think the greatest insult by far would be to call a Welshman a *Sais*," Morgan said, straight-faced. He began to laugh, though, when Guilhem wanted a translation, admitting that *Sais* meant "Englishman."

"That does not offend me," Guilhem said with a grin, "for I'm Norman. I have some new Arabic curses for you, if you're interested?" Morgan was, and so was Renier de Maron's nephew, Walter, who moved closer to hear better; it puzzled both Morgan and Guilhem that so few of the *poulains* bothered to learn any Arabic. Unhooking a wineskin from his belt, Guilhem shared it along with his new-found store of profanities. "*Ya ibn el kalb* means 'You son of a dog,' which is a serious insult since the Saracens think dogs are unclean. To say *In'al yomak* is to curse the day you were born; I like that one myself. And *In'a'al mayteen* means 'Damn your dead.' But my *turcopole* friend Adam says the deadliest insult in Arabic is to call a man a *fatah*, even worse than calling someone a *Sais*."

"Are you going to keep us in suspense? What does it mean?"

Guilhem's grin had now spread from ear to ear. "It means 'foreskin'!" he declared, roaring with laughter at the baffled expressions on their faces. When he got his breath back, he explained that the Saracens practiced circumcision as the Jews did, and the foreskin was the fold of skin cut off and cast aside.

Morgan and Walter recoiled in mock horror, bringing their knees up to protect their family jewels, and soon all three were laughing so loudly that they attracted annoyed glances from others trying to nap. Reaching for Guilhem's wineskin, Morgan pretended to ponder this new curse and then shook his head. "I cannot see that being a useful insult once we go back to our own lands. Now 'Damn your dead,' mayhap. But if I were to call a man a 'foreskin' in a tavern brawl, he'd just stare at me in bewilderment."

"But whilst he puzzled over it, you could hit him!" Guilhem insisted, and that set them off again. This time they made enough noise to vex all of the men who'd wanted to sleep, and Richard ordered the culprits to take turns standing guard. Walter volunteered to take the first watch, and Morgan and Guilhem drew further back into the shade. Soon they, too, were dozing.

Morgan's languid dream-state was broken by a sudden shout. He jerked upright just as an arrow thudded into the tree trunk, so close he actually felt the rush of air on his skin. He instinctively ducked, hearing the high-pitched thrumming as another arrow sped over his head and, then, a muffled cry as it struck its target. All around him was chaos. Richard was yelling for them to mount up, the enemy bowmen screaming *"Allahu Akbar!"* as the men scrambled to their feet. But as the knights hastened to follow Richard's example—he was already astride Fauvel, his sword drawn—the Saracens broke off the attack. As Richard charged after them, Morgan ran toward his stallion. As he swung up into the saddle, he heard his name called out, and he glanced back to see Guilhem stooping over a man who'd taken an arrow in his shoulder.

"Fulk? How bad is it?" He'd directed the question at Guilhem, but it was the wounded knight who answered, saying he thought he could ride if they'd help him up onto his horse. Morgan quickly dismounted and between the two of them, he and Guilhem managed to boost Fulk into his saddle. His face had contorted and he was sweating profusely, obviously in considerable pain. He assured them, though, that he could make it back to Jaffa on his own, and they had to take him at his word, for they thought Richard's need was more urgent since they were all lightly armed, not having taken shields, lances, or helmets to go hawking. "Have them send a patrol out," Morgan flung over his shoulder to Fulk as he and Guilhem spurred their mounts to catch up with the other knights.

Their companions were already out of sight, having disappeared into a copse of trees up ahead. Morgan made sure his sword would be easy to slide from its scabbard, for they could hear sounds of combat by now. But nothing had prepared him for the sight that met his eyes when they rounded a bend in the road. A savage battle was in progress. Bodies lay on the ground, a horse was down and screaming, another galloping in circles, his rider slumped over the saddle, and Richard and his knights were surrounded, fighting desperately against overwhelming odds.

"Mother of God," Morgan whispered, horrorstruck, for it was obvious to him that they'd not be able to escape this trap; there were too many Saracens. But he could not ride away and leave his cousin the king and the others to die. As he unsheathed his sword, he saw Guilhem had made the same choice, for his sword was out now, too. Their arrival had been noticed and some of the Turks were turning their way. Morgan cried out, "Holy Sepulchre, aid us!" and charged toward them.

Guilhem did the same. But it was no battle cry he was screaming. As he closed with two of the Saracens, he shouted, *"Anaa Malik Ric! Anaa Malik Ric!"*

The reaction of the Saracens was immediate and dramatic. Heads whipped around in his direction and he was encircled within moments, men snatching at his reins, others leveling swords threateningly at his chest. He did not struggle, dropping his sword to the ground and raising his right hand in the Syrian gesture of surrender. Having taken him prisoner, his guards yelled to their comrades as they bore him away. And as suddenly as that, the battle was over, Richard and the other crusaders watching in stunned disbelief as their foes shied off and raced away, leaving them alone on a field with their dead and wounded.

Morgan was the only one who understood what had just happened and he was still in shock. There was no time for fear when men were fighting for their lives, but now they could acknowledge it, could admit they'd been doomed and then given an inexplicable reprieve. Once they were sure the Saracens had truly gone, they turned their attention to the men on the ground. Richard swung from the saddle, dropping to his knees beside Renier de Maron. The *poulain* lord's eyes were open, but they did not see him. Blood trickled from the corner of his mouth and his breath came in rasping gulps as the king grasped his hand. After a moment, Richard made the sign of the cross, closed those staring eyes, and rose to his feet. "How many?" he asked huskily, and winced when a shaken Warin Fitz Gerald told him they had four dead and several more were wounded.

Gazing down at the bodies of the L'Etable brothers, who'd been throwing dice with him and joking less than an hour ago, Warin found himself shivering despite the stifling heat. "Renier de Maron's nephew is dead, too. His head was bashed in. Gilbert Talbot's wound seems the worst. . . . And one of the horses broke his leg. God and His good angels looked after us this day, sire. But why? Why did they stop the fight?"

"I do not know," Richard admitted, sounding just as mystified, "I do not know. . . ."

"I do." As they all turned toward him, Morgan slid from his horse and leaned for a moment against the stallion's heaving side, for he knew the blow he was about to inflict upon Richard. "It was Guilhem de Préaux who saved us, my liege. He shouted out that he was *Malik Ric*. The Saracens rode off because they thought they'd captured our king."

There were exclamations from the men, cries of admiration for Guilhem's courage mixed with fear for his likely fate. Richard said nothing, but all the color had drained from his face. It was only when he realized that they were looking to him for guidance that he pulled himself together and began to issue orders. They had to make the difficult decision to leave their dead for later retrieval; the slain knights' horses had been seized and led off by the Saracen soldiers. After putting the thrashing stallion out of his misery, they assisted their wounded to mount and rode toward Jaffa at as fast a pace as the injured could endure.

They'd only covered a mile or so before they saw plumes of dust along the horizon. As the riders came into view, Morgan gave thanks again to the Almighty, for not only had Fulk gotten to their camp, he'd sent out a rescue party. André and Henri were in the lead, with the Earl of Leicester and Guillaume des Barres close behind. They were greatly relieved to see Richard was unhurt, but he cut off their rejoicing with a terse account of Guilhem's capture, and as soon as the wounded were sent on to Jaffa, the others followed Richard as he wheeled Fauvel and led a pursuit of the Saracens that all knew was futile. But after glancing at Richard's bone-white face, none of them argued with him and they continued on until he was ready to admit defeat.

By the time they got back to Jaffa, the camp was in an uproar, and they were mobbed by men wanting to see for themselves that the king was unharmed. The wounded knights had told of Guilhem's heroic sacrifice and there was much talk of his bravery, but it was sorrowful praise, for all knew what had happened to Christian prisoners in the aftermath of the massacre of the Acre garrison. As soon as Richard dismounted, he ordered Guilhem's brothers to be found and brought to his tent. He'd only taken a few steps, though, before the Duke of Burgundy blocked his path.

"Beauvais was wrong when he said you were lusting after the gold of Egypt. It is martyrdom you are lusting after, for there is no other explanation for the way you keep courting your own death!"

Richard's eyes blazed with such fury that some of the other men instinctively drew back. "Christ, what a hypocrite you are, Burgundy! You expect me to believe your sudden concern for my well-being? We both know you'd like nothing better than to spit on my grave."

"Not so. I'd much rather piss in your open coffin. But you cannot keep up this mad behavior, not when your death would likely end our hopes of recovering Jerusalem."

"Get out of my way," Richard snarled, and when Hugh held his ground, several of the bystanders hastily stepped between the two men, Guillaume des Barres pulling his duke away while the Bishop of Salisbury sought to calm his king's rage. Henri was pushing through the crowd to reach his uncle's side. He paused, though, as he heard Guillaume's low-voiced urgings, telling Hugh that Richard was indeed too careless with his own safety but this was neither the time nor the place to argue that point. Agreeing wholeheartedly with the French knight, Henri sighed and hastened after Richard as he stormed off toward his tent.

RICHARD HAD ALLOWED his squires to remove his mail shirt, then slumped down on a coffer. He'd not worn his gambeson under his hauberk and he'd been badly bruised by blows that had gotten past his sword's defenses, but he ignored Henri's plea that he be checked out by his doctor. He looked up only when Pierre and Jean de Préaux were ushered into the tent. It was obvious that they had already been told of their brother's capture, for they had the dazed look of men torn between pride and grief.

"I want you to know," Richard said, "that I will do all in my power to gain Guilhem's freedom. I swear this upon the very surety of my soul and all my hopes of salvation."

Jean murmured an almost inaudible "Thank you, my liege." Pierre swallowed with an obvious effort and then managed a sad smile.

"You must not blame yourself, sire. My brother sacrificed himself for his king and for the Holy City, and there can be no greater honor than that. But we know there is no hope. We've heard what those Bedouin spies have reported, that Saladin has put to death all Christians unlucky enough to fall into his hands. At least we have the comfort of knowing Guilhem will soon be blessed with Life Everlasting, able to look upon the Face of Almighty God."

"No," Richard said, so urgently that they exchanged confused glances. "Saladin will not execute Guilhem, for he understands how much Guilhem's life matters to me. He knows I will pay any ransom he demands. Your brother is too valuable a hostage to be beheaded, worth far more alive than dead."

They were hesitant at first to believe him, afraid to embrace false hope. But Richard's certainty was so compelling and their need so great that by the time they departed the tent, they were no longer convinced that their brother was doomed. Once they'd gone, Henri filled two wine cups until they were in danger of overflowing. Sloshing one into Richard's hand, he said, "Do you truly believe that, Uncle?"

"I have to, Henri," Richard said, "I have to. . . ." As he turned away, Henri thought he caught a suspicious glimmer in the other man's eyes and he hastily drained his wine cup, while he, too, blinked back tears.

RICHARD'S FRIENDS WAITED five days before bearding the lion in his den.
Henri and André were the ringleaders and they'd carefully selected crusaders the
king was most likely to heed—Baldwin de Bethune, the Earl of Leicester, the
Bishop of Salisbury, Morgan ap Ranulf, Jaufre of Perche, Guillaume des Barres,
and the Grand Masters of the Templars and Hospitallers. And so on a Friday evening at twilight not long after Richard had returned from a scouting mission, he
found himself confronted by men whose opinions he could not dismiss as easily
as he had Hugh of Burgundy's.

"As much as it pains me to say it," Henri began, for he'd been given the dubious
honor of being their spokesman, "there were a few grains of sense midst Hugh's
ranting." Seeking to head off the gathering storm clouds, he said hastily, "Uncle,
even a blind pig can find an acorn occasionally. And whilst none of us believe his
charge—that you are courting your own death—we do fear for your safety. The
line between courage and recklessness is not as blurred as you seem to think."

"I lead by example," Richard said flatly. "Our men are so willing to risk their
lives on a daily basis because they see that I am risking mine, too."

None could argue with that, for Richard had just uttered a basic truth of war,
one noncombatants did not always understand—that men fought for one another
as well as for causes or profit, theirs a solidarity that only the battlefield could
forge. Henri did not think this was going as they'd hoped and he glanced toward
the others for support.

"Yes, our soldiers greatly admire your courage, Cousin. But they also fear for
your safety as we do," André said bluntly. "Last Sunday was the third time you've
nearly been killed or captured in a Saracen ambush, the very same ambushes you
warn us to avoid. It was foolhardy to chase after those Turkish archers, especially
since you all were so lightly armed. You would have been wroth with any of our
men for taking such needless chances. Can you deny it?"

Few would have dared to speak so candidly with a king, especially this one. But
André knew that Richard had inherited more than his father's notorious Angevin
temper; he had Henry's innate sense of fairness, too. Neither man had always
heeded it, of course, not a welcome thought as he waited tensely now for Richard's response.

Richard started to speak, stopped himself, and scowled, for he could not deny
it. He would indeed have berated others for ignoring the dangers of an ambush.
"One of the benefits of kingship," he said at last, "is that we get to break the rules

from time to time." Even to him, that was a lame defense, but he really didn't have one. He did not fully understand himself why he felt this compulsion to be the first into the breach, the last to retreat. What of it, though? It was part and parcel of what made him the man he was, after all.

"I do not doubt that is true, sire," the Bishop of Salisbury said, with his usual aplomb. "Kings do indeed get to break the rules. And we have not dared to reproach you for your boldness until now. But we can keep silent no longer, not when the fate of the Holy Land balances so precariously upon the blade of your sword."

"None would argue that all men's lives are of equal value," Guillaume des Barres said quietly. "Your life, my liege, is precious in God's Eyes, and not just because you are a king. You are the man chosen to defeat the infidels and restore Jerusalem to its former glory. You cannot risk such a destiny in needless skirmishes with Saracen bowmen."

As he glanced around the tent, Richard saw that same belief on the other faces, too, a conviction strong enough to risk his anger, even though theirs was a world in which the king's favor counted for all. "It is not fair to make God your ally," he said, half seriously, "for how am I supposed to dispute His Will? I understand your concern, I do. I can promise you this much, that I will try to be more careful in the future. But in all honesty, I cannot promise more than that, for you may drive nature out with a pitchfork, but it will still return."

Most of the men hadn't expected much more from Richard and they reasoned that a qualified promise was better than no promise at all. They hoped to continue the conversation, though, wanting to make sure that he fully understood the depths of their anxiety. But it was then that Warin Fitz Gerald hastened into the tent with news that couldn't wait.

"My lord, King Guy is back! His ship has just dropped anchor in the harbor." Warin paused then, realizing that a council was in progress. "Forgive me for interrupting, sire. I thought you would want to know straightaway. . . ."

Richard had dispatched Guy to Acre with instructions to bring back the truants still enjoying themselves in the city's taverns and whorehouses. He did indeed want to know that Guy had returned, but he was also glad of an excuse to end this uncomfortable lecture. "No, we are done here, Warin. How many ships are with him?"

"Only the one galley, my liege."

"What? You mean he failed to bring any of those laggards back with him?" Richard was incredulous; how could Guy fail at such a simple task? He was halfway across the tent before he remembered the other men. "This cannot wait," he explained. "I have to find out what happened."

They agreed politely that this took precedence, and as soon as Richard had gone, they, too, began to disperse, relieved that at least they'd gotten him to listen. Only Henri and André lingered, helping themselves to some of Richard's wine, for they thought they'd earned it.

"That comment about a pitchfork . . ." André paused to take a deep swallow. "Does it mean what I think it does?"

Henri's mother had made sure he'd received an excellent education, no less thorough than Richard's, and he'd recognized the quote. "It was from Horace," he said, adding when he saw André's blank look, "a Roman poet. Yes, it does mean what you think—that a leopard cannot change his spots, and God help us all, but neither can a lion."

JOANNA AND BERENGARIA had spent the afternoon with Prior William, an English cleric who'd come to Outremer to establish a church and hospital in honor of the martyr St Thomas of Canterbury. He'd arrived during the siege and set up his chapel outside the walls, but now that Acre was in Christian hands again, he hoped to move into the city. Since Richard had promised to endow the hospital, he'd taken the women to see a suitable property near the gate of St Nicholas. Their lives were so different from what they'd experienced back in Sicily and Navarre, when royal duties had kept them busy from dawn to dusk, that they were pleased to be able to function again as queens and they gave the prior permission to purchase the building. They then visited the covered market street, where they bought perfumed soap to assuage Anna and Alicia's disappointment; the girls had wanted to accompany them, for an excursion into the city was much more appealing than their daily lessons. So it was dusk before Joanna and Berengaria returned to the palace, their household knights good-naturedly complaining about being loaded down with their purchases like pack mules.

As soon as they entered the courtyard, Anna and Alicia flew out the door to meet them. "Where have you been?" Anna scolded. "We did not think you were ever coming home!"

"We told you we'd not be back until Vespers," Berengaria said, puzzled, while Joanna studied the girls with sudden suspicion. They were flushed with excitement, had clearly been up to something, and she hoped they hadn't been playing pranks again. The timid Alicia had blossomed under the bolder Anna's tutelage and they'd been chastised in the past week alone for smuggling a mouse into the bed of the Lady Uracca, giggling uncontrollably during the morning Mass, and sneaking a roast from the kitchen to feed to Joanna's dogs.

"We have a gift for you. But it is a surprise, so you must first cover your eyes," Anna insisted, producing two silk scarves for that purpose. Joanna was game, but Berengaria balked.

"I am not going to put on a blindfold," she protested, and was holding firm despite the girls' entreaties when she glanced across the courtyard and saw the man watching in amusement from the door of the great hall. "Richard!" Her dignity forgotten, at least for the moment, she gathered up her skirts and ran into his arms, followed by a delighted Joanna and the disappointed Anna and Alicia.

"You were supposed to wait, *Malik Ric*," Anna pouted, but Richard was too occupied with kissing his wife and then hugging his sister to pay her much mind.

DINNER WAS THE MAIN MEAL of the day and so supper was usually a more modest affair. But Richard, Baldwin, Morgan, and the other knights he'd brought with him proclaimed the lamb stew to be utterly delicious, regaling the women with stories of the dubious victuals cooked over their campfires. Richard did not find the conversation as appealing as the food, though. Guy de Lusignan had often boasted that he'd kept no secrets from his queen, and Richard discovered now that Guy had been as forthright with Berengaria and Joanna as he'd been with Sybilla. He'd told them all about the deprivations and dangers of the march, including Richard's narrow escapes and his crossbow wound. Richard did his best to gloss over the perils they'd faced, and then turned the talk to lighter fare, telling the women about their comic encounters with jerboa, strange rodent-like creatures that hopped like rabbits, and relating the story of Baldwin's disastrous attempt to ride a camel, thankful that at least Guy had not mentioned the Michaelmas ambush.

He was soon to learn otherwise. After they'd consumed the final dish of dates, almonds, and honey, his wife and sister steered him toward the relative privacy of a window-seat. "We were deeply sorry to hear of Jacques d'Avesnes's death," Joanna said somberly. "It is almost as if his Flemish hounds know that he is not coming back, for they have been very subdued and eating poorly." She hesitated, exchanged glances with Berengaria, and then plunged ahead. "Had you been slain at Arsuf, too, Richard, it would have been a grief almost beyond bearing for us. But how much worse it would have been if you'd died in that Michaelmas battle;

then we'd have been tormented with 'what if' and 'if only,' even the guilt of blaming the dead, for how could we not be angry with you for taking such needless risks?"

Richard was at a rare loss for words. "Anyone who thinks women do not speak their minds has never met you, Joanna," he said ruefully. "I am sorry Guy told you about that, for I know you both worry enough about my safety as it is. What Guy did not know is that Henri and André and others have already taken me to task for it. They reminded me that my death could guarantee victory for Saladin, and I promised them that I would try to remember that in the future."

"Will you promise us, too, Richard?"

"I will, Berenguela," he said, and she took comfort from the fact that he sounded utterly serious for once.

"Just remember," Joanna warned, "that if you do not mend your ways, Richard, I will have no choice but to write to Maman about your rash behavior."

"Jesu forfend!" he exclaimed, and when they grinned at each other, Berengaria felt a pang, for their easy camaraderie stirred memories of her brother Sancho, so far away in Navarre.

Joanna's expression soon sobered, for they'd not yet spoken of Guilhem de Préaux. Her gratitude to the Norman knight was magnified by grief; she'd liked Guilhem, remembering how kind he'd been in Cyprus, quickly concocting a lie to shield Berengaria from Richard's neglect. "Guy did not think there was much hope of ransoming Guilhem de Préaux. Is Guy right about that, Richard?"

"I am beginning to wonder if Guy de Lusignan has been right about anything in his life," he said, with an exasperated grimace. "He is most definitely wrong about Guilhem. He has not been executed, nor harmed in any way. But Saladin is refusing to ransom him because he knows how much I want his freedom. That makes him a very valuable bargaining counter, so Saladin means to hold on to him for now."

"But the Saracens must have been sorely disappointed to find out that they did not capture you, after all. Would they make Guilhem suffer for his deception?"

"No, al-'Ādil assured me that he is being treated with respect, Berenguela. The Saracens value courage and loyalty as much as we do."

Joanna's relief was so great that she leaned back in the window-seat, closing her eyes. Berengaria smiled and squeezed Richard's arm. "Al-'Ādil is Saladin's brother, no? But are you sure you can trust him?"

"Yes," he said, "I am. I resumed talks with him not long after Arsuf, and I think he is a man of honor. Of course, Burgundy and that bastard Beauvais would swallow their tongues if they ever heard me say that! To hear them tell it, I came to Outremer for the sole purpose of betraying the kingdom to the Saracens. Meanwhile, their ally, Conrad of Montferrat, is said to be trying to strike a deal with Saladin that would enable him to hold on to Tyre and Sidon."

Both women were so indignant that it was a while before Joanna remembered she had a surprise for Richard. "I almost forgot! A troubadour from Aquitaine arrived in Acre last month. Whilst he may not be as celebrated as Gaucelm Faidit, he is very good, and I arranged for him to entertain us tonight."

"Mayhap tomorrow, *irlanda*. Tonight I think I'll let Berenguela entertain me," Richard said, giving his wife a sidelong smile. As he expected, her creamy skin took on a deep-rose tint and her lashes fluttered downward. But the corners of her mouth were curving as she murmured demurely that it would be her pleasure. "I hope it will not entirely be yours, little dove," he said and pulled her to her feet.

Joanna stayed in the window-seat. Across the hall, Morgan and Mariam were playing chess, but there was an intimacy in their laughter that told Joanna their ongoing flirtation was becoming something more. Her gaze shifted to her brother and his bride, who were exiting the hall with unseemly haste, and she leaned back against the cushions again with a soft sigh. She was happy whenever Richard paid Berengaria the attention she deserved, and she was pleased, too, that Mariam seemed to have found a man she could care for, but she could not suppress a twinge or two of envy. She would soon be twenty-six, too young to be sleeping alone.

"Is this the crossbow wound?" Getting a drowsy confirmation from Richard, Berengaria asked then about a scar on his hip and traced its path with her fingers when he said it was an injury from his early years as Count of Poitou. "What of this scar on your wrist?"

"I do not even remember how I got that one," he yawned. "What are you doing, taking inventory of all my wounds?"

"Not all of them," she said softly, for she'd kept her eyes averted from the ugly yellowing bruises on his shoulder and chest, still very visible eight days after the Michaelmas ambush. Seeking a safer topic of conversation, she said, "You seem so different with such short hair, Richard!" She thought his scalp looked like a hedgehog's bristle, assuming there were red-gold hedgehogs, but she wasn't sure he'd take that as a compliment and kept it to herself.

"It just seemed easier to cut it off and let it all grow back at the same time." He yawned again, but she refused to take the hint, determined to make the most of this unexpected reunion, for she had no way of knowing how long it would be until she'd see him again.

"I was so glad to hear that Guilhem is safe. I owe him a debt that can never be repaid."

"So do I," he said, so low that she barely heard him. "I'd give half of all I own if only I could relive that day. . . ."

She was deeply touched that he trusted her enough to make such an admission. "I do not know war as you do, Richard, but I am sure Henri and André and your friends would tell you what I am about to say now, that those deaths were not your fault. If you had not followed the Saracens, they would likely have still attacked since you were so outnumbered."

"But I ought not to have gone out with such a small escort. I knew better, Berenguela. It is just that scouting is so important. . . ."

She did not dispute that, but she suspected that he went out scouting himself because he enjoyed it, too. "I shall hold you to your promise," she said, and offered up a silent, fervent prayer that these Michaelmas memories would curb some of his recklessness in the future. "How long can you stay, Richard? Joanna would be greatly pleased if you could remain for her birthday."

"I cannot spare that much time, little dove. I will have to go back to Jaffa as soon as I drag those sluggards out of Acre's bordels and hellholes. Guy's leadership leaves much to be desired if he cannot even get a bunch of lazy drunkards to obey him. At least he is not secretly conspiring with the Saracens like that Judas in Tyre. It is pitiful, though, that the best to be said of Guy is that he is not a traitor."

She was only half listening to his complaints, so great was her disappointment that he'd be returning to Jaffa so soon, for she didn't doubt that he'd round up all of his fugitive soldiers in a matter of days. "I will miss you," she said, and he propped himself up on his elbow to look down into her face.

"Well . . . I was thinking of taking you and Joanna back to Jaffa with me. I will understand, though, if you'd rather remain in Acre, for Jaffa would not be as comfortable as the palace here—"

"Richard, of course I want to come with you! How could you ever doubt it?"

He hadn't, for by now he knew the mettle of the woman he'd married. "Actually, I was just being polite and giving you a choice," he said with a grin. "I took it for granted that you'd want to come, one of the many reasons why I consider myself a lucky man."

Berengaria blushed again, this time with pure pleasure, and was emboldened to flirt a little. "May I hear these reasons, my lord husband?"

"The first one is that you are not Alys Capet," he said, so promptly that she realized he'd given this some thought. "Alys could never have coped with the storms at sea and Isaac Comnenus as you did. I doubt that she could even have adapted to life in an army camp, much less in the midst of a siege." He shifted so she could cradle her head in the crook of his shoulder. "You want more reasons? Women are never satisfied, are they?" He gave a loud put-upon sigh, but she knew he was teasing, and after a moment, he said, "Well, I am grateful that you are so sweet-natured. And undemanding; men like that. You have never complained about my snoring, you smile whenever you see me, and you let me have that last helping of dates and almonds tonight."

This playful litany of her virtues was hardly a passionate declaration of love, but she'd not expected one. It was enough for her that he seemed so content with their marriage, that he could offer affection and respect, for she knew not all wives were so fortunate. And when he continued, saying that she had more courage than the vast majority of her sex, with an admirable measure of steel in her spine, she felt such a surge of happiness that she could not speak, knowing that, for Richard, this was the ultimate accolade.

She'd not dared to hope that Richard would bring her to Jaffa, and she felt like a child again, given a wonderful gift when she'd least expected it. In four days, they'd have been wed for five months, and every time her flux came, it was a wound to her heart. Joanna had reminded her that a crop could not be harvested unless seed was planted first. But she could take no solace from her sister-in-law's commonsense admonition, so eager was she to give Richard the son and heir a king so needed. Now, though, she'd be able to share his bed again. The Almighty had often shown His Favor to Richard, sparing his life time after time. Why should He not show His Favor, too, by letting her conceive and bear his child here in the Holy Land? Richard was already sleeping. That was such a comforting thought that she soon slept, too.

JOANNA WAS ELATED when Richard and Berengaria broke the news the next morning. Anna and Alicia were so excited that they forgot they were supposed to act like well-behaved, modest maidens of thirteen and fourteen, shrieking with glee instead, and while Mariam said nothing, she glanced toward Morgan with a secret smile. But most of the women reacted with dismay or horror, for none wanted to trade the luxuries of the royal palace for a tent in another army encampment. Richard had said they were rebuilding Jaffa's walls; it would be months, though, before the city would revive, and it was unlikely ever to offer the markets, diversions, and security of life in Acre.

Sophia and Beatrix were too resilient and too realistic to share the consternation of the younger ladies-in-waiting, and they merely exchanged looks of resignation. Taking their breakfast wine, fruit, and bread to a corner table, they watched with detachment as the other royal attendants struggled to hide their unhappiness. "Only two kinds of women would want to follow men off to war," Beatrix grumbled, "one too adventuresome for her own good or one determined to be a dutiful wife come what may. It is just our bad luck that Joanna is the first kind and Berengaria the second, so we can expect no voice of reason from either of them."

Sophia was wryly amused and chuckled between bites of melon. "That is certainly true for your lady and for my Anna, too, but it is not duty that is drawing Berengaria to Jaffa. Heaven help the lass, she practically glows whenever she looks at him. I suppose it is only to be expected; a man acclaimed as the savior of Christendom is bound to turn female heads. It would be better for her, though, if she were not so smitten. The happiest marriages are those uncomplicated by passion or, God forbid, love."

Beatrix had been a widow for many years, but most of her memories of that long-ago marriage were pleasant ones. "You do not think that is a harsh assessment? Of course, your husband . . ." She stopped, for there was no tactful way to suggest that Isaac Comnenus was one of Satan's minions.

"Oh, my husband was a monster," Sophia said, so blithely that Beatrix blinked. "But I've seen enough of other marriages to realize that men, even the good ones, cannot be trusted with something as fragile as a woman's heart. They are much too careless." Glancing across the hall, she said dryly, "Lionheart is probably lucky, though, that his bride is still bedazzled. How many other queens would be so willing to become camp followers?" Beatrix joined in her laughter, and then they rose and made ready to play their parts, to act as if they shared Joanna, Berengaria, Alicia, and Anna's eagerness to accompany Richard back to Jaffa.

CHAPTER 28

OCTOBER 1191

Camp of Al-'Ādil, Near Lydda, Outremer

ahā' al-Dīn had been with his sultan at Latrun. When he received the summons from Salah al-Dīn's brother, he presumed it meant there'd been new developments in the ongoing talks with the English king. Once he was escorted into al-'Ādil's tent, his surmise was confirmed, for it was to be a rare private audience; the only other person present was Sani'at al-Dīn ibn al-Nahhal. The latter was al-'Ādil's scribe, and so trusted despite his unusual background—he'd converted to Islam from Christianity—that he'd been the one conducting the negotiations on his lord's behalf.

Ordinarily, Bahā' al-Dīn would have been offered a cooling drink, an iced *julab*. But this was the twenty-ninth day of *Ramadan*, their month of fasting, and Muslims were expected to refrain from eating or drinking from sunrise to sunset. So after greetings were exchanged, Bahā' al-Dīn sat cross-legged on cushions and politely waited to learn the reason for his presence. They spoke casually for a time about various subjects: the welfare of their respective families, the escape from Acre of one of their emirs, who'd climbed down a rope from a privy window, and the troubling news that the local peasants were providing the Franks with large quantities of food. But al-'Ādil soon got to the point of the visit.

"You are familiar with the first offer made by the English king?"

"I am, my lord," Bahā' al-Dīn assured him. Richard had sent a remarkably candid letter to Salah al-Dīn, saying that both sides were suffering great losses and they needed to find a way to end the war. He'd asked for the lands west of the River Jordan and the city of Jerusalem. He'd further argued that the True Cross ought to be returned, as "to you it is nothing but a piece of wood, but it is very

precious in our eyes." Salah al-Dīn had rejected all three demands, insisting that
the Holy City was more sacred to Muslims, "for it was the place of our Prophet's
journey and the place where the angels gathered." The lands in question belonged
originally to them, and the possession of the cross "is a great advantage to us and
we cannot give it up except we could thereby gain some advantage to Islam." The
talks had stalled after that and Bahā' al-Dīn was quite curious to find out what the
infidels were offering now.

"We've often agreed that the Franks are a predictable people," al-'Ādil said
with a faint smile. "But that cannot be said of the English king, for he has come
up with a truly surprising proposal. He suggests that we resort to a tried-and-true
method of making peace—a marriage."

Bahā' al-Dīn was astonished. It was true that in the Christian and Muslim
worlds, wars were often settled by marital alliances. But this was a holy war, both
to the Franks and the Saracens. "Whose marriage, my lord?" he asked warily.

Al-'Ādil's dark eyes shone with amusement. "Mine. The English king has
offered me his sister, the widow of the King of Sicily."

Bahā' al-Dīn prided himself on his inscrutability; that was an essential skill for
a diplomatic envoy and a useful one for any man who must deal with princes. But
his discipline failed him now. He gasped audibly, his mouth ajar, so obviously
flabbergasted that the other men burst out laughing. "Surely he was joking!"

Al-'Ādil glanced toward his scribe, indicating that he should be the one to
answer. "It is not always easy to tell with him, my lord, for he has a bantering
manner, often speaking half seriously, half in jest. But I do not think this was a
joke."

"If so, it is a remarkably detailed joke," al-'Ādil commented. "The Lady Joanna
would be crowned Queen of Jerusalem, which would become the capital of our
realm. My brother would give me the lands between the River Jordan and the sea,
making me its king, and Richard would give his sister the coastal cities of Acre,
Jaffa, and Ascalon as her dowry. Jerusalem would have no Christian garrison, just
priests and monks, but Christians would be free to visit or dwell there. The villages would be given to the Templars and the Hospitallers, and my wife and I
would hold all the castles. Our new kingdom would still remain part of the sultan's dominions. Their holy cross would be returned to them, and there would be
an exchange of prisoners on both sides. And after the peace treaty was signed,
Richard and the Franks from beyond the sea would return to their own lands.
Presumably, then, we would all live in peace."

Bahā' al-Dīn found himself agreeing with al-'Ādil; this was exceptionally explicit for a joke. Surely it was not a serious offer, though. So what did the English king hope to gain by it? Was this a test of their will to continue the war? Or something more sinister? Were the Franks seeking to drive a wedge between the sultan and his brother? Seeing that al-'Ādil was waiting for his response, he equivocated, saying with a smile, "But would you be willing to wed an infidel, my lord?"

"Well, this infidel is said to be quite beautiful," al-'Ādil said with a smile of his own. "And the *Qur'an* does allow a man to wed a chaste woman amongst the People of the Book, though a Muslim woman cannot marry out of her faith, of course. I do not know if the Christians' holy book permits such marriages. I would be surprised if so. But all of this comes as a surprise, no? Say what you will of the English king, he is far more interesting than most of the infidels. Can you imagine Guy de Lusignan or Conrad of Montferrat making such an outrageous proposal?"

"They may not have available sisters conveniently at hand," Bahā' al-Dīn pointed out, and they all laughed. He was not misled, though, by al-'Ādil's wry, mocking tone. The sultan's brother was a shrewd player in that most dangerous of games, the pursuit and acquisition of power, deftly balancing his own ambitions against his loyalty to Salah al-Dīn. He was not a man to be easily outwitted or beguiled, and was naturally suspicious of this extraordinary offer. But Bahā' al-Dīn could see that he was intrigued, too, possibly even tempted by it, and why not? What man would not want a crown of his own?

"What is your wish, my lord?" he asked cautiously. "Should this be passed on to the sultan?"

"We have no choice. Even if we could be sure it was a ruse, we'd still have to inform my brother, for if nothing else, it is a revealing glimpse into the English king's mind. I have summoned Alam al-Dīn Sulaymān ibn Jandar, Sābiq al-Dīn, and several other emirs to join us after the noon prayers so we may discuss it. Then I want you to go to the sultan and tell him this—that if he approves of the proposal, I will agree to it. But if he rejects it, say that the peace talks have reached this final point and he is the one who thinks they should not be pursued further."

"I understand, my lord," Bahā' al-Dīn said, for indeed he did. Al-'Ādil was treading with care, as well he should. He was the sultan's most trusted adviser. But he was also a potential threat, for he was far more capable than any of Salah al-Dīn's sons, and despite the deep abiding affection between them, the sultan must occasionally wonder if his brother's loyalties would be as steadfast after his death. "I understand," he repeated, thinking that this infidel English king was more subtle than they'd realized and, therefore, more dangerous.

"You did what???"

"Joanna, will you let me explain? And for God's sake, lower your voice." It was not easy to find privacy in an army camp; Richard had done the best he could, seeking out his sister in her own tent and dismissing her ladies and servants. But his precautions would be for naught if she continued shrieking at him like a wrathful fishwife.

"Explain?" she echoed incredulously. "What possible explanation could you offer that I'd accept?"

Before he could respond, the tent flap was drawn aside. "Richard? Joanna? Whatever is wrong? I could hear the shouting all the way outside!"

Richard was not pleased by Berengaria's intrusion, preferring to discuss this alone with his sister. But he could hardly dismiss her as he had Joanna's attendants, and even if he'd tried to do so, he suspected that Joanna would, in her present contrary mood, insist that her sister-in-law remain.

"Do you want to tell her, Richard, or shall I?" Joanna glared at her brother, looking eerily like their mother in one of her imperial rages. "Your husband has bartered me to Saladin's brother! He has proposed peace terms based upon my marriage to al-'Ādil."

"Richard!" Berengaria was staring at him, horrorstruck. "How could you?"

"You make it sound as if I offered to trade you for a couple of camels! All I did was to suggest that a marital alliance might be one way of ending the war. I did not—"

"You were outraged when Philippe flirted with me at Messina, would never have even considered a marital alliance with France. But now you are content to marry me off to an infidel, an enemy of our faith? I think you have well and truly lost your mind!"

"I never said I intended to marry you off to al-'Ādil! I simply said I'd suggested it to him. And as I tried to tell you, I have three very compelling reasons for making such a proposal." Seeing that she finally seemed willing to hear him out, he said hastily, before she changed her mind, "First of all, Saladin is about eight years older than his brother and not in the best of health, so he likely expects to die first. Secondly, al-'Ādil has proved himself to be a man of great abilities, as skilled at statecraft as he is at winning battles. He is highly regarded by Saladin's emirs and the sultan well knows it. Finally, Saladin's first-born son is just one and twenty, his other sons much younger, and none of them have so far shown al-'Ādil's gift for command. From all I've heard, there is a close bond between the brothers. But Saladin would have to be a saint, assuming Muslims have them, for him not to worry about what happens to his empire after his death."

Pausing, he saw that his wife still looked aghast. Joanna, though, was listening. "Go on," she said. "So you are seeking to stir up discord between Saladin and his brother. How does this marriage proposal do that?"

"Because it is not one al-'Ādil can dismiss out of hand, for it would make him a king. And you a queen, in case you're interested." Seeing that she was not amused by his attempt at humor, he continued, telling her of the peace terms he'd proposed to al-'Ādil. "So you see," he concluded, "this marriage proposal is actually a trap of sorts."

"With me as bait," she said tartly. "You expect Saladin to accept this offer?"

"No, I expect him to refuse."

"You'd best hope that he does, Richard," she warned, "for I would never consent to it."

"Not even to become Queen of Jerusalem, *irlanda*?" he teased, and she frowned.

"Not even to become Queen of Heaven. I am not about to join a *harim*. Yes, I know that Muslims can have four wives, Richard. I grew up in Sicily, remember?"

"But you'd be a queen, which would surely give you greater status than his other wives," he said and ducked, laughing, when she snatched up a cushion and threw it at him.

While Berengaria was greatly relieved that Richard had not truly intended to marry Joanna to an infidel Saracen, she was troubled that he was treating it so blithely instead of with the seriousness it deserved. "I do not understand. Why would Saladin's brother believe you could dispose of the Jerusalem crown as you pleased? And why would he believe that the other Christian lords would accept this?"

Richard patiently explained that no one but Guy wanted him to remain as king and Isabella could be said to have forfeited her right to the crown because of her bigamous marriage to Conrad. "And whilst some of the *poulains* might balk, most of the men who'd taken the cross would not, for they could then visit the Holy City and its shrines, fulfill their vows, and go home."

Joanna had listened intently, her eyes narrowing. "So," she said, "you offer al-'Ādil a crown, Saladin refuses it, al-'Ādil feels cheated, and they begin to regard each other with suspicion. Is that how it is supposed to go, Richard?"

"More or less," he agreed. "Needless to say, this cannot become common knowledge. By the time Burgundy and Beauvais got through with it, they'd have me converting to Islam and launching a *jihad* to set all of Christendom ablaze."

Joanna waited until he'd kissed them both and made ready to depart. "Just out of idle curiosity, Richard, what happens if Saladin and al-'Ādil accept your proposal? What will you do then?"

He paused, his hand on the tent flap. "I'll think of something," he said with a grin and disappeared out into the night.

Once he was gone, Berengaria sat down wearily on Joanna's bed. "Sometimes I fear Richard can be too clever for his own good," she confessed. "I see the value in sowing suspicions between Saladin and his brother, but if word of this got out . . ." The mere thought of that was enough to make her flinch. "I expected the war against the Saracens to be so much more . . . straightforward. Instead it is like a quagmire, poisoned with petty rivalries, personal ambitions, and shameful betrayals. The French hate Richard. The *poulains* are at one another's throats. Guy is not fit to rule, but Richard supports him anyway because of his feuding with the French king. Philippe not only abandoned a holy war, he is likely to launch attacks on Richard's lands in Normandy in utter defiance of the Church. And Conrad is the worst of the lot, for he is actually willing to side with the infidels against his fellow Christians. It is all so ugly, Joanna."

Joanna wondered if she'd ever been as innocent as Berengaria, as trusting of men and their motives. Most likely not, she decided, but then it would have been difficult to cling to innocence in a family known as the Devil's Brood. She sat beside her sister-in-law on the bed, thinking about her father and brothers. It was not just Richard; they'd all been too clever by half, so sure they could outwit their enemies and get their own way by sheer force of will. And where had it gotten them? Papa died alone and abandoned, cursing the day he was born. Hal had been no better than a bandit in his last weeks, raiding churches to pay his routiers. Geoffrey's plotting with the French king had brought suffering upon his wife and children, for his untimely death had made them pawns in the struggle between Brittany and its more powerful neighbors. Johnny had already proven that he could not be trusted, betraying the father who'd sacrificed so much for him. As for Richard, not only did he have his full share of the Angevin arrogance, he had a reckless streak that she found deeply disturbing, for what could be more reckless than contemplating a marital alliance with an infidel prince? Why was it that Maman seemed to be the only one to learn from past mistakes?

"Joanna . . . you look so troubled." Berengaria reached over and squeezed her sister-in-law's hand. "Not that I blame you for being distraught about this scheme of Richard's. He ought to have found another way, ought not to have entangled you in it. Even knowing that he never intended for you to wed Saladin's brother, it still had to be disturbing . . ." She did not finish the thought, faltering at the skeptical expression on Joanna's face. "Surely you do not think he was lying? I cannot believe he'd ever coerce you into a godless marriage. He loves you dearly, Joanna."

"I know he does. I never feared that he'd try to wed me to al-'Ādil against my wishes. Mind you, most men are all too willing to accept *female* sacrifice for the greater good, but my happiness does matter to Richard. Yet you are deluding yourself, Berengaria, if you think this is merely a sleight-of-hand to deceive Saladin and al-'Ādil. Had I reacted differently, had I been excited at the prospect of becoming Queen of Jerusalem—and there are women who'd wed the Antichrist if there was a crown in the offing—I'd wager Richard would have begun to take the marriage proposal somewhat more seriously. If he thought I was willing to make the match, he'd have been willing to see it done."

"I do not believe that," Berengaria said stoutly, doing her best to ignore the insidious inner voice whispering that Joanna knew Richard better than she ever would. "He said it was just a stratagem. What would make you think otherwise?"

"Because it is so well thought out, so thorough. Because he believes that if the Kingdom of Jerusalem is to survive, it is necessary to come to terms with Saladin. Because those terms are fair enough that both sides could live with them. Because he sees the Saracens as his enemies, but not as evil incarnate the way most of his army does. Because he truly seems to respect al-'Ādil and probably thinks he'd be a good husband to me, aside from the small matter of his infidel faith and other wives, of course."

Joanna's smile was sardonic, but a smile nonetheless, for she was beginning to see the perverse humor in it all. It was obvious that her sister-in-law did not, though; Berengaria looked so dismayed that she regretted having been so candid. But was it so bad if Richard's halo tarnished a bit? If Berengaria was to find contentment as an Angevin queen, she needed to become more of a realist, both about their world and the man she'd married.

Patting the younger woman reassuringly on the shoulder, she said, "It does not matter what Richard might or might not have done had I shown myself willing to consider the match. I am not, so that puts an end to it."

It was not that easy for Berengaria, and she later found herself lying awake until dawn, watching the man asleep beside her. How could it even have occurred to Richard to suggest such an unholy alliance? Why was he so willing to treat with these pagans as if they were Christian princes? How could he not see that he was making needless trouble for himself? She never doubted that he was a devout son of the Church, but he had enemies beyond counting who were eager to believe the worst of him. There was so much about these Angevins that she would never understand, and that included Joanna, who, like Richard, could find unseemly amusement in matters of the utmost gravity. Her husband stirred in his sleep, and she carefully tugged at the long strand of hair trapped under his shoulder; she did not braid it on the nights he shared her bed, knowing he preferred it loose. Reminding herself sternly that she was far more fortunate than most wives, she stretched out and closed her eyes. But she still felt unsettled, perplexed, and suddenly very lonely, for she could hear the echoes of her beloved brother Sancho's voice, giving her that gentle warning back in Pamplona. *They are not like us, little one.* Indeed they were not.

WHEN BAHĀ' AL-DĪN carried Richard's proposal to Salah al-Dīn, the sultan at once accepted it, for he was convinced the English king would never carry it out, that his latest gambit was either a joke or a deceitful trick. Richard responded with a regretful message that Joanna was resisting the marriage, but he hoped to persuade her there was no other way to end the war. Although the Saracens remained highly skeptical, the secret negotiations resumed.

RICHARD CONTINUED to give his family, friends, and army reasons to fear for his safety; encountering some Saracen scouts near Jaffa, he forced a battle, killing an emir, taking prisoners, and shrugging off criticism afterward. The following day, All Hallow's Eve, he entrusted Jaffa and his women to the Bishop of Evreaux and the Count of Chalons, and moved the army four miles to Yāzūr, where he camped midway between the Casal of the Plains and Casal Maen, two Templar fortresses that had been razed by Salah al-Dīn. He instructed the Templars to repair the first castle while he set about rebuilding the second one, and despite daily harassment by the Saracens, they made enough progress to excite his men, who were impatient to begin the march upon Jerusalem and saw this as a first step.

SIX DAYS LATER, a small group of squires ventured out to forage, guarded by Templar knights. They had filled bags with fodder and were collecting firewood when a troop of Bedouin horsemen came swooping down upon them. The Templars came to their aid, but they were outnumbered and soon found themselves surrounded. The knights then resorted to a desperate maneuver, dismounting and standing back to back as they prepared to sell their lives as dearly as possible;

their order prided itself upon never surrendering or paying ransom. It was then that André de Chauvigny and fifteen of his household knights arrived upon the scene, drawn by the commotion. Their charge temporarily scattered the Saracens, but they surged back in greater numbers, and the Franks realized this was a battle they were not going to win.

TWO MILES AWAY, Richard was supervising the rebuilding of the stronghold at Casal Maen, pleased by his men's enthusiasm for their task. It helped that the days were cooler now, although still much warmer than November temperatures back in their homelands. They were lugging bags of sand and lime and barrels of water toward a trough, making ready to mix a new batch of mortar when the sentries began to yell for the king.

The boy seemed unhurt, but he was reeling from fatigue and had collapsed upon the ground as soon as he'd blurted out his news. He was too weak to rise as Richard broke through the throng of men encircling him, panting so heavily that his narrow chest heaved as if he were having convulsions. Richard could barely hear his gasping words, and one of the first sentries to reach the squire stepped forward. "An attack by the Turks, sire, near Ibn Ibrak. He said there were too many of them for the Templars. Then other knights rode up, but they are outnumbered, too. It sounds as if they need help straightaway."

"Get him water," Richard ordered, his eyes searching the crowd of bystanders for knights who were already armed. He directed the Earl of Leicester and the Count of St Pol to lead a rescue mission, and then ran toward his tent, calling for his squires. They armed him with record speed. It still took awhile, though, for him to summon his own knights and fetch their horses, so by the time they rode out of camp, they dreaded what they might find.

It was to be even worse than they'd feared. They could already hear the familiar clash of weapons, the screams that indicated men and horses were dying up ahead. As they galloped toward the clamor, they were hailed by several Flemish squires from the foraging party, who'd been hiding in the underbrush by a dry riverbed. The youths were almost incoherent and none of them spoke fluent French, but they managed to communicate the one word that mattered, "Ambush." The attack upon the Templars had been bait for a trap, and Leicester and St Pol had ridden right into it.

Richard spurred Fauvel toward the sounds of combat, the others strung out behind him. Ahead of him was a surging mass of men and horses, a wild mêlée in which it was obvious that the Franks were greatly outnumbered. As Richard drew rein, his knights caught up with him, crying out in horror at the sight meeting their eyes. One glance was enough to tell them that the embattled knights were doomed, but they could not dwell upon that now, for they owed a greater duty to their king than to their cornered comrades. Gathering around Richard, they began to urge him to retreat, arguing that they did not have enough men to rescue the others and if Richard died in a futile attempt to save them, their hope of defeating Saladin would die with him.

Richard angrily cut off their entreaties. "I sent those men out there, promising that I would follow with aid. If they die without me, may I never again be called a king." And with that, he couched his lance and charged the Saracens, shouting the battle cry of the English Royal House, *"Dex aie!"*

He impaled the first man to challenge him, flinging him from the saddle with such force that he was dead before he hit the ground. Dropping his broken lance, Richard then unsheathed his sword and urged Fauvel into the fray again, attacking so furiously that the enemy soldiers shied away, seeking easier prey. By now his men knew he was there, fighting with them, and not for the first time the presence of a king turned the tide of battle. They rallied, seizing the momentum Richard had given them, and drove the Saracens back, long enough for them to manage a retreat from the field.

It was not a victory, but for the men sure they were facing death or capture, it was even sweeter—a reprieve, a rescue against overwhelming odds. When word spread of Richard's defiant vow that he'd never let them die alone, even those who usually disapproved of his bravura exploits were impressed, and to the disgust of Richard's most implacable foes, the November 6 battle burnished the growing legend of the Lionheart even more brightly.

RICHARD HAD so exhausted himself with his exertions, though, that he had to be bled by his physicians the next day, and so it was not until the following day that he was able to meet with al-'Ādil at the latter's camp.

ANDRÉ AND HENRI were among the very few whom Richard had taken into his confidence about the proposed marital alliance, and they accompanied him to the meeting. André was not completely comfortable to be drinking and eating with men who may have been among those seeking to kill him two days ago at

Ibn Ibrak, but the bizarre aspects of the event appealed to Henri's quirky sense of humor and he enjoyed himself thoroughly.

Al-'Ādil welcomed the English king and his companions as graciously as if they were esteemed allies and not men who'd shed so much Saracen blood. Richard had earlier sent al-'Ādil a magnificent stallion, and the sultan's brother now reciprocated with seven camels and a splendid, spacious tent. The Saracens took the obligations of hospitality seriously and Henri would later tease Joanna that she'd be well fed if she married al-'Ādil, for he set a sumptuous table. He explained that he could not offer them wine, as it was *haraam*, forbidden by the *Qur'an*, but they were served delicious fruit drinks cooled with snow and rosewater *julabs*. His guests politely hid any disappointment over the lack of wine and complimented the variety of dishes put before them, grateful that al-'Ādil had remembered they could eat no meat, it being a Friday, and savoring cuisine they'd never tasted before: yogurt, couscous, a fried pistachio crepe called *qatayif*. Richard had brought samples of the food found on Frankish tables, assuring his host that he'd included no meat dishes since he knew their dietary laws held that animals had to be ritually slaughtered. Henri thought there was always some rivalry in any encounter involving royalty, and it amused him that his uncle and al-'Ādil seemed to be vying with each other to show how well they'd prepared for this occasion.

Humphrey de Toron was again acting as interpreter, seated between Richard and al-'Ādil so they could converse easily. He had one awkward moment early on, when Richard protested about his men being ambushed at a time when the two sides were conducting peace talks and al-'Ādil responded with a matter-of-fact reminder that they were at war, mentioning that they'd lost three Mamluks dear to Salah al-Dīn at Ibn Ibrak. Humphrey knew Richard had himself killed one of them during the battle, but he thought it wise to keep that to himself; nor did he translate al-'Ādil's comment about the slain men.

Otherwise, he thought the discussions were conducted with remarkable cordiality. He'd not expected the two men to have such a rapport, but for this one day at least, what they shared—a love of horses and hawking, a mutual respect for each other's courage and battle skills, a similar ironic sense of humor—was enough to bridge the great gap that separated Christians and Muslims, men sworn to holy war and *jihad*.

They had a lively conversation about horse breeding and the different riding styles of the Franks and the Saracens, followed by a discussion of hunting; Richard was fascinated to learn al-'Ādil used trained cheetahs. Eventually, of course, the talk turned to a more controversial topic—the marriage proposal.

430   SHARON PENMAN

"I was desolate," al-'Ādil said blandly, "to hear that your lovely sister is loath to become my wife."

"All is not lost," Richard assured him. "But she does have qualms about wedding a man not of her faith. Mayhap there is a way to resolve this, though. Would you consider becoming a Christian?"

Al-'Ādil nearly choked on his *julab*, but recovered quickly. "Mayhap the lady would consider becoming a Muslim," he parried, and when his gaze met Richard's, they shared a smile of perfect understanding.

"Alas, there have been further complications," Richard confided. "Our bishops and priests are adamantly against the match, so it will be necessary to secure the approval of the Pope in Rome. It will take about three months to get his response, but if he consents and my sister is happy about it, then well and good."

"And if he refuses?"

"We can still get it done. My sister, as you know, is a widow, and so we need papal consent for her marriage. That is not true, however, for a virgin maid. So I could offer you my niece as a bride. She is very young still, but of high birth, the child of my brother and the Duchess of Brittany."

"I will pass your message on to my brother," al-'Ādil promised, and Humphrey sighed with relief, hoping this would be the end of the marriage talk, for he'd been hard put to remain impassive as Richard lied about the supposed outrage of their clerics, none of whom knew anything about the marriage proposal, and then proceeded to rewrite Church canon law to suit his own purposes. Despite his fluency in Arabic, Humphrey had not often been called upon as a translator in such high-level conferences, and he feared he might inadvertently give something away by his reaction to what was said. It was fortunate, he thought, that al-'Ādil and Richard were having too much fun with their verbal swordplay to pay him any mind.

Al-'Ādil finished his drink. "I hope we can come to terms, *Malik Ric*. For if we do not, the sultan may have to listen to other offers."

Richard wished he knew precisely what that Judas in Tyre was offering. "Tell me this, my lord. Would you ever disavow your God?"

Al-'Ādil was no longer smiling. "No, I would not."

"Nor would I. But a man who'd turn upon those of his own faith is doing just that. So why would you or your brother trust such a man?"

"An interesting question," al-'Ādil said noncommittally. "I will pass that on to the sultan, too."

"If we could meet as I've requested, I could ask him that myself," Richard suggested.

"Ah, but as my lord brother has told you, kings ought not to meet with other kings until peace has been made between them."

"Yet you and I are meeting."

"I am not a king," al-'Ādil pointed out amicably.

"You could be, if you accept my peace terms."

The other man merely laughed, and clapped his hands, for Richard had earlier expressed an interest in hearing Saracen music. Much to the surprise of the Franks, their entertainment proved to be a young woman, carrying a harp. Richard had been told the Saracens were very protective of their women, shielding them from the eyes of other men, and he was curious about her appearance, unveiled, in their midst. He leaned over to ask Humphrey if there was a tactful way to find out, but the *poulain* had no need to put such a question to al-'Ādil, for he already knew the answer. "She is a slave, my liege," he explained, so nonchalantly that Richard and his companions exchanged glances, reminded again that the Christians of Outremer were closer in some ways to the Saracens than to their European brethren.

Richard was delighted with the girl's songs, and the visit ended on a high note, with an exchange of compliments and a promise to meet again. On the ride back to their camp, Henri speculated aloud about the lovely slave's fate, suggesting that one of them ought to buy her and grinning when Richard asked if he'd have been so sympathetic had she not been so fair. He retaliated by teasing his uncle about his offer of a substitute bride, wondering aloud whom Constance of Brittany would find more objectionable as a husband for her young daughter—a Saracen or an Englishman.

"We are talking of a crown, Henri. What woman would not want to be Queen of Jerusalem?"

"Aunt Joanna," Henri retorted, and they both laughed.

Humphrey was close enough to hear their conversation, but he found no humor in it. He'd been stunned when Richard had first confided in him, and then euphoric, for this was the first glimmer of hope he'd been given in two years. If Joanna were to wed al-'Ādil and become queen, then Isabella's claim would be superseded. Since Conrad had twice discarded wives when they no longer were of use to him, surely it was possible that he might repudiate Isabella, too, if she could not secure him the crown. For a fortnight, Humphrey had allowed himself to believe in miracles—the restoration of his wife and his stolen life. But he'd slowly come to doubt the sincerity of Richard's offer, and he'd found the sudden mention of the king's niece to be troubling. It was true that Saracen girls could be wed at very young ages, with consummation usually postponed until she'd begun her flux, just as in Christian realms, so a marriage between al-'Ādil and the little Breton princess could still quash Conrad's claim to the throne. He had not been reassured, though, by the tone of the colloquy between Richard and al-'Ādil, for it had not seemed to him that either man was taking the marriage proposal seriously.

Humphrey did not dare to question Richard directly about his intentions, but he'd always found the Count of Champagne to be very affable, and upon their return to Yāzūr, he sought Henri out. "May I ask you something, my lord count? Do you think the Lady Joanna's marriage to al-'Ādil will ever come to pass?"

Henri had an unease of conscience where Humphrey was concerned. He'd supported Conrad's marriage to Isabella because he'd been convinced by the *poulains* that the kingdom was doomed as long as Guy de Lusignan ruled over them. He could not help pitying Humphrey, though, for it had been obvious to anyone with eyes to see that he'd been in love with his beautiful young wife. It was obvious, too, what had motivated Humphrey's question, and he hesitated, finally deciding that honesty was the greater kindness now.

"No," he said, "I do not." He turned away, then, giving Humphrey the only solace he could—privacy to grieve for a shattered dream.

THE FRENCH WERE NOT the only ones displeased by Richard's cordial dealings with the sultan and his brother; many of his soldiers were also unhappy about it, and after his day-long visit with al-'Ādil, some were emboldened to speak out, saying it was not proper for a Christian king to exchange gifts and courtesies with the enemies of God. When he became aware of the growing criticism, even from men who'd always admired his prowess on the battlefield, Richard was both frustrated and angry, but he realized the danger in letting this sore go untreated. If it was allowed to fester, it could undermine his command. He chose to reassure his army with his sword, by adopting a bloody custom that had long been followed by both sides in the Holy Land. The chronicler of the *Itinerarium Peregrinorum et Gesta Regis Ricardi* would report approvingly that "To remove the stain of disgrace which he had incurred, he brought back countless enemy heads to display that he had been falsely accused and that the gifts had not encouraged him to be slow in attacking the enemy." But although he'd calmed the furor for now, the backlash had brought home to Richard a disturbing truth—that a holy war was indeed unlike other wars and he could not rely upon this motley mix of crusaders to give him the unquestioning loyalty he'd come to expect from his own vassals and lords.

THREE DAYS AFTER Richard's meeting with al-'Ādil, Salah al-Dīn summoned his brother and his emirs to a council of war at Latrun. He told them that Conrad had offered to take Acre from the Franks in return for Sidon and Beirut and a guarantee of his possession of Tyre. He then informed them of Richard's latest peace proposal. When he asked for their views, they concluded that if peace were to be made, it was better to make it with *Malik Ric*, for they were more likely to be betrayed by Conrad and the Syrian Franks. It was agreed to send word to the English king that they were not willing, though, to accept his niece in lieu of his sister as a bride for the sultan's brother. The peace talks continued then, but so did the killing.

CHAPTER 29

DECEMBER 1191

Ramla, Outremer

When Richard moved the army to Ramla, Salah al-Dīn withdrew to Latrun and then, on December 12, to Jerusalem, leaving behind his advance guard to harass the Franks. The winter weather had set in by then, and the crusaders suffered greatly, forced to endure torrential icy rains, hailstorms, high winds, and the constant threat of flooding. The damp rusted their armor and their clothes rotted. Food went bad; biscuits crumbled, flour mildewed, and salted pork spoiled. Their pack animals sickened and died and soldiers came down with fevers, catarrh, and colic. But morale remained surprisingly high, for they were now less than twenty-five miles from Jerusalem.

FRIDAY, DECEMBER 20, dawned with an overcast, ashen sky. But it was the first day in over a week that they'd not awakened to heavy rain, and Richard seized the opportunity. South of Ramla were the ruins of Blanchegarde, a castle razed by Salah al-Dīn after the fall of Acre, and he thought it would be a good site to lay an ambush. His nephew Henri and some of his household knights rode off with him, but most of the men were content to remain in camp, repairing their rusted hauberks, getting deloused by the laundresses, and playing games of chance.

Morgan had recently adopted the *poulain* clean-shaven fashion, for it reminded him of home; the Welsh were beardless, confining their facial hair to mustaches. After shaving, he played chess with Warin Fitz Gerald, half listening as the men nearby discussed the women they'd encountered since leaving Marseille a year and a half ago. The consensus was that the whores of Outremer were younger and prettier than their wanton sisters in Naples, Sicily, and Cyprus, and they agreed it was a pity the king had made them stay in Jaffa. Morgan's thoughts were turning toward Jaffa, too. Richard had decided his wife and sister were safer behind its newly rebuilt walls, but Morgan had heard he might fetch them for his Christmas court, and if so, Mariam would accompany them. He was eager for their reunion, though it would have to remain circumspect; there was no privacy in an army camp, not the sort a highborn lady like Mariam would expect.

Warin had just put the chess set away when the raid was launched. The Saracen bowmen did not actually invade the camp, but they fired off a shower of arrows, accompanied by taunts and catcalls. The Earl of Leicester and some of his knights had been about to go on patrol. Now they hastily mounted their horses and rode out to chase the intruders off. Warin and Morgan were members of Richard's household, not Leicester's, but they were bored and so they hurried to arm themselves, as did other men eager for adventure.

The Saracens retreated before Leicester's charge, withdrawing across the River Ayalon and heading back toward the Judean hills. This had become a ritual by now, with both sides knowing their roles, and the young earl prudently halted pursuit as they approached the west bank of the stream. But three of his men had forged ahead, caught up in the exhilaration of the chase, and they suddenly found themselves surrounded by the enemy. When another knight alerted the earl that they'd been captured, Leicester let out a scalding burst of profanity that even Richard might have envied, calling the knights bloody fools, misbegotten dolts, and accursed half-wits. He still felt honor bound to rescue them and gave the command to advance. By now Warin and Morgan had caught up, and they exchanged troubled glances, the same thought in both their minds, their Michaelmas skirmish that had actually been bait for an ambush.

The crusaders overtook their foes on the other side of the river and for a brief time, it looked as if they'd be able to free their men and retreat to safety. But then the trap was sprung. More Saracens swept in behind them, cutting off escape. Almost at once, a well-aimed arrow brought down Leicester's stallion and as he scrambled to his feet, he stumbled and slid down the bank into the water. It was not deep, but as he splashed to the surface, he was struck by a Saracen wielding a mace and went under. He came up sputtering, only to be hit again. By then, several of his men had reached him, and as they held off his attackers, another knight performed an act of loyalty that none would ever forget. Robert de Newburgh dismounted and offered the earl his own horse.

Leicester had already won himself a reputation for courage; indeed, he'd surprised some by his prowess, for he'd not been blessed with the physical advantages that men like Richard and Guillaume des Barres enjoyed. Never had he fought as fiercely as he did now, wielding his sword so savagely that he managed to keep his enemies at bay. But they were greatly outnumbered, and all around the earl, his men were being struck down. Warin Fitz Gerald had been unhorsed at the same time as Leicester, and he'd slumped to the ground after taking several blows by Saracens brandishing flanged maces. Fighting his way toward Warin, Morgan leaned from the saddle and held out his hand. "Swing up behind me," he urged, for a man on foot was surely doomed.

Before Warin could reach him, a Saracen was there, thrusting at Morgan's stallion with his spear. The horse reared up, hooves slipping on the muddy bank, and he and Morgan went over backward. Morgan managed to fling himself from the saddle, but his helmet's chin strap snapped and it flew off as he fell. While his mail coif absorbed some of the impact, his temple struck the edge of a dropped Saracen shield. When he recovered his senses, Warin was pulling him to his feet, the battle was lost, and he was bleeding profusely from a deep gash above his eye.

THEY'D BEEN DISARMED, their reins cut, and their horses were being led on ropes by their captors. The Earl of Leicester had no fears for his own life, for he'd make a valuable hostage. His household knights did not doubt that he'd do his best to ransom them, too, just as Warin and Morgan knew Richard would pay whatever was demanded for their freedom. There were several Flemish knights among them, though, and their lord lay dead in an Arsuf church. Without Jacques d'Avesnes to pay for their release, they might end up in the slave markets of Damascus or Cairo, and their dazed expressions showed that they understood how precarious their future was. Yet all of them were concentrating upon staying in the saddle, for any man who could not keep up was a liability.

This was Morgan's greatest concern. Despite applying pressure to his wound with the palm of his hand, he'd been unable to staunch the bleeding and he was feeling very lightheaded. If he lost consciousness, he could expect no mercy, and he clung to his saddlebow so tightly that his fingers grew numb. He was seeing the world through a red haze when he attracted the attention of one of their guards. He signaled a halt and reined in beside Morgan's horse, drawing a dagger from his boot. The closest knights began to shout and Morgan froze, trying to brace himself for the coming blow. The Saracen ignored the protests of the other prisoners.

Reaching out, he grabbed the edge of Morgan's surcote. With one deft slash of his blade, he cut off a wide swatch of cloth and handed it to the stunned Welshman. Morgan folded it and clasped it to his wound, huskily giving thanks, first to his God and then to his captor, surprising the latter by expressing his gratitude in halting Arabic.

While it was difficult to gauge direction without the sun, Morgan guessed they were heading south toward Latrun, for that was where the Saracen advance guard was camped. The makeshift bandage had finally stopped the bleeding, but his head was still spinning and he found himself fighting off nausea. Although he was beginning to doubt that he'd be able to hang on until they reached Latrun, he refused to despair. He was not going to die on this desolate, muddy plain so far from home. Surely God had not brought him all the way to Outremer only to deny him even a glimpse of the Holy City.

During the summer, dust clouds would have warned of approaching riders before they could actually be seen. Now both captors and captives were taken by surprise. The Saracens tightened their grips on their spears and the hilts of their swords. The earl's men no longer slouched in their saddles. All eyes were upon those distant horsemen. Were they Turkish reinforcements? Or a Frank rescue party? They were almost within recognition range now, moving fast. A sudden glimmer of sun broke through the cloud cover, illuminating the scarlet and silver colors of a streaming banner, and a knight with keener eyesight than the others let out a joyful shout. "It's de Chauvigny!"

The Saracens did not recognize André's cognizance, but their captives' excitement told them all they needed to know. A tense, terse discussion followed, the prisoners assuming they were arguing whether to fight or flee. When they unsheathed their swords, it was obvious the decision had been made.

"St George!" The battle cry was still echoing on the chill December air when the knights couched their lances and charged. Men were yelling in Arabic and French, but the noise seemed oddly muffled to Morgan, for there was a strange ringing in his ears. From the corner of his eye, he saw Leicester try to grab a Saracen spear. When one of the knights' horses bolted, Morgan's mount shied sideways, almost unseating him. He felt a jolt of fear, for he knew if he fell under those plunging hooves, he'd likely be trampled to death; as weak as he was, he'd never be able to regain his feet. His head was throbbing and the dull morning light was suddenly so bright that he had to squint. Someone was beside him. He felt a hand clamp down on his arm, and after that, nothing.

MORGAN HAD BEEN LOST in a shadow world of strange, fragmented dreams, none of which made any sense to him. Waking up was not much of an improvement, for he felt wretched. His head ached, his mouth was dry, and his stomach was heaving as if he were back on a galley in the middle of the Greek Sea. Most troubling was his confusion; he wasn't sure at first where he was or how he'd gotten there. As he studied his surroundings, he realized he was in a hospital tent. All around him, injured men were lying on blankets, some of them moaning. Others were sitting on stools or walking around. He could hear a familiar voice close at hand; after a moment or so, he recognized it as André de Chauvigny's. André was seated on a coffer, arguing with the surgeons. But as Morgan watched, his shoulders slumped and he nodded. He went white as they manipulated his right arm, biting his lip until it bled while they realigned the bones and then applied pulped comfrey root to the fracture. One of the surgeons was bending over Morgan now. He started to speak, but instead slid back into sleep.

When he awoke again, the scene was calmer, quieter, lit by flickering oil lamps. As soon as he stirred, a voice said, "About time! I thought you were going to sleep all day."

This voice seemed familiar, too; after a pause, he said tentatively, "Warin?"

"Who else?" The other knight was stretched out on a pallet beside him. He shifted toward Morgan and then winced. "Holy Mother! They say I cracked a couple of ribs. But the way it hurts, I think every blasted one of them could be broken. How are you feeling?"

"I've . . . been better. . . ."

"We can all say that. At least your skull was not fractured. When the doctor examined you, he said there were no indentations, no protruding bone. So he just applied an ointment of feverwort ere he bandaged . . ." Seeing the blank look on Morgan's face, he stopped. "You do not remember any of that?"

Morgan started to shake his head, discovered that was a bad idea. His memories were hazy, as elusive as drifting smoke. "I remember the battle . . . at least, most of it. . . ."

"The doctors said you might be forgetful, that it ofttimes happens with head injuries. I assume you remember André de Chauvigny's rescue? You looked like you were about to pass out, so I grabbed you and got us both clear of the fighting. Some of our men were eager to join in and indeed did so as soon as weapons began to litter the field. But I figured you and I would be more of a hindrance than a help. It was a fierce struggle. Say what you will of the infidels, they do not lack for courage."

Morgan slowly propped himself up on his elbows, his gaze searching the tent until he found the man he sought. "André was hurt, then? I thought I may have dreamed it. . . ."

"He blames himself, has been fuming about it for hours." Warin glanced admiringly toward André, who was seated on a narrow bed, scowling at his splinted forearm. "He killed the emir leading the Saracens, but the man was still able to stab him with his spear." He anticipated Morgan's next query. "Leicester is battered and bruised, but he has no serious hurts." He gestured across the tent, where the earl was having his numerous cuts and contusions tended to. "God was indeed smiling upon him this day, for he charged back into the fray and had a second horse killed under him."

A memory floated toward the surface and Morgan frowned, troubled that he could not remember the name of a man he knew well. "The knight who gave the earl his mount . . . he survived?"

"He is in better shape than either of us," Warin said with a smile. "As for you, they think you'll soon be on the mend since you showed none of the signs of a fatal injury; no seizures or fever and you can obviously talk, though you insisted upon doing it in Welsh and none of us could understand a word you said!"

"Were there prisoners taken?" When Warin nodded, Morgan resolved to see if the Saracen Good Samaritan was amongst them once he was able to do so, for he owed the man a few comforts. He still had questions, but sleep was beckoning again. Before he could answer the call, a sudden din erupted outside, and Warin grinned. "Either we're under attack or the king has just ridden in and been told of the ambush!"

It was not easy to make a dramatic entrance into a tent, but Richard did it. He headed straight for André, stood gazing down at his cousin and shaking his head. "How in the world did you manage to get injured by a man you'd unhorsed and mortally wounded?"

André's smile was sour. "How in the world did you manage to miss a battle? But I suppose you can ask Saladin to refight it for your benefit."

Richard gave a shout of laughter. "What an excellent idea!" Sitting down on the corner of the bed, he lowered his voice for André's ears alone. After exchanging a few words, he clasped the injured man on the shoulder and then made the rounds of the tent, pausing before each wounded knight to ask a question or offer a joke. He congratulated Morgan upon having such a hard head, teased Leicester for

losing two horses in a single day, and spent so much time with Robert de Newburgh that it was obvious he'd been told of the knight's heroic sacrifice.

Henri had entered almost unnoticed in Richard's wake, and after brief visits
with André and Leicester, he paused by Morgan's cot. From him, Morgan and
Warin learned that they'd abandoned their mission because Richard had an odd
premonition of danger. "It is like another sense, one given to soldiers, at least the
good ones. As it turned out, it is fortunate that my uncle heeded it, for on our way
back to camp, we encountered two of our Saracen spies and they said Saladin had
sent three hundred of his elite troops to Blanchegarde. We'd have run right into
them."

Henri stayed for a while, asking Morgan and Warin questions about the battle
and rescue, for he knew men often needed to talk afterward, and then telling
some comic stories to cheer them up, for he thought life would not be much fun
for them as they healed. Their brief weather respite had already ended and they
could hear the renewed drumming of rain on the roof of the tent.

Henri did succeed in cheering Morgan up, for he'd confided that Richard
planned to return to Jaffa on the morrow and bring the women back with him.
The young count was usually a reliable source and that proved to be the case
again. Morgan awoke from a nap on Sunday evening to find himself the envy of
the hospital tent, for two queens and the Damsel of Cyprus were at his bedside.
Berengaria expressed flattering concern for his injury, Anna gave him a Cypriot
good luck charm, and Joanna contributed an amusing account of their ride over
the very muddy Jaffa road, making it sound as if their fifteen-mile trip had been
an epic trek for the ages. But her real gift to Morgan was the screen that now
enclosed his bed. Rising to leave, she explained that she thought he'd sleep better
if he had a bit of privacy, and winked.

With a rustle of skirts and a fragrance that evoked memories of moonlit, summer gardens, Mariam slipped around the screen, leaned over the bed, and gave
Morgan a kiss that was very different from those they'd shared in the past.

"That," he said, "was worth—"

"Do not dare tell me it was worth getting your head bashed in!"

"Of course it was not worth that much," he said with a grin. "But it was worth
waiting for, *cariad*."

His blanket had slid down to his waist, and her eyes were drawn to the ripple
of muscles, a triangle of golden chest hair, and the skin that she knew would be
warm and firm to the touch, unlike the soft, flabby body of her late husband, a

good man but one well past his prime by the time they'd wed. "I think," she murmured, "that we have been waiting too long, Morgan ap Ranulf, far too long."

He reached for her hand, entwining his fingers in hers. "My sentiments exactly, my heart. Alas, our timing could not be worse, could it?"

"I know," she agreed and sighed. "I know. . . ."

"I am about to blaspheme," he admitted, "for as much as I yearn to see the Holy Sepulchre, I am even more eager now to visit Jerusalem's fine inns."

"Oh, yes," she breathed, "one with a spacious, soft featherbed, clean sheets, a flagon of spiced wine, and a sturdy latch to bar the door."

But they were miles and months away from that enticing vision and they both knew it. Kissing the face upturned to his, he brushed his lips against the lashes that shadowed her skin like silky fans, tasted the sweetness of her mouth, and found he could pretend no longer, even to himself. "Mariam . . . I have to warn you, *cariad*. I am falling in love with you."

She slanted a mischievous glance through those long, fringed lashes, her eyes shimmering with golden glints. "It certainly took you long enough," she complained, but when she added, "*Ana behibak*," he needed no translation for that alluring Arabic whisper.

"*Rwy'n dy garu di*," he said softly, and she needed no translation, either.

ON DECEMBER 23, Richard moved his command headquarters eight miles south to the ruins of the Templar castle called Toron des Chevaliers by the crusaders and Latrun by the Saracens, and there he celebrated Christmas in royal style, or as regal as festivities could be when conducted in tents during relentless rainstorms.

TWO DAYS LATER, Richard observed the holy day of St John the Apostle by holding a dinner for the *poulain* lords who'd not thrown in their lot with Conrad of Montferrat. He did not remember that it was also the twenty-fifth birthday of his youngest brother, John, not until reminded of it by Joanna, and he was sorry she had. Philippe was surely back in his own domains by now and the French king would inevitably reach out to John, try to coax or bribe him into a seditious alliance. Richard had been very generous with his brother and he ought to be able to rely upon the younger man's loyalty. But John was something of an enigma to his family, and Richard would have felt much more confident of his fealty had he not been more than two thousand miles away. No ships had arrived from Europe for months and for all he knew, Philippe was ravaging Normandy with John's heart-felt help. But he resolutely pushed these concerns aside, for "Sufficient unto the day is the evil thereof." It would be foolish to borrow fresh troubles when he was already fighting a war on three fronts—with his French allies and Saracen foes and the vile winter weather.

The dinner was a success, even if it was a Friday fast day, with lively entertain-ment provided by troubadours and musicians, and even livelier conversation. The guest of honor was Raymond, eldest son of the Prince of Antioch. Although Raymond had been an enthusiastic supporter of the crusade, his father had so far remained aloof and Richard thought it politic to make sure the son knew he was a valued ally. But the guest who shone the brightest during dinner was Hugues, Lord of Tiberias and Prince of Galilee.

Hugues was in his early forties, his shrewd, hooded eyes a startling blue against skin weathered by years of exposure to the Outremer sun, a man as resilient and enduring as the land of his birth. He'd fought at Ḥaṭṭīn; in his youth, he'd sur-vived four years in a Saracen prison; he knew Salah al-Dīn personally; he was one of the few barons of the kingdom who'd not defected to Conrad. These were all reasons why Richard considered him to be a man worth listening to; it was an added bonus that Hugues now revealed himself to be knowledgeable about one of the great mysteries of the Holy Land, the secret killing sect known as the *Assassins*.

Richard had heard of them before his arrival at Acre, for their notoriety had spread even as far as Europe. They were led by a chieftain known as "the Old Man of the Mountain," and it was said he promised his young followers an afterlife of eternal pleasure in return for a martyr's death. The Franks had told Richard their name was derived from the Arabic word for "hashish," for they were believed to imbibe it before their missions. They'd been in existence only a hundred years or so, yet there were already so many legends and lurid tales circulating about these shadowy, sinister figures that it was almost impossible to separate truth from myth.

Richard was very pleased, therefore, to discover Hugues was such a treasure trove of information about the *Assassins*. He'd even met the Old Man of the Mountain himself, Rashīd al-Dīn Sinān. Upon learning that Richard already knew Islam was split into two warring camps, *Sunnis* and *Shi'ites*, Hugues then explained that the *Assassins* were a separate *Shia* sect that originally took root in Persia, and were viewed by other Muslims as heretics. They used murder as a political weapon—and to great effect. They were willing to wait months, even years, for an opportunity to get close to their quarry, and excelled at deception and subterfuge. The *Assassins* used daggers and always committed their killings in public so that as many people as possible would learn of the deaths. But their victims were almost always their fellow Muslims. Amongst them, Hugues enumerated, were two grand viziers in Persia and the caliphs of Cairo and Baghdad. The only Frank they'd slain, he said, was a Count of Tripoli about forty years ago.

His audience had hung on his every word, fascinated and horrified in equal measure. Richard was the first to inject a note of skepticism. "It does not seem likely to me that these *Assassins* could be regular users of hashish. How could they manage to deceive their prey, to blend in so well that none suspected them if their wits were addled with this potion?"

Hugues gave the king an approving smile. "Very true, my lord. Frankly, I never believed that myself. I think it is just one of the many rumors that swirl around them. They attract such stories the way Acre attracts sinners. I am not even sure their name is derived from the word 'hashish.' I was once told that it comes from *'Hassassin,'* which means 'a follower of Hassan,' who was the founder of their sect. So who's to say? The only certainty is that the mere mention of that name causes even brave men to glance uneasily over their shoulders."

Joanna had leaned forward, so intent upon the conversation that she was unaware she'd propped her elbows on the table. "What I do not understand, my lord Hugues, is why they so rarely attack Christians. Do they not see us as the enemy?"

"They view us as foxes, my lady, more of a nuisance than a real threat. They reserve their greatest hatred for the *Sunni* wolves, who return it wholeheartedly."

"I've heard that they've tried to murder Saladin numerous times," Richard commented. "Is that true?"

"In part, my lord king. I know of at least two attempts upon his life. Both times they penetrated his camp, and once he was saved only by his armor. He began to take great precautions for his safety and eventually he decided to strike at Rashīd al-Dīn Sinān himself, laying siege to his castle at Masyāf. But he called off the siege after just a week. I've heard various reasons offered for that, including a story that the Old Man of the Mountain threatened to murder Saladin's family if he did not withdraw. It would be hard not to take such a threat seriously after what happened with the sultan's bodyguards. . . ."

Hugues had an innate sense of drama. He paused now to sip his wine, building suspense as his audience eagerly urged him to continue. "Well," he said, "as I heard it, the *Assassin* chieftain sent one of his men to Saladin with a message, insisting it must be delivered in private. Saladin finally agreed to see him, but would not dismiss two of his most trusted bodyguards. Sinān's man looked at them and asked what they would do if he bade them in the name of his master to kill the sultan. They at once drew their swords and declared, 'Command us as you wish.' He then rode out of Saladin's camp with the two bodyguards, the message having been delivered."

There were gasps of delighted horror. This time it was André who took on the role of resident cynic. He was in a surly mood, in pain and frustrated by his clumsy attempts to cut his fish with his left hand, and so he eschewed tact in favor of brusque candor. "That is rubbish. If the *Assassins* could place their own men so close to Saladin, why did they not strike when they had the chance? Why settle for scaring him when they could so easily have killed him?"

Hugues was annoyed by André's derisive interjection. But as he glanced toward Richard, he saw the king looked amused, and so he merely shrugged. "Make of it what you will, my lord de Chauvigny. I can only tell you that Saladin and the Old Man of the Mountain obviously reached some sort of understanding, a truce if you will, for the attempts upon the sultan's life ceased."

Henri, ever the diplomat, took it upon himself to steer the conversation into more placid waters and the awkward moment passed. He personally thought André was right, but logic rarely could compete with legend and he saw that many of the guests preferred to believe Hugues's chilling tale of *Assassins* with diabolical powers beyond the ken of mortal men.

After the meal was done, Richard beckoned to the Grand Masters of the Templars and Hospitallers; he greatly admired the courage, stoicism, and discipline of both military orders and did what he could to show others that they stood high in royal favor. He was soon approached, though, by the Lady Uracca, the youngest— and to his mind, the most foolish—of his wife's attendants. The queen was departing for her own tent, the girl reported, a message that was puzzling on several levels. Why had Berenguela not come over herself? And why was she leaving so soon?

While Richard tended to take the behind-the-scenes activities of the women for granted, rarely stopping to consider how much preparation went into festivities like this, he did know his wife had a strong sense of duty, and it wasn't like her to abandon her obligations as his hostess. Uracca, of course, was unable to provide any answers, but as he searched the crowded tent, he caught a glimpse of Berengaria's new fur-trimmed mantle.

Moving swiftly to intercept her, he was thinking back to her behavior during the meal. The other women had actively engaged in the conversation about the *Assassins*, but Berengaria had remained silent. Now that he thought about it, he realized she had been subdued even before the dinner began, uncommonly quiet and withdrawn for a queen on public display. And she did look pale, he thought, with a stirring of unease, for disease was always hovering over an army encampment and it was so cold the guests had been forced to remain bundled in their cloaks even while they ate. With so many of his soldiers laid low by sickness, how much more susceptible must a delicately reared lass like Berenguela be to the alien, noxious maladies of Outremer?

Drawing her aside, he looked intently into her face. "Uracca told me you were leaving. Are you ailing, little dove?"

"No, I am quite well. I am just . . . just tired. But I will stay if that is your wish."

Relieved, he bent down and kissed her on the forehead. "No, there is no need for that; Joanna can act in your stead. I was merely concerned that you might be ill. Go and rest. In fact, that is a good idea," he said with a smile, "for you are not likely to get that much sleep tonight."

He'd expected her to blush and laugh, as she always did. He did not expect the reaction he got. "No, not tonight!" she cried, and then clapped her hand to her mouth as if she could call her words back.

Richard blinked in astonishment. While he might have agreed in theory that a wife ought to have the right of refusal, it had not occurred to him that his own wife would ever invoke it. "Are you sure you are not sick, Berenguela?"

"I . . . no, I am not ill," she assured him, although she no longer met his gaze, her lashes coming down like shutters to shield her thoughts.

He was momentarily at a loss, but then he understood. "Oh, of course! Your flux has come," he said, pleased with himself for solving this minor mystery so easily, and reached for her hand. Again, he got more than he'd bargained for. She gasped and tears suddenly welled in her eyes. Jerking free of his grasp, she whirled and fled—there was no other way to describe her precipitate exit. Heads turned in her direction and her startled ladies and knights hurried to catch up, while Richard stared after her in consternation.

"Richard?" Joanna materialized at his side as if by magic. "Whatever did you say to her?"

He was usually amused by her protectiveness, even if it did mean she invariably took Berengaria's side whenever they had a difference of opinion. Today he was not amused. "I said nothing," he protested. "We were talking and suddenly she ran off. Go after her, Joanna, and find out what's wrong."

"Richard, she's your wife! You're the one to go after her."

"You'd be better at it than me," he insisted. "I am not good at dealing with female vapors or tears—" Warned by the look on her face, he stopped himself, but not in time.

"'Female vapors'?" she echoed incredulously. "When have you ever seen Maman or me succumb to 'female vapors'? When have you ever seen Berengaria give way to an emotional outburst of any kind? Has she even shed a tear in your presence? If she is distraught, she has a damned good reason for it—and it is your responsibility to find out what it is!"

When Richard didn't reply, she read surrender in his silence. She stayed where she was, though, watching him with an implacable expression until he turned and started for the tent entrance. Only then did she clap her hands, signaling for the musicians to resume playing and for the guests politely to pretend that the queen's flight had been nothing out of the ordinary.

RICHARD WAS NOT HAPPY with his sister. But a sense of fairness that he thought often surfaced at inopportune times compelled him to admit that he'd wronged his wife. Berenguela had none of the vices he attributed to many of her sex; she was not flighty or overly sensitive or sentimental. He still thought Joanna would have been better at offering comfort or ferreting out womanly secrets. Since she'd balked, he had no choice, though, and he entered Berengaria's tent with the reluctant resolve of a man venturing into unknown terrain. His appearance created a predictable stir among her attendants. Thinking they were fluttering about like hens that had just spotted a hawk, he started to dismiss them; remembering in time that it was pouring rain, he settled for waving them away from the screen that afforded Berengaria her only privacy.

She was lying on the bed, but she rolled over when he said her name, looking so surprised to see him that he felt a twinge of guilt. She'd obviously been weeping, for her eyes were red and swollen. "I am sorry," she said, "for making a scene."

"Have you forgotten my family history, Berenguela? By our standards, you'd have to fling a glass of wine into my face to make a scene." Sitting beside her, he reached over and wiped her wet cheeks with a corner of the sheet. "Tell me what is wrong."

"You were right," she confessed; her voice was muffled, as if she were swallowing tears, but she met his gaze steadily. "My flux did come today . . . almost three weeks late."

"Ah . . . I see. You'd thought you might be with child."

"I'd never been late before, Richard, never." A solitary tear trickled from the corner of her eye, slowly flowed down her cheek, and splashed onto his wrist. "I was so sure, so happy. . . ."

"Berenguela . . . I have no doubts that you'll give me a son. But it must happen in God's time."

"That is what my confessor keeps telling me, too," she said, and it was obvious to him that she took no comfort in this truism. He was quiet for a few moments, trying to decide what to say.

"I think it might be for the best if you do not conceive whilst we are in Outremer," he said at last, and saw her brown eyes widen. "Think about it, little dove. You have already experienced more discomfort and danger than most queens could even imagine. Think how much worse it would be if you had to endure all this whilst you were great with child. Then what of the delivery itself? Do you truly want to give birth in a tent? And afterward . . . you'd be fearful every time the baby sneezed or coughed. This is not a kind country for infants, for women and children. Hellfire, lass, it is no country for any man not born and bred here; we all sicken and die much easier than we would back in our own lands."

Her eyes searched his. "You truly would not be disappointed if I do not conceive until we go home?"

"I'd be relieved," he admitted. "Had I known what it would be like here, I doubt that I'd have taken you and Joanna with me. You could have waited for me at Tancred's court in safety and comfort. Now . . . now I must worry about you both whilst I also worry about my men and our chances of defeating Saladin." He smiled, but it held little humor. "There are good reasons, little dove, why men do not usually bring their women with them to war."

"I cannot deny that those are thoughts I've had, too," she confided. "I would not add to your burdens if I could help it, Richard. But . . . but I am still glad that you brought me with you."

Leaning over, he kissed her. When he started to rise, though, she caught his hand. "Will you still come to me tonight? Even though we cannot . . . ?"

"I will," he promised, and kissed her again. She sat up once he'd departed, but she was not yet ready to face the world and she decided to indulge herself for a while longer, safe from the stares and speculations. It was not long, though, before her sister-in-law arrived, and none of Berengaria's ladies dared to deny her entry.

"I know Richard was here," Joanna said forthrightly, "but I was not sure how helpful he'd be. Even the bravest of men seem to become unnerved by a woman's tears."

Berengaria looked fondly at the other woman, thinking how lucky she was to have Joanna as her friend. "My flux came today," she said. "It was so late that I'd dared to hope . . . but it was not to be."

"Berengaria, I am so sorry." Joanna climbed onto the bed and enfolded her in a hug. "You'd been so happy the past few weeks that I'd suspected as much. You told Richard?" She hoped her brother had been sympathetic to his wife's needs, but she did have a few misgivings, for she thought men were the unpredictable and impulsive sex, not women, and they could be insensitive at the worst possible times.

"Yes . . . he was very sweet about it."

Joanna hid a smile, thinking that this was surely the first and only time that anyone had used that word to describe Richard. "I am glad to hear that, dearest."

"He said he'd rather it does not happen until we are safely back in his domains, that it would be too dangerous. He is right, of course, and it is a great relief to know he does not blame me. It is just that . . . that it means so much, Joanna. Every woman surely wants children, but it is so much more urgent for a queen. What could be worse than to fail to give Richard the heir he needs?"

Joanna said nothing, but Berengaria had become adept by now at reading her sister-in-law's face. "Oh, Joanna, I am sorry! Can you forgive me?"

"There is nothing to forgive. I know you did not mean to diminish my loss. My son died, and yes, that is a hurt that will never fully heal. But I've had years to come to terms with it, Berengaria. That is part of my past. I am sure that in time Richard will find me a suitable husband—preferably Christian," she added with a faint smile. "And when that happens, I will have other sons. As will you, my dearest sister. I truly believe that, want you to believe that, too."

She half expected her sister-in-law to soften the presumption of that prediction with a cautious "God willing." Berengaria surprised her, though. "I want to believe it, too, Joanna, and I will endeavor to do so. Why should it not happen, after all? How could the Almighty deny a son and heir to the man who will free Jerusalem from the infidels?"

Joanna opened her mouth, shut it again. During one of his last visits to Jaffa, Richard had confided in her about his constant struggles with Hugh of Burgundy and the French, admitting how exhausted and disheartened he was at times, even confessing that he doubted Jerusalem could ever be taken by force, that their only chance of regaining access to the Holy City was by a negotiated settlement with

Saladin. He'd told her that he knew that would not go down well with his army, that his men would be bitterly disappointed if they failed to recapture Jerusalem. She wondered now if he realized his own wife would share that bitter disappointment. She briefly considered alerting him, but decided against it, for why add one more worry to the many burdens he already labored under?

RICHARD MOVED his army headquarters after Christmas to Bait Nūbā, just twelve miles from Jerusalem. The winter weather remained wretched, yet skirmishing continued. Richard interrupted a Saracen ambush on the third day of the new year, but they fled upon recognizing his banner. Not long afterward, he escorted his wife and sister back to the greater safety of Jaffa. By now he was convinced that it would be madness to advance upon Jerusalem under the circumstances and, upon his return to Bait Nūbā, he confronted the issue head-on.

THEY MET in Richard's command tent during yet another pelting hailstorm, the wind keening in an eerie accompaniment to the rising voices. As soon as Richard broached the subject of turning back, he was assailed by his French allies, accused of betraying their holy quest. Determined to hold on to his temper, he sought to counter their passion with what he saw as irrefutable facts.

"Look at this," he demanded, pointing toward the map he'd laid out upon a trestle table. "I asked men personally familiar with the city's defenses to draw it for us. Jerusalem's walls are more than two miles in circumference and enclose an area of over two hundred acres. We do not have enough men to securely encircle the city. We'd be stretched so thin that they'd be able to send out sorties and break through our lines whenever they wanted. Saladin has been preparing for a siege for months, so I daresay they have food stockpiled. Nor are they going to run out of water; their cisterns must be overflowing by now!" he said, with an angry, ironic gesture toward the rippling walls of the tent, billowing with each powerful gust of the storm battering Bait Nūbā. "Even if we had an army twice as large, it would be sheer folly to begin a siege in weather like this!"

"I cannot believe that you are balking again!" Hugh of Burgundy glanced disdainfully at the map, shaking his head. "We are twelve miles from the Holy City—only twelve miles!"

"Our men did not come so far to turn tail and run." The Bishop of Beauvais had not even bothered to look at the map, keeping his eyes accusingly upon Richard. "Why did you take the cross if you were not willing to fight God's enemies?"

Henri and André both jumped to their feet. But for once the Angevin temper did not catch fire. Richard did not even bother to defend himself, overwhelmed by the futility of it. Christ's Blood, he was so bone-weary of all this. No matter what he said, they'd not heed him. It was as if the past four months had never been and they were back at Jaffa, making the same arguments and aspersions that they'd made then.

He was wrong, though; this was not to be another repeat of their Jaffa confrontation. Hugues de Tiberias had been standing in the rear, but now he pushed his way to the front of the tent. "It is ridiculous to accuse the English king of lacking the heart to wage war against the Saracens," he said scornfully. "If I thought you truly meant that, my lord bishop, I'd wonder if you'd been afflicted by some malady that scrambles a man's wits. Who got us safely to Jaffa? Who won the battle of Arsuf? Not you, my lord bishop or you, my lord duke. Why must we constantly waste time with these petty squabbles instead of talking about what truly matters? Can we take Jerusalem?"

When they would have interrupted, he flung up a hand for silence. "No, by God, you'll hear me out! Some of you use the term *'poulain'* as an insult, at least behind our backs. Well, I am proud to call myself *poulain*. I know far more about fighting in the Holy Land than men who've lived all their lives in the fat, green fields of France, and I say the answer is no. We cannot take Jerusalem. Now are you going to accuse me, too, of not wanting to win this war? This is my home, not yours, and after you've all gone back to your own lands, I'll still be here, struggling to survive against a foe who is not going anywhere, either."

"We do not doubt your good faith or your courage," Hugh insisted. "But we cannot give up now. Jerusalem is within our grasp!"

"No, my lord duke, it is not." Garnier de Nablus remained seated on a coffer, arms folded across his chest, but his voice carried; the Grand Master of the Hospitallers was accustomed to dominating gatherings of other men. "The problems we faced in September are still unresolved. We still risk having our supply lines to the coast cut by Saladin, finding ourselves stranded in enemy territory, caught between Saladin's army and the garrison in Jerusalem. Nothing has changed since we last discussed this, except to get worse. Now we have an army weakened by sickness and desertions and we are in the midst of one of the most severe winters in memory. There is a reason why fighting in the Holy Land is seasonal, and you need only stick your heads out of this tent to understand why that is so."

Before he could be refuted, the Grand Master of the Templars added his voice in support of Garnier. Robert de Sablé argued that even if they somehow managed to capture Jerusalem, they could not hope to hold it, for all the men who'd taken the cross would then depart, their vows fulfilled. "We'd be gambling more than the lives of our men. We'd be risking the very survival of the kingdom, for if our army suffers another defeat like Ḥaṭṭīn, Outremer is doomed. I say we withdraw to the coast and rebuild Ascalon, as the English king wanted us to do last September."

The French were not convinced. They infuriated all the Templars by implying that Robert de Sablé was Richard's puppet because he was a vassal of the English king. They dismissed the concerns of the Hospitallers and *poulains* by arguing that a holy war was not like ordinary warfare, insisting it was God's Will that they besiege Jerusalem and He would reward them with victory. This was the reasoning that had carried the day at Jaffa. But on this cold January night at Bait Nūbā, it did not. Much to the dismay of the French, their fellow crusaders were no longer willing to disregard their military training and experience in favor of such a great leap of faith. It was agreed that the army would not attempt to capture Jerusalem now and instead would seize the ruins of Ascalon, rebuilding it to threaten Saladin's power base in Egypt.

The French departed with dire predictions of disaster and veiled and not-so-veiled threats to abandon the crusade. Hugh of Burgundy paused in the entrance of the tent to glare at Richard, whom he saw as the architect of this shameful surrender. "Our men will never forgive you for this," he warned, "for they will never understand why we did not even try to seize the Holy City."

Richard said nothing, for although he truly believed they'd just averted a calamity that would have reverberated throughout Christendom, he knew that Hugh was right. Their men would not understand and he would be the one they blamed.

CHAPTER 30

JANUARY 1192

Ascalon, Outremer

When they were told there would be no attack upon Jerusalem, the army's morale plummeted. Men had been willing to endure severe hardships if their sacrifice would mean the recapture of the Holy City. Now they were shocked, bewildered, and angry to be told they were returning to the coast, for their suffering suddenly seemed pointless. Richard was no less troubled, feeling that he'd let them down even as he'd saved their lives. He did what he could for them, providing carts to transport all the sick and wounded back to Jaffa, and the eyewitness chroniclers took note of it. Ambroise reported that many of "the lesser folk" would have been left behind if not for the English king, and the author of the *Itinerarium* acknowledged that the ailing would otherwise have died since they were unable to care for themselves. But they also reported that each man "cursed the day he was born," that the heartbroken soldiers could not be comforted.

When the dispirited, bedraggled army reached Ramla, it fell apart. Most of the French refused to serve under Richard's command any longer and scattered, some heading to Jaffa, others to Acre, some even vowing to join Conrad at Tyre. Henri and his men remained loyal, though, and they accompanied Richard on a grim march to Ascalon along roads so mired in mud that they'd become death traps. Battered by the worst weather of the winter—snow, hail, and icy, torrential rains—they finally reached Ascalon on January 20. There the exhausted men sought shelter midst the wreckage of this once thriving city, the storms so intense that Richard's galleys dared not enter the dangerous harbor for more than a week. Just as their food was running out, the raging sea calmed enough for a few ships to land and unload provisions. The weather soon turned foul again, and when supply galleys attempted another landing, they were dashed upon the rocks, most of their crews drowning.

Richard somehow managed to keep the crusaders from utter despair, and put them to work clearing away the stones and rubble. They all shared the labor, the king, his lords, bishops, and knights joining the men-at-arms in carrying away rocks and debris and slabs of sandstone. After hiring local masons out of his own dwindling funds, Richard then sent word to Hugh of Burgundy, urging the French not to abandon the crusade. Hugh was also pressured by some of his own men, those who'd not decamped for Acre or Tyre, and reluctantly agreed to come to Ascalon, although he refused to commit his troops beyond Easter. Richard was infuriated with Hugh's intransigence, but he took what he could get.

HENRI HAD TAKEN some of his disheartened knights to Jaffa for a few days of rest and recreation with the whores who'd relocated from Acre. While there, he visited with Joanna and Berengaria, assuring them that Richard would fetch them as soon as they'd made more progress in the rebuilding. He made it sound as if all was going well at long last, in part because he did not want them to worry and in part because he was an optimist by nature. But when he returned to Ascalon, he discovered that Richard and Hugh's fragile détente had already ruptured. The French duke had asked Richard for another loan, and when the English king refused, Hugh had gone back to Jaffa in high dudgeon, heading along the coast road just as Henri's galley had cruised south.

THE DAY AFTER Henri's return to Ascalon, Richard decided to reconnoiter Dārūm, a Saracen castle twenty miles to the south; if the crusaders could control both Ascalon and Dārūm, they'd be able to clamp a stranglehold upon Salah al-Dīn's supply lines to Egypt. Henri volunteered to come along, and seized his first opportunity to learn the gory details of Hugh and Richard's latest quarrel.

"So . . . what happened? Say what you will of Hugh, he has brass ballocks. I can scarcely believe he dared to ask you for more money. The man has done his utmost to thwart you at every turn!"

"He claimed his men were insisting upon being paid and he did not have the money. I told him I could not afford to give him any more. He's not repaid a denier of the five thousand silver marks I lent him at Acre, and I'm already covering three-quarters of the cost of rebuilding Ascalon. He did not want to hear that, said he was going to Acre and we could go to Hell."

Henri said nothing and they rode in silence for a time. He did not like Richard's uncharacteristically calm recital of yet another desertion; his uncle should be raving about Burgundy's sheer gall, drawing upon his considerable command of invective and obscenities to curse the duke till the end of his wretched days. To Henri, Richard had always been a force of nature, immune to the fears and misgivings that preyed upon lesser men. But it seemed to him now that the English king was being worn down by the constant strife with his own allies, losing heart and hope, and that alarmed Henri exceedingly. What would befall them if Richard gave up the fight and went home as Philippe had done?

He was racking his brain for a conversational gambit that might dispel his uncle's morose mood, and when his gaze fell upon Richard's sleek dun stallion, he had it. "I hear you were busy adding to your legend whilst I was in Jaffa," he said breezily. "I was in camp less than an hour ere I was told about your latest adventure. But surely the part about jumping over that boar cannot be true!"

As he'd hoped, Richard took the bait, for he was never averse to boasting about his exploits. "Well, actually it is," he said with a smile. "I rode out with some of my knights to scout around Blanchegarde. On our way back, we encountered a very large wild boar. It stood its ground, making ready to attack. I used my lance as if it were a hunting spear and embedded it in the beast's chest. But it broke in half and the boar charged right at me. So I did the only thing I could—I spurred Fauvel and he soared over it as if he had wings. The only damage done was a rip to his rear trappings where the tusks caught the material. That gave me time to draw my sword and when it charged again, I struck it in the neck, which stunned it enough for me to complete the kill."

Henri burst out laughing. "You make it sound like just another hunt. But I can tell you for certes that not one man in a hundred would have dared to jump over an enraged boar! That is quite a feat of horsemanship, Uncle, even for you."

"Let's give credit where due, Henri . . . to Fauvel." Richard leaned over to pat the stallion fondly, and Henri laughed again, pleased that he'd been so successful in raising his uncle's spirits. But it was then that one of their scouts came into view, with several Saracens in close pursuit.

They reined in at sight of the crusaders, wheeled their mounts, and made a hasty retreat. The scout, one of the Templar *turcopoles*, headed toward Richard. "There is a large infantry force camped outside the walls, my lord king, between the castle and the village. There seemed something odd about them, though, so I came closer to see—too close, obviously," he said with a wry smile. "I cannot be sure, for I was still some distance away when I was spotted. But I think they are Christian prisoners."

"Let's go find out, then," Richard said, and signaled to his knights to array in battle formation. Riding stirrup to stirrup, lances couched, they soon saw Dārūm Castle looming against the horizon. There were a number of white tents and smoldering campfires, some Saracen horsemen milling about in obvious agitation, but no sign of any Christian captives. "God curse them, we're too late," Richard swore. "They were taken into the castle." For an angry moment, he considered an assault upon it, but they had no siege engines with them. At least they could exact vengeance on behalf of the prisoners, and they charged their foes, shouting the battle cry of the English Royal House.

The Saracens rode out to meet them, an act of undeniable courage, yet a foolhardy one, too, for they were badly outnumbered. When the fighting was done, several Muslims were dead and twenty of them had been compelled to surrender. While all were disappointed that they'd missed a chance to rescue some of their Christian brethren, the knights were pleased that they'd profit so handsomely from this scouting mission, already counting the horses seized and speculating about the ransom demands. Richard was puzzled, though, that the castle garrison had not sallied forth to join in the fray. He was searching the battlements for signs of activity when one of his men let out a shout, pointing toward the village.

It had appeared deserted, for its inhabitants, both Muslims and Christians, had either fled at their approach or barricaded themselves in their houses. But now the door of the church opened and men burst out, laughing and weeping. Some of them had managed to cut their bindings; others were still roped together. They were ragged and dirty and gaunt, but they were also euphoric, all talking at once, thanking God and Richard for their deliverance. When he dismounted, he was mobbed, and it took a while before he could make himself heard above the din.

"Choose one to speak for you," he ordered. "Are any of my soldiers amongst you?"

A few men shouldered their way toward him, identifying themselves as sergeants captured during a foraging expedition near Ramla in December. Gesturing at the others, they said these were men taken during the siege of Acre, unlucky pilgrims, and local Syrians.

"All Christians, though, my lord, even the ones who follow the Greek Church," one of the sergeants assured him. "We've been held in Jerusalem, forced to labor for the infidels, digging ditches and strengthening the city walls. They no longer needed us for that and we were being taken to Egypt to be sold in the slave markets there. . . ." His voice thickened. "I admit I'd given up hope. But God had not forsaken us. . . ." He choked up then, unable to continue, and Richard raised a hand for silence.

"I do not understand why you were not taken into the castle. How did you get away from your guards?"

"It was because of you, sire." Richard knew this new speaker was a soldier, too, just by the look of him; he bore too many visible scars to be a civilian. He'd obviously been a prisoner for some time, for he was noticeably thinner than the sergeants captured near Ramla. But his smile was bright enough to rival the sun. "They recognized your banner, came racing back into camp screaming, 'Malik Ric! Malik Ric!' The next thing we knew, most of our guards bolted. They mounted their horses and fled into the castle, leaving us to fend for ourselves. You ought to have heard what the other Saracens called them, the ones who had the guts to stay and fight you!" He laughed hoarsely, and gratefully accepted a wineskin from one of the knights. "So we ran—stumbled is more like it—and took shelter in the church, where some of us were able to cut our bonds."

Others were pressing forward, eager to tell their stories, too, to bear witness. Many of them were weeping joyfully and it proved contagious; some of the knights had begun to tear up, too. Henri shoved his way to Richard's side, unashamedly swiping at his eyes with the back of his hand. He was not surprised to see that his uncle was one of the few not overcome with emotion. He'd beckoned to several of the *turcopoles*, was instructing them to take word back to Ascalon that they'd be returning with twenty Saracen captives, some wounded knights, and at least a thousand freed prisoners, so they'd need horses and carts sent out to meet them. Turning toward Henri, he said, "I want to get us away from the castle ere some of those fugitive guards have second thoughts and decide they'd rather face me than explain their flight to Saladin."

"What an amazing day, Uncle." Henri was so exhilarated that he embraced the older man exuberantly, undeterred by the fact that they both were splattered with blood and mud. "I was so happy when Acre fell, but I think this is an even more glorious victory. When I'm an old man, I'll be bouncing my grandsons on my knee and boring them to tears as I relate yet again the story of the great Dārūm rescue!"

Richard glanced at Henri, then at the jubilant men still clustered around them. "It was a good day's work," he acknowledged. "But do you know why we were successful?"

To the freed prisoners, it was a puzzling question, for they thought the answer was obvious—God had wrought a miracle on their behalf. Richard's knights agreed with them, although they felt they'd also benefited from the growing legend of *Malik Ric*. But when they said as much, Richard shook his head.

"We prevailed," he said bitterly, "because there were no French here to hinder us."

RICHARD'S NEXT MOVE was an attempt to reach an understanding with Conrad of Montferrat, again asking the marquis to join the army. Conrad flatly refused to come to Ascalon. He did consent, though, to talk with Richard, and it was agreed that the two men would meet at Casal Imbert, halfway between Tyre and Acre.

ANDRÉ WAS NOT THERE to insist that Richard take a safe escort with him on his way to the rendezvous with Conrad. He'd been gone for more than a fortnight, having volunteered to make a risky January sailing to Italy. Since he could not fight whilst his blasted arm healed, he'd grumbled, he might as well do something useful and see what he could learn at the papal court. Richard was reluctant to let him go; in the parlance of soldiers everywhere, he and André had always had each other's backs. But his need for information was urgent, especially now that Philippe was back in France, and he could not very well object to the dangers of the sea voyage when André faced equal dangers on a daily basis in Outremer. So he'd agreed, but his cousin's absence was one more discontent in this winter of so many.

After passing a few days in Jaffa with his wife and sister, he headed north, accompanied by a large contingent of knights and a sizable force of Templars, for he'd learned that his nephew could be as blunt-spoken as André when it came to berating him for taking needless risks. Their coastal journey stirred memories of their march to Arsuf nigh on six months ago; to all of them, it seemed much longer.

By February 19, they'd reached Caesarea. Back in September, it had been deserted, its mainly Muslim population fleeing before the approaching crusader army. Salah al-Dīn had not ordered it razed, though, as he had with Ascalon and other castles and towns in Richard's path, and they found that it was partially occupied again, some of those abandoned houses and shops claimed by the native-born Christians. It had once been home to five thousand people; it was only a ghost now of its former self, but the town was slowly coming to life and Richard's men were delighted with its rebirth. For one night at least, some of them could sleep under roofs in real beds, even visit the baths and wash off the grime and muck of a very muddy road.

Henri was one of the first to enjoy the baths, luxuriating in the sweating room that was heated by a furnace, the hot air coming in through earthenware pipes. He'd quickly embraced the Frankish custom of frequent bathing, but he'd discovered he was more prudish than he'd realized and he'd never been willing to have a bath attendant shave his pubic hair as some of the *poulains* did; now he instructed the man only to remove his beard. Afterward, he wandered about the streets, for this ancient city had been founded before the birth of the Lord Christ. He went into the church of St Peter, and struck up a conversation with one of the canons, who told him the pagan temple of Jupiter had once stood on this site, and then a mosque that had been the scene of a bloodbath when the city had been captured by the Christians over ninety years ago; it was now the cathedral of the Archbishop of Caesarea. As he left the church, a light rain began to fall, and that dampened his interest in further sightseeing.

Despite the rain, Henri was in good spirits when he reached the castle, looking forward to food cooked in a kitchen instead of over a campfire. Unfortunately, Lent had begun, but he was assured they'd have fresh fish, not the salted herring that dulled so many Lenten appetites. They had just been served an eel pie, with oysters and scallops also on the menu, when the meal was interrupted by the unexpected arrival of Stephen Longchamp, brother of Richard's chancellor and one of Acre's co-governors.

He did not wait to be formally announced, hastened toward the dais and knelt. "Thank God I found you, my liege! We knew you were on the way to meet Conrad, but we did not know how far you'd gotten and I feared having to sail as far as Jaffa."

Richard gestured for him to rise. He'd already pushed his trencher aside, for Longchamp's news was obviously urgent. Knowing the other man's weakness for verbosity, he said, "Never mind that. Tell me what is wrong, Sir Stephen."

"You must get to Acre straightaway, my lord, for the city is under attack!"

Richard's gasp was echoed down the length of the table. He'd been braced for bad tidings, but nothing as bad as that. "How can that be? Saladin has dispersed the bulk of his army till the spring campaign!"

"Not Saladin, my liege. Acre is under siege by that whoreson Conrad of Montferrat and his lackey, Burgundy."

By now the hall was in an uproar and Richard had to shout them down. Like his father, he could bellow with the best when the need arose, and a tense silence ensued as Longchamp began to speak again.

"You know how much animosity there is between the Genoese and the Pisans, my liege. They're always at one another's throats, eager to take offense at the slightest excuse. I think their feuding goes back to—"

"No history lessons, Sir Stephen," Richard interrupted impatiently. "Just tell us what happened."

"Well, their latest street brawl got out of hand, and suddenly they were fighting in earnest. Bertrand de Verdun and I did what we could to restore order, of course. But—" Catching Richard's warning eye, Longchamp hastily condensed his narrative. "The Genoese got the worst of it and barricaded themselves in their quarter of the city. What we did not know was that they'd sent one of their galleys up the coast to Tyre, seeking assistance from Conrad. And then Hugh of Burgundy arrived. The Genoese decided not to wait for Conrad and hurried out to the camp he'd set up outside the walls."

He paused, rather enjoying being the center of such undivided attention. "Burgundy was only too willing to assault the city. The Pisans were too quick for him, though. As he was arraying his troops, they attacked him first. His horse was slain in the skirmish and he was thrown head over heels into a mud hole." A reminiscent smile tugged at the corners of his mouth. "The Pisans then retreated back into the city and slammed the gates shut. But the next morning Conrad's fleet sailed into the outer harbor. We've held out for three days so far, and the Pisans entreated us to send word to you that we need help. So . . . I set out to find you," he concluded. "The Caesarea harbor is so dangerous that I almost continued on, for I was not sure that you'd gotten this far yet. Thank God I did not pass on by!"

By now no one was paying any attention to him. Richard was already on his feet. At first incredulous, he was now so outraged that some of the men had begun to give him space, almost as if he were radiating heat. "Saladin will laugh himself sick when he hears this," he said, practically spitting the words. His eyes raking the hall, he beckoned to Robert de Sablé, the Templar grand master, and to Henri, then glanced back at Longchamp. "I want you to return to Acre tonight, tell them that I will be there on the morrow."

Longchamp's face fell at the prospect of more hours onboard ship, but he dutifully agreed. After a moment to reflect, though, he frowned in perplexity and said to the closest man, who happened to be Henri, "How can he get there so quickly? It is nigh on forty miles between Caesarea and Acre."

Henri looked wistfully at the tables holding the first course of their meal. "We'll be riding all night," he said with a sigh, and then hurried to catch up with his uncle.

———

AS HE PROMISED, Richard reached Acre the next day. But by then word had spread that he was on the way, and he discovered that the siege was over. Conrad and Hugh had decided discretion was the better part of valor and hastily retreated to Tyre. Richard set about patching up a peace between the Pisans and Genoese, and managed it by a combination of eloquence, logic, and threats. He then insisted that Conrad meet him at Casal Imbert as originally planned. Conrad had never lacked for temerity and agreed.

Richard's success with the Pisans and Genoese was not repeated at Casal Imbert. Conrad again refused to join the army at Ascalon, and in Richard's view, he added insult to injury by citing the defection of the French as one reason for his lack of cooperation. Richard returned to Acre in a rage and called a council, which deprived Conrad of his half of the kingdom's revenues. This was an empty gesture, though, for it could not be enforced as long as Conrad retained the support of the French and most of the *poulain* lords. In fact, it would later backfire upon Richard, for Conrad would retaliate in a way that was far more effective.

Richard ended up remaining at Acre through March, wanting to make sure that the port city would not be vulnerable to another surprise attack. He also renewed negotiations with Salah al-Dīn, requesting that al-'Ādil be sent to engage in peace talks, offering terms based upon a partition of the kingdom and the Holy City which were very similar to those he'd posed back in November; no mention was made this time of a marriage between Joanna and al-'Ādil. The talks were so amicable that just before Palm Sunday Richard knighted one of al-'Ādil's sons, and Salah al-Dīn and his council were inclined to accept these terms.

But the talks were abruptly broken off when Richard left Acre unexpectedly in late March. His spies had alerted him that he was not the only one struggling with internal dissension. Salah al-Dīn's troops were even more war-weary and disgruntled than Richard's soldiers, for they'd been fighting much longer. More significantly, Richard had learned that Salah al-Dīn's great-nephew was threatening rebellion, apparently on the verge of joining forces with one of the sultan's enemies, the Lord of Khilāt.

Richard decided, therefore, to bide his time and see what developed, hoping that Salah al-Dīn's increasing vulnerability would compel him to accept peace terms more favorable to the Franks, for he knew Ascalon was a huge boulder on the road to peace, with neither man willing to surrender claims to it. Stopping off at Jaffa, Richard collected his wife and sister and returned with them to Ascalon. Easter was the most important festival on the Christian calendar and he meant to celebrate it in grand style, setting up special tents to provide food and entertainment for his soldiers. But three days before Easter, Conrad exacted payment for that council condemnation, sending an envoy to Ascalon to demand that the remaining French troops join him and the Duke of Burgundy at Tyre.

RICHARD WAS HOARSE, for he'd been pleading with the departing knights for over an hour, to no avail. Some looked shamefaced, others obviously miserable, but they felt they had no choice. Conrad had reminded them that their king had appointed Hugh of Burgundy as commander of the French forces and this was a direct order, one given in Philippe's name. Even Richard's offer to pay for their expenses did not sway them, and he withdrew to his tent, discouraged by this latest setback. Henri found him alone soon afterward, a rare state for a king, slumped on a coffer, his head in his hands.

"Uncle . . ." Not wanting to intrude, the younger man hesitated. "You sent for me? I can come back later. . . ."

"No, come in. I promised the French knights that I'd provide them with an escort to Acre, and I want you and the Templars to see them safely there." Richard straightened up and accepted the wine cup Henri was holding out. "Over seven hundred knights lost, plus their squires, their men-at-arms, crossbowmen, their horses and weapons . . . Christ Jesus, Henri, the timing could not be worse. I truly thought we had a chance to put enough pressure upon Saladin to exact better terms. But now this. . . . Even men like Guillaume des Barres and the Montmorency lad feel obligated to return to Tyre rather than disobey a direct order from their king and liege lord. They apologized profusely, promising to return if they can persuade Hugh to release them. That is about as likely as my taking holy vows."

Richard paused to drink, but even the wine tasted sour. He was putting the cup aside when an awful thought struck him and his hand jerked, spilling liquid as red as blood. "What of your knights, Henri? I know you'll stay with me, but will your men?"

"They will, Uncle," Henri assured him, "they will. I've never been so proud of them, for they laughed at Conrad's command. 'Yes, Philippe is our king,' they said, 'but our liege lord is Count Henri and we take our orders only from him, not the damned Duke of Burgundy.' Bless them all, for nary a one was willing to heed Hugh or Conrad. Of course, they know I'll protect them from the French king's wrath." *Assuming we ever get back to France.* Henri left that thought unsaid. There were times when his beloved Champagne seemed as far away as the moon in the heavens, but he did not think his uncle needed to hear that now. If he felt so discouraged at times, how much worse it must be for the man who bore the burden of command upon his shoulders.

"Thank God," Richard said. That was all, but to Henri those two words spoke volumes about his uncle's state of mind. Wishing André was here, for he always seemed to know what Richard needed to hear, he sat down on the carpet at Richard's feet, his eyes searching the older man's face. Henri had suspected for some time that the hellish Outremer climate and the constant stress were having a detrimental impact upon his uncle's health, sapping some of his energy and stamina. He could see now that Richard's color was too high, a flush burning across hollowed cheekbones, and his eyes were very bright, obvious evidence that he was running a fever. But he was not likely to admit it, and so Henri bit back the words hovering on his lips. As hard as it was to keep silent, he could only hope that Richard did confide in Master Ralph Besace, his chief physician.

"What I cannot understand," Richard said after a brooding silence, "is why so many of the local lords can stand aloof from this war. How can men like Balian d'Ibelin and Renaud of Sidon refuse to fight with us when their very world is at stake?"

"Uncle . . ." Henri paused, marshaling his thoughts. He'd not been able to help Richard bridge that great gap separating him from so many in his army. Men inflamed with holy zeal were bound to mistrust their commander's pragmatism, and too often Richard had failed to take that into account. Would he have any more luck now in addressing what he saw as his uncle's one major mistake since arriving in the Holy Land?

"Whilst it is true that to the French, this war is about you more than Saladin, that is not true when it comes to the *poulains*. To them, it is all about two men and only two men—Conrad of Montferrat and Guy de Lusignan. I think you erred in backing Guy, Uncle." Seeing Richard's head come up sharply, he said quickly, "I know you do not like to hear that. And I am not defending Conrad. He'll never be a candidate for sainthood. But it is a crown he seeks, not a halo, and the very qualities that may damn him to Hell—his ruthlessness, his lack of scruples, his ambition—make him a good choice to rule over a troubled land like Outremer.

The *poulains* see his flaws as well as you do. But they need a strong king, a man who will be able to defend his kingdom to the death if need be, and they trust Conrad as they cannot trust Guy. They know that Guy is a puppet king, your puppet, and he can be propped up only as long as you are here to support him. Once you leave, he'll collapse like a punctured pig's bladder, and that is why they have held 'aloof' as you put it. Guy will never be forgiven for Ḥaṭṭīn, Uncle. It is as simple as that."

"There is nothing 'simple' about life in Outremer," Richard scoffed. But Henri was heartened by that relatively mild response, and he dared to hope he'd planted a seed that might eventually take root, for he was convinced that peace with the Saracens would not ensure the survival of Outremer—not if Guy de Lusignan was still its king on the day they departed its shores for their own homelands.

ON APRIL 15, Richard finally got a message from his chancellor, carried by the prior of Hereford. Soon thereafter, he met with Henri, the Earl of Leicester, and the Bishop of Salisbury, men who stood high in his confidence, and they remained secluded for much of the afternoon. By now Joanna and Berengaria had learned of the prior's arrival, and they grew more and more uneasy as the hours passed. Richard had already gotten unwelcome news earlier in the week—word of a rebellion in Cyprus against the heavy-handed rule of the Templars. They had put down the revolt, but the situation on the island remained volatile; the Templars had made themselves quite unpopular, so this was just one more worry for Richard to deal with. The women fervently hoped that the news from England would not be troubling, too. They took turns reassuring each other that Eleanor was quite capable of maintaining peace in her son's kingdom, but they both knew that Philippe's return was akin to setting a wolf loose in a flock of defenseless sheep.

They'd been discussing whether to wait further or to seek Richard out; Berengaria did not want to risk interrupting his council and Joanna wanted to head straight for his tent. The debate was ended by Richard's sudden arrival. One glance at his face and they both tensed, for it was as if they were looking at an engraved stone effigy, utterly devoid of expression.

"Good—you're both here," he said, and his voice, too, was without intonation. "I'd not want to have to tell this twice. Send your ladies away."

Once they were alone, Richard seemed in no hurry to unburden himself. He sat down on the edge of Berengaria's bed, only to rise restlessly a moment later. By unspoken consent, both women remained quiet, waiting for him to begin. At last he said, "Prior Robert brought a rather remarkable letter from my chancellor ... my former chancellor, I should say, since Longchamp was deposed and sent into exile last October. I'll spare you the depressing details, for they do none of the participants much credit. My brother Geoff crossed over to Dover in mid-September and Longchamp saw that as a breach of his oath to remain out of England whilst I was gone, claiming not to believe that I had absolved Geoff of that oath. The chancellor was not in Dover at the time, but his sister is wed to the constable of Dover Castle and they took it upon themselves to order Geoff's arrest. He of course refused to submit and instead took refuge in St Martin's Priory, which they encircled with armed men. He then proceeded to excommunicate the Lady Richeut and all others who were participating in this siege of the priory. This impasse lasted for several days, ending when Richeut and that idiot she'd married sent armed men into the priory to take Geoff out by force. He resisted and they dragged him, bleeding, through the town to the castle, with him hurling excommunications left and right like celestial thunderbolts."

They'd listened, openmouthed, to this incredible story. Berengaria was appalled that they'd dared to lay hands upon a prince of the Church. It sounded almost farcical to Joanna, but she saw the serious implications, too, and marveled that a man as clever as Longchamp could have made such a monumental miscalculation. "What happened, then, Richard?"

"What you'd expect. When word got out of Geoff's arrest, people were horrified, all the more so because it stirred up memories of Thomas Becket's murder in Canterbury Cathedral. With that one foolish act, Longchamp united all of the other English bishops against him. And Johnny was suddenly aflame with brotherly love for Geoff, whom he'd detested up until then, sending knights to Dover to demand Geoff's release. With the entire country in an uproar, Longchamp finally realized how badly he'd erred and he ordered Geoff freed on September 26. By then it was too late. He'd managed to transform Geoff into a holy martyr for Mother Church, giving Johnny all the weapons he needed to bring Longchamp down. The final outcome was inevitable. Urged on by Will Marshal and the other justiciars, the Archbishop of Rouen produced the letters I'd given him in Sicily, which authorized him to depose the chancellor if Longchamp ignored their advice—as indeed he had. It got so ugly that Longchamp took refuge in the Tower of London and seems to have lost his head altogether for a time. He tried to flee England disguised as a woman, only to be caught, shamed, and maltreated. He eventually was allowed to sail for Flanders, where he wasted no time in appealing to the Pope. The Pope reacted with predictable outrage, for Longchamp is a papal legate, after all, and at Longchamp's urging, he proceeded to excommunicate the Archbishop of Rouen, the bishops of Winchester and Coventry, and four of the other justiciars, amongst others."

"Dear God!" This exclamation was Joanna's; Berengaria was speechless.

"You've not heard the half of it yet," Richard said, and for the first time they could see the fury pulsing just beneath his surface composure. "I think the lot of them have gone stark, raving mad. Let's start with our new archbishop. Once Longchamp had gone into exile, Geoff went to his see in York, where he resumed his feuding with the Bishop of Durham, Hugh de Puiset. When Durham refused to come to York to make a profession of obedience, Geoff publicly excommunicated him. Durham ignored the anathema and so did Johnny, who chose to celebrate Christmas with Durham. So Geoff then excommunicated Johnny for having eaten and drunk with one who must be shunned by other Christians."

"Richard . . . can you trust what the prior says, though? If he was sent by Longchamp, naturally he'd try to cast Geoff and Johnny and his enemies in the worst possible light."

Richard had been pacing back and forth. At that, he turned toward his sister with a smile that held not even a hint of humor. "Prior Robert is adept at swimming in political waters. He did indeed carry Longchamp's letter. But he also brought one from our mother, having alerted her that he would be making that dangerous journey from France to Outremer on Longchamp's behalf. I do not ordinarily approve of such blatant self-seeking, but in this case, I am glad the prior was so eager to curry favor with both sides. I might otherwise have doubted Longchamp's vitriolic account of Johnny's double-dealing with Philippe."

Joanna winced, for she'd truly hoped that her younger brother would not fall prey to the French king's blandishments. "What did Johnny do?"

"Philippe offered Johnny his unfortunate sister Alys and all of my lands in France in return for his allegiance. Johnny was untroubled by the inconvenient fact that he already had a wife, and was planning to sail for France when Maman arrived in the nick of time. She kept him in England by threatening to seize all of his English castles and estates as soon as he set foot on a French-bound ship."

Berengaria was shocked by John's disloyalty, for she could not imagine either of her brothers ever committing such a shameful act of betrayal against one of their own blood, much less a king who'd taken the cross. But as she struggled to think of a way to offer Richard comfort, she could not help remembering Sancho's warning. *They are not like us, little one.*

Joanna was not shocked, merely saddened. "When did Prior Robert leave

France?" she asked, and Richard gave her a grimly approving look, for she'd gone unerringly to the heart of the matter.

"In February," he said, "so God alone knows what has happened since then. Maman made it quite clear that Johnny cannot be trusted now that Philippe has begun to whisper treasonous inducements in his ear. She says others have been loath to oppose Johnny, for they fear I will not be coming back; it seems half of England is convinced I'm sure to die in the Holy Land. And Longchamp has made a bloody botch of things. I ought to have listened to her about him. But I valued his loyalty so much that I overlooked his arrogance and unpopularity. To her credit, Joanna, she refrained from saying 'I told you so.' She did say that I need to come home—and soon. She fears that if I do not, I may not have a kingdom to come back to."

Berengaria could not suppress a gasp, stunned that Richard's mother would urge him to abandon the crusade. "But if you leave, Richard, there is no chance of recovering Jerusalem!"

Joanna was more concerned with the loss of the Angevin empire. She started to speak, stopping herself before the words could escape, for this was a decision only Richard could make. "What will you do?" she asked quietly, and he glanced toward her, for a brief moment dropping his defenses and letting her see his anguish.

"I do not know," he admitted. "God help me, I do not know."

AFTER A SLEEPLESS NIGHT, Richard called a council meeting the next day. As the men crowded into his tent, he could see from their faces that they'd heard the rumors sweeping the camp; they looked apprehensive. "Most of you have heard that I've had word from England," he said. "The news was very troubling. My kingdom is in turmoil, threatened by the French king and my own brother. I do not know how much longer I can remain in the Holy Land. But I will not compel any man to act against his conscience. Each one of you can decide for yourself whether you wish to return home with me or stay in Outremer."

Even though some of them must have been anticipating an announcement like this, they all reacted with dismay, insisting that the war could not be won without him and entreating him to stay. Richard let them have their say before responding. "I will not just walk away. I promise you that. If I do have to return to my own domains, I will pay for three hundred elite knights and two thousand men-at-arms to stay in Outremer. I do not want to depart whilst the war continues. But I may have no choice, not if my kingdom is at stake."

Eventually the protests died down, but he could still see reproach and recrimination in the faces surrounding him. He'd wondered which of the *poulains* would be the first to raise the issue of kingship. As it turned out, it was the Grand Master of the Hospitallers, Garnier de Nablus. "We do understand, my liege," he said, "that you find yourself torn between your obligations. One of my Spanish knights ofttimes quotes an old proverb: '*Entre la espada y la pared.*' That is where you find yourself now, between the sword and the wall. You must do as God directs. But ere you go, we must know who will lead us once you're gone."

There was a sputtered objection from Guy de Lusignan, who hastily reminded them of the Acre agreement that had recognized him as king for life, with Conrad and Isabella as his heirs. No one paid him any mind.

"I know," Richard said. "I think you ought to discuss it amongst yourselves, for it should be a decision made by the men who'll have to live with it, not those who'll soon be on their way home. So that my presence will not inhibit a candid exchange of opinions, I will leave whilst you deliberate."

RICHARD HAD HEADED in the direction of Berengaria's pavilion, but at the last moment he veered off. He knew his wife would not berate him or even implore him to remain, but her brown eyes would reveal her bewilderment and her deep disappointment. His sister offered a safer harbor and he made for her tent, instead.

"I told them," he said tersely, "and now they are deciding their future once I'm gone."

He was obviously in no mood for conversation, so Joanna did not press him further. Beckoning to one of her knights, she gave him low-voiced instructions, all the while watching as her brother slouched on her bed, absently petting the Sicilian hound who'd hopped up beside him. The knight was soon back, having retrieved a musical instrument from Richard's tent. "Here," Joanna said, "occupy yourself with this."

Richard was strumming a melancholy little melody when Henri entered and pulled up a stool. "What is that . . . not a lute?"

"It is called an *oud*. Al-'Ādil gave it to me after I expressed interest in Saracen music."

Henri leaned closer to see. "You do not pluck the strings with your fingers like a harp?" Richard explained that a quill was used for the *oud*. His face was hidden, his head bent over the *oud*, and Henri watched him for a while, not sure what would better serve his uncle—silence, sympathy, or candor. Finally deciding upon the latter, he said, "You know they will choose Conrad?"

"I know."

"And . . . and you are all right with that?"

Richard's shoulders twitched in a half-shrug. "You recently reminded me that Guy is a puppet king at best, and could not hope to survive without my support. Since I do not know how much longer I dare remain in Outremer, that can no longer be ignored."

"It is the right decision, Uncle."

"Only time will tell. But compared to the other choice I'm facing, this was a relatively easy one."

"Of course the de Lusignans will not take it well."

"No," Richard agreed, "I do not suppose they will." He said no more, and Henri decided not to probe any further. He yearned to know what Richard would decide to do, for it would affect them all, but he was not sure his uncle even knew, not yet.

The *poulain* lords determined the fate of their kingdom with surprising speed; within an hour, the two Grand Masters, Hugues de Tiberias, and his younger brother were being ushered into Joanna's pavilion. "We have discussed it, my lord Richard, and we are all of one mind, save only Humphrey de Toron and the de Lusignans. We want Conrad of Montferrat as our king."

Richard nodded. "I expected as much."

"And you accept our decision?"

"I said I would, did I not?"

"Yes, my liege, you did." Hugues de Tiberias hesitated. "As you know, I am no friend to Conrad. But under the circumstances, it was the only choice we could make."

Richard nodded again and they soon withdrew, so obviously relieved that Henri thought Conrad would begin his reign with one great advantage always denied Guy—a united kingdom. Richard had picked up the *oud* again, signaling that he had no interest in discussing it further, and Henri took the hint. But almost as soon as the men had departed, Guy de Lusignan burst into the tent, trailed by his brothers, Joffroi and Amaury.

"How could you let this happen? How could you abandon me like this?"

"I did all I could for you, Guy. But I could not change the fact that none of them wanted you as king. I am not going to 'abandon' you, though."

"What . . . you mean to give me a stipend? I am not one of your knights to be paid wages or a pension now that I'm no longer of any use. I am an anointed king!"

"No," Richard said, "you *were* a king. But I have more in mind than a stipend. I cannot give you the kingdom of Jerusalem. I can give you Cyprus."

Guy's mouth dropped open. "Cyprus? But you sold it to the Templars."

"You've heard of the rebellion in Nicosia on Easter Eve? Well, Robert de Sablé told me that they have decided the island is more trouble than it's worth to them. They'd agreed to pay me one hundred thousand bezants and so far have paid forty thousand of that sum. If you reimburse them the forty thousand, Cyprus is yours."

Guy's brothers were listening avidly, eyes gleaming, the sort of predatory glint that Henri had seen in the eyes of falcons when they first sighted their quarry. But Guy seemed more ambivalent, his face displaying both interest and uncertainty. "I cannot afford one hundred thousand bezants," he objected, earning himself scowls from both Joffroi and Amaury.

"If you can come up with the forty thousand for the Templars, that will be enough."

This was such a generous offer that Guy's brothers began to lavish praise upon Richard, thanking him profusely. Guy's gratitude was more restrained. "Thank you, my liege," he said. "But it is just that—" He gave an odd "oof" sound then, and Henri realized he'd been elbowed sharply in the ribs by Amaury. He refused to be silenced, though, glared at his brother, and then looked earnestly at Richard. "I appreciate your kindness, I do. I just find it hard to accept—knowing that Conrad has won. He is the least worthy man in Christendom to wear a crown, sire, for he is deceitful, selfish, puffed up with pride, and ungrateful—yes, ungrateful! Did you know I saved his life once? During the siege of Acre, he was unhorsed and I came to his rescue—me, the man he betrayed!"

This time both of his brothers stepped in, interrupting his harangue with more expressions of appreciation, and then practically dragging Guy away, as if they feared Richard might change his mind at any moment. Once they were gone, Henri smiled at his uncle. "That was adroitly done. Not only do you placate Guy, you give his quarrelsome brothers a reason to stay away from Poitou!"

"Not Joffroi; from what I've heard, he is thinking of renouncing his lordship of Jaffa and going home once the war is over. But with a little luck, Amaury will put down roots in Cyprus with Guy . . . provided that they do not make the same mistakes the Templars did."

Joanna had been a very interested witness to the scene with the de Lusignans. Leaning over, she gave Richard's shoulder a gentle squeeze. "You ought to be proud of what you did today. Now you can go home with a clear conscience, sure that Outremer is in the hands of a capable king." Wrinkling her nose, she added, "Not a likable one, but he is what they need."

Richard inclined his head. Reaching again for the *oud*, he glanced over at his nephew. "You can be the one to let Conrad know he's gotten his accursed crown."

"I'll leave on the morrow." Henri thought this would be an enjoyable mission, for it was always pleasant to be the bearer of glad tidings, and Tyre would erupt in joyful celebrations, revelries that would put both Christmas and Easter in the shade. "Now that Conrad is to be king, the rest of the *poulains* will join us, Uncle. He might even be able to bestir the French into fighting again."

"That is what I am counting upon," Richard said. "This is Conrad's kingdom now. So it is time he defended it. And then, God willing, I can go home."

CHAPTER 31

APRIL 1192

Acre, Outremer

fter lingering a few days at Tyre to enjoy the revelries, Henri and his delegation had sailed to Acre to lay the groundwork for Conrad and Isabella's coming coronation. Here, too, they'd been welcomed as heroes, so great was the universal relief that their kingdom would have a strong hand on the helm once Richard returned to his own lands. Henri and the knights accompanying him planned to depart for Ascalon by week's end, for they were eager to bring Richard good news for a change, a promise that Outremer's new king would soon be leading an army south to join him. But on this Wednesday afternoon, a lavish feast had been given in their honor and they were more than willing to embrace all the pleasures, comforts, and sins that Acre had to offer before returning to the harsh realities of holy war.

Henri had not enjoyed such a delicious repast in months. After the last course had been served, he rose to salute his hosts. He had a felicitous way with words and offered a graceful tribute to the governors Stephen Longchamp and Bertrand de Verdun, to Bishop Theobald, Acre's elderly prelate, and to the other churchmen beaming at him down the length of the linen-clad tables. He singled out the leaders of the Pisan colony for special praise, much to Morgan's amused approval; he thought Henri had a surprisingly deft political touch for one so highborn. Every now and then, Henri reminded him of his dead lord, Geoffrey, for Morgan had first pledged his loyalties to Richard's brother, the most complex and subtle of the Devil's Brood.

Having expressed his appreciation for their hospitality, Henri raised high one of the ruby-red glass goblets that had once adorned the table of the Saracen commander al-Mashtūb. "Fortune's Wheel can spin with a vengeance. But some men seem blessed, destined to soar whilst others fall. Let us drink to the Marquis of Montferrat and his lovely consort, the Lady Isabella. May they rule well and long over your kingdom and may their child be a son."

Not all of the guests had heard that Isabella was pregnant and Henri's toast created quite a stir. He was kept busy for some moments answering the excited questions coming his way, confirming that the marquise was indeed with child, and confirming, too, a rumor heard by the Bishop of Bethlehem, who wanted to know if it was true that Conrad had asked God to approve his elevation to the throne.

"Yes, my lord bishop, he did. Upon being told that he was to be king, he first gave thanks to the Almighty. He then raised his hands toward Heaven and declared, 'I beg You, Lord, that You allow me to be crowned only if You judge me worthy to govern Your kingdom.' It made a profound impression upon his audience, who were deeply moved by his piety," Henri said blandly. But once the trestle tables had been taken apart and the guests began to mingle, he offered a more worldly critique for Morgan and Otto de Trazegnies. "Conrad has a natural flair for high drama, one that even Richard might envy. Little wonder my uncle Philippe was so discontented at Acre, a waning moon trying to compete with two blazing suns."

They both joined in his laughter, but then glanced around to make sure they'd not been overheard, for some of the guests might have felt Henri's comments were indiscreet. While most would have agreed that Conrad and Richard were adroit scene-stealers who thrived on center stage, it was not something to be said aloud. Henri was in high spirits, though, and in no mood to be circumspect. "Do you know how I see Conrad's coronation? As a golden key, opening a door that has been bolted and locked for months. Now that he and my uncle will finally be working together, they'll soon compel Saladin to accept peace terms. We may well be able to sail for home ere the first frost!" He started to add the formulaic "God willing," but moved by mischief, he went with a murmured "*Inshallah*" instead.

Otto was accustomed to Henri's insouciance and merely rolled his eyes. Morgan was no longer paying attention, looking toward the far end of the hall. "I wonder what is going on," he said. "Stephen Longchamp and Bertrand de Verdun just dashed for the door as if they'd been told the palace is afire."

Henri shrugged. "As long as the city is not under assault again, I refuse to worry. And since it is now Conrad's by right, we need not fear him swooping down in another stealth attack. Did I tell you that the Saracen commander has finally been freed? Bertrand said he managed to pay his ransom."

"That is passing strange." Morgan was still gazing over Henri's shoulder. "Why would Balian d'Ibelin follow us to Acre? He knows you brought Conrad's instructions for the coronation, does he not?"

"Balian is here?" Henri turned toward the door, no less puzzled than Morgan. But as he got his first glimpse of Balian's face, his mouth suddenly went dry. He'd seen such a benumbed, dazed expression before. His mother had looked like that when she'd come to tell him that his father was dead and their world forever changed.

Balian was trailed by the two governors, whose stricken faces were attracting as much attention as the *poulain* lord's unexpected appearance. Ignoring the questions and comments that churned in his wake, Balian headed straight for Henri. Already sure that he did not want to hear whatever the older man had come to tell him, Henri forced himself to step forward.

Balian seemed to have aged decades in the few days since Henri had last seen him. "There is no easy way to bring news like this, so I'll just say it straight out. Conrad is dead. He was murdered yesterday afternoon by two *Assassins*."

BALIAN'S SHOCKING REVELATION had unleashed turmoil that bordered on hysteria, for many believed that the Kingdom of Jerusalem had died when Conrad drew his last breath. Leaving Bishop Theobald and the other prelates to try to calm the crowd, the governors escorted Balian from the hall as soon as he'd given a terse account of Conrad's murder. Followed by Henri and the knights who'd accompanied him to Tyre, they retreated to the greater privacy of the solar. Once wine had been fetched by frightened servants, they staggered toward the closest seats like men whose legs could no longer sustain the weight of their bodies. Otto de Trazegnies and William de Caieux slumped onto a nearby bench and Morgan withdrew into a window alcove, almost as if he hoped he could somehow distance himself from the looming disaster. Bertrand de Verdun was no longer a young man and he collapsed into a high-backed chair that he ought to have offered to Balian or Henri, but protocol was the last thing on his mind at that moment. Stephen Longchamp appropriated one of the wine flagons, apparently intending to drink himself into blessed oblivion. Balian sank down on a wooden coffer, staring into the depths of a gilt cup as if it held answers instead of spiced red wine. Henri hovered beside him, too restive to sit still, wanting to demand answers and yet dreading to hear them. He managed to wait until Balian had drained his cup, for it was obvious that the other man was utterly exhausted, physically and emotionally, and then he said, "Tell us the rest, Balian, what you did not tell the men in the hall. Give us as much detail as you can. Mayhap then we can begin to believe it."

Balian set his cup down upon the carpet. "Isabella had gone to the baths," he said dully, as if struggling to comprehend how such a mundane matter could have such monumental consequences, "and when she did not return by midday, Conrad decided he could wait no longer. He said to tell her he'd gone to dine with the Bishop of Beauvais. He had only two knights with him, none of them wearing their hauberks. He . . . he never worried about his physical safety, no more than your English king does. When he got to Beauvais's house, he found that the bishop had already eaten. Beauvais offered to have a meal prepared, but Conrad refused, saying Isabella ought to be back by then and he'd go home to eat with her."

While Balian was looking directly at Henri, his eyes seemed focused upon a scene far from the solar at Acre's royal palace. "It happened after he'd passed the archbishop's dwelling. As he turned into a narrow street near the Exchange, he saw two men waiting for him. They would have looked familiar, Christian monks who'd attached themselves to our households—mine and Renaud de Sidon's—and when one of them approached with a letter, he likely assumed it was from me or Renaud."

Balian paused to press his fingers against his throbbing temples. "When he reached down for the letter, the killer stabbed him. At the same time, the second *Assassin* leapt onto his horse and plunged a dagger into his back. I was told it happened so fast that no one could have saved him. He was carried back to the citadel, still breathing, but it was obvious his wounds were mortal. . . ."

"Was there time to give him the Sacrament of the Faithful?" When Balian nodded, Henri exhaled a ragged breath, grateful that at least Conrad had been shriven of his sins. "What happened to his attackers? And how can you be sure they were *Assassins*?"

"One of them was slain on the spot. The other fled into a nearby church, where he was seized and turned over to the Bishop of Beauvais. Under torture, he admitted he'd been sent by the Old Man of the Mountain. He was then dragged through the streets to his death." Balian picked up his wine cup again, seemed surprised to find it empty.

Henri refilled it for him. "I do not understand. Why did the *Assassins* seek Conrad's death? Had they a grievance against him?"

"Yes . . . last year he'd seized a merchant ship belonging to Rashīd al-Dīn Sinān and then refused to return the cargo and crew. Conrad could be stubborn, and threats made him balk all the more. I'd warned him that one day his pride would play him false, but of course he just laughed. . . ." Balian's voice trailed off, and the other men remembered that his was a double loss, as much personal as political, for Conrad had been wed to his stepdaughter.

Balian took several deep swallows before continuing. "You'd best brace yourselves, for you are not going to like what comes next. Beauvais and Hugh of Burgundy are claiming that ere he died, the second *Assassin* confessed that Conrad's murder had been done at the behest of the English king."

As Balian expected, that got an explosive reaction. They were all on their feet within seconds, bombarding him with infuriated denials, raging against the French accusations so loudly that he thought the men below in the hall could hear. He said nothing, for it seemed easier to let their fury burn itself out; he was too tired to engage in a shouting match. When they at last paused for breath, he said, "I did not say I believed it, Henri. As it happens, I do not. I cannot say I share your conviction that Richard would not be capable of such a crime. I grant you he's much more likely to commit his own killings, but men do sometimes act in ways that we'd not expect. What they never do, however, is act against their own interest. Your English king is desperate to get back to his realm ere he loses it, desperate enough to embrace Conrad's kingship. Not only does he not benefit by Conrad's death, it is a disaster for him."

They subsided, somewhat mollified, and Bertrand de Verdun then suggested Saladin as a far more likely candidate than Richard. Balian started to remind them that Saladin had no motive, either, for he had accepted Conrad's peace terms just days ago, but he remembered in time that they were unaware of this. As soon as he'd learned that he was to be king, Conrad had sent an urgent message to Saladin, saying that he and Richard were no longer enemies and a full-scale war was inevitable now unless the sultan made peace, a threat Saladin had taken seriously. Balian had assumed Conrad meant to break the news upon his arrival at Ascalon. It would be greeted with great relief by the *poulains* and most likely by Richard, too, for the terms were similar to those he himself had offered Saladin, and a peace settlement would free him to return to defend his own kingdom. The common soldiers, those still burning with holy zeal to retake Jerusalem, would have felt betrayed, of course, but Conrad would not have lost any sleep over their anguish. This was the most bitter of Balian's regrets, that they'd come so close to ending this accursed war on terms both sides could live with, only to see those hopes bleed to death along with Conrad.

He would have to tell Henri about Conrad's secret dealings with Saladin of course, but not now. "Saladin had no reason to arrange Conrad's murder," he said, "for he knew Conrad preferred to settle the war over the bargaining table, not the battlefield." When Otto de Trazegnies then offered up Guy de Lusignan as a plausible suspect, Balian could only marvel at how little these newcomers knew of his world. "Can you truly imagine Guy as the mastermind behind a conspiracy like this? He has not the brains, no more than Humphrey de Toron has the ballocks. Besides, your king has cleverly defanged the de Lusignan snakes by giving them Cyprus. Moreover, the *Assassins* are not routiers; their daggers are not for hire to the highest bidder."

Balian hesitated and then decided it was best not to hold back, for they would have to know. "That is what the French are saying, though," he admitted. "Not only are they blaming Richard for Conrad's death, they are also alleging that he sent four *Assassins* to France to murder Philippe." This set off another infuriated outburst, and again he waited until their indignation had run its course. "You've not heard all of it," he warned. "Conrad's body was not yet cold ere Beauvais and Burgundy demanded that Isabella yield Tyre to them, claiming it in the name of the French king."

"Christ Almighty!" Henri stared at the other man in horror. "Are you saying that the French now control Tyre?"

"No, rest easy, they do not. Isabella told them that she was willing to turn Tyre over to Philippe—as soon as he returned from France to claim it."

They stared at him in astonishment and Henri gave a shaken laugh. "Good for her!" After a moment to reflect, he said, "I suppose I ought to be thanking you."

Balian shook his head. "No, it was none of my doing, for I was not there. They took care to seek her out whilst neither I nor my wife nor Renaud of Sidon were with her, doubtless expecting to easily intimidate her into submission. But much to their surprise, they discovered that even kittens have claws. Having reminded them that Philippe had deserted Conrad and turned his back on God's kingdom, Isabella declared that she meant to obey her husband's dying wish—that she surrender Tyre only to Richard or the rightful lord of the land."

The other men exchanged startled looks. Was Conrad capable of such deathbed generosity, putting the welfare of the kingdom before the sea of bad blood that lay between him and the English king? Had he even been capable of expressing such sentiments? "I'll not deny that comes as a surprise," Henri conceded. "You made it sound as if Conrad was well nigh dead by the time he was taken back to the castle, beyond all mortal concerns."

A smile flickered across Balian's lips, one of paternal pride. "I daresay Beauvais and Burgundy have their doubts, too. But who is to call the bereaved widow a liar? She said Conrad gave her these secret instructions ere he died, and how are they to prove otherwise? Isabella then shut herself up in the castle and put the garrison on alert."

Henri suddenly remembered that it was the Bishop of Beauvais who'd wed Isabella to Conrad. Beauvais ought to have remembered that, too, he thought, and felt a surge of sympathy for this beleaguered girl. He'd always been impressed by her beauty, but until now he'd not realized that she had such courage. God knows she'd need it in the dark days to come. She'd already been forced into one unwanted marriage, and it was all too likely to happen again. A young, pregnant woman could not rule a war-torn land on her own. She'd need another husband as soon as possible, need to be wed again with indecent haste, for political necessity always triumphed over propriety. He hoped she'd be given some small say in the matter, although he thought it unlikely. But whom could they choose? Who would be acceptable to all warring factions and yet also be capable of defending the kingdom as stoutly as Conrad would have done?

"What now, Balian?"

The older man shook his head wearily. "We can only deal with one crisis at a time. Right now the greatest danger lies in Tyre, for the people are on the verge of panic and the French will grasp any opportunity to seize control of the city. I want you to come back with me to Tyre, Henri. Mayhap your presence will reassure the citizenry and remind Beauvais and Burgundy that Conrad may be dead but Richard of England is still a force to be reckoned with."

"When do you want to leave?"

"Now," Balian said, and that succinct reply, so fraught with urgency, told them more about the *poulain* baron's state of mind than a torrent of words could have done. They were teetering upon the edge of the abyss and who would know it better than a man born and bred in Outremer?

To Balian and Henri's mutual frustration, the winds had died down, delaying their voyage for hours. They considered riding the thirty miles to Tyre but by then twilight was approaching and it made more sense to keep waiting for favorable winds, as a ship under sail could cover three times that distance in a single day. They were eventually able to raise anchor that night. The winds continued to be contrary, however, becalming them at the midway point, and so it was almost sunrise before their galley was within sight of Tyre's formidable walls and soaring towers. The massive iron chain was lowered to allow them entry into the harbor, and they were soon at the wharf by the Sea Gate. The castle was situated on the eastern harbor mole, and Henri's gaze kept coming back to it; he wondered if Isabella was still abed, if she dreaded each dawning day now as one sure to bring more trouble and grief.

Henri politely declined Balian's offer of hospitality, not wanting to intrude into a house of mourning, and instead chose to return to the archbishop's palace, where he'd lodged on his earlier visit. Rather than wait while a servant was sent to Balian's stable to fetch horses, they decided to walk, glad to be on firm ground after so many hours aboard ship. The city was beginning to stir, people opening their shops, street vendors preparing to start their rounds, windows being flung open and voices echoing on the early-morning air. But there was none of the usual bustle and cheer, and the subdued atmosphere reminded Henri of a town under siege.

The archbishop's palace was unusual in that it was not situated near the Cathedral of the Holy Cross; instead it was next to the hall of the Genoese commune, so after passing the church of St Mark, they turned west. By now the streets were not as deserted and they soon attracted attention. Suddenly people were flocking around them, bursting out of their shops and houses, cheering and laughing. Henri was not surprised that the despairing citizens of Tyre would embrace Balian as their savior. All knew he'd saved the inhabitants of Jerusalem from Saladin's wrath after the battle of Ḥaṭṭīn, so it made sense that they'd feel more secure if he was in the city. Their emotional welcome showed Henri just how raw their nerves were, how badly they'd been shaken by Conrad's murder.

There were so many in the street now that they were unable to make much progress. Glancing at the other man, Henri essayed a small joke. "Since you're Tyre's new patron saint, you might try parting the crowd like Moses parted the Red Sea."

Balian turned to stare at him. "They are not cheering for me, Henri. If Tyre has a new patron saint, it is obviously you."

Henri started to scoff, but then he listened more closely and, to his astonishment, they were indeed shouting his name. Before he could ponder this unexpected development, a priest broke through the throng, seized his hand, and kissed it fervently. "You are our salvation, my lord count, the answer to our prayers! Tell us you'll save our city and our kingdom!"

Henri was rarely flustered, but he was now, and he extricated his hand with difficulty from the priest's frantic grip. As he studied the eager faces of the men

and women surrounding them, a memory stirred—Dārūm and the freed prisoners mobbing Richard, acclaiming him as their savior. An alarming suspicion was
taking form in the back of his brain even before he heard a man cry out in a loud,
booming voice, "Promise us, my lord, promise you'll wed our queen and be our
next king!"

It took them almost an hour to reach the archbishop's dwelling, fighting their
way through crowds every step of the way. Archbishop Joscius hastened out into
the courtyard to bid them welcome, and it was only when they'd been ushered
inside that Henri could draw an unconstricted breath. His heart twisted with pity
for these poor, despairing souls, but he was aware, too, of an instinctive unease,
and he told the archbishop that he needed to rest for a few hours ere he went to
make his condolence call upon the Lady Isabella. The archbishop was a gracious
host even in the face of calamity, and Henri and his squire were soon escorted to
one of the best bedchambers in the palace. His need had been for solitude, not
sleep, but he'd been awake for fully a day and night, and once Lucas had helped
him remove his boots, he stretched out on the bed.

While he hadn't meant to sleep, he soon slipped into that shadow state between
the borders of slumber and wakefulness, and although he would remember none
of his dreams, he knew they'd not been pleasant. He had no idea how much time
had passed when he opened his eyes to find Lucas bending over him, reporting
that the archbishop needed to speak with him as soon as possible.

Henri was still groggy and stumbled to the table, where a basin and towel had
been laid out for his use. Splashing his face with cold water, he shrugged when
Lucas announced dolefully that he could not find a brush. Henri prided himself
upon lacking vanity, although Joanna had once pointed out that only the good-
looking could afford to be indifferent to appearance. Remembering his aunt's
astute observation now, he smiled, for she'd been right, of course; he'd been
blessed with his share of his grandmother Eleanor's beauty, and since childhood,
he'd known there were almost as many advantages in being pleasing to the eye as
there were in being highborn. But he did want to look presentable when he called
upon the Lady Isabella and he was attempting to smooth his curly, fair hair with
the palm of his hand when another knock sounded on the door.

"Tell them I'll be down straightaway, Lucas." A soft cry of surprise from his
squire spun him around, his scabbard not yet buckled. The boy stepped aside,
hastily making an obeisance as the Archbishop of Tyre moved into the chamber,
followed by Balian and at least a dozen others. Henri instantly recognized the
undeniably ugly visage and intelligent dark eyes of Renaud Garnier, Lord of

Sidon, one of the kingdom's most powerful barons. Beside him stood two men Henri had met on his prior visit, Aymar de Lairon, whose recent marriage had made him Lord of Caesarea, and Rohard, son of the newly deceased Pagan, Lord of Haifa. Behind them were Ansaldo Bonvicino, Conrad's chancellor; Atho de Valentia, the citadel's castellan; and Guglielmo Burone and Bonifacio de Flessio, the most influential members of the local Genoese commune, as well as several bishops and a few men unfamiliar to Henri.

After greeting them, Henri asked warily, "What is so urgent that it could not wait until I came down to the great hall?"

"Our need is more than urgent, my lord count." Archbishop Joscius had apparently been chosen as their spokesman. Coming forward, he put a hand on Henri's arm and then said, in the grave, sonorous tones reserved for the pulpit, "We have come to offer you a crown, a bride, and a kingdom."

Henri took a quick backward step, his eyes narrowing. But it was Balian he addressed. "Is this why you wanted me to come to Tyre? Did you know this would happen?"

Balian was neither disturbed nor defensive. "I did not lie to you, Henri, when I told you why you were needed here. But yes, I did hope you would be acclaimed by the people, and I make no apologies for that. We do not have the luxury of mourning Conrad and I make no apologies for that, either, not when the very survival of our kingdom is at stake."

"And Isabella does not get to mourn, either? Does she know that you are planning to marry her off within days of her husband's funeral?"

Balian gave Henri an odd smile, one that managed to convey sadness, sympathy, and an implacable resolve. "She knows," he said, and Henri shook his head angrily, for anger was the safest of the emotions he was struggling with.

"Why could you not be honest with me, Balian? Why could you not tell me that the lot of you had decided I'd make a satisfactory suitor for Isabella's hand?"

"Would you have come back if he had?" the archbishop asked. "We needed a chance to talk with you, to make you see that you are not just a 'satisfactory suitor.' You are the only one whom we can rally around, the only one deemed worthy by us all. You are a man of courage and common sense, a man of good birth and—"

The archbishop was not often interrupted, but Conrad's chancellor was growing impatient that they'd not yet gotten to the heart of the matter. "That is all well and good," Ansaldo Bonvicino said brusquely. "Yes, men respect you, Count Henri, and you've proven yourself in battle, so you can be trusted to lead an army. But none of that makes you indispensable. What does is the blood flowing in your

veins. You are the nephew of two kings, the one man able to command the support of both the English and the French. You are known to stand high in Richard's
favor, but you'd also be acceptable to the Duke of Burgundy, for you are the son
of Philippe's sister. Even after peace is made with Saladin, we will need the continued support of the other Christian kingdoms, need money and men. And we
are much more likely to get it if you are the one ruling over us."

Not all of them were pleased with Ansaldo's interference. They would have
preferred that the case be made by their urbane, eloquent archbishop. They
looked to him now to repair any damage done by the other man's brash candor,
and Joscius was quick to step into the breach.

"I'll not deny that your kinship to the kings of France and England is important to us. But we'd not seek you out if we did not think you'd make a good king,
for we cannot afford another Guy de Lusignan. In you, my lord count, we are
confident we will have a ruler able to meet the great challenges that lie ahead. I
understand that you did not expect this. None of us did. But God's Will is not
always comprehensible to mortal men. 'For now we see through a glass, darkly,
but then face to face.' We can only do our best, and for now that means arranging
a marriage between you and the Lady Isabella, our queen." He smiled then, giving
Henri a look that was both avuncular and earnest. "In truth, you are being offered
a remarkable gift—the Kingdom of Jerusalem and a wife who is highborn, beautiful, and biddable."

Henry could not deny there was truth in what the archbishop had just said.
But at the moment he felt more like a fox run to earth by baying hounds than a
man who'd had a "remarkable gift" bestowed upon him. "I will need time to think
upon it," he said, and then he saw a glimmer of light in this dark tunnel. "I could
not accept the crown without my uncle's consent, so I must talk to Richard ere I
can give you an answer."

There was murmuring from some of the men, but the archbishop was wise
enough to know Henri could not be coerced or pressured into cooperating. "We
can send a message to the English king within the hour."

"No, I must tell him myself," Henri insisted, "and I ought to leave straightaway
so no time will be lost."

This was not well received. The jut of Henri's chin and the taut line of his
mouth did not encourage argument, though, and they reluctantly acquiesced,
even more reluctantly departed the chamber. Joscius, Balian, and Ansaldo lingered after the others had gone so that each man could deliver one last appeal.
The chancellor reminded Henri that most men would thank God fasting for such

an opportunity. Balian sought to assure Henri that Isabella was indeed willing to wed him. But it was Joscius's final comment that would stay with Henri, haunting his peace in the days to come.

"What you decide, my lord count, will matter far beyond the borders of our kingdom. It will affect all of Christendom, for the loss of the Holy Land would inflict a grievous wound upon Christians everywhere. I know you feel overwhelmed at the moment. But if you entreat the Almighty, I am sure He will give you the answers you seek and make His Will known to you."

CHAPTER 32

MAY 1192

Plains of Ramla, Outremer

n May 2, Richard had another of his celebrated narrow escapes. He'd been camped with a small force at La Forbie south of Ascalon and they awoke to find themselves under a surprise dawn assault. Snatching up his sword and shield, Richard charged out of his tent, and he and his knights were able to beat back the attack. Later that day, he sent the Templars to reconnoiter around Dārūm, where they came upon a number of Saracens reaping barley. They took over twenty prisoners and escorted them to Ascalon to assist in the repair of the city walls; both the Templars and Hospitallers relied upon slave labor for building projects. Meanwhile, Richard rode north into the plains of Ramla, where he spent the day chasing off Saracens and fretting why he'd not heard anything yet from Tyre. Common sense told him that Conrad would cooperate now that the kingdom was his. He could not utterly banish a few lingering qualms, though, fearing that the French would try to persuade the marquis to hold aloof, for he was convinced that Burgundy and Beauvais would rather sabotage him than defeat Saladin. He had no doubts whatsoever that Philippe, taking his ease back in Paris, was praying fervently that the war would end in a spectacular failure.

They were only about ten miles from Jaffa, but he decided to pass the night on the plains, and they were setting up camp when telltale puffs of dust were sighted on the horizon. Shading his eyes against the glare of the setting sun, Richard watched as the riders came into view, hoping that this might be the word he'd been awaiting. But the new arrival was even more welcome than a messenger from Tyre. As André dismounted, Richard smiled, more relieved than he'd ever admit that his cousin had safely completed that long and arduous journey to Rome.

A few of his knights had brought down a gazelle, and as the men gathered around their campfires to eat, André shared with Richard what he'd learned at the papal court. The news was not good. On his way back to France, the French king had been spreading stories that Richard was hand in glove with Saladin. In January, he'd met with the Holy Roman Emperor, and from what André had heard, they'd passed much of that meeting maligning Richard. Philippe had also attempted to get the Pope to absolve him of the oath he'd sworn not to attack Richard's domains while he was in the Holy Land.

"The Pope refused," André said, "for that was a bit too blatant even for him."

"'Even for him'? You think he favors the French?"

"It is not that. He is very elderly, almost as old as God, and has neither the backbone nor the desire to offend powerful rulers like Philippe or Heinrich. But some of his cardinals were outraged that Philippe would even contemplate warring upon a man who'd taken the cross, so Celestine was emboldened to deny Philippe's petition." André paused to stab a piece of meat with his knife. "We made for Jaffa since I did not want to chance the harbor at Ascalon, and that's where I was told you were roaming around out here, adding to your collection of Saracen heads. I also heard that Guy is out and Conrad is in." Dropping his facetious tone then, he gave Richard a searching look. "The word from England must be truly terrible if you've embraced that whoreson in Tyre."

"It was and is," Richard admitted. "They probably told you in Jaffa about the prior of Hereford's news. And two more letters came last week, this time from Will Marshal and the Archbishop of Rouen, both warning me that it may cost me dearly if I tarry in Outremer. . . ." Richard paused, having heard a guard's shout that riders were coming in. Handing André his plate, he got to his feet. "Mayhap this is Henri's messenger. If Conrad still balks at joining the army, so help me Christ—" He got no further, having recognized the man on a lathered bay stallion.

Well aware that he was bringing Richard shocking news, Henri had not wanted to hit him with it all at once, and had been mentally rehearsing his account all the way from Tyre. But at sight of his uncle, it was forgotten. Sliding from the saddle, he ran toward Richard, breathlessly blurting out, "Conrad is dead, they are blaming you, and they want me to marry his widow!"

THE TENTS USED on scouting missions were much smaller and Spartan than the spacious pavilions set up back at Ascalon. Richard and Henri sat cross-legged on the blankets that served as the king's bed, shadows encroaching upon the feeble light cast by a single oil lamp. Richard had been stunned to hear of Conrad's murder, although at first he'd seen it only in terms of his own need to depart Outremer as soon as possible. He'd taken the news that the French were blaming him much better than Henri had expected, saying dismissively that no one who knew him would believe so outrageous a falsehood. Henri was not as sanguine, for he feared those who did *not* know Richard could be susceptible to lurid tales of this sort, and his uncle had as many enemies as the Caliph of Baghdad had concubines. But that was a worry for another time; now he could only focus upon his own crisis of conscience, for that was how he saw the Draconian choice being forced upon him.

They'd brought wine and plates of roast venison into the tent; the food remained untouched but they'd not been neglecting the wine. Reaching for his cup, Richard said, "That would be a sight to behold, though—Philippe skulking around Paris, as jumpy as a stray cat, sure *Assassins* were lurking around every corner. He is just fool enough to believe it." He regretted indulging in that bit of black humor, though, when he glanced over at Henri's unhappy face. He'd never seen his nephew, usually so high-spirited and carefree, as distraught as this.

"Well, that is neither here nor there. Obviously we need to talk about this offer of a crown. Do you want to tell me what you think of it, Henri?"

"I'd rather hear what you think first, Uncle."

"Fair enough. You'd be a good king, Henri, most likely a better one than Conrad. So yes, I would like to see you accept it. But I'd advise against the marriage. Unfortunately, that is not an option open to you, is it? The lady comes with the crown. Even if the *poulain* lords were desperate enough to agree, any man she later married would be eager to advance a claim to your throne, following in Conrad's footsteps." Richard shook his head before saying dryly, "A pity she could not be reconciled with Humphrey de Toron, surely the only soul in all of Outremer who has no interest whatsoever in becoming king."

Henri knew why he had such misgivings about wedding Isabella. Curious to learn why his uncle harbored misgivings, too, he said, "I confess it surprises me to hear you say this, for Isabella is your cousin."

"I do not blame the girl for her predicament; none of it is her doing. And how can I not admire her for standing up to Burgundy and Beauvais like that? But my greater loyalty is to you, lad, and I fear such a marriage would be invalid under canon law. The aforementioned Humphrey is alive and well and still her husband in God's eyes, for that so-called annulment was a farce from first to last. If you wed her, Henri, you risk having your children declared illegitimate, for your marriage to Isabella would be no more valid than Conrad's."

"Truthfully, that is not a worry of mine, Uncle, for who would challenge the marriage? The bishops of Outremer supported the annulment and are the ones urging me now to wed Isabella. They are a pragmatic lot, the *poulains*. But it is more complicated than even you know. Isabella is pregnant."

"Ah . . . I see. No wonder you are so uncertain. If she gives birth to a son, he'll inherit the throne. Of course she may have a daughter, in which case any son of yours would take precedence."

"Are you suggesting I go ahead and roll the dice?" Henri asked, with such a sad smile that Richard felt a stab of pity.

"It is understandable that you might be reluctant to marry the girl under the circumstances. But leave that for now. Let's talk about the crown. I do not sense any great enthusiasm for that, either. Why not?"

"It would mean lifelong exile, Uncle. Most likely I'd never see my mother again, or my brother and sisters." Henri gnawed on his lower lip, not sure how candid he could be. But his uncle ought to understand if any man could, for all knew the close bond he had with Eleanor. "I was not yet fifteen when my father died. I assume you know the story? He was seized by the Turks on his way back from the Holy Land, held for ransom, and finally freed after my mother persuaded the emperor of the Greeks to pay it. We were so overjoyed when he finally came home. . . . But his health had been ravaged by his stay in prison and he died soon afterward. My mother took it very hard, and she said she'd have to rely upon me to be the man in the family, to help her protect my little brother and sisters. If I were not to come back to Champagne, I think it would break her heart. . . ."

Richard was not at his best in discussions like this; he preferred to deal with emotions by ignoring them. He was very fond of his sister, though, and he suspected Henri was right, for Marie was fiercely devoted to the welfare of her children. A thought occurring to him then, he brightened. "Might it not console her to know you now ruled a kingdom?"

Henri gave him another sad smile. "The Counts of Champagne consider themselves the equal of kings, so she'd not see that as much of an elevation."

No son of the Duchess of Aquitaine could argue with that, but Richard tried. "You may just need some time. My sisters were all sent away when they were very young to wed foreign princes, but they'd been taught that would be their fate and so did not think to question it. For you, it is different, of course. You expected to rule Champagne till the end of your earthly days. But once you've come to terms with it, it might be easier . . . ?"

Henri took no comfort in that possibility. Never see his beloved Champagne again? Trade its lush greenwoods and river valleys for this arid, inhospitable land with its searing summers and noxious maladies? Trade the family he loved for a life with an unwilling wife and another man's child? "I must sound like such a fool," he mumbled, "whining about having a crown and a beautiful woman forced upon me. Thank you, Uncle, for hearing me out without laughing in my face."

With that, he started to rise. Richard waved him down again. "We are not done yet, lad. I understand now why the prospect of a kingship brings you so little joy. So let's talk about Isabella. Why are you so loath to wed her? Is it because of the baby? Do you fear you might not be able to care for another man's son?"

Henri was grateful for Richard's blunt speaking. "That is part of it, yes. But it is not just that. Conrad did not care that he had an unhappy, unwilling wife. I do. Mayhap it would not matter so much if we were back in Champagne, but here . . ."

"I thought you said you'd been assured she was willing to wed you?"

"What else are they going to say, Uncle? Tell me she has taken to her bed, weeping, cursing her lot in life? How can she be willing? Christ, this is the second time she'd be wed against her will! For all I know, she still loves Humphrey de Toron."

"I find that highly unlikely," Richard said, with unkind candor. "I take it, then, that you have not talked to Isabella yet?"

Henri looked somewhat embarrassed. "No, I insisted upon leaving straight-away, saying I could make no decision until I'd consulted with you. I suppose I should have gone to see her ere I left, but in truth, I did not want to face her. I did not know what to say. . . ."

Neither did Richard. "It seems to me," he said after a long pause, "that she might well see you as a considerable improvement over Conrad. So . . . you've told me why you are reluctant. Tell me now why you would consent."

"For the same reason you are still here in Outremer, Uncle, even though you now know your own kingdom is at great risk."

After that, they lapsed into silence, each man preoccupied with thoughts that were none too pleasant. "I have not been much help, have I?" Richard said at last, and Henri gave him his first real smile.

"No, not much," he agreed. "I do not suppose you'd be willing to forbid me . . . ?"

It was a joke, but not entirely. "I am sorry, Henri," Richard said, with a rueful smile of his own. "No one can make that decision for you."

"I know. . . ." Henri leaned back so that he was cloaked in shadows. "But you do think I ought to accept it."

"Yes," Richard said, "I do."

TWILIGHT IN THE HOLY LAND never lingered, offering a brief interlude between the dramatic acts put on by daylight and darkness. On this Monday in early May, it unobtrusively slipped onstage after a sunset that had been magnificent even by Outremer standards, spangling the cresting waves in crimson and gilding the occasional cloud in a crown of gold. Dusk soon muted those garish, resplendent colors, a soft lilac haze blurring the outlines of the shore. But by the time Henri's galley was within sight of Tyre, the sky was shading from dark blue to ebony and he could hear the city's churches ringing in Compline.

The iron chain had already been stretched across the harbor, but it was lowered with record haste as soon as the ship's master identified his passengers. Some of Henri's knights nudged one another and grinned, already anticipating the royal privileges that their lord would soon be enjoying. Others were subdued and silent, those already in mourning for their lost homeland. Henri meant to offer them all a choice, just as Richard had done, but he knew a strong sense of duty would compel many of them to stay with him. It was a two-edged sword, able to cut both ways—duty.

Morgan had joined him in the bow, and they watched together as a star streaked toward the distant horizon. "If you died tomorrow," Morgan said in a low voice, "they would still find a husband for the Lady Isabella."

"And I should be happy about that because . . . ?"

"I was just reminding you that being the 'ideal choice' and being the 'only choice' are not one and the same."

"I know . . . but I cannot disappoint Richard and God, too. Mayhap one of them, but both?" Henri glanced at the Welshman, a smile coming and going as fast as that shooting star, and his wan attempt at humor brought an unexpected lump to Morgan's throat.

Henri sent a messenger to the archbishop to request horses, for he hoped to avoid a repetition of that earlier mob scene. Curfew had not yet rung and as word spread of his arrival, crowds began to gather. But he was not kept waiting long. Many torchbearing riders soon came into view, and Henri resigned himself to a royal procession through streets thronged with cheering citizens. As they approached the archbishop's palace, Henri could not help looking toward a nearby narrow lane, deep in shadows now, for it was there that Conrad had met the untimely death that would change the lives of so many.

Archbishop Joscius was waiting to welcome him, as were Balian, Renaud of Sidon, and the chancellor, Ansaldo. Henri had expected as much, sure the archbishop would send word to them even before he dispatched an escort to the harbor. At first Joscius was preoccupied with playing the host, offering to have a meal prepared for Henri and his men. Henri politely declined for himself, but accepted on behalf of his travel companions. When Joscius began to make the usual courteous queries about Henri's voyage, Ansaldo could contain himself no longer and demanded eagerly, "Well? Did you see the English king?"

Henri hadn't the heart to drag out the suspense and told them then what they were so desperate to hear, that Richard had given his consent. They were too seasoned as diplomats to show the intensity of their relief. It was more subtle, an easing of a rigid posture, a soft expulsion of a held-in breath—except for Ansaldo, who said fervently and forthrightly, "Thank Almighty God!" That broke the tension and Henri soon found himself surrounded, knights, canons, priests, and servants all jockeying to get closer, wanting to share in so significant a moment in the history of their kingdom.

Henri had to acknowledge their congratulations, well wishes, and expressions of gratitude, and it was a while before he could request that the archbishop send a messenger to the castle. "Please convey my respects to the marquise and ask if I may call upon her on the morrow." Feeling then that he'd done his duty, he confessed to fatigue from his journey and was escorted up to his bedchamber by the archbishop himself.

Privacy was always at a premium in their world and he realized that it was an even rarer luxury for a king. This night might be the last time he would be free of constant scrutiny, able to be alone with his thoughts. After sending his squire down to the hall to eat, he sat on the edge of the bed. It was too early to sleep and he could not very well ask the archbishop to lend him a book when he'd just pleaded exhaustion. Finally, inspiration struck and he opened the door quietly, following the stairwell up to the roof.

As he expected, it was laid out like a sky-top garden, with benches, large flowering planters, and even a trellised arbor to provide shade from the sun. Sitting on a bench, he gazed up at the sky. The moon was in its last quarter and the roof was bathed in a silvery glow. The Holy Land seemed to have more than its share of stars, those remote, pale lights "offering mankind our only earthly glimpse of infinity." The thought wasn't Henri's, but the musings of a childhood tutor. He hadn't thought of Master Roland in years, but his memories of Champagne were close to the surface tonight.

He soon rose and began to pace. His eye was caught by a flash of color, and when he squinted, he could make out the triangular shape of a yellow sail. For a time he watched that distant vessel, speculating upon its destination. Was it heading for Cyprus and Guy de Lusignan's new kingdom? Or the fabled city of Constantinople? Mayhap even France? Two months from now, God willing, it could be dropping anchor in the harbor at Marseille. He was trying to remember how many miles lay between Marseille and his capital city of Troyes when the door banged behind him.

"My lord count, we were so worried! We could not imagine where you'd gone." The man hastening toward him was vaguely familiar and, after a moment, Henri recognized Archbishop Joscius's steward. Henri's normally equable temper had begun to fray around the edges in the past week and he opened his mouth to send the steward away. He wasn't given the chance, though. "I am so sorry to disturb you, my lord, but you have a visitor!"

Henri's brows rose. "At this hour? Say that I've retired for the night and suggest he come back on the morrow."

"But . . . but my lord, it is the queen!"

Henri said a very rude word under his breath, for the last person he wanted to see tonight was Balian's strong-willed wife. It was nigh on twenty years since King Almaric's death had left Maria Comnena a young widow, but Henri thought she remained convinced her handsome dark head was still graced with a crown. His mouth tightened and he started to say that his instructions stood. He remembered just in time that Maria would soon be his mother-in-law. "I will, of course, see Queen Maria," he said with a resigned sigh. "Tell her that—"

"No, my lord, it is the Lady Isabella!"

The steward's consternation would have been comical under other circumstances; it was obvious he thought Isabella had committed a serious breach of etiquette. Henri had hoped to put off this meeting until the morning, but he was not truly surprised that his plans had gone awry; that seemed to be the developing pattern of his new life in Outremer. "Tell the marquise that I will be down to the hall straightaway."

"There is no need for that." This voice came from the stairwell, and as both men spun around, Isabella stepped from the shadows onto the roof. Henri was the first to recover and came forward swiftly, kissing her hand with his most courtly flourish. She murmured, "My lord count," and then dismissed the steward with a smile. He made a sound like a strangled squawk and Henri realized he was appalled that they'd be alone and unchaperoned. Just then, another form emerged from the stairwell, and the steward's shoulders sagged in relief at the sight of Isabella's lady-in-waiting. Reassured that the proprieties would be observed, he bowed and hastily withdrew.

Isabella introduced her companion as the Lady Emma, saying fondly that Emma had been with her since her childhood. Emma reminded Henri of Dame Beatrix, his aunt Joanna's mainstay, ever poised to guard her lamb from prowling wolves, and when he smiled at her, he was faintly amused by her cool response. She would not easily be won over; sheepdogs never were. He was expecting her to hover protectively by Isabella's side, but when Isabella suggested they sit upon a marble bench, Emma took a seat some distance away.

Isabella seemed to sense his surprise. "I trust Emma with all my secrets, with my very life," she said matter-of-factly, and he realized she was reassuring him that Emma would be telling no tales or relating choice gossip about anything she saw or heard on the roof this night.

"You are fortunate to have such a faithful confidante," he said, thinking that at least she'd had one ally in Conrad's household. He'd occasionally felt a few conscience pangs for the part he'd played in bringing that marriage about. He'd been convinced by Balian and Conrad that it was a matter of Outremer's very survival, but he was still chivalrous enough to feel sympathy for that eighteen-year-old girl, tearfully insisting that she loved her husband, did not want to be separated from him. He'd been pleased, then, by what he'd seen when he'd dined with Conrad and Isabella before his departure for Acre. They'd appeared comfortable together, and he'd noticed no overt signs of stress in Isabella's behavior toward her husband. Even though it had gotten off to the worst possible start, he thought their marriage seemed no worse than many and probably better than some; at least he'd hoped so. In their world, women were always the ones to make the concessions, and he supposed that was true even for queens.

"I owe you an apology," he said. "I ought to have seen you ere I left to consult my uncle. That was not only bad manners, it was cowardice."

"I was not offended," she assured him, "truly I was not. Like me, you'd been tossed without warning into deep water and you were struggling to stay afloat." She glanced at him from the corner of her eye and then said, "Mayhap I ought to be apologizing to you? For coming to you like this, I mean. No one wanted me to do it. Not my mother, nor Balian, for certes not the archbishop. When I was announced, he looked dumbstruck, and even tried to convince me to return to the castle, saying it was not proper for me to seek you out like this. I think it makes them nervous when I show that I have a mind of my own," she said with a smile, and Henri caught his breath.

When she'd emerged from the stairwell, his first impression was one of fragility and loss. She was clad in a plain, dark-blue gown with a high neckline, wearing no jewelry but her wedding band, her hair covered by a simple linen wimple. Her skirts hid any evidence of pregnancy, for she was still in the early stages; Henri was intensely aware that she was with child, though, and that made her seem even more vulnerable in his eyes. But then she'd smiled, a bewitching, luminous smile that gave him a glimpse of the young woman beneath the somber widow's garb, and suddenly he saw her not as a tragic figure, not as his fellow victim in a bizarre twist of fate, but as a very desirable bedmate.

"I am glad you came," he said, with enough sincerity to bring a faint flush to her cheeks.

"I had to . . . Henri. I know you do not want to stay in Outremer." When he started to speak, she stopped him with a light touch of her hand. "I understand, for this is my home, not yours. And I also understand your reluctance to wed me. How could you not have misgivings about such a marriage—a reluctant wife carrying another man's child, not the best of beginnings."

Her lashes swept down for a moment, and then she raised her head and met his eyes without artifice or coquetry. "I cannot ease your yearning for Champagne. But at least I can ease your mind about me. I am not being compelled to marry you, Henri. I will not deny that I am being urged to it on all sides. But I am in a stronger position than I was when they insisted I wed Conrad. The laws of our realm offer me protection against an unwanted marriage, for the Assizes provide that a widow may not be forced to wed for a year after her husband's death. So at the risk of being shamelessly bold, you need not fear that I'll be an unwilling wife."

Henri very much wanted to believe her. "I know you have a strong sense of duty. You proved that when you agreed to marry Conrad."

"I am so glad you understand that!" She leaned toward him, that enchanting smile flashing again. For all that she'd been twice wed, she still seemed like an innocent, and he felt sure she did not realize the impact her physical proximity was having upon him. "Not everyone does," she confided. "I loved Humphrey, did not want to leave him. But I was not browbeaten into agreeing to marry Conrad as so many think. Yes, I was greatly pressured by Conrad, by my mother, my stepfather, Archbishop Joscius, almost all of our lords and bishops, even the papal legate. I did not yield, though, until I realized that this was the only way to strip Guy de Lusignan of his kingship."

"I think you showed commendable courage . . . Isabella."

"I never expected to be queen. Why would I, for my sister had two children already and was still young enough to have many more. I was content with Humphrey and the life we had together. But the deaths of Sybilla and her daughters changed everything."

"Just as Conrad's death has."

She nodded. "At least he died happy. He so desperately wanted to be king. I'm glad he had those few days. . . ."

Henri was surprised both by the sentiment and by the ironic undertones, coming from a girl with the face of an angel. "Conrad . . . you and he were able to . . ." He did not know how to ask so probing and personal a question, but he needed to know. If she'd been maltreated, it might well affect their own marriage.

"Yes," she said simply. "When I agreed to marry him, I realized that I could not do so with hatred in my heart. It was not always easy, not at first. But I did my best to be a dutiful wife and if I could not give him more, I do not think he missed it. He had what he wanted most, a claim to the crown. It may be that our child might have brought us closer together. He very much wanted a son."

Now that they'd come to it—the baby in her womb that was both a blessing and a curse—he did not know what to say, not sure how honest he dared to be. How much easier it would have been if only she'd not been pregnant!

Isabella proved to be the braver of the two. "We need to talk about it, Henri, about the fact that I am with child, Conrad's child." Instinctively her hand moved to her abdomen, a protective gesture that caught at his heart. "The welfare of my baby matters even more to me than the welfare of my kingdom. Not many men would be willing or able to accept another man's child. I know it can be done, though, for Balian did it. I was just five when he married my mother and he always treated me as if I were his flesh-and-blood, even after they had their own children. Conrad could never have done that, not when a crown was at stake. But I think . . . I hope you can, Henri. The others chose you for your courage and royal blood, your kinship to the kings of England and France. What matters more to me is that you are honorable and have a good heart."

They were very close now on the bench. Her eyes looked almost black against the whiteness of her face, and he found himself thinking that a man could drown in their dark depths. "Isabella . . ."

"I know you think we are both trapped," she said softly, "and I suppose we are. But if you wed me, I promise you this—that I'll do all in my power to make sure you never regret it."

He reached for her hand, entwining their fingers together. How fearful she must have been and how brave she was now, putting her pride aside to offer herself to him like this. He could see the pulse throbbing in her slender throat, and suddenly knew he could not bear to think of her wedding another man, one who might not treat her and her baby with the kindness, tenderness, and respect they deserved.

"I will be honored to wed you, Isabella," he said, and when she lifted her face, heartbreakingly lovely in the moonlight, he kissed her soft cheek, her closed eyelids, and then those full red lips. He'd meant it to be a pledge, a reassurance, but her mouth was so sweet and her body flowed into his arms so naturally that he forgot she was so newly widowed, forgot she was pregnant, forgot all but the passion that blazed up between them with an intensity, a hunger he'd not experienced before. When he finally ended the embrace, he saw that she was as shaken as he was. Her dark eyes were starlit, her breathing uneven. "This is not the destiny either of us expected," he said. "But it is one we can forge together."

ON TUESDAY, MAY 5, 1192, Henri and Isabella were wed in Tyre by a French bishop, a week to the day after Conrad of Montferrat's assassination. Henri at once set about mustering an armed force to assist Richard in an assault upon Dārūm Castle. When he and the Duke of Burgundy moved the army to Acre, the chronicler of the *Itinerarium* reported that "The count took his wife with him, as he could not yet bear to be parted from her."

CHAPTER 33

MAY 1192

Ascalon–Dārūm Road

Upon his arrival at Ascalon, Henri learned that Richard had grown impatient with waiting and had ridden south to begin the siege of Dārūm Castle on his own. Henri set out at daybreak the next day, his men soon complaining of the oppressive heat. It was Pentecost Eve, the weather already much hotter than it would have been back in Champagne. Henri wondered if he'd ever get accustomed to the sultry Syrian climate, and he was relieved when the seventeen stone towers of Dārūm eventually came into view. Raising his hand, he signaled for a halt so they could assess the situation. By now he could see Richard's tents in the distance, and the siege engines he'd brought by ship from Ascalon, but they were strangely silent. A swirl of dust heralded the approach of the Duke of Burgundy, and Henri coughed when he inhaled a lungful, hoping the other man did not plan to ride beside him for the rest of the way. That was apparently Hugh's intention, though.

"What did he think he could accomplish with only his household knights? Sometimes that man has not a grain of sense, just an insatiable hunger for fame."

Henri had never liked the duke, feeling he'd done nothing but obstruct their progress, and he was still angry at the way Burgundy and the Bishop of Beauvais had attempted to browbeat Isabella when they thought she'd be most vulnerable. Yet he knew Outremer needed French support and so he contented himself with saying mildly, "You do remember, Hugh, that Richard is my uncle?"

"A man cannot pick his kinsmen," Hugh said, generously absolving Henri of that tainted family bond. "But you cannot deny that Richard is a lunatic on the battlefield."

"I'll not deny he is reckless about his own safety." Henri ignored Hugh's snort. "But he is never reckless when it comes to the lives of his men."

"And I am? Why—because I am urging an assault upon the Holy City? That is why we are here, Henri, why so many good men took the cross. We swore to retake Jerusalem. If we do not even try, we dishonor the memories of all those who died for their faith."

It was obvious to Henri that Conrad had not confided in his French allies, for Hugh did not appear to know of the marquis's secret talks with Saladin. "Do you truly believe it is worth putting the very survival of the kingdom in jeopardy, Hugh? I've yet to talk to a single *poulain* who thinks we ought to take so great a risk. To a man, they say another loss like Ḥaṭṭīn would doom Outremer."

"You know what I think? That the disaster at Ḥaṭṭīn has sapped them of their will to fight for the True Faith. They no longer have the stomach for battle, even if it means humbling themselves before the enemies of God."

Henri turned in the saddle to stare at the other man, incredulous. "The Templars have no stomach for battle? I'd not say that in their hearing if I were you."

"I am not saying they lack courage. But living in the midst of pagans and infidels and unbelievers corrupts the soul, and not even the Templars are immune to it. Nor am I surprised that the *poulains* are so willing to yield Jerusalem to Saladin. They still attend Mass, but they live like Saracens, luxury-loving, decadent, and effeminate—"

"And we take frequent baths, too. What greater proof of depravity can there be?" Neither Henri nor Hugh had noticed as Balian d'Ibelin had reined in his stallion within earshot. Balian was accustomed to hearing criticism like this from suspicious newcomers, those who thought the Syrian Franks were too much at home in this alien environment, and he no longer reacted with youthful anger or indignation, for it served no purpose. He'd long ago acknowledged the irony of it, that the survival of Outremer depended upon men who judged its inhabitants to be unworthy to dwell in God's Kingdom.

Balian's sly raillery was not lost upon Hugh, who gave him a suspicious scowl, but the *poulain* lord was pleased to see that Henri looked amused. He wanted Isabella to be happy with her new husband, wanted the young count to be content with his new life. "As interesting as this discussion is," he said, with just a hint of sarcasm, "you might want to direct your attention to the castle battlements."

It took a moment or so for them to see it, and when they did, they could only stare in disbelief at the red and gold banner flying from the keep—the royal lion of England.

RICHARD SAUNTERED FORWARD to greet them, looking justifiably proud to Henri and insufferably smug to Hugh. He was quite willing to regale them with the details of his capture of Dārūm, and most of the men were eager to hear, for it was a remarkable feat to seize a castle in just four days, especially with such a small force. Those like Hugh, who took no pleasure in hearing of Richard's exploits, prudently kept silent, aware that a lack of enthusiasm would seem like the worst sort of sour grapes, and Richard soon found himself surrounded by admiring knights; to Hugh's annoyance, many of them were French.

They could see the evidence of the brief siege all around them. The gate was smashed, the broken wood blackened by fire. The walls had been seriously damaged by the trebuchets Richard had brought from Ascalon. Hugh was not surprised when some of Richard's knights boasted that their king had pitched in when they carried the dismantled siege engines over a mile from the beach, and when they said that he'd taken personal command of one of the trebuchets, Hugh muttered, "He would."

No one paid him any heed, for Richard was explaining that he'd noticed a weakness during an earlier scouting mission. The deep ditch before the great tower was cut out of natural rock on one side, but on the other, it was reinforced with a layer of paving. Richard put his sappers to work, renegade Saracens from Aleppo whom he'd hired at Acre, and they soon broke through the paving, then stuffed the tunnel with combustible matter and set it afire, causing part of the tower wall to collapse. After they'd destroyed a Saracen mangonel mounted on top of the keep, the garrison sent three men out to seek terms. First they'd asked if they could have a truce while they consulted with Saladin, and then they offered to surrender the castle if they and their families could depart in freedom. "I told them," Richard said coolly, "to defend themselves as best they could," making clear his disdain for foes who'd yield so easily.

Henri blinked. While commanders often insisted upon an unconditional surrender, especially if they'd been put to the time and trouble of storming a castle or town, he would have accepted the qualified surrender offer had he been in Richard's place. He forgot sometimes how ruthless his uncle could be when it came to waging war. Thinking unwillingly of the Acre garrison, he said, "What happened when you took the castle?"

"They did not offer much of a fight." Richard sounded both disapproving and disappointed. "When we broke through yesterday, they fled into the keep, and

soon offered to surrender unconditionally. We took about three hundred prisoners." Richard gestured toward the castle, and Henri saw a group of men lined up
in the bailey, hands bound behind their backs, surrounded by guards.

The others had begun to exclaim indignantly, for Richard had just revealed
that the garrison had hamstrung all of their horses when defeat seemed inevitable; to knights, deliberately crippling a horse was a far worse sin than slaying a
man. But Henri continued to study the prisoners. A much smaller group huddled
nearby, looking forlorn and frightened, the wives and children of the garrison.
Henri knew he was not supposed to feel pity for them; they were the enemy, after
all. But he did. As hard as war could be for soldiers, it was always harder for the
noncombatants, for the women, the young, the elderly. At least back home, there
were periods of peace when people could go about their daily lives, not fearing
that men would swoop down upon their villages and towns, burning and looting
and killing. He wondered if there would ever be peace in the Kingdom of Jerusalem. Somehow he doubted it.

With an effort, Henri shook off these dismal thoughts; it was both dangerous
and hurtful to keep making comparisons between Champagne and Outremer,
the world he'd lost and the one thrust upon him. His uncle was still accepting
congratulations from the other men, who were delighted to learn that they'd
found and freed forty Christian prisoners in the castle dungeon. After some of
the French lords began to praise Richard, too, Hugh forced himself to mumble a
grudging "Well done." He was unable to resist adding, "You always did have the
Devil's own luck."

"A man does not need luck when he knows what he is doing," Richard shot
back, and then glanced toward Henri. "We'd planned to celebrate Pentecost on
the morrow and send the prisoners and wounded on ahead to Ascalon. Does that
meet with your approval?"

Henri was startled to be treated as an equal; he'd have to get used to that, too.
"And Dārūm?"

"That is up to you. Dārūm is yours now."

Henri was taken aback. "Mine? That is most generous of you, Uncle!"

Even the French were impressed by such a magnanimous gesture, except for
Hugh, who looked as if he wanted to spit into the dust at Richard's feet. Richard was
obviously taking a grim pleasure in the other man's vexation. But when he turned
again to Henri, grey eyes searching blue ones, he was conveying a message that went
beyond mere words. "After all," he said, "this is your kingdom now, is it not?"

Henri held his gaze. "Yes," he said, "it is."

IN LATE MAY, one of Richard's spies warned him that the Saracens were fortifying a stronghold with the euphonious name Castle of the Figs. The garrison fled at his approach, though, and by May 29, he was camped near a reed-choked river about twelve miles south of Ascalon. It was here that another messenger from England found him. John d'Alençon was the Archdeacon of Lisieux, a former vice chancellor of England, a man Richard trusted, and the news he brought was deeply disturbing.

The archdeacon's report made it sound as if England was descending into chaos. Richard's half-brother Geoff was still feuding bitterly with the Bishop of Durham, rejecting the efforts of Eleanor and the council to make peace between them. Richard's exiled chancellor, Longchamp, had laid an interdict upon his own diocese after the Archbishop of Rouen had confiscated the revenues of his bishopric of Ely, and the people were suffering greatly, for no Masses could be said, no confessions heard, no weddings performed, and bodies were left unburied in the fields. Eleanor had intervened, persuading the archbishop to restore Ely's revenues to Longchamp and insisting that Longchamp revoke the interdict and lift the excommunication he'd placed upon the archbishop. But the situation remained volatile, made worse by the arrival of two papal legates who laid the duchy of Normandy under interdict after being refused entry by Richard's seneschal, and then took refuge at the French court.

Even more alarming was the archdeacon's account of the ongoing conspiracy between the French king and Richard's own brother. Philippe had attempted to launch an invasion of Normandy, thwarted only by the reluctance of his French barons to attack the lands of a crusader. After Eleanor had prevented John from joining the French king in Paris, John then seized two royal castles, Windsor and Wallingford, and continued to circulate rumors that Richard was dead, which made men loath to antagonize the man likely to be their next king. The archdeacon had also brought letters from Eleanor, the Archbishop of Rouen, and the council, conveying the same urgent plea—that Richard return home as soon as possible, for he was in danger of losing his throne if he did not.

Richard was badly shaken by these latest warnings. It seemed as if all was slipping away, both in Outremer and his distant, beleaguered domains. He was convinced the French were determined to sabotage any chances of a military victory against the Saracens, and now his own kingdom was in grave peril. For a man accustomed to being in command, it was intolerable to feel so helpless, to be at the mercy of forces beyond his control. He responded by withdrawing into a dark, brooding silence, saying nothing about his intentions, and that silence only fed his army's unease. Many soldiers blamed Richard for his unwillingness to lay siege to Jerusalem, but only the French commanders wanted him to depart, for few believed victory was possible without him. When rumors spread throughout the camp that he planned to go home, morale plummeted.

RICHARD HAD BEEN SECLUDED in his tent for several days, wrestling with the competing demands of king and crusader, fearing they might be irreconcilable. If he remained in the Holy Land, he could lose his crown. But how could he violate the sacred oath he'd sworn to Almighty God? He'd always been very decisive, both on and off the battlefield, quick to assess risks and reach conclusions, never one for second-guessing himself. But now he was faced with an impossible choice and, for the first time in his life, he did not know what to do.

He'd prayed for guidance, to no avail. God had given him no answers. Instead he was confronted with more bad news, delivered by Henri, André, and the Bishop of Salisbury.

Richard had never seen his nephew so angry. "Last night the Duke of Burgundy and the Bishop of Beauvais held a secret council with the other lords, including some of your vassals from Poitou, Anjou, England, and Normandy. None of us were invited, for obvious reasons, nor were the Templars, the Hospitallers, or any of the *poulain* barons. They decided that they will march upon Jerusalem whether you stay or not, Uncle. They then leaked word of their decision to the army, and men reacted as you'd expect—with great joy." Shaking his head, Henri said bitterly, "They are going to lay siege to the Holy City even if it means they all die in the attempt and, unforgivably, even if Outremer dies, too. They may well have doomed every man, woman, and child in the kingdom and we did not even have a say in it."

Richard's own temper had caught fire as he'd listened. "So be it, then. If that is their decision, I now know what mine will be. They can neither take nor hold Jerusalem, the fools! Why should I sacrifice my own kingdom for nothing?"

None of them argued with him. As much as Henri wanted to, he could not. He was convinced that Hugh of Burgundy could no more defeat Saladin than he could fly to the moon. Whatever hopes they had of success would end when Richard sailed for home. Yet how could he ask his uncle to remain when none would heed his voice? Even if victory was impossible in Outremer, the Angevin empire could still be saved. But not if Richard remained in the Holy Land.

THE ARMY MOVED NORTH to Bethgibelin, camping by the stark ruins of a Hospitaller castle. Here the men encountered swarms of the tiny flies they called "cincelles" and "flying sparks." The insects swarmed incessantly, stinging every inch of exposed flesh and raising such lumps that their victims resembled lepers; despite the searing heat, the soldiers wrapped themselves in cloths and masked their faces to fend off these winged assaults. Yet the men remained determined to reclaim Jerusalem from the infidels, while Richard remained tormented by doubts, for he'd soon begun to question a decision made in anger. Could he truly turn his back upon the Holy Land? Could he sail away as Philippe had done, abandoning Henri and his Christian brethren to a war they could not win? Was that what God would want him to do?

A solitary figure had been keeping vigil for hours outside Richard's tent, swatting ineffectively at the flies, refusing to leave his post even for meals or to answer nature's call. Father William had entered the English king's service when he was Count of Poitou, and when Richard had taken the cross, William had done so, too, for the army would need chaplains, and what better death could a man have than to die in the Holy Land, doing God's Work? He had been devastated by Richard's refusal to besiege Jerusalem. It was far worse, though, to think Richard would abandon them, abandon their sacred quest, abandon the Almighty and the Lord Christ, and as he watched over the king's tent, he wept.

When Richard finally emerged, his attention was drawn to the chaplain, just as William had hoped. But he lost his nerve then, and agreed to speak candidly only if the king promised him that he'd not be angry. Having extracted an impatient reassurance from Richard, the chaplain still hesitated, searching for the right words. "My lord king, it is the talk of the camp that you intend to leave us. May that day never come. God forbid that mere rumors keep you from conquering the Holy Land, for we fear that would bring you eternal disgrace."

He saw Richard stiffen and momentarily faltered. Emboldened when the king did not rebuke him, he pressed on. "Lord king, I entreat you to remember all that God has done for you. Never did a king of your age accomplish such glorious deeds." The words were coming quickly now, slurring in his haste to get them said. He reminded Richard of his past victories as Count of Poitou, spoke of how

Richard had taken Messina and seized the island of Cyprus and sank that great Saracen ship. Such triumphs were proof of divine favor, as was his miraculous recovery from the scourge of Arnaldia, which had killed so many others. "God has committed the Holy Land to your protection. It is your responsibility alone, now that the French king has cravenly run away. You are the sole defender of Christendom. If you desert us, you will have abandoned it to be destroyed by our enemies."

He fell silent then, tears continuing to streak his face, swollen from multiple cincelle bites, his eyes fastened imploringly upon his king. His disappointment was almost too much to bear when Richard turned away without answering.

ON THE FOLLOWING AFTERNOON the army reached Ascalon and made camp in the orchards outside the city walls. Henri then met privately in Balian's tent with some of the other *poulain* lords and the Templar and Hospitaller Grand Masters, holding a strategy session in which they all urged Henri to try to convince Richard to stay. When he balked, they politely but firmly reminded him that his first loyalties now must be given to Outremer. He returned to his own pavilion at sunset in a grim frame of mind, only to find Joanna and Berengaria anxiously waiting for him. Richard was always closemouthed, Joanna conceded; she'd never seen him like this, though. He was obviously greatly troubled, but he'd brushed aside all their questions and concerns, pulling back like a turtle retreating into its shell. "What has happened, Henri? What do we need to know?"

Henri told them about the dire news from England and then about the decision to march on Jerusalem. He had just finished when a summons came from Richard. Joanna and Berengaria accompanied him; he wasn't about to rebuff his aunt and decided it was up to Richard to dismiss the women if he did not want them present. Richard did not seem disturbed to see them; he did not even seem surprised. Seeing his uncle through Joanna and Berengaria's eyes, Henri could understand why they were so worried. Richard looked haggard, even haunted, like a man who'd become a stranger to sleep. His gaze flicked from face to face, his own face inscrutable, his thoughts shielded. When he did not speak, Henri prompted, "You wanted to see me, Uncle?"

Richard nodded then, almost imperceptibly. "I have decided not to return to England. Whatever messages come, whatever happens, I pledge to remain in the Holy Land until next Easter."

Henri felt a great surge of relief, followed by guilt. Joanna's emotions were less ambivalent; she did not think it was fair that Richard should be asked to sacrifice so much more than the other crusaders. Berengaria crossed to her husband's side, looking up at him with a smile so joyful that she seemed to be glowing; at that moment, Henri thought she was beautiful. "Does this mean you will be laying siege to Jerusalem, Richard?"

"Yes," he said, sounding very weary. "I will tell the others tonight and then have my herald proclaim it to the rest of the camp on the morrow."

Henri kept silent, not sure what to say. Nor did he meet his uncle's eyes, for he knew what he'd see in them. It would have been like looking into his own soul on the night he'd returned to Tyre, knowing his choices were illusory, knowing he was trapped.

RICHARD DISPATCHED HENRI to Acre to corral the last of the deserters and to find reinforcements in Tyre and even Tripoli, for if they were going to march on Jerusalem, they would need every single soldier they could round up. Because Richard did not think it was safe for the women to remain at Ascalon without him, he asked Henri to escort them back to Acre. He then led the army to Bait Nūbā, the village that was just twelve tantalizing miles from the Holy City. There they set up camp to await Henri's return and to fend off Saracen raids and hit-and-run attacks.

THEY'D BEEN AT BAIT NŪBĀ two days when one of Richard's spies reported that Saracens were lying in ambush at the spring of Emmaus. Richard set out at dawn with some of his knights, took their foes by surprise, and in the fight that followed, twenty Turks were slain and Salah al-Dīn's own herald captured. When the surviving Saracens retreated, Richard set off in pursuit. He was mounted on Fauvel and soon overtook a man on a rangy bay stallion. Fauvel screamed a challenge, lengthening stride, and the Saracen swung his horse around to meet the attack. He charged, wielding a spear that was deflected by Richard's shield, and took the full thrust of the king's lance. Reining Fauvel in, Richard leaned from the saddle to make sure the other man was dead. When he looked up, his eyes widened. "Jesu!"

It was then that André caught up with him. He'd seen Richard go chasing off after the Saracens and followed, for even Richard's lethal skills could be overcome by sheer numbers. Pulling up alongside his cousin, he barely spared a glance for the body sprawled nearby; in the fifteen years he'd fought at Richard's side, Death had ridden with them so often that they'd come to take its presence for granted. He was more concerned with Richard's odd immobility; he seemed frozen, scarcely breathing.

"Richard? Are you hurt? I do not see any blood. . . ."

"Look," Richard said huskily, never taking his eyes from the dream-like vision that seemed to be floating on the horizon, shimmering in a golden haze of heat.

André raised his hand to shield the glare. "Is that . . . ?"

"Yes . . . it is Jerusalem." Richard had not expected to be so moved, yet as he gazed at those distant limestone walls and towers, it struck him with utter and awful certainty that this was as close as he'd ever get to that most holy and hallowed of cities, the cradle of Christendom. His eyes filled with tears, which André tactfully pretended not to see.

MORGAN, WARIN FITZ GERALD, Pierre de Préaux, and a few other knights and Templars had been out scouting and decided to detour to Ramla before heading back to Bait Nūbā, for the former site had a cluster of barrel-vaulted cisterns. As they approached, they were startled to see dozens of white tents set up near the castle ruins. Advancing warily, they were delighted to discover that this was Henri's camp; he was on his way to Bait Nūbā with fresh troops from Tyre and truants from Acre. Morgan was not surprised that Henri had been more successful than Guy in conscripting the sluggards; the count's easy affability concealed a strong will. They were happy to accept Henri's invitation to stay the night, and they repaid Henri's hospitality by catching him up on all that had occurred since his departure for Acre.

They gave him the most momentous news first—that it had been decided not to besiege Jerusalem. During a heated council the week before, Richard had argued passionately against it, as he'd done in the past, citing the threat to their supply lines, the scale of the city's defenses, and the danger that they'd be trapped between the Jerusalem garrison and Saladin's army. The French had responded as they'd done in the past, too, and accused Richard of caring only for his own honor and glory. He'd been honest about that, Morgan told Henri, candidly admitting he did not want to be blamed for another Ḥaṭṭīn and the loss of the kingdom. He accused the French in turn of seeking his disgrace and insisted he would not sacrifice his army in a rash enterprise that had no hope of success. They countered that it was not his army. He again urged an attack upon Egypt or Damascus, insisting that was the strategy best calculated to bring Saladin back to the bargaining table. And the French rejoinder was that Jerusalem was not negotiable.

"It was," Morgan said, "basically the same argument we've been having since last September at Jaffa. This one did have a different ending, though. It was agreed upon to choose a jury of twenty men, whose decision would be binding upon all. They selected five Templars, five Hospitallers, five *poulains*, and five French lords. Richard insisted that the men who actually lived in Outremer ought to have the greater say. Of course he knew what the verdict would be—fifteen to five in favor of launching an attack upon Egypt. And of course the Duke of Burgundy was furious that he'd been outmaneuvered and repudiated the agreement, saying it was Jerusalem or nothing."

"The king did his best to win them over," Warin chimed in, "offering his fleet for the expedition, pledging to pay for seven hundred knights and two thousand men-at-arms out of his own coffers, even promising to assume the expenses of French knights. All to no avail. And when word got out, the common soldiers were distraught, outraged that Jerusalem would be denied them yet again."

Henri could not help sympathizing with them even though he was sure Richard was in the right. It would have been better never to have raised their hopes, and he could not help wondering if his uncle had ever really intended to assault Jerusalem. But he felt a touch of shame upon hearing what Morgan said next, that Richard had declared before the vote that he'd not desert the army even if they insisted upon the siege. He would not take command, though, saying he refused to lead men to their deaths when it served for naught. No, Henri decided, it was unfair to accuse Richard of bad faith. Their quest had been doomed before Richard and Philippe even reached Outremer, poisoned by the embittered rivalry between the two kings, the two countries. But as tragic as this outcome was for the soldiers who'd been willing to offer up their lives for the Holy City, it was a blessing for the kingdom. Their army would not be sacrificed in vain, and even if the French deserted them, there was still hope of reaching a settlement with Saladin, who had his own troubles.

"I suppose Burgundy is now threatening to pull out and go back to France," Henri said, making a face. No, they told him, the army had been temporarily distracted from their feuding by the arrival of one of Richard's spies, a native Syrian who went by the name "Bernard." He brought news that set the entire camp into an uproar. A supply caravan was on its way from Egypt to Jerusalem, laden with treasure, weapons, and thousands of horses and camels. It would be an incredibly rich prize if they could take it, and its loss would deliver a great blow to Saladin. Richard had ridden out that very night to intercept it, taking five hundred knights and a thousand men-at-arms, as well as the French. They laughed at Henri's startled expression, explaining that Hugh of Burgundy had actually agreed to take part in the raid, but only if the French were allotted fully a third of the booty.

"If that man had not been so highly born, he'd have made a good outlaw," Morgan said with a grin. "But at least for now, the excitement over the caravan has united us, for Richard promised that the spoils would be shared with all, whether they took part in the raid or stayed behind to guard the camp."

"So now we're waiting with bated breath to hear if it was successful. The timing has to be perfect. Fortunately, our king is good at this sort of thing." Warin laughed and began to tell Henri the rest of their news, what he blithely described as "the usual bloodshed."

"We had two fierce skirmishes with the Saracens," Warin reported between bites of bread. "The first one occurred on June twelfth when the Saracens lured some French troops away from camp. Things were going badly for them until the Bishop of Salisbury and the Count of Perche rode to their rescue. The second one began when the Turks ambushed one of our supply caravans from Jaffa." He paused to finish his food before relating a sad story about Baldwin de Carew, who'd been unhorsed in the battle and commandeered his squire's mount, only to see the squire struck down and beheaded soon thereafter.

Henri had no liking for Baldwin, who'd been one of the two knights who'd broken formation at Arsuf, forcing Richard to commit to a premature charge. Henri would have offered his own horse to his uncle in a heartbeat; he'd even do it for Philippe, who was his liege lord. But he hoped he'd not accept another man's horse, knowing it could mean the other man's death. Because he considered Morgan, Warin, and Pierre to be friends, he felt comfortable enough to say as much. They looked at him in surprise before Morgan reminded him, as gently as possible, that he'd be shirking his royal duty to refuse such an offer, for a slain king was the worst of calamities. Henri frowned into his wine cup, wondering how long it would take for him to feel at ease with his new rank.

By now the meal was done, but they lingered by the fire, savoring the simple pleasures of wine and conversation. They commiserated with Pierre de Préaux, whose heroic brother Guilhem remained in captivity, for Saladin still refused to ransom him, and Henri good-naturedly endured the usual bridegroom jests. They were lamenting the recent deaths of two knights from snakebites when the sentries warned that riders were approaching.

They got quickly to their feet, reaching for weapons in case it was a Saracen raid. But they soon heard cries of "The king!" and so were ready to welcome Richard and his men when they rode into the camp. There was no need to ask if the ambush had been successful, for it looked as if thousands of beasts—camels, horses, mules, asses, and donkeys—were being herded by downcast Saracen drovers. The pack animals were heavily laden, and Richard's elated knights were eager to boast of their plunder. They told Henri that they'd seized gold, silver, brocaded silks, spices, sugar, purple dye, wheat, barley, flour, Saracen mail shirts, weapons, and large tents, all intended for Saladin's army at Jerusalem. They'd captured almost four thousand camels, they bragged, and as many mules and donkeys, also taking five hundred prisoners and killing many, men now lost to the sultan. It was, they proclaimed to Henri with what he thought was pardonable pride, a great victory for the Franks, a great defeat for the Saracens.

Henri soon realized that Richard was not joining in the jubilation. He answered questions readily enough, accepted their compliments with a smile, and agreed that it had been an outstanding success. But he seemed to be doing what was expected of him, not really sharing in the rejoicing. His behavior was so out of character to Henri that he seized the first opportunity to draw Richard aside for a private word.

"The celebrating is likely to go on far into the night. Even the French are well satisfied; it is the first time I've seen Burgundy smile in months. So why are you not better pleased about it, Uncle?"

"I am pleased," Richard insisted, and Henri shook his head.

"You ought to be triumphant. You dealt Saladin a grievous wound, gained enough pack animals for a campaign in Egypt, and gave the Saracens another story to tell around their campfires about *Malik Ric*."

"But it has changed nothing, Henri. I could have captured every blessed beast from Dārūm to Damascus and it would not matter, for the French will never agree to a campaign in Egypt and I cannot convince them of their folly."

Henri could not dispute that. "At least you've kept them from besieging Jerusalem."

"And half the army will never forgive me for it."

Henri started to speak, then stopped himself, for he could not dispute that either.

RICHARD DISTRIBUTED the camels to his knights and the donkeys to the men-at-arms, and the chroniclers reported that all rejoiced. The euphoria did not last long, though, and soon some were complaining because such a large number of pack animals had sent the price of grain soaring. But the underlying cause of their discontent was the decision not to besiege Jerusalem, and the Duke of Burgundy and the Bishop of Beauvais seized the opportunity to argue again for an assault upon the Holy City. The debate ended when Richard's Syrian spies reported that Salah al-Dīn had poisoned the wells and destroyed all the cisterns within two leagues of Jerusalem in anticipation of a siege, for no army could hope to prevail without water. The French then set up their own camp apart from the others, and Hugh wrote a satiric song about Richard, annoying the latter so much that he retaliated in kind and composed a mocking song of his own. By now it was obvious to all that such deep divisions could not be healed, and the decision was made to withdraw from Bait Nūbā and head back to Jaffa. It was July 4, the fifth anniversary of the calamitous Christian defeat at Ḥaṭṭīn.

HENRI SPURRED HIS STALLION to catch up to Richard. The day was utterly still, with not even a vagrant breeze, the sky devoid of clouds or birds and leached of color; it seemed almost white to Henri every time he squinted up at the blinding blaze of the sun. The heat was brutal, but they no longer needed to fear burns and peeling; by now even men as fair-skinned as Richard and Henri were deeply tanned. He could hear the drone of insects, the plodding of hooves, but no other sounds, for the army was marching in eerie silence. He found himself thinking that it was as if these thousands of unhappy men had become ghosts, trapped in a waking dream. He knew it was not a good sign when he was getting so morbidly fanciful and he glanced over at his uncle. "What now?" he asked, his mouth and throat so dry that the words emerged as a croak.

Richard kept his eyes on the road ahead. "We reopen talks with Saladin," he said, "and hope that he is as war-weary and discouraged as we are."

HUMPHREY DE TORON was very busy for a fortnight, going back and forth between Jaffa and Jerusalem. Richard and Salah al-Dīn had been able to agree upon the basic terms fairly quickly, for they were not that different from those Richard had originally proposed to al-'Ādil. The land was to be divided, with the Saracens retaining the "mountain castles" and the Franks holding on to Richard's coastal conquests, with the area in between to be shared by both. Salah al-Dīn and his council were willing to give Richard the Holy Sepulchre and to allow Christian pilgrims free access to Jerusalem, the sultan promising "to treat your sister's son like one of my own sons." But Ascalon was to be the rock upon which the peace negotiations foundered, for Salah al-Dīn insisted that Ascalon be destroyed, and Richard was not willing to agree to this.

RICHARD HAD DISPATCHED Humphrey back to Jerusalem in one last attempt to reach an accord. Learning that Richard had returned to Jaffa that afternoon, Henri was heading for the castle. It heartened him to see how much progress the city had made in the nine months since they'd ridden into desolate ruins. Once they'd rebuilt the walls, many of the former residents came back; at least the Christians did. It was Henri's hope that the day would come when Saracens and Franks could once more dwell in the towns and countryside in relative harmony, for the kingdom could not survive without cooperation between the various peoples who laid claim to its hallowed, blood-soaked soil. It had happened before, so why not again? Henri tried to convince himself that eventually they'd have to end the war, if only because both sides were too exhausted to keep fighting. But by then, what would be left of Outremer?

There was a reassuring air of normalcy about the recovering city: women marketing, children playing in the streets, vendors hawking their wares on spread-out rugs. There was also a thriving traffic in sin. The contingent of prostitutes who'd followed the crusaders from Acre to Jaffa had stayed even after the army left, for there were always plenty of soldiers there—men convalescing from wounds and sickness, deserters, those in need of a brief respite from the war. Leaning out of upper-story windows, some of these ladies of ill repute called out to Henri and his escort as they rode by, promising all sorts of carnal delights for the right price. Henri just laughed and called back, "Sorry, sweethearts, I'm a married man now," but a few of his knights cast wistful looks over their shoulders as they passed.

When they reached the castle, Henri was told Richard was abovestairs in the solar, and he headed in that direction. But as he opened the door to the stairwell, he found himself face-to-face with Humphrey de Toron. They both came to an abrupt halt. Henri had done his best to avoid just such an encounter, and he'd been so successful that he suspected Humphrey had been dodging him, too.

Deciding the least awkward approach would be to ignore the obvious, Henri said, as nonchalantly as he could, "I'd heard you were back from Jerusalem. Is Saladin still demanding that we raze Ascalon to the ground?"

"I regret so. With neither of them willing to compromise on this, the chances for peace do not look good. I did what I could to persuade the sultan, explaining the vast sums King Richard had spent on Ascalon, but to no avail. . . ."

Humphrey sounded as if he were blaming himself for the failure of the negotiations, and Henri wished he could assure him that he'd done the best he could under difficult circumstances, but he feared that Humphrey would take it as condescension. "My uncle has complete faith in you," he said at last. He would have continued up the stairs then, but Humphrey was still blocking his way.

"Is she . . . well?" he asked, no longer meeting Henri's gaze.

"Yes, she is." Henri would have preferred to leave it at that, but he understood Humphrey's concern. Deciding he owed it to the other man to ease his mind if he could, he said, "She is no longer troubled by early-morning sickness and her midwives have assured her that she is young and healthy and the pregnancy and birth ought to go as expected."

Humphrey had lashes a woman might have envied, long and thick, veiling his eyes. But he could not control his face. Henri thought, *Hellfire and damnation,* and suppressed a sigh. "Humphrey . . ."

Humphrey's head came up. "No," he said, "I do not blame you. The man I blame is dead and deservedly so." He started to squeeze past Henri, but then stopped, the words coming out low and fast, as if escaping of their own will. "I will pray the child is a girl. I would not want to see a son of Conrad of Montferrat rule over Outremer."

He didn't wait for Henri's response, was already gone before Henri said, very softly, "Neither would I." He stood there for a time, thinking upon the odd turns and twists of fate that had brought him and Humphrey de Toron to this moment, and then took the stairs two at a time, his spurs striking sparks upon the stone grooves of the steps.

Richard and André were alone in the solar. "I was about to send word to you," Richard said. "It will not be to your liking, though."

"I know. I just met Humphrey de Toron downstairs. He said Saladin would not budge about Ascalon."

"Neither will I," Richard said, his voice flat and hard, "so the talks are done. On the morrow I want to send three hundred knights to Ascalon to strengthen its defenses and to destroy Dārūm. Is that acceptable to you, Henri?"

"Of course." Henri looked around for a wine flagon, didn't see one. "What is your plan?"

"Are you so sure I have one?"

"You always do."

That earned him a fleeting smile from his uncle. "As it happens, I do. There is only one coastal port still under Saladin's control. So let's take it away from him."

"Beirut?" Henri considered for a heartbeat or two and then smiled. "Beirut it is."

"I thought you'd like that idea," Richard said dryly. Glancing over at André, he explained, "I daresay my nephew would agree to lay siege to Constantinople as long as it meant we'd be heading to Acre first."

Understanding then, André grinned. "Of course, his bride is waiting for him at Acre!" Shaking his head in mock regret, he said, "Ah, youth . . . when a man is utterly in thrall to his cock."

They both laughed, but Henri did not mind their teasing. He knew there was no malice in it. And because he was a secret romantic at heart, he even felt a twinge of sympathy for his uncle, sorry that Richard would never be as eager to be reunited with Berengaria as he was to see Isabella again.

CHAPTER 34

The last Sunday in July was unusually hot even for an Outremer summer, but in late afternoon a westerly wind began to stir the fronds of palms and to rustle the silvery-green leaves of the ubiquitous olive trees. To take full advantage of it, Isabella, Berengaria, Joanna, and their ladies retreated to the palace roof, sheltering from the sun under a canvas canopy as they enjoyed the feel of a cooling sea breeze on flushed, sweltering skin.

Isabella had made herself as comfortable as her pregnancy would allow, resting her feet upon a footstool, easing her aching back with several small pillows. She'd been stitching a chrysom robe for her baby while Mariam read aloud to them from Chrétien de Troyes's *Lancelot, the Knight of the Cart*. She put her sewing aside when Mariam excused herself to go belowstairs, and Anna at once hastened over. She was always eager to engage Isabella in conversation, and Joanna and Berengaria suspected it was because a faint scent of scandal trailed in Isabella's wake. So far Isabella had good-naturedly indulged the girl's curiosity, but the older women kept a watch on her, knowing Anna's exuberance could be misread as impudence.

"I only had one brother," Anna said sadly, "and he died. I still miss him. Do you have brothers or sisters?"

"Yes . . . I had an older half-brother and sister from my father's first marriage, who are both dead."

Anna mulled this over, for she found the genealogy of the kingdom's Royal House to be rather confusing. "Oh, of course! Your brother was the Leper King!"

Joanna winced, and Berengaria and Sophia frowned. But Isabella did not lose her composure. "Yes, Baldwin was sometimes called that. There are people who believe leprosy is divine punishment for sin. The Pope even declared that Baldwin's leprosy was the judgment of God. In Outremer, we know better. My brother was well loved by his subjects and greatly admired for his courage and gallantry."

Seeing then that Anna was distressed by her faux pas, Isabella deftly changed the subject, saying, "And I have four younger siblings, two brothers and two sisters born to my mother and Balian. They've lived in Tyre since Balian's lands were captured by Saladin—" She stopped so abruptly that she drew all eyes. Letting out an audible breath, she summoned up a smile when she saw that she was the center of attention. "My baby is active today. If I did not know better, I'd think there was a game of camp-ball going on in my womb."

Those who'd borne children shared knowing smiles, remembering their own pregnancies. Berengaria had avoided this subject whenever possible and she felt a twinge of remorse; it was rude, after all, to ignore Isabella's coming motherhood. "When is the baby due?" she asked, as warmly as she could.

"My midwife says early November, most likely around All Saints' Day, but definitely ere Martinmas."

Anna had thrown a cushion on the ground and settled herself comfortably at Isabella's feet. "Have you selected any names for the baby?"

"No, I've not had a chance to discuss it with Henri yet. We'll probably name a daughter Maria, for that would honor both our mothers. If it is a son, I think I'd like to call him Henri." Isabella raised her chin, meeting the eyes of the other women with a trace of defiance. If any of them thought that unseemly, they were wise enough to hide it. Seeing no disapproval on their faces, she leaned back against the pillows and addressed the issue head-on. "Balian told me the Saracens are scandalized that I would wed Henri whilst carrying Conrad's baby. One of them asked him, 'But whose child will it be?' And my stepfather, bless him, said, 'It will be the Queen's child.' They found that impossible to understand."

Joanna had come to admire Isabella's courage and she proved that now by saying emphatically, "Well, we understand and that is all that matters. You did what a queen must always do—put the needs of your kingdom first." She paused to make sure the other women got the message—that gossip would not be tolerated—for she'd heard several of Berengaria's handmaidens and even her own Lady Hélène doing just that.

"I agree," Berengaria said, just as staunchly, her gaze singling out the worst offender, who blushed and averted her eyes.

Isabella was pleased that both queens had spoken out so forcefully, for she'd noticed some tension lately between her own attendants and a few of their ladies-in-waiting, and she suspected careless or malicious chatter was at the heart of it. Her sense of mischief soon asserted itself, though, and she could not resist pointing out the obvious with an impish smile. "I did indeed do what I believed to be my duty. Of course few women would see it as a great hardship to wed the Count of Champagne."

Midst the laughter that followed, Anna took advantage of the mellow mood. "May I ask a question, Lady Isabella?"

The fact that she'd felt the need to ask warned Isabella that it was likely to be intrusive. "You may ask, Anna. I cannot promise that I will answer."

"I was wondering . . . Did you ever think of reuniting with your first husband after Conrad was slain?"

She was at once rebuked by Sophia for asking something so personal, but Isabella decided it was best to have it out in the open. "The past is like an impregnable castle perched on a sheer cliff, visible to all for miles around, but impossible to enter. There is no going back, Anna. Nigh on two years ago, the barons and bishops of Outremer made it quite clear that they would never accept Humphrey as king, and nothing has changed since then."

Anna nodded, satisfied. "Humphrey is good-looking," she acknowledged, damning him with faint praise. "But Henri is handsome, too, and he is very dashing, as well, almost as brave as *Malik Ric*. I hope I can find a husband like him." This last comment was delivered with artless abandon, as if the thought just happened to pop into her head. It was actually calculated to nudge the conversation in the direction she wanted it to go. "I have another question," she confided, meeting their eyes innocently, "this one for those who've been married. Can you tell me what it is like to lie with a man?" Before she could be reprimanded again, she said quickly, "I have the right to know, for I will be wed myself one day, and surely you'd not have me learn from the prattle of servants. I've heard the first time is supposed to hurt, but after that? Is it pleasant?"

Joanna was wryly amused when all eyes naturally turned toward her. She did indeed think Anna had a right to know; ignorance posed its own dangers. "Yes, it is pleasant," she said, adding prudently that it must be enjoyed within the sacrament of marriage.

Anna leaned forward, blue eyes shifting from Joanna to Berengaria to Isabella, then back to Joanna again. "But what does it feel like?"

Joanna found that was not easy to explain. "It is . . . pleasurable," she said, giving the other women a "help me" look.

Sophia remained conspicuously silent, confirming their suspicions about her years as Isaac's wife, but Berengaria did her best. "It is an act of great intimacy, Anna. Most women find it very comforting to share such closeness with their husbands."

Isabella had listened in growing surprise, not expecting them to use such bland, benign phrases for an experience so awesome. She opened her mouth to offer a far more vivid and compelling description of love-making, but caught herself in the nick of time, suddenly comprehending the reason for their caution.

Anna was disappointed, hoping for more specific answers, but she saw this was all she was going to get and, after a few moments, she wandered off with Alicia, who was obviously impressed by her friend's boldness, for they were soon giggling together. Once the girls were out of hearing, Isabella leaned closer and lowered her voice. "At first I could not understand why you both were being so reticent, so reluctant to tell her the truth, but then I—"

"Reticent?" Joanna echoed, genuinely puzzled. "I *was* truthful with her, Isabella. It is important that young girls know it is not a sin to find pleasure in the marriage bed. If they are not told that by other women, they may pay heed to the wrong voices, to those who would have them believe that the loss of their virginity is to be mourned even within the sacrament of marriage. From childhood, they hear our priests preach that not even God can raise up a virgin once she has 'fallen.' Little wonder so many girls go to their marriage beds in such dread. Far better that Anna or Alicia should listen to us than to—"

"A Padre Domingo," Berengaria interjected, and she and Joanna exchanged smiles, as if sharing a private joke.

Isabella was embarrassed now that she understood the magnitude of her mistake, and she was not sure what she was going to say if they questioned her about her "reticent" comment. Fortunately at that moment, Joanna cried out, "Anna! You and Alicia are too close to the roof's edge."

"There are men coming up the Jaffa Road, lots of them!" Anna shaded her eyes, balancing on tiptoe as she strained to see the distant banners, and then she turned back toward the women with a radiant smile. "It is *Malik Ric*!" Adding for Isabella's benefit, "And your husband, too!"

⁂

ISABELLA WAS SOMEWHAT self-conscious about disrobing before Henri, for in the six weeks they had been apart, her body had changed dramatically, at least in her eyes. Her face seemed fuller, her slender ankles no longer so slender, her breasts larger than they'd ever been, blue veins vivid against the fairness of her skin. She supposed that many women felt like this as their pregnancies advanced, wondering if their husbands would continue to find them desirable. But few of them went to their marital bed carrying another man's child. Would Henri still be able to see the woman behind that distended belly?

Her ladies had undressed her and she was already in bed when Henri entered. He was obviously eager to be alone with her, but he still took the time to greet her women courteously before he ushered them out; she'd been struck by his good manners from the time of their first meeting, when she was still Humphrey's wife. Watching as he stripped with flattering speed, she felt desire stirring at the sight of his naked body. She'd been more fortunate than most women, for she'd been wed to three uncommonly handsome men, but she'd never wanted Humphrey or Conrad the way that she wanted Henri, and had since their first kiss upon the roof of the archbishop's palace. She'd gloried in their love-making during their brief time together, experiencing sensations that were new and overwhelming, and she caught her breath when he turned, for he was offering indisputable physical proof of his need for her.

"You are so beautiful," he said, his voice husky. "No troubadour or trouvère would ever praise flaxen locks again after seeing you with your hair loose, flowing down your back like a midnight river."

As he slid into bed beside her, she put her hand upon his chest, over his heart. "Thank you for that, Henri, for making me still feel desirable. I'm as swollen as a ripe melon, and I was not sure you would—"

She got no further, for he stopped her words with a kiss. "Melons," he said, "are my favorite fruit." He was nuzzling her throat, his breath warm on her skin. "But is it safe for the baby . . . ?"

"I asked the midwife," she assured him, "and she said it was quite safe until the last month."

The bed curtains were open and she could see the candle's golden light dancing in his eyes; they were the blue of a harvest sky, she thought, for she was still in that sweet, bewitched state where everything about her lover was a source of pleasure and fascination. "So you asked the midwife," he murmured, tightening his arms around her. "Dare I hope that means you missed me as much as I missed you?"

"I missed you very much, my darling." She wasn't sure she'd have confided so readily in Humphrey or Conrad, for she'd played a more passive role with them, as an innocent and then a dutiful wife. With Henri, honesty came easily, for with him, she felt free to be herself, free to admit that she'd been eager to have him back in her bed. "I was so glad when Dame Helvis told me our love-making would not endanger the baby. But . . ." She paused and then sighed when he kissed her breast; they were so close now that she could feel his arousal, hot against her thigh.

"But what, my love?"

"Well . . . look at my belly, Henri. How are we to . . . ?"

"Is that what is worrying you, Bella?" He laughed softly. "That is easy enough to remedy." And he proceeded to prove it.

ISABELLA HAD REACHED her climax first, and so she was able to watch as Henri enjoyed his. Now she lay in the circle of his arms, marveling that the simple act of love-making could be so different. Their first couplings had been urgent and impassioned; they'd usually left a trail of discarded clothing scattered about their bedchamber and remained abed so late each morning that they were greeted with sly smiles when they eventually appeared in the great hall. Tonight, though, it had been less intense, slower and more deliberate. She knew he'd held back, and was touched that he was so protective of the baby, so protective of her. Surely a man capable of being both lustful and tender would be a good father.

"So . . ." he said, giving her a drowsy smile, "did you like being the one in the saddle?"

She had; this new position had given her greater freedom to move, and knowing it was prohibited by the Church was somehow exciting in and of itself. "Will I have to do penance for it?"

"Only if you tell your confessor. Have you never wondered, Bella, at the oddity of it—that the men who decide what comprises sins of the flesh are the same ones who shun such sins themselves? My uncle once said it was like asking a holy anchorite to lead an army into battle."

"Which uncle—Richard?"

"No, Geoffrey, the one who was killed in a tournament outside Paris. Although I'm sure Richard would agree—as most men would. Few would argue that adultery is not a serious sin. But why is it sinful for you to mount me or for us to lie together during your pregnancy or even when you will have your flux? Granted, that might be untidy, but why sinful? Above all, I do not understand why the Church cautions men against loving their own wives too well, insisting that they sin if their lust burns too hot. If that be true, I am doomed," he said cheerfully, "truly doomed!"

"I am, too, then," she confessed, propping herself up on her elbow so she could watch the amusement playing across his face. She loved the intimacy of conversations like this, loved the way they could shut their bedchamber door and shut out the rest of the world, at least for a while. "That reminds me," she said. "I had a very interesting and surprising discussion about carnal matters with your two aunts this afternoon."

He cocked a brow in feigned shock. "Women talk about carnal matters?"

"As if you men do not!"

"Well, yes, we do that," he conceded, grinning. "But men tend to boast about the vast number of their bedmates, and I would hope that is not true for royal wives like Joanna and Berengaria!"

"Speaking of that, you've said very little about your past. I know nothing of the women you've bedded."

"And I intend to keep it that way," he said firmly, although the corner of his mouth was twitching with suppressed laughter. Sitting up, he swung his legs onto the floor and returned a moment later with a cup of spiced wine. Offering her the first sip, he took several swallows before setting the cup down on the carpet. "So what do women say, then, when they talk of the marriage bed?"

"Well, it began with Anna asking us what it felt like to lie with a man. She wanted to know if it was 'pleasant.'"

"It is only natural that she'd wonder about it," Henri said with a chuckle. "What did you tell her?"

"Joanna assured her that it was indeed 'pleasant,' and Berengaria agreed, saying the intimacy was very comforting. I could scarcely believe my own ears, for they made it sound so . . . so tame, so downright dull! I started to speak up, but then it occurred to me that they were deliberately understating it, lest Anna be too intrigued."

"That makes sense. Anna is a handful, and if they'd dwelled too much upon the delights of the flesh, she might be tempted to try them for herself."

"So I thought. But when I said as much once Anna was out of earshot, they looked at me in perplexity. Joanna said Anna deserved an honest answer and they'd given her one. It was only then that I understood, Henri. To them, love-making is indeed pleasant, enjoyable, intimate. But they know nothing of what else it can be, what you taught me it can be!"

"I am not sure I want to hear about my uncle's bedsport, and for certes I do not want to envision my aunt Joanna in the throes of passion. They are my family, after all, and I still remember how discomfited I was as a lad when I realized that my own parents did the deed, too!"

They both laughed and she wished she'd known him then; she did not doubt he'd been a happy child and she thought that she must do all in her power to make sure that he would be no less happy in Outremer than he'd been in Champagne. Henri leaned over and gave her a soft, seeking kiss. "Well? Are you not going to tell me 'what else it can be,' Bella?"

"I do not know if that would be wise. I'd not want to puff up your male pride too much. . . ." She let him persuade her, though, with a few caresses. "It is not easy to find the words. When you make love to me, I stop thinking. I just . . . feel. It is as if my very bones are melting, as if every nerve in my body is afire. It is a little scary to be so out of control, but it is very exciting, too, the way it must feel to be drunk. Only I'm not drunk on wine, Henri, I'm drunk on you."

Henri kissed the hollow of her throat, brushing back a strand of her long black hair. "How did I ever get so lucky?"

"By letting my stepfather lure you back to Tyre," she said with a smile. "Your turn now. When you make love to me, how does it make you feel?"

"Blessed," he said, with a smile of his own, "truly blessed."

"Silver-tongued devil," she said lightly, but the candlelight caught a suspicious sheen in those wide-set dark eyes. "All those troubadours and trouvères at your mother's court taught you well— Oh!"

"What?" His immediate alarm revealed the intensity of his protective instincts. "Are you hurting?"

"No, the baby just kicked, and quite a kick it was, too." Remembering that her womb had not quickened until he'd gone to join Richard at Bait Nūbā, she said, suddenly shy, "Would you . . . like to feel it?" When he nodded, she placed his hand on her abdomen, with a stab of regret that her pregnancy must be so complicated, not the source of pure joy it ought to be.

Henri's eyes widened. "I felt it move!" He laughed, fascinated, for the first time seeing the baby as an individual in its own right, not just part of Isabella's body. "Do you think it swims around in your womb like a tadpole? I wonder what it thought was happening whilst we were making love?"

"I daresay the rocking motion put it to sleep. At least I hope so, for it is well past its bedtime." She managed to keep her tone playful, no easy task, for her throat had closed up.

"Speaking of sleep . . . Richard is likely to roust me out of bed at dawn to plan our assault upon Beirut. Once he makes up his mind to do something, he wants it done yesterday." Deciding to let the candles burn themselves out, he kissed her again, saying, "Good night, my love." Lifting the sheet, then, he leaned over to drop a kiss on her swollen belly. "Good night, little one."

The first time he'd done that, he'd acted on impulse, but she'd been so moved by the gesture that he'd incorporated it into their bedtime ritual. She gave him a dazzling smile now, then nestled against his body, her head cradled on his shoulder. To his amusement, she was soon snoring; she'd never done that before and he assumed it was yet another symptom of pregnancy. He shifted his position with care, not wanting to disturb her sleep, and let his hand rest lightly upon her rounded abdomen. Whenever he entreated the Almighty to keep Isabella safe and well, he always included the baby in his prayers. But he also prayed that the child she carried would be a girl.

MORGAN WAS WATCHING from the shadows as Mariam and two men-at-arms approached the Cathedral of the Holy Cross. He could not hear what she said, but it was obviously welcome to the men, who beamed and bowed respectfully before leaving her alone on the steps. She waited until they were on their way before entering the church. When Morgan materialized silently beside her, she did not speak, either, following as he opened a side door that led out into the cloisters. None of the secular canons were about, for they were getting ready for the None Mass; Morgan and Mariam had chosen their time with care. Morgan had already scouted out the cathedral precincts and when he said, "This way," she nodded and slipped her arm through his, pausing first to draw her veil across her face, leaving only her eyes visible. He knew it was a trick of the light, but they looked golden, as lustrous and gleaming as a cat's eyes in the dark, and he was glad he'd found an inn so close to the cathedral.

"How much time do we have?" he asked once they'd safely merged into the usual street traffic of pedestrians, carts, vendors, beggars, and an occasional horseman.

"I told them to meet me back at the cathedral when the bells sounded for Vespers. They were delighted to have the rest of the afternoon to themselves, are likely headed for the nearest tavern or bawdy house."

"Vespers . . . then we have three hours."

She nodded and her eyes crinkled at the corners, as if she were smiling. "I am supposed to be meeting Bishop Theobald and Prior William of the Hospital of St Thomas the Martyr to discuss donations for the poor, and I told them to take me to the cathedral first so I could offer up prayers for those who died during the siege of Acre. It would have seemed strange if I'd made it later than Vespers, for they know I'll be expected back for the evening meal. I could not leave the castle without an escort, though. A king's daughter—even one born to a *harim* concubine—cannot go wandering about the streets by herself, after all. Sinning would be so much easier if only I were not so highborn!"

Morgan halted so he could look directly into those glorious golden eyes. "Do you think that we are sinning, *cariad*?"

"No, I do not," she said, without hesitation. "Fornication is surely a venial sin at worst. So unless you have a wife hidden away in Wales that you've failed to mention, I do not think we are putting our souls in peril." They resumed walking and she rested her hand again in the crook of his elbow. "If I'd said yes, that I did think we were about to commit a mortal sin, would you have taken me back to the castle?"

He considered the question. "No, I'd have tried to convince you it was not a sin," he said honestly, and when she gave a low, throaty laugh, he wanted to stop and kiss her then and there. Fortunately, they did not have far to go, for the inn was already in sight. He'd planned it as thoroughly as a military campaign, arranging access to a back entrance so she'd not have to pass through the common chamber. Even though she was veiled, he did not want to subject her to the stares of other men. She teased him that a man did not get to be so adept at trysts without having had a lot of practice, but her footsteps were as quick as his as they mounted the stairs.

He'd deliberately rented a chamber on the top floor so they could leave the windows unshuttered, and the room was aglow with late-afternoon sun. Mariam had worried that there might be some initial awkwardness once they were alone, but as soon as he slid the door's bar into place, Morgan unpinned her veil and kissed her the way he'd wanted to kiss her out in the street. "Let's do this right," he murmured and swept her up into his arms. But as he headed for the bed, his boot slipped on the floor rushes and her weight kept him from regaining his balance. With a startled oath, he pitched forward, tumbling them both onto the thin straw mattress, and only his agility in twisting aside at the last moment kept him from landing on top of her.

Before Mariam could say a word, he burst out laughing, "Good, Morgan, very good! What better way to impress a woman than to drop her onto the floor? What else can I do to bedazzle you, my lady? Step on your skirt, kick over a chamber pot?"

By now she was laughing, too, for if he'd truly been trying to impress her, his mirthful reaction to his mishap could not have been better calculated to do just that. From their very first meeting, she'd been charmed by his inability to take himself too seriously, a trait she found to be as appealing as it was rare. "It was not as bad as that," she protested. "You did not really drop me onto the floor. And at least you did not blame me for the fall, claiming I was too heavy to lift."

"Good God, woman, I am clumsy, not stupid!" he said with a grin, and she realized how much she'd missed in her marriage to a decent, dependable man who'd known nothing of the joys of laughing together in bed. She traced the shape of his mouth with her finger and he caught her hand, pressing a hot kiss into her palm. After that, they could not get their clothes off fast enough.

Morgan genuinely liked women, in and out of bed, and because many of them found him very attractive, he'd had more than his share of liaisons in his twenty-seven years on God's Earth. He knew that initial couplings were not always all they were hoped to be; sometimes a man and woman needed time to learn each other's rhythms, to listen to what their bodies were telling them. He was aware, too, that disappointment was more likely because he'd been waiting so long for this, having had months to imagine what it would be like to make love to Mariam. He'd actually sought to lower his expectations for their first time, and he would soon recall that with amusement, for he'd had no reason to worry. Delay had honed their desire to a feverish pitch, generating so much heat that he'd later joke it was a miracle the bed had not caught fire. They trusted each other enough by now to abandon any inhibitions and what followed was a sexual experience so powerful that it left them both exhausted, astonished, and awed.

"Will it be like this every time, Morgan?" Mariam asked once she'd gotten her breath back. She started to sit up, decided her bones were not strong enough to support her yet, and sank back on the pillow, regarding him in wonderment.

He jerked the sheet off, for he was soaked in sweat. "I wish I could say yes, *cariad*, but this was . . . it was as close to perfect as we can hope to get."

"You mean we peaked already and it is all downhill from now on?" That struck them both as wildly funny and they laughed until tears came to their eyes. "What is the name of your famous Welsh sorcerer . . . Merlin? I think I'll start calling you that," she said, giving him a cat-like smile of utter contentment, "for you cast a potent spell indeed."

"Merlin? I cannot argue with that," he said, so complacently that she poked him in the ribs. He defended himself with the pillow and they enjoyed an erotic wrestling match that ended abruptly when they rolled dangerously close to the edge of the bed.

They were still euphoric, still riding the crest of the wave, and neither was ready to return to the reality waiting beyond that barred door. But Mariam had a sudden unwelcome thought. "How will we know when Vespers is nigh? If I am late, the men may seek me out at the bishop's palace."

"I bought one of those candles marked with the hours," he said, and forced himself to rise from the bed, crossing the chamber and fumbling with flint and tinder until the wick caught fire. She'd never been in an inn before, but as she looked around, she realized how much he'd done to make their tryst as comfortable as possible, for it was much cleaner than such a rented room ought to be, with fresh, fragrant rushes scattered about on the floor and no trace of the usual dust and cobwebs. In addition to the candle, there was a washbasin, towels and sheets too costly to be found in any inn, a pillow, wine cups, a flagon, and a bowl of fruit; he'd even thought to provide a brass chamber pot.

Holding out her hand, she beckoned him back to the bed, saying in a soft, purring voice, "It is lonely over here without you, beloved." He brought the wine and fruit with him. He was practical enough to bring the towels, too, and took his time blotting the damp sheen from her body, marveling that her skin was as tawny as her eyes. As he began to rub himself down, she watched with pleasure, sipping her wine. "I wish it were not so complicated to arrange a tryst, Morgan. We cannot keep using Bishop Theobald as my excuse or people might start to suspect me of having a liaison with him!"

"He should be so lucky," he said, feeding her a slice of mango and licking the juice as it trickled down her throat. She was wearing her hair in two long braids, a style no longer popular in the western kingdoms but still fashionable in Outremer, and he tickled her cheek with one of the plaits, wishing he could see her hair loose, as a husband would. But how could they manage an entire night together when it was so difficult to find even a few stolen hours?

"Joanna once told me that her mother's enemies claimed Eleanor had been unfaithful to the French king," she said, returning the favor by popping an orange section into his mouth. "As if a queen could ever vanish from sight long enough to commit adultery! Her disappearance would cause a panic in the palace. Servants are always underfoot, eyes are always watching, and not all of them friendly, for spies are everywhere. At least a widow has a bit more freedom, for her chastity is no longer as important as a wife's fidelity or as valuable as a virgin's maidenhead.

Since I am a widow and not under such constant scrutiny, we ought to be able to find some way to take advantage of that."

"Well, we're likely to have time to think about it. From what I've heard, Richard plans to set out for Beirut in the next day or two."

"So soon? You've only been here two days!" She sounded so disappointed that he leaned over and kissed her; she tasted of wine and mango and smelled of perspiration and an exotic sandalwood perfume. "I hope it will not be tomorrow," she said, "for Isabella's sake as well as mine. It is Henri's twenty-sixth birthday and she is planning to celebrate it in grand style. Who would have imagined such an ill-omened marriage would bring them both so much joy? But it is obvious to anyone with eyes to see that they are utterly besotted with each other."

"And I'm utterly besotted with you, *cariad*," he assured her, and she laughed, Henri and Isabella forgotten, content to have her world shrink to an inn chamber, a bed, and the man in it. They shared secrets and memories as the afternoon passed. He told her more about his parents and their remarkable love story, a king's bastard son and his blind Welsh cousin who'd defied the odds and carved out a life together in the mountains of Eryri. He told her, too, of his service with Geoffrey of Brittany and the old king, and the conflict between his love of Wales and his love of adventure. She spoke of her husband, whom she'd respected but never loved, and of the Saracen mother she barely remembered, talking of her life in Sicily, growing up with Joanna, her brother's child-bride. She confided that she'd let go of her anger over the massacre of the Acre garrison, for she'd not wanted to poison her friendship with Joanna, and she admitted that she'd come to see it truly had been a military decision, albeit a brutally cold-blooded one.

"I'd assumed that Richard saw Saracens as so many of our Christian brethren do," she explained, "as godless infidels better off dead. But I no longer believe that." When he asked what changed her mind, she swore him to secrecy and then told him about Richard's plan to marry Joanna to al-'Ādil. He was not as surprised as she'd expected, reminding her that Richard had knighted al-'Ādil's son and several Mamluks and emirs he'd become friendly with during his negotiations with Saladin.

"That drove the French well nigh crazy," he laughed. "But Richard never cares what others think of him, which is both his strength and his weakness. He respects the courage of his Saracen foes and so it seems natural to him to honor it, even if others see it as heresy or treason."

They finished the wine and fruit and talked of their siblings. He told her of Bleddyn back in Wales, who'd repudiated his Norman-French blood, and his sister Mallt, named after the Empress Maude, happily wed to a Welsh lord. In turn, she talked of her half-sister Sophia, the ultimate survivor, and William, who'd been a better brother than a king. But they never spoke of the future, for no man in Richard's army had any tomorrows promised to him, and so it was wiser to live just for today, especially for secret lovers unlikely to have more than what they had found on this hot July afternoon in an Acre inn.

MORGAN AND MARIAM had fallen asleep, were awakened by the bells chiming for Vespers, and dressed almost as hastily as they'd undressed earlier. They got to the cathedral just before Mariam's escort arrived. Out of breath and very apologetic for being late, they were greatly relieved when she magnanimously forgave them. Morgan planned to return to the inn later to retrieve his sheets, towels, and pillow, for he hoped to be able to use them again. But now he trailed inconspicuously after Mariam and the men-at-arms, wanting to be sure they got safely back to the castle.

He'd always had an observant eye and he was not long in realizing that something was amiss. The outdoor markets were deserted, the vendors doing no business. The normal noise of the city was hushed and there was fear on the faces of the men and women he passed in the streets. As the palace came into view, he could see a crowd had gathered before the gatehouse, and it was then that Acre's church bells began to peal—not to summon laggards to Vespers, but to sound the alarm.

Morgan grabbed the first man he saw, an elderly greybeard who must have seen decades of bloodshed in the course of his long life. "What is wrong? What has happened?"

"Jaffa—it has been taken by Saladin!"

THE CASTLE GATE WAS CLOSED, unusual during daylight hours, but Morgan was known by the guards and had no trouble gaining admittance. He found the great hall was packed with agitated men and shocked women. Isabella was seated upon the dais, flanked by Joanna and Berengaria, as if they were offering moral support in her kingdom's moment of crisis. It was so crowded that Morgan did not even try to reach the women and searched instead for a familiar face. Finding one, he shoved his way toward Warin Fitz Gerald.

Warin wasted no time giving him the bad news. A ship had arrived a few hours ago from Jaffa, its passengers dispatched for help when they saw Saladin's army descending upon them.

To Morgan, that was better news than he'd expected to hear, though. "Then the city has not yet fallen to them?"

Warin looked at him bleakly and then gave a half-shrug. "That was three days ago," he said. "The king and Count Henri rode off to the French camp to tell Burgundy and Beauvais. King Richard will want to leave as soon as possible. Every hour that we delay . . ." He did not bother to finish the sentence, did not need to do so.

By now Mariam was beside Joanna on the dais. As her eyes met Morgan's, the same silent thought passed between them, gratitude that they'd had a few private, precious hours before the storm broke. Whatever happened, at least they'd had that much.

Isabella had been joined by Bishop Theobald of Acre and Joscius, the Archbishop of Tyre; both men were worried about the Bishop of Bethlehem, newly elected as the Patriarch of Jerusalem, for he'd recently ridden down to Jaffa, which came under his ecclesiastical control. But his fate was only one fear midst so many. If Jaffa was retaken by Saladin, any chance for a negotiated peace would be gone, and the fighting and dying of the past year would have been in vain.

Soon after dark, Henri returned with the Grand Masters of the Hospitallers and the Templars. Ignoring her aching back and fatigue, Isabella rose to her feet and waited as he strode toward her. By now she knew him well enough to see the signs—the taut line of his mouth, the clenched muscles along his jaw, the set of his shoulders—and she braced herself for more bad news, even though she could not imagine what could be worse than the loss of Jaffa.

"They refused," Henri said in lieu of any greetings, his voice still throbbing with remembered rage. "Burgundy and Beauvais, they will not ride with us to rescue Jaffa. Their hatred of Richard matters more to them than the fate of their own countrymen. There are French soldiers at Jaffa, but they'll let them die, they'll let them all die ere they lift a finger to help us!"

Isabella was stunned, as were all within earshot. Beauvais's fellow prelates were incensed that he'd turn his back upon his Christian brethren, and they at once declared their intention to go to the French camp and confront him. Henri knew there was no point in it and he took Isabella's elbow, drawing her aside. "I think Richard wanted to kill them," he said. "I know I did."

"What now?" she asked quietly, for she was determined not to give in to any emotional outbursts which would benefit neither Henri nor her baby nor their kingdom.

"Richard has gone to the harbor. He plans to sail tonight for Jaffa. He wants me to lead a land force on the morrow, the Templars, Hospitallers, *poulains*, and as many others as we can get. I'd better tell Berengaria and Joanna," he said, steering her back to her dais seat before he headed toward Richard's wife and sister, who were standing a few feet away, not wanting to intrude upon his time with Isabella.

Isabella could not remember when she'd felt so bone-weary. She watched as Henri spoke with the other women, and although it did not seem right to worry about personal cares in the midst of such a calamity, she could not help being grateful that she'd have one more night with her husband. She felt a touch of pity for Berengaria, who could not even be sure if Richard would return to bid her farewell, but she felt admiration, too, for the other woman's courage. How did she face each day, knowing she could go from wife to widow in the thrust of one well-aimed sword? Isabella, who'd gone from widow to wife in the span of a week, hoped that she'd be able to endure the waiting with Berengaria's stoicism and grace. But with so much at stake, she could only pray that the Almighty would give her the strength she would need, as queen, wife, and mother-to-be.

When Henri came back to her, she reached out and entwined her fingers in his. "Without the French, you will be greatly outnumbered," she said, as steadily as she could. "Can Jaffa be saved?"

He'd just been asked that very question by Berengaria and Joanna, had responded with a confident smile, reminding them that Richard thrived on such challenges. But as much as he wanted to reassure Isabella, too, he could not bring himself to lie to her. "I do not know, Bella," he said at last. "God help us all, I do not know."

CHAPTER 35

JULY 1192

Off the Coast of Haifa

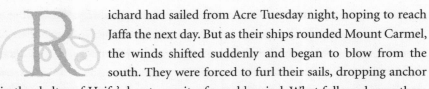ichard had sailed from Acre Tuesday night, hoping to reach Jaffa the next day. But as their ships rounded Mount Carmel, the winds shifted suddenly and began to blow from the south. They were forced to furl their sails, dropping anchor in the shelter of Haifa's bay to await a favorable wind. What followed were three of the worst days of Richard's life. He was accustomed to facing death with utter sangfroid, was famed for his cool head in a crisis. By Friday, though, his nerves were fraying like well-worn hemp, for each passing hour made Jaffa's downfall all the more likely.

As he strode the deck, he was being watched with sympathetic eyes. Yet few of the men dared to approach him, for he put them in mind of a smoldering fire, one that could flare up at any moment. But the Préaux brothers were deeply grateful that Richard had taken such pains to bolster their spirits in the months since Guilhem's capture, periodically summoning them to offer reassurances that he still lived and promising to find a way to secure his freedom. They felt they owed it to Richard to try to ease his troubled mind, and when he finally halted his pacing, they moved to his side.

"Jaffa still holds out, sire. Their faith in you will give them the courage to resist, for they know nothing short of death could keep you from coming to their rescue."

They'd meant well, but their comfort only salted Richard's wounds. Jaffa's fall would be a devastating blow to Outremer's survival. Its loss would cut the kingdom in half, shattering crusader morale and causing Saracen spirits to soar, resulting in the swelling of Saladin's army just as the French were defecting. Richard was well aware of that, for he'd always been one for strategic planning. For now, though, what he found hardest to bear was that he'd failed the men who'd trusted him. Would they pass up chances to make a peaceful surrender, sure that he was on the way as Jean de Préaux insisted? God help them if so, for if the town and castle were then taken by storm, they could expect no mercy. Their faith in him could doom them all.

It was then that André lurched into Pierre de Préaux; he rode like a centaur, but he was always clumsy on the deck of a pitching ship. "May I have a private word with you, my liege?" He didn't wait for a response, turning toward their tent, and Richard had no choice but to follow. As soon as they were inside, André said, "I have a favor to ask of you, Cousin. For the love of God, lie down and try to get some rest. Since we left Acre, you've slept less than a cat treed by a pack of dogs, and not only are you wearing yourself out with all this pacing and fuming, you are wearing us out just watching you!"

Richard objected, more from contrariness than anything else. But André was right; he *was* tired. Sitting down on the bed, he rubbed his eyes and then his temples, hoping to head off a dull, throbbing headache. When he looked up again, André was gone. After a time, he dropped to his knees by the bed. *"In nomine Patris et Filii et Spiritus Sancti."* The Latin phrases came unthinkingly to his lips, but what followed was not so much a prayer as a desperate cry from the heart.

"Lord God, why dost Thou keep me here when I am going in Thy Service?"

There was no answer, of course. He knew what the priests said, that the Ways of the Almighty were beyond the understanding of mortal men. But why would God not send the winds to bring him to Jaffa? How could He want Jaffa to fall to the Saracens? And why had He ever allowed Jerusalem to be lost? Getting to his feet, Richard lay down on the bed, bringing his arm up to shield his eyes from the sun streaming through the open tent flap. *Not my will, but Thine, be done.* Easy enough to say, but so hard to accept. And yet such acceptance was the cornerstone of their Christian faith. *Thy Will be done.*

He hadn't expected to sleep, but after a while, he dozed, lulled by the rocking movement of the ship and the rhythmic splashing of waves against its hull. When he awoke, André and the Earl of Leicester were bending over the bed, their faces so joyful that he knew at once what they'd come to tell him. Sitting up, he heard what was surely the sweetest of all sounds—the flapping of canvas as the sails were unfurled. "The winds have changed!"

"Yes, they are blowing now from the north!"

"Thank God!" Richard closed his eyes for a moment. "Thank God and all His good angels!"

BY SEA, IT WAS ONLY forty-six miles from Haifa to Jaffa, and the ship's master assured Richard that they'd be there sometime that night. The wind continued to pick up, though, and within hours, their small fleet was scattered. Richard refused to despair; at least they were being swept in the right direction. After midnight, the moon rose. It had been full upon their arrival at Acre and half of it was still visible, casting a soft glow upon the cresting waves as they rolled shoreward. The harbor of Jaffa was an anchorage on the northwestern side of the castle, sheltered by reefs, and it was not yet dawn when they saw the silhouette of the most famous one, Andromeda's Rock. It was Saturday, the first of August, four days since the Saracens had launched their surprise attack upon the city.

They anchored just north of the harbor and began the tense vigil until sunrise. Jaffa was divided into a lower town, the faubourg, and the citadel, located on higher ground to the southwest. From their galleys, they could not see the landward side, which would have borne the brunt of the Saracen assault, and so they could not tell if the walls were still intact. The city remained shrouded in shadows, giving up none of its secrets.

They had only three galleys at first, but by the time the horizon finally began to lighten off to the east, four more had straggled in. Dawn in the Holy Land was usually resplendent, the sky splashed with molten gold as the sun began its celestial arc. This morning the men had eyes only for the looming walls of Jaffa. As the dark retreated, they squinted until the banners flying above the city slowly came into focus—streaming in the wind, the bright saffron colors of Salah al-Dīn.

A muffled sound swept the decks of the galleys, a groan torn from multiple throats as they understood what they were seeing. Some cursed, most stared in stricken silence. Richard had been standing motionless in the prow of his galley, scarcely breathing as he awaited the moment of truth. When it came, he let out a hoarse cry. "We're too late!" He slammed his fist down upon the gunwale, again and again. "Too late!"

His men had never seen him so anguished and did not know what to do. Only André moved, stepping forward to catch his wrist before he could strike again. "Not your sword hand," he said, his voice oddly gentle. "You did all you could, Richard, all any man could do."

Richard saw nothing but those swirling golden banners. "Tell that to the dead of Jaffa."

As the sun rose in the sky, they could see the tents of the Saracen army. Their little fleet was soon noticed and men on the beach began to jeer and shout, waving weapons, a few aiming arrows although they could penetrate armor only at close range. But most of them seemed unconcerned by the appearance of the enemy ships. Jubilant cries of *"Allahu Akbar!"* wafted across the water to the miserable men in the galleys. Even if Richard had not seen the sultan's banners, he'd have known the town had fallen, for theirs was the swagger of the victorious.

Some of his knights felt a shamed sense of relief that they'd arrived too late, for few operations were as dangerous as a sea landing in enemy territory. It was true Richard had managed it in Cyprus, but then they'd been confronted by the incompetent, hated Isaac Comnenus and his poorly trained routiers. Here at Jaffa, they faced the tough, battle-proven troops of Saladin, the victor of Ḥaṭṭīn. So there were men in the galleys who felt they'd been reprieved, even as they grieved for their slain brethren. By nine, the third hour of the day, their ships numbered fifteen, yet it was obvious to them all that they were still greatly outnumbered. They did not fear for their safety as long as they stayed offshore; Richard had controlled the sea since his seizure of Saladin's fleet at Acre. It was not easy, though, to look upon their triumphant enemy, strutting along the beach, their laughter echoing on the wind, all the while knowing what horrors were hidden by the town walls, and many of them wished that Richard would give the order to depart.

Richard had not moved for hours, unable to tear his gaze from the crowded beach and those banners flying proudly over the captured city. He seemed to see everything on a battlefield and had soon noticed that no flags flew over the castle itself. That wan hope quickly ebbed, for there was no sign of life, no indication that the citadel still resisted. Jaffa had held about four thousand souls, many of them convalescing soldiers, as well as the inevitable noncombatants caught up in siege warfare—merchants, priests, women, and children. How many of them had died when the town had fallen? Would any of them be able to avoid the slave markets in Cairo and Damascus by offering ransoms? Saladin had been vengeful on occasion, as when he executed the Templars and Hospitallers after Ḥaṭṭīn. But he was also known to be merciful, and Richard kept reminding himself of that as he watched the sultan's soldiers celebrating a well-earned victory, one that would have reverberations throughout Christendom for years to come.

When the Earl of Leicester and André finally joined him in the prow and asked what he wanted to do, he could not bring himself to give the order to raise their anchors, not yet. André, who knew him better than he knew himself, thought that by remaining on the scene, he was doing penance for failing to get there in time. He did not try to persuade Richard to go, though; that would be for naught.

"Look!" Richard said suddenly, pointing toward the castle. Turning, they saw the figure of a man balancing upon the wall, waving his arms frantically; he was shouting, but his words were drowned out by the pounding of the surf and the cries of the Saracens on the beach. He appeared to be wearing a priest's habit. As they watched, he made the sign of the cross and then leaped from the wall. Fortunately, his fall was cushioned by the sand and he scrambled to his feet, apparently unhurt. Pulling his ankle-length garment over his head, he sprinted toward the water. By now he'd been noticed by some of the Saracens. They seemed amused by the sight of this paunchy, pallid enemy clad only in braies and a shirt, and just one made an attempt to stop him, sending a poorly aimed arrow his way as he plunged into the sea and began to swim toward the ships.

Richard whirled, but there was no need to give the command; they were already hauling on the anchor chains. His galley shot forward, the sailors straining at the oars. The priest's flailing arms showed that he was not a strong swimmer and he had begun to tread water as the galley drew up alongside, grabbing gratefully at an outstretched oar. Once he'd been hauled aboard, he collapsed onto the deck, shivering so violently that one of the knights hastily fetched a blanket and draped it around his trembling shoulders.

"My lord king, save us!" he gasped. "You are our only hope!"

Richard's hand closed on the priest's arm in a grip that would leave bruises. "Some are still alive? Tell me—and quickly!"

"You'd have been proud of them, sire, for they fought valiantly. For three days, we held them off. Even when part of the wall fell by the Jerusalem Gate, we built a bonfire in the gap to keep them out. But yesterday their sappers and trebuchets brought down a large section of the wall. We retreated into the castle and agreed to surrender today if no help had come by then. After your galleys were spotted this morning, Saladin said we must leave the citadel straightaway and some of the men agreed, for they did not think there were enough ships to make a landing. When you stayed offshore, the patriarch and castellan went to see Saladin, thinking all hope was lost. But then I realized why you'd not tried to land—you did not know the castle was still held by the garrison! So I . . . I committed myself to the Almighty's Keeping and jumped from the wall," he concluded, sounding astonished by his own courage.

"You are a brave man. God will reward you for what you did today and so will

I." Richard had knelt to hear the priest's story. As he rose to his feet, his eyes swept the deck, moving from one face to another. "I cannot promise victory," he said. "But I will either prevail or die in the attempt. Eternal shame to any man who balks, for glory or martyrdom awaits us. God's Will be done." He gestured then to his trumpeter. The man at once blew the signal to advance, and as it echoed out across the water, the decks of the galleys erupted into frantic activity. Forgotten now, the priest huddled in his blanket and began to pray.

Richard's royal galley was as conspicuous as he could make it, painted a red hue brighter than blood; the canopy tent was crimson, too. Even the surcote Richard wore over his hauberk was a deep scarlet. Just as no one could ever overlook his presence on the battlefield, the *Sea-Cleaver* would draw all eyes, proclaiming that the English king was aboard. It led the way toward the shore and soon had the attention of the men on the beach. They did not seem alarmed; their faces reflected amazement and disbelief that the Franks would dare attempt a landing. There was something oddly lethargic about their reaction, but Richard did not have the time to puzzle over it, for the ship had reached the shallows.

When he judged it safe, he leaped over the side into the sea. Water rose to his hips. Paying his knights the ultimate compliment—never once glancing back to be sure they were following—he began to wade toward the shore, a crossbow in one hand, his drawn sword in the other. As he emerged from the water, a man ran forward, shouting in a language he did not know; he thought it might be Kurdish. Richard was not fully armed, for there'd been no time to put on his mail chausses; this made his bare legs vulnerable to attack. He had been taught to watch his adversary's eyes and he caught that quick downward glance as the Saracen soldier came within striking range. He was ready, therefore, when the man lunged, pivoting and then slashing at that outstretched arm. There was a scream, blood spurted over them both, and he turned to face his next foe. There was none. Men were standing as if rooted, staring at him, but none moved to the attack.

For the first time, he looked back, saw his knights and crossbowmen struggling ashore. Pierre de Préaux was just a few feet away. Panting heavily, he had no breath for speaking and gestured with his sword. Richard spun around to see a horse and rider bearing down upon him. He'd dropped the crossbow when he'd confronted the Kurdish soldier and he quickly snatched it up. It was already loaded; he had only to aim and fire. The bolt hit the other man in the throat and he tumbled from the saddle. Richard made a grab for the reins, but the rider's foot had caught in the stirrup, and as his body slammed into the horse's legs, the animal panicked and bolted.

Richard swore, for they had no horses with them. By now several knights had reached his side, offering lavish praise for that remarkable shot, laughing when Richard admitted he'd been aiming for the man's chest. They were all a bit giddy, most not having expected to get this far, thinking they'd be cut down while they were still in the water. Some of the Saracens had begun to shoot at them, but their arrows were embedding themselves in the armor of the knights, doing no real damage. Richard's Genoese and Pisan arbalesters, just now coming ashore, were much more effective. Taking turns, one man shooting while another loaded, they unleashed a barrage of bolts that soon had their foes in retreat. Richard still marveled at the half-hearted resistance they'd encountered so far, but he wasted no time taking advantage of it. Now that they'd established a beachhead, they needed to hold it, and he gave orders to scavenge driftwood, planks, barrels, wood from the half-buried hulks of wrecked galleys, whatever they could use to erect a barricade.

Leaving his crossbowmen and men-at-arms to put up a makeshift shelter, Richard then led some of his knights toward the northeast wall, saying he knew a way into the town. None thought to question him; after their amazing success so far, they'd have believed him had he said they were going to fly over the walls. He had something more prosaic in mind—a stairway cut into the rocks that led up to a postern gate. The steps were so narrow that only one man at a time could climb them, making him so vulnerable to defenders up on the wall that it was easy to see why no Saracen had attempted it. Not having to fear an aerial assault, Richard and his men quickly reached the postern gate. A few blows with a battle-axe shattered the wood and they found it gave entry into a house built against the town wall. It belonged to the Templars, Richard said, his statement soon confirmed by the discovery of a body propped up in bed, still clutching a sword, his brown mantle with the red cross signifying him to have been a brother of the order, not a knight. His splinted leg explained why he'd died in bed, and the bloodstains on the bedding and floor gave evidence of the fight he'd put up, for they were obviously not all his. The men paused, honoring his sacrifice with an instinctive moment of silence, and then followed Richard as he headed for the outer door.

What struck them first was the stench of death. It was an odor they were all familiar with, but it seemed particularly foul in such sweltering summer heat. The street ahead of them was littered with the bodies of men and animals. By the Templars' door, a large dog was sprawled, lips still frozen in a snarl. A man was floating in a nearby horse trough; another lay curled up beside an overturned cart, his entrails spilling into a puddle of clotted dark blood. The air hummed with the droning of feasting insects, while two vultures circled overhead, waiting to resume their interrupted meal. And everywhere were the rotting carcasses of pigs. But there were no Saracens in sight, raising immediate suspicions in Richard's mind of ambush.

They advanced cautiously. All around them were the signs of a violent assault. Many of the houses had damaged roofs and a few of the trebuchet rocks had dug craters in the street. Doors had been smashed in by men in search of plunder, and arrows carpeted the ground. There were incongruous sights, too. A basket of eggs left on a bench. A woman's red hair ribbon snagged on a broken wheel. A costly mantle discarded, soaked in blood. A child's toy dropped in the dirt. Someone's pet parrot, shrieking from the wreckage of its owner's home. Evidence of disrupted lives, ill fortune, the human suffering foretold in Scriptures—*Man born of woman is of few days and full of trouble.*

After glancing around, Richard summoned Henry le Tyois, his standard-bearer, and told him to unfurl his banner where it would be visible to those in the castle. Henry scrambled up onto the wall, tossed down the sultan's eagle, and replaced it with the golden lion of the English king. One of the knights hastened over to snatch up the Saracen banner, thinking it would make a fine keepsake. Just then a young man emerged from a mercer's shop, heavily laden with bolts of expensive silks and linens. It was hard to say who was the more surprised, the knight or the looter. For a moment, they gaped at each other, and then the Saracen sensibly dropped his booty and fled.

"Christ Jesus," Richard said softly, suddenly understanding. No commander as astute as Saladin would have allowed his soldiers to continue looting the town in the midst of an enemy rescue mission. That plundering was still going on could have only one meaning—the sultan had lost control of his men. "Close ranks," he ordered, and they continued on.

As they turned into Jaffa's main street, they halted abruptly, staring at the red liquid filling the center gutter. There were gasps, for many of them knew the story of the capture of Jerusalem in God's Year 1099; the Christian army had slaughtered most of the Muslim and Jewish inhabitants of the Holy City, killing men, women, and children alike, boasting that their men had waded in blood up to their ankles. But after a closer look, Richard was able to reassure them. "Not blood, wine," he said, pointing toward the pyramid of smashed kegs.

There were murmurings of relief, and one of Richard's Poitevin knights, Raoul de Mauléon, evoked edgy laughter by saying loudly, "I can forgive a lot, but not the waste of so much good wine!" The laughter stopped, though, when they saw what lay ahead. A group of Saracens waited for them, swords unsheathed, arrows nocked and bows drawn.

Richard's men already had their own swords out. After a quick look to make sure they were ready, he gave the command and they charged forward. Most of them shouted "Holy Sepulchre, aid us!" though a few invoked "St George!" or the *"Dex aie!"* of the English Royal House. But it was André's battle cry that swiveled Richard's head in his direction, for he was bellowing *"Malik Ric!"* at the top of his lungs. As their eyes met, he grinned. "I thought it only fair to warn the Saracens that they're facing Lionheart," he explained, and Richard felt a surge of affection for this man who'd fought beside him for so many years, who was able to jest as they were about to engage the enemy.

They could hear the words *"Malik Ric"* rippling through the Saracen ranks. But they held fast and a furious mêlée ensued, the street seething with thrashing bodies and flashing blades. It was then that what Richard had hoped would happen, did. The castle gate opened and men raced out, attacking from the rear. Caught between the garrison and Richard's knights, those Saracens who could not flee were slain or surrendered, and it was soon over.

Once they realized they'd retaken the town, Richard's knights erupted in wild cheering, and Richard himself was mobbed by the grateful garrison. They were all flying high, drunk on the sweet nectar of salvation, having expected to die in defense of the castle or as they staggered out of the surf. Richard shared the euphoria. He did not have the luxury of giving in to it, though, and once some of the jubilation began to ebb, he drew André and the Earl of Leicester aside.

"This is all well and good," he said, "but it is no victory to celebrate. We're trapped by Saladin's army in a town that is in ruins, with not enough men to hold off another assault."

"That is still better than bleeding to death on the beach," André pointed out, "which seemed all too likely to me. If I may say so, my lord king, that was not one of your more rousing speeches to the troops. Follow me if you lust after martyrdom?"

Leicester's eyes widened. Despite his own impressive exploits in the Holy Land, he still felt like a green stripling when measured against the battlefield fame of the older men, and he was too much in awe of Richard to treat him with André's easy familiarity.

"I'll try to do better next time," Richard said dryly. He smiled, yet he was not altogether joking when he added, "Let's hope that Henri does not loiter along the way, for if he does not arrive with the rest of our army soon, I'll have no choice but to make that martyrdom speech again."

As HIS GALLEY headed south, its sails billowing in the wind, Henri stared at the passing shoreline, but he was not really seeing the rocky sea cliffs or the distant hills. He was so tense that he felt as if even his eyelashes were clenched, and he'd not eaten for hours, not trusting his stomach. Their march had gone well—until they'd reached Caesarea on Saturday. There they'd learned that a large Saracen force blocked the road ahead, commanded by Salah al-Dīn's new ally, the son of the *Assassin* chieftain, Rashīd al-Dīn Sinān. After much heated discussion, it was decided that they dared not advance farther, for the loss of their army would be more calamitous to the kingdom than the loss of Jaffa. It was a painful lesson for Henri in the harsh realities of life in Outremer and the need to defer to the opinions of more experienced men, in this case the *poulain* lords and the Grand Masters of the Hospitallers and Templars. He understood their caution; the disaster at Ḥaṭṭīn had left them all with scars. But he could never have waited at Caesarea, not without losing his mind, and after he discovered a galley in the harbor, he filled it with knights and sailed on Sunday morning for Jaffa.

He was dreading what they would find, and by the time they passed the ruins of Arsuf, he was pacing the deck like a man possessed, for they were less than ten miles now from Jaffa. Did the town still hold out? Had his uncle launched an assault, thinking he had reinforcements on the way? His mental musings were so dark that he felt a rush of gratitude when Morgan joined him, hoping the Welshman's voice could drown out his own thoughts. But Morgan's mood was none too sanguine, either, and he said morosely, "Forget the threat of Hell's infernal flames. The true torture would condemn a man to wait and wait and wait—for an eternity."

"You'll get no argument from me on that." The hollow sensation in Henri's stomach got worse, for the church of St Nicholas had come into view. Jaffa lay just ahead. Closing his eyes, Henri said a silent prayer—for his uncle, for those trapped in the besieged city, for his new homeland.

One of the sailors had gone up into the rigging to keep watch and he suddenly let out a yell, standing precariously upon the mizzenmast. His words were incomprehensible to most of those on the deck below; only his fellow Genoese crewmen could comprehend the Ligurian dialect. But his excitement was so obvious that the knights crowded to the gunwale to join Henri's vigil. And then they all were laughing and hugging and shouting, for the red and gold banner flying over Jaffa was Richard's.

Midst the clamor, Morgan had to shout, too, in order for Henri to hear him. "I confess that I've always been somewhat skeptical of miracle claims. But by God, no more!"

Henri's smile was incandescent, brighter than all the gold in Montpelier. "You do not have to believe in miracles, Morgan. Just believe in my uncle."

AS SOON AS THEY BEACHED their galley and waded ashore, Henri was surrounded by soldiers, eager to know when they could expect the rest of the army. He gave them a smile and a noncommittal "soon" and then asked for Richard. None seemed to know where he was, so when they said André de Chauvigny was in the town, Henri headed for the shattered Jerusalem Gate, trailed by his knights.

He'd never seen a city that had come so close to dying and he was shaken by the extent of the destruction. Even worse than the sights were the smells; it was like stumbling into a charnel house. He was not surprised that the men loading bodies into carts had their noses and mouths muffled by scarves. He found André by the east wall, climbing over the rubble to inspect the damage done by Saracen sappers and trebuchets. At the sight of Henri, he scrambled down so hastily that he turned his ankle and treated nearby bystanders to a burst of colorful cursing. Grabbing the younger man by the arm, he pulled Henri into the closest structure, a ruined, ransacked shop that had once been an apothecary. Standing in the wreckage of mortars, pestles, and smashed bottles and jars, Henri gave him the bad news, not even trying to soften his words for there was no way to make it palatable. The light was not good, but André seemed to lose color.

"Well, at least Richard will have his speech ready," he muttered, kicking the broken glass and crockery aside to clear a path to a wooden bench. Sinking down upon it, he saw Henri's puzzled look and forced a smile. "A private joke, lad." Unhooking a wineskin from his belt, he drank deeply. "I suppose it is too much to hope that you brought wine with you? God curse them, the Saracens poured out every drop in the town." He drank again before tossing the wineskin to Henri, and then got reluctantly to his feet. "We'd best get this over with. Let's go find Richard."

Henri was not looking forward to that conversation and took a long swallow before handing the wineskin back. "I could scarcely believe my eyes when I saw Richard's banner. How in God's Name did he do it, André?"

"Damned if I know," André said with a crooked smile, "and I was there. I used to joke that men would follow him into the depths of Hell. Yesterday they did."

As they stepped outside, the stench caused Henri to gag. He soon saw why; another cart was lumbering by, loaded with bodies. But as he glanced into the cart, he frowned. "What in the world . . . ?"

"Oh, that." André brought up his aventail flap to cover his lower face until the cart had passed. "The Saracens killed every single pig in the town, for their holy book says swine are unclean. They dragged most of them into a churchyard and then the whoresons threw the bodies of slain Franks in with them. It was meant to be a mortal insult, so our lads are returning the favor. We're burying our own, but we're dumping the pigs outside the walls with the corpses of any Saracens we can find."

Henri watched the cart rumble down the street toward the Ascalon Gate. His father had liked to quote from Ecclesiastes, that *there was a time for every purpose under the sun. A time for war and a time for peace.* The Holy Land had seen more than its share of war. When would the time for peace come? "How many died, André?"

"We do not know yet. There is always much bloodshed when a town is taken by storm. Those who were able to get into the castle, survived. Those who could not, died. Saladin did not seek a bloodbath, for he wanted the castle garrison to surrender ere Richard could come to their rescue, and he tried to rein his men in, without much success. But I'll let Richard tell you about that."

He was clambering over the rocks toward a gaping hole in the wall and Henri followed. "Where is he?" When André said he was in his command tent, Henri felt a chill of alarm. "Is he ailing?" he exclaimed, for it was very unlike Richard to be in his tent in the middle of the afternoon. He was greatly relieved when André shook his head, for he thought a man could sicken merely from breathing the fetid air that overhung Jaffa. It was, he thought with a shudder, like a plague town.

"He's well enough," André said and then glanced over his shoulder with a grin. "He has guests." And he laughed outright at the baffled expression on Henri's face, refusing to explain as they made their way toward the camp set up outside the walls.

As they approached Richard's tent, Henri could hear animated voices coming from within. When they entered, he was confronted by a scene that was surreal, for his uncle was entertaining some of Saladin's emirs and Mamluks, seated cross-legged on cushions as they laughed and shared platters of figs, dates, pine nuts, and cheese. Richard sprang to his feet with a delighted cry. Welcoming Henri with an affectionate embrace, he took advantage of the hug to murmur a question pitched for his nephew's ear alone, and flinched at the whispered answer. But when he turned back to his Saracen guests, his smile was steady, utterly unrevealing.

"You know my sister's son, the Count of Champagne," he said genially, "now the Lord of Jerusalem."

Henri had met them all before, for these were men who'd remained on amicable terms with the English king even in the darkest days of the holy war between their two peoples. Abū-Bakr was the chamberlain of Saladin's brother al-'Ādil; he and Richard had become quite friendly during the off-and-on peace talks. Aybak al-'Azīzī was a Mamluk who'd been escorting the caravan Richard had raided, but he apparently held no grudges. Sani'at al-Dīn was al-'Ādil's scribe and Badr al-Dīn Dildirim al-Yārūqī was the lord of Tell Bāshir, an influential emir who stood high in the sultan's favor. They greeted Henri affably and, not for the first time, it struck him that his uncle got on better with his Saracen enemies than he did with his French allies.

"I was just telling them that Islam has no greater prince than their sultan," Richard explained to Henri, "so I did not understand why he'd departed as soon as I arrived. I said that I'd not even been fully armed, that I was still wearing my sea boots."

"And how did they respond to that?" Henri asked, for he knew not all appreciated the Angevin sense of humor. For certes, Philippe had not.

"Oh, they laughed," Richard said, and Henri marveled that they could be trading jests when yesterday they might have been trading sword thrusts. He found it heartening, for surely mutual respect was a good foundation for building a peace, and he very much wanted peace for Outremer, convinced that it was the only way to ensure the survival of the Kingdom of Jerusalem.

The conversation continued in this vein, half joking, half serious, Geoffrey, the Templar *turcopole* whom Richard used when Humphrey de Toron was unavailable, translating for both sides. Richard expressed concern when told that al-'Ādil had been taken ill and wished Abū-Bakr a speedy recovery when he revealed that his limp was due to an injury he'd suffered during the siege. They in turn complimented Richard upon the prowess he'd displayed in retaking Jaffa and joked that they'd have spared a few kegs of wine for him had they only known he'd be arriving so soon. The mood in the tent was polite and playful and held so many undercurrents that Henri thought a man might drown in them if he made a misstep.

But when his Saracen guests made ready to depart, Richard became serious. Turning to Abū-Bakr, he said, "Greet the sultan for me and tell him we must make peace. My lands over the sea are in peril and I know his people are suffering, too. This war is harming us both and it is up to us to put an end to it."

Abū-Bakr responded with equal gravity, promising that he would convey

Richard's message to his sultan, his courtesy as polished as any courtier's, his dark eyes giving away nothing of his inner thoughts, and it occurred to Henri that this was like watching a chess game come to life, one played for the highest of stakes.

As soon as they had gone, Richard exhaled a deep breath, then seated himself on a coffer. Now that he was no longer playing the role of gracious host, Henri could see how weary he looked. "So," he said, "tell me what happened to your army." He listened without interrupting, and after Henri was done, he ducked his head for a moment, his face hidden. When he finally glanced up, it was with a faint smile. "So you left them at Caesarea and hastened to Jaffa to die with us?"

"Well, when you put it that way, it sounds quite mad," Henri acknowledged wryly. "But I do not know how much longer I can endure the suspense. What happened here, Uncle?"

Over a light meal of bread, cheese, and fruit, Richard told him. "They fought fiercely, like men with nothing left to lose. But after the wall collapsed on Friday, they sought to save themselves and their families. Saladin agreed to let them surrender the next day and set terms for their ransom. Soldiers were to be freed for an imprisoned Saracen soldier of equal rank. For the townspeople, he demanded the same sums that he'd negotiated with Balian d'Ibelin when Jerusalem yielded: ten gold bezants for a man, five for a woman, and three for a child. But by then his men were running wild in the town, and he told them to remain in the citadel for their own safety."

"Was the death toll very high?"

Richard nodded bleakly. Many of the dead were wounded or ailing knights and men-at-arms who'd remained behind in Jaffa to regain their health. Yet he knew his army would have done the same had their positions been reversed. War was war and soldiers were the same the world over, although killing came easier to some than others.

Henri decided that he and Isabella would found a chantry to pray for the souls of those who'd died in the Jaffa siege. "I cannot even imagine their joy when your sails appeared on the horizon," he said, reaching for a chunk of cheese, his first food of the day.

"I wish it had been that simple. Saladin got word Friday eve that I was on the way and, according to several prisoners, he tried to get his men to take the castle ere I arrived. They balked, though, some exhausted by the fighting and their wounds, others more interested in plundering the town, especially once they discovered that many of the caravan's goods had been brought there. When Saladin heard that my ships were approaching the next morning, he sent Bahā' al-Dīn—you remember him from our first meeting with al-'Ādil—to coax the garrison out. By now they'd seen the ships, too. There were only three galleys at first, so forty-seven men and their families agreed to come out. The rest of the garrison decided to resist now that rescue might be nigh. But as the morning wore on and we stayed offshore, they despaired, and the patriarch and castellan went to entreat Saladin to restore the original terms of surrender."

Anticipating Henri's question, Richard explained that they'd thought they were too late. "But then a brave priest swam out to my ship. We landed on the beach, cleared it, and I led men up a Templar stairway into the lower town. Once the garrison saw my banner, they sallied forth and we soon had them on the run. With his army in such disarray, Saladin had no choice but to withdraw to Yāzūr, taking the patriarch and castellan with him as prisoners. A pity about Bishop Ralph. But I was told the castellan had tried to flee at the start of the siege, had to be shamed into coming back and doing his duty, so he well deserves to end up in a Damascus dungeon."

Henri started to ask how Richard had known about the stairs, but then remembered something Morgan had told him—that when they took Messina, Richard had led them to a hidden postern gate he'd discovered during an earlier reconnaissance of the city. Much of his uncle's success as a battle commander was due to his meticulous preparations, his eye for the smallest detail. But that still did not explain how a small force of knights had been able to prevail against such overwhelming odds. "You make it sound like just another day's work, Uncle. I wonder if Caesar or Roland or Alexander the Great were equally casual about their conquests."

Richard laughed, always pleased to have his military skills lauded. "I will gladly take full credit for our victory at Jaffa, especially if there are any French within earshot. But we benefited greatly from the low morale of Saladin's army. His men have been campaigning for years, are tired, homesick, and frustrated, for they've had few opportunities for booty since my arrival at Acre, and even soldiers fighting a holy war still expect to profit from it."

Leaning over, Richard helped himself to a handful of pine nuts. "The men we faced had no interest in fighting, Henri, were so busy ransacking the town that they did not even realize we'd gotten ashore. We were lucky in so many ways yesterday, but I do not know how long it will hold. Jaffa's defenses could now be overrun by a band of determined monks!"

"Not if *Malik Ric* stands astride the battlements," André joked. Getting a skeptical look from Richard, he insisted, "No false modesty, Cousin. You've earned such a reputation for lunatic courage and battlefield mayhem that no sensible man wants to take you on. Even I would not!"

"I'd rather not wager our survival on that, André. The truth is that we're in a deep hole and we can only pray Saladin's own woes will keep him busy as we try to dig ourselves out." Richard shifted uncomfortably; like all of his men, he was stiff and sore, his body bruised and battered from yesterday's struggles. Catching the troubled expression on his nephew's face, he acted quickly to reassure him. "I'm nothing if not stubborn, Henri. I'll find a way to make this right—for you, for me, for my men. I have no intention of failing or of dying in the Holy Land. I'd never give those French malcontents that satisfaction!"

ABŪ-BAKR BROUGHT Richard's message back to Salah al-Dīn and the bargaining began. The sultan argued that since Jaffa was now laid waste, Richard should have the lands only from Caesarea to Tyre. Richard countered with an imaginative proposal, explaining that the Frankish custom was for a lord to give land to a vassal, who then agreed to serve him in time of need; if he held Ascalon and Jaffa from the sultan, he would promise to return if requested and offer his military services, "of which you know the value." Salah al-Dīn then offered to share the two towns, Jaffa for Richard and Ascalon for himself. Richard thanked him for agreeing to cede Jaffa, but insisted he must hold Ascalon, too, for he'd spent a king's ransom to rebuild it. Moreover, if the sultan would agree to this, he promised that peace could be made in just six days and he would leave then for his own lands. But if not, he would have to remain through the winter and the war would go on. Salah al-Dīn responded that he could not agree to yield Ascalon. And if Richard was willing to be far from his family and homeland when he was a young man in the flower of his youth, at a time when he sought his pleasures, "how much easier is it for me to spend a winter, a summer, then another winter in the midst of my own lands, surrounded by my sons and my family." He was an old man, he said, and he'd had his fill of worldly pleasures. He could outwait the English king, for he was serving God and what could be more important than that?

With Ascalon still blocking the road to peace, the talks sputtered to a halt. By now the sultan had learned that the Frank reinforcements were at Caesarea, with no plans to advance farther. When he was told that Richard was camped outside Jaffa with a small force of knights, he realized that he was being presented with a rare opportunity. If the English king were to be captured or killed, their war would be won.

CHAPTER 36

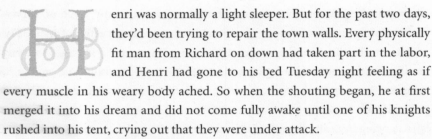

enri was normally a light sleeper. But for the past two days, they'd been trying to repair the town walls. Every physically fit man from Richard on down had taken part in the labor, and Henri had gone to his bed Tuesday night feeling as if every muscle in his weary body ached. So when the shouting began, he at first merged it into his dream and did not come fully awake until one of his knights rushed into his tent, crying out that they were under attack.

Henri had never armed himself so quickly, not bothering with his mail chausses in his rush to put on his gambeson, hauberk, and helmet. Hastening outside, he came upon a chaotic scene. Men were dashing about, some half-dressed, a few not even wearing their braies, clad only in their padded aketons, all clutching their weapons and looking about frantically for the enemy. Catching sight of Morgan and Raoul de Mauléon, Henri ran toward them. As they fumbled to fasten their aventails and buckle their scabbards, they told him what little they knew. Morgan had heard that a Genoese crossbowman had ventured from camp to take a piss and saw the dawning sun reflecting off the helmets and shields of an approaching army. Raoul reported rumors that the Saracens had split into two bands, one intent upon capturing the king, the other meaning to retake Jaffa and deny them that refuge. They were joined now by the Préaux brothers, who said Saladin himself was leading his troops, so many thousands that they were surely doomed. Henri did not know whom to believe and he began to search for his uncle.

He finally found Richard surrounded by crossbowmen and men-at-arms. Like Henri, he was bare-legged, but that was the only evidence that he'd been torn rudely from sleep. He seemed to be an island of calm in the midst of a storming sea, and his composure alone drew men to him, straining to hear what he was saying.

"This is what I want each one of you to do. Brace yourself with your right knee on the ground, your left leg bent. Hold your shield in your left hand, your spear in your right hand. Drive the butt of the shaft into the ground so it is anchored at an angle with the spearhead aimed at the height of a horse's chest." Richard directed his attention then to his arbalesters, addressing himself to the Genoese and Pisan sergeants who could translate for their men. "I want a crossbowman standing behind each two spearmen so he can be sheltered by their shields, and another of your men right behind him, both of them with their bows spanned. As soon as the first man shoots, he'll switch bows so he can keep shooting."

Richard would not normally have spelled out his orders in such detail, but he knew men's wits could be clouded by fear, and their only hope of survival depended upon them understanding exactly what was expected of them. That seemed to be the case; they were exchanging glances and nodding, some even smiling as they grasped what he had in mind. He was turning to summon his knights when a quavering voice from the ranks of the spearmen cried out, "Will . . . will this truly work, my lord?"

Glancing back impatiently, Richard saw that the speaker was very young, so pale that his freckles stood out like scars, round blue eyes filled with entreaty and barely controlled panic. "Of course it will work, lad," he said heartily, as if surprised the question could even be raised. "Horses have eyes and brains, do they not? You think they'll want to impale themselves on your spear? If you were a horse, would you?" Clapping the youngster on the back with a wink and a grin, he was relieved when the boy mustered up a weak smile of his own, for nothing was as contagious as fear.

As he swung away from the arbalesters and spearmen, he was thankful to see André, Leicester, and Henri standing a few feet away, for there was no time to search for them; every passing moment brought Saladin's army closer to their camp. "You heard, then? I want the knights to array themselves like the spearmen and those who are mounted to anchor our line near St Nicholas Church—" They were staring at him so oddly that he paused. "What?"

"A barricade of bodies, bristling with spears. That is bloody brilliant." André was looking at Richard as if seeing a stranger. "How did you ever come up with it?"

"I did not. It is a Saracen defense tactic." Richard smiled grimly. "I am not too proud to learn from an enemy." Beckoning them to step in, he lowered his voice.

"We have fifty-four knights, but only eleven horses. The ones taken from Saracens are battle-worthy, but the others are palfreys, cart horses, and nags. Still, better than nothing. I want them to go to the best riders. You three, of course, then Hugh de Neville, Guillaume d'Etang, Raoul de Mauléon, Gerard de Furnival, Roger de Sathy . . ."

He reeled off the names without hesitation and Henri marveled at his powers of concentration; his own thoughts were darting hither and yon like swallows at dusk. Richard was mounted now, gesturing and shouting as he sought to rally his troops, and Henri hastened to mount his own horse, adding his voice to his uncle's even as his eyes kept straying toward the horizon. The dawn sky was scattered with clouds; they'd absorbed the vibrant hues of sunrise, several as red as Richard's galley, *Sea-Cleaver*, a few reflecting the deep lilac that was Isabella's favorite color, and he could not help wondering if he'd be alive to see the sunset.

THEIR SHIELDS AND SPEARS firmly rooted in the dry Outremer dirt, their backs protected by the sand cliffs leading down to the sea, the men turned toward their king, astride a restive black stallion. With all eyes upon him, Richard tore his own gaze from the dust clouds being kicked up to the east; time was running out. Raising his hand for quiet, he began to speak. "I know you are fearful. But we are not defeated. If we hold fast, we can prevail over our foes. Yet to do that, every man must do his part. If even one of you gives in to your fear and tries to flee, you doom us all. Rather than let that happen, I will personally kill anyone who seeks to run."

He paused to let his warning sink in. "We are all going to die, but in God's Time, not Saladin's. For most people, their deaths have no meaning. If we die this day, we die for the Lord Christ and the Holy Sepulchre. Can there be a greater glory than that?" Again he paused, his gaze moving intently from man to man. "When we took the cross, we pledged our lives. In return, we were promised remission of our earthly transgressions. It does not matter how dark your sins are—and I'd wager some of them are very dark indeed." As he'd hoped, that bit of gallows humor elicited some tight smiles. "So our salvation is assured. But our defeat is not. If we hold firm, they will not be able to penetrate our defenses. You are brave men and I am proud to fight alongside you. I know you can do this. You need only have faith—in God, in your own courage, and in me."

In the past, when he'd sought to embolden his men before combat, they'd often responded with raucous cheers, their blood already surging with the apprehensive excitement of battle-seasoned soldiers. This exhortation was met with a subdued silence, but he was encouraged by what he saw on their faces—they looked resolute. Still fearful, yet eager to clutch at hope, and desperate. That was good, for he knew desperate men would fight like fiends. "Holy Sepulchre, aid us!" he shouted and they began to shout it, too, the war cry of the third crusade echoing on the humid August air like a defiant, despairing prayer.

RICHARD HAD WARNED the men to take their waterskins, saying they'd have need of them as the day wore on. Morgan unhooked his and took a sip, just enough to wet his dry mouth. They could see the enemy in the distance, their approach heralded by so much dust that it seemed as if a vast army was swooping down upon them. An unnatural silence had settled over their ranks, each man alone with his own thoughts. All around Morgan, knights were getting into position, securing their shields and lances. He was sure that they felt as he did, wishing they were on horseback. He glanced toward the mounted knights, his gaze lingering upon Henri as he silently repeated the latter's words. *You do not have to believe in miracles, Morgan. Just believe in my uncle.* God knows, he wanted to. But Henri had told him they only had fifty-four knights, four hundred crossbowmen, and two thousand men-at-arms. By any calculation, they were greatly outnumbered. How could they hope to hold out against such odds?

As he looked around, he wondered how many of these men were doomed. He very much doubted that Richard would be taken alive; the only way to overcome him would be to kill him. But Henri was likely to be captured, for he was too valuable a hostage to be slain. On impulse, Morgan called out "My lord count!" and moved toward the other man. "I've a favor to ask," he said as Henri turned in the saddle. "If I die today, will you tell the Lady Mariam that my last thoughts were of her?" He'd had enough combat experience to know that would not be true; a man would be thinking only of how to save himself. And Mariam was shrewd enough to know that. But the message might still be of some comfort to her. "You know how women are," he said with a self-conscious smile. "They are sentimental creatures and set a store by such things."

"They do, indeed." Henri nodded in agreement, striving to match Morgan's light tone. "I will convey the message should it come to that. And I'd have you convey the same message to my wife should the need arise." They chuckled, affectionately indulgent of the foibles of their ladies, but neither man met the other's eyes, shuttering the windows to the soul. And then Morgan hastened back to his fellow knights.

The waiting was over. They could see the golden banners of Saladin, could hear the ominous drumbeats that reminded them of their wretched march to Arsuf nigh on a year ago. The Saracens halted as they realized they'd lost the element of surprise, but they wasted no time in getting into battle formation. The crusaders blinked back the sweat trickling down into their eyes, took white-knuckled grips upon their weapons, and sought reassurance in their king's undaunted demeanor. "Hold fast!" he urged, sounding coolly confident. "We can do this!"

The Saracen drums had picked up their tempo, and then, with wild yells and the blare of trumpets, they charged. Morgan was accustomed to fighting on horseback; he discovered now that the ground beneath his feet actually vibrated with the thudding of thousands of hooves. The enemy bowmen were shooting arrows, displaying their remarkable proficiency at a skill the Franks had never mastered. But most of the arrows bounced off their shields. Richard waited until his arbalesters were squirming with impatience, their fingers twitching toward the triggers. When he gave the command, the air hummed as the bolts were loosed. Horses shrieked and stumbled; men were slammed back against their saddle cantles, crying out in pain. Still they came on and the crusaders braced for the impact, continuing to kneel behind their shields as horses and riders thundered down upon them, even though their every instinct was to run.

But at the very last moment, the Saracens veered off. Not a single man tried to breach that barbed wall. They swerved aside, racing their horses down the line of spears and shields, seeking in vain for a weak link in the defensive chain, and then they were in retreat, with the crossbowmen's bolts continuing to find targets until they were out of range.

There was a stunned silence, broken by a burst of triumphant laughter. "Did I not tell you how it would be?" Richard exclaimed. "We need only hold fast, lads, and victory will be ours!"

Men began to breathe again, to measure their lives in more than minutes. They thanked God and laughed and looked at Richard with awestruck eyes. He let them savor the moment and then reminded them that it was not over yet. "We must not let down our guard. They'll be back."

RICHARD WAS RIGHT; a second charge soon followed. It was no more successful than the first, the men and horses either unable or unwilling to brave that menacing barricade. A third try to dislodge the crusaders failed, too, and even at a

distance they could see the mounting frustration and fury of the Saracen commanders. The marksmanship of their arbalesters was taking a high toll; the field
was strewn with the bodies of wounded or dying men and stricken horses. Their
crossbowmen had none of the knights' affection for horses and gleefully targeted
them, for a dead one meant an injured or stranded rider.

Their own losses so far had been very light, men hit by the enemy's shower-
shooting tactics, which rained arrows down upon them but did not do serious
damage because of their shields and armor. The temperature had soared as the
sun climbed in the sky and their hair became matted and sodden underneath
their helmets, their bodies drenched in sweat, their voices hoarse from breathing
in so much dust. Steaming piles of manure from the knights' mounts fouled the
air, mingling with the smell of urine, for men had to relieve themselves where
they were. They were all thirsty, rationing their water at Richard's insistence, constantly slapping away buzzing insects and shifting to ease their cramped muscles.
But none complained, for they were still alive.

Around noon, the Saracens tried another stratagem. During a lull in the fighting, Richard got an urgent message from the castle garrison. The enemy had
gotten into the town, they reported, and people had panicked and were fleeing
to the ships. Leaving Henri and Leicester in command, Richard took André, a few
knights, and some crossbowmen, and hurried off to deal with this new crisis.
With him gone, his men suddenly felt vulnerable again, but no attacks were
launched; as far as they could tell, the Saracen forces seemed to be in disarray.

To no one's surprise, Richard was soon back, with three captured horses, a
fresh supply of bolts for his arbalesters, and bloodstains on his surcote that were
not his. The crossbowmen who'd accompanied him were happy to boast about it
to their comrades, saying the Turks had fled as soon as they saw him take on and
defeat three Mamluks; he'd then hastened to the shore, where he convinced the
fugitives to return to the town and dispatched most of the galley crews to help
defend Jaffa, leaving only five men to watch over each ship. And on the seventh
day, he rested, they chortled, for their brief respite from the claustrophobic confines of their cordon had greatly improved their morale.

The Saracens were taking longer and longer to muster their men for another
assault, and when it did come, it lacked the energy or intensity of the first charges.
It was becoming apparent to the crusaders that the enemy was growing discouraged, upset by their lack of success against a much smaller force, and fatigued by
their exertions under a hot sun. This was what Richard had been waiting for, and
he called his mounted knights to him.

"They've worn themselves out," he said. "Look how lathered their horses are. They are being prodded on by their commanders, but they have no more heart for it. It takes a lot out of a man to watch his friends die, and all for naught. So . . . now it is our turn."

Despite the audacity of what he was proposing—their small band of knights against Saladin's army—his men did not even blink, for they'd known that sooner or later, their king would take the offensive. And any doubts were easy to drown in the rising tide of enthusiasm; after having to remain passive for nigh on nine hours, they were eager to hit back. Once they were lined up, stirrup to stirrup, lances couched, Richard signaled to his spearmen, who hastily cleared an open space, and under cover of heavy crossbow fire, the knights charged.

They caught their foes by surprise, never expecting that they'd dare to go on the attack. They hit the Saracen lines with such force that they broke through, scattering men like leaves on the wind, and actually penetrating as far as the Turkish rear guard. To those left behind, it was an odd experience, war transformed into a spectator sport. Accustomed to being in the midst of the fighting, they'd been relegated to the status of bystanders and that did not come easily to them. But they were under orders to hold the line, and so they could only watch from a distance and pray that their king had not overreached himself.

Richard was easy to pick out, identified by his crimson surcote, his loyal standard-bearer, and the way so many of his adversaries would sheer off rather than cross swords with him. At one point, he disappeared from view and his soldiers were faced with an impossible choice: rushing to his aid or obeying his command to maintain their formation. His discipline held and they waited anxiously until he eventually fought his way free. By now, they were cheering like men watching a tournament mêlée, and when they saw the Earl of Leicester's horse stumble and throw him, they began to shout warnings as if they could be heard. Richard noticed Leicester's plight, though, and rode to his rescue, holding their foes off long enough for the earl to remount. Again and again he recklessly charged into the Turkish lines, yet somehow he always emerged unscathed. When Raoul de Mauléon was surrounded and captured, Richard was the one who saved him. When the Saracens sought to rally around one of their emirs, it was Richard who spurred to meet him. And after Richard struck with such ferocity that his sword decapitated the other man, he soon found himself alone on the field with his knights and the dead.

Once they realized the battle was over and they'd actually won, Richard's men went wild. Their jubilant celebration stopped abruptly, though, when they saw

Richard galloping his stallion toward the enemy. As they watched, first in alarm and then in delighted disbelief, he rode the entire length of the Saracen line and none dared to accept his challenge.

———

ALL AROUND HENRI, men had slumped to the ground. Soon they would tend to the wounded, put any suffering horses out of their misery, search the bodies of the slain Saracens for valuables, and eat and drink their fill while cursing their enemy anew for smashing all of those wine kegs. But for now, they wanted only to rest their weary bodies and to give thanks to their God and their king, for this was a victory even more miraculous than their successful landing upon Jaffa's beach four days ago.

Henri was willing to defer the duties of command, too, and just exult in their deliverance. He and Morgan and several other knights were seated on the trampled grass, sharing waterskins and trying to motivate themselves to move. Every now and then someone would mention the battle, marveling at Richard's bravura performance and their own survival. They laughed loudly when Henri speculated how the French would react once they heard that the English king had saved Jaffa without their help. They did not stir, though, until Richard and André rode up.

Sliding from the saddle, Richard took a step, staggered, and sank to the ground. When Henri offered him a waterskin, he drank as if he could never quench his thirst, then unfastened his helmet and poured the rest of the water over his head. His face was etched with exhaustion, his eyes bloodshot, and his hauberk was bristling with arrows, so many that André joked he looked like a human hedgehog. He grimaced, for he'd not be able to remove his armor until they'd been extracted. "They are going to have to bring my tent to me," he confessed, "for I could not stir from this spot even if a dagger were put to my throat."

"I'm glad to hear that, Uncle," Henri said with a grin, "for some of your feats today had us doubting that you are mere flesh-and-blood like the rest of us."

"Oh, I am flesh-and-blood, Henri," Richard said with a tired smile, and then showed them the evidence. Knights sought to protect their hands by wearing mail mittens called "mufflers," usually attached to their hauberks, with split leather palms so a man could slide his hand out when not fighting. As Richard did that now, they saw that the muffler had been of little use, for he'd wielded his sword so constantly that his hand was swollen, the skin cracked and blistered and bleeding from the force of his blows.

HENRI OCCASIONALLY FELT as if he'd inherited another man's life, for he had claimed Conrad's wife, Conrad's crown, even Conrad's child. He'd also acquired Conrad's espionage system and was delighted to discover that his spies were even better informed about Saladin's court than those who served his uncle. On this Wednesday, a week after their narrow escape, he'd learned some fascinating details about that thwarted attack and was looking forward to sharing them with Richard.

As he walked through their camp, he could not stifle memories of that day; they came upon him unexpectedly, like sudden flashes of lightning in a clear sky. He found himself remembering his fear, a visceral dread of death that he'd not experienced before, despite facing constant danger since his arrival in the Holy Land. It had taken him a while to understand that it was because of Isabella, that she was his hostage to fortune now and he would always fear for her future and that of their children as much as he feared for his own safety. He would never be able to emulate Richard's last gesture of defiance—gallant, glorious, and quite mad.

After a moment to reflect upon that, he began to laugh, realizing that he'd never have done it before his marriage, either. What man would? Only the Lionheart, whose Angevin empire now encompassed the realm of legend, too. Like all of the soldiers who'd watched Richard's prowess that afternoon, Henri had been bedazzled. Nothing was more admired, more valued in their world than bravery on the battlefield. War was a king's vocation, and at that his uncle excelled. But as he went in search of Richard on this August afternoon, Henri could not help thinking that even if a man did not fear Death, he still ought to accord it some small measure of respect.

Just then he heard his name called and paused for André to catch up with him. "Wait until you hear what I've learned, Cousin! We truly were in God's Keeping last week. Saladin meant to strike whilst we were still sleeping. But his Kurds began to quarrel with some of his Mamluks over who should go in on foot to seize the king and who should remain on horseback to make sure none of us could escape into Jaffa's castle. By the time they came to an agreement, dawn was nigh and that sharp-eyed Genoese with a full bladder caught sight of them." His amusement ebbing, Henri said somberly, "Think how it would have turned out had they attacked in the middle of the night."

André, ever the pragmatist, merely shrugged. "You might as well ask why

Richard did not die when he was afflicted with Arnaldia back at Acre. Or what would have happened if Guilhem de Préaux had not learned a bit of Arabic. Just be glad, Henri, that Richard's luck has so far kept pace with his boldness."

Henri thought that race was often too close for comfort. "I have more to tell you," he said. "As we suspected, Saladin himself was in command last week. He was outraged when his men were unable to break through our lines and kept urging them on, promising that they'd be well rewarded for their efforts. But when they were thwarted time after time, they began to balk. Finally, when he demanded that they charge again, only one of his sons was willing to obey. The others refused, and my spy says that the brother of al-Mashtūb even dared to remind Saladin that he'd sent in his Mamluks to try to stop the looting in Jaffa, saying he should send those Mamluks against us."

André was laughing. "You deny soldiers their booty and they get testy! We were lucky we took that caravan or our lads might have been ripe for mutiny, too."

"That is what my spy said," Henri agreed. "Saladin's men were angry that he'd offered terms for the surrender of Jaffa, feeling cheated of their just due, for they'd not had an opportunity for plunder in many months. He said Saladin was so wroth that some feared he might order the crucifixions of those who'd dared to disobey him. But he realized that he'd lose face if his men continued to be repelled by 'a handful of Franks,' and so he ordered a retreat." Pleased by André's response to his revelation, he said eagerly, "Let's go tell Richard. With luck, he'll not have heard it from his own spies yet!"

As they approached Richard's tent, they stopped to admire two finely boned horses cropping grass nearby. After winning his improbable victory on August 5, Richard had opened peace talks again, and three days later Abū-Bakr had ridden into their camp with a letter from the ailing al-'Ādil and these magnificent Arab stallions. They were a gift from the sultan's brother, Abū-Bakr explained, in recognition of the English king's great courage. Richard had been delighted and his knights envious, for Arabs were superior steeds. Henri had taken one out for a gallop and had been very impressed by the horse's smooth gait and cat-like agility. "I tried to coax my uncle into sharing," he told André, "pointing out that he has Fauvel, after all, but he just laughed at me."

"That's like asking a man to give you his concubine because he has a beautiful wife." André's grin faded as he caught sight of Jehan, one of Richard's squires. The youth was hovering by the entrance of the tent, so obviously worried that André quickened his pace.

As soon as he saw them, Jehan heaved a sigh of relief. "The king is still abed. I know he slept poorly last night, for I heard him tossing and turning for hours. But this is so unlike him, as the sun has been up for hours—"

André parted the tent flap and darted inside, with Henri right behind him. The same disquieting thought was in both their minds; a number of their men had sickened in the past week and they were convinced Jaffa had become as unhealthy as a cesspit because of all the noxious odors. One glance at the man in the bed confirmed that Richard had been stricken, too. His sheet was soaked in sweat, his chest glistening with a sheen of perspiration, and his face was deeply flushed. He struggled to sit up as they approached the bed, and they could see that his eyes were glazed, unnaturally bright. "Jesu," he mumbled, his voice very husky, "I've never felt so wretched. . . ."

"You're giving off enough heat to set the tent afire." André looked around for a washing basin, dipped a towel in the water, and put it on Richard's forehead. "Is it the quartan fever again?"

Richard swallowed with an effort. "Yes. The chills came in the night, then the fever. . . ."

André explained tersely for Henri's benefit that Richard had been laid low by quartan fevers in the past, the last attack happening during their stopover at Rhodes. "I'm not surprised you've taken ill. It is a wonder you're still amongst the living, given the way you push yourself. This is what we are going to do. We're sending a galley to Caesarea to fetch Master Besace. In the meantime, I'll find a Jaffa doctor to tend to you, and yes, you'll have to stay in bed—even if I have to tie you to it, Cousin."

He braced himself then for the inevitable argument. When it did not come, when Richard merely nodded, André and Henri exchanged troubled looks. If Richard, a notoriously difficult patient, was suddenly cooperative and reasonable, that meant he was much sicker than they'd realized.

CHAPTER 37

AUGUST 1192

Jaffa, Outremer

s the distant walls of Jaffa came into view, Henri found himself tensing, just as he had three weeks ago, not knowing what he'd find. Then, he'd feared that the city had fallen; now he feared that his uncle had died during his brief trip to Caesarea, for it had soon become obvious that Richard was gravely ill, so ill that he'd dispatched Henri to convince the French to join them at Jaffa. Henri had done his best, employing all of his eloquence and powers of persuasion; he'd thought it was a hopeful sign that they'd ventured as far as Caesarea, and he could see that some of the French knights wanted to answer the summons. But the Bishop of Beauvais was now in command, Hugh of Burgundy having returned to Acre after falling ill, and Beauvais forbade them to join Richard at Jaffa. Few dared to defy him, for he wielded the French king's name like a club and they all knew he'd pour poison into Philippe's ear upon their return to France. So Henri was sailing back to Jaffa with just a handful of men, those who had the courage to value their crusading vows more than their king's favor. While he was not surprised that Guillaume des Barres was one of them, he was surprised that Jaufre of Perche was one, too, and as he glanced at the young count standing beside him at the gunwale, he wondered if Jaufre realized he'd made a dangerous enemy in the bishop.

"How bad is it?" Jaufre asked, his eyes tracking the sleek forms of several dolphins keeping pace with their galley; every now and then there'd be a silvery splash as they leaped clear of the water. "I'm guessing things must be dire indeed if the king was willing to swallow his pride and seek French aid again."

"We cannot lose Jaffa," Henri said resolutely. "Some of the *poulain* lords arrived by galley in the past fortnight, but we are still greatly outmanned. We have less

than three hundred knights, and Saladin's army is growing by the day. He has gotten reinforcements from Mosul and our spies say more are expected from Egypt.
We've been trying to repair the town walls, but so many are sick. And they've all
been shaken by the king's illness. . . ."

"Does Saladin know the king is ailing?"

Jaufre's naïve question earned him a wry smile from Henri. "He probably
knew it ere Richard did. The man has more spies than there are priests in Rome.
Richard has been yearning for pears and plums, all he seems able to eat, so Saladin has been sending baskets of fruit and snow from Mount Hermon to ease his
fever. If Beauvais and Burgundy knew that, they'd see it as proof that my uncle
and the sultan are partners in a vast conspiracy to conquer Christendom for
Islam."

"They do not care about proof," Jaufre said, with enough bitterness to show
Henri that some of the French crusaders were very unhappy with their commanders. By now they were approaching the harbor and Henri felt a vast relief
when he saw men waving and smiling at the sight of his blue, white, and gold
banner, for there was none of the panic that he'd have seen on their faces if his
uncle had died while he was at Caesarea.

SOME OF THE SOLDIERS still camped in tents, convinced that the air of Jaffa was
unhealthy. But Richard had been moved into the castle for greater safety; they
feared the ailing king might have proven to be an irresistible target for his Saracen
foes. As Henri was escorted into his uncle's chamber, he came to an abrupt halt,
for the atmosphere was stifling. Despite the summer's heat, several coal braziers
were smoldering, and one glance at the blanketed figure in the bed was enough to
explain it. The cycle had begun again—severe chills, to be followed by a high fever
and sweating. Richard was shaking so badly that his teeth were chattering, but he
put out a trembling hand to beckon Henri forward.

"No . . . luck?" The voice did not sound like Richard's at all, slurred and
indistinct.

"I'm so sorry, Uncle. I truly tried. But Beauvais ordered them in Philippe's
name to remain in Caesarea. Whilst I doubt Hugh of Burgundy would have been
any more reasonable, he'd gone back to Acre after taking sick." Hoping it might
cheer Richard up, Henri embellished the truth, saying that he'd heard Burgundy
had been "puking his guts out" and had made the trip to Acre "clutching a chamber pot as if it were the Holy Grail."

The corner of Richard's mouth twitched in what might have been a smile, but he closed his eyes then and Henri took the hint. He knew his uncle did not like others to see him so sick, so helpless, and he thought that was one reason why Richard had forbidden him to let Berengaria and Joanna know of his illness. He'd said Jaffa was much too dangerous for them, and Henri could not dispute that. But as Richard's condition worsened, Henri feared that his uncle's wife and sister might be denied the chance to bid him a final farewell. After exchanging glances with Master Besace, who merely shrugged his shoulders, indicating Richard was in God's Hands, Henri made a quiet departure.

THEY'D GATHERED in a tent close to the Jerusalem Gate to hear Henri's report: the *poulain* lords Balian d'Ibelin, Hugues de Tiberias and his brother William; the Grand Masters Robert de Sablé and Garnier de Nablus; and the men closest to Richard—André de Chauvigny, the Earl of Leicester, and Hubert Walter, the Bishop of Salisbury. While they'd been expecting bad news, a gloomy silence still fell once Henri was done speaking.

"There are rumors that Saladin means to make another assault on Jaffa now that the English king is incapacitated," Garnier de Nablus said bleakly. "Under the circumstances, it would be astonishing if he did not, yet if he does, God help us all."

"His men showed they had no stomach for fighting," Leicester pointed out, but without much conviction.

"They had no stomach for fighting Richard," Balian corrected. "Since he's bed-ridden, they might recover some of their lost courage. Moreover, Saladin has fresh troops now, the reinforcements from Egypt." Balian paused, looking around at the circle of grim faces. "We need to make peace—for all our sakes. And there is only one way to do it. I'm guessing most of you are chess players, no? Well, any chess piece except the king can be sacrificed, and I think it is time to sacrifice one. We must give up Ascalon if we have any hope of winning this game."

The other *poulains* were nodding in vigorous agreement, but Richard's men looked dubious. Henri was the one to give voice to their misgivings, admitting that he was not sure Richard would ever agree.

"We cannot hold it without Richard," Balian said bluntly. "So unless he plans to renounce his own domains and remain here to defend it, it makes no sense to let Ascalon wreck this last chance of peace." He paused again, this time looking directly at Henri and André. "You must convince your king. If he will not consent, the best we can hope for is that the war goes on. But I think it is much more likely that we'll all die in the ruins of Jaffa, unable to fend off another Saracen assault."

RICHARD'S CHILLS had given way to the expected fever, and his doctors were doing all they could to bring his temperature down, coaxing him to sip wine laced with betony, bathing his burning skin with water cooled by the snow from Mount Hermon. Henri, André, and Hubert Walter had gathered in a far corner of the chamber, watching the doctors' efforts as they continued a low-voiced debate about what to do. André thought it best to wait until Richard's fever broke, for he'd become delirious as it peaked earlier in the week. But Henri and the bishop feared that time was running out even as they argued, and they eventually prevailed.

Approaching the bed once the doctors were done, they were relieved that Richard still seemed lucid, and they took turns trying to persuade him that Ascalon must be sacrificed. It was far more important to Saladin than it was to them; he'd never make peace as long as Franks controlled the route to Egypt. Without Richard, it could not be defended. If peace were not made soon, they risked another attack on Jaffa, risked being stranded in Outremer till the following spring, risked the survival of both kingdoms—Jerusalem and England. Richard listened in silence and at last turned his head aside on the pillow, whispering, "Do as you think best...." Overjoyed, they thanked him profusely and hastened off to send word to the Saracens that Ascalon's fate was now open to negotiation.

Richard was not left in peace for long; the doctors returned, insisting he must be bled, and he did not have the strength to object, wanting only for them all to go away and let him be. He dozed for a time, awoke with another throbbing headache. Feeling as if his body were on fire, he sought to throw off the sheet and discovered he had more visitors. The French king and his brother Johnny were standing by the bed, regarding him with smug smiles.

We thought you'd want to know what has been happening back home, Big Brother, although you'll not like it much. I am going to wed Alys, keeping her in the family, Johnny said with a grin. *And I am thinking of taking Joanna as my queen now that you'll not be around to object,* Philippe confided. *But the weddings will have to wait until after we lay claim to Normandy, of course. And England will soon be mine, too,* Johnny boasted, *for none will dare to defy me once they hear you died in the Holy Land.* Richard told them to go away; they just laughed at him. And then Johnny did go, but Philippe still leaned over the bed, whispering in his ear. *Your little brother will be a lamb to the slaughter, Lionheart. How long do you think it will take me to strip Johnny of every last acre? I'll have Normandy, Anjou, Brittany, even your beloved Aquitaine in the time it takes for your body to rot in an Outremer grave. Your Angevin empire will soon be a French one and there is naught you can do to prevent it.*

Richard cried out and his doctors were there at once, stopping him as he attempted to get up, telling him he must stay in bed. Did they not see Philippe and Johnny? Did they not hear the laughter? He tried to tell them, but talking was too much of an effort, and he let them lay him back against the pillows. His head was pounding; so was his heart, sounding as loud in his ears as the Saracen war drums. Had they launched another attack? When he closed his eyes, he could see that dead Templar, propped up in bed, sword in hand. Where was *his* sword? He struggled to sit up, looking around wildly for it. But the chamber was filling with shadows and he could see nothing beyond the bed.

Is this what you want, Richard? A familiar figure emerged from the darkness, holding out Joyeuse, the sword Maman had given him on his fifteenth birthday, when he'd been invested as Duke of Aquitaine; he'd named it after Charlemagne's fabled weapon, said to have flashed lightning in the heat of battle. He reached for it, but his brother pulled it away before his fingers could touch the enameled pommel. *What good will a sword do you when you are as weak as a mewling kitten?* Geoffrey sat on a nearby coffer, tossing the sword aside. *You were so pleased when you heard I'd been trampled in that tournament. Very shortsighted of you, Richard. You'd have been better off with me as your heir, much better off.*

As if you'd not have connived for my crown, too! You'd never have been satisfied with a duchy if a kingdom was in the offing.

He had no energy for speech, but he did not need it, for Geoffrey seemed to pluck his words from the air, saying with a sardonic smile, *Yes, but I would have been willing to wait. Face it, Richard, you'll never make old bones. Other men lust after women. You lust after Death, always have. You've been chasing after her like a lovesick lad, and sooner or later she'll take pity and let you catch her. So I could afford to wait. But Johnny had to entangle himself in Philippe's web, the damned fool.*

You entangled yourself in Philippe's web, too, Richard reminded him. *If you had not been plotting with the French, you'd not have been at Lagny when that tournament was held.*

You know why I turned to Philippe. I got tired of Papa treating us like his puppet princes, tired of him dangling that accursed crown before us like a hunter's lure. So

did you, remember? You did me one better, too, doing public homage to Philippe for
all your fiefs "on this side of the sea" whilst Papa looked on, dumbfounded. But you
could safely make use of Philippe, for you knew you could outwit him and outfight
him. So could I. Johnny cannot, as he'll soon learn to his cost. Ah well, you'll be dead
by then, so mayhap it will not matter so much.

Christ Jesus, Geoffrey, of course it matters! Furious, Richard thrashed about,
trying to free himself from his sheets. *If you've come only to mock me, go back to*
Hell where you belong!

Purgatory, not Hell, Geoffrey said and laughed before fading back into the
blackness. Richard called out to him, but he got no answer. He was alone.

AFTER CONFIRMING that there were only three hundred knights with Richard,
Salah al-Dīn met with his council and it was agreed to attack Jaffa or, failing that,
Ascalon. By August 27, he was at Ramla, making ready for the assault. But it was
then that he got two messages that changed his plans. Abū-Bakr reported that
Richard had asked al-'Ādil to broker a peace, requesting to be indemnified for his
expenses if he had to surrender Ascalon. Salah al-Dīn halted their march and
instructed his brother, "If they will give up Ascalon, conclude a treaty of peace."
The next day the emir Badr al-Dīn Dildirim al-Yārūqī brought word that he'd
been approached by the Bishop of Salisbury, who told him that Richard would be
willing to yield Ascalon without compensation. Salah al-Dīn was uneasy about
making peace, confiding in Bahā' al-Dīn that he feared their enemy would grow
strong again now that they had a secure foothold along the coast. But he had no
choice, he said, for his men were war-weary, homesick, and had shown at Jaffa
that they were no longer dependable. After meeting again with his council on
Sunday morning, August 30, the sultan sent an envoy to the English king with a
draft of the peace treaty.

"No," RICHARD SAID, shaking his head stubbornly. "I did not agree to yield
Ascalon without compensation. I would never do that!"

There was a shocked silence, the other men looking at one another in dismay.
"You did, Uncle." Henri approached the bed, picking up the document that Richard had crumpled and flung to the floor. "André and the bishop and I . . . we came
to you and explained why Ascalon had to be sacrificed—"

"No! I would not do that."

"Richard . . . it happened as Henri says. You do not remember . . . not any of it?"

Richard's eyes searched André's face, then shifted to Hubert Walter. "No . . . I agreed to this? You swear it is so?" When all three of them assured him it was, he sank back against the pillows. It was very disturbing, even frightening, to think he'd made such an important decision and had no memory of it. When he glanced up again, he saw that the sultan's envoy was becoming agitated, asking Humphrey de Toron what had gone wrong. "Humphrey . . . tell him that if I said it, I will honor my word. And tell him to say this to Saladin—that I accept the terms and understand that if I receive any compensation for Ascalon, it will be because of his generosity and bounty."

The envoy was ushered out, obviously greatly relieved that there was to be no eleventh-hour surprise. By unspoken assent, the other men left, too; only Henri and André remained. "This is my fault, Uncle," Henri said unhappily. "André insisted that we ought not to ask you until your fever broke. But I feared to wait—"

"It is your kingdom, Henri. It was your decision to make as much as mine." Richard could not remember ever feeling so exhausted or so disheartened. "I need to sleep now. . . ." He hoped it would come soon, stilling the questions he could not answer, the insidious voice asking what he'd truly accomplished here. So many deaths, and all for what?

WHEN RICHARD AWOKE, it was still light, so he could only have slept for an hour or so. One of his doctors was quickly hovering over the bed, asking if he would like some soup or fruit. He made himself say yes, for he knew he had to eat to regain his strength. He was frightened by his weakness; it was as if he'd become trapped in a stranger's body, not the one that had served him so well for nigh on thirty-five years. A quartan fever recurred every third day, so he ought to be fever-free today, but he was not. If he died here at Jaffa, what would become of his kingdom? What of Berenguela, left a young widow in a foreign land so far from home? Or Joanna? Had he lost the Almighty's Favor by failing to take Jerusalem? Ought he to have tried, even knowing how many men would die in the attempt? "Give me a sign, O Lord," he whispered. "Let me know that I was not wrong. . . ."

He tried to eat the food the doctors brought to him, but his stomach rebelled and he could swallow only a mouthful or two before he was fighting back nausea. He asked for music, for that had always been a source of comfort, but the harpist's

melodies sounded melancholy and mournful, even though he'd requested something lively. He finally slept again, a shallow, uneasy sleep that gave him little rest,
and awoke to find his nephew standing by the bed.

"I've been waiting for you to wake up," Henri said. "I have news you'll want to
hear."

Richard doubted that, almost told Henri to come back on the morrow. But the
younger man's eyes were shining; he did not look like the bearer of yet more bad
tidings. "What?"

"I had a message tonight from Isabella. She says that Hugh of Burgundy died
at Acre five days ago."

Richard stared at him. "I think," he said, "that I've just gotten my sign." Henri
did not know what that meant, but it did not matter; his uncle was smiling, the
first real smile he'd seen on Richard's face since he'd been stricken with the quartan fever.

ON SEPTEMBER 1, Salah al-Dīn's envoy, al-Zabadānī, came to Jaffa with the final
draft of the treaty, waiting in a tent outside the town until Richard was carried out
to meet him on a litter. He was too ill to read it, but said, "I have made peace. Here
is my hand." A truce was to begin on the following day, to last three years and
eight months. The terms were very similar to those discussed in the past, with the
crusaders to hold the coastal areas from Jaffa to Tyre. The peace was to include
the Prince of Antioch, the Count of Tripoli, and Rashīd al-Dīn Sinān, leader of
the *Assassin* sect. Ascalon was to be razed to the ground and to remain so for the
duration of the truce. Richard's reliance upon the sultan's generosity was not mis-
placed; Salah al-Dīn compensated him for the money he'd expended at Ascalon
by agreeing that the Franks and Saracens would share the revenues of Ramla and
Lydda. Both sides would be able to move freely, to resume trade, and Christian
pilgrims would be given access to Jerusalem. The two armies mingled and Bahā'
al-Dīn reported that "It was a day of rejoicing. God alone knows the boundless
joy of both peoples."

Richard remained seriously ill, Bahā' al-Dīn repeating a rumor that he'd died.
On September 9, he sailed to Haifa and then on to Acre to convalesce. He sought
to pay the French back by asking Salah al-Dīn to allow only those Christian
knights who bore letters from him or Henri to visit Jerusalem. But the sultan
wanted as many crusaders as possible to fulfill their holy vows, knowing they'd be
less likely to return then, and he ignored Richard's request. Three pilgrimages

were organized, one led by André de Chauvigny and another by the Bishop of Salisbury. The latter was accorded the honor of a personal audience with Salah al-Dīn, who told him that Richard had great courage but he was too reckless with his own life. While many of his soldiers and knights took advantage of the peace to worship at the Holy Sepulchre, Richard did not.

ANDRÉ WAS HOLDING COURT, regaling a large audience with his account of his pilgrimage to Jerusalem. "It almost ended ere it began," he said, "for the men we'd sent on ahead to get safe conducts from Saladin stopped at Toron des Chevaliers and fell asleep. The rest of our party assumed they'd reached Jerusalem and we passed them by as they slept. When we realized we were arriving without advance warning, we sent word hastily to al-'Ādil and he dispatched an escort to protect us, rebuking us for our rashness." He'd charitably not mentioned the names of the errant envoys, but Pierre de Préaux, William des Roches, and Gerard de Furnival flushed uncomfortably, knowing many were aware they were the culprits. They were grateful when Berengaria distracted attention from them by asking André why they'd needed safe conducts, for she thought the Holy City would be open to all pilgrims.

"Well, we are more than pilgrims, my lady. We're the men who defeated Saladin's army at Acre, Arsuf, and Jaffa, and many of them still bear grudges. We were told some of them entreated the sultan to let them take vengeance for the deaths of their fathers, brothers, and sons. But he refused to allow it, giving al-'Ādil the responsibility of making sure that Christians would be safe during their stay in the Holy City."

André then told them of his visit to the most sacred site in Christendom, the Holy Sepulchre; and as he described the two-story chapel with Mount Calvary above and Golgotha below, Berengaria had to fight back tears. When André said that Saladin had allowed the Bishop of Salisbury to see the True Cross, she bit her lip, thinking that the sultan would surely have done as much for Richard and his queen. André and the other men had seen all the places so familiar to her from her readings of Scriptures: the rock upon which the body of the Lord Christ had lain, the Mount of Olives, the Church of Mount Sion where the Blessed Mary had died and was assumed into Heaven, the room where the Last Supper had taken place, the Valley of Jehosaphat, the Pool of Siloam, where the Saviour had restored a man's sight. Places she would never get to visit.

She bowed her head so none would notice her distress, but it was then that

André leaned over and urged her husband to make the pilgrimage, too. "There is still time, Cousin," he said, "to change your mind." Richard merely smiled and shook his head, but for just a heartbeat, his defenses were down and his naked yearning showed so plainly on his face that Berengaria caught her breath. So he did want to see the Holy City! Why, then, would he not go?

LYING IN BED beside Richard, Berengaria was still thinking of his earlier unguarded moment in the great hall. There were two explanations circulating about Richard's refusal to make a pilgrimage to Jerusalem—that he was still too sick to make the trip or that it was too dangerous. It was true that he was not fully recovered, although he tried to hide it as best he could. She saw how exhausted he was when he went to bed at night, how little he ate, how easily he tired during the day. They'd only begun sharing a bed again in the past few days and he'd not yet made love to her; she was content to cuddle, but his forbearance was further proof that he was still convalescing. She knew, though, that he'd never have let ill health keep him from traveling to the Holy City; like most soldiers, he was accustomed to fighting through pain. And the other rationale was no more plausible. It was ludicrous to think that the man who'd ridden out alone to challenge the entire Saracen line to combat would of a sudden be so concerned for his own safety. She'd reluctantly concluded that a pilgrimage to Jerusalem was simply not that important to him, and her resentment began to fester, for in denying himself that privilege, he was denying her, too. She was Richard's queen; how could she go without him?

But she had been given a glimpse into his heart earlier that evening, and she was now sure it was not lack of interest. "Richard?" When he turned toward her, she shifted so she could look into his eyes. "I need to talk with you. It is important."

He propped himself up on his elbow. "Why do women always want to have these talks when a man is half asleep?" he grumbled, but she saw the smile hovering in the corner of his mouth. "All right, little dove. You have my full attention."

"Why did you not go to Jerusalem?"

He was quiet for so long that she was not sure he was going to answer. "I did not deserve to go, Berenguela. I had not earned that right. When I took the cross, I pledged to free the Holy City from the Saracens, and in that, I failed."

Her throat tightened, for beneath her tranquil surface, her emotions were surging at flood tide. Guilt that she'd so misjudged him. Pride that he would not accept from the infidels what he could not get through God's Grace. Frustration that he confided so little in her, that after sixteen months of wedlock, they were still strangers sharing a bed, that the only intimacy he seemed able to offer was carnal. Unspoken anger that he'd kept her away from Jaffa when he could have been dying. Fear that was with her every moment of every day, the dread that she would become a widow ere she could truly become a wife. She'd been telling herself for months that their life would be different once they returned to his domains, that their real marriage would begin then. But she'd been badly shaken to learn he'd been so desperately ill and had chosen to keep her in ignorance. It had raised doubts she was unwilling to confront, even to acknowledge.

"I think the Almighty will honor your sacrifice," she said softly, and he leaned over, brushing his lips against her cheek. But she lay awake long after he fell asleep, tears trickling from the corners of her eyes as she wept silently for Richard, for herself, and for the Holy City that neither of them would get to see.

SEPTEMBER 29 WAS THE DAY chosen for the departure of Richard's wife, sister, and most of the fleet, which Richard had placed under André's command. Once they reached Sicily, the women would continue their journey overland to avoid the winter storms. André and Leicester would then sail on to Marseille, the same route Richard planned to take once he was able to leave Acre. Berengaria and Joanna had bidden farewell to Isabella at the palace, for her pregnancy was so far advanced that even the short trip to the harbor was beyond her. Escorted by Richard and Henri, they arrived at the wharfs to find a large crowd had assembled to see them off. The women were glad to be going home, although they were uneasy about the long sea voyage ahead of them, none more so than Joanna. She was putting up a brave front, but it was belied by her pallor and the brittle edge to her laughter. Richard was watching his sister with troubled eyes, and as soon as she moved away, he leaned over to murmur in Berengaria's ear. "*Irlanda* is no sailor, suffers more grievously from seasickness than anyone I've ever known. I'm relying upon you to take care of her, little dove."

"I will do my best," she promised, tilting her head so she could look up into his face. She knew why he was not sailing with them; he'd explained that he had important debts still to settle. But she wished so very much that he was not remaining behind. Like his soldiers, she felt safer in his company, and she knew Joanna did, too. And it would be months before they'd be reunited, months in which she could do naught but worry about him. Their departure was

dangerously close to the end of the sailing season; it would be even more dangerous for him if he delayed by another week or two.

And he had more to fear than storms at sea. As a man who'd taken the cross
and fought for Christ in the Holy Land, he was under the protection of the
Church, but she feared that would matter little to his enemies . . . and he had so
many. The French king. The Holy Roman Emperor. The Duke of Austria, said to
still be nursing a grudge over his dishonored banner at Acre. The brother of Conrad of Montferrat, who'd been told that Richard was responsible for Conrad's
death. The Count of Toulouse, an old foe who was conspiring with the French to
do Richard harm. And the Bishop of Beauvais, who'd already sailed and would be
slandering Richard with every breath he drew. Like the trail of slime that marked
a snail's passing, Beauvais would be leaving venom in his wake as he moved from
court to court, and she was not sure the truth could ever catch up to all those lies.

"I wish you were coming with us, Richard."

"I would if I could, Berenguela. But you'll be safe with André and Leicester,
and Tancred will provide you with a large escort on your way to Rome." Richard
knew she was shy of public displays of affection, but when he kissed her, she
returned the embrace with unexpected ardor, hoping that last night God had
finally heeded her prayers and let her conceive. If she could depart the Holy Land
with his child in her womb, it would be proof of divine favor, proof that the
Almighty was not wroth with Richard for his failure to take Jerusalem.

Berengaria and Joanna were not the only ones to be worried that Richard was
delaying his departure. Mariam was very unhappy about it, too, for Henri and
Joanna had asked Morgan to wait and sail with Richard, both of them concerned
that he was still suffering from the aftereffects of that near-fatal bout of quartan
fever. Morgan was trying to coax her into a better humor, joking that it was for
the best. "If we sailed together, think how difficult it would be for me, *cariad*, having you close at hand and yet out of reach. I'd be like a man parched and half mad
with thirst, chained to a keg of Saint Pourçain wine and not being able to drink a
drop of it."

Mariam was not mollified, but they'd already had this argument and she did
not want their last words to be quarrelsome. Morgan squeezed her hand, and
then turned as Joanna approached. "Keep my brother out of trouble, Cousin
Morgan," she said, with strained playfulness. He promised that he would, even
though he thought that was a task beyond his capabilities. But he knew she was
nervous that Richard would be traveling without André, who was probably the
only man able to rein in the king's more reckless impulses.

The lighters were waiting to ferry them out to their ships. But Joanna had been entrusted with a private message for Humphrey de Toron and she drew him aside to say that Isabella had heard he'd accepted Guy de Lusignan's invitation to settle in Cyprus and she wished him happiness in his new life. "Thank you, Lady Joanna," he said, and she found herself thinking again that he was a remarkably handsome man, with one of the saddest smiles she'd ever seen.

Most of the farewells had already been said. André and Richard joked as if they were not facing dangers as daunting as any they'd confronted in the Holy Land, and no one listening to their banter would ever have suspected that Richard might be sailing home to a lost kingdom, a realm in ruins. Henri kissed all the women with great gallantry and Joanna nearly wept, for it was unlikely she'd ever see him again. Richard hugged his sister so tightly that she thought he might have cracked a rib, kissed his wife, and promised they'd all be together to celebrate Christmas or, at the latest, Epiphany. "If Philippe took four months to get home, I can damned well do it in three," he said with a smile, and lifted Berengaria into the lighter before she could ask if he truly meant that.

The barge rocked as it rode the waves out to their waiting ship, and Joanna started to look greensick. Berengaria reached over and squeezed her hand, all the while gazing back toward shore. The sky was free of clouds and the wind blew steadily from the southeast, a Jerusalem wind, surely a good omen. But she'd begun to tremble, chilled by a sudden sense of foreboding, the fear that this would be her last memory of Richard: standing on the Acre wharf next to Henri, smiling and waving farewell.

AFTER STOPPING at the Cathedral of the Holy Cross to offer prayers to St Michael, whose day it was, invoking his protection for their fleet, Richard and Henri returned to the palace in a somber mood. As soon as they dismounted in the courtyard, Balian d'Ibelin appeared in the doorway of the great hall. "I was just about to send for you, Henri. Isabella's birth pangs have begun."

Henri gasped and dashed up the steps, darting past Balian into the hall. Following more slowly, Richard stopped beside the *poulain* lord. "I thought she was not due for another month?"

Balian shrugged. "The midwives may have miscalculated. Or the baby may have decided to come early."

Richard knew little of the birthing chamber, but Henri had told him that Balian had four children with his Greek wife. "Are Isabella and the baby in danger?"

"Early births pose more of a risk to the baby, but it is always dangerous," Balian said quietly, "always. Maria had planned to be at Acre with Isabella when her confinement began, and I'd feel much better if she were here," he confessed. "But wishing will not make it so. We'd best go inside, for Henri will have need of us. It is likely to be a very long day."

MEN WERE NOT PERMITTED in the birthing chamber, but that did not keep Henri from making numerous trips abovestairs to plead for news from the midwives. Emma would come out, tell him cryptically that all was proceeding as it ought, disappear back inside, and Henri would return to the hall to pace and fret. Richard tried to occupy him with a chess game, but he was too distracted to concentrate for long. After he pushed away from the table and headed yet again for the stairs, Balian came over.

"The lad has the attention span of a sand flea right now. I was the same way when Maria was giving birth to our first. Fortunately, it does get easier. May I sit, my lord? I've something to say to you."

Richard gestured to a chair, somewhat warily. Balian had given Henri his full support as soon as he and Isabella were wed, but he'd stayed aloof from the crusade while Conrad lived, and Richard remembered that all too well. "I am listening."

"I thought you ought to know what the Bishop of Beauvais is saying about you."

Richard's mouth twisted in a mirthless smile. "I'm well aware of the lies he's been spreading—that I am responsible for Conrad's death, that I sent *Assassins* to France to murder Philippe, that I am in league with Saladin and the Devil to betray Christendom to the Saracens. I'd not be surprised if he is claiming that I'm a secret Muslim, too."

"But do you know he is also accusing you of poisoning Hugh of Burgundy?"

"Good God Almighty!" Richard shook his head incredulously. "It is a wonder they are not blaming me for the murder of Thomas Becket in Canterbury Cathedral!"

"Or the Great Flood or the expulsion from Eden," Balian suggested dryly, and they found that sharing a laugh dispelled some of the lingering tension between them. "Above all, they are saying that you accomplished nothing, that your campaign was a failure because you did not recapture the Holy City. I daresay they'll find men to believe that. But not in Outremer. Ere your arrival, the Kingdom of Jerusalem consisted only of the city of Tyre and a siege camp at Acre. Because of your efforts, our kingdom now stretches along the coast from Tyre to Jaffa, we will have an opportunity to strengthen our defenses, Saladin no longer controls Ascalon, and Christian pilgrims can worship again at the Holy Sepulchre. That may not sound like much to lazy French burghers back in Paris, but it means a great deal to those who call Outremer home."

Henri and André had been telling Richard this, too, but he discovered now that it meant more coming from a man who was not his friend.

As word spread that Isabella was in labor, *poulain* lords began to arrive at the palace and a palpable air of tension overhung the great hall. Henri was too focused upon his own unease to notice, but Richard did. He knew what they feared and were murmuring among themselves: What would happen to their kingdom if Isabella's child was stillborn and she did not survive? It was a realistic fear, for the birthing chamber could be as dangerous for a woman as the battlefield was for a man. And although Henri had wed their queen, he was not an anointed king, for he'd not yet been crowned. Isabella had not, either, but she had a bloodright to the throne; Henri did not.

Richard found that their anxiety was contagious, and after a cursory supper that went largely uneaten, he slipped out of the hall. Twilight had yielded to night and the air was cool against his skin. The waning moon had not yet risen but the courtyard was bathed in starlight. He sat down upon a marble bench, frustrated by his lingering fatigue; when would he feel like himself again? Not wanting to think of Isabella's ongoing ordeal, nor of his fleet, now at the mercy of the unforgiving Greek Sea, he welcomed a diversion, the appearance of one of Jacques d'Avesnes's Flemish hounds. Joanna had taken her cirnecos with her; Jacques's big dogs had been spared the sea voyage when Isabella and Henri offered to adopt them. Richard fondled the hound's drooping ears, but the dog's presence was stirring hurtful memories of Jacques and all the men who'd died in Christ's Name, gallant ghosts hovering in the shadows, reminding him how many would not be coming home.

He raised his head at the sound of footsteps. Henri was coming toward him, holding a lantern. He did not need it, though, for his smile alone could have illuminated the entire courtyard. "Isabella is resting," he said, "after giving birth to a beautiful baby girl."

Richard's relief momentarily rendered him speechless. "I am so glad, Henri, so glad for you both!"

"I wanted you to be the first to know, but as soon as the others in the hall saw my face, there was no need of words." Henri set the lantern down on the bench, but he was too wrought up to sit. "We're going to name her Maria after both our mothers. I always thought newborn babies were red and wrinkled and bald. Yet Maria looks like a little flower, with a feathery cap of dark hair like Isabella's."

"Our time in the Holy Land has been very different from what we expected it to be. But surely the greatest surprise is that you've become a father," Richard said, smiling, and Henri laughed aloud.

"If any soothsayer had predicted that in Outremer, I'd wed a widowed, pregnant queen, I'd have thought him madder than a woodhound!" Henri laughed again, before saying, "I have a confession, Uncle. I'd been praying that Isabella would give birth to a daughter, not a son."

"You ought not to feel guilty about that, Henri, for it is only natural that you'd want to see a son of your own as king one day."

"I think I could have loved Conrad's son, for I'd be the only father he'd ever know. But what if I were wrong, if I came to resent him for taking precedence over my blood sons? It just seemed so much easier—and safer—if only she'd have a girl. Of course I did not let Isabella know I had these doubts." Henri perched on the end of the bench, still so energized that he seemed like a golden hawk about to take flight at any moment. "But when the midwives finally let me in to see her, she confided that she'd been praying for a daughter, too!"

Richard decided that his cousin Isabella was either deeply in love with his nephew or a very clever young woman; either way, he thought their chances for a good marriage were excellent. "As you say, lad, easier and safer. And I'll wager that by the time I come back to Outremer, you'll have a son of your own to show me."

"'Come back'? You mean that, Uncle?"

"Of course I do." Richard was surprised by Henri's surprise. "I did not fulfill my vow to retake Jerusalem. Nor did we make peace. We agreed to a truce that will last for only three years and eight months. Did you truly think I'd leave you on your own to fend off the Saracens when war resumes?"

Henri was overwhelmed. "You have no idea how much that means to me! I thought that when you sailed for home, our farewell would be final. You believe Jerusalem could be taken?" He tried to dampen down his excitement, then, for he owed his uncle honesty. "But could you come back without putting your own realm in jeopardy?"

"We could not take Jerusalem because the Saracens were united, as they had not been when it first fell to the Christians. Had we not faced Saladin, had we not been subverted at every turn by Burgundy and Beauvais, our chances for success would have improved dramatically. Saladin is a great prince, but as he himself pointed out to me, he is not a young one, and his brother is far more capable than any of his sons. By the time I return, his empire might well be torn asunder. As for my own empire, it will not be easy, but it can be safeguarded. I'll start by putting the fear of God into Johnny. Then I'll teach Philippe that there is a high price to be paid for treachery." Richard's face had hardened as he thought of his disloyal brother and the unscrupulous French king. But after a moment, he smiled at his nephew. "With you as my ally instead of Conrad and without the French to hinder us, think what we can accomplish!"

PIERRE AND JEAN DE PRÉAUX had delayed their departure as long as they could, anguished by the prospect of having to leave Outremer with their brother still a Saracen prisoner. They'd even discussed remaining until the following spring, but they both had families of their own back in Normandy. They'd reluctantly decided to sail with Richard when he left, and that day was fast approaching. Richard had been busy settling all of his outstanding debts and arranging for a horse transport for Fauvel and his Arab stallions. He'd had a public crier proclaim that his creditors should present themselves at the palace and he'd made sure that payments were made to the garrison at Ascalon, to masons for work done on Jaffa's walls, to merchants for supplies provided to his army. After being told by Baldwin de Bethune that Richard expected to leave by week's end, the Préaux brothers paid their own debts and informed the innkeeper that they'd be vacating their chamber in two days. They were heading for the market to buy St Denys medallions, for they'd be sailing on his name day, when the summons came from the king.

They hastened to the palace, hope flickering. In the past Richard had twice managed to relay to them messages from their brother, and at Jaffa, he'd promised to ask al-'Ādil to pass on a message to Guilhem. As painful as it was to leave without knowing his fate, it would be even worse if they had to depart without bidding him a word of farewell. Upon entering the great hall, they were told Richard was awaiting them in the solar and they hurried into the stairwell. To their surprise, Richard himself opened the door. Jean's view was partially blocked by his brother's shoulder. He thought he saw Henri standing behind Richard and he wondered why they had not thought to ask the count to get a message to Guilhem; he was known to have a good heart, after all, and he'd have the time that Richard did not. But it was then that his brother shocked him by pushing past

Richard into the solar. Mortified by such a breach of protocol, Jean started to stammer an apology on Pierre's behalf. Richard just laughed and swung the door open wide, enabling Jean to see the man caught up in Pierre's bear hug. With a hoarse cry of disbelief, Jean lunged forward so he, too, could embrace Guilhem.

What followed was bedlam, with all three brothers talking at once, laughing and weeping and pounding one another exuberantly on the back, while Richard and Henri watched, smiling. Guilhem was noticeably thinner; his once-round face now had angles and hollows. He looked older, too, to their searching eyes. But his humor had not changed, nor had his hearty, loud laugh. "Who'd ever have thought," he joked, "that your little brother would turn out to be worth a king's ransom!"

"Actually an emir's ransom," Henri corrected with a grin, "or ten emirs, to be precise. My uncle freed ten highborn Saracens to gain Guilhem's release."

Guilhem's grateful brothers began to acclaim Richard for his generosity, marveling that he'd have given up such a vast sum for a Norman knight, one who'd merely been doing his duty to protect his king. For Richard, this had been a debt of honor, one that had to be repaid, no matter the cost, and he brushed aside their emotional praise, explaining that he'd said nothing in case the negotiations failed at the eleventh hour. He'd also wanted to surprise them, looking forward to their joy when Guilhem was restored to them. Their reunion was all he could have hoped for; never had he seen three men as happy as the Préaux brothers were on this October afternoon in the royal palace at Acre. But as he looked at their tear-stained, blissful faces, he was taken aback by what he felt—a sharp prick of envy.

After they eventually left, so euphoric they practically seemed to float down the stairs, Richard and Henri shared gratified smiles. Richard then surprised his nephew by asking him if he was close to his younger brother. "I'd say so," Henri confirmed. "I am much older than Thibault, of course; he was born when I was thirteen. So that gave me the opportunity to play the wise elder brother, which I enjoyed enormously," he said, with a reminiscent chuckle. "And when our father died two years later, I suppose I became even more protective of Thibault. He's a good lad, wanted so badly to come with me to the Holy Land. . . ." A shadow crossed his face, but his homesickness was forgotten when Richard began to speak of his own brothers, for he'd never heard his uncle mention them before.

"Hal was no 'wise elder brother,' for certes. He could not find water if he fell into a river. Even worse, he was as malleable as wax, swayed by the slightest breeze. Had he ever become king, it would have been catastrophic for all but the French king. Now my brother, Geoffrey . . . he was too clever by half and, as far back as I can remember, we were at odds. Mayhap it was because we were so close in age—just a year between us—but we were always rivals, never friends."

Richard moved to the trestle table, reached for a wine flagon, and then changed his mind. "With Johnny, it was different. He was nine years younger, and I did not see him much as we grew up, for he spent several years being schooled at Fontevrault Abbey. My parents may have been considering a career in the Church for him; if so, he'd have been spectacularly ill-suited for it. The one time our father entrusted him with any authority—sending him to govern Ireland when he was eighteen—he made an utter botch of it. And when he was seventeen, he joined Geoffrey in invading Aquitaine. I blamed our father for that, though. He'd told Johnny that Aquitaine was his if he could take it away from me. When Geoffrey and Johnny then tried, he hastily recalled them, insisting he'd never meant to be taken seriously. I've sometimes wondered if he said that, too, to the knights who murdered Thomas Becket after he'd raged about being shamefully mocked by 'a lowborn clerk.'"

Henri was fascinated, for his uncle's turbulent family feuding had always been off-limits, and since he was kin to Richard on his mother's side, he didn't have personal knowledge of the Angevins' internecine warfare. "But you were very generous to Johnny once you became king," he interjected, unable to resist adding, "more than he deserved," for he'd always viewed John with a jaundiced eye. "You gave him a great heiress and lands worth four thousand pounds a year!"

"And my mother had misgivings about that," Richard admitted. "But our father had played the same damnable games with Johnny that he had with the rest of us, so I felt he deserved a chance to show he could be trusted."

"And he showed you." Henri was not usually so harshly judgmental, but he thought John's sin—betraying the man who was his brother, his king, and a crusader in God's Army—was beyond forgiving.

Richard nodded grimly. "Yes, that he did."

ON FRIDAY, OCTOBER 9, Richard was ready to go home. The vast army that he'd led to Sicily, Cyprus, and the Holy Land had been decimated by illness and war. Galleys would have been swamped in heavy winter seas, so he'd given the ones that were still seaworthy to Henri, and planned to sail in a large buss. It could hold hundreds of men, but as Henri looked at that lone ship, it seemed like a great comedown from Richard's spectacular arrival at Acre sixteen months ago, and he thought his uncle would be dangerously vulnerable to the violent storms that roiled the Greek Sea at this time of year—and to a host of enemies, some earned, some not, all eager to see him brought low.

He sought to hide his concern, forcing himself to smile as Richard kissed Isabella and then gave him a quick, casual embrace, as if he were merely sailing down the coast to Jaffa. Henri's studied nonchalance did not deceive his wife. Isabella had been dreading this day, knowing how hard it would be for him, knowing how deep-rooted was his ambivalence about his new life in Outremer. He gamely sought to make her believe that he was content, but the fact that in five months he'd done nothing to arrange a coronation spoke volumes to her. It had not escaped her, either, that Henri continued to call himself the Count of Champagne, and she spent a great amount of time trying to find ways to make him feel less of an exile in a foreign land. She'd blessed Richard for promising to return, and it had occurred to her that once Thibault came of age, there was no reason why Henri's mother should not come to visit. She was known to be devout, and for Christians, a pilgrimage to the Holy Land was what the *hajj* to Mecca was to Muslims. Giving Henri a searching look as he watched Richard's lighter row out toward the waiting ship, she vowed that she'd make him happy in this new life that had been forced upon him.

"Henri . . . I want us to be honest with each other, to share the deepest secrets of our hearts. You can tell me anything, can tell me when you yearn for home—"

He tightened his arm around her, stopping her words with a gentle finger against her lips. "I am home, my love."

THEY'D CHOSEN to depart at dusk so they could sail by the stars. Earlier that day, it had been overcast, but brisk winds had scattered the clouds. As the buss raised anchor and headed out of the harbor, most of the men on deck were looking toward the horizon, where the sky was streaking with the dying rays of the setting sun. But Richard kept his eyes upon Acre, slowly disappearing into the distance. "Outremer," he said softly, "I commend you to God. May He grant me the time I need to come back to your aid." He stayed where he was, not moving until darkness swallowed up the shore and all he could see was the endless, rolling sea and the glittering stars, brilliant and cold and eternal.

Afterword

I am not going to include the star players here; the fates of the Angevins are already well-known to us and will be covered in my usual obsessive-compulsive detail in *A King's Ransom*. So I am focusing upon the historical figures who are not as familiar, some of whom might not even surface if Googled.

Philippe Capet will have a major role in *A King's Ransom*. His sad sister, Alys, was finally returned to France in 1195, and Philippe immediately married her to the teenage Count of Ponthieu. Alys was then thirty-five, but she was able to conceive, giving birth to a daughter. Philippe's youngest sister, Agnes, known as Anna after her marriage to the Byzantine Emperor's son, lived for the rest of her life in Constantinople, taking Theodore Branas, a Byzantine general, as her lover and then her husband. She had a daughter, but after that, she disappears from the written record.

The Holy Roman Emperor Heinrich von Hohenstaufen, his consort, Constance de Hauteville, and Leopold von Babenberg, the Duke of Austria, will be appearing again in *A King's Ransom*.

Tancred reigned as King of Sicily for only four years. He struggled valiantly to stave off the threat posed by the Holy Roman Emperor, Heinrich, but his fledgling dynasty was doomed after the sudden death of his eldest son, Roger, in December of 1193. Tancred himself died in February of 1194, leaving as his heir a four-year-old son. His widow, Sybilla, was forced to yield to Heinrich, who was crowned as King of Sicily at Christmas. Soon thereafter, he conveniently claimed to have discovered a conspiracy and brutally executed a number of Sicilian lords. Sybilla and her children were sent to Germany, where she and her daughters were confined to a convent for years; they eventually managed to escape to France. Her little son was taken to a German monastery and was never seen alive again. There are several accounts of his tragic fate; the most credible says that Heinrich had him blinded and castrated, and he died in 1198.

Isaac Comnenus was held at the Hospitaller stronghold of Margat until 1194. Upon regaining his freedom, he began to intrigue against the Byzantine Emperor, Isaac II. He died circa 1196, said to have been poisoned. His second wife, Sophia, returned to Sicily in 1192, but nothing more is known of her after that. Anna, the Damsel of Cyprus, accompanied Joanna and Berengaria back to Richard's domains; her subsequent history will be related in *A King's Ransom*. Neither Sophia's nor Anna's names were recorded by the chroniclers. W. H. Rudt de Collenberg, the author of "L'empereur Isaac de Chypre et sa fille, 1155–1207," an invaluable scholarly article about Isaac and Cyprus, speculated that his daughter may have been called Beatrice, for a Beatrice received a generous bequest in Joanna's will, and several of the Damsel's maternal ancestors bore this name. But two of Joanna's ladies took the veil at Fontevrault Abbey after her death, and one of them was Beatrice, which refutes his theory. So I had to choose names of my own for Isaac's wife and daughter.

Salah al-Dīn's health continued to deteriorate and he died of a fever on March 3, 1193; Bahā' al-Dīn ibn Shaddād reported that he'd given so much to the poor that there was no money to pay for his funeral. His sons fought over the succession, and in January 1200 his able brother, Malik al-'Ādil, was proclaimed the Sultan of Egypt. He had a successful reign and was succeeded by his son in 1218.

Guy de Lusignan did not govern Cyprus for long, dying in 1194. His brother Amaury managed to get the Emperor Heinrich to recognize him as King of Cyprus, a title Guy had not claimed, and the de Lusignan dynasty ruled the island kingdom for over three hundred years. Humphrey de Toron did not remarry; he apparently died soon after following Guy to Cyprus. I hope to deal with Balian d'Ibelin's story at a later date.

Henri and Isabella had five happy years together before he was killed in a bizarre fall from a palace window at Acre in September 1197. Isabella was then wed to Amaury de Lusignan, Guy's brother, now King of Cyprus. Isabella died in April 1205 at the age of thirty-three, having been widowed three times and divorced once. She and Henri had three daughters; one of them, Alice, would later marry a son of Amaury by his first wife and become Queen of Cyprus. Isabella's daughter by Conrad, Maria of Montferrat, ruled as Queen of Jerusalem until her death following childbirth at age twenty.

The Third Crusade was considered a failure in Richard's time because they'd been unable to recapture Jerusalem; Richard himself saw it that way, too. Ironically, successive crusaders adopted the military strategy he had wanted to pursue—assaulting Egypt. Richard did succeed in gaining the kingdom another hundred years of existence, until the fall of Acre in 1291.

AUTHOR'S NOTE

Richard I was never one of my favorite kings, although my knowledge of him was admittedly superficial. I saw him as one-dimensional, drunk on blood and glory, arrogant, ruthless, a brilliant battle commander but an ungrateful son and a careless king, and that is the Richard who made a brief appearance in *Here Be Dragons*. I saw no reason not to accept the infamous verdict of the nineteenth-century historian William Stubbs that he was "a bad son, a bad husband, a bad king."

So I was not expecting the Richard that I found when I began to research *Devil's Brood*. I would eventually do a blog called "The Surprising Lionheart," for after years of writing about real historical figures I'd never before discovered such a disconnect between the man and the myth—at least not since I'd launched my writing career by telling the story of another king called Richard.

The more I learned about this Richard, the less I agreed with Dr. Stubbs. I think Richard can fairly be acquitted of two of those three damning charges. I loved writing about Henry II. He was a great king—but a flawed father, and bears much of the blame for his estrangement from his sons. Certainly both Richard and Geoffrey had legitimate grievances, and it can be argued that they were driven to rebellion by Henry's monumental mistakes; see *Devil's Brood*. I bled for Henry, dying betrayed and brokenhearted at Chinon, but he brought so much of that grief upon himself.

Nor was Richard a bad king. Historians today give him higher marks than the Victorians did. Yes, he spent little time in England, but it was not the center of the universe, was only part of the Angevin empire. After his return from his crusade and captivity in Germany, he found himself embroiled in a bitter war with the French king, and spent the last five years of his life defending his domains from

Philippe Capet. The irony is that he has been criticized in our time for the very actions—his crusading and his military campaigns—that won him acclaim in his own world. By medieval standards, he was a successful king, and historians now take that into consideration in passing judgment upon him.

He was, however, a bad husband, his infidelities notorious enough to warrant a lecture from the Bishop of Lincoln. Note that I say he was taken to task for adultery, not sodomy. I discussed the question of Richard's sexuality at some length in the Author's Note for *Devil's Brood* and will not repeat it here since this note is already going to rival a novella in length. Very briefly, the first suggestion that Richard preferred men to women as bedmates was not made until 1948, when it took root with surprising speed; I myself helped to perpetuate it in *Here Be Dragons*, for I'd seen no need to do in-depth research for what was basically a walk-on role. But the actual "evidence" for this claim is very slight, indeed. I'll address this issue again in *A King's Ransom*, for that is where Richard will have his famous encounter with the hermit. The research I did for *Devil's Brood* inclined me to be skeptical, and I am even more so after finishing *Lionheart*, for I had not realized the intensity of the hatred between Richard and Philippe. The French chroniclers accused Richard of arranging the murder of Conrad of Montferrat, of poisoning the Duke of Burgundy, of plotting to kill Philippe by sending *Assassins* to Paris, of being bribed by the "godless infidels" and betraying Christendom by allying himself with Saladin. So why would they not have accused him of sodomy, a mortal sin in the Middle Ages, and a charge that would have stained his honor and imperiled his soul? If they'd had such a lethal weapon at hand, we can be sure they'd have made use of it.

Berengaria has remained in history's shadows, a sad ghost, a neglected wife. She has not received the respect she deserves because her courage was the quiet kind; she was not a royal rebel like her formidable mother-in-law. She has been called a barren queen, unfairly blamed for the breakdown of her marriage. Since I knew of her unhappy marital history, I was somewhat surprised to discover that the marriage seems to have gotten off to a promising start. Because Richard shunned her company after he recovered his freedom, I'd assumed this was true in the Holy Land, too. But Richard actually went to some trouble to have her with him when he could. It would have been easier and certainly safer to have had her stay in Acre instead of bringing her to Jaffa and, then, Latrun. We cannot be sure what caused their later estrangement, but I have some ideas; as a novelist, I have to, don't I? I think we can safely say, though, that the greater blame was Richard's.

What surprised me the most about Richard the man as opposed to Richard the myth? I already knew he was almost insanely reckless with his own safety, so it came as something of a shock to learn that he was a cautious battle commander, that he took such care with the lives of his men. It is a fascinating paradox, and one which goes far toward explaining why he was loved by his soldiers, who seemed willing "to wade in blood to the Pillars of Hercules if he so desired," in the words of the chronicler Richard of Devizes.

It also surprised me to learn that his health was not robust, that he was often ill, for that makes his battlefield exploits all the more remarkable. The Richard of legend smolders like a torch, glowering, dour, and dangerous. But the Richard who comes alive in the chronicles had a sardonic sense of humor, could be playful and unpredictable; Bahā' al-Dīn reported that he habitually employed a bantering conversational style, so it wasn't always easy to tell if he were serious or joking. And while I'd known he was well educated, able to jest in Latin and write poetry in two languages, I admit to being impressed when I discovered him quoting from Horace. Even his harshest critics acknowledge his military genius; he hasn't always been given enough credit, though, for his intelligence. The mythical Richard is usually portrayed as a gung ho warrior who cared only for blood, battles, and what he could win at the point of a sword, but the real Richard was no stranger to diplomatic strategy; he was capable of subtlety, too, and could be just as devious as his wily sire.

But I was most amazed by his behavior in the Holy Land, by his willingness to deal with the Saracens as he would have dealt with Christian foes, via negotiations and even a marital alliance. As tragic as the massacre of the Acre garrison was, it was done for what he considered valid military reasons, not because of religious bias, as I'd once thought. However serious he was about offering Joanna to al-'Ādil, it was revealing that he'd entertained an idea that would have horrified his fellow crusaders, and it is impressive that he managed to keep it secret; we know of this only because the Saracen chroniclers reported it. He was not the religious zealot I'd expected. The man who was the first prince to take the cross refused to lay siege to Jerusalem, alarmed his own allies by his cordial relations with the Saracens, and although he believed they were infidels, denied God's Grace, he respected their courage. According to Bahā' al-Dīn, he formed friendships with some of Saladin's elite Mamluks and emirs, even knighting several of them. That was the last thing I'd have imagined—knighting his infidel enemies in the midst of a holy war?

I don't expect *Lionheart* to change the public perception of Richard I any more than *The Sunne in Splendour* could compete with the Richard III of Shakespeare. But I do hope that my readers will agree with me that this Richard is much more complex and, therefore, more interesting than the storied soldier-king. Perhaps I shouldn't have been so surprised by what my research revealed. As an Australian friend Glenne Gilbert once observed astutely, "There had to be reasons why he was Eleanor's favorite son."

War was the vocation of kings in the Middle Ages, and, at that, Richard excelled; he was almost invincible in hand-to-hand combat, and military historians consider him one of the best medieval generals. It was in the Holy Land that the Lionheart legend took root, and his bravura exploits won him a permanent place in the pantheon of semimythic heroes, those men whose fame transcended their own times. Even people with little knowledge of history have heard of Caesar, Alexander, Napoleon—and Richard Lionheart. This would have pleased Richard greatly, for he was a shrewd manipulator of his public image.

But if Richard is the best-known medieval king, he is also the most controversial. His was an age that gloried in war and that jars modern sensibilities. The darkest stain upon Richard's reputation is the killing of the Acre garrison. It certainly contributed greatly to my own negative feelings toward Richard, especially after I read in Stephen Runciman's *A History of the Crusades* that the families of the garrison were slain, too. Human beings are conditioned to react to numbers; we find the deaths of two thousand six hundred men more shocking than the death of one man or a dozen. And the deaths of noncombatants is particularly reprehensible. So when I wrote *Here Be Dragons*, I was not at all sympathetic to Richard, repulsed by the blood of so many innocents on his hands.

More than twenty years later, when I began to do extensive research about the man, I was astonished to learn that the story of the killing of the women and children has no basis in fact. It first struck me that Runciman cited no source for his statement, and that really surprised me, for this is such a basic tenet of historical research. I then found that only older books like Runciman's (which was written more than fifty years ago) made the claim that the families were killed, and not a single one offered any evidence to substantiate this accusation. This charge is not found in any of the more recent histories, including those written by historians specializing in the era of the Crusades.

This was of such importance that I put everything else aside and devoted my time to researching all the contemporary sources for the siege of Acre. I read every chronicle I could find that dealt with this tragic episode; I even sought out different translations of Ambroise and Bahā' al-Dīn. In none of them did I find it said that the families of the garrison were put to death. To the contrary, *Arab Historians of the Crusades,* the translation of Bahā' al-Dīn's account of the massacre, refers to the martyrdom of three thousand *men* in chains. I also found a passage in al-Athir's chronicle in which he said Saladin had sworn that all Franks taken prisoner would be killed in revenge for the *men* put to death at Acre; see *The Chronicle of Ibn al-Athir for the Crusading Period from al-Kamil fi'l-Ta'rikh*, Part 2, "Crusade Texts in Translation," translated by D. S. Richards, page 390. So this turned out to be just another one of the myths that trailed in Richard's wake—and a valid reason for not recommending the Runciman book. (Bahā' al-Dīn said three thousand had been slain, Richard said two thousand six hundred, and I decided he was in the better position to know.)

The execution of the garrison remains troubling, though; these were men who'd fought bravely and surrendered in good faith, believing that they would be ransomed. But Richard was ruthless when he waged war, and the matter-of-fact tone of his letter to the abbot of Clairvaux shows that he felt himself justified in executing them after Saladin defaulted on the terms of the surrender. Bahā' al-Dīn admitted that Saladin had been seeking to delay their departure from Acre, although I find it highly unlikely that he expected to have his bluff called in such a brutal fashion. But the Saracens must have seen Richard's action as a military decision, for how else could Richard have formed friendships with so many of Saladin's emirs and Mamluks?

I still found myself feeling enormous sympathy for the slain men and the loved ones they left behind. I felt sympathy for all those who died during the Third Crusade, soldiers and civilians alike. It is not always easy for an instinctive pacifist to wade through so much blood and gore while writing of medieval battles! As a writer and a reader, I am faced with one of the greatest challenges, which is not to judge people of another age by our standards of conduct. The truth is that virtually every medieval ruler committed acts that we would find abhorrent, and that includes Richard, his father, Henry, Saladin, and most of the men I've been writing about over the years, with the possible exception of poor, addled Henry VI. But I never feel too sanctimonious, not when I remember the death toll for civilians in the wars that have convulsed our world during my own lifetime. St Francis of Assissi has always been a lonely voice crying out in the wilderness.

Lionheart was a unique writing experience. I've never had such a wealth of eyewitness accounts of events; the closest I'd come was Becket's murder in Canterbury Cathedral. This was beyond wonderful, spoiling me for other books. I had amazing resources to draw upon—two chronicles written by men who accompanied Richard on the Third Crusade, and three Saracen chronicles written by men who were there, two of them members of Saladin's inner circle. There were other chronicles, too, which I list on my Acknowledgments page, but it was the ones written by the poet Ambroise, the clerk Richard of the Temple, and Bahā' al-Dīn ibn Shaddād that I found absolutely riveting.

Imagine being able to read accounts of battles by the men who actually fought in them. Bahā' al-Dīn watched as Richard landed on the beach at Jaffa, vividly describing his red galley, red tunic, red hair, and red banner. Ambroise's account of the crusaders' march along the coast reads like a battlefield dispatch. The author of the *Itinerarium* compared the fleet Saracen horses to the flight of swallows, and explained how the stings of tarantulas were treated with theriaca, which only the wealthy could afford. Both the crusader and Saracen chroniclers reported Guilhem de Préaux's heroic sacrifice. Occasionally, I had to reconcile differing accounts. Ambroise said the huge Saracen ship was rammed by Richard's galleys when they could not capture it; Bahā' al-Dīn said the captain gave the order to scuttle it. So I went with the most likely scenario that both chroniclers were correct.

Even the random details come straight from the pages of these chronicles: Philippe's lost falcon at Acre. The Saracen slave girl who charmed Richard with her singing during his visit with al-'Ādil. Complaints about the tiny flies called cincelles. The postern gate at Messina and the Templars' stairway at Jaffa. The pears, plums, and snow sent by Saladin to Richard when he was ailing. Richard's one glimpse of the Holy City. The sudden mist that swept in from the sea and cut off Richard's rear guard on the march to Jaffa. The logistics of a medieval army on the move, which I'd never encountered anywhere else. Richard's unfair banishment of Guillaume des Barres in Sicily and their reconciliation after al-'Ādil's attack upon the rear guard. Philippe's unexpected interest in Joanna. Richard's despair as he struggled to reconcile the competing demands of king and crusader. Even the names of the men killed in combat. Dialogue that occasionally came from the mouths of the men themselves. And Fauvel, the Cypriot stallion that so bedazzled Richard and the chroniclers.

Richard did, indeed, break his sword in his squabble with that understandably irate Sicilian villager, and he only had one knight with him at the time; I took the liberty of letting Morgan be the man. He really did arrive in Cyprus just in time to rescue his sister and betrothed, mere hours after Isaac Comnenus had issued his ultimatum to Joanna and Berengaria; no writer would have dared to invent high drama like that. I actually tried to tone down his battlefield heroics, as reported by the chroniclers, not wanting my readers to think I'd gone Hollywood on them. But he truly did ride up and down alone before the Saracen army at Jaffa. If that had been reported by Richard's chroniclers, I'd have been skeptical, but it comes from two of the Saracen chroniclers; Bahā' al-Dīn was mortified that none had ridden out to accept Richard's challenge.

I took only one historical liberty with known facts, in Chapter Thirty-two. Richard did advise his nephew Henri to take the Jerusalem crown while warning him of the perils of marriage to Isabella; Richard was convinced that she was still legally wed to Humphrey de Toron. But Richard and Henri had no face-to-face encounter; it was done via messengers due to the time pressure, for the *poulains* were eager to have the marriage done ASAP. Since this is a novel, though, I opted for the greater drama of a personal discussion between the two men. I also shifted Richard's killing of the wild boar from April to February. And because the chroniclers neglected to describe the palace at Acre, I used the description of the palace at Beirut.

In any historical novel, there are always times when we have to "fill in the blanks." As I've said before, medieval chroniclers could be utterly indifferent to the needs of future novelists. We often do not have birth dates, wedding dates, sometimes not even death dates, and, more often than not, we don't know the cause of death, either. All we know of the demise of King William II of Sicily is that he died of an illness, it was not prolonged, and it was unexpected. So I chose an ailment that was very common in the Middle Ages: peritonitis. I also had to select a birthdate for Isabella's daughter by Conrad of Montferrat. We know Isabella was pregnant when she wed Henri in May of 1192, for one of the Saracen chroniclers was horrified by this, seeing it as proof of the immorality of the Franks. So Maria was born sometime during 1192, and, rather than keep my readers in suspense, I let her be born before the book's end.

Aside from the "poetic license" I took in letting Henri unburden himself in person to Richard, I did not stray from the truth of this remarkable episode in Outremer history. Isabella did indeed defy the French; Henri hurried back to Tyre after learning of Conrad's murder, where he was embraced by the population and the *poulain* lords, who urged him to claim the young widow and the crown; and Isabella did come to him on her own, against the advice of others, as I have her do in *Lionheart*. Henri's reluctance was not at all unusual. Few crusaders intended to remain in the Holy Land; the great majority returned home after fulfilling their vows. Not even the promise of lands and titles was enough to tempt many men into renouncing their old lives. Joffroi de Lusignan had been made Count of Jaffa and Ascalon, but he still sailed for Poitou after the truce with Saladin. When a French churchman, Jacques de Vitry, was elected to the bishopric of Acre, his initial response was horror, for he saw this as lifelong exile. Guy de Montfort, the uncle of "my" Simon in *Falls the Shadow*, journeyed to the Holy Land and wed Balian d'Ibelin's daughter Helvis, but after her death he returned to France. So Henri's ambivalence about the offer made to him at Tyre was not that surprising, and while his marriage to Isabella seems to have been a happy one, it is telling that he never sought to be crowned and continued to call himself the Count of Champagne.

Now, on to the assassination of Conrad of Montferrat. The French did their best to convince the rest of Christendom that Richard was responsible for Conrad's murder, and one of the Saracen chroniclers, Ibn al-Athir, claimed that Saladin had arranged with Rashīd al-Dīn Sinān to have both Richard and Conrad killed, but neither Richard nor Saladin are considered serious suspects by historians. Richard was desperate to leave Outremer in order to save his own kingdom and Saladin had just concluded a treaty with Conrad. The consensus is that the most likely explanation is the one given by one of the chroniclers—that Conrad had rashly offended the *Assassins* by seizing one of their ships.

I have always been glad when readers alert me to mistakes; otherwise, I'd keep on making the same errors instead of going on to new ones. So I was grateful to the readers who told me there were no brindle greyhounds in the Middle Ages, that foxes do not have black eyes, and medieval roses were not ever-blooming. But there is no need for readers to write and tell me that "fire" is a word that should be used only with gunpowder weapons, not crossbows. I am familiar with this argument, but I am a novelist, not a purist, and I found it impossible to write a battle scene with just the one verb, "shoot." And while I'm on the subject of mistakes, Joanna's and Berengaria's belief that they were at their most fertile immediately after their "flux" was in error, but it was theirs, not mine; medieval understanding of the reproductive process was not always reliable.

I was confronted with two mysteries when I began to research *Lionheart*—why it took so long for word of Henry II's death to reach Sicily and why word of the Sicilian king's death did not reach France until the following March. This is rather bizarre as it was quite possible for a messenger to travel from London to Rome in a month. One of Richard's couriers even managed to get from Sicily to Westminster in just four weeks, although that was extraordinarily fast. But four months is beyond slow. Yet when William II died on November 18, 1189, he did not know that Henry had died that past July, and a chronicler specifically said that Richard learned of William's death during his meeting with the French king Philippe, at Dreux Castle, in March 1190. What news could have been of greater significance than the death of a king? Since there is no hope of solving this puzzle, the best I could do was to offer plausible explanations for the inexplicable delay. For readers wanting to know more about the speed of travel in the Middle Ages, I recommend *The Medieval Traveller* by Norbert Ohler.

While writing *Lionheart*, I made an interesting discovery. Henry II is believed to have used two lions as his heraldic device, and I'd assumed that Richard had done the same in the first years of his reign. But Richard's crusader chroniclers referred often to his "lion" banner. So I did some research and found that the chronicles were right; Richard did begin his reign with a single lion rampant. In 1195, he adopted the coat that would remain the royal arms of England: gules, three lions passant guardant or. An excellent account of the evolution of early heraldry can be found in *The Origin of the Royal Arms of England: Their Development to 1199*, by Adrian Ailes. Richard also used a dragon standard at times. It has been suggested that Saladin may have used an eagle heraldic device, so I gave him one in *Lionheart*.

I try to avoid using terms that were not in use during the Middle Ages. So my characters do not refer to the Byzantine Empire, instead calling it the empire of the Greeks. It was even more of an inconvenience not to be able to employ the word "crusade." Medievals spoke of "taking the cross" or "going on pilgrimage"; the first term is unwieldy and the second conjures up peaceful images at variance with the reality of crusading warfare. As always, I do allow myself a bit more leeway when I am speaking in the narrative voice. It is always a challenge to decide whether to use medieval or modern place-names. In *Lionheart*, I went with the latter for geographical clarity; for example, I used Haifa rather than Caiphas, and Arsuf instead of Arsur. And I continue to struggle with the bane of historical novelists—the deplorable medieval habit of recycling the same family names. Thankfully, many names have variations; otherwise, my readers couldn't tell the players without a scorecard. So in *Lionheart*, we have Geoffrey, Geoff, Jaufre, and Joffroi; William, Guillaume, and Guilhem. I chose not to use the name that the crusaders called Malik al-'Ādil—Saphadin—because it is not familiar to readers and could have created some confusion, unlike the much better known sobriquet Saladin. And for the curious, Richard was being called Lionheart even before he became king.

I usually try to anticipate readers' queries, and am doing so now. I also plan to do a blog in which I discuss my *Lionheart* research and material I could not include in the Author's Note. Although the poleaxe did not come into common usage until the fourteenth century, there is a twelfth-century painting in the cathedral at Monreale that shows one, and I thought it would be fun to mention since Richard was very interested in weaponry innovations. Contemporaries of

Berengaria's brother, Sancho, reported that he was extremely tall, and according to Dr. Luis del Campo Jesus, who examined his bones, Sancho was over seven feet in height. And assuming that the skeleton discovered in the abbey founded by Berengaria at Epau is indeed hers, she was just five feet in height. We do not know her exact birth year, although Anne Trindade, the more reliable of Berengaria's two biographers, makes a convincing case that she was born circa 1170. The most quoted comment about Berengaria's appearance came from the snarky Richard of Devizes, who sniped that she was "more prudent than pretty." But he never laid eyes upon her. The chronicler Ambroise, who probably did, described her as very fair and lovely, and the author of the *Itinerarium* claimed Richard had desired her since he was Count of Poitou, which is a sweet story but rather unlikely, for medieval marriages were matters of state, and I doubt that Richard had a romantic bone in his entire body. While only one chronicler, Robert de Torigny, the abbot of Mont St Michel, mentions Joanna and William's son, Bohemond, he is a very reliable source, for he was a good friend to Henry II and was accorded the great honor of acting as godfather to Henry and Eleanor's daughter, Eleanor, who'd later become Queen of Castile. As I explain in the Afterword, we do not know the names of Isaac Comnenus's second wife and daughter, called the Damsel of Cyprus by the chroniclers; Sophia and Anna are names of my choosing. Ranulf and Rhiannon's son Morgan is one of the very few purely fictional characters to make an appearance in one of my novels, as is his love, the Lady Mariam. As I did in *The Reckoning* with Ellen de Montfort's attendants, Hugh and Juliana, I had to create histories for Joanna's ladies-in-waiting, Beatrix and Alicia, for all we know of them are their names and their utter devotion to Joanna. And now a word about Arnaldia, the baffling illness that almost killed Richard at Acre. It was not scurvy, as is sometimes reported. That was known in the army camp, and the crusaders distinguished it from Arnaldia; moreover, scurvy is caused by a deficient diet, and Richard had just spent a month in Cyprus. It remains a mystery, having defied diagnosis for more than eight hundred years.

Even for me, this is turning out to be a very long Author's Note. I'd like to close with a *mea culpa* and an apology. I have a section on my website called Medieval Mishaps. Sometimes apparent inconsistencies in my books are not errors but merely reflect the "accepted wisdom" at the time I was writing. For example, sharp-eyed readers may have noticed that Eleanor has shed two years since *Here Be Dragons* and my first mysteries; it was always assumed she'd been born in 1122, but Andrew W. Lewis convincingly demonstrated that she was actually born in 1124. Sometimes my mistakes are revealed by subsequent research, such as my women wearing velvet in the twelfth century or Richard III having the world's longest-lived Irish wolfhound. Until now I considered my most infamous mistake to be the time-traveling little grey squirrel in *Sunne*. But that squirrel has been utterly eclipsed by the mistake I recently found in Chapter Seventeen of *The Reckoning*, where I have Edward I telling Roger de Mortimer that crossbows were more difficult to master than long bows. I was truly horrified, for just the opposite is true. What makes this so baffling to me is that I *knew* this at the time I wrote *The Reckoning*, and I never drink and write at the same time. So how explain it? I haven't a clue, but it is extremely embarrassing, and I've been doing penance the only way I can—by calling as much attention to this bizarre blunder as I can.

After the *mea culpa*, the apology. In the Author's Note for *Devil's Brood*, I did something well intentioned but foolish—I offered to provide material from my blogs for readers without access to the Internet. I did not anticipate the volume of letters and found it impossible to respond to them all, for I do not have any assistants to help with correspondence, reader requests, research, etc. So I would like to say I am sorry to those who wrote to me and received no response. The sad truth is that e-mail, blogs, websites, and social networking sites like Facebook have become the only realistic means for writers and readers to interact.

I'd initially intended to tell Richard's story as one book, but I soon realized that I'd underestimated the extent of the research I'd need to do, though this is Richard's fault more than mine. The man's travel itinerary would put Marco Polo to shame—Italy and Sicily, Cyprus, the Holy Land, Austria, Germany, France; a pity he didn't have frequent-flier miles. As the deadline loomed and Richard and I were still stuck in Outremer, I began to panic. Fortunately, my friend Valerie LaMont came up with a brilliant idea; why not write two books about Richard? It made perfect sense, for there is a natural breaking point—the conclusion of the Third Crusade. Much to my relief, my publisher was amenable to this approach, and so *A King's Ransom* will pick up where *Lionheart* ended, as Richard sails from Acre for home. Of course he has no idea what lies ahead—an unlikely encounter with pirates, shipwreck, capture, imprisonment, ransom, betrayal, his deteriorating marriage, and an all-consuming war with the French king. *A King's Ransom* will also be my final farewell to the Angevins, surely one of history's most dysfunctional and fascinating families. I will miss them.

S.K.P.

February 2011

www.sharonkaypenman.com

Acknowledgments

My acknowledgments pages must sometimes read like that classic line from *Casablanca*—"Round up the usual suspects." But few writers have been as fortunate as I have been in the course of my writing career, for I have had the same editor and agents for nigh on thirty years, almost unheard of in the publishing industry. So once again I want to thank my editor extraordinaire, Marian Wood, and my wonderful agents, Molly Friedrich and Mic Cheetham. At the risk of embarrassing them, I feel truly blessed. I would also like to thank Kate Davis of G. P. Putnam's, Paul Cirone and Lucy Carson of the Friedrich Agency, and Dorian Hastings for a superb copyediting job. The "usual suspects" list includes Valerie and Lowell LaMont; no writer could ask for a better book midwife than Valerie, and Lowell continues to exorcise my computer demons with his usual finesse. I want to thank my friend and fellow historical novelist Elizabeth Chadwick for pointing me in the right direction as I sought to envision Fauvel, Richard's famed Cypriot stallion. The admiring chroniclers described him as a dun, but there are bay, red, and grey or grulla duns. Elizabeth reminded me that Fauvel was a popular medieval name for chestnut horses, thus giving me a eureka moment—Fauvel was a red dun! I am very grateful to Dr. Larry Davis, Dr. Diego Fiorentino, and Ellie Lewis for their efforts to diagnose Richard's mystery ailment, the mystifying Arnaldia, which has been baffling historians and physicians for over eight hundred years. I allowed Morgan to borrow the evocative phrase "whispers of the blood" from Dana Stabenow, author of the brilliant Alaskan mystery series. And I want to say *Diolch yn fawr* to my friend Owen Mayo for his kindness in vetting Morgan's Welsh, which is Morgan's native tongue but not mine. Lastly, I'd like to acknowledge my Facebook friends and blog readers for their encouragement as I worked on *Lionheart*. Too often, it can seem as if writers operate in a vacuum, but thanks to the wonders of modern technology that is no longer true. Think what Shakespeare could have done with his own Facebook page.

More and more of my readers have been asking me to include a bibliography for my novels. I have begun listing some of my sources on my website and blog, but that doesn't help those readers without Internet access. So I am going to cite here the cream of the crop, those books I found to be most helpful and most reliable. The gold standard for Ricardian biographies remains John Gillingham's *Richard I*, published in 1999 by the Yale University Press; he has also written *Richard Coeur de Lion: Kingship, Chivalry and War in the Twelfth Century*. I am not sure I could have written *Lionheart* without *The Itinerary of King Richard I, with Studies on Certain Matters of Interest Connected with His Reign*, by Lionel Landon; unfortunately, this book is almost as hard to find as the Holy Grail. *The Reign of Richard Lionheart: Ruler of the Angevin Empire, 1189–1199*, by Ralph Turner and Richard R. Heiser, does not address the most consequential and fateful event of Richard's life—the Third Crusade—but it does cover the remainder of his reign, and has an excellent concluding chapter called "Richard in Retrospect," which analyzes the way his reputation has fluctuated over the centuries. Kate Norgate's *Richard the Lion Heart*, published in 1924, has stood the test of time surprisingly well. In all honesty, I have not read the second half of Frank McLynn's *Richard and John: Kings at War*, but the half of the book about Richard is accurate and insightful. I also recommend *Richard Coeur de Lion in History and Myth*, edited by Janet Nelson; *The Legends of King Richard I, Coeur de Lion: A Study of Sources and Variations to 1600*, by Bradford Broughton; and *The Plantagenet Empire, 1154–1224*, by Martin Aurell, translated by David Crouch. And since so many of my readers have seen the wonderful but historically inaccurate *The Lion in Winter*, here are two excellent books about medieval sexuality: *The Bridling of Desire: Views of Sex in the Later Middle Ages*, by Pierre J. Payer, and *Sexuality in Medieval Europe: Doing Unto Others*, by Ruth Mazo Karras; I hope to have a comprehensive bibliography about this subject on my website by the time *Lionheart* is published.

My favorite book about Richard's mother is *Eleanor of Aquitaine: Lord and Lady*, a notable collection of essays edited by Bonnie Wheeler. There are a number of biographies written about Eleanor, more than Henry, which would probably not please him much. Just to list a few of her biographers: Ralph Turner, Régine Pernoud, Jean Flori, D. D. R. Owen, Marion Meade, and Amy Kelly, though the last two authors' conclusions about the so-called Courts of Love are no longer accepted. I also recommend *The World of Eleanor of Aquitaine: Literature and*

Society in Southern France between the Eleventh and Thirteenth Centuries, edited by Marcus Bull and Catherine Leglu, and *Eleanor of Aquitaine, Courtly Love, and the Troubadours*, by Ffiona Swabey.

I was blessed with a treasure-trove while researching and writing *Lionheart*—two chronicles written by men who'd accompanied Richard on crusade and two by members of Salah al-Dīn's inner circle. I felt very fortunate to have access to Helen Nicholson's translation of *The Chronicle of the Third Crusade: The Itinerarium Peregrinorum et Gesta Regis Ricardi*, and Marianne Ailes's translation of *The History of the Holy War: Ambroise's Estoire de la Guerre Sainte*. These wonderful books make fascinating reading and provide invaluable footnotes about the persons and places mentioned in the texts. Another crusader chronicle is *The Conquest of Jerusalem and the Third Crusade: Sources in Translation*, by Peter W. Edbury, and then there is *Chronicles of the Crusades*, edited by Elizabeth Hallam. Bahā' al-Dīn ibn Shaddād wrote a compelling account of his time with Salah al-Dīn; in *Lionheart*, I quoted from the nineteenth-century edition, *Saladin, or What Befell Sultan Yûsuf*, translated by the Palestine Pilgrims' Text Society, but there is a more modern translation by D. S. Richards, complete with valuable annotated notes, titled *The Rare and Excellent History of Saladin*, which I recommend highly. Other contemporary chronicles are *The Chronicle of Ibn al-Athir for the Crusading Period, from al-Kamil fi'l-Ta'rikh*, Part 2, also translated by D. S. Richards, and a chronicle written by one of Salah al-Dīn's scribes, Imad ad-Din al-Isfahani, translated into French by Henri Masse as *Conquête de la Syrie et de la Palestine par Saladin*. There is also *Arab Historians of the Crusades*, translated by Francesco Gabrieli. Non-crusading chronicles include *The Chronicle of Richard of Devizes*, translated by J. A. Giles; *The History of William of Newburgh*, translated by Joseph Stevenson; *The Annals of Roger de Hoveden*, translated by Henry T. Riley; and *History of William Marshal*, translated by S. Gregory and annotated by D. Crouch. The quotation from the Comtessa de Dia's song, "Cruel Are the Pains I've Suffered," in Chapter Eleven, comes from *Lark in the Morning*, translated by Ezra Pound, William De Witt Snodgrass, and Robert Kehew.

Moving on to Sicily and Cyprus, there is *The Travels of Ibn Jubayr*, translated by Roland Broadhurst, a remarkable account of a pilgrimage to Mecca made by a Spanish Muslim in 1183–1184; his description of a deadly storm in the Straits of Messina was my inspiration for Alicia's shipwreck in Chapter One of *Lionheart*. *The Kingdom in the Sun*, by John Julius Norwich, is a beautifully written book about Norman Sicily, although his "take" on Richard is outdated. Another outstanding book about Sicily is *Admiral Eugenius of Sicily, his Life and Work and the*

Authorship of the Epistola ad Petrum and the Historia Hugonis Falcandi Siculi, by Evelyn Jamison. For the history of medieval Cyprus, readers need look no further than Peter Edbury's *The Kingdom of Cyprus and the Crusades, 1191–1374*. There is also George Hill's four-volume *A History of Cyprus;* volume I concerns Richard's conquest of the island.

The best book about the Crusades, IMHO, is Thomas Asbridge's riveting *The Crusades: The Authoritative History of the War for the Holy Land*. Other books on my Favorites List include *God's War: A New History of the Crusades*, by Christopher Tyerman; *Holy Warriors: A Modern History of the Crusades*, by Jonathan Phillips; *Fighting for the Cross: Crusading to the Holy Land*, by Norman Housley; the six-volume *A History of the Crusades*, edited by Kenneth Setton; and *The Assassins: A Radical Sect in Islam*, by Bernard Lewis. The definitive study of Salah al-Dīn is still *Saladin: The Politics of the Holy War*, by Malcolm Cameron Lyons and D. E. P. Jackson. I also recommend *The Crusades: Islamic Perspectives*, by Carole Hillenbrand. Some social histories are *The World of the Crusaders*, by Joshua Prawer; *The Crusaders in the Holy Land*, by Meron Benvenisti; *Medicine in the Crusades: Warfare, Wounds and the Medieval Surgeon*, by Piers D. Mitchell; and *Daily Life in the Medieval Islamic World*, by James E. Lindsay. For books dealing with warfare during the Crusades, a classic study is *Crusading Warfare, 1097–1193*, by R. C. Smail; there is also David Nicolle's two-volume *Crusader Warfare*.

Lastly, for books that cover medieval warfare in general, I have several exceptional books to recommend: *By Fire and Sword: Cruelty and Atrocity in Medieval Warfare*, by Sean McGlynn; *Noble Ideals and Bloody Realities: Warfare in the Middle Ages*, edited by Niall Christie and Maya Yazigi; *Western Warfare in the Age of the Crusades, 1000–1300*, by John France; *Tolerance and Intolerance: Social Conflict in the Age of the Crusades*, edited by Michael Gervers and James M. Powell; and *War and Chivalry: The Conduct and Perception of War in England and Normandy, 1066–1217*, by Matthew Strickland.